CONTENT WARNING: This book is intended for mature readers and contains adult subject matter, including graphic violence, profanity, indirect references to sexuality and childbirth, drug and alcohol use, and scary situations. Reader discretion is advised.

Praise for *The Nightmare Machine*

"I really liked this book! The way the story unfolded kept me engrossed the whole time. The action sequences were nail-biting and kept me on the edge of my seat, but the character development and the way the mystery unfolded were the true treasures in my opinion. I came to understand and care for these characters and thoroughly enjoyed watching the way their thinking and relationships evolved during their adversities and adventures. Would highly recommend for anyone who loves a thrilling adventure with compelling characters. A true can't-put-it-down book!" —Sarah B., Amazon reviewer

"*The Nightmare Machine* is a captivating and thrilling novel. A must-read book that I could not put down. It's very suspenseful and a joy to read. Tim White is a masterful storyteller!" —Josh S., Amazon reviewer

"I absolutely loved this wild emotional roller coaster that took me from 'hell yeah' to 'hopeless' and back. I felt so connected to the characters because they were so real, relatable and someone I would want to be or know in person." —Audrey P., Amazon reviewer

"The characterizations in this novel are rich and as the story progressed, I found myself rooting for the protagonists.... I was impressed that the novel explores compelling moral questions and manages to promote a life-affirming viewpoint—without being didactic or heavy-handed." —Stewart M., Amazon reviewer

"Really, the greatest praise that I can give this book is that I couldn't put it down. Every good book I have ever read has grabbed me by the collar and demanded that I finish it in one go (and I nearly did with *The Nightmare Machine* except for this pesky thing called 'sleep...')." —Nick E., Amazon reviewer

"If you like gripping horror, memorable characters and GUNS, this book is well worth the price of admission." —Hunter D., Amazon reviewer

For more information, visit TimWhiteWriting.com

Copyright © 2023 Tim White

Cover art by Jon Wos

ISBN-13: 979-8-9883299-0-9 (ebook)

ISBN-13: 979-8-9883299-1-6 (paperback)

ISBN-13: 979-8-9883299-9-2 (hardcover)

ISBN-13: 979-8-9883299-3-0 (audiobook)

Library of Congress Control Number: 2023920460

Published by Ocean Scribe Publishing, Gilbert, AZ

THE NIGHTMARE MACHINE

Tim White

"Fairy tales are more than true—not because they tell us dragons exist, but because they tell us dragons can be beaten."

—G.K. Chesterton

For Amy and Tom

CHAPTER ONE
Dreams

December 17, 2021
Bangor, Maine

It was a typical teenage girl's bedroom, if neater than most. Strips of LED lights, switched off for the evening, ran along the edges of the ceiling. The window in the eastern wall had a broad sill, upon which rested several well-tended potted plants, carefully arranged to soak up the morning sun. The posters of actors and bands were perfectly vertical and precisely aligned next to one another.

Similarly, the books and papers on the desk were stacked neatly and arranged at ninety-degree angles. The white carpet was free of clothes and freshly vacuumed. The walls were a soft pink—a color the paint store called Rose Dust.

In one corner, a pair of tangled headphones lay on top of a hastily discarded backpack, the only sign of mild untidiness. On the wall above the backpack, three shelves displayed various awards for academic achievement and community service. The trophies were meticulously polished, the wooden plaques free of dust.

The alarm clock on the nightstand read 10:00 p.m. The girl asleep in the bed looked like the proper owner of the bedroom. Like the room, she was all right angles, one knee drawn up, the other leg straight, one arm down at her side, the other tucked under the pillow. Her pajama top was white, the bottoms light pink, matching the walls and carpet. Her breathing was slow, even, and perfectly consistent. Like the backpack tossed in the corner, her red hair splayed wildly over the pillow was the only thing that suggested disorder.

An hour passed. She remained motionless, perfectly at peace.

Down the hall, her father slept less peacefully. His room was more sparsely decorated but equally tidy. A few framed vinyl records adorned one wall; an autographed bass guitar hung on another.

The bed was big enough for two, but he slept alone. A single framed photo on the nightstand showed a smiling couple on a beach—him and a woman who hadn't slept in his bed for twelve years.

A beautifully hand-painted urn on a high shelf held her ashes.

The man often had vivid dreams. Some nights, he dreamed of his wife, waking with moisture in his eyes and a smile on his face. Other nights, his dreams were plagued by dark forms and whispered promises of perdition.

Tonight, he had no dreams. Even so, he slept fitfully. He always did.

Another hour passed.

His eyes flew open at the sound of an ear-splitting scream from down the hallway. "Sara!" he shouted, as if by reflex, before he'd even come fully awake. His feet hit the floor as he yanked open the nightstand drawer and closed his fingers around the loaded pistol. He was at his bedroom door in a flash. It opened outward, and even though it was unlocked, he shouldered it open forcefully, causing the knob on the opposite side to punch a large hole in the drywall.

His daughter needed him.

At a running pace, her bedroom door was only six steps away. Many thoughts raced through his mind in that brief distance.

At first, he wondered if she had merely had a bad dream, the same sort of bad dream that every teenager has once in a while. He dismissed that notion immediately. Her scream carried discordant notes of heart-wrenching terror far beyond anything that a normal nightmare caused.

Then he thought—hoped—that she'd screamed because someone had broken into the house. That seemed a horrible thing for a father to hope for, that an intruder was in his daughter's bedroom. But he was armed, he was reasonably strong, and he'd been taking Krav Maga classes twice a week for years; so had Sara. They could defend themselves against an intruder.

Deep in his heart, he knew there was no intruder. The gun in his hand would be useless against this threat. In seventeen years, he'd never heard Sara scream that way before.

Only one thing could make her scream like that.

He reached her bedroom door and flung it open. His eyes weren't fully adjusted to the darkness, but he could see her sitting up in bed, clutching the sides of her head as though she were suffering the worst headache imaginable. She screamed again, so loudly that he half-expected the window to shatter. He dropped the gun on the floor and grabbed her shoulders, shaking her.

"Sara! It's okay, I'm here!"

She screamed again. Blood dripped from her nose onto her white shirt. Her eyes were screwed shut so tightly that, in the darkness, it looked like she had no eyes at all. *Jesus, she's still asleep*, he thought. He shook her again, more violently, shouting her name over and over. He fumbled around on her nightstand until he found the small lamp, switching it on so he could see better.

She was turning blue. She just kept screaming, hunched over, hands clapped over her ears. He tried to move her hands so she could hear him, but she resisted with strength that seemed impossible for her petite frame. His mind raced, trying to think of how he could snap her out of it.

An idea came to him. He swept her up in his arms and jogged back down the hall, toward the bathroom. With an elbow, he clicked on the light, then gently laid her in the bathtub, careful not to bang her head on the porcelain. Hesitating only for a moment, he turned on the cold tap full blast.

Frigid water erupted from the shower head, drenching her instantly. The water was barely above freezing, liquid only because the pipes were wrapped.

It had the desired effect. Sara's eyes shot open, and she gasped in a breath, choking off another scream. She spluttered and began to thrash.

She probably thought she was drowning.

Before she could hurt herself, he dragged her out of the tub and sat next to her on the floor. She blinked once, twice, three times, slowly regaining her senses. Her green eyes focused on him, and finally, she saw him.

"Dad?" Her voice was barely above a whisper.

"I'm here, baby," he said, moving her wet hair out of her face.

She collapsed against him, sobbing. He held her and said nothing, letting her come out of it slowly. He didn't ask what had done this to her. He knew.

An icy chill ran up his spine.

She said nothing either, as though it wouldn't be true as long as neither of them spoke it aloud.

Gradually, her sobs tapered off, and she began to shiver violently against him. He realized that she was probably freezing in her soaked pajamas. "Go get changed," he said softly, "before you turn into an ice cube."

She looked up at him. He could see a question in her eyes that she seemed embarrassed to ask.

"I'll wait right outside your door," he said.

That seemed to give her the strength she needed to stand up. He followed her back to her room, retrieved the gun from the floor, and quietly shut the door behind him as he left.

He stood in silence in the dark hallway, his eyes unfocused. He'd known this day was coming, but now that it was here, it seemed unreal.

He wept, silently, just for a minute. It would be the last time he'd allow himself to cry.

His daughter was strong, but she would need his strength as well.

He prayed that it would be enough.

* * *

Sara sat on a bar stool at the kitchen counter, a steaming mug of black coffee in front of her. She was seventeen, but her face was still a blend of girlish and womanly features, so she looked younger—perhaps too young to be drinking black coffee at 12:30 a.m.

She sipped at it, more for the heat than the taste.

Her father paced back and forth in the living room. She could hear parts of his conversation.

"It's Ethan. Yes, I know what time it is…. Right. Yes, I'm sure."

Looking at her, one would never guess that she'd been a sobbing, terrified mess just thirty minutes earlier. The corners of her mouth were turned down in a slight frown, her brow furrowed, her eyes alert but far away. Her countenance was that of an athlete preparing for an Olympic performance: focused and austere.

She came out of her thoughts long enough to overhear another snippet of her father's conversation. "Three others. Two are quite solid, I think. I have some concerns about the third…. Yes, he's very young…. Yes. I understand."

Sara pushed away from the counter and opened the refrigerator, studying its contents.

Grilled cheese. That sounded good. Her eyes darted between shelves. Bread, butter, cheese. All ingredients accounted for. She gathered them and dumped everything on the counter next to the stove.

Her father came back into the kitchen, setting his phone gently on the counter. He arched one eyebrow. "Grilled cheese in the middle of the night?"

With a spatula, Sara flicked a lock of hair out of her face. "Aren't I entitled?"

Ethan's shoulders sagged, and he blushed slightly. "Of course."

She turned back to the stove and began spreading butter in the pan. "Today's Saturday." He remained silent, not understanding what she was getting at. She cleared her throat and went on. "I was wondering if maybe we could go to Wonder World. The new roller coaster opens today."

Ethan came to stand beside her, resting one hand gently on her back. "Do you really think we have time?"

She tossed a buttered slice of bread into the pan, where it sizzled merrily.

She looked up at him. "I think we can spare one day."

He smiled. "Alright."

"Can Dylan come?"

"Whatever you want."

She turned back to her grilled cheese, grinning broadly to herself. Ethan was amazed—and sometimes taken aback—at the way she seemed so much like a grown woman in one moment, only to do something in the next moment that reminded him of the grinning, gap-toothed little girl in pigtails she'd been not that long ago.

CHAPTER TWO
Ghosts

One Week Later
December 24, 2021

Dylan poked his tongue out, concentrating. Holding his right hand steady, he used his left to tighten the vice on the workbench ever so slightly. Satisfied that his bulky, ugly-as-sin prototype battery was secure, he opened a drawer and rummaged through it, coming out with a pair of needle-nose pliers so tiny that they looked fake.

A bead of sweat fell from his forehead and splashed onto the workbench. He wiped his forehead with the sleeve of his hoodie, then paused, set the pliers down, took off the hoodie, and tossed it onto his bed. It was too warm for long sleeves anyway.

He stretched and yawned, exhausted. He hadn't slept well in a week or so. He tried not to think about the bags under his eyes that must be full-on black by now. At least it was winter vacation, so he wasn't struggling to stay awake in class.

Retrieving the pliers, he set about connecting voltage and ground wires to the input pads of a small voltage regulator. Once the wires were loosely connected, he traded the pliers for a soldering iron and carefully soldered the wires into place. That done, he dug around in the drawer for a voltmeter and measured the battery's output: 8.1 volts.

"Hmm," he said aloud. He'd been expecting nine volts. Maybe the concentration of salt in the battery was still off.

His stomach growled, prompting him to glance at the clock above his bed. It was well past dinnertime, and his dad hadn't called him, meaning he hadn't made dinner—again. Sighing, Dylan double-checked that the soldering iron was switched off before heading for the door, leaving his tools strewn around haphazardly.

Before leaving the room, he turned, pulled his phone from his pocket, and snapped a picture of the workbench. He sent it to Sara, along with a single word: *Progress!*

She replied immediately. *Awesome! But next time, zoom in more so I don't have to see your disgusting room.*

He laughed. She wasn't wrong. There were so many clothes and boxes of random electrical parts on the floor that he could barely see the carpet. He was a slob, she was a neat freak, and they teased one another incessantly. It was hardly the only respect in which they were opposites. Most adults couldn't fathom why they spent so much time together.

As Dylan descended the stairs, he could hear the TV in the living room. It sounded like the news.

He wished that his dad would watch something else once in a while.

On the way downstairs, he paused at the landing and turned to look out the window. He hated everything about the tiny apartment—except the window on the landing. He leaned his elbows on the sill and rested his chin in one hand.

Hours earlier, light snow had begun to fall, dusting everything outside. To the right, a cluster of old birch trees, their branches stripped naked for winter, hid the nearby highway from view. On the left, a small creek wound its way through the icy remains of the forest. Sparkles of fading sunlight danced on the surface of the frozen water, making it look as though the creek were still running.

A single northern cardinal perched on the branches of a short bush, a vibrant splash of red against the monochromatic white backdrop. The blanket of snow on the ground was perfectly flat and undisturbed, except for the bird's tiny footprints near the bush. As Dylan watched, the bird looked right at him, its head cocked curiously to one side. After a moment, it ruffled its feathers and flew away, leaving the motionless landscape outside looking like one of his father's photographs.

The old ones, anyway. The good ones.

Dylan descended the stairs the rest of the way and entered the living room. A low fire crackled in the fireplace, providing pleasant warmth. He noticed that one of the ships-in-a-bottle on the mantle was dangerously close to the edge. He crossed the room and pushed it farther back on the mantle so it wouldn't fall and break.

He wished they had a Christmas tree. The room looked naked without one.

Richard Masters was sitting on the couch, poring over a newspaper he'd spread over the coffee table. He looked up over his glasses. "Hey," he said softly.

"Hey, Dad. You hungry?"

Richard glanced at his watch. "Ah, not really."

Dylan crossed into the kitchen and opened the refrigerator, scanning its contents. "You need to eat something. I know you didn't eat the lunch I made for you, it's still in here."

"You're probably right."

Dylan crouched, rummaging in the lower drawers. "I'll make spaghetti. We have sausage and tomatoes in here that are still good." Much of the food was rotten. Spaghetti was about the only thing he could make with what was edible.

His father bent back over the newspaper. "Sounds good," he mumbled inattentively.

Dylan sighed quietly to himself. Without further comment, he brought the tomatoes over to the counter, found a reasonably clean knife, and began chopping them. He worked in silence for a while, dumping a can of tomato sauce into a saucepan and adding some oregano. While he was waiting for the water to boil, Dylan transferred all the rotten food from the refrigerator to the trash can.

Richard came into the kitchen and gave his son a light hug. "How's the science fair project going?" he asked.

Dylan perked up as he dumped the ground sausage into a hot skillet. "Really good, I think. I had a couple ideas that didn't work out, but I think I know what I'm doing now."

Richard smiled, scratching his graying stubble. He hadn't shaved in almost a week. "Tell me."

"I think I can make a nine-volt battery that runs on salt water. I read about the idea in *Popular Mechanics* a little while ago. Some engineers in England made a saltwater battery that shows a lot of promise. Mine is a lot simpler, of course, but I think I can do something they haven't figured out yet."

"Oh?"

"I think I can make one that can also *recharge* itself, just by being immersed in salt water. The capacity is really low, but I see a few possible uses for it, like safety lights at sea. What if boats had lights that didn't need external power? You could keep the emergency lights on just by tossing them in the water, or maybe just the power cells." Dylan scratched his head, again lost in thought about his project.

Richard didn't respond. Dylan looked up and saw that his father was looking at his phone. He sighed again and went back to chopping tomatoes.

A long silence filled the kitchen, offset by the low chatter of the TV in the next room. Dylan added the pasta to the water and stirred the cooked sausage into the sauce. He yawned again, shaking his head to clear the ever-present cloud of fatigue.

Finally, Richard put down his phone and spoke. "Did you see the news today?" His tone was casual. Too casual.

Dylan's eyes narrowed in suspicion. His back was to his father; he tried to keep his tone more neutral than his face. "No, I've been working on stuff."

"They found a woman in Canada, alive. She'd been missing for more than fifteen years."

Dylan spun around, slamming the wooden spoon on the counter. Tomato sauce splashed everywhere, spattering his shirt and the side of the refrigerator.

"Dad, you have to let it go. Mom's gone. She's been gone my whole life, and she's never coming back."

Richard said nothing, but his shoulders dropped a little. He removed his glasses and began cleaning them on his shirt, looking as though he wished he hadn't said anything.

"We're two months behind on rent," Dylan continued, unable to keep a current of frustration out of his voice. "You could be working. You *should* be working. Look, this guy in my class, his older sister is getting married, and she's looking for a wedding photographer. If you call her and tell her you're my dad, I'm sure she'll hire you."

Richard shrugged one shoulder and put his glasses back on. "Maybe."

Dylan raised his hands, then let them drop helplessly to his sides, ignoring the pot boiling over behind him. "Can you just… be my dad? Please? I could use at least one parent."

Richard's face contorted in shock. He looked as if Dylan had slapped him. He worked his jaw, but no words came out.

"I'm sorry," Dylan said, his voice barely more than a whisper. He turned and switched off the burner. "Spaghetti's ready."

Without another word, he left the kitchen and went back upstairs.

* * *

Dylan shut his bedroom door softly, taking extra care not to slam it. He leaned his back against it and shut his eyes, trying to settle his emotions. It wasn't that he was angry at his father. He wasn't even disappointed, not really. He just wanted him to *understand*.

One could only do so much to change things. "So much" usually turned out to be "not much." Dylan's mother had gone missing when he was only a few months old. From day one, Richard had been adamant that Marie would never leave her husband and newborn son, and she would never kill herself. Something had happened *to* her.

Dylan believed him. The beautiful, joyful, loyal woman he'd come to know through photos and home videos would never abandon her family.

At the thought of photos, Dylan opened his eyes and went to his closet. From the top shelf, he retrieved a large box and opened it, revealing several thick photo albums. On top of the stack were the framed photos for which his father had won the Pulitzer Prize so long ago, before Dylan was born.

Gingerly, he picked up the frame, running his fingers lightly over the glass. Richard's winning submission was a set of two photographs, framed side by side. The left-hand photo was black and white, taken just before the advent of fully digital photography. It showed an emaciated Chinese family of three in dirty clothes—a mother, a father, and a son who looked to be about eighteen. The family stood in front of a soulless, whitewashed apartment building, identical to countless others in Communist China. They were slightly in motion, each with one leg extended, as though they were about to get into a vehicle that was just out of frame. Each wore a tattered backpack and held a small cardboard box, presumably containing their most important belongings. Their heads were bowed submissively, their eyes cast downward, lips pressed together tightly in joyless severity. Slightly out-of-focus people walking by in the background also had their heads down, the horrific memory of the then-recent Tiananmen Square massacre undoubtedly still fresh in their minds.

The right-hand photo was in comparatively brilliant color, slightly faded and desaturated, taken exactly six months after the other, with the first commercially available digital camera. The same family stood side by side in front of a small but warmly decorated restaurant in Victoria Harbor, Hong Kong. Despite being six months older, each of them looked younger and healthier. They smiled victoriously at the camera, the father's right arm raised toward the restaurant behind him. The restaurant's door was open, permitting a partial view of the front counter. Barely visible in the photo, a framed HK$10 bank note hung on the wall behind the cash register.

Richard had submitted the winning photo set when he was twenty-one, just five years older than Dylan was now, becoming the youngest-ever Pulitzer recipient.

Dylan gently set aside the framed photos and flipped open one of the albums. Tens of thousands of Richard's photos were collecting dust in his closet. Dylan didn't think he'd looked at any of them since Marie's disappearance.

He'd never asked his father if he could look at the photos. He had no reason to think he wasn't allowed to, and yet he always looked at them in secret. Until he was about twelve, he'd done so with the utmost caution. He would wait until Richard went to sleep or left the apartment before sneaking into his closet to borrow one of the albums. He always paid close attention to where he'd taken it from, so he could put it back in the same exact spot.

Eventually, he stopped returning the albums. His favorites had been in his room for years now, and Richard had never said anything. Dylan doubted he'd noticed. Now, looking at the photos was one of his favorite things to do, especially when he was feeling down. He considered it an intensely private activity. He had never shown the albums to anyone else, not even Sara.

Some things were just for him.

The photos were arranged chronologically, so he knew just where to look. He flipped to the photos from 2004, the year before he was born. The first photo from that year was one of his favorites. It showed Richard and Marie, their smiling faces pressed together, in front of an old New England manor house. Cherry trees, Marie's favorite, were in full bloom in the front yard. Dylan had lived there only for the first few months of his life and had no memory of it.

He touched his mother's face lightly. Behind her in the photo, the sun was just beginning to set, casting a white halo around her face that made her look like an angel. The effect must have been intentional; Richard was certainly capable of preventing the artifact or editing it out if he'd wanted to.

Dylan turned the page. He knew all the photos by heart; he could have reviewed the whole album in his head with perfect accuracy, but there was something irreplaceable about looking at the photos, touching them. He paused on another of his favorites that showed Marie in the process of falling off a Jet Ski in Cancún. In such a situation, most people would be frightened or angry—annoyed, at the very least. Marie was laughing hysterically. He didn't need to look at the back of the photo to know the date it was taken: August 11, 2004. She was already pregnant with him but probably didn't know it yet.

He skipped ahead several pages, pausing on a third photograph. Marie was in bed, looking exhausted, her hair plastered to her head with sweat. The photo was taken from above—Richard must have been standing. Despite looking terribly tired, she had the brightest smile on her face that Dylan had ever seen.

Her adoring gaze was fixed on her newborn son in her arms.

A tear splashed onto the page. Panicked, Dylan hastily scrubbed it away with the hem of his shirt, even though the photo itself was protected by clear plastic.

Suddenly angry, he slammed the album shut. Then, as if apologizing to the book for his outburst, he set it carefully back in the box.

Marie lived only in his memory now, and in Richard's. Neither of them was capable of finding answers, and they definitely couldn't bring her back. The police hadn't found anything, nor had the private investigators Richard had hired with the last of their savings. If there were answers to find, someone would have found them long ago. She was almost certainly dead, and they would never know why or how. Wasting time and energy on it was pointless. There were limits to what they could do, and this task was simply beyond their abilities.

Why couldn't his father see that?

He flopped onto his bed, staring at the ceiling. He still had his pants and shoes on. It didn't matter; he wasn't going to sleep anytime soon.

The minutes ticked by, melting into hours. Occasionally, he heard his father moving around downstairs, but there was no other sound to mark the passage of time. Thoughts and memories drifted through his head in a current of anger and apathy. Like oil and water, the two emotions clashed, refusing to mix, instead alternating, one displacing the other, back and forth.

At some point during his wallowing, Dylan glanced at the half-built battery on his workbench. He considered working on it some more, but his head wasn't in it.

He probably wouldn't be able to finish that, either. Whenever it seemed he was about to achieve something truly incredible, it always went wrong. He'd begun to learn that lesson many years earlier, as promising leads about his mother evaporated into nothingness, time and time again.

The best way to avoid disappointment was to stop trying.

Irritated with himself, he finally stood up and rummaged around for his phone, eventually finding it under a discarded shirt. He glanced at the time. Sara might still be up. He opened the messaging app.

You awake?

A few minutes later, the reply came. *Yeah. What's up?*

Feel like talking?

Sure. I'll call in a few.

He returned to his bed and tried to think of nothing in particular. When the phone rang, he answered.

"Hey," he said.

"Hey," Sara replied.

"Sorry to bug you on Christmas Eve."

"No big deal. Dad went to bed already, I'm just watching TV."

"Anything good?"

"Home shopping channel. Need some steak knives for $19.99? Better hurry, they're almost sold out."

He smiled. "I'm good."

"What's up? Can't sleep?"

He hesitated before answering. "More like don't want to."

"Bad dreams?"

He nodded, then realized she couldn't see him. "Yeah."

"Me, too. I don't want to sleep either."

Dylan rolled onto his side. "What are you having bad dreams about?"

There was a long pause, and Sara's voice was quieter when she responded. "I'd rather not say."

He didn't push it. Another long silence stretched between them, but it was comfortable. With one another, they didn't feel the need to always say something.

Finally, Sara broke the silence. "So, the Hurlitron was cool," she said, referring to the new coaster at Wonder World.

Dylan grinned despite his dark thoughts. "Yeah, one of my top five for sure."

"I never thought my dad would go on it."

Dylan had been surprised as well. Mr. Holcomb—Ethan, as he insisted —was the opposite of a thrill seeker. "Me neither. I thought for sure he'd pass out, but I have to give him credit, he powered through."

"And then you offered him a churro right after, totally serious, like it was no big deal," Sara cackled.

Dylan burst into giggles as well. "I couldn't tell if he was gonna barf or punch me!"

They laughed together, each trying to keep it down, lest a mildly annoyed father come to intrude on the conversation. It was after midnight, and both of them had bedtimes, though they were loosely enforced.

Gradually, the laughter faded into another relaxed silence. This time, Dylan broke it after a few minutes.

"Are you gonna be at the clinic tomorrow?"

"Yeah, Dr. Warner is working, she pulled the Christmas shift. She didn't ask me to help, but I can tell she needs it."

"Mr. Davis said he can take me to the dam around lunchtime. He'll pick me up from the clinic, he said it's more convenient for him. You can just go with us if you'll be there."

"Don't let him hear you call him Mr. Davis, it makes him feel old."

"He is old. He's like, almost fifty."

"He's like my dad, he wants to be called Tom. I have some extra stuff to do before lunch, so I'll meet you at the dam a little later, around one."

"Alright."

"How's your dad?"

Dylan grunted. "Same as always."

Sensing that the change in topic was unwelcome, Sara backpedaled. "I guess I'll see you in the morning, then. We should both try to sleep."

"Sara?"

"Yeah?"

"I don't want to."

"Are the nightmares that bad?"

He hesitated again. "Yeah."

"Same, honestly."

"Will you stay on the phone with me?"

"All night, if you need me to."

CHAPTER THREE
Monsters

Twenty Years Earlier
November 19, 2001

The desert soil outside Kandahar drank in the rain greedily. It began as a light patter, the drops instantly disappearing as they met the barren clay. Within a few minutes, dark green clouds overhead had unleashed a deluge. It was just past noon, but the cloud cover was so complete that it felt like dusk.

Tom Davis press-checked his M4 carbine, pulling back on the charging handle just enough to verify that there was a round in the chamber. He grumbled to himself. The rain was an unforeseen surprise this time of year, but he supposed it had its advantages. It would cover their approach to the village, making it harder for enemy sentries to see and hear his squad.

Manny Ramirez crouch-walked over to Davis's position, moving slowly, keeping the wormwood shrubs between himself and the Taliban-held village. When he reached the rock Davis knelt behind, he lightly tapped his friend on the shoulder and spoke quietly.

"Where do you want me?"

Davis didn't reply right away, scanning the hills to the west. "What do you think?"

"East and west are pretty much the only two choices. There's nothing higher than a few meters on this side, and I don't want to risk going all the way around to the north end of the village. Too many eyeballs."

"Looks to me like that outcrop on the west side has better visibility, but it's also more exposed. On the east side, you'd be less useful, but there's a lot more cover."

"My thoughts exactly. Tell me where to go."

Davis thought for a moment, blinking rain out of his hazel eyes. "Command says to expect fifteen or twenty tangos, so that means thirty to forty. If shit goes sideways, we're gonna need all the firepower we can get, especially toward the center of town where they can hit us from any direction." He pointed toward the area of the village that worried him the most. "You can't see the plaza from the east side. We need you where you can do the most damage. Go west."

"You got it, boss." Ramirez unslung his M24A2 rifle, chambered a round, and disappeared into the tall grass.

Davis flopped onto his belly in the mud and crawled away from the rock until he reached the rest of his team behind the remains of a partially collapsed wall. He rose to his knees and spoke to them in a low voice.

"Alright, give Ramirez about ten minutes to get to that outcrop over there. Everyone triple-check that you're on the encrypted channel. I don't want to get into a firefight because one of them overheard us." The seven other Rangers checked their radios, each flashing a thumbs-up to confirm that the settings were correct. "I have a strong preference about how I want this to go down. What is my preference?" Davis asked.

"Zero shots fired, zero bodies," replied Mark Sampson, squad medic.

"I still don't understand why we're doing this. Stealth isn't really our specialty, we blow shit up," said David Burns, rifleman.

"You know how spread out we are all around Kandahar. The guys who normally do this kind of thing are busy, and command says there's no time to wait for them. We're Rangers. We do whatever needs to be done," Davis said, trying not to sound like he was reprimanding.

A ninth man joined them, crawling silently through the mud until he could rise to his knees behind the wall.

"Jackson, how's it look?" Davis asked.

"Not good. I count twenty-five outside, so figure on another ten or so indoors. The package is in a small house in the northeast corner... I think."

"You think?"

"Most of the buildings are missing walls or roofs, so I could see inside and confirm there's no one in there. But I count four buildings all closed up, he could be in any of them. The one in the northeast has two guys standing outside who never leave the area, so I'm guessing they're his guards."

"Or they're decoys," Burns said.

"Could be. We won't know until we get in there," Davis muttered. "I don't like it."

"What's to like?" asked Sampson.

Davis keyed his radio. "Ramirez, you moved in yet?"

The sniper answered after a slight delay. "All set."

"Gimme a count."

After a minute or so, Ramirez spoke again. "Twenty-six outside."

"Copy. Hang tight, we're going in soon." Davis turned back to the other men. "Okay, three teams. I want to be in and out as fast as possible.

Hartford and Burns, with me. We'll get to that shed at the southeast corner and head straight north. Hopefully, we'll get lucky and find the package on the first try, where Jackson thinks he is. Sampson, you go with Jackson and Fernandez up the west side. Stone, Hayes, and Boyd, you head up the middle, but take it slow, and I mean *slow*. Don't get caught in the middle of the village, it's a death trap. Fall back and try the east or west side if the middle's too crowded."

The other men nodded their understanding and began to check their weapons. Abruptly, the rain started coming down even harder, nearly deafening on their Kevlar helmets. A spear of lightning briefly illuminated the dilapidated collection of huts a few hundred meters away, followed by a violent *crack* of thunder from the north.

Davis keyed his radio so that Ramirez could hear him as he spoke to the entire squad. "This is the final push, and with any luck, our last mission together. Kandahar will fall any day now. I'm going home next month, and I know some of you are done, too. I've had enough war for a lifetime. Keep your heads on straight and stay focused. We're professionals, and we're the best. Don't fuck it up. Let's not make any more widows or orphans today."

"Unless it's on their side," Hayes said with a grim smile, jerking a thumb in the direction of the Taliban stronghold.

"If necessary. But I want all of you to go home, and killing them makes that less likely, so fingers off the trigger if at all possible."

"That was beautiful. I think I'm tearing up a little," said Ramirez over the radio, his voice choked with exaggerated emotion.

"Shut the fuck up, Ramirez," Davis replied. "Let's move."

* * *

Just as Jackson had reported, two guards stood motionless outside the small house in the northeast corner of the village. Unless they moved or turned around, there would be no way to approach them from the side or back. A frontal assault, no matter how quick and quiet, was risky. Davis whispered into his radio.

"Jackson, did you ever see these guys leave their posts?"

"Never. They barely even look around. Real pros, at least by camel jockey standards."

"I've had one eye on them the whole time, too. Like fucking statues, these guys," Ramirez chimed in.

So much for zero body count.

Davis sighed, then turned to face Hartford and Burns. Using hand signals, he instructed both of them to engage the same guard on his command. He then told Ramirez to fire on the second guard once they engaged the first. Davis would stand by, ready to put more rounds on either target if one didn't go down right away.

"Ready?" he whispered. All three men replied that they were. "Go."

In perfect sync, Hartford and Burns swept around the corner, rifle barrels raised, moving forward at a forty-five-degree angle to give Davis room to stay to the left as he followed. Each man's M4 barked sharply as the experienced shooters opened up with short bursts of tightly controlled automatic fire. The suppressed shots echoed with dull *thuds* and flat *cracks*, louder than Davis would have preferred.

The guard on the right never stood a chance. Ten rounds of 5.56 impacted his chest, neck, and face faster than he could blink in surprise. A cloud of red mist ballooned behind him, quickly dissipating in the rain. He rocked on his heels for the briefest moment before falling backward, dead before he hit the ground.

Davis quickly aligned the glowing reticle of his reflex sight on the other guard's forehead, but before he could fire, the man went limp and collapsed, blood and bone fragments spraying from a golf ball-sized hole just above his left eye. A split second later, the muted *thump* of Ramirez's M24 reached Davis's ears, but just barely. He held his breath, hoping that he'd heard the shot only because he'd been listening for it.

All ten Rangers held their positions, waiting, listening for any sign that anyone had heard the gunfire. Alpha team kept their rifles trained on the house's front door and windows. Surely, someone inside had heard the shots. They were so close and so loud.

A full minute passed. No shouts or gunshots erupted from the house or elsewhere in the village. Cautiously, the Rangers relaxed.

"Hartford, Burns, on me," Davis said once the other two men had finished hiding the guards' bodies. "Let's get this over with."

The three men stacked up on the door to the house that hopefully contained the Taliban defector, the man they were here to rescue before his former allies tortured him to death. The windows were boarded up from the inside; there was no way to know what they were walking into. Hartford and Burns exchanged their magazines for fresh ones. Davis took a deep breath and let it out slowly. Few things were more nerve-racking than a blind entry.

He pressed his ear against the splintered wooden door. He heard nothing inside. Even if someone was moving around in there, he might not hear it over the driving rain.

Burns tapped Davis's shoulder lightly, letting him know that the other two men were ready. Ever so slowly, Davis turned the knob, willing it not to make noise. It turned freely. He could only hope that there wasn't another latch or lock on the inside of the door.

Once the latch was fully disengaged, he took one last deep breath, then rammed his left shoulder into the door, hard.

For the briefest instant, the rain-swollen wood stuck in the jamb, then the door broke free and swung inward. Davis swept into the room, rifle raised, his index finger holding four pounds of steady pressure on his rifle's five-pound trigger.

The adrenaline rushing through his body heightened his senses and seemed to slow time. His eyes scanned the room, taking in a scene that made little sense. There was no sign of the defector in the one-room house. Instead, two Taliban fighters, jolted awake by the door crashing open, were blinking sleep from their eyes and fumbling blindly for their weapons. A third man stood with his back to them, bent over a workbench against the far wall. In response to the noise, he began to turn, reaching for something on the workbench.

Davis let his training take over. He ignored the sleeping tangos to his left and right; Hartford and Burns would take them. Only he had a shot on the third man, straight ahead. He depressed the trigger as the target spun to face him. Several rounds struck the man in the chest, climbing up toward his neck as the M4's muzzle rose with the recoil. Blood peppered the wall to the sides and behind him. He opened his mouth to scream, but Davis heard nothing, not even the gunshots, deafening in the enclosed space. He was dimly aware of gunshots behind him as Hartford and Burns lit up the terrorists who hadn't yet brought their weapons to bear.

The man he'd shot began to fall forward. As his body continued to turn, Davis finally saw what he'd grabbed. Davis was a combat engineer—an expert in explosives, among other things. He instantly recognized the device clutched in the dying man's fingers: a homemade clacker used for remotely triggering bombs.

His eyes darted back to the workbench. As the man fell to his knees, Davis could see what was on it: a suicide vest wired with several bricks of plastic explosives, each primed with a detonator.

It was enough to level the house and all the ones around it.

The bomb maker wasn't dead yet. Fighting against the shock and pain of his wounds, he struggled to close his fingers around the clacker.

Davis closed the distance in the blink of an eye. He lunged forward into a kick, putting all his weight and momentum behind it. His aim was true; his heavy boot struck the man's wrist and sent the clacker flying. Reflexively, his eyes squeezed shut, waiting for the explosion. These homemade clackers rarely had safety mechanisms, so if it hit the wall or floor at the wrong angle, it could depress the lever enough to trigger the vest.

A heartbeat passed, then two more. Nothing happened. He opened his eyes to see the clacker lying motionless in the far corner.

Before the bomb maker could cause any more trouble, Davis fired two more rounds into his head, ending the threat. Idly, he noticed that the man was wearing headphones; he could faintly hear the music. That, plus the fact that the other two had been asleep, would explain why none of them had heard the shots outside.

Luck only got you so far. Then it got you killed.

"Clear," Burns said. Davis could barely hear him over the ringing in his ears, made worse by the audible rush of his own blood, driven by his hammering heart.

Somewhere to the southwest, angry shouts and staccato bursts of gunfire ripped through the steady drone of the rain. *And there's the luck that gets us killed,* Davis thought.

Ramirez's voice crackled over the radio. "God dammit. They definitely know we're here now."

Davis didn't respond. He was still trying to work it out. It didn't make any sense.

"Davis," Burns said in a low voice. "Time to go."

Comprehension flashed in the squad leader's eyes. "The defector was never here. Bad intel from minute one. This is just a street-level bomb shop. That's why security was so light—they weren't expecting company."

"Okay, great. Can we go now?" Hartford growled.

Davis removed his right glove and touched the upper receiver on his rifle to discharge any static electricity, then carefully pulled the detonators out of the plastic explosives and tossed them aside. "Yeah, let's."

"Boss, I think it's time to call the taxi," Hartford said. "Hajjis don't have eyes on us yet, but that's gonna change in the very near future."

"Do it." Davis keyed his radio as Hartford switched his to another channel to contact the helicopter waiting several klicks away. They'd planned to exfiltrate on foot, back to the south, but that plan had assumed they'd get in and out undetected. The chopper was plan B.

"Ramirez, start thinning the herd. Everyone else, move to our position, the chopper can land just north of here. Stay in Ramirez's lane as much as possible. No widows or orphans," Davis said, reloading his rifle and storing the partially spent magazine.

"Unless it's on their side," Stone said over the radio, finishing their unofficial squad motto.

* * *

"Boss, I hate to be the bearer of bad news, but I see three vehicles to the north. They're forced to go slow because of the terrain but they'll be here in a few minutes. I also see three tangos on foot thirty meters to the west, they know I'm here somewhere," Ramirez said, his voice garbled by radio static.

"Fuck," Hartford whispered.

"Agreed," Davis said, then keyed his radio. "Ramirez, can you move up to the house in the northeast corner of the village? Chopper's two minutes out."

Ramirez clicked his radio mic twice to indicate that he'd heard. That was a bad sign; it meant he didn't want to talk for fear of being overheard. As much as Davis wanted to rush to his best friend's aid, he resisted the temptation. They needed to hold this position until the whole squad arrived, then move north to the LZ as a team.

More bursts of AK-47 fire erupted nearby. For the moment, no rounds were coming directly toward Alpha team; the enemies seemed to be spraying and praying, hoping to get lucky. They did that a lot.

Davis swore. By his count, they'd killed at least twenty of these goatfuckers, maybe as many as thirty. How many were there? Before he could wonder, the distinctive *thump* of Ramirez's rifle sounded once, twice, three times, with hardly a pause in between. That, too, was a bad sign. If Ramirez was firing as quickly as he could work the bolt, it meant that enemies were dangerously close to him.

A violent blast of thunder rattled the sky, and the rain began to come down even harder, in sheets so thick that it was becoming difficult to see. Davis leaned out of cover just long enough to look west, down the narrow dirt path that passed for a street. After searching for a moment, he saw Ramirez behind a large rock about thirty meters away, reloading his rifle. Three Taliban were steadily advancing on his position from the south, peppering the rock with a constant barrage of bullets. Within moments, they'd pie the corner around the rock, and Ramirez would be cut down.

Davis, always outwardly cool and collected in battle, saw red. These terrorist fucks had already deprived the world of too many good people. Ramirez would not be added to that list.

Fighting to channel his fury without letting it displace his reason, Davis shifted his grip on his M4 slightly, moving his left hand forward to rest behind the trigger of the rifle's underslung M203 grenade launcher. The tangos were unaware of him, bunched tightly together, about thirty meters away, and at a slightly lower elevation.

In other words, the situation had 40mm grenade written all over it.

Davis stepped out of cover and flipped up the adjustable ladder sight on top of his rifle. He aimed carefully, exhaled, and firmly depressed the launcher's heavy trigger.

With a loud *chunk*, the grenade was away. Immediately after it left the barrel, Davis shifted back to his standard shooting grip, ready to spray the hostiles with 5.56 rounds if any survived.

It turned out to be a mostly unnecessary precaution. With a deafening concussion, the grenade detonated just a few paces in front of the group. The two in front were violently ripped apart and killed instantly; the one behind them only lost a leg and most of his abdomen. Red mist and black smoke blossomed outward, both quickly dissipating in the rain. The third terrorist was still clutching his rifle and struggling to aim it at Alpha team, despite being blown nearly in half. Davis put him down with a single, well-placed shot.

"Jesus Christ!" Ramirez shouted.

"You're welcome," Davis hollered back, moving to new cover, closer to his friend.

"You did it. You finally got to use your favorite toy in action," Burns joked in an effort to alleviate the tension.

"Hell yeah," Davis responded, sliding open the grenade launcher's breech to eject the empty casing before slamming a fresh round into place.

"Heard an explosion. You guys alright?" Hayes asked over the radio.

"It was Davis," Hartford responded.

"No shit? With the 203? Congrats, boss," Hayes chuckled.

Despite the air of forced mirth, none of the Rangers found killing the least bit funny—not even killing terrorist scum. It was merely a coping mechanism, a slightly more palatable alternative to raw terror. They weren't out of the woods yet, and all of them knew it. Any of them could catch a stray bullet at any moment—especially if Hajji reinforcements arrived before the chopper did.

Ramirez was about to move toward Davis when a fresh burst of gunfire erupted from the south, raking the rock that had already been mercilessly jackhammered by lead.

"Fucking hell, don't they ever quit?" Ramirez griped, hunkering down again. "I still can't move."

"Hartford and Burns, move to the yellow house and draw fire away from Ramirez. I'll leapfrog around to the south and hit them from behind, then we get out of here. Bravo, Charlie, ETA," Davis barked into his radio.

"Two minutes," came the reply. To the north, a low rumbling sound became audible and gradually grew louder, signaling the Blackhawk helicopter's imminent arrival.

"Make it one," Davis said. He turned, ready to move south and flank the incoming enemies.

He stopped dead in his tracks at what he saw. It took a moment for his mind to process it. North of Hartford's new position, crouched under a rickety wooden table, visible only to Davis and Ramirez, was a scrawny, shirtless boy, clutching a ragged stuffed animal and bawling his eyes out. He couldn't have been older than seven or eight.

"Davis, come on. Get the lead out," Burns yelled, noticing that his squad leader hadn't moved.

"There's a fucking kid," Ramirez called back.

"What?"

"A kid. Right there in the open. Jesus Christ, he's gonna get shot any second."

Davis steeled himself. Instinct told him to go to his friend. "Ramirez, I'm coming to cover you."

"I'm fine. Get the kid," Ramirez shouted over the storm. Only Davis heard him; the others were engaging the enemy.

Davis's heart suddenly slowed. In comparison to how fast it had been hammering before, it felt like it had stopped.

The raindrops seemed to fall so slowly that he could count them. His ears rang with a persistent, low hum from all the gunfire. His teammates' voices faded from his awareness. The only voice he could hear was the boy's, clear as day.

It was the most agonizingly heart-wrenching cry he'd ever heard.

With a final glance toward his best friend, Davis darted out of cover and ran for the boy.

* * *

Tom jerked so violently that he nearly fell out of bed. He sat up, panting, and threw off the covers. The sheets were so drenched with cold sweat that, for a moment, his sleep-addled mind distantly wondered if he'd come down with a fever. From the foot of the bed, his golden retriever, Riley, stared up at him with a deeply concerned expression.

Gradually, his breathing slowed, and his senses came more sharply into focus. He felt his forehead. It was damp but cool. There was no fever.

Just fear.

The clock radio cast a dim orange glow onto the polished mahogany nightstand. The display read 3:12 a.m. His mind automatically put a zero in front of the three, converting it to military time.

The silence of the house was frighteningly complete. Sometimes, he could hear the faint hum of the refrigerator's compressor in the kitchen, but at the moment it wasn't running. The grandfather clock in the foyer wasn't ticking because he hadn't wound it recently. He cleared his throat, just to confirm that he could still hear. The endless barrage of gunfire, so loud twenty years ago, echoed faintly across time, bringing his chronic, low-level tinnitus to the front of his awareness.

Unable to stand the silence any longer, he rose to his feet, wobbling unsteadily for a moment. He padded to the kitchen, only dimly aware of where he was going. Automatically, his right hand found the liquor cabinet in the darkness, opened it, reached inside, withdrew the half-empty bottle of whiskey. His left hand found a glass, and only then did he realize that it would be hard to pour a drink in the darkness.

Fuck it.

He put the glass back, opened the bottle, and drained it. He managed to get most of it in his mouth. As the liquor coated his stomach, its warmth slowly began to radiate outward, into his limbs. Only then did he switch on the light above the stove, banishing the darkness in a small radius. He set the now-empty whiskey bottle on the counter. The glass clinked quietly against the polished granite.

Tom stared straight ahead at the sliding glass patio door, into the night. Several long minutes passed. His eyes kept trying to look to his left. He wouldn't let them. Doggedly, he continued to stare straight ahead, locked in a battle of wills with himself.

Finally, he could stand it no longer. He turned his head to the left, where a framed photo hung on the wall opposite the liquor cabinet. A goofy-looking, nineteen-year-old Ramirez wearing a North High Spartans T-shirt grinned back at him. Beside Ramirez in the photo, Tom sported a woman's bikini top and maintained a severely serious expression, one arm around his friend's shoulders.

The brass plaque below the photo read "Manuel Ramirez, beloved son, brother, and friend. 1975–2001."

Tom sat down on his kitchen floor and began to cry.

CHAPTER FOUR
Demons

December 24, 2021

Alex Warner yawned and clicked her pen rhythmically, every second, like a metronome. When that failed to produce meaningful results after a few minutes, she went back to chewing on it.

Another five minutes went by, and still, the pen stubbornly refused to write. The patient disposition form in front of her remained mockingly blank. She had to write something eventually, but whatever she wrote would irreversibly alter the patient's future.

Court-ordered drug treatment cases were her least favorite. Patients who came to her only when forced to usually weren't interested in overcoming their addictions. In most cases, earning their trust and respect was nearly impossible. And when her staff suffered injuries or abuse on the job, it was usually at the hands of the "mandies," as they called such patients—short for "mandatories."

Alex hurled her chewed-up pen across the room and reprimanded herself for having such selfish thoughts. Mandies weren't easy to work with, but of all her patients, they needed her the most. An addict who found themselves on the business end of a judge's gavel, by that very fact, needed the most help. Clearly, previous interventions hadn't worked.

You didn't become a rehab doc because it's easy, she thought. *Get your shit together and help this person.*

Properly chagrined, she sheepishly went to retrieve her pen. She returned to her computer desk and logged back into the electronic health record system, then pulled up the chart she was looking for.

Dan Reiser, thirty-four. Alex clicked past the demographics page and found the section of his chart that detailed his criminal history. She'd already read the entire file several times, but clearly, she needed to read it again.

Driving while intoxicated, two counts. Child endangerment, one count, for having his son in the car on one of those occasions. Breaking and entering, two counts. Assault, one count. Petty theft, three counts. And of course, the whole laundry list of possession charges. Alcohol and meth seemed to be his poisons of choice.

Never mix uppers and downers, Alex thought with a snicker, and then she grimaced. *That's not funny.*

She clicked over to the medical history section. Dan had never voluntarily sought treatment, but he'd been involuntarily committed to inpatient treatment facilities three times. He'd completed all three programs, if one were to use "completed" in the loosest possible sense.

She noted that the treatment programs to which he'd previously been committed all used a particular twelve-step methodology that had been popular for many decades. Such programs did help some people, but they were largely ineffective, in part because they denied the patient's agency, which also absolved him of responsibility. You couldn't be helpless to stop using and be held accountable for your misdeeds while using; it was one or the other.

And so, Alex again reached the same brick wall she'd been running into all night. The treatment protocol she'd been developing for years was different. It was a brand-new approach to drug treatment; she only had a few years of data, but the early results were promising.

Dan had been under her care for a month, and it was time to submit her recommendation to the court. If she said he was making progress, he would remain out of prison—on parole, of course. If she reported that he was making no progress or actively resisting treatment, it would constitute a parole violation, and he would go back to prison. Probably for a very long time, with his record.

Alex left her desk and moved to the couch, finally kicking off her shoes. Briefly, she thought that it might be a bad idea to sit down. She was exhausted and didn't want to risk falling asleep just yet.

On second thought, there was little chance of that. No matter how tired she was, fear of the nightmares would keep her awake for a while yet.

She clicked her pen once more, then finally started to write with it. On a scrap of notebook paper, she drew two columns. On the left, she began to list reasons to send Dan back to prison.

For one thing, he'd made little meaningful progress in the time he'd been under her care. For another thing, she just didn't like him. She paused, tapping the pen to her lower lip. Why didn't she like him? Was it personal or professional? After a moment, she decided it was both. He'd assaulted her nurses on two occasions. Neither was egregious—mostly shoving and halfhearted kicking—but assault was assault. He'd stolen things from other patients, and sometimes, he was rather belligerent during counseling sessions.

Alex shifted her pen to the right-hand column and began listing reasons to recommend continued treatment. Not often, but occasionally, Dan seemed to have moments of lucidity wherein he expressed genuine regret for the harm he'd done to others. He *could* be rehabilitated.

Maybe.

She wrote "rehabilitation possible," then moved down a line, wrote a number "2," and, unable to think of anything else, wrote the other reason to keep him: "Treatment takes time; Dan needs more exposure to the program."

She laid down the pen. That was horse shit, and she knew it. It wasn't entirely horse shit, but it was more than 50 percent horse shit.

She had a third reason for wanting to keep Dan out of jail, but she couldn't write it down because, medically, it was 100 percent horse shit.

He needed her.

Everyone else had already given up on him, written him off as a lost cause. But even the worst addicts could change. She'd seen it before. It didn't happen often, but when it did, it was the most wonderful thing to behold. It always seemed to happen when she was at her wit's end, driven into the ground by yet another failure, ready to throw in the towel and become a veterinarian.

How much more schooling would I need? I already know people medicine. Cats and dogs are still mammals. Can't be that different.

She'd never said it aloud, but she lived for those rare redemption stories. Losing patients never got easier, whether she lost them to death or the criminal justice system, but her occasional victories almost made all the tears and sleepless nights worth it.

Almost.

Sighing, she stood up and dropped her note paper on the desk, next to the patient disposition form. She glanced at the clock on the stove; it was 10:15. Not as late as she'd feared, but she needed to get to bed soon. She desperately needed sleep—peaceful, restful sleep.

She made herself a promise. One hot bath, one glass of wine, and then she'd make a decision about Dan before bedtime. She couldn't have this hanging over her head at work tomorrow; she had other patients to help.

On her way to the bathroom, she switched on the sound system. Light, airy jazz floated from speakers installed all around the condo. After a moment's consideration, she switched it to nature sounds—a tranquil beach would do for tonight.

In the bathroom, her heart lifted at the sight of the large garden tub, probably her favorite material possession.

God, that's such a typical thing for a single woman in her forties to think. You even have scented candles and an old wine glass in here. Get a couple of cats, and the stereotype will be complete.

She frowned at the out-of-character cynical thought that seemingly had come out of nowhere. She was just tired and venting her work-related frustration at herself. A bath would help.

Hopefully, the bad dreams wouldn't come tonight. For the past week, she'd been haunted by horribly vivid nightmares, more real and terrifying than any she'd ever had. It was getting to the point where she was reluctant to go to bed.

It was probably just stress related to her indecision about Dan. Once she cleared that up, her brain should let her sleep peacefully.

She sat on the edge of the tub and opened the faucet, adjusting the temperature. Once it began to warm up, she brought the wine glass back to the kitchen and refilled it. She double-checked that the front door was locked, then set about packing a lunch for the next day. It was tuna salad, an apple, and yogurt for the third day in a row. She had nothing else in the fridge.

By the time Alex returned to the bathroom, the tub was full. She undressed, threw her clothes vaguely in the direction of the hamper, set her wine on the windowsill beside the tub, and slipped into the water.

Immediately, the hot water began to calm her. She lay back, resting her head on the edge of the tub. Remembering that her hair was still in a businesslike bun, she pulled the bobby pins free and tossed them onto the counter.

For a time, she closed her eyes and just marinated. The original plan was to mull over the Dan situation in the tub, but as the warmth seeped into her tired bones, the prospect of thinking about work rapidly lost its appeal.

Finally, she decided not to fight it. She did her best to clear her mind and simply spend a few minutes relaxing.

Within moments, she'd fallen asleep.

* * *

Alex woke up in her bed.

Strange, she thought.

She blinked sleep from her eyes and tried to focus on the ceiling above her. For some reason, everything was blurry.

She'd just drifted off in the tub for a few minutes. How had she gotten to her bed?

As consciousness returned, she realized several things in quick succession.

One, her back hurt. So did her knees, elbows, and fingers.

Two, no matter how much she rubbed sleep from her eyes, she still couldn't see very well.

Three, the bed she was lying in was not hers.

She threw her legs over the side of the bed and made to stand up, but a sharp pain flared in her hips in response to the sudden movement. She hissed and gritted her teeth, moving more slowly. She looked down at her legs and saw that she was wearing a faded, floral-print nightgown.

She didn't own anything like that.

Alex felt her heart begin to pound. What was happening? She still couldn't see. A small desk lamp on an antique nightstand to her left was on, filling the room with soft orange light, but everything had a hazy quality, as though she were looking through warped, dirty glass. Once again, she made to rub her eyes, stopping when she saw her hands.

The skin was loose, wrinkled, pale, and dotted with age spots. A dull ache throbbed in her knuckles when she flexed her fingers.

"What the hell is going on?" she said aloud, a note of panic rising in her voice.

Only the voice wasn't hers, either. It was quiet, airy, and raspy.

She could see well enough to tell that she wasn't in her bedroom. She lurched to her feet and stumbled to a nearby makeup table, leaning toward the affixed mirror. She nearly had to press her nose to it to see her reflection.

The aged face staring back at her wasn't hers—but she did recognize it.

"Dear god," she whispered.

Somewhere outside the room, something *thumped* loudly. She took a step backward, reflexively reaching for the makeup table to steady herself. Her left hand brushed against something plastic—a pair of glasses. Desperate to see, she snatched them up and fumbled around for a moment, finally managing to put them on. Her vision was still a little blurry, but for the most part, she could see again.

Another *thump* from the next room, followed by a scraping sound. Alex swallowed, suddenly aware that her mouth was painfully dry. Almost unconsciously, as though spellbound, she found herself taking a step toward the door, then another. Her frail, unfamiliar hand reached out, grasping for the polished brass doorknob. It turned easily. Almost against her will, as though someone else were controlling her body—"her" body —she pulled the door open a few inches.

The orange light from the desk lamp spilled a few feet into the hallway, then vanished, choked off by the darkness outside. She listened, trying to tune out her galloping heartbeat. She heard nothing else except for a clock somewhere outside the room, *tick, tick, ticking* away.

She knew what waited out there, in the night. She didn't want to see it, didn't want it to see her. And yet, her feet moved forward anyway, shuffling slowly along carpet that was long overdue to be replaced.

She stopped just outside the bedroom door. A few paces to her left, a staircase descended to a landing, turned ninety degrees, and continued to the ground floor.

It seemed dangerous, the stairs being so close to a door. Someone could hurt themselves.

To her right, the clock continued its rhythmic ticking, somewhere out of view. Somehow, the sound intensified the silence. The stillness and quietness of the house pressed in around her like a physical weight.

A sudden chill washed over her, eliciting a violent shiver. A heartbeat later, a shadow leaped at her from out of the darkness. She flinched hard and tried to scream, but the sound caught in her throat. The shadow slammed into her—no, not exactly, it rushed past her, knocking her off balance as it went.

Her arms pinwheeled, and before she knew it, she was falling backward. It was all happening too fast. Her aged mind and body couldn't keep up. She flailed her arms wildly, trying to catch something and arrest her fall.

Her fingers caught only air. A sharp crack of white-hot pain lanced through her shoulder blades as she toppled over and struck the balusters. She kept falling, waves of pain ripping through her neck, hips, and stomach with each impact. Over and over she tumbled, helpless to stop it.

The back of her head struck the landing with tremendous force. For the briefest fraction of a second, molten agony exploded at the base of her skull.

Then she felt nothing.

* * *

Alex thrashed violently in the tub, splashing water everywhere. Her forehead slammed against the tile backsplash. Her vision dimmed. She saw stars as nausea bloomed in her stomach, each wave more intense than the last. She clutched her head, fighting to remain conscious.

Unable to hold it down, she leaned over the edge of the tub and vomited, retching until her throat burned from the stomach acid. Distantly, she wondered if it was the nightmare or the head trauma. Probably both.

The water in the tub sloshed back and forth, gradually calming. Alex forced herself to remain still and control her breathing, resting her injured head against the cool porcelain, waiting for the pain and nausea to fade. Slowly, they did. She blinked sweat and blood out of her eyes.

Blood? She touched her forehead gingerly, and her fingers came away red. *Fantastic*, she thought.

Carefully, she hauled herself out of the tub, electing to sit on the edge rather than stand up. The last thing she needed was to slip in her own puke and crack her head again. Wouldn't that be a fun sight for the paramedics when they discovered her body the next day? She snatched a towel and pressed it to her head.

Once the bleeding slowed, she carefully stood up and retrieved a first aid kit from the medicine cabinet. She'd stocked it with a few extra items, including a suture kit. Stitching her own forehead in the mirror would be awkward, so she instead ripped open a pack of adhesive wound closure strips. She used a wad of toilet paper to blot away the rest of the blood, then examined the wound.

It looked bad but not horrible. It definitely needed to be closed or it would leave a nasty scar. She pulled a bottle of isopropyl alcohol from the cabinet and splashed some into the wound, screaming as quietly as she could so as not to worry her neighbors. Once that small slice of hell had passed, she stretched the skin taut and applied two strips, pressing firmly to ensure they wouldn't come loose. Lastly, she dabbed a thin layer of antibiotic ointment over the injured tissue.

Well, that was fun.

She took a minute to examine the face in the mirror, taking comfort in its familiarity. Her father had been Persian; her mother, Greek. She had always liked her dark eyes, olive skin, and long, thick hair.

Tonight, she was just grateful to see her own face again, rather than the one that had been haunting her dreams all week.

Alex opened the tub drain and rubbed her arms, shivering. She'd been out of the hot water too long. She hurried into her closet and put on some sweatpants and a light sweater, savoring the warmth.

Slowly starting to feel more like herself, she returned to the bathroom armed with bleach and paper towels to clean up the barf. That done, she brushed her teeth to banish the taste of it.

Oddly, she felt better and more focused, despite the total chaos of the preceding ten minutes. Her gaze slid over to the untouched glass of red wine on the windowsill, which suddenly looked wholly unappealing. She brought it to the kitchen, dumped it out, and put on a kettle for tea instead.

Her cell phone rang. It was past 11:00 now; only one person would be calling her this late. She fished the phone out of her purse and answered it.

"Hey, Gina." Gina Patterson was the clinical director of a treatment center in Portland, two hours away. They'd met during a conference nearly a decade ago and had become close friends in the intervening years.

"Merry Christmas," Gina said.

Alex forced a note of cheeriness into her voice. "You, too."

"I'm just calling to check on you. I have a feeling you're still hung up on that court thing."

"Yeah, I was just about to wrap that up."

"Are you okay? You sound… different."

"It's nothing. I fell asleep in the tub and whacked my head pretty good, that's all. I'm fine."

"Ouch. You sure?"

"Yes, it's alright."

"So, what are you going to do about Dan?"

In that instant, Alex knew exactly what to do. It was so obvious now that her prior indecision seemed unexplainable. "He needs more time."

"Alex…." Gina's voice trailed off, as though she wanted to say more.

"What?"

"Are you sure about this? I know, he's your patient, not mine. But based on what you've told me, he doesn't seem responsive to treatment."

"You're right. He's my patient, not yours," Alex snapped. A long silence stretched between them. She sighed apologetically. "I'm sorry. That was mean."

"You're under a lot of stress. It's okay. I just want to make sure you're being objective about this."

"I can fix him." As soon as the word "fix" was out of her mouth, Alex faltered, as though she could snatch it back before Gina heard it. Doctors didn't "fix" their patients, especially not in rehab.

Gina pretended not to notice. "If anyone can help him, you can."

Alex felt her shoulders relax, only then realizing that she'd been tensing them. She'd known Gina long enough to know that the other woman wasn't just blowing smoke; she really did believe in Alex. "I appreciate you checking up on me. I need to get some sleep. Can I ask a favor?"

"Of course."

"Would you mind… writing me some eszopiclone? Just one or two pills, enough for tonight and maybe tomorrow."

There was another long pause. "Are you sure?" They were both doctors. Gina didn't need to say, "Those are some serious sleeping pills with a high risk of dependency, especially for people with a history like yours."

"Please," Alex said, softly.

"Alright, but just for tonight. Let's find some time to get together after Christmas." Again, there was an unspoken second meaning in Gina's words: *I'm really starting to worry about you.*

"Yes, I'd love to see you soon. There's a twenty-four-hour pharmacy just down the street from my place, Quik-Script."

"I'll look up the number and call it in now."

"Thank you. I'll give you a call on Sunday, and we'll figure out a plan, I can probably come down to Portland for a day or two next week."

"Sounds good. Sleep well."

Alex ended the call and set the phone face-down on the counter. The kettle began to whistle. She turned off the burner and poured herself a cup of chamomile tea.

Hopefully, eszopiclone would knock her out hard enough to ward off any dreams. She just needed one night of restful sleep. After that, everything would be okay.

She sipped at her tea for a few minutes before picking up her car keys to head to the pharmacy. On her way out the door, she paused at her desk, picked up a pen, and checked the box on the disposition form labeled "Provider recommends parole with continued treatment."

CHAPTER FIVE
Incubation

December 25, 2021
Day One

Sara, awkwardly carrying three cups of coffee, extended one pinkie and carefully typed in the access code. The red light turned green, the keypad beeped, and the automatic door to New Horizons Recovery Center slid open quietly. She blinked rapidly as she stepped from the dark parking lot into the brightly-lit hallway, not yet fully awake.

Not that the little sleep she'd gotten had done her much good.

Faint sounds of activity drifted from the hallways to either side as she headed toward Dr. Warner's office near the center of the building. It sounded like the nurses were just rousing the patients and starting to hand out morning meds.

A side entrance door opened ahead of her and Dylan came stumbling in, brushing snow off the shoulders of his jacket. God, he looked awful. His skin was unusually pale, his eyes were half closed and bloodshot, and the bags under them were dark purple. Despite his zombielike appearance, she couldn't help but smile when she saw him. When he noticed her, he returned the smile in kind and fell in to walk beside her.

"Is one of those for me?" he asked.

"Middle one. More sugar than coffee, just like you asked," she said, stifling a yawn.

He took the indicated cup and sipped the hot liquid carefully. "Thanks."

"Go home and spend time with your dad," she said. "It's Christmas."

He shrugged. "He's in his usual trance, he doesn't have time for me. The only thing to do at home is work on my battery project, but I don't think I'd get anything done. It's really hard to focus."

"Still with the bad dreams?" Sara asked. She already knew the answer.

He nodded but said nothing.

The two teens arrived at the office. The nameplate next to the door read "Alex Warner, M.D., Clinical Director." Bangor was a small city, and New Horizons was a small clinic with a tight budget; Alex had to wear multiple hats.

Dylan held the door open for Sara. Like the rest of the building, the office was warmly decorated, more reminiscent of a living room than a medical facility. Dr. Warner had a thing for butterflies, evidenced by a few paintings, sculptures, and toys. The carpet was a soft charcoal color, and the sofa was light blue—a calming, reassuring color. Three diplomas hung on the wall in polished ebony frames: Alex's biology and psychology degrees, and her MD. Holiday decor occupied every inch of available wall or table space, from streamers of tinsel to miniature Christmas trees in pots, complete with tiny ornaments.

Alex spun around on her swivel chair and smiled at the new arrivals. She, too, looked exhausted to the point of near collapse. "Good morning." Her smile inverted into a frown. "Wait, why are you guys here on Christmas?"

"Today's the only day Mr. Davis can show me around the dam," Dylan said. "He said we had to go when no one else was there. It's too busy and dangerous when the normal construction work is going on."

"Dr. Warner, what happened to your head? Are you okay?" Sara said.

Alex reflexively touched the fresh cut on her forehead. "Oh, it's nothing. Bumped it last night, is all. It'll be fine." Her forced smile faltered when Sara and Dylan both took sips of coffee. "You two don't normally drink coffee, do you? Aren't you a little young?"

Sara huffed. "We don't normally need it. And I'm seventeen, basically an adult."

"I'm almost seventeen," Dylan said, quieter but no less defensive.

Alex took the latte that Sara offered her. "Sorry, I know you're not kids anymore. I guess I'm just old-fashioned." She paused, eyeing Sara suspiciously. "I don't usually drink coffee, either. What made you think I'd want some today?"

Sara shrugged. "Seems like everyone is super tired lately."

Alex said nothing, studying their faces carefully. They looked much like her own: terrible. She opened her mouth, then closed it again, debating whether to say it. Finally, she did.

"Nightmares?" Sara and Dylan both nodded. Alex shook her head in puzzlement. "Me, too," she confessed.

The three of them were spared an awkward silence when the door opened to reveal Christine, one of the senior nurses. She stopped halfway into the office as though surprised to find it occupied.

"Dr. Warner, oh, uh, sorry. I guess I assumed you wouldn't be here today."

Alex grunted. "I have some things to wrap up, my holiday break doesn't start until tomorrow. Do you need something?"

"I was just going to grab the secure storage room keys from your safe."

Alex extended a hand toward the safe. "Be my guest." She turned back to Sara and Dylan while Christine got what she needed. "Are you guys sure I can't convince you to go home and spend time with your families?"

"I know there's still a giant pile of referrals and reports that need to be faxed or filed, and I know that you'll lose your mind if it's still there when your break starts. I can take care of it for you, since you refuse to hire more help," Sara said.

"I just don't really want to be home today. I have to meet Mr. Davis here around lunchtime, anyway. I'll help Sara until then," Dylan added.

Alex sighed. "I would love to have one or two more people to help with the office work, but we just can't afford to hire anyone else right now. I really appreciate your help in the meantime." She smiled, grateful for Sara's selfless aid—and feeling a little guilty for accepting it.

Alex noticed Christine hovering off to the side and turned toward her. "What's up?"

The nurse shifted uncomfortably. "Can we talk in private for a second?"

Alex's eyes darted apologetically to Dylan and Sara. They let themselves out.

"It's... about Dan," Christine said.

Alex's heart skipped a beat. "What did he do now?"

Christine held up both hands to implore patience. "No, it's nothing like that. As soon as I saw you, I could tell nobody had told you yet."

This time, Alex's heart sank. "Told me what?"

"Late last night, he escaped. Sucker punched a security guard and ran out the door behind the laundry guy." Alex shot to her feet, panic creasing her features. Christine rushed to get the rest of the words out. "Dr. Warner, I'm sorry, he... he's dead. He somehow got ahold of more meth right after he left, and he overdosed. Cardiac arrest. He was pronounced DOA at the hospital."

Alex sank back into her chair. Her mind was blank. She couldn't think of anything to say. Part of her wanted to be angry, but even in her fog of stunned grief, she knew that wasn't right. New Horizons was a treatment center, not a prison. They had security guards and locked doors, but a patient who was really determined to leave would find a way. She certainly wouldn't want any of her staff endangering themselves trying to stop an escaping patient.

She must have sat in numb silence for longer than she realized because she was suddenly aware of Christine gently shaking her shoulder. "Dr. Warner? Are you okay?"

"Oh, yes, thank you for telling me."

"Please don't be mad. We all agreed that you needed rest and shouldn't be rushing down here in the middle of the night. We called the police right away. There's nothing more you could have done. Once a mandie leaves the building, it's out of our hands, you know that."

"Yes, I know. You're right."

"We're all worried about you. You've been pushing yourself too hard, and...." Christine hesitated, unsure of how brutally honest Alex would allow her to be. She decided to test the boundaries. "You're taking too much personal responsibility for your patients. You're a great doctor, and we all love working with you, but you can't save everyone. No one can."

Alex said nothing. Christine's voice sounded far away and muted, as if she were underwater. Emboldened, Christine knelt in front of Alex and went on.

"Why don't you head home and start your break early? Everyone else is here today, nobody's out sick. We've got it covered."

Finally, Alex met the other woman's eyes. "I have a few urgent things to finish, and I'll need to review the incident report about Dan. I'll make you a deal, half a day. I'll head home after lunch."

Christine nodded and smiled, relieved. Clearly, she'd been expecting Alex to put up more of a fight. "Deal." She stood up, patting Alex's leg reassuringly.

As soon as the nurse left the room, Alex buried her face in her hands, sobbing freely. "I'm sorry," she whispered.

* * *

Alex's tuna salad sat in a Tupperware container on her desk, untouched. She spun lazily around in circles on her chair, staring at the ceiling, trying to decide if she had any unfinished tasks that couldn't wait a week or so.

Someone knocked softly on the door. "Come in," she called.

Tom Davis stepped in, quietly shutting the door behind himself. "Hey, Dr. Warner," he said. When he saw her face, his voice faltered just the tiniest bit. Alex couldn't blame him; she probably looked like a reanimated corpse.

"Hey, Tom, good to see you. But if I have to ask you one more time to call me Alex, I may have to strangle you." She smiled just in case he thought she was serious.

He nodded, scratching his beard. "Right, sorry. Old military habit, you know, calling everybody by their last names. Merry Christmas, by the way." He sat on one of the couches and leaned back, stretching.

"You, too," she said. "It's very nice of you to show Dylan around the dam today." Alex watched him closely. Like her, Dylan, and Sara, he looked as though he hadn't had a good night's rest in weeks. His closely cropped hair, short beard, and clothes were meticulous, as always, but there was little he could do to hide the bloodshot eyes and heavy lids.

He shrugged. "I don't have anyone waiting at home except my dog, and he doesn't care what day it is. Are the kids around here somewhere?" he asked.

"Kids? Haven't seen any kids. If you mean the young adults who have strong feelings about being called 'kids,' they should be here in a few minutes. They're just finishing up."

He laughed, shaking his head. "I have a niece who's the same way, she must be about that age now. Accidentally called her a kid two Thanksgivings ago, and she didn't speak to me for the rest of the day."

Alex picked up a pen and clicked it a few times. "I don't think you've mentioned family before. Do you see them often?" When he didn't answer right away, she added, "Just curious, not asking as a psychiatrist."

"Not often, no. I have one brother, he has a wife and two kids. He lives on the other side of the country, so we usually only get together around the holidays. I won't see them this year, they're in France for a few weeks."

He met her eyes and held her gaze for a long moment. He looked like he wanted to say something else but wasn't sure if doing so might break some unspoken rule. She tried to keep her face friendly and inviting. "Something on your mind?" she asked.

Tom crossed his arms and leaned back against the sofa, away from her. She noted the defensive body language that suggested he was uncomfortable with whatever he was about to say. "Doc—Alex—I don't know that I'd presume to say we're friends, but we're friendly acquaintances, right?"

She shrugged. "Sure." She and Tom both had longstanding relationships with Ethan Holcomb and crossed paths regularly.

"Can I ask you a medical question? Unofficially?"

She nodded and put down the pen. "I won't even take any notes." She was pretty sure she knew what he was going to ask.

"What would you recommend for nightmares? I don't mean the regular nightmares that we all have once in a while." His voice dropped in both pitch and volume. "I mean nightmares so bad you never want to sleep again."

She took a deep breath and employed a risky tactic. "Would it make you feel better or worse to know that you're not the only one?"

He didn't look surprised at the question. She'd seen her face in the mirror a few hours ago; her insomnia was as obvious as his. "Both, I suppose," he said carefully.

"You're not my patient, so I can't give you medical advice, but I'm happy to share some basic info."

He shrugged. "Anything helps."

"Usually, if nightmares are really bad and persist for more than a night or two, it's an indication of unresolved psychological trauma."

"Usually?"

"Hmm?"

"You said 'usually,' meaning, not always. What else could it be?"

Alex leaned back in her chair, chewing her lower lip thoughtfully. "Less commonly, alcohol, drugs, certain medical conditions. Sometimes, the brain just does weird things, and there may not be an obvious explanation. I know that doctors are supposed to have all the answers, but psychology and oneirology—the study of sleep and dreams—are both fairly new fields, only a few generations old. There's still a lot we don't know about how the brain works during sleep."

"Let's say those have all been ruled out."

Alex didn't answer right away. The conversation was beginning to drift toward the blurry line separating casual questions from a privileged doctor-patient relationship.

She knew that Tom had been an Army Ranger, that he'd fought in the early days of the war in Afghanistan. He'd never shared details, but he didn't need to. It seemed pretty safe to assume that he'd seen and done things that would give anyone nightmares.

Finally, Alex decided it was safe to explore a little further. She could always hit the brakes if it became clearly necessary. "You don't drink?" she asked. She'd seen him drink liquor on a number of occasions.

His candor surprised her. "I do. Definitely more than I should, but I'm not an alcoholic. The war broke things in me, I don't deny it, but I dealt with that a long time ago. As much as anyone can deal with it, anyway. So, it wouldn't seem to make sense that any of that could suddenly start causing these god-awful nightmares after everything's been mostly fine for fifteen years."

Alex was surprised to find herself at a loss for words. *Maybe this is getting too personal,* she thought. She, Sara, Dylan, and Tom all seemed to be having the same inexplicable problem. His words made her consider her own situation for a moment. The more she thought about it, the more convinced she became that her distress over Dan wouldn't cause nightmares as horrible as the ones she'd been having. Dan was far from the first patient she'd agonized over—or lost—but she'd never before felt like she was living through a horror movie.

"I'm sorry you're going through this. It sounds awful," she finally said. "I think the best thing to do would be to talk to a professional—someone other than me—who can do a deep dive with you." Tom nodded slowly, his eyes unfocused, as though he were thinking about something else. She went on. "I have a colleague in Bridgton I'd be happy to refer you to if you'd like. He specializes in PTSD—not that I'm diagnosing you with PTSD, or with anything else, of course. I just mean that he works with a lot of vets. I think he might be a good place to start—online or over the phone, if you prefer. I know it's a long drive to get out there."

Finally, Tom looked up at her and forced a smile. "That would be great, thanks."

Alex rummaged around in her desk drawer, found one of her business cards, and began to write the other doctor's information on the back of it. She was glad he hadn't asked her for sleeping pills. There was no way she could do that, and it would have made their otherwise easygoing relationship slightly awkward.

Just after she handed him the business card, there was another knock on the door. Tom nodded to Alex, indicating that it was alright to answer.

"Come in," Alex called. Sara and Dylan entered. This time, they both had energy drinks from the vending machine down the hall. *They're going to give themselves heart attacks at this rate*, she thought.

"Hey, Mr. D—uh, Tom," Dylan said. Tom returned the greeting.

Alex smiled at the teens. "Thanks, guys, I'm sure the outbox is empty now."

Sara beamed. "No problem. Always happy to help."

Tom stood up, twirling his keys around one finger. "You guys ready to go?"

"I am," Dylan said. "Just let me use the bathroom first."

"I have one more thing to do, I'll meet you guys at the dam a little later. I drove myself today," Sara said.

"You're driving now? God help us," Tom said, clutching his chest in exaggerated panic.

Sara deftly hurled a tongue depressor at him. He dodged it and made a ridiculous face at her, chuckling to himself. Dylan laughed, Sara glared at him, and Alex rolled her eyes.

"Boys are stupid," Sara said to Alex.

"Yes, they are," Alex agreed.

* * *

Tom's truck hummed along the highway, leaving fresh tire tracks in the light blanket of snow covering the asphalt. The road was oddly empty. Tom remembered that it was Christmas day; most people were already on vacation.

Like I should be, he thought. He chided himself. Dylan was super excited about seeing the new hydroelectric power plant, and during a normal workday, it was far too busy. A day like today, when only a skeleton crew was present, was a perfect time to show him around.

Dylan had his elbow on the passenger door armrest, his chin resting in his hand, his bright blue eyes fixed on the dam in the distance. Tom hadn't spent much time around him, at least not when no one else was around. Dylan and Sara were practically joined at the hip, and because Tom regularly crossed paths with Sara's father at events hosted by the Chamber of Commerce or Rotary Club, Dylan often floated at the periphery of Tom's awareness.

The boy was noticeably quieter and shyer when Sara wasn't around. So far, they'd ridden the whole way in silence. Tom tried to strike up a conversation.

"So, you seem pretty interested in the new hydro plant."

Dylan turned to face him, clasping his hands together in his lap. A moment ago, he'd looked close to falling asleep, but at the mention of the power plant, he perked up. "Yeah, I really appreciate you showing me around. I'm sure there are some hoops to jump through to get whoever's in charge to sign off on a private tour for someone my age."

Tom chuckled. "I may not have filled out all the forms the bureaucrats want, but my company is building the plant, and I say it's alright. Just keep your hard hat on, stay close to me, and don't stick your hands in anything that moves."

Dylan fidgeted a bit, his smile slightly forced. "I think I can manage that."

"So, you want to go into construction?"

"Engineering, actually."

"Oh, yeah? What kind?"

"I want to double major in electrical and mechanical. There's a school in New Mexico that has a really cool double major program, they even have a job placement program to help you find jobs that use both skills once you graduate."

Tom nodded. "Now I see why you're interested in the plant. It is an engineering marvel, that's for sure."

"Yeah."

Both of them fell silent for a while. The only sounds were the truck's heater and the gentle patter of snowflakes against the windshield. Tom wasn't a great conversationalist, but he did respect ability and enthusiasm.

Clearly, Dylan had some measure of both, but he seemed reluctant to talk about himself. It had always been clear to Tom that Dylan had some self-esteem issues. Whenever Sara was around, Dylan seemed at ease, but she was clearly the leader of their two-man squad. She was a real firebrand, a type-A personality with big plans and the brains to see them through. Yet she was also kind and respectful, even deferent to her elders. She seemed to have her whole life planned down to the last detail. She'd have no trouble getting into any college.

To Tom, Dylan seemed to orbit Sara, content to be pulled along by the gravity of her relentless ambition. She blazed the trail; he followed once the path was clear.

Tom rarely gave conscious thought to Dylan and Sara when they weren't physically nearby, but as he thought about them now, he began to wonder about Dylan's home life. His father, Richard, wasn't exactly a shut-in, but Tom had only met him two or three times; he rarely left their apartment. Ethan Holcomb, Sara's father, had become something of a foster father to Dylan.

Richard's reclusiveness and Dylan's lack of confidence probably both had something to do with the unexplained disappearance of Dylan's mother. As far as Tom knew, the mystery had never been solved. Dylan clearly didn't like to talk about it, so Tom never asked, but he'd collected rare snippets of gossip over the years, here and there at various dinners and fundraisers. Tom had the sense that Richard was obsessed with finding his wife, so much so that he rarely did much parenting.

That's not fair, Tom thought. *I don't know all the facts; I shouldn't assume.*

Still, he doubted that Dylan had much in the way of male role models. Tom was exhausted and desperately in need of a weekend to himself, but if showing Dylan around the dam could bring him some joy and inspiration, then Tom's discomfort was a small price to pay. Tom mentally shook himself, warding off his mounting fatigue with sheer willpower. He'd be home in a few hours. For now, Dylan needed him.

Tom cleared his throat and tried to restart the conversation. "I think I remember from earlier this year, someone from your school won second place at the national science fair, I read about it in the paper. Something about a new way to build magnetic motors that gives them more torque. They had a picture of it, looked pretty cool."

Dylan scratched his head self-consciously. "Yeah, that was me."

"Really? No shit?" Tom genuinely hadn't known. He must have skimmed the article and not seen the winner's name. "You're pretty good, then. I couldn't build something like that. I mean, I could put the parts together if you gave me a schematic, but I wouldn't have the creativity to dream it up in the first place."

Again, Dylan put his hands between his knees and squeezed them together, looking nervous. "You were an engineer in the army, right?"

Dylan had kept the conversation about engineering but deftly redirected it so that he was no longer the subject. Tom noticed the tactic but played along with it. "Yeah, I was a combat engineer."

Dylan grinned like a Cheshire cat. "So, you blew up bridges and stuff?"

Some things were universal to all teen boys, apparently.

Tom hesitated briefly before answering. Now they were getting into things he wasn't particularly fond of talking about. "Sometimes, yes. But combat engineers do other things, too."

"Like what?"

"Well, we disarm explosives, to keep our friends and civilians safe. We're kind of a hybrid of mechanical and electrical specialists, like you want to be. We can also design and build infrastructure on a small scale, if the situation calls for it."

"That's really cool."

"So, if you want to be an engineer, why volunteer at a drug rehab place?" Tom asked casually.

Dylan blinked twice, taken aback by the question. "Well...." He frowned, searching for an answer.

Tom allowed himself a mischievous grin and made sure Dylan saw it. "Definitely not to be close to Sara."

Dylan's face instantly turned beet red. "No! Well, maybe, but so what? She's my friend."

Tom struggled not to laugh. He wasn't mocking Dylan, but he found his embarrassment endearing. "*Just* a friend?"

Dylan crossed his arms and huffed, turning his head to look back out the window. "Yes."

Tom eased up on the teasing. "Alright, I'll stop."

Dylan uncrossed his arms and turned back to face Tom. "It's fine, it's just... not like that." Tom nodded slowly, as though he were mulling over a profound revelation. "Besides, no girl would ever be interested in me."

Tom winced. "That's not true." Something about the way Dylan had said it struck Tom as more than typical teenage mopiness. He hoped he hadn't gone too far. For fear of making it worse, he said nothing else.

* * *

All seemed forgiven and forgotten by the time Tom turned onto the long gravel driveway leading to the dam a few minutes later. Dylan had rolled down the window and was leaning out of it like an excited puppy. Tom didn't especially want snowflakes melting all over the inside of his truck, but he let it slide. He felt like he owed Dylan a small debt for upsetting him earlier.

As soon as Tom parked at the bottom of the concrete stairs leading up to the power plant's main control room, Dylan hopped out. He had to have been freezing—he wore only a light jacket, and his nose and cheeks were cherry-red in the cold—but he didn't seem to notice.

"Here," Tom said, handing over a bright yellow hard hat he'd retrieved from the back seat. Dylan plopped it onto his head and tightened the band so it wouldn't fall off. Tom adjusted his own hard hat and led the way up the stairs. He unlocked the heavy steel door and held it open for Dylan, following and relocking it afterward.

They were alone in the control room. Tom put on his best tour guide voice. "Here in the control room, engineers and power distribution specialists at the Westbriar Hydroelectric Dam deliver power to more than fifty thousand residents in the town of Southampton, just a few miles downstream. Over time, as new turbines are built and the original turbines are optimized, the dam will eventually provide power to approximately ninety thousand people. This will make it the largest hydroelectric power plant in all of New England."

Dylan rolled his eyes at Tom's cheesy impression as he ran his hands over the unfinished control panels. The complexity and ingenuity of it were breathtaking. Thousands of switches and hundreds of status screens would eventually light up the room in every shade of red, green, white, and yellow. From outside, at night, it would look like an endless Christmas party. Dylan smiled at the thought.

He turned to face Tom. "What kind of operating system will it use? It would have to be Linux-based in some way, right?"

Tom held up both hands as if defending himself. "You'll have to ask the software guys about that. There are subcontractors crawling all over the place, but most of them are off today. We just do the walls, the catwalks, the power lines—stuff like that. We leave the specialized parts to experts in those fields."

Dylan supposed that made sense. He felt slightly dumb for asking. A frown darkened his face, but only for a moment. He grinned when, through the thick window behind Tom, he saw a row of enormous generators that would eventually be connected to the turbines. He darted across the room and tugged on the door leading down to that area, finding it locked.

"Open it," he whined, rattling the handle uselessly.

Tom found the right key, shaking his head. "You remind me of Riley."

Dylan made a face. "Who's Riley? Your kid? I didn't think you had kids."

"Riley is my golden retriever."

Dylan rolled his eyes again, then careened down the metal staircase once Tom had opened the door. "Slow!" Tom shouted after him. "If you break your neck, all the paperwork is really gonna ruin my holiday." Obediently, Dylan restrained himself, using the handrail to carefully descend the rest of the stairs.

"Who's there?" A familiar voice floated up from down below, somewhere behind one of the nearby generators. Had they been running, the concrete chamber would have been filled with the steady hum of powerful machinery, but for now, the metal giants stood still and silent. Dylan paused and looked up at Tom, seemingly unsure if he should answer.

"Teddy, it's me, and I've got Dylan with me," Tom called down as he descended the stairs.

"Who?" Teddy's voice came back.

"Dylan Masters, Sara Holcomb's friend."

"Oh, right. Yeah, I remember."

Teddy Jackson stepped out from behind the generator, dusting his hands on his jeans. Tom smiled at the sight of his old friend, now his construction manager. Except for a few new lines on his face and some hints of gray in his black hair, he looked just as he had twenty years ago in the Afghani desert.

"Nice to meet you, Dylan," Teddy said, extending his hand. Dylan shook it awkwardly. He'd warmed up to Tom—at least in the specific context of geeking out about engineering—but he was clearly uncomfortable around strangers.

Tom stepped in. "Dylan, I've known Teddy since my army days, we were in Afghanistan together."

"And some other places," Teddy added cryptically.

Dylan mulled this over for a moment. "I don't think I was born yet."

"You weren't, and thanks for pointing that out," Tom grunted. "You know, if you were to 'accidentally' fall into the reservoir, no one would ever find your body."

Dylan cackled. "Fair enough," he said. Tom felt like he'd won a small victory by learning something about his sense of humor.

"You guys were Rangers, right?" Dylan asked. Tom and Teddy both nodded. Dylan grinned. "Tell me a cool Ranger story."

At this, Teddy glanced sidelong at his old friend and boss. Tom's expression had darkened, and he'd crossed his arms, probably without even realizing it.

"Hey, Dylan," Teddy said. "Tom's got a few other things to check on around here before he heads home for the weekend, but he's too polite to say so. How about I show you around? I know this place better than he does, anyway."

Dylan looked at Tom, seemingly unaware that he'd raised an unwelcome topic. "Um, yeah, I guess that'd be okay."

Tom gave Teddy a single nod of thanks when Dylan wasn't looking. "I'll come back here in two hours, and then we'll head home."

Once Tom had disappeared around the corner, headed for another part of the dam, Teddy took a seat on the edge of the generator's concrete foundation. "Listen, Dylan, I know you didn't mean any harm, but you should know... Tom doesn't like to talk about those days. We saw a lot of stuff during the war—stuff no one should ever have to see." He waited, studying Dylan's face to see if he needed to be more explicit.

Thankfully, he didn't. Dylan nervously rubbed his right arm with his left hand. "Yeah, I understand. I'm sorry. It was a stupid thing to ask."

Teddy smiled to let Dylan know that he wasn't mad. "It wasn't stupid, don't think that. No harm done. He'll forget all about it in the next five minutes. Now, would you like to see how these generators work?"

Dylan's goofy grin returned, and he eagerly followed Teddy around to the back of the enormous machine.

* * *

Tom expertly ran the circular saw along a sturdy white oak board, executing a perfectly straight cut. Setting the saw aside, he lifted the cut piece and carried it to a workbench a few feet away, where he began carefully measuring it and marking out additional cuts.

He heard footsteps approaching behind him, but he didn't look back. Whoever it was would know to wait until he was done.

"Hey, boss."

Tom sighed quietly. *Almost* everyone knew not to interrupt him when he was doing math. He set down his pencil and turned.

"Hey, Gavin. What's up?"

Gavin West was one of Tom's newest employees, a twenty-something ex-con who had finished an eighteen-month sentence for low-level distribution about three months ago. About 15 percent of Tom's employees were parolees. Sometimes, they showed themselves to be diligent, careful workers, eager to prove that their past misdeeds would stay in the past, but sometimes, they turned out to have learned little from their time in prison.

So far, Gavin seemed to be one of the latter. His work was sloppy, and he was often late, according to Teddy.

He grinned, brushing a strand of greasy hair out of his eyes as he eyed the wood on the bench. "Boss man, don't you have better things to do than framing?"

Tom kept his tone civil. "Usually, but I like to stay involved with the hands-on work when I can spare the time. Do you need something?"

"Uh, yeah, actually, next week off, if that's cool." He said it more like a statement than a request.

"We have an HR department; they handle time off and scheduling, not me," Tom said. "But I do know that the terms of your parole stipulate that you have to maintain full-time employment, and that time off is authorized only for verifiable emergencies."

"Yeah man, it's definitely an emergency," Gavin said, laughing.

Tom frowned. "Most people don't find emergencies funny."

Gavin either didn't hear him or didn't care. "Alright, man, I'll check with Debbie in HR."

"Deanna," Tom corrected.

There was that infuriating grin again. "Yeah, that's what I said."

Movement in Tom's peripheral vision caught his attention. He turned to see another familiar face: Dominic Nichols, the parole officer responsible for most of the ex-cons working for Tom's company. As he approached, Nichols kept his right hand on his holstered sidearm and produced a pair of handcuffs with his left. Gavin also turned to see what Tom was looking at.

"Merry Christmas, Gavin. You fucked up one time too many. You're going back to jail."

Gavin blinked twice in surprise, slowly, like a cow. "Huh?"

Nichols did not look amused. "The rules were made clear to you on day one. You report to work on time, every day. You've been late five times in the last month, and I let those slide, against my better judgment. Last night, you missed curfew, which is 9:00 p.m. You didn't sign in until 10:30."

"This is bullshit, man," Gavin griped.

"Turn around. Hands behind your back," Nichols said, flicking open the cuffs.

Tom found himself speaking almost before he realized what he was doing. "Officer Nichols, don't."

Nichols cuffed Gavin and began to pat him down. "Don't what?"

"It's my fault, not his."

Nichols stopped and straightened. He looked at Tom but kept one eye on Gavin. "What's your fault?"

"Gavin missing curfew last night. I kept him late."

Nichols assumed a nonplussed expression. "Mr. Davis, you've been employing my ex-cons for years. You know my rules just as well as they do. Curfew is non-negotiable."

Tom nodded. "Yes, I do. I'm sorry. We're a little behind on this project, and I made most of my guys stay late to catch up. We don't normally work over the holidays, but we've really gotta hit this deadline."

Nichols stared at Tom in silence for a long moment. Gavin fidgeted uncomfortably but wisely kept his mouth shut. Nichols turned to him. "Is that how it happened?"

Gavin nodded vigorously. "Yeah, man, for sure. I told him I had curfew, and he said he would clear it with you later."

Nichols turned back to Tom, his features hardened into a frown of intense displeasure. "Mr. Davis, this is not a game. You don't write ex-cons hall passes for curfew. That's not how it works."

"I know. I'm sorry. It won't happen again."

"Were I so inclined, I could charge you with obstruction."

"Gavin isn't perfect, but he's making progress. I… needed him. I trusted him to do the job right, we were shorthanded last night."

"I find that hard to believe," Nichols said. Tom sighed, unsure what else to say. Nichols went on. "You're ex-army, right?" Tom nodded. "I get it. You feel responsible for those under your command. It's an admirable thing. Just make sure you're not sticking your neck out for scumbags who are gonna drag the rest of your team down."

"No more keeping parolees past curfew. Understood."

With a final scowl, Nichols uncuffed Gavin, spun him around by the shoulder, and poked him in the chest with a finger, hard. "You. No more missed curfews, and no more showing up to work late. You're one minute late, one more time, and you're done."

"Right. Sorry," Gavin mumbled, rubbing his sore wrists.

Nichols spun on his heel and walked out. Tom met Gavin's eyes and held his gaze for a long moment. "That's the last time I lie for you. Get your shit together," he said quietly. Gavin nodded but said nothing, then shuffled away.

Alone once again, Tom went back to what he was doing, having to start his calculations over from the beginning. He worked in silence for a time, enjoying the hum of power tools and the smell of fresh sawdust.

Seemingly out of nowhere, Teddy, Dylan, and Sara appeared next to the workbench as he was measuring and marking more wood. Tom glanced at his watch and grimaced. It was past the time he'd agreed to come back for

Dylan.

"Sorry I'm late, I lost track of the time," he said.

"No worries," Dylan said cheerfully.

"See some cool stuff?" Tom asked, pulling off his hard hat and safety glasses.

Dylan nodded enthusiastically, like a baby bird. "There's so much cool stuff here, I'd have to come back ten more times to see it all."

"Kid's a sponge, and he knows more about engineering than some of our project managers do," Teddy put in. "You should hire him."

Tom smiled. "Come back after you finish school. If you want a job, it's yours," he said to Dylan. "But with your skills, I suspect you'll have grander ambitions."

Dylan beamed. "I'm not sure what I want to do yet, but I really appreciate the offer."

"Hello again, Sara," Tom said to her. She'd been waiting patiently off to the side.

"Hey, Tom. I wanted to catch you before you left," she said.

"What's up?"

"Do you have dinner plans tonight?"

Tom blinked, caught off guard. "No, nothing special," he said.

"Will you join us for dinner at our home? My father has something important he'd like to discuss with you, Dr. Warner, and Dylan."

Tom blinked again, even more surprised now. "Something about business?"

"Partly."

Tom scratched his beard and had to make an effort to suppress a yawn. Now that he'd stopped moving around, his fatigue was rapidly coming back. "I don't know. Normally, that would be fine, but I'm pretty tired. I was hoping to hit the sack early tonight."

"Please. It's important. I hate to impose, and I'm sorry it's so last-minute, and I'm double sorry that it's on Christmas day, but it would mean the world to us. We'll make it up to you somehow." She offered him a warm smile. Her tone was a perfect blend of apologetic and assertive. *She'll be a hell of a negotiator one day,* Tom thought.

"I'm guessing you've already roped Dylan and Alex into this, so if I say no, that makes me the bad guy."

Sara grinned. "Correct."

Tom sighed internally. His dream of a restful night's sleep was probably just that, anyway—a dream. He supposed he would rather be awake and exhausted at Ethan's dinner table than suffering another bout of nightmares.

"Alright. Let me head home, shower, change, and then I'll come over."

Sara bowed in a gesture of gratitude that was somehow both exaggerated and sincere. "Thanks! See you there."

Sara and Dylan rushed off toward the parking lot, whispering and laughing about something. Tom shook his head in wonderment.

"I feel sorry for whatever guy she ends up with. He doesn't stand a chance," Teddy mused.

"Feel sorry for me. I have to see her again in two hours," Tom said.

CHAPTER SIX
Induction

Tom rang the doorbell. It played a pleasant excerpt from the second movement of the *Moonlight* sonata. A moment later, Ethan opened the door, all smiles. He wore a lavender button-down shirt with the sleeves rolled up to his elbows and a burgundy silk tie, loosened for comfort after a long day of work. Snippets of conversation and laughter drifted out the open door from somewhere farther back in the house.

"Tom! Great to see you, and thanks so much for coming." Ethan paused, and his smile inverted into a concerned frown. "Jesus, you look exhausted. I'm sorry, Sara said you were tired, but I didn't know it was that bad."

Tom waved a hand dismissively. "It's alright, I'm here now. I have plenty of time to catch up on rest over the long weekend."

Fat chance, he thought.

Ethan nodded. "Okay. Come in, come in." He stepped aside and held the door open, one arm extended in invitation.

Tom stomped snow from his boots and stepped over the threshold. He'd only been inside Ethan's home a few times before, but he appreciated its warmth. It was tastefully decorated without being snobby. Art from all over the world covered the walls, but each print was an affordable reproduction in a modest frame. Colorful fish darted back and forth in a large tank along one wall, and family photos adorned every flat surface. A beautiful, silver-leafed Christmas tree draped in tinsel, lights, and ornaments stood in the corner near the front window, guarding a pile of brightly wrapped presents that any dragon would be proud to roost on.

Ethan gently raised a hand in front of Tom, imploring him to pause. "Forgive me for asking so bluntly, but are you armed?"

Tom's hand moved instinctively toward the H&K P30SK subcompact 9mm under his shirt. "Yes, is that a problem?"

Ethan smiled apologetically and opened a drawer in a nearby table. "Would you mind? It would make Sara and me feel a bit better. It's a silly thing, I know. We're both working on feeling more comfortable around guns."

Tom had no reason to object. "Sure thing," he said. He carefully removed the holstered pistol, placed it in the drawer, and slid it closed.

"Thank you," Ethan said. "Right this way." He strolled through the kitchen, into the dining room.

Tom followed to find Sara, Dylan, and Alex already seated around a small, round wooden table stained a magnificent shade of dark brown, almost black. Several pots simmered on the stove, and Tom smelled a strong but pleasant aroma—fish? Something from the ocean, undoubtedly.

"Lobster Alfredo," Ethan said, as if he'd read Tom's mind. "And garlic bread, plus a lovely chardonnay for those old enough to partake." He checked each pot, stirring one of them. "Your timing is perfect, it's just about ready."

"It smells delicious, thank you for having me," Tom said as he slid into a vacant chair between Alex and Dylan. He was somewhat surprised to see Ethan cooking. Tom knew that he ran two nonprofit organizations with combined revenue in the hundreds of millions of dollars; he had always assumed that the Holcomb family had chefs and servants. The house was large but not extravagant, so maybe Ethan was one of the few nonprofit executives who paid himself a reasonable salary.

"Nice to see you again," Alex said to Tom, raising her glass in greeting. "Wine?" She reached for a half-empty bottle in an ice bucket.

Tom waved a hand, politely declining. "I'd love a beer, if there is any," Tom said. Alex shrugged and removed her hand from the bottle.

"Sara, sweetheart, find a drink for Tom," Ethan called from the stove. Obediently, she scurried to the kitchen and began rummaging in the refrigerator.

Dylan watched Sara for a moment, then turned to Tom. "Thanks again for showing me around the dam, Mr. Da—ah, Tom. I'd love to go back sometime. Whenever it's not too much trouble, of course."

Tom tapped his hand to his forehead in a quick salute. "Anytime."

Sara returned and plunked down a bottle of beer on the table in front of Tom. He thanked her and took a sip as she returned to her seat. Everyone made aimless small talk for a few minutes until Ethan appeared next to Alex and began distributing steaming plates of pasta and garlic bread. Tom wasn't especially hungry, but it did look wonderful. Hot food was always welcome in the dead of winter when it often took half an hour to fully warm up after coming in from the cold.

The small talk continued for a few minutes, and everyone praised the delicious food until Ethan, sympathetic to his guests' tiredness, got to the point. "Tom, Dylan, Dr. Warner. Thank you all for coming on such short notice, and on Christmas, no less. I apologize for the invitation that must have seemed a little cloak-and-dagger. I have some big news to share with you all that cannot wait until after the new year.

"Tonight's guest list is no accident. As all of you know, I run two nonprofit endeavors: one in education, Jumpstart International; and one in health care, Haven Recovery Outreach. What you may not know is that HRO has been working on a massive project for some years now, right here in Maine. This new project is much bigger and much more important than anything we've done before," Ethan fell silent for a moment, letting the suspense build.

Finally, he went on. "HRO will be building a new drug treatment center about twenty miles from here—the largest in Maine. And it will save lives using Dr. Warner's revolutionary new treatment protocol—assuming she's willing, of course."

Alex's fork fell from her hand and clattered onto her plate. She, Tom, and Dylan all stared at Ethan in shock. Only Sara, undoubtedly briefed beforehand, seemed unsurprised.

"Way to go, doc," Tom said.

"I—what?" was all Alex managed to get out.

"You heard me," Ethan said to her. "I believe in what you're doing. In just three years, you've blown most traditional treatment models out of the water, and I don't think it's a fluke."

"What exactly are you asking me to do?" Alex said, slowly regaining her composure.

"I want you to run the place. You'll have four other doctors at your disposal, all chosen by you, and each of them will supervise a small team of therapists and nurses. Funding will be far from unlimited, though. In the early years, frugality will be the name of the game. You'll have to do a lot with a small team, at least for a while. But if anyone can do it, you can.

"Because this is a nonprofit facility, you don't need to worry about investors' portfolios. Construction costs and the first five years of operating capital are already in an account, ready for use. After five years, future donations, grants, and other revenue should be no problem at all, provided you continue to optimize the program—which I'm sure you will. I'm not at liberty to discuss dollar amounts at this early stage, but suffice it to say that with the number of established donors already on board, and considering the size of the checks they've written to us in the past, I'm confident that this new treatment center will continue to grow and thrive long after you've retired."

Alex stared at Ethan in stunned silence. Dylan finally swallowed a bite of garlic bread he'd been slowly chewing since Ethan started talking.

Finally, Alex managed to speak. "I'm sorry, I'm just... overwhelmed. It's an incredibly generous offer, and the potential to help so many patients—it's amazing. I'm not sure what to say."

Ethan's smile widened. "How about, 'I accept?'"

Alex's eyes darted back and forth as she struggled to process the news. "Well, yes, I mean, I would love to, it's just that, it's such a big change. There are so many things to think about."

Ethan's smile didn't falter. "Of course, I understand. I don't mean to pressure you; I was only kidding."

Sensing that Alex was having a hard time gathering her thoughts, Tom stepped in to give her a break. "Ethan, that's wonderful news, and I'm sure your confidence in Alex is well-founded. But, if I can be blunt, what does it have to do with me?"

Ethan turned his gaze to Tom. "I apologize again for my rudeness, Tom. I know you're exhausted and probably eager to get home. I will cut right to the chase. I'd like you to build the new treatment center."

Now it was Tom's turn to drop his fork. "Excuse me?"

"Your construction company has been a pillar of this community for almost twenty years. You may not know this, but I've been watching you grow your business from day one. As a Rotary Club member, the development of our lovely city is a responsibility I take very seriously. I watched you start with little more than a beat-up old truck, a toolbox, one employee, and the willingness to work as long and hard as it took to earn your customers' trust. Now look at you. How many employees do you have now?"

"One hundred sixty, but most of them are contractors," Tom said, feeling a bit dizzy.

Ethan waved a hand at the trivial distinction. "So, you're feeding 160 families, growing our community—and giving ex-cons a second lease on life. I've vetted you very carefully. Every single one of your clients has heaped praise on you for the speed, quality, and affordability of your work. In short, you're admirably selfless, you pride yourself on doing the job right, and you can stay on budget. I know of no other construction company around here that can check all three of those boxes."

That wasn't entirely true. Tom did hold his employees to an exceptionally high standard of workmanship, but some—especially some of the parolees—never seemed to get the message. He paid out a lot of overtime, much of it in service of redoing poor-quality work, but he usually managed to hit deadlines and keep clients happy. Still, the impact on his bottom line was substantial. Without those extra costs, the company probably could have been 50 percent bigger by now.

Tom noticed that everyone was staring at him and realized that he'd been lost in his thoughts for a time. He cleared his throat and spoke. "It is a wonderfully generous offer, Ethan, thank you. But, like Alex said, it is a lot to think about. After we finish up our part of the new hydro plant, we're lined up to start a very lucrative contract that will help us grow substantially. It's not official yet, but I have a handshake agreement with the client, and we expect to sign the papers next month."

Ethan nodded slowly. "Yes, I figured as much. I don't have specific knowledge of that project—I'm not spying on you—but I assumed that, with your reputation, you would have all the work you can handle."

Tom chose his next words carefully. "Then you must have a pretty persuasive offer in mind."

Alex, Dylan, and Sara watched the exchange, each of them motionless, as if afraid to upset some delicate balance.

Ethan pushed his plate aside and rested one foot on the opposite knee, assuming a more casual posture. "I realize it's perhaps somewhat inappropriate to ask you to discuss the details of your business in front of others. And the same to you, Dr. Warner," he said with a nod in her direction. "But I ask for your forgiveness, your patience, and your understanding. I need both of you for this to work. One or the other, alone, is insufficient."

Tom frowned. This was not how business negotiations were done, nonprofit or otherwise. Ethan must have a powerfully good reason to play his hand so openly, with such willing vulnerability.

Ethan went on. "You're right. I do have a persuasive offer, one I would make to no one else except the two of you. But before I get to that, I have one more thing to confess." Tom waited while Ethan took a deep breath. "I'm asking you to do this project at cost."

Tom blinked. Surely he'd misheard. "As in, I can expect to break even, but not much more." Ethan nodded. Tom crossed his arms, making a conscious effort not to be insulted. "And why would I do that when I have a project lined up that will secure my company's future for at least the next decade?" An edge of anger crept into his voice.

Ethan's voice was perfectly calm. "Because you, Tom—and you, Dr. Warner—have something this project desperately needs, something it can't get anywhere else."

Tom still wasn't hearing what Ethan's project could offer *to* him. "And that is?"

Ethan locked eyes with him, then with Alex. "You both have exceptional ability—and the willingness to use it for the benefit of those who lack it."

Tom hadn't known what answer he was expecting, but that was not it. Before he could respond, Alex cut in. "Ethan, you want us to do this solely because it's the right thing to do? Because addicts need help, and we're in a unique position to give it to them?"

"What nobler reason is there?"

Neither Tom nor Alex had an answer for that. Dylan looked like a deer caught in the headlights, his eyes wide, undoubtedly wondering what any of this had to do with him. Sara leaned back in her chair and sipped at a can of orange soda, cool as a cucumber.

Ethan stood up, placed his hands flat on the table, and leaned forward, lowering his voice. "Dr. Warner, I'm not sure that even you fully realize how important your program is, but I do. Extrapolating from the results you've achieved at New Horizons in just three short years, you could increase long-term recovery rates by as much as 50 percent, with the proper funding and support. Fifty percent! Think of the benefit to mankind, how many lives you'll save, how many broken families you can heal.

"New Horizons is a small, privately owned clinic, with investors to satisfy. It's played an important role in your career—it's given you a place to test a radical new methodology, a set of ideas that no established corporation or nonprofit would roll the dice on—but it's served its purpose. It's time for bigger and better things. I believe that your achievement is one of those that only comes along once in a generation—once a century.

"Tom, the incredible strength of Dr. Warner's program—its novelty, its ingenuity—is also its Achilles heel. It challenges virtually every established pillar of modern drug treatment. It slaughters too many sacred cows and takes too many risks. Investors and donors won't touch it, not on a national —an international scale—not without real, solid proof that it works.

"But once they see that proof, once we can show them that Dr. Warner's ideas work on a level far beyond anything we've ever seen in this field before, she'll go from counterculture underdog to the most widely esteemed expert on drug treatment in the world, overnight. Treatment centers using her methodology will spring up all over the world.

"To get there, we need data. To get the data, we need more patients. To get more patients, we need a much bigger facility, with more staff who understand Dr. Warner's ideas. To get all of that, we need money—and that's the bottleneck. As I said, we have some donors on board, some true believers who see Dr. Warner's genius, as I do—but even with their donations, we only have so much money. To get this done—to get it done right, on the scale necessary to show the world five years of irrefutable, statistically significant data—we have to stretch our initial budget as far as possible.

"I can't pay you as much as the dream client you have lined up. It's probably not even close. But I ask you to consider the once-in-a-lifetime spiritual value you'll get from this project. You'll be the man who built the best, the most effective, the most groundbreaking drug treatment center in the world. You'll be helping Dr. Warner save more lives than you can imagine. When this program becomes the global standard in addiction medicine—and it will—you'll share credit with Dr. Warner for saving millions of lives—tens of millions, stretching generations into the future.

"Tom. Dr. Warner. You can do this. You're the *only* ones who can do this. We have a very small, very limited window of opportunity. If we let it close, all of mankind will suffer an incomprehensible loss. There may never be another chance to show the world the magnitude of Dr. Warner's achievement."

Tom suddenly felt very small. A few minutes ago, he'd felt his anger mounting. He'd been incensed that Ethan would ask him to not only forgo an incredible opportunity for his company but to halt its growth for years, maybe a decade or longer.

But as Ethan spoke, Tom began to see his point. If Alex's program really did have that kind of potential to save lives, it seemed inarguable that he had to help make it happen, if he could. He had ability and resources, and he was in a unique position to use them for the benefit of others—to improve countless lives.

Very softly, Tom asked, "You rehearsed that speech, didn't you?"

Ethan straightened his tie. "Was it obvious?"

Alex pushed her chair back and stood up. "Ethan, I… I need some air. May I step outside for a moment?"

"Of course, my dear." Ethan hurried to the sliding glass patio door and opened it for her. "There are heaters outside, let me switch them on so you don't freeze to death."

Alex escaped to the patio, and a moment later, Tom stood up. "I think I'll join her."

Ethan nodded. "Take all the time you need."

* * *

Alex gazed out over the Holcombs' property, rubbing her arms to ward off the cold. It was well below freezing, but the powerful heaters made it tolerable.

Snowflakes drifted silently among the naked birch trees. A small forest stretched across the back half of the property, dark and still. Alex guessed it must cover twenty acres. To the east, a pond that housed koi fish in the summer was drained and covered for the winter.

It was a lovely home to grow up in. Alex was glad that Sara had a father who could give her such a wonderful childhood.

Tom appeared next to her, his breath forming white clouds in the air. For a while, they stood next to one another in silence, watching the snow come down.

"I just had to get out of the house for a minute," Alex confessed, unsure why she felt the need to say something. "I get claustrophobic sometimes, especially when I'm stressed out."

"We all have our phobias," Tom said. "I can't stand snakes, personally. Even though I know most of them are harmless."

Another long silence stretched between them.

"Is he right?" Tom asked.

"About my treatment protocol?" Alex replied. Tom nodded.

Alex didn't answer for a long time. Tom waited, letting her sort it all out in her head. To some extent, he knew how she felt.

"Yes, he is," she finally said. "It's hard to be objective about something like this, something you've created that defies what all your peers are doing. When someone attacks your baby, your instinct is to defend it at all costs.

"But I can say, honestly and truthfully, that this baby needs to be defended. It's only been a few years, and like Ethan said, I don't have many patients. But from what I've seen, this could be the future of addiction treatment. No program has anything close to a 100 percent success rate, but my patients, in general, do so much better than anyone else's. Sometimes I have trouble believing it myself."

Tom smiled at her. "You really are a genius, then."

She snorted. "Not sure I'd go that far."

"Do you really believe everything he said? Even the part about saving the world? Could it get that big?"

Again, Alex hesitated for a long moment. "I want to believe it."

"You want to believe it because of the evidence, or because you want to believe it?"

She looked directly at him. "The evidence is there. The protocol works."

Tom held her gaze, studying her eyes. She meant it. "I'm in if you are," he said.

Alex smiled and gave him a single, firm nod.

* * *

After Alex and Tom had gone outside, Ethan turned to Dylan. "Let's talk about something less stressful for a bit, shall we?" Dylan shrugged agreeably. "Did Sara show you the pictures from our scuba diving trip in Cancún a few months ago?"

"Yeah, she did." Dylan forced a smile. "It looked like a great time."

"We're still a little sad you couldn't join us," Ethan said.

"It's not that I didn't want to, I just...." Dylan trailed off.

"Dad," Sara said, a note of mild agitation in her voice.

"Hmm?"

"Dylan can't swim," she said quietly. Dylan felt himself blushing furiously.

"Oh, I didn't know. I'm sorry, Dylan, I didn't mean to put you on the spot like that," Ethan said.

"It's alright," Dylan mumbled. Taking a deep breath, he summoned the courage to ask the question he'd been suppressing for nearly an hour. "Mr. Holcomb?"

Ethan stood up and put his hand on Sara's shoulder. "You're going to ask me what the hell any of this business stuff has to do with you."

Dylan blushed again. He'd rarely heard Ethan swear, even so mildly. "Yeah, I guess."

"Well, nothing, at least not directly. But Sara and I have something very important to discuss with you, too—something that calls for a celebration, I think—and we thought it would be nice to make one big party out of it. I've done enough talking for now, I'm sure everyone's tired of hearing my voice. Sara, why don't you bring Dylan up to speed?" With that, Ethan started collecting plates and taking them back to the kitchen.

Sara scooted her chair closer to the table and reached across it, placing her hand on Dylan's. "Dylan, how are you going to pay for engineering school?"

He made a face. "What's that got to do with anything?"

She smiled patiently. "Just answer the question."

"Student loans, I guess. Does it matter?" They both knew that Richard, although not destitute, wasn't far from it.

"What if you could get a full ride?"

He pulled his hand away, slightly irritated. "I probably won't get one. I'm not good enough for anything like that."

"What if you could? I mean, what if you could get a *guaranteed* full ride? Now. Tonight."

Dylan stared at her. Rather, he stared *through* her, not understanding what she was saying.

Ethan came back into the dining room. "She means it."

"How?" Dylan asked, dumbfounded.

Ethan sat back down, resting one arm on the table. "Tom and Dr. Warner aren't the only ones here tonight who are very good at what they do." Dylan, who never felt worthy of compliments, looked down at his lap and fidgeted. Ethan glanced at his daughter. "Tell him, Sara."

"Dylan, you're so smart. I swear you could invent, build, or fix anything. Dad's other nonprofit, Jumpstart International—you remember me talking about it?" Dylan nodded. "Among other things, they give scholarships to high school students who show great promise in various fields. Like engineering."

Dylan swallowed. Was this going where he thought it was?

"Dylan, this year's award for engineering innovation is yours. For the motor you built earlier this year when you were still a sophomore," Ethan said quietly.

Dylan was stunned. "Really?" was all he could say. Ethan nodded. "But... isn't that, like. What's the word when you give things to your friends and family?"

"Nepotism?" Ethan asked.

"Yeah, that," Dylan said.

Ethan laughed merrily. "No, Dylan, it's not nepotism, but I can see why you'd worry about that. I don't choose the scholarship winners, but I can make recommendations to the people who do. I recommended you, yes. But the board voted unanimously for your motor. They all agreed that it's an incredible achievement for someone your age. The fact that you're my daughter's friend had nothing to do with it."

"I... don't know what to say. That's incredible. You'd really do that for me?"

"Gladly," Ethan said.

"It's a scholarship?"

"That's right. A full ride to any engineering program of your choosing, anywhere in the world. Tuition, books, housing, food—all paid for."

Dylan's head was spinning. He'd never dared to even dream of something like this. "But I don't graduate for another year and a half."

"The money will be waiting for you when you're ready. You have up to three years after graduation to choose a program."

Dylan locked eyes with Sara. "What about you?"

"What about me?" she asked.

"Have you decided what you're doing after graduation?"

She nodded. "I'll be working with Dr. Warner to help her get her new program off the ground. Assuming, of course, she and Tom both agree to make it happen."

"I think they will," Ethan mused.

"For how long?" Dylan asked.

"I'm not sure," Sara said. "But I definitely want to stay with Dr. Warner for a while. I'm excited about her program. I can't imagine anything more fulfilling than being a part of it."

Dylan fell silent. He had a handful of double major programs in mind—he'd already done the research—but none of them were in Maine. The closest one on his list was the one in New Mexico that he'd told Tom about. Surely there were others, maybe even one within a day's drive, but if he were in school full-time, hours away, he'd hardly ever get to see Sara.

"Mr. Holcomb?" Dylan finally said.

"Yes?"

"I really can't tell you how grateful I am for this. It's so generous, and it's nice that someone thinks I'm good at things."

Ethan raised an eyebrow. "But... there's a 'but' coming."

Dylan inhaled, then let it out slowly. "I think I'd rather stay here. In Maine, I mean. After school."

Ethan stared at Dylan for a long moment, then his gaze darted to Sara, and finally, back to Dylan. Comprehension flashed in his eyes. "I see."

"You think I'm ungrateful." Dylan pulled his head into his shoulders, feeling like a turtle. Sara stared at him. She seemed completely stunned by what he'd said.

"No, Dylan, not at all. You're one of the finest young men I know. I'd never think such a thing about you," Ethan said, patting Dylan's shoulder reassuringly. "Listen, you still have a year and a half of high school anyway, like you said. We can do something called a conditional award, which means we set the money aside until you finish high school, and then you can decide if you want it. If you don't, we can give it to someone else. How does that sound? You don't have to decide anything right now."

Relieved, Dylan smiled at Ethan. "That sounds great. Thank you so much," he said.

"You're very welcome. Now, there's one more important thing," Ethan said, standing up.

"What's that?" Dylan asked.

"Cake," Ethan replied with a grin before disappearing into the kitchen.

Dylan watched him go, then turned back to Sara. He balked when he saw her face. Her brow was furrowed, her mouth twisted in confusion. Her bright green eyes were fixed on his with an intensity that she rarely directed at him.

"Dylan, are you nuts?"

"Huh?"

"Why would you just stay in Maine? There's nothing here for you."

He stared back at her, dumbfounded. "You're here."

She slumped in her chair, finally breaking eye contact. "Yes, but... you can't get the future you want here. Be brave, Dylan. You can do this without me."

"How do you know what future I want? I don't even know that yet," he retorted, annoyance creeping into his voice.

"I just want what's best for you," she said softly.

"I know, Sara. But like your dad said, I have a year and a half to decide. That's a ton of time."

Finally, the smile came back to her face. "You're right. It's plenty of time."

The patio door opened, letting a small flurry of snowflakes rush into the dining room. Tom and Alex came back in, shut the door, and rubbed their hands together to banish the lingering cold. A moment later, Ethan returned, bearing a beautifully decorated white cake in one hand and a stack of small plates in the other.

"Tom, Dr. Warner, you're just in time. If you can stand us for another twenty minutes or so, we'd love to offer you some heavenly buttercream cake, with fresh strawberries."

"I think we've reached an agreement," Alex said, glancing sideways at Tom. He nodded in confirmation.

"Oh?" Ethan said, pausing halfway to the table.

"We're in. Tentatively, of course. We want to see the numbers, and I need to learn more about Alex's program—the usual due diligence. Assuming it all checks out, we'll do it," Tom said.

Sara beamed. Ethan broke into the widest grin any of them had ever seen on his face. He rushed to the table, gently set down the cake, then stepped over to Tom and Alex and wrapped them both in a fierce bear hug.

"Whoa, hey, usually a handshake is fine," Tom joked.

"Not for this, it isn't," Ethan said, finally breaking the hug to look at both of them. "We're going to change the world together."

"Now you *have* to have some cake," Sara said, retrieving a knife to cut it with.

"And some more wine," Alex said, raising her empty glass. She felt at peace for the first time in weeks, maybe months.

Or rather, she felt as though she *should* be at peace—but there was some nagging, ethereal doubt in the back of her mind. She pushed it aside.

Tom was having similar thoughts. He, too, ignored them.

"More wine, of course," Ethan said. "Help yourselves."

Sara began to pass slices of cake around the table. Tom, Dylan, and Alex each took several bites. Ethan was right—it was splendid.

"Thank you all, again, for coming tonight. We won't keep you any longer.

Once we finish dessert, I'm sure you're all keen to get home and see to your own holiday plans," Ethan said.

"Yes, let's find some time after the new year to get together and start the ball rolling," Alex added.

Dylan suddenly slumped forward, falling face-first onto the table. The fork in his hand clattered to the floor.

Alex immediately leaped to her feet. "Dylan! What's wrong?" she cried, rushing around to his side of the table. She shook him, but he didn't respond.

Tom also shot to his feet. "What's wrong with him?"

"I don't know," Alex said. "Help me lay him on the floor, I need to examine him."

Tom came around to help her, carefully lowering the boy to the floor. He then noticed that Alex had her eyes closed and was clutching her head, not paying any attention to Dylan.

"Alex? What's wrong?" Tom asked, increasingly concerned.

"I—don't...." Before she could say anything more, she pitched forward, falling across Dylan's motionless body.

Tom looked up at Ethan, suspicion flaring in his eyes. "What the fuck is this?" he snarled.

Ethan and Sara both stared back at him calmly. Tom noticed that the cake slices in front of both of them were untouched.

Did they...? No. It can't be, Tom thought, rising to his feet. He suddenly felt lightheaded, and his vision dimmed.

"Did you... poison us?" he choked out, his voice hoarse. Tom ran for the living room, struggling to move in a straight line. His vision was getting darker by the second. He felt drunk. Very drunk.

Somehow, he managed to find the table where he'd stored his gun. He ripped the drawer open, feeling around inside.

It wasn't there.

He turned back to the kitchen, but the sudden motion disoriented him even further, and he fell backward, onto the floor. His vision was so dark that he could barely see Ethan and Sara standing in the kitchen doorway, watching him. "He's the biggest one. I thought it might take the longest to work on him," Ethan said, his voice sounding far away. He held up Tom's gun, still holstered.

"Good thinking," Sara replied.

Tom struggled to stand but couldn't make his legs work. A moment later, darkness and silence took him.

* * *

Sara descended the stairs into the finished basement that also served as the den where she sometimes did homework or read fantasy novels. Once there, she approached a flat-screen TV mounted on the wall, reached behind it, and felt around with both hands until she found two small bumps about eighteen inches apart. To anyone who didn't know what they were, the carefully concealed switches looked and felt like normal sections of textured drywall. She pressed them both at the same time.

A bookcase on the opposite wall swung open silently, revealing a large room beyond. Six strong, young men in black suits waited inside. "It's time," Sara said to them. Without a word, they followed her upstairs.

In the kitchen, the silent men paired up and began to carry Alex, Tom, and Dylan back down to the basement, taking care not to injure them. Sara and Ethan followed.

"Are you ready?" Ethan asked. Sara gave a single nod in response. "You're sure? I know you know this, but a single mistake ruins everything. You're sure everything is ready? I don't need to remind you what's at stake."

"You're right—you don't need to remind me. We're ready. I promise," Sara said, keeping her tone gentle.

Ethan sighed and took a moment to compose himself. He took a handkerchief from his pocket and wiped his eyes. "I can't tell you how much I wish there were another way," he said. His voice trembled ever so slightly.

"Me too, Dad. But there isn't."

"I'm so sorry to place this burden on you." This time, his voice cracked badly.

Sara took his hand and squeezed it. She couldn't bring herself to say anything.

The silent helpers carried their unconscious charges into the room behind the bookcase. It was about the size of a four-car garage, dug into the earth outside the house's normal footprint. It didn't appear on any blueprints, and no one would have any reason to suspect it was there.

The room's walls, floor, and ceiling were reinforced concrete, sealed but unpainted. Four twin beds were lined up against the north wall, each with an IV pole and a cart of medical supplies next to it. Along the east wall, a low counter held assorted medical lab equipment, attended by four middle-aged women in lab coats. In the west wall, a heavy steel door blocked passage to another area.

On the floor in the center of the room, two large, concentric circles were drawn in thick, red chalk. Seven short lines, evenly spaced around the perimeter, connected the two circles. In the center of the design, a small fire burned inside a ring of stones, its smoke pulled safely out of the room by a dedicated ventilation system.

The six helpers carefully deposited Dylan, Tom, and Alex into three of the four beds, then stepped aside, making way for three of the women to begin taking vital signs and drawing blood.

"How are they?" Ethan asked, worried that the sedatives may have been too strong.

"At a glance, they seem fine. The woman's breathing is a little slower than I'd like, but it's within an acceptable range. We'll know more when we finish the tests," said one of the doctors, a woman named Atwood.

"Alex," Sara said softly.

"Hmm?" Dr. Atwood responded, not really paying attention.

"You said 'the woman.' Her name is Alex, and she's about to do you the mother of all favors," Sara said.

Dr. Atwood blinked in surprise, then turned to face Sara. "Yes, Sara, you're quite right. I apologize."

Another of the doctors finished drawing blood from Dylan, applied a bandage to his arm, and took the samples to a centrifuge across the room, where they would need several minutes to spin down.

"How long to finish the tests?" Ethan asked, pacing slowly back and forth. He glanced at his watch, muttering about being behind schedule.

"About twenty minutes."

"I'll get ready," Sara said. She took off her pastel-pink sweater and tossed it aside, then retreated to the northeast corner of the room and drew a small curtain for privacy while she changed. A few minutes later, she emerged wearing a plain black T-shirt, rugged canvas pants, and heavy hiking boots. She crossed the room to the door in the western wall and entered a six-digit code on the keypad beside it. With a metallic groan, the door popped open. Sara slipped inside and was gone for several minutes, leaving Ethan to continue pacing as he waited anxiously for the doctors to finish their tests.

When Sara came back, she'd donned a lightweight level II armored vest capable of stopping pistol rounds as large as .357 Magnum. Several MOLLE pouches on the vest held a small first aid kit, two M67 fragmentation grenades, and extra magazines for the heavily customized M61C rifle she carried in both hands. A thigh holster on her right leg held a .32-caliber Walther PPK and two extra magazines. She wore a small, heavy-duty backpack containing a few other essential supplies, and her vibrant red hair was tucked carefully under a black fleece watch cap.

"That hat makes you look like a boy," Ethan said, trying to be funny.

"Thanks, Dad. Just what every daughter likes to hear. It also keeps my hair out of my face so I don't, you know. Die."

"Yes, let's avoid that," he said, his voice barely above a whisper.

"Mr. Holcomb, all three Wardens are medically cleared," Dr. Atwood said as she walked toward Ethan and Sara. "No active infections or clotting disorders. The man—Tom—his triglycerides are a bit high, but that's to be expected for someone his age. Nothing to be concerned about."

"And you cross-checked these findings against their medical records?" Ethan asked, folding his arms.

"Of course. All four of us agree they're in perfect health."

Ethan nodded. "Good." He turned to Sara. "Go ahead."

Letting the rifle hang from its sling against her chest, Sara opened a nearby cabinet and withdrew a small black box, then walked to the middle of the room and set the box and the rifle on the floor near the fire. She approached Dylan and stood next to the bed. She watched him for a moment. His chest rose and fell evenly. His tired face looked peaceful. He looked to be getting the first restful sleep he'd had in weeks.

It wouldn't last long.

Sara bent down and lightly kissed his forehead, then whispered in his ear. "Dylan... I'm so sorry."

From a sheath on her belt at the small of her back, she drew a sharp, single-edged survival knife. With a short, quick jerk, she pulled the blade across her left palm, then did the same to Dylan, pressing her hand against his to allow the welling blood to mix. She repeated the procedure with Alex and Tom, then allowed one of the doctors to bandage her hand. Throughout the process, she made no sound, nor did her face betray any hint of pain. Ethan, the other three doctors, and the six silent men watched from the far corner of the room.

That done, she returned to the fire and knelt in front of it. She opened the black box and withdrew several glass jars filled with mixtures of rare herbs that she'd prepared several days earlier. She opened each in turn, casting handfuls of dried herbs into the fire. Each time, the flames flared higher and briefly glowed different colors—first the bright blue of a clear sky, then the deep purple of twilight, and finally obsidian black.

Sitting so close to the fire was making her sweat. She wiped her forehead with the back of one arm.

Sara closed her eyes and began to speak in a language that few could read and fewer still could speak aloud. Her voice was suddenly two full octaves lower than normal. Had the occasion not been so deadly serious, Ethan might have joked that she now *sounded* like a boy. He dared not say a word. Sara needed to concentrate.

The slightest mistake in her inflection or pronunciation of the words would instantly snuff out her life.

Time dragged on. Everyone in the room remained still and silent as Sara continued to chant. For a full hour, she went on, reciting the words perfectly and without hesitation. Ethan knew the words and knew what they meant; he'd first taught them to her more than twelve years ago and had made her practice them endlessly ever since.

And he hated himself for doing it.

Abruptly, Sara stopped and opened her eyes. Sweat dripped from her face and the exposed skin of her arms. Her breathing was uneven and ragged. The invocation was done. There was only one step left.

Dr. Atwood moved to the low counter, where she picked up a portable ultrasound unit and a long biopsy needle. As she did so, Sara lay on her back on the cold floor near the fire. Dr. Atwood approached and knelt beside her. "Ready?" she asked.

Sara nodded, pulling her armor and shirt partway up to expose her waistline. Dr. Atwood applied a thin layer of conductive gel, then gently moved the ultrasound wand against Sara's skin until she found what she was looking for. "Exhale, then hold," Dr. Atwood commanded. "You know the rules, I can't use any anesthesia. I'm sorry."

Sara took several quick, sharp breaths, then pushed all the air out of her lungs, held her breath, and nodded. Without ceremony, Dr. Atwood plunged the long needle into Sara's lower abdomen, guided by the image on the ultrasound display. She felt Sara's muscles contract violently, but the girl didn't move and made no sound. Dr. Atwood's heart broke for her. No woman should have to endure such a thing, much less a girl not yet out of high school.

But it was necessary.

As gently as she could, Dr. Atwood withdrew the needle with a small piece of tissue lodged in its bevel. Sara inhaled and finally relaxed a bit, tears streaming from her eyes. Dr. Atwood handed Sara a bandage to tape over the small spot of blood on her abdomen and waited patiently for her to recover.

When Sara felt steadier, she sat up and, using two fingers, gently took the piece of tissue from the end of the needle. Turning back to the fire, she uttered a single word in that strange language and dropped the tissue into the flames.

With a loud *pop*, the flames turned pure white and flared higher, nearly reaching the ceiling. A moment later, the fire returned to its normal size and color.

"It's done," she said hoarsely.

Another *pop* echoed through the room, even louder this time. This sound came not from the flames but from the electric lights as several bulbs burst in their sockets while others dimmed, darkened, and finally came back to life. In a matter of seconds, the temperature dropped sharply, raising goosebumps on Sara's bare arms. She ignored the momentary discomfort and shakily rose to her feet.

One of the other doctors approached and held her hand out. In her palm lay four syringes, each bearing a yellow warning label. Sara opened a pouch on her vest, withdrew a hard-sided case, put the syringes inside, then closed the case and returned it to the pouch.

Sara retrieved her rifle, then walked over to the empty fourth bed and sat on it. Ethan came to stand beside her. "Be strong," he said simply. "And be careful." She closed her eyes and answered with a single nod.

Ethan stepped aside to make room for Dr. Atwood, who produced a syringe from the pocket of her lab coat. Sara lay back on the bed, situated her head on the pillow, and carefully laid the rifle at her side, keeping one hand on it.

"Sara?" Dr. Atwood said, waiting for the teen to meet her eyes. "Thank you."

Again, Sara gave a single nod of acknowledgment, then held out her arm. Dr. Atwood palpated the skin, found a suitable vein, and expertly injected the drug.

Within moments, Sara slipped away.

CHAPTER SEVEN
Invocation

December 26, 2021
Day Two

Dylan screamed, but a rushing wind ripped the sound away. For some reason, he was falling—fast.

It was dark, and with the fierce wind in his eyes, he couldn't see much.

He crashed violently into something hard, landing on his back. The impact forced the air from his lungs, rattling his shoulders, neck, and teeth with dizzying pain that nearly knocked him unconscious. Reflexively, he gasped, trying to draw a breath.

Instead, he got a mouthful of brackish water.

He tried to cough, instead sucking in more water. Suffocating panic banished all rational thought from his mind. He still couldn't see. It was so dark, so cold. He couldn't tell which way was up.

He flailed his arms and legs madly. He couldn't swim. He didn't know how to move his limbs to get his head above the surface. He tried to keep his mouth closed, tried to stop swallowing water, but water was already in his lungs, and his body insisted on coughing it out—which only let more in.

His vision dimmed. The pain and panic were so overwhelming that his heart felt like it was trying to tear its way out of his chest. His shoes felt so heavy. They were dragging him down.

At the edge of his awareness, just before he lost consciousness, he felt the fingers of his left hand close around something solid. His dwindling flame of self-preservation nearly extinguished, he rallied one last burst of determination. He clutched the object and pulled with what little strength he had left.

His head broke the surface. He hacked and retched, flailing blindly, still unable to see anything more than a few feet away. The thing he was holding onto felt like wood, and it was large. He pulled it closer; it was flat and buoyant. Weakly, he heaved his chest up onto it, his legs still trailing in the water.

He turned his head to one side and vomited. Spit, snot, water, and partly digested lobster came up in waves, and he nearly choked on that, too. He gasped a few breaths of precious air.

Before he could begin to recover, something snatched at his right leg and pulled hard.

It was probably a good thing that he was too weak, dizzy, and terrified to scream. Had his mouth been open when he went under the second time, that surely would have been the end of him.

Dylan had no doubt that whatever was pulling him down was alive. It was big and strong, and it moved with purpose. He'd only managed to draw half a breath before going under, and in his exhausted, panicked state, that air wouldn't last long.

A thought came to him with perfect clarity.

If I die now, I'll never see Sara again.

His panic didn't fade, but it moved to the back of his mind, far enough to allow him to concentrate, to choose what he did with his few remaining seconds of life. He forced himself to open his eyes. The frigid salt water stung, but he needed to see.

It was terribly dark. He could see only muted shafts of moonlight, clouds of bubbles, vague shapes and shadows, hints of movement all around. The thing still had a firm hold on his right leg, and at some point, it had grabbed his left arm as well, but it was no longer actively dragging him down.

It seemed content to wait for him to drown.

Summoning his last shred of willpower, he forced himself to look down, nearly paralyzed with fright at what he might see. An enormous yellow eye loomed out of the depths, rising to meet him.

Dylan finally screamed, unable to contain it. Most of his remaining air escaped, and he slammed his mouth shut, biting his tongue hard in the process. He tasted blood. His chest burned in agony. He knew that he had only a few moments of air left.

The eye drew close to his face, hovering inches away. It was gargantuan, easily the size of a truck tire. He couldn't make out what the eye was attached to, only that it was a large, pulsing, irregular black mass. Below the eye, a yawning maw studded with flat, dull teeth opened, beckoning him.

Dylan frantically glanced to each side and finally saw what was holding him. He had expected to see the great tentacles of some dreadful leviathan, like the kind that haunted the nightmares of Lovecraft and Verne.

Instead, he saw a dozen vaguely humanoid arms. They were enormous, disproportionate, and covered in sickly tumors, but they were unmistakably arms, with misshapen hands and twisted fingers.

The arms began to pull him toward the mouth. Dylan pushed and kicked, struggling to break away, but he was hopelessly outclassed in strength.

As the maw opened wider, something metallic glinted inside. At first, he thought it was another set of teeth, but after a moment he saw that it was a long, jagged shard of steel driven into the back of the creature's throat.

As Dylan was pulled ever closer to the creature's mouth, pounding his fists uselessly against the arms, a memory came rushing back to him—a scene from only a few minutes ago, it seemed.

"Be brave," Sara had told him at the dinner table.

Dylan knew that he was going to die. His father would never know what had happened to him. The loss of his son, on top of Marie's inexplicable disappearance, would surely destroy whatever was left of Richard Masters.

A fiery core of anger erupted in Dylan's chest.

No.

Fuck this monster, he thought.

Conserving his last remnants of strength, he stopped fighting. Instead, he pulled himself along the creature's bulbous head, willingly feeding himself into its mouth.

It welcomed him.

He needed to make sure he went in headfirst. If he'd kept fighting, he'd have been swallowed feet first, and then there would be nothing he could do.

Despite being inside the beast's mouth, Dylan felt strangely calm. He reached out with his right hand and grabbed the exposed end of the metal shard. It cut into his flesh, his blood staining the water in red swirls. He ignored the pain. He had bigger things to worry about.

With all his might, he pulled. The shard loosened. He yanked again, and this time, it came free. He immediately slammed it upward, through the roof of the creature's mouth.

He didn't know if the thing had a brain, but if it did, he intended to stab the ever-living shit out of it.

The monster roared in fury, ejecting Dylan from its mouth. The sound, muted by the water, came to his ears as a deep *thump*, so powerful that it rattled his teeth.

Wasting no time, Dylan plunged the shard into the yellow eye. He felt something inside burst, and dark green fluid squirted into the water.

That seemed to convince the creature that this meal was too much trouble. It shoved him away with amazing force, sending him rocketing through the water for what felt like fifty feet. He lost his grip on his weapon, and it spiraled down into the black depths.

His vision was fading again. The struggle had lasted less than twenty seconds, but now he was really out of time. Wildly, he kicked his feet, reaching for the surface.

Fortunately, the creature hadn't dragged him too far down. He broke the surface for the second time, thinking of nothing except keeping his head above the water. He hacked, coughed, and vomited some more, expelling what felt like a gallon of seawater.

As his sight slowly returned to normal, he saw another large piece of driftwood a few feet away and flailed over to it. For a minute, he treaded water, holding onto the wood.

Finally, with agonizing slowness, the panic and nausea began to subside. His bleeding hand throbbed. He wondered if the creature would come back for him, then decided that it didn't matter. If it did come back, he was finished. He didn't have the strength to fight it off again.

When he felt strong enough, he hauled himself up onto the driftwood, still panting. He lay still for some time, gasping great lungfuls of salty air, not realizing that he'd closed his eyes at some point. When he opened them, he immediately shut them again, shaken to the core by the delayed realization of where he was.

Somehow, he was in the ocean, but *what* ocean? It looked… wrong, somehow. Mustering scraps of courage he didn't know he still had, he forced himself to open his eyes and look again.

Thick clouds the color of rotten olives scudded low and fast across a charcoal sky. Somewhere behind them, a rumble of thunder rolled, so deep and low that it was barely audible. Here and there, thin, spidery fingers of lightning darted toward the surface of the water before retreating back to the clouds with an odd sort of slowness, like snakes withdrawing to their hiding places after snatching unwary prey.

It took Dylan a moment to realize that it was raining, and then another, longer moment to realize that it was raining upside-down. Rain droplets lifted themselves out of the gently rolling waves and rose into the sky, creating concentric rings on the surface that started big, then constricted to nothing.

Dimly, Dylan felt a muted need to scream, to cry for help, to sob in primal fear. He resisted these urges only because he was stunned into a frozen stupor, not comprehending what was happening, or how, or why.

Willing himself to do something, he looked around. The piece of wood he was floating on looked like part of a wrecked ship—an old one, like the Spanish galleons pictured in his school history books.

In most directions around him, there was nothing to see except more sickly green water, although he thought he could see land to his right. It was far away, but he was pretty sure it was there.

He let his arms hang off the sides of the wood and began to slowly paddle. Before long, he began to shiver violently. There was a chilly edge to the wind that would be merely uncomfortable if he were dry, but soaked as he was, he'd probably freeze to death soon.

If he didn't get knocked off his makeshift lifeboat and drown first.

It was impossible to measure time. He didn't bother trying to check his phone; there was no way it worked anymore. He might have paddled for five minutes, or fifty. He wasn't sure.

As he slowly drew closer to land, he became increasingly convinced that his awkward paddling wasn't accomplishing much. More likely, the small waves were doing most of the work. He stopped paddling to let his aching muscles recover.

When he finally drew close enough to shore that he could stand up in the water, he silently thanked the driftwood that had saved his life and slogged the rest of the way up to dry land. He collapsed to his knees in gray sand that looked and felt more like wet ashes.

Idly, he noticed that his fingers were turning blue. Still shivering so hard that using his hands was difficult, he wormed his way out of his sodden hoodie and tossed it aside. He felt slightly warmer without the heavy mass of soaked cotton pressing against him, but it wasn't enough. He needed heat, and shelter from the rain—the upside-down rain that was now pulling itself from the very earth to ascend into the clouds, as though he were watching a movie in reverse.

Forcing himself to stand, Dylan looked around, studying the beach more closely. As far as he could see in both directions, there was nothing along the shore except more driftwood, a few blue-gray crabs wandering about —and the shattered hull of a large wooden boat.

A shiver ran up Dylan's spine, but this time, it wasn't from the cold. He thought about the wood he'd ridden to shore and the jagged metal in the creature's mouth.

He had a feeling he knew what had happened to the boat.

Farther inland, he could see something that looked like it might be a small clump of buildings. Eager to get far away from the water, he began walking in that direction, and once the soggy sand gave way to firmer earth, he started to run. Dylan hated running, but he needed warmth, and the only way to get warm at the moment was to get his heart rate up.

As he ran, his breath coming in ragged pulls, one thought began to crowd all others out of his mind.

Where was Sara?

* * *

Alex sat up with a gasp, panting. She tried to open her eyes, then realized that they were already open—she just couldn't see anything because it was pitch black.

She sat still, afraid to move. She was sitting on something hard and cold, maybe stone or concrete.

Where am I?

She tried to think. The last thing she remembered was Dylan falling unconscious at the dinner table. What had he been doing before that?

Eating cake.

She gasped. Had Ethan and Sara poisoned Dylan? Had they poisoned her and Tom, too?

It didn't make any sense. Why would they do such a thing?

Yet, she could think of no other explanation.

Alex searched her mental archive of pharmacology knowledge as she tested her limbs and checked her pulse, gathering information that might help her figure out what she'd been dosed with. She felt weak and sleepy, but other than that, she seemed to be alright, and her vitals were within normal limits. It was probably some kind of pre-op sedative designed to wear off after a few hours, maybe midazolam or something similar.

Cautiously, she stood up, feeling around. As her eyes adjusted, she realized that it wasn't quite pitch black, just nearly so. Very faintly, she could make out four walls and a ceiling, and several large, rectangular objects about waist high. Feeling them gingerly, she found that they, too, were made of smooth stone.

She felt around in her pocket. Her phone was still there. She pulled it out and tried to unlock it, but the screen wouldn't turn on. After fiddling with it for a minute, she realized that it wasn't on and wouldn't turn on. It wasn't damaged, as far as she could tell, and the battery should be more than half full. She couldn't understand what the problem was. She put the phone back in her pocket.

Looking up, she noticed a small sliver of silvery-white light filtering in through a crack in the ceiling. She stared at it hard, trying to discern more detail. It looked like a loose piece of stone in the ceiling.

Kicking off her heels—trying to climb in those would kill her for sure—she carefully stood on top of one of the rectangular stone blocks. Stretching her arms, she could just barely reach the ceiling.

There was indeed a loose stone. It felt like the mortar holding it in place was old, much of it having flaked away over many years. She shoved at the loose stone, and it fell away, just barely missing her head as it crashed to the ground. She yipped, startled.

That was dumb, she thought. *Probably shouldn't have been standing right under it.*

At least she could see now. Moonlight illuminated most of the small room.

Alex realized she was standing on a sarcophagus. There were three in total. Suddenly uneasy, she hopped back down to the floor.

"What the hell am I doing in a mausoleum?" she asked aloud. Her voice came back to her with a ghostly echo, bouncing off the highly polished walls.

She turned to the door. It, too, was made of stone, and it looked like it probably weighed hundreds of pounds. Bracing her feet against the floor, she leaned against the door and shoved with all her might.

It didn't budge. *Wonderful,* she thought. It was probably locked from the outside—many mausoleums were, to prevent theft and vandalism.

Her next thought made her stiffen and sent a frigid chill of fear up her spine.

That means someone locked me in here.

Panic began to rise in her throat. She had known Ethan and Sara for years. They were some of the kindest, best people she knew—or were they? What possible reason could they have for doing this to her? And to Dylan and Tom, wherever they were?

"Help!" she shouted, as loudly as she could. "Someone help me!" She clambered back on top of the sarcophagus and screamed toward the hole in the ceiling, trying to send her voice as far into the night as possible.

After several minutes of shouting, her throat started to hurt. She forced the panic down, locking it away. She needed to think. Yelling wasn't helping. If anyone could hear her, they'd have come by now. Step one was getting out of here. Her questions could wait.

She looked around again. The ceiling was too high. Even if she could knock more stones loose and make a hole big enough to climb through, she didn't have the upper body strength to haul herself out that way. Forcing the door open would never happen in a million years. That left the walls.

Alex carefully did a lap around the room, trailing her fingers along the stone and carefully inspecting every crack, searching for openings or weaknesses. She found none.

"Well, shit," she said to herself. Clasping her hands behind her back, she began pacing back and forth.

After several minutes, she had nothing.

There's no way out. I'm going to die in here. Slowly but surely, her claustrophobia was beginning to flare up. The mausoleum wasn't exactly tiny, but the more she thought about being trapped inside, with no way out, the more strongly the panic came rushing back.

Again, she forced it down. *Work the problem*, she told herself. Telling herself that there was no solution wouldn't help anything. There had to be some way out. She just had to find it.

"The floor," she said, snapping her fingers. She knelt and began crawling back and forth, inspecting the stone tiles. As she covered more ground and found the floor to be just as solid as the walls, the wave of panic and hopelessness crested again. Once more, she fought it back, trying to stay focused on the task at hand. As long as she was doing *something*, she was gathering new information, learning more about her situation. There was no reason to freak out yet.

Finally, in the far corner, near the door, she found a broken piece of tile about the size of her hand. Once she'd pried it free, she could feel cool dirt underneath.

An idea came to her. She retrieved the stone that had fallen out of the ceiling and brought it back to the corner. It was a good size, and quite heavy. Raising it high in both hands, she hurled it at the broken tile as hard as she could. A spiderweb of cracks appeared in the floor. She picked up the stone and smashed it down again, and again, and again.

After a few minutes, she was panting and sweating, but she had something she could work with. She tossed broken pieces of stone aside and began to dig in the loose dirt with her hands. The soil was thick, wet, and cold. She suddenly realized that she, too, was freezing—she could see her breath forming clouds in the air, but she'd been too focused on other things to notice. Now, though, the cold was starting to seep into her bones, despite her intense workout.

After nearly an hour, Alex had removed several buckets worth of dirt, which now sat in a pile a few feet away. She'd discovered something under the ground she hadn't expected. Along with the dirt, pieces of old clay had started to come out of the hole. Now that she could see inside, she finally realized where the clay was coming from.

Flooding was a problem in most cemeteries, so robust drainage systems were a high priority. Alex was staring at the top of an old drainage tunnel. She vaguely recalled from her college anthropology class that clay was not an ideal material for drainage systems; modern societies rarely used it. Wherever she was, the graveyard must be hundreds of years old.

Her heartbeat quickened. The tunnel was three feet in diameter, at most. Her claustrophobia wasn't too bad in reasonably open areas, but she was not at all prepared to squeeze into a space that tight.

Part of her fear morphed into anger. What kind of sick joke was this?

Alex sat back on her heels and tried to think. What other option was there? None, as far as she could tell. A rectangular room had only six possible exits: floor, ceiling, four walls. Five of those six were firmly ruled out.

Maybe there was something useful inside the sarcophagi. She approached one of them and tried to shove the lid open. It didn't move at all; it was far too heavy for her. She tried the other two with the same result. She looked around for something she could use to lever the lids open, but there was nothing.

Out of options, she turned back to the hole. She swallowed hard, trying not to think about what she had to do.

She couldn't sit around in here forever. She had no reason to think help was coming.

And if someone did come for her, they may not be coming to help.

That thought got her moving. Diving deep into her dwindling reserves of willpower, she forced herself to lie down and start worming into the hole.

I have no way of knowing where this goes. Maybe it doesn't lead anywhere. Maybe it'll just collapse and crush me to death.

"Not helping," she said aloud to herself.

Once she was fully inside the tunnel, her panic returned in full force. Frigid water and sticky mud squished into her sleeves, her shirt, the waistband of her jeans. Her shoulders were wedged tightly against the sides. She could turn her head, but just barely. She lay still for a moment, trying to control her breathing.

Stop hyperventilating. You need oxygen, and you need to stay calm. If you pass out in here, you're done.

Mentally, she visualized slamming a door and locking it, shutting her fear away. She inched forward, pulling with her fingers, pushing with her toes, and wiggling her shoulders to crawl along like a snake. She felt like a sardine.

Never before have I been so grateful to have small boobs, she thought, then laughed aloud. Oddly, she felt a little calmer. *That's it. Stay focused on something else, something not terrifying.*

Inch by inch, she pressed forward. It was now impossible to see anything ahead, so she closed her eyes. Somehow, the darkness was a little less paralyzing if she kept her eyes shut. It seemed a comforting lie to tell herself, that it was dark because she chose to make it so.

Before long, she was exhausted. Each minuscule increment of progress took a lot out of her. She was moving her muscles in ways they weren't meant to move, and it was rapidly taking a toll on her stamina.

Suddenly, she stopped moving forward. She tried to pull with her hands and push with her feet, as she'd been doing, but it was no longer working. She could barely breathe. Every time she tried to inhale, the tunnel wouldn't allow it. Her chest and back were both tightly wedged. Her ribs were compressed. She couldn't get a full breath. Her open mouth was hardly an inch from the surface of the muddy water.

The fear came roaring back and she started to hyperventilate. At some point, the pipe must have narrowed. She was wedged firmly in place.

Okay, okay, it's fine. Chill out. Just go back. Get back to the mausoleum and think of something else.

She tried to back up, pushing with her hands.

She didn't budge.

The wall of reason and willpower holding back the fear collapsed. She began to cry, trying in vain to breathe, to move, to do anything that would improve her situation.

None of it was working.

"Help!" she shouted. Her voice echoed ahead of her, fading into the distance. She screamed over and over, sobbing freely now.

No one could hear her. No one was coming.

She struggled to control herself, but it was no good. Her chest burned, her lungs were on fire. She couldn't breathe. She was starting to feel lightheaded. She shook her entire body furiously, raging against the very earth, trying to move with enough force to dislodge herself.

This drainage tunnel would be her tomb.

She heard a noise somewhere above her. She choked off her sobs, trying to listen. Had she imagined it?

There it was again. Very faintly, but it was there. Somewhere above and ahead of her.

It sounded like someone calling her name.

"Help! I'm here!" she shouted with renewed hope. She hollered over and over, using what precious little air she had, trying to be as loud as she could.

Several minutes passed. She began to think she'd imagined it. She was dying. Her dying brain had conjured a fantasy of being rescued, that was all.

But then, suddenly, she could see. A small square of moonlight appeared a few feet ahead of her. Steadily, it grew bigger. Someone above was hitting the roof of the tunnel with something heavy. Bits of broken clay and dirt fell into the tunnel, and then a large rock.

A pair of hands grabbed the rock and shoved it aside. A face appeared ahead of her, upside-down. In her state of oxygen-deprived delirium, it took her a moment to realize who it was.

"Tom?" she whispered hoarsely.

"Alex!" he said. "Holy shit, what are you doing in here?"

She didn't know what to say. Instead, she began to cry again. "Please help me."

"Okay, yeah, right. I'm gonna help you. Just try to calm down." His head disappeared, and a moment later, his arm came reaching toward her. "Stretch as far as you can, grab my hand," he yelled.

Alex stretched, reaching as far ahead as she could. With the greatest effort, she managed to grab his hand, but hers was so slick with mud that it slipped away. She tried again, got a better grip, and pulled as hard as she could. She could feel him pulling as well, but he was upside down and in an awkward position. He didn't have much leverage.

Still, she didn't budge.

"Alex, I'm gonna let go of your hand, but just for a second. Stay calm. I'm not leaving you," Tom said, poking his head back into the hole. "Alex, look at me." She looked at him. "We're gonna get you out of here, but you're gonna have to do something you don't wanna do."

Her heart, already hammering, began to race even faster. "What? What do you mean?"

"The tunnel gets even tighter about a foot ahead of you, but then it opens up again. We just need to get you past that part."

"How? I can't...." She trailed off, unwilling to contemplate forcing herself into an even tighter space.

"Listen. You can, and you have to. I'm gonna help. I'm not leaving until you're out of there. But you're stuck. We're gonna do this together. I'll take your hand again, and I'll pull, but you need to push all the air out of your lungs. You need to make yourself as small as possible."

Once again, the panic tightened its grip. "I can't! I already can't breathe! I'll get stuck, and I'll suffocate!"

"No, you won't. I won't let that happen."

"Just break the pipe above me! You broke it to get in here!"

Tom shook his head. "I can't. There's a mausoleum right above you, I can't get in there. This is as close as I could get. You've gotta come to me. You can do it."

She had no answer. She felt like she was close to passing out. Each breath was so shallow. She was getting so little air.

"Alex. If you die in there, it's gonna make me feel like shit for the rest of my life. Come on. Don't do that to me," Tom said softly.

Alex blinked. What an odd thing to say. And yet... he wasn't wrong. It wasn't only her life at stake here.

She couldn't die knowing that her death would ruin someone else's life.

"Okay," she said weakly. "Okay."

"Good. Let's do it. Once I grab your hand again, I'm going to count to three. On three, you push all the air out, and then you let me do the rest. I'll pull. It's gonna take more than one try. Every time you hear me say 'three,' you exhale. That's all you need to focus on. I'll do the rest."

He reached down and took her hand again. Alex tried to do what he'd said, tried to focus on her one job.

It was easier said than done.

"One, two, three," Tom called.

Against every instinct of self-preservation, Alex exhaled as hard as she could. Tom pulled, nearly ripping her shoulder out of its socket.

She felt herself slide forward. Not much, maybe an inch. But she moved.

"One, two, three," Tom yelled again.

Again, she exhaled, and again, she moved forward a tiny bit.

She was getting dizzy. She hadn't had a full breath in so long.

"I can't stay conscious much longer," she said.

"Almost there. Come on. One, two, three."

Suddenly, she jerked forward several inches. The pressure on her back eased up just a bit, allowing her to draw perhaps one-quarter of a full breath.

After several more repetitions, Tom pulled her up, through the hole, and out into the cool night air, falling onto his back as he freed her. Alex collapsed on top of him, sobbing, gasping for air. He held her, letting her recover.

After several minutes, the fear slowly began to fade. Once she was breathing normally again, she pushed herself away and sat up.

"Tom... thank you."

He smiled, stood up, and offered his hand to her. "Buy me a beer sometime."

She took his hand and stood. As she looked into his eyes, she noticed something odd about them. "Your eyes...," she said, trailing off.

"Do they look weird?" he asked. She nodded. "Kind of glassy and far away, like I'm on something?"

Alex nodded again. "How did you know?"

"Yours look the same way."

She blinked, expecting her eyes to feel different somehow. They didn't. "I don't understand what's happening. Where are we? How did we get here?"

Tom shook his head. "No idea."

"Did Ethan and Sara do this to us?"

"I think so."

"Why?"

"Again, no idea."

"How did you find me?"

"I heard you yelling for help a while ago. Well, I didn't know it was you, but I heard someone yelling. I came to about half a mile that way," he said, pointing.

She looked in that direction. The small cemetery was surrounded by a tall iron fence. Outside the fence, she could see low, grassy hills, and a beach far in the distance. In the opposite direction, farther inland, there was a small cluster of run-down buildings, maybe half a mile away.

"What happened to you?" she asked.

Tom grimaced. "Snakes." He said nothing more, and she didn't press him.

"God. Were you bitten?"

"No, I don't think so. I should have been. There were so many of them. I got lucky."

"Earlier tonight, when we were outside, you said you were afraid of snakes," Alex said. Tom nodded. "I'm claustrophobic, and...." She gestured weakly at the broken pipe.

"Alex," Tom said, waiting for her to look at him. When she did, he went on. "I don't know where we are, but there's something wrong with this place. Very wrong."

"What do you mean?"

"When I tell you, you're gonna think I'm crazy."

She forced a weak smile. "We don't use that word in my profession."

"You will now."

Her smile faded. "What happened?"

"When I woke up, it was raining. It stopped just a little while ago."

That explained the wet grass under her bare feet. "So?"

"It was raining upside-down." Alex blinked, unsure what to say. "I swear it's true. Water was coming up out of the ground and rising into the sky," he said, pointing up.

"Tom, that's—"

"Not possible? I'm well aware."

Before Alex could respond, Tom suddenly spun around, as though he'd heard something. Alex saw his right hand move to his hip. He then brought his empty hand up to his face and stared at it in confusion for a moment, before muttering, "Shit."

"What is it?" Alex whispered.

"Who's there?" Tom called, toward some bushes outside the fence. "Come out."

After a long pause, a familiar voice drifted toward them. "Mr. Davis?"

"Dylan!" Alex called. "Yes, it's us!"

The bushes rustled, and Dylan emerged. He grabbed the iron bars, resting his forehead against them. "I'm so glad to see you," he said. He looked on the verge of tears.

"Dylan, are you okay? Are you hurt?" Alex asked, rushing to the fence. She noticed that his eyes had the same glassy, faraway look as Tom's.

"Yeah, I'm okay. Well, mostly," he said, holding out his right hand. Alex took it gently. There were several long, deep gashes in his palm. Dried blood, black in the pale moonlight, covered his entire hand and the lower half of his forearm. When she gently touched the injury, he winced in pain.

Alex then noticed a small, cleaner cut on his left palm. While examining it, she saw a similar cut on her left hand as well. It didn't hurt. She must not have noticed it earlier. She looked at Tom. He held out his left hand, displaying an identical cut.

"What happened?" Tom asked.

"You would never believe me in a million years," Dylan said, his voice wavering.

"More unbelievable than upside-down rain?" Tom asked.

"You saw that, too?" Dylan gasped. Tom nodded.

"This is insane," Alex said, releasing Dylan's hand.

"You think we're both lying? Or that we both imagined the same thing?" Tom asked.

"No, but—it can't rain upside-down. It just can't," she said, surprised at the uncertainty in her own voice.

"Dylan, you're soaked," Tom observed.

"Yeah, I... fell in the ocean," he mumbled, shivering.

"You *fell* into the ocean? From where?" Alex asked.

"I don't know. Nowhere, I think. Just, somewhere up in the air. Like I just appeared there."

Alex folded her arms. "Next you're going to tell me there was a sea monster."

Dylan burst into tears and fell to his knees. Alex stared at him, stunned by his reaction. "Dylan, what's wrong?" she asked.

"Come on," Tom said. "Let's get over to him. The gate's this way."

"Dylan, just sit tight, we'll be right there," Alex said, unsure what she'd said to upset him but feeling guilty, nonetheless.

A minute later, Tom and Alex had exited the cemetery and reached Dylan on the other side of the fence. He was still sobbing, holding his face in his hands. Alex knelt next to him.

"Dylan, honey," she said, trying to sound maternal. "Tell me what happened. I'm sorry if I upset you. We need to help each other figure out what's going on."

"You won't believe me. I'm not even sure I believe it," he choked out.

Tom knelt beside Alex. "Jesus, there really was a sea monster," he whispered. Dylan began to cry even harder. "I'll take that as confirmation," Tom said softly, placing a hand on Dylan's shoulder.

Alex didn't believe it for a second, but this wasn't the time to point that out. Instead, she reached out and pulled Dylan into a hug. "It's alright, we'll figure this out. But for now, let's try to get out of here and get back home, or at least somewhere we know. Okay?"

Dylan looked up at her, his filthy face streaked with tears. When he noticed her eyes, he blinked in surprise. "What's wrong with your eyes?"

"I don't know, Dylan. Yours look the same way. So do Tom's. I don't think it's anything to worry about just now."

"Have you seen Sara?"

Alex didn't know how to answer that. She realized that because Dylan was the first one to fall unconscious, that probably meant that the drugs had hit him the hardest. He may not remember much.

He may not realize that Sara was the one who had done this to them.

Alex glanced at Tom. He held her gaze for a long moment, then gave an almost imperceptible shake of his head.

"No, sweetie, we haven't seen her," Alex said. Tom nodded his agreement. "Maybe she's nearby."

"Come on," Tom said, gently pulling Dylan along. "Let's go check out those buildings over there. Maybe there's a car or a phone, something we can use."

"A landline maybe? My cell won't turn on," Alex said.

"Mine neither," Tom said.

"Mine's probably broken," Dylan said meekly. "It's soaked."

"Let's go," Tom said again. "I'm sure we'll find something helpful."

With that, he set off toward the buildings at a brisk walk, Alex and Dylan following closely behind.

* * *

Tom, Alex, and Dylan stood shoulder to shoulder, each confused by what they were seeing. The cluster of buildings looked like a village pulled straight out of eighteenth-century Europe.

Most of the simple buildings were a single story, and none were taller than two. All had clapboard siding that may have been white once upon a time but was now faded with age. The window glass was warped and had visible imperfections, as though it had been glazed by inexpert hands. Some of the buildings looked like small homes. Others appeared to be old-timey taverns, general stores, or tradesmen's shops.

The buildings were arranged roughly in a circular pattern, with a large plaza in the center. In the middle of the plaza stood a multitiered stone fountain decorated with naked, frolicking cherubs. It was filled with rancid water and looked like it hadn't worked for a long time.

There was no sign of electricity anywhere. Tall, wrought-iron lampposts held glass-sided oil lanterns that swayed gently in the breeze. Some of the windowsills held half-melted wax candles, all extinguished.

"Did we go back in time?" Dylan asked, rubbing his arms against the cold. Alex could hear his teeth chattering.

"Given what else I've seen today, it wouldn't surprise me," Tom muttered. "Stay close to me and be quiet. I want to find out if anyone's here."

Tom led Dylan and Alex to the nearest building, a squat house not much bigger than the one-room huts he'd seen in Afghanistan. He stopped next to a low stone wall outside the house. Decorative iron bars with pointed ends topped the wall, probably to stop birds from perching there.

One of the iron bars was broken and lying on the ground. Tom picked it up and hefted it, feeling the weight. It was about three feet long, heavy, and sharp on one end.

In the absence of his gun, it would do.

Feeling better now that he was armed, Tom slowly approached the house's front door, listening. When he reached it, he pressed his ear against it, staying as far to one side as possible. He couldn't hear anything inside. He wasn't sure that meant anything. The door was pretty thick, probably decent at blocking sound.

He turned to the others. Alex was chewing her lip, trying to stay cool. Dylan had that deer-in-the-headlights look again, his eyes huge and darting nervously.

"Stay here," Tom said, keeping his voice low. "I'm gonna take a quick look inside. If you hear anything that doesn't sound good, or if I'm not back in two minutes, run. Get as far away as you can and try to find somewhere safe."

"Are you sure about this?" Alex whispered.

"No, but we need information, resources, something. I didn't see anything else in the distance, just empty grass fields. If you have a better idea, I'm listening."

She didn't have a better idea. Tom looked at Dylan. He, too, shook his head.

"Two minutes," Alex said.

"Two minutes," Tom confirmed.

The bargain struck, Tom turned back to the door. Instead of a knob, it had a heavy iron ring. Gingerly, he tugged on it. The door opened silently on well-oiled hinges. It was dark inside. The faint moonlight only illuminated the floor in the entryway, an open doorway a little farther inside, and part of a wall. The floorboards were rough and irregular, probably cut by hand.

He didn't bother taking out the small flashlight he always carried with him. It didn't work. He'd tried using it as soon as he woke up here. The batteries were fresh, and the bulb wasn't damaged, but it wouldn't turn on.

Silently, walking heel to toe, Tom crept into the house. He held his makeshift weapon in both hands, low at his right side. Keeping his back to the wall, he peeked through the open doorway.

It was a small kitchen, minus any electric appliances. It had a wood stove, a straw mat on the floor, even an old-fashioned butter churn.

On the opposite side of the small kitchen was another open doorway, with a dining room beyond that. In the dim light, Tom could just barely make out a human shape sitting at the table. He squinted. The person had long hair. It looked like a girl or a young woman.

Her back was to him. She wasn't moving.

Tom inhaled, then exhaled slowly. *This is a bad idea*, he thought.

Before he could change his mind, he stepped around the corner, keeping the iron bar behind his back to appear nonthreatening. "Excuse me," he said quietly, trying to sound more apologetic than terrified. "My friends and I are lost. Can you help us?"

At the sound of his voice, the girl whipped around so violently that Tom took a step back, startled.

Nothing could have prepared him for her face.

She had no lower jaw. It looked to have been ripped clean off by some unspeakable violence. Bits of rotting flesh clung to her cheekbones, and a blackened tongue lolled wildly from her open throat. Her left eye was missing. The right eye hung halfway down her face, dangling by a thin bunch of nerves.

Before Tom could process what he was seeing, she lunged for him, screeching like some feral beast.

His training and instincts took over. Skills he hadn't used in two decades came out with only a heartbeat of delay. Unconsciously, and with lightning speed, he noted that the narrow kitchen wouldn't permit a horizontal swing with the bar—he'd hit the wall, and then he'd be dead. Thrusting attacks were best in tight spaces.

He lunged forward to meet her with a powerful front kick. The heel of his heavy boot caught her in the nose, and she stumbled back with a sickening crunch. Ribbons of thick black fluid sprayed over his boot, his lower pant leg, the nearby wall.

In the back of his mind, Tom knew that he couldn't afford to respond with anything less than unrestrained violence. The kidnapping, the upside-down rain, the snakes, Dylan's impossible encounter with a sea monster—whatever was going on, Tom was not in the world he knew, and playing by that world's rules would get him killed. He couldn't worry about things like use-of-force laws. He didn't know what all the pieces of this fucked-up puzzle added up to, but he knew with crystal clarity that if he gave this girl —this *thing*—so much as a heartbeat of time to mount an attack, it would kill him.

And then it would tear Alex and Dylan apart, too.

Following the momentum of his kick, Tom stepped forward, shifted most of his weight to his front leg, and stabbed with the iron bar, using the pointed end like a spear. With shocking agility, the creature leaped aside, dodging the attack entirely. Tom stumbled forward, trying to recover his balance.

In a flash, his opponent was behind him. He didn't spare the time to turn around. It was faster than he was—it had just proven that. Instead, he drove his right elbow back as hard as he could, hoping he'd estimated his point of aim correctly.

He felt and heard another nauseating crunch, suggesting that he'd hit it in the face again. Stepping forward and away from the creature to get some distance, he turned, raising the iron bar over his right shoulder.

Incredibly, the creature was already on him. Tom had always thought he was quick, in terms of both agility and reflexes.

Not quick enough, apparently.

His weapon clattered to the floor as the creature leaped on top of him, driving him down. The back of his head smacked the wall as he fell, and he nearly blacked out. He fumbled blindly and managed to seize the creature around the throat with both hands.

It was impossibly strong. Even pushing with all his considerable strength, it was all he could do to keep its jagged yellow teeth away from his neck. It wouldn't need a lower jaw to rip open his jugular. The black tongue thrashed around crazily, licking his face.

The taste of his sweat seemed to intensify the creature's fury. It beat at him with both hands, trying to pummel him into submission. Its strength was out of all proportion to the size of its spindly arms and body. Each blow hit his face and chest like a hammer, but he dared not let go of its throat.

He had to get back on offense. Kicking up his right leg, he struggled to wedge his knee under its left thigh, but the gap was too tight. He tried again, failing again. The teeth and tongue were scant inches from his throat.

Its breath smelled like rotten meat.

Finally, he was able to get his knee under its thigh. He pushed his leg up with all his might, widening the gap. As soon as there was enough room, he whipped his other leg around its waist and bucked his hips to the left, throwing the creature off balance. He rolled with it, his stamina rapidly waning, and managed to secure an awkward mount.

The creature continued to strike and punch at him while simultaneously trying to find exposed flesh to bite. He still didn't dare take his hands off its neck. Turning his head left and right, he searched for a weapon.

There, on a short bookcase, just in front of him—a cross that looked to be made of heavy stone. Keeping his left hand where it was, he reached out with his right and snatched the cross, immediately bringing it down on the monster's forehead with a wet crunch. He struck again and again, dealing devastating damage, but the creature seemed unfazed and kept up its relentless thrashing.

Finally, the cross broke into pieces. For the briefest instant, the creature slowed. It may not have been feeling pain, but the sheer trauma Tom had inflicted on its face seemed to have some effect.

Wasting no time, he jumped to his feet and scooped up the iron bar. With all his strength, Tom swung it down, aiming for the floor underneath the creature's head. The heavy bar destroyed what remained of the creature's forehead, cracking the thick bone into several pieces.

Finally, it went still. Tom knew better than to assume it was dead. He pressed the attack, bringing the heavy weapon down on its pulverized face over and over, reducing the head to black mush.

He stopped swinging only when his chest began to heave with exertion. Panting, he looked around, scanning the area for other threats. He saw no other deformed monster girls, but what he did see made his stomach churn.

On the floor, on the far side of the dining room, were the partially eaten remains of a person. The body was so badly mutilated that he couldn't even tell if it was a boy, girl, man, or woman—or even another one of the creatures with damaged faces.

Tom had seen a lot of violence and depravity, but none of it had prepared him for that. He doubled over and vomited.

"Tom!" Alex cried as she ran up to him. He held out a hand, warning her to stay back. He wiped his mouth, desperate to talk before she came into the dining room.

"Alex! Stop! Stay there," he managed to get out. Thankfully, she obeyed. "Don't come in here. For the love of whatever god you believe in, don't come in here." His words and his shaking voice changed something in her face. She looked down. The creature he'd killed had collapsed across the kitchen doorway. When she saw its destroyed head, she took a step back, covering her mouth with her hands.

"Tom, what—"

"Get out. Back outside. Move," he said, stepping toward her. He grabbed her arm firmly enough to pull her along, but he took care not to hurt her.

Dylan met them at the front door. "We heard—"

Tom cut him off. "It's not safe here. We have to leave, now."

Dylan opened his mouth to say something but closed it again when he saw the smoldering rage in Tom's eyes—and the barely controlled fear in Alex's.

As the three of them jogged across the plaza, doors of other buildings began to open. Within seconds, a dozen emaciated figures with terribly injured faces were sprinting toward them.

Tom quickly sized up their options. A narrow alleyway to the right looked clear. He hated the thought of getting boxed in back there, but he couldn't see a better exit. The creatures were closing in from every other direction.

"Run!" Tom shouted. Dylan and Alex didn't need to be told twice. "Don't get separated!" He sprinted to the alley, glancing back to make sure they were following. The alley ran straight for about twenty paces, then curved sharply to the left. As soon as Tom rounded the corner, he saw that there was no way out. A ten-foot wall blocked further passage.

"God damn it!" he swore as Alex and Dylan skidded to a halt beside him. "Get behind me," he said, putting himself between them and the entrance. "Dylan, help Alex over that wall, then I'll help you. Do it fast."

Dylan stared at him, his mouth hanging open. "I'm not—I can't—"

Tom shoved him, hard. "Now!"

"Dylan, come on, I need your help," Alex said, pulling him by the hand. Finally, he went, all color drained from his face.

Tom turned to face the alley entrance. Creatures were already sprinting toward him, mindless violence in their eyes—those that still had eyes. Fighting one of those things had been hard enough. If more than one ganged up on him, he was done. He looked around, searching for other options. To his right, a few feet ahead, was a tall stack of large wooden crates.

He darted toward them and crammed the iron bar between the topmost box and the wall behind it, using the heavy piece of metal as a prybar. He shoved hard, and the box toppled to the ground. He quickly did the same with two more boxes, creating a half-assed barricade. It wasn't much, but it was better than nothing.

It did at least slow them down a little. The first few creatures scrambled over the boxes, but as they did so, they couldn't use their hands. Tom took full advantage of that fact as he laid into them.

He abandoned any thought of killing them. There were too many. He only needed to keep them at bay long enough to get over the wall. The best thing to do would be to create as much chaos as possible. He stabbed at the first creature, knocking it back into the others. He swung the bar and took out the next one's ankles, causing it to crumple. A third leaped over the first two, and Tom aimed a vicious side kick at its knee. He felt bone snap, and the creature went down, sprawling across the others.

Each monster that fell made it harder for those behind to get past them. Tom risked a glance back to see how Alex and Dylan were doing. Surprisingly, Alex was already on top of the wall, leaning down with her hand extended. Dylan jumped, grabbed her hand, and awkwardly tried to pull himself up, but he wasn't making much progress.

Tom looked back at the advancing wave of horrors. Within another few seconds, the sheer weight of their numbers would roll right over the temporary bottleneck he'd created.

It was time to go.

He turned and booked it. When he reached the wall, Dylan was still only halfway up, flailing his legs. Alex simply wasn't strong enough to pull him up. Tom dropped the bar and pushed Dylan's feet up. He and Alex both toppled over the wall, neither one prepared for the sudden boost. Dylan managed to land on his feet, but Alex landed on her back, smacking her head on the ground. She screamed in pain, clutching her head, fighting to remain conscious as her vision swam. With Dylan's help, she managed to get to her feet and start moving again.

Wasting no time, Tom jumped for the top of the wall, managing to grab it on the first try. He pulled himself partway up, then grunted in surprise, suddenly feeling his age. *This was a lot easier when I was twenty-five*, he thought. Slowly, with great effort, he managed to get his chest on top of the wall, taking some of the strain off his arms.

Something grabbed his left foot and bit into the flesh above his ankle, hard. Tom howled in rage and slid partway down the wall, resisting with all his might, his biceps burning. If they pulled him down, he'd be shredded in seconds.

Looking back to aim, he kicked awkwardly with his right foot. He struck the thing in the face, but it held fast, trying to rip his calf muscle clean off the bone. He kicked it again, and again, but still, it refused to let go. The others were closing in, the next one only a few steps away.

Finally, on the fourth kick, he made solid contact and managed to pull his other foot away. Adrenaline surged through him, granting him a fresh burst of strength. In a moment, he cleared the wall and dropped to the ground on the other side. Under normal circumstances, his aging knees might have been able to withstand the fall, but when he hit the ground, the deep bites in his leg pulsed with white-hot pain, and he toppled over.

Dylan and Alex were already running and were well ahead of him. *Good*, he thought. *Get clear.* He hobbled to his feet and started to run. Each step made the pain in his leg flare again. He ignored it.

Before he caught up to them, another wave of monsters came flooding down the street to his left. He cut right, shouting at Dylan and Alex to do the same. They heard him and changed course.

Ahead of them, the door of the last house on the lane opened. Tom braced himself, expecting another wave of creatures to come pouring out.

Instead, Sara stepped out onto the porch, waving at them.

"Here! In here!" she hollered.

Tom was shocked, not only to see her there but by what she was wearing: black body armor, and a thigh holster with some kind of small-caliber sidearm in it. She was holding an AR-15.

Now I've seen everything, he thought.

He quickly considered their options. He could see only two: Trust the girl who had drugged them and hope she wasn't planning to do worse—or keep running, out into the open plains, where the relentless creatures would surely overtake them even if his leg weren't injured.

There was no time to think about it. Option one was clearly not a good one, but option two was off the table. "Go!" he shouted to Alex and Dylan, waving them toward Sara. They went without argument, sprinting through the open door.

When Tom cleared the door, Sara slammed it behind him, dropping a heavy wooden beam in place to secure it.

"Sara, what is happening? Why do you have guns?" Alex panted, doubled over with her hands on her knees.

"There's no time," Sara said. She was right—the creatures were already pounding on the door. It was sturdy, but it wouldn't hold forever. Tom held his questions for the moment. They needed an exit strategy. Everything else was secondary.

Sara stepped toward them and held out her hand. In the dim light, it took a moment for the others to see what she was holding: four autoinjector syringes, each bearing a yellow warning label.

"What are those?" Alex asked, still out of breath.

"There's no time. Take one. Inject it in your thigh," Sara said. Her eyes had the same glassy look as theirs.

"Sara—" Dylan took a step toward her, but she cut him off.

"We have less than a minute, I'm guessing. Take it," she said again, her voice oddly calm and commanding.

"Why, so you can poison us again? You already did it once," Tom spat angrily. Dylan stared at him, not understanding why he'd said that.

So, he doesn't remember, Alex thought.

"You have no reason to trust me. I don't blame you. But those things are gonna get in here soon," Sara said.

"How is a shot supposed to help? What's in the syringes?" Alex growled, clenching her fists at her sides. In Tom's experience, she was usually pretty passive—she must be really pissed to be showing it outwardly.

"It's how we get out of here. Time's running out. Take it, or we all die," Sara said.

Her voice was too calm. The door was beginning to buckle. The heavy beam holding it shut was starting to splinter and crack. Somewhere else in the house, a window shattered.

They were coming.

Tom hated to admit it, but Sara was right about one thing: He didn't have any other ideas. Leaving the house some other way wouldn't help. Those things would certainly run them down outside.

"We're not done talking about this," Tom snapped, grabbing one of the syringes.

"No, we're not," Sara agreed, a hint of sadness in her voice.

Tom removed the safety cap and rammed the autoinjector into his thigh as she'd instructed. He felt the needle deploy with a brief prick of pain.

And then he disappeared.

"What the fuck!" Dylan screamed, falling over. "Where did Tom go?"

"Dylan, please!" Sara shouted, shoving a syringe toward him.

"Dylan, we're out of time," Alex said, trying to sound calm for his sake. "Here, I'll help you." She closed her fingers around two of the syringes, one for each of them.

CHAPTER EIGHT
Illumination

In Alex's next moment of awareness after injecting the mystery drug, she was in another strange place she didn't recognize—a large concrete room with beds, medical equipment, and a whole bunch of other people crowded into the far corner. She noticed Dylan next to her, but she didn't think he was there a moment ago. Did he just *appear* next to her? She put an arm around his shoulders protectively. She noticed that her heart was racing—faster than two hundred beats per minute, it seemed.

Then, right in front of her eyes, Sara *did* appear out of thin air. Alex could only stare in stunned silence. She couldn't believe it. It was like a Vegas magic show—Sara was not there one instant, and the next, she was.

Near the center of the room, next to the cold ashes of a dead fire, Ethan lay on his back on the floor, rubbing his jaw. Tom stood above him, looking pissed. Tom grabbed Ethan by the collar and hauled him up, pulling his fist back to hit him again.

Sara stepped forward, still holding the rifle down at her side. "Tom! Stop!"

Tom glanced at her. "Why should I?"

"Because, Tom," Ethan said, spitting out a mouthful of blood, "as much as you want to hit me, I think you want answers more, and you may find that I have a hard time giving them without teeth."

Tom paused, his fist still drawn back. "I see your goons in the corner over there. They haven't tried to stop me. They'd really just let me wail on you?"

"If you insist, yes."

"Why?"

"Because I told them to."

"That doesn't make any sense."

"I think you'll find that it does, if you give me time to explain."

Tom lowered his fist but didn't release his grip on Ethan's shirt. Ethan pulled something from behind his back: Tom's holstered pistol. Alex gasped when she saw it. Ethan held the weapon out, grip first. Tom took it and stuffed the holster back into his waistband.

Then he drew the pistol, cocked the hammer, and placed the barrel directly against Ethan's forehead. None of the suited men in the corner moved, nor did the women in white coats. They all just stood there, watching the scene unfold.

"Tom!" Sara shouted, raising her rifle. She aimed it directly at Tom's back.

Alex felt sick. Dylan had his arms wrapped around her, his face buried in her shoulder. Alex felt like she had to stop this before someone got killed, but she had no idea what to do. She was afraid that, if she interfered, she would make it worse.

Ethan raised a hand toward Sara, palm up. "Sara, lower the weapon. Tom's not going to kill me."

"You sound pretty sure," Tom growled. Reluctantly, Sara lowered her rifle, pointing it at the floor.

"You're a hell of a warrior, Tom. But you're not a cold-blooded murderer," Ethan said.

"There's a first time for everything."

"Kill me, if you really think that's the right thing to do. No one will stop you. Including Sara."

Alex glanced at Sara, who looked less than fully convinced about that.

A tense silence filled the room. It probably lasted only a few seconds, but to Alex, it felt like an hour. Sensing an opening, she took a small step forward. "Tom," she said softly. "You saved my life just a few minutes ago, and Dylan's. You're a better man than this."

Tom didn't respond or move. Ethan remained still as well, waiting for Tom to make a decision.

Finally, Tom decocked the pistol and lowered it to his side. "Talk."

"First, let's have the doctors check you out."

"Doctors?"

Ethan waved a hand, and the four women began to approach. Tom raised the handgun again, not aiming it at anyone, but clearly expecting trouble.

"Tom," Sara said, with surprising compassion in her voice. "We tricked you. We lied to you. We hurt you. And I can't tell you how much it hurt us to do it. I beg you to let us explain. I hated doing it, and so did my father. But we had no choice, and we had a reason. We don't want to hurt you anymore. Look how outnumbered you are. If we wanted to do you further harm, we've had a dozen chances in the past five minutes alone." To make her point, she crouched and laid her rifle on the ground, then stepped away from it, holding out her empty hands.

"Explain. Your. Selves," Tom said, enunciating each word, his voice low and threatening.

"You're injured," Ethan said. "These women are all doctors, just like Dr. Warner. Let them treat your wounds. Please, take a seat, and rest for a minute. All of you probably feel very on edge right now. Racing hearts? Sweating? Increased irritability?"

Alex realized he was right. "What did Sara give us?"

"Adrenaline," Sara said. "Two milligrams."

"That's four times the normal adult dose," Alex said, her eyes wide with shock. "It could've killed us."

"Yes, it could have, and it still might. It was also the only way to bring us back," Sara said.

"Back from where?" Tom asked, irritation creeping back into his voice.

"Everyone, please. In due time. We will explain everything. For now, just rest a moment," Ethan cut in.

Reluctantly, Tom sat on the nearest bed, but he kept his weapon drawn. Alex took a seat on the next bed. Instead of going to an empty bed, Dylan sat next to her. Alex knew that his heart must be racing like hers was, and he was sweating badly, but he nonetheless looked exhausted. His eyes were half closed and unfocused.

Alex realized that he might be in shock, or dangerously close to it. She placed a hand on his arm reassuringly.

Two of the women in white lab coats approached Alex and Dylan. Each was holding another syringe. "What are you giving us?" Alex asked, her suspicion flaring again. She couldn't entirely blame Tom for his outburst.

"Labetalol to counteract the adrenaline, and a very low dose of lorazepam to help you relax a little. We've dosed it carefully for each of you, based on your body weight. It won't make you sleepy," one of the doctors said.

Alex relaxed a little. The explanation made sense. "Dylan, honey, it's okay. Let her give it to you. We need to bring your heart rate down." He looked up at her but said nothing. After a long delay, he held out his arm, his dirty face still blank and pale. The two doctors bent over to administer the injections. Another did the same to Tom, and the fourth gave an injection to Sara.

Ethan rolled over to them in a wheeled office chair he'd brought in from the den. "Starting to feel better?"

"Yes," Alex said. Tom nodded his agreement as well, obviously trying hard to keep his anger in check. Dylan had finally stopped sweating, although he still hadn't said anything. Alex gently squeezed his wrist to check his heart rate. It was still too fast, but it was starting to come down.

Each of the doctors then set about examining her respective patient, disinfecting, suturing, and bandaging as needed. They were surprisingly gentle and reassuring. Tom and Dylan each received a cocktail of intravenous antibiotics because they'd both had their skin broken. Alex and Sara had suffered only bumps and bruises but were instructed to let a doctor know right away if they began to feel unwell.

"Alright, Ethan," Tom said when the doctors were finally finished. "Start explaining." He still held his sidearm tightly in his right hand, but it was pointed toward the floor, and his finger was off the trigger. Sara handed bottles of water to Tom, Alex, and Dylan, then pulled up another chair and sat next to her father. She removed her watch cap and tucked it behind her belt, letting her hair down.

"Tom, Alex, Dylan," Ethan said, looking to each of them in turn. "Every man, woman, and child on Earth needs your help."

* * *

"Say again?" Dylan said, finally coming out of his trance.

"Sara and I will tell you everything, but it will take some explaining. It won't make sense at first. You will undoubtedly think we're insane. When considering what's possible or impossible, I ask you to think about what you've just experienced, which must seem to defy explanation," Ethan said.

"You could say that," Tom said dryly.

"The place we just came back from—the place my father and I sent you to—it's called the Twilight. Very roughly translated from ancient Sumerian, it's 'the twilight land beyond the horizon of this world, forsaken by mother and father.' So, 'Twilight' for short," Sara said.

"As you've probably guessed but aren't yet willing to fully accept, the Twilight is not Earth. At least, not exactly. At the risk of massively oversimplifying it, you can think of it as a separate dimension, overlaid onto and intertwined with this one. It has a close relationship to sleep and dreams," Ethan added.

"The next time you go to sleep, no matter what, you'll return there. All of you," Sara whispered, casting her eyes down at the floor.

"I agree with the first thing you said," Tom interjected.

"Which thing?" Ethan asked.

"You're insane."

"Maybe. If so, how would you explain what you experienced?"

"Some kind of elaborate hoax. A dream. A hallucination. Three possibilities, off the top of my head," Tom said. It sounded more like a plea than a statement.

"What technology or trickery can make rain fall from the ground to the sky, right before your eyes? Can the best actors and makeup artists on the planet create creatures like the ones we barely escaped from?" Sara asked.

"And if that's true... if they were actors or something...," Alex said, trailing off.

"Then I killed a person," Tom said quietly.

"But you know it wasn't a person," Ethan said. Tom didn't answer, but Alex and Dylan both saw doubt in his eyes.

"Tom, your leg was injured. Dylan's hand. Alex's head. The wounds on your bodies right now—did you dream them into reality?" Sara asked. Each of them touched their respective injuries, vividly recalling how they'd gotten them.

"Did you all share the same dream? See one another in that dream? See, hear, and feel the exact same things—in a dream?" Ethan pressed the attack.

Tom stood up and began pacing. As he did so, he holstered his pistol. Alex breathed a small sigh of relief at seeing that. Tom was clearly still angry, but he was no longer on the brink of killing someone, at least. She turned her head to check on Dylan. His expression was unreadable, but he seemed to be listening.

"You said we would go back there the next time we go to sleep," Dylan said. Even though he wasn't looking at Sara, Alex got the impression he was directing his words at her. "So... we *were* asleep? It was a dream, but... a dream that was real somehow?"

Sara nodded. "That's one way to put it."

"But it's like *The Matrix*," Dylan said, referencing one of his favorite movies. "If you die there, you really die."

Sara nodded. "Yes." Her reply was so quiet that the others could barely hear her. "But unlike *The Matrix,* there's no separation of your mind and body. We were physically in the Twilight."

"That's why our eyes looked weird. We were asleep. I saw a documentary about people who sleepwalk. Their eyes looked like that."

Ethan offered Dylan a sad smile. "That's right. You're clever and observant, Dylan. That's one reason we need your help."

"You've said 'we need your help' a few times now. Who is 'we,' and what do you want our help with? And did it ever occur to you that drugging, kidnapping, and endangering people isn't the best way to ask for their help?" Tom said.

Ethan nodded. "All perfectly fair questions, Tom. Let me answer them one at a time, starting with the last one. Had there been any other way—*any* other way—to enlist your help, we would have done so. Once again, you have our deepest apologies for forcing it on you in this way, whatever such an apology is worth. I hope that, as we answer your other questions, you will begin to understand why this deeply regretful approach was necessary.

"As to who we are, Sara and I represent an organization known as the Circle of Mercy. Not to sound self-aggrandizing, but we are protectors of mankind, for some five thousand years now."

"Protectors of mankind," Alex repeated flatly. She felt numb with disbelief. She still wasn't convinced that any of this was real. Perhaps it was simply the latest and weirdest nightmare her sleeping mind had decided to torture her with.

Ethan went on. "The Twilight is home to a... deity, for lack of a better word. This deity, this god—whom we call Ardu—sleeps there, in a great cathedral far from the village you just visited. Every so often, he stirs and begins to wake. When that happens, it's our responsibility to put him back to sleep. Should he awaken fully, the consequences would be cataclysmic for mankind.

"I say 'would be' as though such a situation were purely hypothetical, but in fact, Ardu has awakened a number of times throughout human history. I take it you've heard of the Plague of Justinian? The 1887 Yellow River flood?"

"Two of the deadliest disasters in recorded history," Alex said, incredulous at what Ethan seemed to be implying.

"Why would this 'god' do such a thing? Surely, he'd have reasons beyond destruction for its own sake," Tom said. His tone suggested that he was asking as a way of poking holes in the story, not because he believed it.

"In ancient Akkadian, 'Ardu' means 'servant,'" Sara said.

"He serves us by killing us en masse?" Alex scoffed.

"In a way, yes," Ethan said so quietly that, at first, the others thought they'd misheard him. Raising a hand to forestall further questions, he went on. "You may be getting the impression that the Circle of Mercy's goal is to ensure that Ardu stays asleep in the Twilight. That is, in fact, our secondary objective. Our primary objective is broader than that: to buy time."

"Time for what?" Tom asked. He glanced at Dylan to see how the boy was doing. He was looking at the floor and picking his nails.

"For mankind to earn salvation," Sara put in before Ethan could answer.

Tom raised both hands in a gesture of surrender. "Alright, I give up. This doomsday cult shit is not my scene. Peddle your crazy somewhere else, I'm all full."

Alex stood up and fell in beside Tom. "I have to agree. I can't deny that we've seen some things that seem to defy explanation, but... gods? The apocalypse? Saviors of mankind?"

"I understand that it seems insane to the core. Believe me, I had the same reaction when my parents first told me this, more than forty years ago,"

Ethan said.

"So, your whole family is nuts," Tom grunted.

"Going back countless generations, I'm afraid," Ethan said in a conciliatory tone.

"Well, good luck with your Jonestown thing," Tom said as he headed for the basement door.

"If you require further proof, I can provide it," Ethan called after him. "Or rather, my daughter can."

Tom almost kept walking. The slightest pinprick of doubt made him stop, but he didn't turn back around.

"You've been having nightmares for a week now," Sara said, looking at Dylan, Alex, and Tom in turn. "So have I."

Tom turned to face her. "What is that supposed to prove? It's no secret that none of us have been sleeping."

A long, heavy silence filled the room. Sara turned her eyes down and heaved a deep sigh, reluctant to go on.

But she had to. The others weren't buying it. She had one last ace up her sleeve, and it was time to play it.

"I know what you've been dreaming about," she said, sounding tired and much older than she was.

"Is this the part where you read my horoscope?" Tom snarled, crossing his arms impatiently.

Sara looked him dead in the eye. "Manny Ramirez," she said, in a flat, matter-of-fact tone.

For a moment, Tom was stunned into silence. When he spoke, Alex half-expected his words to physically cut Sara's skin somehow, so sharp was the barely restrained fury in his voice. "Where did you hear that name?"

Sara didn't back down. "From you."

"I've only said that name to a handful of people, and none of them have ever said it to you, that I'm sure of," Tom said. "Besides, it doesn't prove anything about your batshit god story. Maybe one of my friends did mention Manny to you, for some reason—in which case, I owe them a very harsh conversation. Or you just ran a background check on me. It wouldn't be hard to find records of Manny in my life somewhere."

"How many people know his last words to you?" Sara asked. Alex, still not sure what was unfolding in front of her, was surprised to hear Sara's voice choked with emotion.

Tom said nothing. Dylan looked up, a mixture of fear and curiosity on his face. Alex held her breath. Sara kept her eyes firmly fixed on Tom's.

"'I'm fine. Get the kid,'" she finally said. A single tear fell from her eyes as she squeezed them shut.

Alex had no idea what that meant, but it pained Sara to say it, that much was obvious. For some reason, Alex expected Tom to run across the room and hit Sara. A few hours ago, the idea of Tom assaulting a teenage girl would have seemed nothing short of ludicrous. The fact that it now seemed plausible suggested that Sara had crossed a line that could never be uncrossed.

Tom did not run toward Sara, but he did walk toward her, slowly. He stopped inches from her face, reached out both hands, and grabbed the straps of her armor. Alex could see the muscles in his arms straining as he lifted her clear off the floor, her heavy boots dangling. Sara made no move to resist him. She held his gaze and kept her arms at her sides, ready to endure whatever he would do.

Tom's voice was ice. "No one knows that except me. No one." His jaw was clenched so tightly that Alex's own began to ache.

"Exactly," Sara said.

For a long moment, Tom looked like he was considering snapping her neck. Ethan watched silently. He made no move to help his daughter.

Finally, Tom lowered Sara to the floor, gently. Without another word, he walked through the open door to the basement and disappeared from view.

Alex must have zoned out for a moment. The next thing she knew, Sara was standing right in front of her, holding both of her hands. "'I forgive you. You have a lot of healing to do. Better get to it,'" she said, another tear rolling down her freckled cheek.

Alex's knees gave out, and she fell backward, barely managing to break her fall with her hands. She felt like she'd been punched in the stomach. Sara couldn't possibly have heard those words anywhere but in her dreams. Not like that, not verbatim.

Dylan scrambled backward on the bed until his back hit the wall behind it. His eyes were wide with raw terror as Sara approached him. "Sara, no," he begged. "Please."

She didn't stop. She sat on the bed next to him. His hands were balled into tight fists against his chest. She reached for them, and he resisted. She didn't fight him. She simply clasped his fists in her hands.

She waited. Dylan's lower lip trembled. He said nothing, but his face bore an unmistakable plea for mercy.

Still, Sara said nothing. Still, she waited.

Finally, Dylan seemed to deflate. His shoulders slumped, and he opened his fists. His dirty, ragged nails had dug angry red marks into his palms.

Once Sara was holding his open hands in hers, she began to sing to him, very softly.

Slumber time is drawing near,
Night is gath'ring round us.
Stars will all be bright and clear,
When the sandman has found us.
Dream sweet dreams the long night through,
Mother will be near to you.
Go to sleep, my dear one.

Dylan raised his head. Alex had seen Dylan cry a number of times in the past few hours, and she fully expected to see him crying now.

His eyes were red but dry. "Tell me what you want me to do," he said to Sara.

* * *

"I thought you might be out here," Alex said as she shut the patio door behind her. "Déjà vu, huh?"

Tom was standing with his arms folded and his back to her, in exactly the spot she'd been standing not too long ago. He was watching the snowflakes dance their silent waltz in the moonlight, as she had done during dinner, earlier that evening. He didn't turn around. "Did she mindfuck you, too?"

"That's another word we don't use in my profession, but in this case, I can't think of a better one," she said.

"And Dylan."

"I think so."

"I don't understand."

"Neither do I."

"Whatever she said to you—was it something no one else could ever possibly say to you?" Finally, Tom turned to face her. "Think carefully before you answer. Is there *anyone* else who knows whatever words she said to you? Anyone at all?"

Alex was certain that she knew the answer, but she took a moment to think it over anyway. Finally, she shook her head. "Not a soul."

"So... Sara can see our dreams. But that's not possible. Help me come up with some other explanation for this."

Alex raised her hands, then let them fall back to her sides helplessly. "When I think of one, you'll be the first person I share it with."

"No one tried to stop us. I don't think there's even anyone in the house right now, they're all downstairs in that weird room. What's to stop us from going back to our cars and leaving?"

"Nothing, as far as I can tell."

"Is Ethan that confident that he's got us trapped?"

"Maybe."

Tom studied her face. "You don't think that's the reason."

"No, I don't think so. It's more like...." She trailed off.

"More like what?"

She frowned, searching for the words. "I have this sense that, whatever 'help' he needs from us, he needs us to give it freely. I think we could leave, and he wouldn't try to stop us. That would be his answer, if not the one he's hoping for."

Tom nodded slowly. "I think you're right."

"I know we've heard a lot of strange things tonight. I have another to add to the pile."

"You want to go back and hear what else he has to say."

"Not so much 'want.' I feel like I have to."

"Then I must be just as crazy as you are." Alex opened her mouth to say something, but he cut her off. "I know, you don't use that word in your profession. Can you think of a better one?"

Alex pulled open the patio door. "No, I can't."

"You're that eager to go back down there, huh?"

She shot him a sideways glance. "No. I lost my shoes in a graveyard, if you recall, and I'm standing in the snow in my bare feet. I just want to feel my toes again."

* * *

Alex sat on the bed next to Dylan, who had regained a little of his color. She smiled as warmly as she could manage and patted the space between them. He scooted over to sit next to her, still staring at the floor.

Tom sat down on a folding chair that had appeared next to Ethan and Sara.

"Convinced?" Sara asked. Her tone was regretful rather than smug.

"Keep talking," Tom said quietly.

"As I indicated earlier, the Circle of Mercy is at least five thousand years old," Ethan said. "The oldest known written records of our order date back to 3000 BC. They are written in Sumerian, one of the earliest known written languages. Somewhat more recent records exist in Akkadian and Hittite, but they are woefully incomplete. Thankfully, our record keeping started to get much better around the time of Christ."

"This god, Ardu. How does he 'serve' us by killing us?" Alex asked.

"Mankind is impure, selfish, egotistical. There have always been moral paragons among us, but by and large, people are more concerned with their own petty dreams and dramas than they are with the well-being of their fellow men," Ethan said, taking on a tone and posture that reminded Alex of Sister Gretchen, her Catholic grade-school teacher. "It may seem hard to believe in light of what little we've told you so far, but Ardu does have mankind's best interests at heart. He wants to see us reach our full potential, to live as we were always meant to: every man his brother's keeper."

Sara chimed in. "Simply put, Ardu serves us by giving us a choice: redemption or annihilation. He hopes we will choose the former but is prepared to punish us with the latter if necessary."

Tom, Alex, and Dylan all stared at her. "You say this like you're talking about parents taking their kid's phone away for getting bad grades," Tom said, incredulous.

"The difference is one of degree, not of kind. In Ardu's eyes, anyway," Ethan sighed. "The goal of true brotherhood among men is a worthy one, of course, but if you're asking whether I believe the ends justify the means —no, I don't. However, our feelings on the matter are irrelevant. These are our two choices. We don't worship Ardu—we certainly don't sanction his methods. But it is what it is. The only choice we have to make is whether or not we will shield humanity from his wrath. Someday, people will finally learn to place others before themselves—not because they're expecting a reward, but because it's the right thing to do. That day is still a long way off. Our job—the Circle's job—is to keep mankind alive for as long as it takes for most of us to learn that lesson."

Alex frowned. "You really think that's possible? Everyone on Earth becoming Mother Teresa?"

"Honestly? I'm not sure. All we can do is buy time. As to when we, as a species, cross the finish line, Ardu will be the final judge," Ethan said. "We'll know we're there when the Maidens stop dreaming."

"Pardon?" Tom said.

"Sara is a very special girl. The three of you knew that already, but you didn't know just how special she is. Sara is what we call a Maiden—a young woman chosen to put Ardu back to sleep, to buy mankind another generation of life, another few decades to learn and grow," Ethan said, smiling proudly at his daughter. She smiled back, her eyes moist.

"And how is she supposed to do that?" Tom sighed. Alex thought he was showing remarkable patience.

"There is a veil between this world and the Twilight, a barrier that prevents passage in either direction. But when Ardu begins to stir, as his power slowly begins to grow, the veil weakens, becomes thinner. At that time, all Maidens of the Circle begin having unmistakable nightmares. That is our signal that another cycle is ending. Her first nightmare begins a countdown. It tells her that, from that day forward, she has seven days to prepare. After that, the veil weakens enough to allow passage in both directions by means of an ancient ritual. She then has another seven days to enter the Twilight, reach the cathedral, and put Ardu back to sleep," Ethan explained.

"How long is a 'cycle?'" Alex asked.

"For most of recorded history, each cycle was roughly eighty years long," Sara said. "But sometime around the late eighteenth century, they started getting shorter—a lot shorter. No one knows why. Today, each cycle is fifteen to twenty years long."

"You said 'all Maidens.' There is more than one? And they're all girls—er, women?" Dylan said, avoiding Sara's gaze.

Sara nodded. "Yes, Maidens are always women. There are hundreds of Circle families all over the world, and at any given time, about a quarter of them have women between the ages of sixteen and thirty—Maidens who may one day be called, as I've been. We are trained for this mission—called a Pilgrimage—from the age of four. From that day on, we prepare.

"Every so often, all of the Circle families meet to assess each Maiden's qualifications and readiness. We are rated on a complex scale that considers discipline, compassion, intelligence, and many other factors."

"Like combat readiness," Tom said, shaking his head in disbelief as he stared pointedly at Sara's rifle.

She smiled sadly. "That's right."

"Based on the rating system that Sara described, each Maiden is assigned a position in a queue. When the final seven-day countdown begins—as soon as passage to the Twilight becomes possible—every Maiden tests her Wardens at the same time, in a different version or 'instance' of the village you all just returned from," Ethan said.

"Her Wardens. You mean... us," Alex said, her words coming out in a hoarse whisper.

"And by 'tests her Wardens,' you mean she dumps them into a nightmare, unarmed and unprepared, and sees if they come out alive," Tom said, shaking his head in disbelief.

Alex shot to her feet, comprehension flashing in her eyes. The pieces were beginning to fall into place. "You want us to protect her? From that hellish place that nearly killed all three of us? How do you expect us to do that? And why us?"

Ethan and Sara both waited patiently as Alex sputtered and fumed. Tom cut in. "That's the part that still doesn't make sense." He paused. "Let me rephrase. *None* of this makes sense, but that part makes the least sense of all. Assuming you're telling the truth about all this—which is one big fucking assumption—why us? Why drag a bunch of strangers into this? If this whole 'Pilgrimage' thing is something you spend your whole lives getting ready for, why not use your own people? Like your meatheads in the corner over there, they look like they're good at hurting things," Tom said, jerking his thumb toward the six stern-faced men who still hadn't said a word.

Sara nodded as though she'd been fully expecting the question. "Combat ability is one consideration when a Maiden chooses her Wardens, yes. But it's not the only consideration. It's not even the most important one." She paused.

"Okay, I'll bite," Alex sighed.

"The most important predictor of a Maiden's success, by far, is the strength of the bond of trust she shares with her Wardens," Sara said with grave finality, as though she were pronouncing some solemn verdict.

Tom scoffed. "Bond of trust? How exactly does kidnapping people, drugging them, and dumping them into an exceedingly lethal nightmare facilitate trust?"

"I don't expect any of you to ever forgive me for this," Sara whispered. "I don't deserve your forgiveness. I would have given anything not to have to do this to you. But you aren't just pawns to me. I chose you because you are the best, the brightest, the kindest and most selfless people I know. As I've gotten to know each of you over the years, I've done so with full sincerity. I was sizing you up as potential Wardens, yes, but that's not all you are to me. I respect and care for you as individuals. If I didn't have this burden to bear, I would still hope to have all of you in my life," Sara said, her voice wavering on the last few words.

"Ethan, why aren't you one of Sara's Wardens, then? You raised her in this... organization of yours. Seems like the least you could do would be to protect her," Alex said, trying not to sound too accusatory.

Ethan grimaced. "Occasionally, Maidens do choose their fathers as Wardens, but it's generally ill-advised. Someone needs to stay behind and take care of the logistical concerns while the Pilgrimage is in progress. I'll make sure the doctors and other support staff get what they need, and I'll stay in touch with the other Circle families to update them on Sara's progress, and to ask for advice when they might know something helpful."

Suddenly feeling a pressing need to change the subject, Tom asked, "If there are Maidens all over the world, does that mean we'll have help?" Alex wasn't sure if he'd meant to say "we'll have help," as though he'd already decided to go along with this insane fever dream.

Ethan shook his head. "Unfortunately, no. Excluding the trial you just experienced, only one Maiden and her Wardens can enter the Twilight at a time. At this very moment, every other Maiden in the world is having a conversation with her Wardens similar to the one we're having now, but Sara is first in line. No one else can enter the Twilight unless we make a certain phone call, which will only happen if one or more of you refuse the burden of a Warden. With the utmost seriousness, I implore you not to do that. If you refuse this calling, it falls to another, less qualified Maiden. That will significantly damage humanity's chances, and we need every advantage we can get."

Dylan looked up. "We can refuse?"

"Yes," Sara said simply. "There's nothing we can do to force you."

"You mean, other than drugging us and putting us at extreme risk of death. Other than that kind of force," Tom snapped.

Neither Holcomb took the bait. Instead, Ethan went on in a soft, reassuring voice. "This is all part of a pattern that's been refined into a well-oiled machine over millennia. This cycle is the way it is for a reason. The whole point of the Pilgrimage is to prove that mankind is willing to do better, willing to freely *choose* a better path, willing to walk the moral high road without coercion. Regrettably, force is necessary to demonstrate that the path is real, but no Maiden or Warden can be forced to walk it. If any of you refuse, Sara will undo the binding ritual, allowing you to return to your lives and sleep normally. You'll never enter the Twilight again."

"All of you have been free to leave from the moment we returned from the Twilight," Sara said. "If even one of you refuses, the next Maiden in line will be called, and so on, until one full team answers the call."

"And if none do?" Alex asked.

Sara hung her head. "Then Ardu will take that as a sign that mankind is beyond redemption. He will… put us out of our misery."

Tom stood up and began to pace. "You're not making a very compelling argument as to why *we* should do this. You said any one of us can refuse. It doesn't need to be unanimous? I could just say 'I'm out,' and then you make a phone call, even if Alex and Dylan are crazy enough to drink the Kool-Aid?"

Ethan nodded. "That's right. But before you do so, there's one more thing you should know."

Tom threw up his hands. "Of course there is."

"Sara is first in line for a reason. Of all the Maidens, she is best equipped to walk the path. You've all been evaluated by similar standards as well, for years now. Collectively, all of the Circle families around the world have decided that the four of you stand the best chance of success."

"Why only four of us? Why not send a whole army?" Alex asked.

Ethan thought for a moment. "Have you ever tried to rub your stomach and pat your head at the same time?"

Alex blinked. "What's that got to do with anything?"

"Humor me."

"When I was a kid, I guess."

"Try it now."

"Are you serious?"

"As a heart attack."

Alex sighed and began to rub her stomach and pat her head. At first, her hands kept getting confused, failing to do what her brain wanted. Eventually, after a bit of practice, she was able to keep it going. Dylan and Tom watched the display in mixed disbelief and confusion.

Ethan continued. "You can do it, but it's tricky, right?"

"I suppose."

"The Maiden is the anchor, the vital connection between our world and the Twilight. You can go there only because Sara has bonded you to her. When she travels to the Twilight, she needs to pat her head to bring one person along. To bring a second person along, she must also rub her stomach at the same time. To bring a third, she must do both while standing on one foot. Not literally, of course, but you get the idea. Most Maidens can only bring two Wardens along. A few, like Sara, can manage three. In exceedingly rare cases, a Maiden may manage four, but never more than that."

"What do you mean Sara 'bonded' us to her?" Alex asked.

Sara held up her bandaged left hand. "By blood."

Tom, Alex, and Dylan each reflexively glanced at their own left hands, each of which bore a fresh, shallow cut. Alex looked back up at Sara. "You mixed our blood?"

"We screened all of you for bloodborne diseases first," Ethan said, raising his hands defensively.

"Oh, in that case, by all means. Put your blood in my body while I'm unconscious," Tom said with acidic sarcasm.

"Sara," Dylan said, breaking his long silence. Everyone else turned to look at him. "Those things in the village. The ones that almost killed us. They used to be people, didn't they?"

Sara shook her head. "No, if that makes you feel any better. It's a bit complicated, and I don't think we need to get into it just now. But they were never 'real' people from here, from our world. They're from the Twilight. They manifest there, for lack of a better word."

"What about the sea monster?" Dylan said, trying not to relive the encounter in his mind.

"Dylan, I don't know exactly what happened to you. I'm sorry. I would give you answers if I had them. I'm sorry I wasn't there to help you," Sara said. This time, it was she who failed to meet his eyes.

"Yeah, about that," Tom cut in. "You're supposed to be 'the anchor.' If you can ferry us back and forth, why did we all end up in different places?"

"The first time is different," Sara said. "It's a bit like manually scanning radio frequencies to find a signal. The first time you enter the Twilight, I have no control over where you end up. It will be somewhere near that village, but other than that, it's out of my hands. Now that we've all been there together, I can guide you more precisely next time."

"Why always the village? Does it mean something?" Alex asked.

"Everything in the Twilight means something, but that's a question for another time. Most of the Twilight changes over time. The geography, the weather, the... creatures you might encounter. Even the very laws of physics. The village and the cathedral where Ardu sleeps, those two places rarely change, but everything in between is in a constant state of slow flux. In other words, the start of the Pilgrimage is always the same, as is its end, but what you encounter along the way largely depends on you. The journey is long and difficult, but other than that, we can't tell you what to expect," Ethan said.

"Once we reach any given place in the Twilight, I can then take us directly there the next time we go back," Sara said. "But I need to see it with my own eyes first."

"Naturally," Alex and Tom said in unison.

"The Pilgrimage isn't seven straight days in the Twilight, thankfully. A Maiden and her Wardens leave the Twilight to take breaks as needed, to rest and recover in safety."

"How often do people survive this nightmare safari?" Tom said.

Sara sighed. "As we said, it's extremely dangerous. Some Wardens survive the Pilgrimage and return to their normal lives. Some... don't."

"How many don't come back?" Tom said, his voice low and dangerous.

"About half," Sara replied, very quietly.

"Half," Tom repeated. He shook his head, incredulous.

"And the young women? The Maidens?" Alex pressed.

"They're just as vulnerable, but a Maiden must survive until the end of her journey—at all costs. It is her Wardens' job to protect her," Ethan said with grave finality. He stood up, dusting his hands on the back of his pants.

"I know that you have many other questions, but the clock is already ticking, and time grows short. We can answer your other questions later. But we must know your decision now."

Abruptly, Dylan walked straight out the door, into the basement. Sara heard the bathroom door open and close a moment later. "Let's give him a few minutes," she said.

Tom approached Ethan and pulled him aside, lowering his voice so the others couldn't hear. "Listen, to some extent, I guess I can understand why Sara would pick me—I suppose I'm halfway decent at killing things, and there will clearly be a need for that. I also get why she'd pick Alex, a healer of both mind and body. But why Dylan? He's just a scared kid."

Ethan was already nodding conspiratorially before Tom finished speaking. "Yes, I share your concern. Dylan is a wonderful boy. He and Sara have been best friends for most of their lives, but he has some growing up to do. Ultimately, it's not up to me. The Maiden, not her father, chooses her Wardens. It's not my place to second-guess her."

"Most dads don't trust their seventeen-year-old not to crash the car. You trust yours with the fate of the entire planet?"

"Fully," Ethan said, without hesitation.

* * *

Once Ethan and Tom had rejoined Alex, Tom asked, "You expect us to do this suicide mission—sorry, 'Pilgrimage'—unarmed?"

"Hardly," Ethan said. As he spoke, he began walking toward the steel door in the west wall, beckoning Tom and Alex to follow. "Any equipment you might require is at your disposal." Ethan punched in an access code, then hauled open the door, revealing an armory that made even Tom's jaw drop.

The room behind the door was capable of arming a small nation. Wire racks covering every wall held an enormous variety of weapons. Body armor in several different types and sizes lay neatly arranged on shelves. Olive drab ammo cans held every caliber of ammunition, thousands of rounds each.

"You are free to use whatever you deem necessary, or to provide your own equipment, if you prefer," Ethan said.

"Hold on," Alex said, turning to Tom. "You're talking like you've already decided to do this. You're talking like you believe it."

He turned to her. "You don't?"

"It's crazy."

"I agree. But what else could explain everything we've been through tonight?"

Alex sighed in frustration. "I don't know. You really believe what they're saying?"

Tom shook his head. "It's not like I want to. It's not like I'm excited about it. But...." He trailed off.

"But what?"

Tom pulled her aside, as he'd done to Ethan a few minutes earlier. Ethan respectfully moved farther away. "Let's assume, just for a minute, that everything Ethan and Sara said is true. I'm not saying I believe all of it, but just assume with me."

"Okay, I'm assuming, for now."

"Are they wrong about it being the right thing to do?"

Alex had been contemplating that question for some time now. "I want to hear your answer first."

"Don't get me wrong, it's insane, but maybe it's not as insane as we first thought. What if, somehow, we *can* do this? I'm good at violence. I'm not proud of that, but it's part of who I am. Violence is clearly an unavoidable part of this Pilgrimage, or whatever.

"You fix people, and by all accounts, you're really good at it. If we're going into battle, I definitely want a doctor nearby. And you know how to heal the mind, not just the body. Think about Dylan. Can you think of anyone more in need of therapy after what he's been through tonight? If he has any chance of coming through this as anything more than a broken husk, you're gonna have to be there for him in ways that Sara and I can't be.

"And think about what Ethan said, about taking the moral high road. If we really are capable of pulling off something like this—and I mean *if*— don't we have a duty to give it our best shot? If the entire human race is really depending on us, who are we to refuse?"

Alex regarded Tom with an unreadable expression. She said nothing.

Tom thought back to the graveyard, to when he'd freed her from that cramped drainage tunnel. He remembered Alex's reluctance to free herself, how her courage had dwindled in the face of a seemingly insurmountable obstacle.

He remembered what he'd said to change her mind, and then he rolled the dice.

"Alex, you can say no. Ethan and Sara already said that. If even one of us backs out, the whole thing is off. But if you do that, you pass on this horrible burden to some other girl and the confused, scared people she's chosen to protect her. Can you live with that?"

Her answer was so quiet that Tom could hear it only because he already knew what she would say. "No. No, I can't."

Tom nodded once, then waved to Ethan, signaling that it was alright to rejoin them. "I don't know whether I speak for Alex, but let me be clear about something: We're not friends. Not anymore. I'll never forgive you for this."

Ethan nodded his understanding. "I deserve no less."

"Even so, I'll do what I can to help. I'll protect Sara to the best of my ability."

"As will I," Alex said, her heart sinking. Slowly but surely, she could feel the familiar wave of cold fear building in her chest again.

"I'm relieved and pained, in equal measure, to hear that," Ethan said. "But we're still missing one vote."

"Mine," Dylan said, coming around the corner. Sara followed on his heels, her face stoic. He stopped a few paces away, his hands stuffed in his pockets.

"I don't know how much help I will be. Probably not much. I'll probably never understand why Sara thinks I can do something like this. But I can see how determined she is." Dylan turned to face his best friend. "Sara, I've never met anyone as brave as you. I'll never be that brave, but you make me want to try. I'll protect you if I can."

Ethan clasped his hands in front of him. "And so, the Wardens pass the final test," he said. "Take a few hours to gather your thoughts. Go home and gather any supplies you may need. Return here by sunrise. And whatever you do, you must not fall asleep before then."

CHAPTER NINE
Genesis

Dylan paused in front of his apartment door with one hand on the knob. Tom had dropped him off and promised to return an hour later. Neither of them had spoken during the ride. Dylan had spent the time coming up with various lies to tell his father about where he was going to be.

He wouldn't be gone for seven straight days, at least. Sara had said that they would come back from the Twilight as needed.

Dylan tried not to think about the crushing, insane reality of what he was walking into. After the song Sara had sung to him—the song she couldn't possibly have known—all lingering doubts about the truth of her story had evaporated. As long as he didn't think about the fear or the danger, he could keep putting one foot in front of the other.

As long as he didn't contemplate the possibility of never seeing his father again, of Richard never knowing what had happened to his son.

Finally, Dylan decided that it didn't really matter what cover story he came up with. Richard probably wouldn't notice anything out of the ordinary. Dylan was usually in one of three places: with Sara, at school, or locked in his room for long periods. He'd once been in his room for a full twenty-four hours, except for bathroom breaks, and Richard had thought he was at Sara's house the whole time.

He turned the knob and pushed open the door. "Dad, I'm home," he called, trying hard to make his voice sound normal.

Silence.

Dylan went into the kitchen. There was a half-eaten sandwich on the counter. It wasn't even on a plate.

Richard must be asleep. It was after midnight. Dylan checked his phone to see if his dad had called or texted, then remembered that it no longer worked after his unplanned swim. He placed the phone on the counter and left a scribbled note next to it. *Dad—dropped my phone in the sink, sorry :(*

Dylan quietly climbed the stairs and entered the bathroom. He took a hot shower, mostly to keep his mind distracted from what he was about to do. He felt a little better once he was clean.

Once he was in his room, it got harder to ignore the reality of his near future. He put on an old pair of cargo pants, thinking that the heavier fabric and extra pockets might be wise choices. He chose a plain white T-shirt and a black hoodie for warmth. Finally, he pulled on his running shoes.

He expected he'd be doing a lot of running.

Picking up his backpack, he dumped its contents onto his bed and started filling it with supplies. Ethan and Sara hadn't given him a packing list. He packed two small toolkits, one for electrical stuff and another for mechanical problems. He grabbed a plastic organizer box filled with miscellaneous parts and stuffed that in the backpack, too. Finally, he added a few sets of clean clothes to leave at Sara's house. He would surely be getting dirty again.

He paused, unsure what else to bring. Nothing came to mind. Ethan had said he would provide whatever equipment they needed.

Tom would surely have some thoughts on what they would need.

Dylan zipped up the bag but left it in his room for the moment. He crept down the hall to Richard's bedroom and cracked open the door. Richard was asleep on his side, facing away from the door, snoring quietly. Dylan stood there for a long moment, staring, not sure what he'd been planning to do.

Finally, he turned away and started to close the door. Richard suddenly rolled over and sat up, blinking. The light from the hallway must have woken him.

"Sorry, Dad," Dylan said.

"Dylan? What time is it?"

"Late. I just wanted to let you know that Sara's having a… family thing, and I'll be staying there for a bit, maybe a day or two. If that's okay."

Richard rubbed the sleep from his eyes, still gathering his wits. He mumbled something about "the holidays."

"Can I go? I can stay here if you want me to." It was a gamble, but it was a reasonably safe one. Richard hadn't expressed a single strong opinion about Dylan's whereabouts in years.

"No, that's fine if you want to go there. I'll be fine." It wasn't a guilt trip. He would be too busy hunting for clues about Marie to notice Dylan's absence.

"My phone's broken, but you have Mr. Holcomb's number, call him if you need me." Ethan surely had prepared plenty of convincing lies.

"Okay."

"Dad?"

"Hmm?"

"I love you."

Richard blinked, taken aback by the sudden confession. "I love you too, kiddo."

"Go back to sleep. I'll see you soon."

Before he could lose his wavering courage, Dylan quietly shut the door.

* * *

Tom was the last to arrive back at Sara's house. He parked his truck in the driveway and shut off the engine. *If you're gonna drag my ass to hell, the least you can do is give me a parking spot*, he thought.

Before he got out, he pulled out his cell phone—which had worked normally ever since he'd returned from the nightmare world—and composed a message to Teddy.

Teddy, sorry to text so late. I've had a family emergency come up and I'll be out of town for a week or two, I'm about to catch a flight now. Please hold down the fort for me and ask the girls at the office to forward my calls to Greg. And please drop by once a day to check on Riley while I'm gone. Thanks, and sorry for the short notice. I'll buy you dinner when I get back.

It wasn't likely to set off any alarms for Teddy. Similar things had happened a handful of times before, and Teddy had always kept the ship afloat in Tom's absence. After confirming that the message had been delivered, he shut off the phone and put it in the glove box.

Stepping out of his truck, Tom pulled a large duffel bag and a backpack from the back seat. He'd changed into heavy-duty canvas EMS pants, tan army boots, and a long-sleeved combat shirt designed to resist abrasion and tearing.

One of Ethan's mute goons opened the front door as Tom approached. Tom breezed past him without a word and headed down to the basement. When he entered the "doom room," as he'd started to think of it, Alex, Dylan, Sara, and Ethan were already there. Alex and Dylan both recoiled when they saw him, and he realized that he probably had on his murder face.

He made a conscious effort to soften his expression.

He noted that Dylan had on a backpack—his school bag, by the looks of it—and Alex was wearing a bright orange EMS bag on her back. Both had changed into clothes heavier and more durable than what they normally wore, with long sleeves and pant legs. Tom nodded his approval silently to himself.

"Tom, thank you for coming," Ethan said. Tom resisted the urge to make a smart-ass crack about not having much of a choice. "We're ready if you are."

"Ready for what?"

"Training, I expect. I thought you would want to start by sharing some of your martial knowledge with the others."

Martial knowledge, Tom thought with some irritation. Why did Ethan always have to talk like an asshole?

"How much time do we have?" Tom asked.

"From here on out, that's ultimately up to Sara," Ethan said, resting a hand on her shoulder. "But I know my daughter. She will defer to your expertise in matters of combat."

Sara thought for a moment. "I'd say we have eight hours before we should go in. As of now, we have"—she checked a watch she'd put on —"five days and eighteen hours to finish the Pilgrimage. It's not as much time as you might think. The cathedral is a long way from the village."

"Sara," Dylan said, fidgeting nervously. "What are you gonna do when we get to this church, or whatever? You have to put Ardu back to sleep? What does that mean? Is it dangerous?"

Sara smiled warmly at him and touched his arm reassuringly. "Thankfully, that's the least dangerous part of all. It's a ritual, mostly chanting and drawing weird symbols. Nothing to worry about. If—when—we get that far, we're done. I only need a few minutes to do the ritual."

Dylan nodded, looking somewhat relieved.

"Dr. Warner, my dear, you look like something is bothering you," Ethan said.

Alex stared at him incredulously. "What could possibly be bothering me?"

"Of course. Forgive me."

"Do you *seriously* think we can do this? It seems impossible and suicidal. We're just regular people," she said, her shoulders slumping.

"You're far from the first. As I said, this cycle has been repeating for at least five thousand years. Hundreds of Maidens and Wardens before you have done this. If any had failed, we wouldn't be having this conversation right now. Sara and I have every confidence in you."

"Yeah, about that," Tom said, shifting the duffel bag on his shoulder. "Earlier, you said this god has woken up a few times before and killed a whole shitload of people. That would mean someone else *did* fail. How are we still here?"

Sara grimaced. "It has happened a few times. There is an... emergency option we can deploy in that case."

"Emergency option?"

"A different ritual, one that can interrupt Ardu's rampage, return him to the Twilight, and put him back to sleep. But it's complex, dangerous, and not guaranteed to work," Ethan said. "This emergency ritual is a Hail Mary, and we've been fortunate that it worked the few times it's been necessary. I'd not like to tempt fate in that way again, given a choice. The Pilgrimage, fraught with peril as it is, remains the most reliable option with the greatest chance of success."

"And unlike Ardu's presence in our world, the Pilgrimage doesn't put billions of innocent lives at risk," Sara added.

"Right. Only four, in this case," Tom said matter-of-factly. Not missing a beat, he turned to Ethan. "You have some land behind the house? Twenty acres or so?"

Ethan nodded. "About that."

"Any neighbors to the north, west, or south?"

Ethan shook his head. "Not for at least a mile. All the houses around here are far apart from one another."

"Good." Tom turned to Sara, Dylan, and Alex. "Follow me." He pulled open the armory door and led the others inside. "You know how to use that thing?" he asked, pointing at Sara's rifle.

"I do," she said.

"Show me."

"How?"

"Field strip, reassemble, and function test."

Without hesitation, Sara raised the rifle into a low ready position, taking care not to point the barrel at anyone else. She removed the magazine, stored it in a pouch on her vest, and worked the charging handle to eject the chambered round. She flipped open a small storage compartment in the buttstock, took out a thin metal rod, and used it to loosen the retaining pin in the lower receiver.

Separating the rifle into two pieces, she deftly removed the bolt carrier, the bolt itself, and the firing pin. She held the smaller parts in her hands, showing them to Tom, and he nodded. Sara then reversed the process and reassembled the rifle. When she was done, she locked the bolt open, closed it again, moved the selector switch from safe to semi, and squeezed the trigger, producing a soft *click*.

She did it all in under a minute. Dylan watched the display with wide eyes and an open mouth. Alex looked queasy.

"Good," Tom said. "But not good enough."

"How so?"

"You know your weapon, and I'm assuming you've been taught to fire it with some competence." Sara nodded. "How many men have you killed?"

She blinked. "None."

"How many monsters? How many of those things from the village?"

"None. Passage to the Twilight wasn't possible until yesterday."

"That's what's going to get us killed. Shooting a gun at a paper target is nothing like firing at someone—or something—that's trying to knife you in the ribs or rip your throat out." Tom turned, addressing the group. "I can't train any of you to handle combat, not psychologically and emotionally. I sure as hell can't do it in eight hours."

Ethan was watching silently from the open doorway.

"There is a deadline," Sara said softly, trying not to sound confrontational. "More time would be great, but we can't make more time."

Ignoring her, Tom pointed at Dylan. "Ever fired a gun before?" Dylan shook his head. Tom turned his raptor-like gaze on Alex.

"I fired a .22 a few times at summer camp thirty years ago," she said.

If Tom was disappointed, he didn't show it. His demeanor had changed radically. This was not Tom, the small business owner, the builder, the civil engineer, pillar of the community. They were meeting Staff Sergeant Davis of the 75th Ranger Regiment, a man with thirty-eight confirmed kills and no tolerance for bullshit.

He went on. "Every fight we get into is a fight we might lose, a fight that might end in my death, or yours, or yours, or yours," Tom said, pointing at each of the others in turn. "We're headed into enemy territory, a place where everything wants to kill us; that much is clear. I still don't know what to think about all this business involving gods and rituals, but I do know that seven days from now, I would like to be back home, alive. And I want you guys back home, alive, as well.

"Our best chance of making that happen is to avoid threats whenever possible. If running is an option, we run. If sneaking around a threat is an option, we do that. We stand and fight only when there is no other choice."

Alex and Dylan both felt a little relieved to hear that.

"However, I'm guessing that, at some point, we're going to have to fight for our lives." Tom pointedly looked at Sara.

She nodded gravely. "Almost certainly."

"I'll do my best to teach you the fundamentals, the bare basics of what you need to know and do when that happens," Tom said. "If we have to fight, all of you will follow my lead and my orders. That is not negotiable. This is not a democracy. Make no mistake, I don't enjoy being in charge of others in life-or-death situations. If I had my way, I'd be at home right now, frying up some eggs and bacon. But Ethan and Sara roped me into this insanity for a reason. I have experience that none of you have. We're all good at something. In your respective areas of expertise, I will listen to what you have to say, as long as what you say makes sense. You have my word on that.

"In combat, there is no time for discussion. There is no time to evaluate better options. You make the right moves at the right time, or you die. It's that simple. If I tell you to do something—or not do something—I'm telling you because it's what you need to do in order to not die. In that moment, you listen to me. No exceptions, no hesitation, and no arguments. Are we clear?"

"Clear," Alex said, her head spinning.

"Clear," Dylan echoed, far more quietly.

Tom had his game face on, but inside, it was killing him to speak this way to two kids and a woman he respected. None of them were ready for something like this—not even Sara, despite whatever training and preparation she'd undertaken for most of her life.

He sure as hell wasn't ready for something like this.

But he had no choice. He needed to make the reality of the situation and the consequences of mistakes crystal clear to them. If he didn't, they would die, and it would be his fault.

"Now," Tom said, approaching Alex, "we need to get each of you equipped with gear that you can use comfortably." He looked Alex up and down, sizing her up. She held his gaze and kept her chin up, trying to look braver than she felt. After a moment, he stepped in front of Dylan and did the same. Dylan kept his eyes on the ground.

"Look at me," Tom said quietly. Dylan raised his head. "I know it doesn't seem like it, but it'll be okay. We'll get through this, together, one step at a time." Dylan gave a single, timid nod in response.

"I think submachine guns would be a good fit for you two," Tom said. "Medium-caliber, something not too difficult to control, something that doesn't require a lot of arm strength." He walked over to the racks of weapons lining the walls and began looking them over. After several moments, he turned to Ethan. "You've got some excitingly illegal hardware here."

Ethan smiled without humor. "If anyone has a legitimate need for it, we do."

Tom turned to Sara. "What can we expect in terms of opfor?" She gave him a blank stare. "Sorry, opposing forces. What kinds of enemies are we likely to run into?"

She shrugged. "There's no way to know. As I said earlier, the Twilight changes over time, except for the village and the cathedral. We have reports from previous teams, but they're helpful only in a very general sense. We probably won't see many—if any—of the same things they dealt with."

"If this has been going on for five thousand years, why does the village look like something from the 1700s? Five thousand years ago, no one could build anything more complicated than a mud hut."

Sara nodded. "For most of recorded history, the village looked much older than it does now. Something changed around the end of the eighteenth century, and the village took on its current appearance at that time. We're not sure why."

"Any idea whether we'll run into anything with ranged capabilities? Guns? Spears? Arrows?"

Sara shook her head. "I doubt it; we've rarely read reports like that. The creatures in the Twilight take many forms, but most of them aren't capable of using tools or weapons; that seems to be consistent. But anything is possible."

Tom thought for a moment. "Then we don't need long-range weapons, other than your rifle. If there's something dangerous more than a hundred meters away, we should be able to avoid it entirely. We shouldn't be engaging targets at that distance. How far can you shoot that thing?" Tom asked, gesturing at Sara's rifle.

"Accurately? About three hundred meters."

"Good enough for this purpose. I hope," Tom said. He turned back to the wall of guns and selected one that, to Alex's untrained eye, looked like a smaller version of Sara's rifle. Tom opened the action and verified that the chamber was empty before handing it to Alex. "Keep your finger off the trigger," he cautioned.

Reluctantly, Alex accepted the weapon. It wasn't as heavy as she expected. She held it awkwardly, afraid to move.

"This is a SIG MPX, a 9mm submachine gun. The 'sub' in submachine gun means it fires pistol-caliber rounds—in this case, bullets larger but slower than what Sara's rifle shoots. The 'machine gun' part just means it'll keep firing as long as you hold the trigger down. A 9mm sub-gun is relatively easy to control, so you don't need to be strong to hold onto it."

"Just what I always wanted," Alex said, unable to hold back the sarcastic remark.

"Sit tight for now. I'll show you how it works once we get outside," Tom said. He then took a similar-looking gun from the wall and handed it to Dylan. "This is an H&K UMP, .45 caliber. UMP means 'universal machine pistol.' Same basic idea as the one I gave Alex, but the bullets are bigger, so they're more powerful. You're stronger than she is, so I think you can handle the recoil."

Dylan inspected the chamber and worked the action a few times, getting a feel for it. The UMP had an unusual design that featured a charging handle near the end of the barrel, but Dylan knew how to manipulate it without Tom having to tell him.

"I thought you said you'd never fired a gun," Tom said.

"Not a real one, but I play lots of video games," Dylan said, his cheeks reddening. Tom closed his eyes and pinched the bridge of his nose but held his tongue.

Over the next several minutes, Tom selected sidearms for Dylan and Alex, then helped them choose armor, holsters, slings, and other basic gear.

"I will admit, this would be kind of cool under other circumstances," Alex said, inexpertly adjusting her armor and trying to sound casual.

"You brought your own gear?" Sara asked Tom.

Tom nodded as he opened the duffel bag and began retrieving his equipment. "Benelli M4 12-gauge shotgun, exceptionally good at making things dead at close range." He held up a comically large revolver. "460XVR Magnum. This thing will blow the engine block right out of a truck, or drop a grizzly bear, if your aim is good."

"Not the weapons I would have expected you to choose," Ethan said from the doorway.

"I like to shoot things once, and only once," Tom replied dryly. "It takes an experienced shooter to handle massive calibers. I figured we should have some real stopping power somewhere in the squad."

Halfway through the process of strapping on a dark brown plate carrier, Tom stopped, staring at something. Dylan and Alex followed his gaze. He walked over to a chunky, odd-looking weapon on the wall and picked it up gingerly.

"Is this what I think it is?" he asked.

"No. It's better," Ethan said, walking over to him.

"It looks like a China Lake," Tom said, staring at Ethan in disbelief.

"As I said, it's more than that. The China Lake 40mm grenade launcher is exceedingly rare, only a handful still exist in private collections. This is a later Trident model that we acquired and modified at significant expense. Given where you're going, I think the cost was justified. You'll find that its mechanical reliability is greatly improved compared to the original design."

"If the ATF ever found this room, you'd go away for life."

"A necessary risk."

"May I?" Tom asked, hefting the grenade launcher.

"Everything in this room is at your disposal. Use whatever will maximize your ability to protect my daughter and yourselves."

Needing no further convincing, Tom slung the heavy weapon over his back, then began filling a bandolier with 40mm grenades.

* * *

Dylan moved his head away from the sights to look at the row of tin cans set up on a sheet of plywood. He'd managed to hit two of them.

In ten shots.

"Good," Tom said, "but you're still flinching. When you squeeze the trigger, try to let the shot surprise you. Apply steady, even pressure, keep your muscles relaxed, and don't anticipate the shot. You're afraid of the gun going off—which is normal, it's okay—but when you flinch, you jerk the gun just before it fires, which causes your shot to miss. Load ten more rounds and try again."

Tom shuffled through the snow until he reached Alex, several meters away. He stood behind her and watched as she struggled to load a magazine. It kept falling out of her weapon. "What am I doing wrong?" she asked.

"You're just not using enough force, that's all." He picked up the magazine, dusted the snow away, and pointed to the top of it. "This bit of metal here locks into a latch in the magazine well, but when the bolt is closed, it takes a bit of muscle. Just ram it in there. Don't worry about breaking anything, the gun can take it."

Alex nodded and tried again, inserting the magazine with more force. This time, it stayed put. She shouldered the sub-gun, put her eye behind the rear sight, and exhaled. Tom watched her squeeze the trigger.

Nothing happened.

"Safety's on," he said gently. Mumbling to herself, Alex flicked the selector to auto, reacquired her sight picture, and squeezed the trigger again.

Still, nothing happened.

"I'm going to get us killed," she said, obviously frustrated.

"Think it through. Remember the steps I showed you. You can figure this out without me," Tom said.

Alex stared at the weapon for several moments, turning it around in her hands, inspecting its various parts. Tom noted with satisfaction that she was careful to keep the barrel pointed downrange. Through his electronic hearing protection, Tom monitored the *cracks* of Dylan's and Sara's weapons, listening for anything out of the ordinary.

"Aha!" Alex suddenly exclaimed. She pulled back the charging handle and released it, chambering a round. This time, when she shouldered the weapon and squeezed the trigger, she sent a burst of automatic fire downrange. A single can went flying.

"Good," Tom said, "You're getting it. Just remember to pull your weapon in tight to your shoulder and use the foregrip to control the recoil, especially on full auto."

Tom trudged over to Sara. The sun was high overhead, its rays glittering in the fresh snow. He checked his watch.

It was almost time.

Sara was halfway through a magazine of 5.56 when he reached her. He watched without comment. She was firing about once per second at targets one hundred meters away. Tom counted. In fifteen rounds, she didn't hit a single can.

The bolt on her M61C locked back, and she growled in frustration. "I'm usually better than this," she mumbled, dropping the empty mag and reaching for a fresh one.

"Slow is smooth, smooth is fast," Tom said.

"Huh?"

"We're almost out of practice time, unless you want to stay longer. You know the timetable."

She shook her head. "No, we need to go soon."

"Then there's only one thing I want you to focus on if you have to fire that weapon. Slow is smooth, smooth is fast." Sara cocked her head, waiting for him to explain. "You're firing way too quickly. It doesn't matter how many rounds you send downrange if none of them hit anything. When we go in there, and you're shooting at something horrible—something that's trying to take your life, or Dylan's—I want you to fire *slowly*. Don't pull the trigger until you know you have a solid shot, no matter how long that takes. I don't care if you only fire once, as long as that one shot hits. Show me accuracy. Speed comes later."

Sara opened her mouth, looking like she was going to argue, then closed it and nodded. "Okay."

"Everyone on me," Tom hollered, loud enough for Dylan and Alex to hear. Once they drew near, Tom pointed to Alex. "I want you to wear a watch cap, like Sara's."

"Why?"

"Long hair is a liability. If something grabs your hair, it gains a lot of control over you."

"Alright," Alex agreed. It made sense.

Tom turned back to Sara. "What can we expect in terms of weather? Are we dressed appropriately?"

"I think so," she said. "The Twilight is usually cold but not freezing. We're ready."

Tom locked eyes with her, but he spoke to all of them. "Let's get one thing clear. We're not ready for this. I'm not sure anyone could ever be ready for something like this. If you think you're ready, you get confident, and it's a short leap from confidence to cockiness. Cockiness gets all of us killed."

Dylan fidgeted. No one said anything.

"We're going to a goddamned scary place. Don't think you're better than the fear. You're not. Fear is the only thing that might keep us alive, but you can't let it paralyze you. Feel it. Acknowledge it. Don't try to block it out—that's impossible. Instead, you need to use it. Let the fear be a reminder to have respect for everything we're up against. Channel the fear into anger, when appropriate. Anger will be very useful where we're going, but never let it take over, never let it cloud your judgment. A warrior's strength comes from here," Tom said, lightly touching Sara's chest with one finger, over her heart, "but only when tempered and directed by this." He moved the finger to her forehead.

"That all sounds easier said than done," Alex said.

"It is. But the second you start acting with your emotions instead of your head, we all die."

* * *

Back in the doom room, Sara, Tom, Dylan, and Alex checked their gear, then double-checked each other, ensuring that they had enough ammunition and medical supplies. Sara found a spare watch cap for Alex.

"What about food and water?" Tom asked.

"There's a bit of a silver lining there. You don't need to eat or drink in the Twilight. As long as you're fed and hydrated when you go in, you can survive there indefinitely," Sara said.

"Until something else kills you," Dylan griped.

"Not helping," Tom admonished.

"Here, take these. And don't lose them, they're really important," Sara said, pulling four hard-sided plastic cases out of a nearby drawer. She handed one to each of the others and kept the last for herself.

Alex opened the case. Inside were two autoinjector syringes, one with a yellow sticker, one blue. "The yellow is more adrenaline?" she asked. Sara nodded. "That reminds me of something else I wanted to ask. Why didn't natural adrenaline wake us up last time? Our bodies are flooded with it when we're running or fighting."

"It's a question of dosage," Dr. Atwood cut in. "Rarely, if ever, does the body naturally produce enough adrenaline at one time to sever the connection to the Twilight."

"What's in the blue syringe?"

"Sedatives," Dr. Atwood said. "Drugs injected into muscles usually need a few minutes to start working, but both the adrenaline and the sedatives are custom blends designed to take effect within seconds. The safest way in and out of the Twilight is to fall asleep naturally—it's much less of a shock to the system. But sometimes, that's not an option. If you need to leave the Twilight immediately, take the adrenaline. It's dangerous—potentially fatal—so use it in life-or-death emergencies only. The sedatives are for quickly entering the Twilight from our world, if necessary."

"What happens if you use the blue one when you're already in the Twilight?" Dylan asked, his eyes wide with concern.

"Don't do that. At best, you won't be able to return here for hours, because the drugs will deepen your sleep and make it much harder to wake up. At worst, it could put you in a coma."

"Hang on," Alex said. "You said the best way in and out is to fall asleep naturally. If you fall asleep in the Twilight, you come back here? I thought we were already asleep, that that was the only way to get there."

Sara chimed in. "When you fall asleep in the Twilight, you're actually falling asleep in reverse, if that makes any kind of sense, so you're actually waking up, and you return here, to our world."

"So, once we're there, we fall asleep to wake up, even though we're already asleep?"

"Basically."

"Our gear goes with us?" Tom asked. "It had better, or else why bother having it?"

"It does," Sara said. "Anything you can reasonably carry on your person will go back and forth with you. There seems to be a size limit."

"Which is why we can't just fall asleep in a truck and drive the whole way," Tom mused.

"Ardu would probably consider that cheating," Sara said dryly. "Also, there's no point in bringing that," she said, tapping the SureFire flashlight mounted on the handguard of Tom's shotgun.

"Why not?" he asked.

"Electronics from here don't work over there. No one is sure why, but there are some theories about electromagnetic fields or something."

"That's why our phones didn't work," Dylan said. Tom detached the SureFire light and stored it in a pouch on his belt, along with several others he'd brought for the rest of the team.

"Right. Some teams have reported finding electronics in the Twilight; those work because they originated there. And there's one more thing," Sara said. "Nothing from the Twilight can come back here; it's a one-way street. Anything you pick up there has to stay there. As for light, I put a torch in each of your packs, along with some oil and a lighter."

Tom stared at her. "You mean actual torches. Not the British kind, but the kind that you set on fire."

"Unless you know another way to make light without electricity. I also packed us glow sticks for emergencies, but they're not very bright."

"You're wearing a watch," Alex pointed out. "Won't that stop working, then?"

"Not this one," Sara said, tapping it. "This one's old-fashioned, purely mechanical. No battery. You just have to wind it every day." With that, she pulled another three watches just like it from her pocket and handed them out.

"There's one more thing you should be aware of," Ethan said from off to the side. "The electronic guidance chips in the 40mm grenade rounds won't work, either."

"Meaning they'll detonate at any range, so I'll have to be extra careful not to blow myself up. Noted," Tom said.

"Anything else we need to know?" Alex asked, strapping on the watch Sara had given her.

"Plenty, but we can cover the rest later," Sara said. "We need to get going."

Now that the unavoidable was upon them, Tom, Alex, and Dylan each felt a spike of fear. Until now, it had all seemed hypothetical. Each of them had a moment of private panic. Each of them considered backing out, considered running home to hide under the covers and let it be someone else's problem.

None of them could do that.

Dr. Atwood came into the room. Sara nodded to Dr. Atwood, indicating that it was time.

"Please, lie down," Atwood said, gesturing to the beds. Nervously, each of them complied. Only Sara was rock steady—outwardly, at least.

"I'll be the last one in and the last one out," Sara said. "You may hear me talking quietly in a language you don't understand. Listen to my voice, but don't try to understand the words. I'll guide us back to the village."

"But those things will be there, waiting to get us," Dylan said, his voice trembling.

"No, Dylan, they won't. I promise. You'll see. I'll explain once we get there," Sara said.

"I'm going to give each of you a mild sedative, much milder than the one Sara gave you for emergencies," Atwood said. "It won't put you to sleep, but it will help you to relax and make it easier to fall asleep naturally."

"We're all exhausted. Try to focus on that," Sara said. "Try to lose yourself in how tired you are. Once the sedative starts to work, you should be able to fall asleep."

"Sara," Dylan said, barely above a whisper, "I can't do this."

"You can. I'll be right there with you."

Alex noted how calm and maternal Sara sounded. She really had been preparing for this day all her life.

Tom had a different thought. He still didn't understand why Dylan was here. He was a smart kid, but he wasn't cut out for something like this. He was supposed to protect Sara, but it looked more and more like she'd be protecting him.

Each of them felt a slight pinch as Dr. Atwood moved down the line of beds, administering injections. At some point, Ethan appeared nearby. "Thank you," he said to them. "That may not mean much. I know you didn't have much of a choice. But thank you, nonetheless, on behalf of the entire human race."

Tom thought he should say something, but he was suddenly having a hard time focusing. Sara was mumbling something in a low, guttural language that sounded too aggressive and masculine to be coming from a teen girl's mouth. Dimly, he thought about Riley, hoping he'd left enough food and water out for him.

Alex thought about her patients, hoping that her team wouldn't be too upset with her for calling out sick at the last minute.

Dylan thought about his mother.

Sara's strange chanting had a paradoxically calming effect. Within minutes, the concrete room faded away.

CHAPTER TEN
Crucible

The village was different. For one thing, it was quiet. No horribly disfigured people rushed out of houses to attack. The only sound was a rhythmic creaking as the metal lanterns swayed in a slight breeze. The fountain looked newer, cleaner—and it was running. Dirty water, almost black, spilled over the top bowl in thin sheets, cascading several layers down in intricate patterns.

The surrounding countryside had changed entirely. Before, there had been nothing to see in any direction except the graveyard and the beach beyond it. Now, gargantuan trees with gnarled black trunks rose a hundred feet into the air all around. Their leafless branches terminated in razor-sharp points. Some of the trees were so huge that it would take ten men to join hands around one of them.

At the edge of the plaza, beyond the fountain, a massive iron gate, easily forty feet tall, blocked passage to a gloomy forest beyond. The trees to either side were so dense, their branches so tightly interwoven, that they formed an effectively impassable fence stretching as far as the eye could see in both directions.

The air had a damp chill to it, leftover humidity from the upside-down rain. The only light came from the silvery moon high above.

"It was early afternoon just a minute ago. Is it always nighttime here?" Tom asked.

"Yes," Sara said, without further explanation.

"I thought you said the village never changed," Alex said in a low voice. She was gripping her weapon so tightly that her knuckles were turning white.

"It doesn't. Not really," Sara whispered back. "It has two states. The version you saw before is a proving ground. Much like the Twilight is layered on top of and interwoven with our world, the proving ground is a separate, more superficial layer of the village. You only see it the first time you come here. Once you pass the test and come back, you see this version —the real version, if you want to call it that."

"How many layers are there?" Dylan asked, standing unnaturally close to

Sara.

"Four," she responded. "The proving ground is the topmost, 'shallowest' layer—the one closest to our world. Most of the rest of the Twilight resides in the second layer, almost like a deeper level of sleep. Eventually we'll reach the Hollow, which is a third, even deeper layer."

"What's the fourth layer?" Alex asked.

Sara visibly shuddered. "The Deep Nothing. Don't worry about it. We don't need to go there."

"I take it that's where we need to go now," Tom said, raising one hand to indicate the forest beyond the enormous gate.

"That seems like a safe bet. The path to the cathedral is long and dangerous, but it should be fairly obvious. Ardu wants us to succeed, after all—he wants us to walk the path and prove ourselves. I don't think he wants us to get lost," Sara said.

"Let's go take a look. Stay close," Tom said, leading the way.

* * *

The four of them stared up at the enormous gate, contemplating their options. A thick chain connected to an ancient gearbox ran vertically along one side of the gate, but the entire mechanism had long since rusted over and wouldn't move. The gate itself was covered with an intricate pattern of gears—more than a hundred, they estimated. Each gear was a different size and color, as though each was made of a different material.

None looked to have moved in a very long time.

Tom let his shotgun hang on its sling and rubbed his chin. "This design doesn't make any sense. It looks like all these gears eventually disengage these two locking pins, at the top and bottom, but you don't need a hundred gears to do that. It's needlessly complicated."

"Welcome to the Twilight," Sara said, scratching her neck. "A lot of things about this place don't work the way you'd expect them to. We need to be prepared for... strangeness."

"Dylan? Any ideas?" Tom said, glancing sideways at him.

"Um... no, sorry." Tom thought that Dylan looked a little smaller and a little younger than before. He seemed to be gradually shrinking into himself, like a turtle trying to hide from predators. He had barely said anything ever since Tom and Alex had found him at the graveyard.

A minute later, Alex shook her head and sighed. "I'm going to regret this," she said.

"Sounds like you have an idea," Sara said.

"I do. A bad one."

Tom tapped his watch, which he'd synchronized to Sara's. "A bad idea is better than no idea. Let's hear it."

"I used to be a rock climber when I was younger."

"You're right—that is a bad idea."

"You never told me that," Sara said, looking mildly offended.

"You really want to talk about who's been keeping secrets?" Alex shot back. When Sara cast her eyes down in shame, Alex softened her voice. "Sorry."

Tom lightly touched Alex's shoulder, refocusing her attention. "Can you do it?"

Alex looked up at the gate again, thinking. "My mind remembers the techniques, for the most part. It's my body I don't trust. I haven't gone climbing in thirty years."

"I brought some nylon rope. If you can get to the top and tie it off, the rest of us will have a much easier time," Tom said.

"I was hoping I might see a way to open the gate once I get up there," Alex said.

"Doesn't seem likely. There's so much rust all over this thing that it probably wouldn't move even if we could unlock it. And look, some of the gears have broken or missing teeth, so the mechanism wouldn't work as intended anyway."

Alex sighed. "If someone has a less stupid idea, I'd love to hear it."

No one said anything.

Tom pulled a coil of black rope from his pack and handed it to Alex. "Listen, if anything attacks us while she's up there, we'll handle it. Cover Alex at all costs. Alex, while you're up there, you don't worry about anything going on down here. You focus on not falling."

Sara gave Alex a nervous grin that probably was meant to be reassuring. "We shouldn't have to worry about that. Nobody's ever been attacked in the village after the first trial."

Tom gave her a dubious look. "That means exactly nothing to me. We prepare for the worst."

Sara crossed her arms, her rifle clacking against the rest of her gear. "Really, it will be fine. We don't have to worry until we're past the gate." Tom's frown morphed into a heated glare, and Sara raised her hands defensively. "Alright, alright, you're in charge of tactics." There was a hint of smugness in her voice.

"Do me a favor and stow the teenage rebellion bullshit, at least while we're in constant mortal danger," Tom said.

"Guys," Alex cut in, "seriously. We're supposed to be a team, right? Let's act like it." She slipped the coiled rope over her shoulder and approached the gate, touching it in various places, assessing the structural integrity of the gears she could reach. The others watched in silence, letting her concentrate.

Alex turned back to Tom. "Hold this? I can't climb with it banging around." She unslung her MPX and handed it over.

Tom accepted it, then turned to Sara and Dylan. "You guys, put your backs to the gate over there and watch the plaza. I'll take the other side. Stay away from the trees."

The two teens moved to comply as Alex chose a handhold and started climbing. Almost immediately, she ran into a problem. Most of the gears did, in fact, turn—not enough to disengage the locks, but enough to throw her off balance every time it happened. Barely five feet above the ground, she was already struggling to find reliable handholds and footholds.

"This is gonna be harder than I thought," she called to the others.

"Just stay focused and take your time, don't worry about us," Tom called back.

As Alex slowly made progress, Tom scanned the tree line to his right, keeping one eye on the plaza. Even from here, he could feel an oppressive aura of dread radiating from the forest. He had no doubt that they would find unpleasant things in there, but he couldn't see another way forward. The forest looked like it covered a massive amount of land, and Sara had said the timetable was pretty tight. Going around the forest would take days—time they didn't have.

He tried not to dwell on how surreal and impossible the whole situation was.

On the other side of the gate, Dylan tried to keep his attention from wandering. He couldn't understand why Sara would think he could do something like this, and he *definitely* couldn't understand why she would knowingly put him in danger. His heart was heavy with the crushing weight of betrayal. Friends didn't dump friends into living nightmares. He easily could have died in the ocean when that horrible creature attacked him.

He *should* have died, statistically speaking. He knew better than to attribute his survival to anything but luck.

He tried to shake himself out of it. Sara needed him, or at least, she seemed convinced that she needed him. He understood why she'd done what she'd done, but that didn't make it hurt any less. He just didn't get what made her think that he was capable of saving the world. He hadn't been able to find his mother or to convince his father to do any real parenting. He couldn't even drive; he always felt nervous behind the wheel.

Maybe some people could change the world, but not him. That notion used to bother him, but not anymore. Acceptance was easier. It was pointless to rail against the way things were.

Alex had reached an impasse. She was two-thirds of the way up, but the only two gears she could reach from her position both spun freely. If she tried to climb either one, her weight would just pull her to the bottom of the gear's arc.

She wedged both knees tightly between two gears that were rusted firmly in place and leaned back, taking some weight off her thigh and calf muscles so she could think for a minute. She was breathing heavily and sweating badly. She wiped her forehead and dried her hands on her pants.

She didn't often yearn for her twenties, but she did now.

A thought that she'd had and dismissed several minutes ago came creeping back. The only way forward that she could see was a third gear above the next two, but there were two problems: It was out of reach, and although it *looked* heavily rusted and therefore probably immobile, she couldn't be sure without touching it.

She looked all around, to her sides, and below. Climbing back down and finding another path would be tiring, but it might be safer than what she was contemplating. After a minute of searching, she sighed and stayed where she was. There was no other way up. All possible routes converged at the third gear above.

She stayed put for a time, her heart pounding. The only way up had a good chance of sending her plummeting to her death, or at least a bunch of broken bones. Fear paralyzed her mind and her muscles, stopping her from trying it.

But everyone else—*everyone* else—was depending on her. This insane Pilgrimage had just barely begun. If they couldn't get past this gate, then millions, possibly billions of people would pay the price for Alex's cowardice.

That thought gave her a tiny sliver of courage. Her stamina was fading; she needed to get moving. Against every instinct of self-preservation, she carefully pulled herself into a standing position on top of the gear she was resting on. Moving ever so slowly, taking great care to keep her weight evenly distributed, she pressed her stomach against the gate, refusing to look down.

The gear she was standing on had a bit of free movement in both directions. If she shifted her weight to either side, it would spin enough to throw her violently back to the ground.

She looked up. It was a vertical jump of about three feet—doable on solid ground, but she was not on solid ground.

She was getting very tired. It was now or never. Before she could change her mind, she bent her legs and jumped as hard as she could.

At the last instant, the gear she was standing on lurched to the right, screwing up her balance and impeding her jump. Her heart plummeted and her stomach lurched. *This is it, I'm dead*, she thought.

Somehow, she caught the bottom rim of the gear above with her left hand. She swung crazily, slamming her right shoulder into the gate. Thankfully, the gear she'd grabbed didn't move, but she was rapidly losing her tenuous grip.

"Alex!" Tom shouted from below. He ran toward the bottom of the gate, preparing to try to catch her if she fell. Dylan and Sara moved to join him, but he yelled at them to hold their positions and stay alert for threats.

"Hang on!" Sara called, a note of helpless frustration in her voice.

Awkwardly, Alex managed to spin herself around and grab the gear with her other hand, but she still had a problem. Climbing was mostly done with the legs, especially for women. She didn't have the upper body strength to pull herself up by her arms alone.

She knew that she could hold on for another ten seconds, at best. Rocking her hips, she swung her legs left, then right, then left again. She kicked her left leg out, trying to wedge her foot between the teeth of another nearby gear, but she missed. Wasting no time, she tried again, swinging back and forth to build momentum.

This time, she managed it. The muscles in her arms ached with relief as some of her weight shifted to her leg. She scrambled awkwardly, finally managing to worm her way into a mostly standing position on top of the gear to her left. She panted from fright and exhaustion.

"You okay?" Tom called.

"Never better," Alex yelled back. "Now be quiet so I can concentrate."

Once she'd rested for a minute, the climb to the top of the gate wasn't too bad. Still, out of respect for how high she was, she went slowly. A forty-foot fall would not end well. Once she was on top of the gate, she found that it was wider than she'd guessed—the gate itself was nearly two feet thick—so keeping her balance wasn't too difficult.

She slipped the rope off her shoulder, looped one end around the massive locking pin, and carefully tied it off with a trace-eight knot. She silently thanked her seventeen-year-old self for mastering the knot well enough that she still remembered it three decades later.

That done, she tossed the rest of the rope back down to the others. "Pull on it as hard as you can to make sure it's solid before you climb up," she shouted.

Tom dug around in his pack and produced a mechanical rope ascender he'd taken from the Holcombs' armory. He showed Dylan and Sara how to use it, then pulled rear security while they made their way to the top of the gate one by one. Dylan was visibly shaking as he started gaining height, but he choked off his fear and shoved it down. He'd already made Sara think he was a coward; he didn't want to make it worse.

Once all four of them were balanced on top of the gate, Alex pulled up the rope and tossed it down the other side, leaving it tied in its original position. "We'll have to leave the rope here," she said. "There's no way to untie it from the bottom."

After another few minutes of careful descent, one by one, they reached the ground on the far side. "Alex, that was amazing," Sara said breathlessly, hugging the older woman around the waist.

"Yes, well done," Tom agreed.

Dylan smiled nervously. "Yeah, it was pretty cool, no way I could have done that," he said.

"Thanks, but once is good for me, I'll be fine if I never have to do that again," Alex said, the adrenaline slowly fading as her breathing evened out.

The four of them turned to study the forest ahead. The ground was hard-packed dirt the color of old bricks. Other than the twisted, ominous trees, there was no vegetation except for a few scraggly, thorned weeds defiantly clawing their way up through the parched earth.

Straight ahead, the lower branches of the hulking black trees began to move. At first, the four of them all thought it was a trick of the dim moonlight, that they were imagining it. But as they watched, the branches continued to stretch outward, untangling themselves to reach across the dirt path.

Tom raised his shotgun and flicked off the safety. He wasn't sure what shooting trees would accomplish, but he wanted to be ready if harm was coming their way. "Sara, what's happening?" he asked in a low whisper.

"I don't know," she replied. She didn't seem as concerned as Tom was; she kept her rifle at the low ready. "Let's just stay still and see what happens."

As they watched, the branches on the right side of the path began to intertwine with those on the left, forming a pleached alley that extended into the distance as far as they could see.

"That would be pretty if the trees didn't look like they came from hell," Dylan whispered, shifting his weight back and forth nervously.

Slowly, Tom lowered his shotgun. "It's almost like...."

"The trees themselves are showing us the way," Sara finished.

"Is that a good thing?" Alex asked.

"Nothing here is good," Tom said. "Assume that everything in this place is trying to kill us until proven otherwise."

"In any other circumstance I'd call that cynical, but here, I think it's probably good advice," Alex said.

* * *

The group walked in silence for a time, weapons gripped tightly in hands that trembled occasionally. They could barely see the path. They'd considered lighting torches, but Tom had advised against it, pointing out that light and heat attract predators.

The others had needed no further convincing.

The sharp black branches overhead were interwoven so tightly that hardly any moonlight made it to the ground. The air was heavy and stale. The forest was unnaturally quiet. No sound or movement broke the stillness, not even the chirp of night bugs.

Sara idly wondered if there were any bugs in the Twilight.

"Does anyone else feel... paranoid?" Alex asked, careful to keep her voice quiet. Tom raised an eyebrow as if to suggest that not feeling paranoid would be noteworthy. "Yes, I know, this is insane, and it's probably going to get worse. I mean, does anyone else feel *disproportionately* paranoid? More unnerved than you should be?"

"Yeah," Sara admitted without shame. "Nothing bad has happened yet, except for Alex almost falling, but I still feel really anxious, like...." She frowned, searching for the words.

"Like something is watching us?" Alex finished.

As soon as Alex said that, it clicked in Sara's mind. She *did* feel like there were unfriendly eyes on her.

"Tom, you were a soldier. You've been to war. I'm sure you can tell when someone is out there watching you. You'd tell us if you saw something, right?" Alex said.

Tom didn't answer right away. "It depends," he finally said.

"It depends?" Sara echoed, her voice rising with restrained shock. "What could it possibly depend on?"

"I'd tell you if I thought the benefit of telling you outweighed the risk," Tom said.

"What risk? Why would you keep something like that from us?" Alex asked.

"Any number of reasons. For example, running is the worst thing you can do when there's a predator stalking you. If I thought that warning you about a predator would cause you to run, then I wouldn't tell you."

"Are there predators out there watching us now?" Sara whispered, hunching her shoulders unconsciously as if trying to make herself smaller. Her eyes darted left and right, trying to see into the darkness beyond the path.

"No, I don't think so," Tom said. "But something does feel off."

"But you just said you may not tell us if there were predators. How do we know you're telling the truth now?" Alex said.

"You don't," Tom responded coolly.

"So far, this is not the trust-building exercise I was hoping for," Alex grumbled.

"Trust is secondary," Tom said. "We do need to trust one another, to the extent possible. Sara and her father didn't exactly start us off strongly in that department, but if I ever have to choose between your trust and keeping you alive, if it's one or the other, I'm going to choose the latter. That goes for all of you."

"Hopefully, it doesn't come to that," Alex said.

"Dylan," Tom said. "Eyes up."

Dylan shook himself out of his thoughts and looked at Tom. "Huh?"

"You're moping. Ever since we cleared the gate, you've been walking with your head down, not paying attention. This whole thing sucks, I get it. But we need every advantage we can get, and you're 25 percent of the team. Pay attention."

Dylan said nothing, but even in the pale moonlight, Tom could see his cheeks reddening. Whether it was anger or embarrassment, Tom didn't know—nor did he care.

They walked on in silence for a while. Tom watched Dylan closely. The boy kept his head up for a few minutes, but before long, he was staring at the ground again, shuffling along rather than walking. Tom said nothing but made a mental note to have a serious one-on-one chat with him later.

Sara was the first to notice that Dylan wasn't there anymore. One moment, he was beside and slightly behind her, and the next, he was gone.

Sara spun around. For a split second, she thought he'd simply disappeared, but then she saw him—or at least, the top half of him. "Dylan!" she cried, far too loudly. She rushed toward him, trying to process what her eyes were seeing. Finally, she understood—he'd fallen into some kind of mud or quicksand just off the path. He was up to his waist and sinking quickly.

"Dylan!" Alex echoed, rushing to Sara's side.

"What happened?" Tom said, turning back to join them. "Keep your voices down," he admonished.

"Help!" Dylan screamed, completely ignoring Tom's command. Panic carried his voice through the trees. "I'm sinking!"

"Alex, wait," Sara said, thrusting her right arm out to stop Alex from taking another step. "The mud, or whatever, it blends in with the path, it's hard to see. Look, you almost fell in."

Alex saw that Sara was right. Another step and she would have joined Dylan.

"Dylan, we'll get you out, but you have to be quiet," Tom said, kneeling at the edge of the mud. "If you bring something down on us, you're gonna turn a small problem into a really big one."

"O—okay," Dylan stammered, more quietly this time. "Please, pull me out. I'm sinking really fast."

He was right. He was already up to mid-chest.

"Here, grab my hand," Tom said, setting his shotgun on the ground as he leaned forward. "Sara, Alex, grab my other hand so I don't fall in."

Dylan reached out, stretching as hard as he could, but he couldn't reach Tom's hand. "Please, help," he whined.

"Dylan, it's gonna be fine, just relax. Take a few steps toward me," Tom said, keeping his hand extended.

"I can't, my feet aren't on the bottom. If I move my feet, I just sink faster," Dylan said, starting to hyperventilate.

"Let go of my hand for a minute," Tom said to Alex and Sara. When they did, he picked up his shotgun and racked the bolt, ejecting the chambered shell. "Okay, hold me," he said.

Holding the shotgun by the barrel, Tom leaned forward again, holding the stock out toward Dylan. "Dylan, grab the stock but *do not pull.* Look at me." Tom waited until Dylan controlled himself enough to meet his eyes. "If you pull, I'm gonna end up in there with you. Just get a good grip on the stock, but don't pull. Let us do that part."

As soon as Dylan grabbed the stock, panic flashed in his eyes. He was too far gone to listen to reason.

He pulled.

Alex and Sara tried to hold Tom steady, but he was heavy, and he was precariously balanced at the edge of the mud pit. They weren't strong enough to hold him. Both of them screamed helplessly as Tom slipped away and splashed into the mud right beside Dylan.

He went in head first.

Sara screamed again, but this time, it was because something grabbed her —something in the trees.

In the blink of an eye, Sara vanished into the shadows.

"Sara!" Alex shouted, raising her MPX. For a moment, she spun back and forth, paralyzed with fear and indecision. Dylan and Tom were both drowning, but something had snatched Sara and dragged her away. They all needed her. She couldn't help everyone.

Somehow, Tom had righted himself in the mud. His head was above the surface, but just barely. "Help Sara!" he shouted. "If she dies, it's all over!"

He was right. "Hold on!" Alex yelled. "I'll come back!"

Her heart pounding, Alex slowly took a step off the path. The trees were already so thick that she could barely move between them. Her gun shook violently in her hands. She took several deep breaths, trying to steady herself.

Somewhere not far ahead, a horrific scream ripped through the night.

"Sara!" Alex shouted again. The knowledge that Sara was in mortal danger temporarily suppressed Alex's fear. She charged ahead recklessly, sharp branches ripping shallow cuts in her face and arms. Within moments, there was blood in her eyes and running over her fingers. Her hands were slick with it. It was hard to keep hold of her weapon.

But keep hold of it she did. Alex had never held any strong opinions about guns one way or the other, but she was glad to have one now. Her weapon was a lifeline, some small measure of safety and reassurance in a nightmare that was rapidly spiraling out of control.

Suddenly, Alex stumbled into a small clearing. Blinking blood and sweat from her eyes, she raised her weapon, remembering to hold the stock firmly against her shoulder, as Tom had shown her.

Her jaw dropped.

Sara was on her back, shielding her face with her arms. *Something* was on top of her. It was unmistakably not human.

At first, Alex thought it was a small tree. It was made of wood—the same black, rough wood as the trees around her. But it wasn't just wood; parts of it gleamed a dull yellowish-white in the moonlight. Once she finally understood what she was looking at, her heart began to hammer even faster.

The white parts were human bones.

The thing on top of Sara was some unholy fusion of wood and bone. Instead of arms and legs, it had thick branches that moved in fits and jerks. Instead of a head, smashed fragments of a human skull were held in place by thick roots that snaked in and out of the mouth and eye sockets. Broken rib bones were embedded all over the monstrosity, in places where ribs didn't belong.

Its heavy arms were raised high.

It was about to cave in Sara's face.

A sudden well of anger surged forth in Alex's chest, mixing with her fear. She squeezed the trigger of her MPX, hard.

Nothing happened.

"God dammit!" Alex shouted, shaking the gun in frustration.

The tree thing swung. Sara screamed and twisted her head away, her neck bending at an unnatural angle. The thick branches slammed into the ground barely an inch from her forehead, sending geysers of dirt into the air. The creature raised its branches, preparing to attack again.

Finally, Alex realized the problem. She would have smacked herself in the head for being so stupid, but now wasn't the time. She used her thumb to flick the selector switch from safe to auto, then held down the trigger.

In two seconds, thirty rounds of 9mm Parabellum peppered the creature. Some of the rounds flew harmlessly into the trees behind; Alex had aimed high for fear of hitting Sara. Alex had a pair of shooter's earmuffs hanging around her neck, but she hadn't taken the time to put them on. The rapid *cracks* of gunfire were astonishingly loud. Immediately, her ears began to throb painfully, and a dull ringing sound muffled her hearing. Distantly, she thought that being outside had saved her hearing; if she'd been in a confined space, she might be deaf already.

The bullets did no appreciable damage to the creature, but they did get its attention. Slowly, it turned to face Alex, its movements accompanied by the sound of creaking wood.

"Oh, shit," Alex muttered. Suddenly aware that her gun was empty, she fumbled for the magazine release. The empty mag clattered to the ground as she groped for a fresh one.

Moving faster than she would have thought possible, the creature rose and took several steps toward her. Alex retreated until her back hit a tree. She finally pulled a new magazine free and tried to load it, but she missed the magazine well. The full magazine squirted out of her bloody, sweaty fingers like a melon seed and spun away into the darkness.

"Fuck!" Alex screamed. The thing was nearly on her.

She quickly considered her options. Running was out—she wouldn't leave Sara. She glanced left and right. The trees to either side were so thick and so close together that she'd never get between them. The only way out was forward—past the creature.

Alex remembered something Tom had said during their one-day crash course in guns and small-unit tactics: When time was short, when you had only a few seconds to respond to danger, switching to your sidearm was usually quicker than reloading your primary weapon.

She dropped the MPX, letting the sling catch it. With her right hand, she drew the Glock 17 from the holster on her thigh. Before she could raise it, the cursed thing reached her. It swung a thick branch directly at her head.

Alex was not particularly quick, and she certainly wasn't trained in hand-to-hand combat. Her saving grace was that, although the creature's legs were deceptively fast, its arms were comparatively slow. She ducked just in time, evading the attack so narrowly that she felt a rush of air over her head.

The monster struck the tree behind her with devastating force. A loud *crack* echoed through the night air as the blow tore away a chunk of wood the size of a cinder block.

Alex tried not to visualize what such a powerful impact would have done to her head.

She shuffled to the right and stood up again, turning to face the creature as she continued backing away, trying to gain some distance. She brought the Glock up in one hand and squeezed the trigger as quickly as she could. The pistol jumped in her hand, and she could see that most of the rounds were missing.

Again, Tom's voice came into her mind. *Never fire one-handed if you can help it.*

Alex brought her left hand up, adopting a steadier, two-handed grip. She got off three more shots, all of which struck the head area and sent pieces of shattered bone flying off into the night—but once again, she underestimated the creature's speed.

Before she could leap aside, it was on her. With sharp, wooden fingers, it grabbed her throat, choking off her air. It squeezed so violently that her vision immediately dimmed, almost fading to black as the carotid arteries on either side of her neck were pinched shut, cutting off the blood to her brain.

Even as she fought for her life, Alex couldn't help but analyze the situation medically. With the incredible force being applied to her neck, one of three things would happen. Best case scenario, she would pass out within the next few seconds, and the creature could then murder her at its leisure. Alternatively, it might crush her trachea, condemning her to a slow, agonizing death by suffocation.

Or maybe it would just snap her neck like a dry twig. It certainly seemed strong enough.

Somehow, she still had the Glock in her right hand. With the last of her strength, she raised it toward the creature's bullet-pocked face and hammered the trigger. Round after round dug splintered channels into the wood, none of which deterred her executioner in the slightest. Amber sap oozed from the bullet holes like thick blood. The Glock's slide locked back. The empty pistol fell from her fingers, which were becoming increasingly hard to control.

Just before Alex slipped into unconsciousness, she was suddenly free, falling onto her butt. She gasped in a breath, color rapidly returning to her vision.

The monster was on fire. Orange and yellow flames engulfed its upper half. Sparks flew into the air in all directions, and through the muted ringing in her ears, Alex could hear popping sounds, like those made by fresh wood tossed into a roaring campfire.

The creature shrieked. It sounded like a thousand tormented children wailing in unison, with a ghostly, echoing quality. She couldn't imagine how it made such a sound with no vocal cords, but she knew that the horrific scream would haunt her dreams for the rest of her life.

However short it might be.

Still not in full control of her muscles, Alex awkwardly scooted away, driven back by the heat of the flames. She didn't understand what was happening. Her right hand bumped into her empty pistol.

Never lose your weapon, Tom said in her head. She picked it up and finally managed to stagger to her feet.

Then she understood. Sara stood behind the abomination, gripping a blazing torch like a club. Alex remembered her saying that she'd put a torch in everyone's backpack.

Good girl, Alex thought.

"Let's go! More are coming," Sara cried, waving the torch as she darted into the trees, back the way Alex had come from.

More? Alex thought. *Christ almighty.* She followed Sara, running as fast as she dared in the darkness, guided by the bobbing flame of the girl's torch.

When they reached the path again, Tom and Dylan were still struggling to escape the quagmire. Based on the way Tom was holding his head, Alex guessed that he must be just barely tall enough for his feet to reach the bottom. He was doing his best to hold Dylan's head above the surface, but Dylan was still flailing in panic.

"Little help!" Tom shouted. Alex saw his shotgun lying on the ground—he must have managed to toss it clear of the mud as he'd fallen in. She considered trying to use it as he had, but she and Sara weren't strong enough to make that work, nor were their arms long enough.

"I have an idea," Sara said as she turned toward a tree just off the path. She raised her rifle and aimed it at one of the lower branches. At first, Alex thought she'd seen another of the wooden creatures, but the tree Sara was aiming at looked like all the others.

Alex managed to clap her hands over her ears just before Sara unleashed a long burst of automatic fire. The rifle rounds were much louder than those fired by Alex's MPX. A moment later, Alex finally understood Sara's plan. She'd used bullets as an improvised long-range chainsaw, blasting a long, heavy branch right off the trunk of the tree.

"Help me!" Sara called to Alex. Together, they dragged the heavy branch over to the mud pit and held it out. It was more than long enough, and even the thinner end was sturdy enough for Tom to grab without much fear of breaking it.

Alex admired Tom's selflessness. Even though Dylan had fallen in because he'd been ignoring Tom's orders about paying attention, and even though he'd pulled Tom in with him by panicking, Tom still made sure Dylan got out first. Spitting out great mouthfuls of sticky mud, Tom helped Dylan find the branch, then gave his butt a mighty shove to help him escape the pit. Straining with all their limited strength, Alex and Sara hauled the branch out with Dylan attached to it, then passed it back over to Tom. He was heavier, but he was also doing a much better job of keeping his cool than Dylan was, so it wasn't too much harder to pull him free.

All four of them collapsed to the forest floor, panting raggedly.

"What were you shooting at?" Tom gasped.

"One of those," Sara said, raising her arm to point with a trembling finger.

A dozen more of the living trees were shambling toward them out of the darkness.

"What in the fucking fuck are those?" Tom yelled, leaping to his feet. He found his shotgun lying several feet away and snatched it up.

Dylan shrieked in raw terror. He was done with puberty, but in that moment, he sounded very young.

"Don't bother shooting them," Alex said. "Run."

Tom spun on his heels, trusting that Alex knew what she was talking about. He took two steps, then stopped.

Dylan was still on his back, frozen in fear. Tom reached toward him.

"Dylan! Time to go!" Tom shouted.

Dylan didn't respond. He was staring at the advancing monsters, which were rapidly closing the distance.

"Dylan, come on!" Sara shouted. Her voice seemed to snap him out of it. He blinked twice, his eyelashes throwing off flecks of mud. Suddenly noticing Tom's hand, he took it and allowed himself to be pulled up.

"Go!" Tom shouted. "I'm last!" Once the others were ahead of him, Tom fell in behind.

"The torch!" Sara cried, starting to turn back. She'd dropped it to use her rifle. It burned brightly on the ground, twenty paces behind.

"Leave it!" Alex said. "Run!" She grabbed Sara's shoulder as she ran and spun her back around. Thankfully, Sara seemed to realize that going back for the torch would be suicide, and she didn't resist.

The four of them ran down the path, chests heaving, driven by terror and adrenaline. Tom risked a glance back to see how far behind their pursuers were.

He missed a step, nearly crashing to the ground. The tree things were right behind him and gaining ground.

"How are they so fast?" he shouted. "Run faster!"

Until now, the four of them had been running but not sprinting, trying to conserve their stamina. Clearly, that was no longer an option. They all turned up the speed, holding nothing back.

Gradually, the path ahead began to widen, and the trees to either side became thinner, with more space between them. "Look out!" Sara cried, pointing to the right. More tree things were coming out of the forest on that side, trying to cut them off.

"Go left!" Alex yelled.

In unison, they all veered left, off the path and into the brush. They were panting fiercely, running on fumes, but they dared not slow. They leaped over large rocks, dodged around crooked tree trunks, and ducked under low branches. The sounds of crashing wood grew louder behind them.

The monsters were getting closer.

Suddenly, Sara skidded to a halt, her chest heaving. The others slid to a stop as well, turning back toward her.

"Sara, we gotta go, there's no time!" Tom shouted.

"They're herding us!" she shouted, struggling to draw enough breath to get the words out.

"What?" Alex said.

"They want us to go this way! We gotta go back!" With no further explanation, Sara darted back the way they'd come.

"God dammit! What is she thinking?" Tom roared.

"We can't leave her!" Alex shouted, taking off in the same direction.

Tom shoved Dylan to get him moving again. He swore under his breath. "Punch through!" he yelled ahead. "Don't stop for anything! If we stop, we're dead!"

Seconds later, dark shapes loomed out of the shadows as the tree things met them head-on. Tom was surprised at how few there were. *Maybe Sara is right*, he thought.

Sara was in the lead. She deftly squeezed between two of the creatures, hardly losing any momentum. They turned to swing at her, but she was already gone. Alex, Tom, and Dylan followed her lead, staying as far away from the monsters as they could, slowing only as much as necessary.

Sara led them back across the path, into the trees on the far side. The ear-splitting shrieks of the tree things began to fade. It sounded like they were falling behind, but they were definitely still in pursuit.

"There!" Sara yelled, looking back so the others could hear her. With her left hand, she was pointing through the trees at something they couldn't see yet. She angled that way, and her Wardens followed.

Soon, they saw what she'd seen. In the pale moonlight, the base of a large hill loomed toward them. It was easily fifty feet tall. A massive iron fence ringed the entire hilltop. Beyond the fence, the roof of a large house reached toward the sky.

At first, Tom, Alex, and Dylan could see no way up to the house. There was no staircase and no obvious path winding up the hillside. Then they saw Sara skid to a halt in front of a rickety wooden platform, its upper crossbeams supporting a large pulley. From the pulley, a thick, ancient-looking rope ascended into the trees.

It was an elevator.

The others caught up to Sara and joined her on the platform. Under any other circumstances, all would have expressed serious doubts about the elevator's structural integrity, but they were far past the limits of their stamina, and their tireless pursuers were again closing in.

Sara tugged on the fat wooden lever that must have engaged a counterweight system somewhere above. It didn't budge. With a growl of frustration that sounded almost feral, she rammed her shoulder into it. This time, it moved; with agonizing slowness, the elevator began to rise.

They were only a few feet off the ground when the tree things began to arrive. Tom raised his shotgun but didn't fire, waiting to see if it would be necessary.

When the first creature took a running swipe at the elevator, it missed by inches. Sara and the others shared a sigh of relief as more tree things gathered below, howling in fury as they stretched futilely for prey now safely out of reach.

No one said anything. They all panted, trying to catch their breath, trying to resist the urge to sit down and rest. When the elevator broke through the canopy, snapping branches as it went, the moonlight suddenly became brighter. For the first time since entering the forest, they could see one another clearly.

Each thought that the others looked terrible. Tom and Dylan were covered in reddish-black mud and countless scratches from sprinting headlong through the trees. Alex still had dried blood all over her face and arms, and a purplish-black ring of bruises was beginning to form around her neck where the creature had grabbed her. Sara had only minor bumps and scrapes, but she was disheveled and exhausted. Strands of her red hair poked out from under her watch cap, and her face was caked in dirt.

When the elevator finally creaked to a halt at the top of the hill, they all shuffled quickly onto solid ground, unwilling to trust the rickety contraption any longer than necessary. The great, dark house loomed before them, silent and menacing. A gate in the fence stood open, beckoning them onward.

"Look," Sara said, so quietly that the others almost didn't hear her. They turned to see what she was looking at.

In the forest below, they could see a large clearing, about the width of a football field. There was something in the clearing, something huge that took up most of the available space. It took several long moments to understand what they were seeing.

"Dear god," Alex said.

The edges of an enormous pit ran right up to the tree line all around the clearing. The pit was filled with a writhing mass of wood and bone. Tendril-like branches as thick as semi trucks reached angrily toward the sky, lashing back and forth in search of prey. Hundreds of the smaller bone-and-wood creatures burst out of the trees and hurled themselves into the great, pulsing mass, joining with it until they could hunt once more.

The clearing was not far from where they'd been heading when they first left the path.

"Sara was right," Tom said, his voice hoarse. "They were herding us—toward that."

"If we'd come out of the trees at a dead sprint, we'd have had no time to react," Alex whispered. Her voice trembled. The others could hear that she was making an effort not to cry.

"Sara… you saved us," Dylan panted.

"She saved my ass, too," Alex said. "One of those things was about to break me in half. Sara set it on fire. Apparently, they don't like fire."

Abruptly, Tom turned toward Dylan and grabbed one strap of his armor. Tom drew back his other hand, making a fist. Dylan flinched and tried to cover his face with his hands.

"Tom! What are you doing!" Alex shouted.

Alex and Sara were both sure that Tom would knock Dylan's teeth out. He looked like he wanted to, but his fist didn't move. It hung motionless in the air behind his head. Dylan trembled like a leaf, waiting for it.

Finally, Tom dropped his fist and let go of Dylan. When he spoke, his voice was low and dangerous. "You almost got yourself killed. Then, you almost killed me. Then, because you and I were both stuck in that pit, you almost got Alex and Sara killed."

Dylan hung his head. "I know," he said.

"I'm trying to be patient here. I know you're scared. It may not seem like it, but I'm scared, too. We're all scared. We almost got ripped apart by tree zombies because you were feeling sorry for yourself and not looking where you were going. Get your head in the fucking game here."

Dylan said nothing. In the moonlight, the others saw a single tear wind its way down his mud-caked cheek. "I'm sorry," he whispered.

"Don't be sorry. Be better," Tom said, the anger in his voice now tempered with a surprising note of compassion. He turned to Sara and Alex. "Let's get moving," he said.

As the other three followed Tom through the gate and into the mansion's courtyard, Dylan stopped. He looked at the house, frowning. "Does this house look familiar to any of you?" he said.

Tom, Sara, and Alex studied the house for a moment, then turned back to Dylan. "No. Should it?" Tom said.

"I don't recognize it either," Alex said.

"Me neither," Sara said.

Dylan stared at the house for another long moment, his mouth twisted in thought. Finally, he shook his head. "I dunno. I just thought it looked familiar for some reason."

"Look, there's a cable car over there," Sara said, pointing to the yard behind the house. There was indeed an ancient-looking cable car waiting silently at the edge of the hill. The cable stretched far into the distance, farther than any of them could see, rising at a gentle angle into snow-capped mountains beyond the edge of the forest.

"Is that the direction we need to go?" Tom asked Sara.

"More or less," she said. "There's no north, south, east, or west here, at least not in the way we normally understand directions. But the moon never moves, and it hangs directly over the cathedral. So, we just follow the moon."

"So, it's either the cable car or back down and through the forest, for what looks like another five or ten miles, at least," Tom observed.

"I vote cable car," Alex said.

"No argument here. I'm not eager to see those tree things again," Sara agreed.

"Yeah, the cable car would be faster for sure, and probably safer—assuming it doesn't just fall and kill us that way," Tom said.

"It's always nighttime in the Twilight, but at least we have you for sunshine," Sara quipped.

"There's a fence blocking the backyard, but it looks climbable enough," Alex said. "Certainly much easier than the last thing I climbed." She took a few steps forward and reached for the fence.

Tom grabbed her shirt and yanked her back. "Hold it," he said. "Look."

Alex followed his gaze until she saw the faded sign, reading: "DANGER: HIGH VOLTAGE."

"The fence is electrified?" Sara said. Tom picked up a stick and tossed it at the fence. It bounced away with a small shower of sparks.

"Wood has very low conductivity," Tom said. "If a stick creates sparks, there's some serious juice in those bars."

"Nothing is ever easy," Sara sighed.

"Hey," Alex said to her. "This is your road trip, not ours."

"So… we have to go through the house," Dylan said.

"Looks that way," Tom said. "It's a big house, but it's still just a house. Should be a straight shot."

"Nothing is ever easy," Alex said, echoing Sara.

As the party of four moved cautiously toward the front door of the dark manor house, four pairs of eyes watched them silently, from far away —far enough that they surely couldn't be detected.

What do you think? whispered a ghostly, feminine voice, like tinkling icicles.

Too early to tell, said another that sounded like running water. *We must wait and see.*

CHAPTER ELEVEN
Escalation

"Alex," Tom said softly.

"Hmm?" she said.

"Your primary weapon and sidearm are both empty."

He was right. She'd never gotten a chance to reload them after the struggle in the clearing. She did so now.

"You're missing two magazines for your MPX," Tom said.

"I dropped them when I was trying to help Sara. It was... intense," she said.

"Try not to lose ammo, this shit's gonna be hard enough," Tom said. When he saw Alex's incredulous expression, he cleared his throat and tried again. "Sorry. I didn't mean to be a dick about it."

"It's okay," she said. "You're not wrong. It's just that none of us are used to this. You're the only gunfighter here."

Tom nodded. "I'll do my best to remember." He turned slightly so he could speak to all of the others. "Alright, everyone, hearing protection on. Electronic hearing protection is a godsend, but electronics don't work here, so we're stuck with old-fashioned earmuffs that block all sound indiscriminately. Once we get inside, try to communicate nonverbally whenever possible. If you have to talk, talk loud. If you're too quiet, the rest of us won't be able to hear you. It's not ideal, but it's better than rupturing an eardrum, which is likely if you fire a gun indoors without protection."

"I can attest to that," Alex said. Only now was the ringing in her ears finally beginning to fade. All four of them donned their earmuffs and adjusted them for comfort.

"I'm on point—I always will be when we go indoors," Tom said. "Stay behind me, stay alert, and don't leave my side unless I tell you to. Hopefully, we'll be able to cut through the house quickly with no issues."

No one voiced any doubt for fear of jinxing it.

Tom press-checked his shotgun and flicked off the safety, keeping his trigger finger straight along the receiver, away from the trigger. He'd loaded his weapon with four rounds each of double-aught buckshot and lead slugs, alternating in the magazine tube. Buckshot was devastating to soft tissue over a wide area, whereas 12-gauge slugs would punch right through a human target—and the person behind, and several walls behind that person.

Anything that got within twenty meters of Tom was going to have a bad day.

They stacked up on the front door, with Tom in the lead and Sara behind him, followed by Alex and Dylan.

"Go red," Tom said to the others, instructing them to verify that their weapons were loaded and ready to fire. "Don't shoot me in the back, pretty please. Ready?"

"No," Dylan said flatly. Alex reached behind and touched his arm gently. That seemed to calm him a bit.

"Me neither, if it makes you feel any better," Tom said. "Let's get it over with." Testing the doorknob, he found it unlocked. Slowly, silently, he pushed the door open.

* * *

Tom swore quietly as he crept through the foyer. He'd been planning to turn right, toward the backyard, but the hallway in that direction was crammed wall to wall, floor to ceiling with furniture and random items. He pivoted left, aiming his shotgun down the opposite hallway. He saw several closed doors but nothing out of the ordinary, except for a long runner carpet the color of red wine. It was badly rumpled.

As though something had recently run across it at top speed.

He turned to the others and lifted one earmuff away from his ear, indicating that he wanted them to do the same. When they did, he whispered, "Moving all this shit would be way too noisy, and I don't wanna be here that long anyway. Let's find another way." The others all nodded and fell back into position.

The house reminded Tom of many he'd built in New England. A particular style of manor was popular there, reminiscent of southern plantation houses in some ways. The house they were in now was built in the same basic style, but it was old and dusty. It had soaring, vaulted ceilings, polished hardwood floors, and large rooms decorated with elegant simplicity.

If not for the clutter and the pervasive feeling of foreboding, it would be a nice place.

Tom moved silently down the left hallway, hugging the right-hand wall. When he reached the first door, he shifted to a left-handed shooting grip and carefully tested the knob. Finding it locked, he moved on, testing each subsequent door. The next two were also locked; only one was left on this side of the hall. He was reluctant to try the doors on the other side because they probably didn't lead to the backyard.

He had the distinct impression that they were being funneled, just like in the forest.

The last door on the right was unlocked. Cracking it open a few inches, Tom could see nothing inside—it was pitch-black. Cautiously, he peeked into the room. He had a vague impression that it was fairly large. The floor tiles he could see were alternating squares of black and white marble, conjuring images of an old-time ballroom.

Sara tapped his shoulder. When he looked at her, she mimed sparking a lighter in her hand, asking if she should light a torch. Tom shook his head. Walking into a dark room with a blazing beacon of light would make them easy targets, and it would make it harder for them to see anything outside the radius of the firelight. He didn't want to do that unless it was unavoidable.

For now, he'd rather take his chances in the dark and try to remain undetected.

Tom waved to get everyone's attention, holding up two fingers on his right hand and two on his left. He then moved his hands away from one another. The others nodded their understanding; Tom and Sara would go right, Alex and Dylan would go left. Slowly, Tom crept into the room, keeping his back to the wall and his shotgun ready. Sara followed close behind, trying not to let Tom see how nervous she was.

Even though Sara had dragged him into a hellhole worse than any in the Middle East—without his permission—he felt responsible for her safety. Everyone else seemed to think he was some kind of Terminator, a singularly effective killing machine who could keep them safe while reading a book and brushing his teeth at the same time. In reality, he was just a guy who knew how to make stuff dead. He was far from superhuman, and he was acutely aware of that fact now. His heart pounded like a jackhammer in the darkness. Sara gave him a reason to act braver than he felt.

Alex and Dylan made a similar pair. She was glad that he was there because she felt that falling apart in front of him would set off a chain reaction of panic throughout the whole party, akin to the keystone falling out of an archway. She was pretty sure that she was the main reason he hadn't yet had a complete breakdown. He seemed to think that she had some idea of what she was doing, some kind of knowledge or experience that made her qualified to be here. She didn't, but as long as Dylan believed it, she could make herself believe it.

Kind of.

Once all four of them had entered the room and moved partway around the perimeter, Tom caught the distinct scent of blood.

The door slammed shut with a loud bang. Soft, wicked laughter echoed from somewhere deeper in the room.

"Sara and Dylan! Light! Now!" Tom shouted, holding his position, straining to see and hear. It was so dark. He could only see shadows and vague suggestions of shapes.

Tom and Alex heard the teens frantically scrambling for torches and lighters. The seconds dragged on. All of them braced themselves, expecting something horrid to pounce at any moment. Nothing happened, but gradually, another faint sound became audible, somewhere near the middle of the room.

It sounded like someone crying.

Finally, the torch that Sara had taken from Tom's pack flared to life, followed by Dylan's a moment later, on the other side of the room.

Sara gasped. Alex let out a clipped scream. Dylan cried out in terror and revulsion. Tom stared in shocked silence.

A tapestry of gore and malevolence hung from the walls and ceiling, covering the entire back half of the large room. Strands of rusted barbed wire crisscrossed every which way, forming an impenetrable wall of pain.

Suspended in the middle of it was a middle-aged woman.

Her head sagged forward, ribbons of spit and snot dripping to the floor. She wept quietly, out of her mind with pain and fear. The barbed wire pierced the skin of her shoulders, her back, her sides, her ankles, holding her several feet off the floor. She shuddered violently, like a fly caught helplessly in a spiderweb. With each jerk and twist of her muscles, the barbed wire tore more of her flesh, sprinkling the floor with crimson drops.

"Please," she whispered, her voice ragged with torment. "Kill me."

"Sara," Tom said, rooted to the floor, unable to make his muscles move. "What have you gotten us into?"

Alex dropped her MPX onto its sling and rushed forward.

"Alex, wait!" Dylan called, reaching out a hand to stop her. She was already gone.

Seeing Alex rush headlong into danger finally unlocked Tom's muscles. He charged forward and managed to snatch the strap on the back of her armor just before she reached the woman. "Alex, stop!"

With surprising force, she spun around and shoved Tom away. "I'm here for a reason, aren't I? I'm a doctor. This woman needs help!"

Again, Tom grabbed her armor, from the front this time. "And you can't help her if you're up there with her, or worse!" he said through gritted teeth. Sara ran up behind him and tried to help pull Alex away. The older woman stood firm, resisting with strength that surprised the others.

"Let go! If you want to stop me, then shoot me!" she yelled.

Sara glanced at Tom. She could see in his glassy, faraway eyes that they were thinking the same thing. Alex was committed to a foolhardy course of action, but they couldn't afford the distraction of wrestling with her. They both released her at the same time and moved a few steps to each side to cover her. Because Sara was holding a torch, she couldn't use her rifle. She drew her .32 Walther with her free hand instead.

"Dylan, get over here and cover the door," Tom called, aiming his shotgun toward the rear of the room. He couldn't see much back there; the torchlight didn't extend far enough.

Thankfully, Dylan obeyed, if timidly. Dropping his torch and raising his UMP in shaking hands, he fell in back-to-back with Sara, aiming at the door they'd come in.

The tortured woman continued to cry quietly, her blood-soaked hair hanging in front of her face. There was so much blood that Alex couldn't even tell what color her hair was. Gingerly, she touched the woman's cheek. "It's okay," Alex said. "I'll help you, I'm a doctor. Just try to stay calm, don't move. What's your name?"

"D—Daniela," the woman managed to croak out.

Tom heard Sara gasp.

Alex turned to Dylan. "Do you have any tools we can use to get her down?"

Without looking back, Dylan said, "I have some wire cutters in my pack. It might take some extra muscle, but they could work."

"Sara," Alex said.

"On it," Sara replied. She holstered her sidearm and began digging in Dylan's pack so he could keep his weapon trained on the door.

Alex turned back to the woman and began touching her chest and stomach as gently as possible, trying to examine her wounds to see if any were immediately life-threatening.

"Oh, fuck me," Tom whispered.

An enormous shape materialized out of the shadows behind the woman, behind the wall of barbed wire. Alex hadn't seen it yet; she was too focused on her patient. Sara and Dylan were both facing the other way. Only Tom saw the monstrosity.

It was the size of a large truck, its rubbery flesh a pale yellow-gray color and flecked with dried blood. The top half was vaguely human, with two muscular arms and a face.

A smiling face.

A dirty cloth was tied around its head, covering its eyes like a blindfold. Its lower half was a powerful, serpentine tail. The creature moved with grace that seemed impossible, walking on its muscular arms as its tail slithered along behind.

Tom fired. The powerful semi-automatic shotgun kicked hard against his shoulder with a thunderous *boom* dampened to tolerable levels by his hearing protection. The gas-driven action cycled smoothly, ejecting the spent shell and chambering another in the blink of an eye. Tom tapped the trigger twice more, sending a slug and another volley of buckshot directly toward the horror's grinning face.

Suddenly, it wasn't there anymore. An instant later, it reappeared in the same spot, then darted to the right. Tom shifted his aim and fired twice more, but again, somehow, he missed. He didn't understand. His aim was dead-on, he was sure of that. Was the thing really that fast?

The beast reappeared, again in the same spot. Tom fired his last three shells as fast as he could work the trigger. Again, he hit nothing but air. The creature blinked back into view, then retreated into the shadows.

Tom had fired all eight rounds so quickly that Alex, Sara, and Dylan were only just now reacting to the shots. Alex flinched but kept trying to free the woman, using Dylan's cutters to snip away at the barbed wire. Dylan panic-fired a burst of .45 ACP randomly into the darkness, hitting nothing.

"Alex, back up!" Tom shouted. With his left hand, he rotated the shotgun ninety degrees and laid the buttstock on his right shoulder with the loading port facing outward. With his right hand, he grabbed a single shell from his plate carrier, slapped it into the open chamber, and slammed the bolt release with the side of his fist, chambering a fresh round. He then grabbed four more shells, palming them two by two. In one fluid motion, he shoved two shells into the tube, then the other two. Snatching three more shells, he repeated the procedure, reloading the gun from empty to full in under five seconds.

"Cover me!" Alex screamed. "I'm not leaving her!"

Tom considered dragging her away with as much force as necessary. He understood her desire to help, but this was not the time. Her rash judgment was going to get them all killed.

Before he could make a decision, the creature loomed out of the shadows, reaching for Alex. Tom fired four shots in quick succession. Once again, the creature vanished, unharmed, then reappeared and immediately retreated. When it scurried back into the small ring of torchlight, it was hanging from the ceiling, and only Sara could see it. Her heart felt like it was about to beat its way out of her chest. Gritting her teeth, she tossed her torch aside, shouldered her rifle, and aimed.

Her perception of time slowed as her adrenal gland flooded her system with adrenaline. The creature began reaching its bulging arms toward Alex, as though it meant to pick her up and carry her off to a grisly fate. Sara could see individual beads of sweat on Alex's face as she yelled at Tom, her mouth moving in slow motion. She could see each dexterous movement of Tom's fingers as he expertly loaded more shells into his shotgun.

Sara's right eye searched for the target beyond her front sight post. As soon as she found it, she began to squeeze the trigger, intending to pepper the beast with a long burst.

She stopped, the trigger millimeters from its breaking point. The creature continued to descend on Alex in slow motion. Sara's mind raced, her thoughts turbocharged by adrenaline. Her target was moving in an odd, jerky pattern. It would be hard to hit.

Slow is smooth, smooth is fast, Tom said in her head. *I don't care if you only fire once, as long as that one shot hits. Show me accuracy. Speed comes later.*

It felt wrong to hold her fire as the monster's arms drew ever closer to her friend and mentor. Sara wanted to shoot now, to help Alex.

Instead, she lowered her point of aim, placing the front sight barely a foot above Alex's head. Her right thumb flicked the selector switch from auto to semi. She held her breath and waited.

There. For just a moment, the creature paused.

She squeezed the trigger once. The rifle kicked against her shoulder.

She expected a spray of blood, or a roar of rage—some kind of confirmation that she'd hit the target. Instead, it simply disappeared, just as it had when Tom had fired at it.

She growled in frustration.

At least she'd stopped it from snatching Alex.

Several steps away from Sara, Dylan saw the thing blink away and reappear. It quickly swung to the side, to a position directly behind the suspended woman. He didn't think Sara could see it from her angle. Misshapen yellow hands reached out, snaking through the barbed wire, reaching for Alex.

He didn't think she had noticed the threat. She was consumed by her desperate struggle to cut her patient free.

Tom was still reloading his shotgun, not yet ready to fire again.

It was all happening so fast. Too fast.

No one except Dylan could both see the creature and possibly do something to stop it from grabbing Alex.

He didn't consciously decide to move, but suddenly, he was running. His UMP bounced on its sling against his chest and his mud-caked sneakers pounded on the marble floor. He dived forward, slamming into Alex like a linebacker. The two of them tumbled away a fraction of a heartbeat before the yellow hands closed around her.

Seemingly unbothered, the monstrosity simply chose a new target, instead wrapping one gigantic hand around the helpless woman's torso, the other around her legs. It did so tenderly, almost lovingly. Tom raised his shotgun, preparing to fire again. Now able to see her target, Sara shifted her aim as well.

With no fanfare, the creature pulled in opposite directions, ripping Daniela in half.

A fountain of blood erupted, spattering the Maiden and all her Wardens. Sara tasted some of it in her mouth, hot and coppery. Entrails slopped across the floor in a wet pile. Casually, the abomination tossed the two halves of the woman aside. Her torso crashed to the floor near Tom's feet.

Good fucking god, she's still alive, he thought in numb revulsion, his heart breaking with sorrow for her. Daniela's eyes blinked up at him, filled with shock and disbelief. Her mouth moved, but no words came out.

Tom and Sara fired at the same time. Once again, the creature vanished, unharmed, then reappeared and quickly retreated into the shadows. The same soft, wicked laughter they'd heard earlier echoed faintly from the back of the room.

Then, finally, blessedly, all was silent.

Dylan rolled over onto his stomach and started to push himself to his feet. He slipped in the woman's guts and crashed back to the floor. When he saw what he'd put his hands in, he promptly threw up.

"No!" Alex screamed. "No! Fuck!" She rushed to Daniela's side. "I'm sorry. I'm so sorry. I tried," Alex stumbled on her words, tears falling freely. She grabbed the woman's hand, trying to comfort her.

Daniela stared up at the ceiling with lifeless eyes.

* * *

Sara and Tom retrieved the discarded torches and managed to drag the others into the next room through an unlocked door on their side of the barbed wire. It resembled a small library or study, with bookshelves and an old writing desk. Alex looked catatonic, staring vacantly ahead, saying nothing. Dylan didn't look much better. The front of his armor was spattered with gore and his own puke.

After quickly scanning the room for obvious threats, Tom knelt in front of Alex. "Listen to me," he said. "You've gotta snap out of it. You did your best, but you can't save everyone. That woman died knowing you were giving everything you had trying to save her. That's something, at least. She's not suffering anymore."

Sara knew that that wasn't true, but she didn't say so. Instead, she turned to Dylan. "Dylan, Tom is right. That woman is gone. I know it's horrible, I feel sick, too. But she's dead; she doesn't need help anymore. We're not dead, Dylan. We still need help. We need you."

That seemed to bring him out of his trance, at least partly. Alex also started to come around.

"Let's move before that thing comes back," Tom said. "Somehow, it can dodge bullets. I don't think any of us hit it."

Tom and Sara helped their respective charges to their feet. Woodenly, numb with shock, the group pressed on. Tom took point again, leading them through several more rooms. Thankfully, there was no further sign of the creature. They emerged back into the foyer, now on the other side of the barricade. From there, they passed quickly through a cluttered kitchen and into the backyard. Each of them felt a heavy weight of dread lift from their shoulders as they stepped out of the house of horrors and into the chilly night air.

In a small patch of dark soil underneath the kitchen window, a dozen white lilies bloomed vibrantly, their petals bright and brilliant in the moonlight. The lovely flowers seemed strangely out of place, especially in light of the horrific carnage that had just unfolded inside the house.

Anxious to leave, Sara and the others jogged across the yard to the ancient cable car. Alex and Sara tossed handfuls of dirt onto the torches to extinguish them, then stowed them. "Let me go first and make sure it's not about to fall," Tom said, holding up a hand. He stepped into the car and paused for a moment, waiting to see if it would crash to the forest floor, far below. It swayed a bit under his weight, but it seemed solid enough. He stepped over to the small control panel and pulled the lever that presumably started the car.

Nothing happened.

Frowning, Tom examined the control panel more closely. There was a green bulb labeled "POWER," but it was dark. He tapped the oil gauge with a finger. The needle rested on "E," for empty.

Tom exited the car. "No power and no oil," he said. Turning to Dylan, he asked, "Can you fix it?"

Dylan didn't respond. He was staring off into the distance. Tom shook him by the shoulder to snap him out of it.

"Huh?" Dylan said.

"The cable car. It needs power and oil. Can you fix it?"

"I don't know. Can't you?"

Tom bit back an angry reply. "No, probably not. My specialties are construction and explosives. You're the one who builds motors." Tom thought that he might be able to fix the cable car, but even if he could, it would probably take hours, and a lot of trial and error.

Dylan broke eye contact with Tom, looking at Sara instead. She gazed back at him with a small, sad smile. Dylan's heart broke when he saw that her face was spattered with so much blood that, in the moonlight, he couldn't tell the blood from her freckles.

Swallowing hard, he tried to be brave for her.

"I... I'll try," he said, his voice breaking a bit.

"Good," Tom said. "We'll cover you. There's an access panel in the floor of the car. I think you can get to everything from there."

Shrugging off his backpack, Dylan flipped open the access panel and went to work. Within a few minutes, he was in his element, muttering to himself and pawing through his box of spare parts. Sara sighed with relief at seeing Dylan finally acting somewhat like himself, even if only for a little while.

Tom, Alex, and Sara watched the house in silence, weapons at the low ready. They were all too drained and numb to speak. That poor woman's grisly death replayed over and over in their minds. Even if they survived this twisted nightmare, they would be condemned to watch her being ripped in half in their dreams for the rest of their lives.

Sometime later, Dylan came out of the cable car, shouldering his pack and wiping his grease-stained hands on his mud-stained pants. "All set," he said. "It still has some oil, I think the gauge is just broken. As for the power, I—"

"I don't care, as long as it works," Tom said, cutting Dylan off.

"Let's give it a try," Sara said, ushering the others inside. She pulled the lever. With a mechanical sigh, the cable car lurched and began to move.

For the first time since watching Daniela die, Alex's face showed some hint of emotion. She smiled tiredly at Dylan, squeezing his arm. "Nice job," she said.

Sara smiled at him as well. "Like I said last night, you can fix anything."

Alex and Sara looked pointedly at Tom, who so far had said nothing since entering the car. Dylan looked down at the floor, fidgeting. Tom frowned. Clearly, Alex and Sara expected him to say something.

"Yeah, right. Thanks, Dylan," he said. The boy shrugged self-consciously, reluctant to acknowledge the compliments.

Exhausted, the four of them sat down heavily on the two small benches inside the car. It creaked along for a while, swaying back and forth. It was moving slowly but consistently. The mountains were far away. It would be a long ride.

After an extended silence, Tom cleared his throat. "Did you guys hear about the two Egyptian pharaohs who farted at the same time?"

The others stared at him in open astonishment. "Excuse me?" Alex said, not quite sure she'd heard him correctly.

"They had a Tutankhamun," Tom said with a perfectly straight face.

A heavy silence filled the cable car.

"A toot in common," Tom repeated, more slowly.

There was no sound save for the creaking of the motorized pulley.

Dylan was the first to laugh. He collapsed into a fit of giggles, holding his stomach.

His laughter seemed to infect the others. Sara and Alex found themselves joining in, unable to stop it. Tom cracked a smile for the first time in days, relieved to see the tension lifting.

Finally, the laughter began to die down. "That was the stupidest joke I've ever heard," Sara said, wiping tears from her eyes.

"And yet you laughed," Tom countered.

"I never thought I'd hear a fart joke from Tom, the mighty warrior," Dylan wheezed.

"Me neither," Alex agreed, clutching her aching sides.

"Believe it or not," Tom said, "I'm not always a humorless grump. There was even a time when I briefly pursued a career in comedy."

"I don't believe it," Sara said.

Alex studied Tom for a moment. "I do," she said quietly.

"You do?" Dylan asked, surprised.

Alex nodded. "I can see it. Tom is a hard man sometimes, but only because he has to be. Look at the role he's had to fill. What else would you expect?"

Tom said nothing but offered her a small smile of appreciation.

The cable car continued its slow journey, and the group again fell into silence for a time. It was Alex who finally broke it.

"Sara," she said. "You saved my life in that house, didn't you." It didn't sound like a question.

Sara shrugged. "Dylan saved you, too."

Alex smiled at Dylan and patted his leg. "That's right, he did. Thanks, Dylan. You were very brave, and chivalrous." He blushed.

"I only heard Sara fire one shot while I was reloading," Tom said.

Sara looked at him. "Slow is smooth, smooth is fast," she said.

Tom gave her a single nod. "I'm glad you took it to heart."

"Not as glad as I am," Alex said, putting her arm around Sara's shoulders and pulling her into a side hug. "I'm sorry I was stupid. I'm sorry for putting us all in danger."

The others expected Tom to say something like, "Yeah, you fucked up. Don't let it happen again." Instead, he said, "You wouldn't be who you are if you didn't give your all to help that woman. Never lose that compassion. Don't let the senseless violence of this nightmare kill that fire inside you. Fight with everything you have to keep it burning."

"I guess our heartless killer really is full of surprises," Dylan said.

"You're still on thin ice. Don't push your luck," Tom grunted.

"Who was that woman, anyway? She said her name was Daniela," Alex wondered aloud.

"She was a Maiden," Sara said. The others looked at her, waiting for her to explain.

"Did you know her?" Dylan asked.

Sara shook her head. "Not personally. I was just a baby when she came here. I was taught the names of every Maiden and Warden who came before me so that I would never forget the great service they did for me, and for all of mankind. Daniela Esperanza, from Córdoba, Argentina, was the first Maiden of the last cycle.

"Some Pilgrimages end in failure. Some Maidens and Wardens are killed before they reach the end of the path. Some simply go missing." None of the others found that hard to believe. "When that happens, the next team in line must go in, but they do so at a severe disadvantage. They start at the beginning, at the village, but the seven-day timer doesn't reset."

"So, some people had it even harder than we do," Tom mused.

Sara nodded. "Daniela's team disappeared after two days, and the next was successful. Barely."

Alex balked. "You mean she's been alive, and stuck here, for... what, something like twenty years?"

Again, Sara nodded. "Sixteen."

"Jesus," Tom whispered. "I can't imagine how she survived that long. And then... to die just when it seemed help had finally come."

Alex wiped away another tear. The others could tell that she was being eaten alive by guilt.

"I don't understand why that blindfolded thing didn't kill us," Dylan said softly.

"The Stalker?" Tom said.

Alex stared at him. "You gave it a name?"

Tom nodded. "I don't think we've seen the last of it. We need to call it something, and we need to be ready when it comes back."

"Why 'the Stalker,' though?" Sara asked.

"Because it didn't kill us."

Alex scratched her head. "I don't follow."

"Why didn't it kill Daniela? Right away, I mean, when it first captured her," Tom said. "Why would it go through all that trouble to do… that… to her, and then just leave her there on the edge of death?"

There was only one answer that made sense. "It takes pleasure in making us suffer," Alex said, her voice barely a whisper.

"Which is why it didn't kill us," Tom said. "It could have, easily. It can dodge bullets. We can't hurt it, at least not in the conventional way. It knows we can't hurt it. It has nothing to fear from us. It didn't kill us because it knows it can take its time. It'll be back, but it won't kill us until it's broken us with fear and pain."

"Hence, 'the Stalker,'" Sara whispered.

The four of them contemplated that unpleasant thought. After a long silence, Alex changed the subject.

"Sara," she said. "How were you able to see into our dreams?"

Sara shrugged. "I don't know, I just can. All Maidens can see their Wardens' nightmares when the end of a cycle draws near. We aren't sure where the ability comes from, but it's probably meant to be used the way we always use it: to convince our Wardens that this crazy story is true."

"So, you can read our minds?" Dylan asked. He looked decidedly uncomfortable about that.

She shook her head. "No, I promise. Only your nightmares, and only those you had during the initial seven-day period."

"That's comforting… I guess," Tom said.

Dylan swallowed. He looked like he felt compelled to ask a question despite not really wanting to know the answer. "What did you see? In my nightmares?"

Sara hesitated. "Well, I didn't 'see' much. Your dreams weren't very clear, visually. I saw something like a human shape, but it was indistinct, hard to make out. I mostly remember the sound—the song."

"The song my mom used to sing to help me fall asleep when I was a baby," Dylan whispered. He was staring at the floor again. "The song nobody else knows, except my dad."

Alex could tell that Dylan was deeply uncomfortable talking about his mother. She redirected the conversation to give him a break. "Something else is bothering me," she said.

"I'll answer any questions I can," Sara said.

"The dinner party, just before you drugged us." Tom bristled at the memory. "Why go through such an elaborate ruse? And why make up such a detailed story about a new treatment center if you were just going to drug us anyway?"

"The treatment center is real," Sara said, "as was the offer to run it—if, by some miracle, you still want to once this is over, after all that we've put you through. If not, my father will change the plan as needed."

"It was another test," Dylan said as it began to dawn on him.

"Yes," Sara whispered.

"So many tests," Alex said, shaking her head.

"That one was the most important test of all," Sara said. "It was the last one before the physical test, the proving ground where you each faced your worst fears and survived. Before putting you through that, we had to be sure that each of you had the most important ingredient of all."

"Which is?" Tom said.

"The willingness to selflessly put your own desires aside to serve others —to shepherd all of humanity to safety, no matter the cost to yourselves."

A stunned silence filled the cable car.

"If I was willing to put my company in stasis for a decade to help people I'd never met, then it was at least pretty good odds that you'd be able to convince me to escort you through hell itself," Tom said, shaking his head in disbelief. Sara nodded in confirmation.

"At first, I thought I'd failed some kind of test when your dad offered me a scholarship and I turned it down. He seemed so disappointed, and you seemed so shocked," Dylan said to Sara. "But he wasn't disappointed, and you weren't shocked. It was all an act. I didn't fail the test; I passed it. You wanted to know how far I was willing to go to protect you. So, you offered me everything I'd ever dreamed of on a silver platter, just to make sure I'd turn it down in favor of staying close to you."

Sara offered her best friend a sad smile. "That's right," she said.

"But I don't fit the pattern," Alex cut in. "You didn't ask me to give up my dream; you *handed* it to me on a silver platter, like Dylan said."

"Did we?" Sara said. There was no hint of uncertainty in her voice. Obviously, the question was meant to be rhetorical. When Alex didn't respond, Sara went on. "Is a new treatment center really what you wanted most? Truly?"

Alex fell silent for a long time. Finally, in a strained whisper, she said, "No."

Tom blinked. "No?"

Alex sighed. "Truth be told, New Horizons is where I belong. Of course, I want my new protocol to take off and grow, and of course, I want it to save as many lives as possible. But I don't want to captain that ship myself. I can't go much higher up the ladder without becoming a full-time administrator, and I can't think of anything I want less. I want to be on the ground—in the field, as it were—helping patients with my own hands, at least some of the time. I...." She trailed off, unsure how to finish the thought.

"You couldn't bring yourself to leave your patients. Not unless it was the only way to make amends, the way in which you could best serve them— regardless of what you wanted for yourself," Sara filled in.

Tom and Dylan both desperately wanted to ask the same question: Make amends for what? Both held it back, sensing that Alex wasn't ready to share that openly.

Alex put her face in her hands and began to weep softly.

Tom stared at Sara. "You are the most dangerous seventeen-year-old I've ever heard of," he said.

"I wish I didn't have to be," she replied.

CHAPTER TWELVE
Consumption

Snowflakes began to alight on the cable car's filthy windows as it creaked along, climbing ever higher. Finally, the Maiden and her Wardens were approaching the mountain. They huddled together for warmth as their teeth began to chatter.

"I thought you said we shouldn't need winter coats," Dylan said, rocking back and forth in a vain effort to keep warm.

"I also said the Twilight changes, and I didn't know what to expect," Sara griped. She was the smallest of them, so she was having an especially hard time with the biting cold.

"Maybe we should go back and get some warmer clothes," Dylan said. Tom drew his .460 Magnum and cracked open the cylinder to verify that it was fully loaded.

"I think that's a good idea," Alex said.

"I think we should push on a little longer," Sara countered. "We're all tired now, but it will get worse later. We should cover as much ground as we can now, while we still have some energy."

"That won't matter if we freeze to death," Alex pointed out.

"I don't think we need to worry about that. Even in blizzard conditions, you don't go straight from walking around to dead, right? You fall asleep first, then freeze to death in your sleep."

"And if we fall asleep, we'll just return to your house," Alex said, catching on. "Are you sure about that?"

Sara hesitated briefly. "Mostly."

"Well, we're here now," Tom put in. "I think Sara's right. As tired as we are, it's gonna get worse. I think we should at least try to find somewhere warm before we rest."

Alex sighed, clearly not happy about it. "Let's make sure we keep moving, then. That's the best way to stay warm and stay awake."

The cable car reached its destination and shuddered to a halt, lurching back and forth as its momentum dissipated. Silently, the door swung open on its own.

"That's not creepy at all," Sara grumbled.

Taking point, Tom leaned out the open door and looked around. There wasn't much to see. They were stopped at a small wooden platform covered in several inches of snow. A narrow footpath wound its way steadily up the mountain. There was no other way to go.

"Looks like we're going up. It's gonna get colder," Tom reported, stepping outside. The others followed, voicing their displeasure.

"No point standing around. Let's get going," Sara said, starting off.

Tom put an arm in front of her. "I know you're the expert here, but let me stay in front," he said. Sara nodded, allowing him to move in front of her. They began to walk single-file along the path—it wasn't wide enough to travel any other way. There was nothing to the left but open air and a drop of a thousand feet or more. A fierce, icy wind threatened to tear them away from the rock and hurl them down the mountain. They went slowly, hugging the wall to the right for support.

Before too long, Tom called back, "I see a cave or tunnel up ahead. It might go back a ways. Maybe we'll get lucky and be able to cut through the whole mountain without having to go much higher."

Just as he'd reported, they came to the mouth of a cave a few minutes later. They hurried inside, eager to be out of the frigid wind.

"Dark in here," Dylan observed. "Maybe we can light a torch? The heat would be nice, too."

Alex nodded. "I think it's worth the risk."

"I suppose it's unavoidable. We can't very well stumble along blind, it'll be pitch black once we go a little farther," Tom said.

Alex already had her torch out. She sprinkled some oil on the wick and lit it carefully. The others gathered around it, soaking up the heat for a minute.

"The walls in here are strange," Sara said, running her hands over the rock. "They're weirdly smooth. The ground, too."

She was right. The rock was an odd color, a dark reddish-brown, almost black, and it did feel too smooth—more like ice than stone. Tom stamped his boots, testing his footing. "The ground is pretty slick. It'll be easy to slip, so let's take it slow," he said.

The heat from Alex's torch kept her left hand nicely thawed out, but her right became numb and stiff in short order. As they ventured farther into the cave, the flame illuminated odd shapes in the walls. After a few minutes, the walls began to change, fading in a gradient from opaque reddish-black to a lighter, translucent red.

"Uh-oh. Not good. Look at this," Sara said a few minutes later, beckoning Alex to bring the torch closer. She pointed to a spot on the wall where the stone was almost perfectly transparent.

Embedded within was the upper half of a human skull.

"How... how did that get there?" Dylan stammered. Alex couldn't tell if he was stuttering because he was freezing or terrified. Probably both. She rubbed his back reassuringly.

Tom drew a stout combat knife from his belt and stabbed at the wall a few times. Small chunks fell away. "It's not stone," he said. "It's ice."

"But why is it red?" Alex wondered aloud. She let her MPX hang on its sling and held the torch in both hands to defrost her fingers.

"Dunno. Let's keep moving. This place feels wrong," Tom said.

He took another few steps and suddenly pitched forward. Luckily, Sara was right behind him. With speed that surprised all of them, even her, she snatched at the back of Tom's armor and managed to grab his shotgun sling. As Alex rushed over to help, the circle of flickering light cast by her torch illuminated the edge of a deep, yawning pit, nearly invisible in the darkness.

"Help! He's heavy!" Sara yelped. Tom was beginning to pull her over the edge with him. Alex grabbed his shotgun sling and, together, they pulled him back.

"Thanks," he breathed, visibly shaken. "What is it with falling into surprise holes around here?"

Alex arched an eyebrow. "It's almost like it could happen to anyone."

Her insinuation wasn't lost on Tom. He shot her a look of annoyance. Dylan wasn't paying attention and didn't hear the exchange. Tom held out his hand, and Alex passed him the torch so he could see where he was going.

Farther down the passageway, more clear patches of ice became visible, most with bones embedded inside. Some contained pieces of equipment instead—scraps of fabric, pieces of rope, even a few knives and handguns. Some of the weapons looked a hundred years old. The ice that wasn't clear was a consistent shade of dark red.

"I'm still not sure what this means, but I'm sure I don't like it," Tom said. "Watch your step up here, there are lots more holes in the ground. Everybody stay close to me so we can all see."

The tunnel widened into a large cavern. As Tom had said, there were nearly a dozen holes of varying sizes in the ground, and even a few in the walls. All were lined with the same reddish ice.

None had a visible bottom.

Carefully, they picked their way across the cavern toward the opposite wall, staying well clear of the dangerous pits. "Look here," Sara said. "I think I see light." Sure enough, a fist-sized hole in the wall was letting in a shaft of moonlight.

"We're almost out, but which way do we go?" Alex wondered.

"Three passages, not counting the one we came from," Tom said, pointing out each one. "It could be any of them. I guess we'll have to try them one at a time."

"Dylan, what are you doing?" Sara called softly. Tom and Alex turned to see where he was.

Dylan was standing dangerously close to one of the holes. He picked up a small chunk of ice from the ground and tossed it into the hole. They heard it clacking against the sides as it fell.

"Quit screwing around," Tom growled. "And get away from there before you fall again."

"Come on, honey, let's get out of here," Alex said as she stepped carefully over to Dylan.

A deep, low rumble shook the ground under their feet.

"God dammit, what did you do!" Tom shouted at Dylan.

Before Dylan could raise a defense, the rumbling rapidly grew in intensity. Spiderwebs of thin cracks began to appear in the ice all around, in the ground, walls, and ceiling.

"Let's get out!" Sara yelled, waving them toward the closest passageway.

Great sheets of ice began to shatter into pieces all around the cavern, revealing pulsing, red tissue underneath.

Living tissue.

Before Alex and Dylan could move away from the hole, an enormous, muscular tongue erupted from it and wrapped around Alex's waist. In the blink of an eye, it dragged her down into the hole.

"Alex!" Sara yelled, running to help. She took a single step and slipped on the ice, crashing to the ground.

"Help!" Dylan screamed. "I can't hold her!" Tom could see Dylan lying on his stomach, his arms extended into the hole below. He must have managed to grab Alex as she was pulled in.

"The *mountain* is alive?" Tom shouted. Movement in the corner of his eye caught his attention. More gargantuan tongues were snaking toward them from all four of the cavern's exits. "Sara, Dylan—get Alex!"

"Dylan, hold on!" Sara cried, struggling to maintain her footing. The rumbling grew stronger.

Tom tossed aside the torch, shouldered his shotgun, and began firing at the four advancing tongues. He fired two rounds at each in quick succession. All but one of the shots struck home, and the tongues recoiled in pain.

But they recovered, and they kept coming.

He reloaded the shotgun as fast as he could, but he was out of practice, and his hands were freezing. Two shells slipped out of his numb fingers and rolled away.

He realized that he wouldn't have time to fully reload the shotgun. Two of the tongues, dripping yellowish saliva, were about to strike at Dylan and Sara. Tom dropped the M4 onto its sling and drew his revolver, cocking the hammer as the heavy gun cleared its holster.

The bright orange front sight post was easy to see, even in the flickering torchlight. He fired two shots, one at each monstrous tongue. The Magnum's recoil was incredible, and it took time to bring the gun back down after each shot. Still, he was glad he'd brought it. The writhing tongues definitely felt the massive bullets. They flapped grotesquely and twisted around one another, momentarily denied their prey.

Tom quickly shifted his aim and blasted another two tongues snaking toward Dylan from the opposite side of the cavern, emptying the revolver. He snapped open the cylinder and slammed the ejector rod, dumping the smoking, empty casings onto the frozen ground. Each was nearly the size of a Chapstick tube.

He reached into a pouch on his belt and found a fresh speed loader of .460 rounds. He inserted the new rounds, twisted the knob on the speed loader to release them, and smacked the cylinder closed with the palm of his hand, ready to fire again.

Quickly reassessing the situation, he fired four more .460 rounds, once again driving all four tongues back just before they reached his allies. That bought him a few seconds, enough time to finish reloading the shotgun.

Suddenly, Dylan was at his side, tugging on his arm. "Tom! Come help!"

Tom was utterly floored to see Dylan standing beside him instead of helping Alex. "What the fuck are you doing? Go help Alex!" he roared, shoving Dylan away.

Dylan was undeterred. He scrambled back to Tom's side, clasping his hands together in supplication. "I'm not strong enough! We need your help to get her out!"

Tom shoved Dylan away a second time, harder, deliberately knocking him down so he could raise his shotgun and fire two rounds at the tongue that had been about to snatch Dylan from behind. "If I stop shooting, we're all dead! Go get Alex! Now!"

Thankfully, Dylan listened, but his eyes were wide with fright and self-doubt. He ran back to Sara, falling twice as powerful tremors continued to shake the cavern.

At the edge of the hole, Sara was straining with all her might, trying to pull Alex free. The walls of the pit were alive with throbbing red tissue that gripped Alex in a suffocating cocoon, trying to swallow her down into the mountain's bowels. Sara was not strong, and without Dylan's help, she was quickly losing the struggle.

Alex heard Tom firing and reloading with astonishing speed. She realized that he must be trying to keep more of the tongues away from her, Dylan, and Sara. The gunshots were so loud in the enclosed cavern that she couldn't even hear Sara screaming her name just a few feet away. Alex panted in fright, hardly able to draw a breath as the repulsive, wet tissue squeezed her like a vise from the chest down. Her panic exploded out of control as memories of being stuck in the drainage tunnel came rushing back to her. At the time, she had thought that there was no worse way to die.

She had been wrong.

Slowly but surely, Alex could feel the horrid mouth drawing her in deeper. At some point, Dylan had returned and was trying to help Sara pull Alex free, but even together, they weren't strong enough. The fact that they were lying down didn't help, either—they couldn't get much leverage. But if they stood up, they'd never be able to maintain their footing on the slick ice.

The suffocating panic in Alex's chest gave way to grim acceptance. They couldn't save her. Maybe with Tom's help, but he couldn't stop shooting. All he could do was buy time.

But no amount of time would be enough. Alex made her decision. She wouldn't let Sara or Dylan be devoured along with her.

"Sara, Dylan, it's okay. Let go," she yelled.

Either they didn't hear her, or they didn't listen. They kept trying, futilely, to pull her out. Within another few seconds, they would both be pulled in, too.

Resigned to her fate, Alex twisted her wrists and jerked her hands away as hard as she could, breaking free from theirs.

Dylan and Sara screamed in unison, their faces frozen in shock. Within a heartbeat, Alex disappeared, swallowed by the living mountain.

Tom was still shooting as fast as he could, barely keeping the relentless tongues at bay. Sara stood up, the stunned sorrow on her face quickly giving way to anger. Grabbing the back of Dylan's shirt, she hauled him to his feet and shoved him toward Tom. "Go!" she yelled at him. "Be ready!"

Dylan had no idea what he was supposed to be ready for, but he obediently started making his way back to Tom.

Struggling to keep her balance as the ground continued to tremble, Sara moved to a different hole a few paces away. "You like to eat things, huh? Eat this, then," she growled. She reached into pockets on her armor and pulled out both of her M67 fragmentation grenades, one in each hand. She pulled the pins out, first one, then the other. Then, simultaneously, she shifted her grip, letting both safety levers spring free, igniting the fuses. Her face an iron mask of fury, she dropped both grenades into the pulsing pit. It swallowed them hungrily.

Tom was once again reloading his shotgun when the grenades went off. A terrific concussion rocked the cavern, stronger than any of the tremors so far. He and Dylan were both knocked to the ground. All the tongues seized and began thrashing in unison, hammering the walls and ceiling with wet thuds.

With a disgusting burbling sound, the hole that had swallowed Alex ejected her, along with a geyser of gore and bone fragments. Covered in organic sludge, Alex soared through the air and crashed to the ground on her side. She skidded on the ice for several feet, nearly falling right back into another hole. Sara was already there, helping Alex to her feet.

Tom breathed a sigh of relief that Alex seemed to be okay, only mildly surprised at the manner of her return. They had no time to waste. The tongues were recovering from the explosion, resuming their tireless advance. His weapons were doing visible damage, blasting great craters in the putrid flesh, but he'd be out of ammo long before he destroyed any of the tongues.

"Everyone on me!" Tom shouted as loudly as he could so the others could hear him over the cacophony. "Pick a direction and cover me. Keep these things away from us!"

Relieved that Tom seemed to have a plan, the others fell in around him and opened fire. None of them would have been able to hold all the tongues at bay on their own—Tom was a far faster and more precise shooter, with much bigger guns, and defending the entire team by himself had tested the limits of his considerable skill. But working together as something vaguely resembling a coordinated squad, Dylan, Sara, and Alex were each able to cover a third of the cavern, at least for a short while. It was hard to see much in the wavering light of the abandoned torch.

Tom turned to the small hole in the cavern wall and took off his backpack. From it, he pulled a large block of Semtex and began stuffing it into the hole, packing it as tightly as he could. Given a choice, he would have carefully selected a few different locations to place the explosives for maximum effectiveness, but time was a luxury they didn't have. He'd have to make up for precision and efficiency with sheer volume of explosive material.

Once he'd packed the hole with as much Semtex as he dared, he yelled at the others to move along the wall, into the far corner. They complied, moving slowly enough that they could keep firing. Tom needed to finish his task quickly; the others were all firing on full auto and chewing through their ammunition. They couldn't have much left.

Tom uncoiled the Nonel nonelectric shock tube detonator that he'd prepared at the Holcombs' house and shoved the blasting cap into the Semtex, then joined the others in the far corner. Alex and Dylan were both out of ammo for their primary weapons and were firing their sidearms crazily, their eyes wide with fear, any semblance of coordinated tactics gone.

"Cover your ears and sit down!" Tom shouted. Thankfully, the others all heard him and obeyed without hesitation. The tongues surged forward, closing on them with alarming speed. Tom pulled his earmuffs over his ears, flipped open the safety cap on the detonator, and depressed the switch.

An absurdly powerful explosion rocked the mountain. Titanic chunks of ice fell from the ceiling, and more were blasted clear across the cavern, smashing into the walls with such force that Tom half-expected a full cave-in to follow. One tongue was crushed into bloody pulp under a block of ice the size of a bus. Had any of them been standing, they almost certainly would have been hurled several feet, possibly right into one of the waiting mouths. The remaining tongues, now only an arm's length away, recoiled again, striking blindly in all directions.

Tom grabbed Alex's arm and began pulling her along the wall toward the gaping hole he'd created. Dylan and Sara followed, firing wildly at any tongue that got too close.

When Tom saw the steep slope outside, his stomach flip-flopped. A snowy hill dropped away at a severe angle. He couldn't see the bottom.

The fall alone might kill them.

But there was no choice. "Tuck and roll!" he shouted into Alex's ear before unceremoniously shoving her through the hole. He did the same with Sara and Dylan, then dived after them.

A lashing tongue reached for Tom's boot as he jumped, missing by inches. Denied their meal, the bleeding tongues thrashed in impotent fury.

The four of them bounced and skidded down the steep slope, trying to protect their heads. The thick snow made the experience somewhat less lethal, but even so, each impact was painful, driving the wind from their lungs. Dylan's head missed a sharp rock by less than a foot. Alex's MPX bounced up and smacked her in the chin, but somehow, it didn't break any of her teeth.

Finally, they slid to a halt as the slope leveled out. Curses and groans of pain were snatched from their lips and carried away on the frigid wind. Less than twenty feet ahead, the hill simply stopped, transitioning abruptly to a sheer vertical drop.

"Please tell me we're almost done with this," Dylan moaned.

"I wish," Sara replied, heavily winded. "We still have a long way to go."

"Dylan," Tom said once he'd managed to stand up.

"Yeah?"

"I'm just about done with your shit."

"Tom," Alex said, helping Sara to her feet. Tom held up a hand to cut her off.

"That's the second time in eight hours you've nearly gotten us all killed," Tom said, his voice as cold as the icy wind. "There will not be a third. I told you to help Sara. Instead, you left her, and Alex, to come tell me to do the thing I'd just told *you* to do. What did I say yesterday during training?"

Dylan didn't answer. He was the only one still sitting on the ground. He was shivering and hugging himself, avoiding Tom's furious glare.

"Tom, he—" Sara began. Tom cut her off as well.

"What did I say?" Tom asked again, never taking his eyes off Dylan.

"That we need to do whatever you say, no questions."

"Do you get it yet? Do you understand why I said that? Do you see what happens when you hesitate, when you pity yourself instead of paying attention, when you wait for someone else to take action instead of doing it yourself?"

"Yes," Dylan whispered.

"I don't think you do," Tom said. "I don't think you've learned anything."

"Tom!" Alex finally shouted. Her tone made it clear that she would not be silenced again. "That's enough!"

Ignoring Alex, Tom turned to Sara. "Can you kick him out?"

Sara blinked. Ice crystals were starting to stick to her eyelashes. "What?"

"Can you cut Dylan out of the team somehow? Undo his part of the spell, or whatever?"

Sara crossed her arms and met Tom's hard stare with one of her own. "No, and even if I could, I wouldn't."

"Your funeral," Tom said. "Except, it's not just your funeral. It's Alex's, and mine, and Dylan's, and everyone else's, too. Right?"

Alex stepped in between Tom and Sara. "This is not the time to have this conversation."

"Alex is right," Sara said. "It's freezing, we're exhausted and out of ammo. Each of us is covered in a different disgusting substance, and there's no way down from this cliff. It's time to head back."

"There's an overhang over there, it looks like it's mostly protected from the snow," Alex said, pointing. "Come on."

Too drained to be bothered by the awkwardness of it, the four of them burrowed close together under the shelf of rock, sharing their remaining reserves of body heat. Tom stayed as far from Dylan as he could manage but said nothing more. As exhaustion quickly took hold, they nodded off and disappeared, one by one. Sara made sure that she was the last.

CHAPTER THIRTEEN
Insight

December 27, 2021
Day Three

"Good heavens," Ethan said, staring openly. "Is everyone alright?"

"No, but thanks for asking," Tom said, shrugging out of his armor.

"Yes, your things, they're... well used. Please, just leave your gear in a pile, we'll have it cleaned and repaired while you rest."

"I'm still tired, but not as tired as I thought I'd be," Alex noted with surprise.

"Me, too, now that I think about it," Tom agreed.

"Like I said, we're asleep while we're in the Twilight," Sara explained. "It's not as restful as normal sleep, but it's better than nothing. Once we return here, we should feel somewhat rested. The reverse is true as well—spending time here, while we're awake, recharges us to return to the Twilight."

"I think I get it," Dylan said, tossing his filthy armor into the pile on the floor. Some of the silent bodyguards came in from the basement and began collecting the discarded gear.

"I'm glad everyone seems to be more or less intact," Ethan said. "I'll need a report, of course."

Tom blinked in surprise when he saw that all four of them were still covered in Daniela's blood, but the mud that had previously caked him and Dylan from head to toe was entirely gone. Then he remembered what Sara had said earlier: Nothing that originated in the Twilight could come back to the normal world. He supposed that made sense, and it explained why the blood remained—Daniela wasn't from the Twilight.

"Can I please, please take a shower?" Dylan begged.

"Of course, Dylan. You can use the upstairs bathroom, between my room and Sara's. Tom, Alex—feel free to use the first floor and basement bathrooms as you prefer."

* * *

An hour later, Alex found Tom back in the doom room as she was drying her hair. He, too, looked somewhat human again, wearing clean clothes and with the blood finally scrubbed away. He was talking to Ethan.

"Shouldn't we keep going with the mission? Time is short, right?" Tom was saying.

Ethan shook his head. "As Sara said earlier, it's critical that you take time to rest—without falling asleep, of course. If you stay in the Twilight for too long, you'll become exhausted, which puts all of us in even more danger than we're already in. Besides, you need breaks from... the things you've seen and done there. Don't worry too much about the deadline; hundreds of Wardens who came before you have completed the Pilgrimage, and they all took time to rest."

Tom noticed Alex waiting off to the side and turned toward her. "Do you need something?"

She nodded. "I think it's time for me to start pulling my weight around here."

"How do you mean?"

"None of us are badly hurt, thankfully—not yet anyway. But that doesn't mean we're in good shape." Tom frowned at her, unsure of what she was getting at. "Come with me," she said, tossing her towel into the pile of dirty clothes.

Alex led Tom upstairs, pulled him into Ethan's empty office, and shut the door. Tom crossed his arms. "You wanted a private place to lecture me about Dylan," he said.

"Shut up and listen to me for a minute," Alex said. Tom's eyebrows went up at hearing her tone, but he said nothing. "Do you know what I do for a living?"

Tom studied her face for a moment, suspecting a trap. "You help drug addicts."

"More basically than that."

Tom was silent for another long moment. Finally, he shook his head. "I give up."

"I help people learn to live with themselves, and with each other. I'm guessing that's one of the main reasons Sara dragged me into this. We're all still alive right now partly because of you, and partly because of me, and partly because of Dylan and Sara. But the lion's share of the credit goes to luck, and I think you know it. I don't need to be a soldier to know that the four of us were not exactly a well-oiled machine out there."

Tom's features hardened into a frown. "Of course not. I had eight hours to train you. That's barely enough time to show you how to not shoot yourselves in the foot."

Alex stared right back at him, unruffled. "That's exactly my point. We're not soldiers, and you're not back in Afghanistan. Sara and Dylan may not be children anymore, but they're not all grown up, either. Sara's been steeped in this madness for her entire life, but Dylan was just tossed into it like a lamb being thrown into a wolf's den."

"I know that," Tom said. "I'm not being hard on him because it's fun, I'm trying to keep him alive. He's in no way ready for something like this. His only chance of surviving it is listening to me."

Alex held up a finger to emphasize her next point. "I'm not questioning your intentions, Tom—only your methods."

Tom almost argued with her. Instead, he decided to hear her out. "Go on."

"Why is Dylan acting the way he is?"

"How am I supposed to know?"

"Think about it. You're a smart guy. It's not hard to figure out."

Tom thought for a moment, digging up various memories of Dylan and stitching them together, looking for patterns. He recalled the boy's reluctance to talk about himself on the way to the dam, his conviction that girls weren't interested in him, and the way he always seemed to fade into the background, rarely speaking unless someone spoke to him first.

"Well," Tom finally said, "he clearly has self-esteem issues."

Alex cocked her head. "And why is that?"

"You wouldn't be asking me unless you thought I already had enough information to put it together."

"No, I wouldn't."

Tom turned away from her and studied a painting on the wall behind him, an idyllic country landscape. He wasn't really looking at the painting, just giving his eyes something to do while he thought it over. Finally, he turned back to Alex. "His mom disappeared right after he was born. Dylan eventually gave up the search, but his dad never did. Dylan's always talking about how he can't do this or can't do that, he's never smart enough or strong enough or good enough. His failure to find answers about his mom broke him in some way. Now he doesn't want to try difficult things because he's terrified of failure, especially when the stakes are high."

Alex folded her arms. "That's what I think."

"But he *can* do things, that's what frustrates me about him. When it comes to engineering, he's a borderline genius. He just needs to get off his ass and try."

"Think back to when you were sixteen. How did you respond to adults telling you to get off your ass and try?"

Tom grunted. "Point taken."

"The bottom line is, Dylan doesn't think he's effective. When you tell him how useless he is, do you think that makes the problem better or worse?"

Tom sighed. "I thought I wasn't your patient."

"I think you, Dylan, and Sara all became my patients yesterday, regardless of how any of us feel about it."

"None of this changes the fact that Dylan's going to get someone killed, or all of us killed, if he doesn't snap out of it," Tom pushed back.

"No, it doesn't. But the way you interact with him needs to change."

"What do you suggest?"

"He needs to start believing that he is effective, that he can achieve things, at least sometimes. He gets some of that from Sara already, but he needs to hear it from you. He's only ever known you as a no-nonsense businessman who hangs out with his friend's dad sometimes. But over the past day, he's seen Tom, the warrior, cool as a cucumber in the face of death. You're the one he's scared of. I think you might even scare him more than the Twilight does."

"I'd never hurt him," Tom said defensively.

"No? You almost knocked him out at the house," Alex reminded him.

"I was upset. I wouldn't have hit him."

"You beat up Ethan right in front of him."

Tom threw up his hands. "If there was *ever* an extenuating circumstance."

"None of that is what worries him, Tom. He's not afraid of you physically hurting him. Not really."

"What, then?"

"Why is he here?"

"He's loyal to Sara. To a fault, I think."

"So, his two strongest convictions are: He needs to protect Sara—and he's not capable of protecting Sara. He's in a constant state of conflict, trying to reconcile a contradiction. And then along comes Tom the action hero, kicking ass and taking names."

Tom shook his head, finally beginning to understand. "I make him feel even more useless."

"I don't like this any more than you do, but we're in it now, and all we have is each other. Like you said in the forest, Dylan is one-quarter of the team. We need him to do the things that only he can do, and he needs to believe that we can't do this without him. And guess what—we can't. I don't just mean that we need his engineering skills, either. He's Sara's emotional lifeline just as much as she's his. I think she's keeping her cool largely because Dylan's with her."

"He did fix the cable car, and he saved you at the house," Tom mused.

"Tell him that," Alex said. "Tell him that you appreciate him and give him credit for the things he's good at. If he doesn't start to believe in himself at least a little bit, and very soon, this little expedition won't last much longer. He needs to see you as someone he can look up to, learn from, and depend on, not a judge waiting for him to screw up again."

Tom nodded slowly. "The soldier in me wants to tell you to cram it and let me do this my way. But you're right."

Alex put a hand on Tom's shoulder. "That's how I know we're going to get through this. When the chips are down, you see reason, and you'll do the right thing."

"'Truth is not what you want it to be; it is what it is. And you must bend to its power or live a lie,'" Tom said, half to himself.

Alex smiled at him. "Somehow, it doesn't surprise me that you're a Musashi fan."

* * *

When Alex and Tom returned to the doom room, Ethan, Sara, and Dylan were there, talking quietly. Dylan had changed into fresh clothes, a light blue T-shirt and jeans. He was staring at the floor, and he had his hands stuffed into his pockets. "I don't think I can go back there," he said, his voice trembling.

Sara put a hand on his shoulder, her face displaying mixed emotions. "Dylan, I'm so sorry for putting this terrible burden on you. But remember, you're in control. The Pilgrimage is a path that we must walk of our own free will or not at all. If you want to back out, now's the time. Nobody will blame you."

Alex's heart broke at the look of abject fear and indecision on Dylan's face. Clearly, he was giving serious thought to calling it quits.

He wasn't the only one, she was ashamed to admit to herself.

Tom cut into the conversation, partly to give Dylan a minute to collect himself. "Ethan, whatever doubts I still had about the truth of your story are gone."

"I'm both glad and sad to hear that," Ethan said. "Sad because I wish the story weren't true, and because you had to see the nightmare for yourselves to believe it."

"Sara handled herself well out there," Tom went on. "She kept her cool and got creative under pressure." Ethan smiled at his daughter and rested a hand on her back. "Alex was also indispensable. She's not a born fighter, but she rose to the challenge and pulled the rest of our asses out of the fire more than once. And she's already proven her ability to make cranky old men admit when they're wrong." Ethan and Sara both frowned in puzzlement but said nothing, waiting for Tom to explain.

"Dylan," Tom said. "Come here." Dylan hesitated for a moment, then shuffled forward like a dog waiting to be punished, dragging his feet. He kept his eyes down the entire time. "Look at me," Tom said, his voice firm but not unkind.

Dylan lifted his head and met Tom's eyes. Tom could tell that it was a real effort for him. "You made some big mistakes out there, and you've got a lot of learning ahead of you. I expect you to make your absolute best effort to learn from those mistakes and to not repeat them," Tom continued. Dylan immediately lowered his head again. Tom reached out and gently lifted his chin with two fingers, reestablishing eye contact. "That said, we would all be dead without you, most likely. Alex, for sure."

Dylan blinked, taken aback. "What?"

"I'm sorry I was so hard on you. Sometimes I forget that not everyone is a soldier. The army drilled that mind-set into me pretty hard, and I guess I still carry it around to some extent. You can do things none of us can do. We need you. Sara needs you most of all. I know you're thinking that you can't do this. I know you want to quit. So do I, if that makes you feel any better. But I also know that you want to do whatever it takes to protect Sara. Remember that if any of us back out, it doesn't fix the problem—it just passes the problem on to someone else, someone less qualified to fix it. Sticking with the Pilgrimage is the best way to protect Sara because we've got the best chance of finishing it—or at least, Ethan and a bunch of his friends seem to think so. We have a duty to everyone on Earth, including Sara. Will you help us get through this thing and put it behind us as nothing more than a bad memory?"

Dylan's lower lip trembled. "I'll do my best," he said.

Tom extended his hand. "When men make promises to one another, they shake on it. A handshake is a big deal. Don't shake my hand unless you really mean it."

After a moment's hesitation, Dylan reached out and grasped Tom's hand firmly.

"Together," Tom said.

"Together," Dylan echoed.

CHAPTER FOURTEEN
Siege

The snowstorm had intensified since they'd left. Now equipped with more climbing gear and heavier clothing, they searched the area, looking for a solid anchor point.

"I'm not sure I can do this," Dylan yelled over the howling wind, peering over the edge of the cliff at a descent of several hundred feet.

Tom held back a harsh reply. "Remember what we talked about?" he hollered back.

After a delay, Dylan responded, "I'll try." He still didn't sound confident.

"Over here," Sara called. "What about this root?"

The others trudged over and saw that she'd found a thick, gnarled tree root sticking out of the snow. The tree it had belonged to must have fallen over the cliff at some point. Tom kicked at the root and pulled on it as hard as he could, testing its strength. "I think that should work, as long as we go one at a time," he said.

While Alex got to work tying off several ropes, Tom turned to Dylan, showing him a self-braking rope descender that he'd retrieved from the Holcombs' stockpile. "Just pull slowly on this lever to go down," Tom said. "The more you pull on the lever, the faster you'll descend. There's no rush, so take it slow—and don't look down. Close your eyes if that helps. You can keep them closed until your feet touch down. Don't worry about falling—if you let go of the lever, you'll stop automatically. Then you just keep going when you're ready."

"O–okay," Dylan said.

"If it makes you feel any better, I think I'm going to hate this part even more than you will," Sara said, giving Dylan a supportive side hug.

Alex joined them. "I'll go first to show you how. It's pretty simple," she said. She began to strap on a climbing harness. "The harness attaches to the descender, and it's more than strong enough to hold you. You'll also have a second rope attached to your harness for safety. That rope is anchored up here, and I've tied it so that it will gradually let out slack as you descend. If you fall—which you won't—the safety line will snap tight and catch you."

Alex sounded more confident than she felt, but she needed the others to believe that this was a breeze for her. In terms of physics, it was—the gear they'd brought was more than capable of getting them to the ground safely. Still, she hadn't dangled herself off a cliff in a long time.

Before she could chicken out, Alex hooked herself to the descender and had the others double-check her knots. Once she'd gotten thumbs up all around, she carefully lowered herself over the edge and began to descend. Almost immediately, the wind began to push her back and forth. She tried to ignore it, reminding herself that climbing gear was designed to handle these kinds of conditions. She descended slowly, maintaining a steady pace, keeping her eyes straight ahead.

Before too long, her boots touched powdery snow. She breathed a sigh of relief, then tugged sharply on the rope twice, letting the others know she was safe. She detached the descender and safety line and watched them disappear into the snow flurry as they were pulled back up.

A few minutes later, Dylan came into view and touched down beside her. He was hyperventilating, but he recovered quickly enough once he saw Alex standing next to him. Sara was next, and she'd been telling the truth—she looked even more nervous than Dylan had. Finally, Tom came down, looking like he'd rappelled down cliffs a hundred times before.

He probably had, Alex realized.

From there, the descent down the mountain was reasonably safe, if physically grueling. Slowly, they picked their way down steep slopes and wound circuitously between giant boulders, their footprints quickly filled in by new snow. The exertion helped ward off the biting cold. There wasn't enough spare oxygen to fuel any conversation.

About halfway down the mountain, the snow abruptly stopped. It didn't stop falling from the sky—it *froze*. Individual snowflakes hung motionless in the air as though each was suspended by an invisible wire. Somehow, the snowflakes ignored the howling wind and stayed still, hovering in fixed positions.

"More weird weather," Tom murmured.

"Yesterday, that would have been the strangest thing I'd ever seen," Alex said. "How quickly we grow accustomed to the absurd once it becomes common." She reached out and touched a snowflake hanging right in front of her. It stuck to her finger until she brushed it away.

The endless night wore on. After a few hours, they reached the foothills. The unmoving snow thinned out and eventually disappeared as the air gradually warmed. Heavy coats became unnecessary and were stuffed into packs. Another few hours later, the slope began to level out, and the snow on the ground gave way to mud. Finally free of the blizzard, the Maiden and her Wardens found some flat rocks and sat down to catch their breath.

"Well, that was a nice workout," Sara said.

"If only the rest of the trail were that easy," Tom said.

"It's weird to not be thirsty or hungry after all that," Alex observed.

"Look, there are some buildings over there," Dylan said, pointing. He was right. It looked like a small town far in the distance, bigger than the village they'd seen earlier. The terrain between was a flat, muddy plain, with sparse vegetation and clear visibility in all directions.

"For the first time in two days, I see something I like," Tom said. "We can see for miles out here. Nothing should be able to sneak up on us."

"Weren't you the one who told me to always expect the worst?" Sara asked.

"That's right," Tom admitted. "We can hope for a break, but we shouldn't expect one."

"Looks like the town is our next stop," Sara said, pointing to the moon directly over the buildings. "Ready when you guys are."

Conversation was sparse as they crossed the plain. They kept up a slow jog, not quite running, trying to make good time without exhausting themselves.

Tom found himself lost in his own thoughts. The longer he spent in this hellhole, the more he hated it. In many ways, it reminded him of Afghanistan—both were hotbeds of evil where death and terror lurked around every corner. *But even Afghanistan has some good people*, he thought.

The two places had something else in common: He was bound to each by duty. He didn't want to be here any more than he'd wanted to be in Afghanistan twenty years ago. But as much as he was loath to admit it, Ethan and Sara had a point. In this case, it didn't matter what he wanted. The list of people who had any chance of making it through the Twilight in one piece was a short one, and Tom was on it. Who was he to simply say "no" when billions of people needed him to say "yes"?

A few hundred meters outside the town, Tom halted and raised a hand. "Do you hear that?" he asked, keeping his voice low.

The others listened. "No," Alex finally said.

"Me neither," Sara agreed. "I don't hear anything."

"The ground...," Dylan said, trailing off. He took several steps back, raising his UMP.

Suddenly, Alex and Sara felt it. The ground was trembling slightly. Over the next few seconds, it rapidly got stronger.

A huge column of earth exploded skyward just behind Tom, showering all of them with mud. Tom was the fastest to react, but even he wasn't fast enough. As he turned, readying his weapon, he was knocked sprawling by a violent impact.

Alex, Dylan, and Sara stood frozen in fear and disbelief. A gargantuan snake, covered in rusted chains nearly six inches thick, reared its head to the sky, hissing viciously. Fangs as big as swords gleamed in the moonlight.

Quick as lightning, it descended on Tom, closing its mouth around his abdomen with bone-crushing force.

Tom screamed. It was the first time the others had heard him vocalize raw pain and fear. The snake shook him like a ragdoll, trying its best to chew him in half.

Sara and Alex opened fire, followed by Dylan a second later. They all aimed for the snake's midsection, afraid of hitting Tom. The .45, 9mm, and 5.56 rounds all pinged harmlessly off the chains, creating sparks as they ricocheted.

The whole damned thing was armored. Except for its eyes and the inside of its mouth, there was no exposed flesh to shoot.

None of them dared aim for either spot while it still had Tom.

Tom cried out again, struggling mightily, trying to reach his sidearm. He couldn't. The pain in his chest and stomach was astounding. He couldn't understand how he hadn't been bitten in half. He expected his neck to snap at any second from being whipped back and forth so violently.

As Sara dropped an empty mag and reached for another, she saw Dylan out of the corner of her eye. He wasn't firing. Instead, he had his right hand pulled back behind his head.

He was holding a grenade.

Before Sara could wonder what his plan was, Dylan heaved the grenade. He wasn't especially athletic, but he had a large target. The grenade bounced and rolled through the mud, coming to a rest just a few feet from the place where the snake's midsection met the ground.

"Down!" Sara shouted. She dropped to her stomach, yanking Dylan and Alex down along with her.

They flattened themselves just in time. The grenade detonated, astonishingly loud even in the open air. The snake jerked. The chains around its midsection were still intact, but it had clearly felt the concussive force of the explosion. Tom flew from its mouth, hit the ground hard, and rolled a few times before coming to a stop.

He wasn't moving.

"Keep its attention!" Sara called to Alex and Dylan. As they raised their weapons to fire at the beast, Sara sprinted to Tom, falling to her knees beside him.

She gasped when she saw the damage. The ceramic plates in his armor were shattered into pieces. Blood ran from several puncture wounds in his chest and stomach.

His eyes were closed.

"Tom!" Sara shouted, shaking him. "Tom! Come on! Get up!"

He didn't respond.

Growling in fury, Sara rolled him over and pulled the China Lake grenade launcher's strap over his head, freeing the heavy weapon. She'd only fired it once, but she remembered how to work it. She pulled the stock tight into her shoulder and sat back on her heels, bracing for the recoil.

She saw Dylan dive wildly to the side, his limbs flailing. The snake's fangs slammed into the ground where he'd been standing just a second earlier.

"Get clear!" Sara shouted. Dylan, on his stomach, saw her aiming the grenade launcher. His eyes went wide, and he tried to stand up, but he kept slipping in the mud.

Alex, still on her feet, ran to Dylan and helped him up. Together, they ran toward Sara.

The behemoth's fangs were wedged firmly in the soft earth, temporarily pinning its head in place. But Sara had no doubt that it would free itself any moment.

She pulled the heavy trigger. The first grenade missed, sailing over the snake's head by several feet and detonating harmlessly in the mud far away. She pumped the launcher, chambering another high-explosive round. As small as she was, it took some effort. She lowered her point of aim and fired again.

This time, the grenade struck the snake squarely in the side of the head. The force of the explosion freed its fangs from the mud, and the whole creature rolled over onto its side, hissing furiously.

Another of Tom's lessons replayed in Sara's mind. *When your life is on the line, there's no such thing as overkill. Terrify and overwhelm your enemy with unrestrained violence. Anything less gets you and your friends killed.*

The China Lake had two rounds left. Sara pumped it and fired again, then once more. The first round hit the snake just below its jaw, and the second impacted the ground under its head. Somehow, the heavy chains covering the beast remained intact, but the snake was not entirely unaffected. It struggled to right itself, shaking its head back and forth as if trying to clear its vision.

With the same lightning speed it had displayed during its initial ambush, the snake burrowed its way into the ground, sending up more fountains of dirt and mud. A heartbeat later, it was gone, leaving no evidence of its presence other than the fresh craters.

"Tom!" Alex shouted, trying to assess the damage. He still wasn't moving.

"Is he poisoned?" Sara asked, slinging the launcher over her back. "What can I do to help?"

"Envenomated," Dylan said, wringing his hands with worry.

"What?" Sara asked, staring at him in confusion.

"Envenomated," he said again. "Poisoned is when you eat it. If it bites you, that's venom, not poison."

Sara stared at him incredulously. "Thank you, Dylan. Very helpful," she said.

"Jesus, I think he is," Alex said. Tom's breathing was noticeably faster now, and the exposed skin on his stomach, around the puncture wounds, was beginning to turn green. "Dylan, you're stronger than we are. Can you carry him?"

"I—I'll try," he stammered. Grunting with effort, Dylan picked Tom up, managing an awkward fireman's carry.

"The buildings," Sara said. "Let's go."

Alex nodded. "We can't do anything out here."

It wasn't far to the edge of the town, but the journey felt like it took forever. Alex's mind raced as she tried to think of possible treatments.

"Why is he still here?" she asked.

"Huh?" Sara responded.

"Why is Tom still here? Shouldn't he have gone back to your house?"

Sara shook her head. "Only if he went to sleep. Being unconscious is different."

"I figured that would be too easy," Alex panted. "We need to find some kind of medical facility."

"It looks like an old mining town," Sara said as they passed the first buildings. One building had a tall bucket lift rising from its roof, and another had two crossed pickaxes over the door. It looked like a store that sold mining equipment.

"Then there should be some kind of medical building," Alex said. "At least, there would be in our world. Mining towns are pretty self-sufficient."

"There," Dylan wheezed from behind them. It was obvious that he couldn't go on much longer. He was pointing to a three-story building about a hundred paces ahead. A faded, rusted sign had mostly fallen to the ground. The letters that remained read: ITAL.

"Hospital," Alex said. "Good. Let's hurry."

*　*　*

"God dammit!" Alex roared. She ripped open one cabinet after another, hurling boxes of medical supplies to the floor. All of it looked decades old. None of it was what she needed.

She didn't even know what she needed. Antivenom, obviously, but what kind? Antivenom was snake-specific; there was no universal antidote.

She was pretty sure that there was no antivenom for snakes the size of subway trains.

"What can we do?" Sara asked, fidgeting anxiously. Tom was stretched out on an exam table, looking worse by the minute.

"I don't know. I'm thinking, I'm thinking," Alex said, pacing back and forth like a caged tiger.

"What if one of us goes back? To Sara's house, I mean," Dylan said. "We can get whatever medicine he needs and come back."

"Sara, you and your father have stockpiled all kinds of supplies in preparation for this. Do you have any antivenom? Any kind at all?"

Sara shook her head. "No, I'm sorry. There aren't any venomous snakes in Maine, and I don't think any teams have reported running into one here. Not in the last hundred years, anyway."

Alex snapped her fingers. "Dialysis," she said, half to herself.

"What's that?" Dylan asked.

"It's a machine that takes your blood out, removes toxins, and then puts the blood back into you," Sara said.

"Would that work?" Dylan asked, a glimmer of hope in his eyes.

Alex knew the answer. "No," she said, pulling her hair in frustration. "I don't think it would work for snake venom, and it takes hours, anyway. Tom doesn't have hours."

"We have to do *something*," Sara said.

"You think I don't know that!" Alex snapped. "Just let me think."

A terrible silence filled the room. Tom's breathing, previously too fast, was now very slow and shallow. He was hardly breathing at all. He was so awfully pale.

Alex's mind was blank. She was out of ideas. Tom was dying, and she couldn't stop it. She felt useless. She was a goddamned doctor—that was the whole reason Sara had brought her—and she could do nothing to help Tom.

Suddenly, Dylan's expression changed from anxiety to determination. Ripping open one of the pouches on Tom's armor, he pulled out the hard plastic case, then the adrenaline injector inside it.

Before Sara or Alex could interfere, Dylan slammed the injector into Tom's thigh.

Alex lunged across the room and grabbed Dylan by the shoulders. "What the hell do you think you're doing!" she shrieked. "Do you have any idea what adrenaline could do to him right now?"

Dylan shoved her away. "At least I'm doing *something!*" he shouted back.

Tom was still there, motionless on the table. Dylan lunged across his body, grabbing at Alex's chest. She tried to shove him away, not sure what he was doing, but then he let go—and she saw that he was holding her adrenaline injector.

Again, Dylan rammed it into Tom's thigh.

"Dylan, you're gonna kill him!" Sara yelled, trying in vain to pull her friend away from Tom.

"He's already dying! What am I gonna do, kill him twice?" Dylan countered. He shoved Sara back, then pulled out his own adrenaline and, once again, injected Tom.

Alex was furious. She couldn't believe Dylan's recklessness. Apparently, he'd taken Tom's pep talk too far and was now wildly overcompensating.

"There! Look!" Dylan panted, his chest heaving. He pointed at the table.

Tom was gone. Alex and Sara both stared in shock, mouths agape.

"He's gone," Alex managed to get out. "Where did he—"

"He should be back at my house," Sara said. "When you leave the Twilight, you return to the same place you entered from."

"The doctors there can help him. Better than we can, anyway," Dylan said.

"If he's even still alive," Alex hissed. "You just gave him a massive overdose of adrenaline. You probably stopped his heart."

"At least I did something! You were just standing there, watching him die!" Dylan shouted, his hands clenched into fists at his sides.

The exam room door suddenly buckled under a heavy impact. Screeching and scrabbling sounds, like nails on metal, echoed in the hallway outside. Alex instinctively reached for her adrenaline shot—then remembered it was gone. The door rattled in its frame again, the wood beginning to crack and bow.

They were cornered, on the third floor, without their best shooter.

"Ears!" Sara shouted, quickly donning her hearing protection. Dylan and Alex followed her example, but they were still fumbling for their weapons when the door splintered into pieces. Luckily, Sara was ready. She fired several short bursts.

Disfigured monstrosities like those they'd barely escaped in the village were pouring in.

Sara's first volley of rifle rounds went high, striking the wall, but the second burst struck a creature in the head. It dropped like a sack of bricks, viscous black fluid splattering the ceiling and floor. Dylan and Alex joined in as more abominations filled the doorway, tripping over one another to get at their prey. Brass casings rained to the floor by the dozens. Dead creatures fell one after another, creating a waist-high pile of mutilated bodies just inside the room.

As suddenly as the onslaught had started, it stopped. No more battered or bisected faces appeared in the doorway, but more shrieking howls were coming down the hall outside. Dylan rushed to the door, leaning out to look in both directions.

"Holy hell, there are so many," he said, his voice quavering. He began to shove bodies out of the doorway, trying not to retch as their hot, sticky fluids coated his hands.

Sara saw what he was doing. "Help us," she said to Alex. "We need to block the door."

Together, they dragged bodies out of the way and shoved a heavy bank of freestanding metal lockers in front of the shattered door. As soon as the makeshift barricade was in place, it pitched forward as more creatures assaulted it from the other side. Alex and Sara threw all of their weight against it, trying to stop it from falling over. Their boots slipped in the black blood.

Dylan ran to the window, the only other possible exit, and looked down. There was nothing outside except a twenty-five-foot drop to hard ground. He ripped off his pack and dug through it. "Rope!" he yelled. "Does anyone have rope left?"

"No," Sara said, grunting with effort.

"We left most of it at the cliff, there was no way to untie it," Alex shouted. "Tom had the last of it."

Of course, he did.

Dylan ran around the room, ripping open drawers and cabinets, looking for bedsheets, hoses, clothesline—anything they could use to escape by the window. There was nothing.

Alex and Sara were beginning to lose the struggle. They were becoming fatigued, and the wave of creatures crashing into the lockers over and over was relentless.

Suddenly, with perfect clarity, Dylan knew what he had to do.

Detached and numb, as though watching his own body from far away, he grabbed Sara from behind, wrapping one arm around her neck in a clumsy choke hold.

"Dylan! What the hell are you doing!" Alex screamed, nearly fainting in disbelief.

He didn't answer. There was no time. Sara hadn't reacted yet, undoubtedly because she was still processing what had happened, but she would start elbowing him in the ribs any second. With his free hand, Dylan reached into the pouch on her armor, withdrew the plastic case, and popped it open. Just as Sara was beginning to fight back, he flicked the safety cap off the adrenaline injector and rammed it into the side of her leg.

"You're the one who needs to survive," he whispered into her ear.

A heartbeat later, she was gone.

Dylan took her place, throwing all his weight against the lockers. Alex, finally understanding what he'd done, gave him a single grim nod. Even though Dylan was stronger than Sara, it wouldn't be enough of a difference. The lockers were slowly but surely being pushed out of the doorway, farther back into the room. Blue-gray hands covered with cuts and bruises were reaching through the gap, grabbing wildly for prey. The feral howls were so close and so loud.

So hungry.

"I think this is it," Dylan said, his voice choked with heartbreak.

"You were very brave," Alex said. "I'm proud of you."

CHAPTER FIFTEEN
Hope

"Sara, thank god," Ethan said, pulling her close. "What happened? Are you alright?"

Sara shook her head, still dazed. Her heart was pounding like a jackhammer. Under her watch cap, her hair was soaked in sweat.

"Dad?" She sounded confused.

Ethan gripped her shoulders to steady her. "Sara, you're back home. You're safe. What happened? Are you hurt?"

"No, I... I don't think so." She patted herself, checking for injuries.

"When Tom came back, we thought he was dead. We feared the worst."

We thought he was dead. Sara looked up. "Tom's alive?"

"For now, yes. What happened to him?"

All four of the Circle doctors were crowded around one of the beds, talking to one another in hushed tones. Bandage wrappers, empty syringes, and medication vials littered the floor.

"A... snake," Sara managed to get out.

"A snake? What kind of snake—never mind. Go tell the doctors everything, hurry."

Sara dropped her rifle to the floor as she ran to Tom's side.

* * *

Sara sat in a chair next to Tom's bed, watching him. The doctors had done all they could for now. As they'd said, the rest was up to him.

It was hard to know exactly what was wrong with him. Without knowing what the venom was or how it was attacking his body, it would be nearly impossible to counteract it. All they could do was manage his symptoms and provide supportive care. Hopefully, they could keep him alive long enough for the venom to gradually lose its potency and work its way out of his system.

Footsteps approached from behind, stopping beside her chair. "I need to go back," she said. Her voice was tired, her throat dry.

"Sara," Ethan said. "From what you told us, Alex and Dylan are either not at the hospital anymore, or they're...." He trailed off.

"I have to look for them," Sara said.

"By yourself? Absolutely not," Ethan said with uncharacteristic assertiveness.

Sara stood and turned to face him. "There's still time."

Ethan shook his head. "No, there isn't. Even if you could convince me to let you go back there alone, which you can't, there's no point. Sara, honey, I need you to be completely objective about this. Do you really think Alex and Dylan could still be alive?"

She was silent for a long time, her face blank. Finally, she collapsed against her father, sobbing.

"Sweetheart, I'm so sorry," Ethan said. His heart broke for her. He held her close, unsure what else to do. "It's time to send in the next team."

"The hell it is," croaked a hoarse voice.

Sara spun around. Tom was sitting up in bed, propped up on one elbow. His chest was covered in bloody bandages, and he had a black eye from when the snake had hurled him to the ground.

"Tom!" she shouted. She threw her arms around him.

"Holy shit, that hurts so bad," he wheezed.

"Sorry! Sorry," Sara said, backing off.

"Tom!" Ethan said. "Take it easy, you're not in great shape."

"What happened?" Tom asked, shaking his head slowly as if trying to clear a thick fog from his mind. "I remember... something big."

"It was a snake," Sara said. "A really big one."

Tom blinked. "How big?"

"Like... a couple of city buses."

Tom touched his heavily bruised stomach, wincing. "How am I not dead?"

"We're not entirely sure," said Dr. Atwood as she approached, having seen Tom moving around. "You were bitten with tremendous force, that much is obvious. The fangs must have been huge. They penetrated your skin, but only a little—your armor mostly stopped them. You're one lucky man. Without that armor, the fangs alone would have mulched most of your internal organs, and the venom wouldn't have had a chance to kill you."

Tom grunted. "Remind me to send a fruit basket to the guys who made the armor."

"You were... envenomated," Sara said, recalling Dylan's pedantic correction.

"That explains the massive headache," Tom said, rubbing his temples.

"Wait a minute. You said I 'was.' I'm better now?"

"I don't know that we can jump to that conclusion yet," said Dr. Atwood. "The Twilight is a strange place. Its laws and properties are always changing. You seem to be recovering, but we don't know what the venom is or what its effects are. It could still be slowly killing you."

"Tom," Ethan said, gently cutting into the conversation. "Sara and I are both tremendously relieved that your condition seems to be improving, but I need to send in the next team. Without Alex and Dylan...." He trailed off.

Tom looked up sharply. "What do you mean, 'without Alex and Dylan?' What happened to them?" At that, Sara hung her head and began to cry again, more softly this time. "No," Tom said. "They're not...."

Sara was too upset to speak, so Ethan recounted the story as she'd told it to him. He spared no detail; Tom needed to fully understand the reality of the situation. When he'd finished, Tom pushed himself up to a full sitting position, ignoring the stabbing pain in his chest and sides.

"But you don't know for sure. They could have made it," he said.

"I wish it were so, but I don't see how," Ethan said, hanging his head. "I'm sorry."

"How long has it been?"

Ethan checked his watch. "About six hours."

Tom let out a heavy sigh. "They would have used their adrenaline by now, or they would have found a safe place to sleep and come back that way."

Sara shook her head and wiped away her tears. "Even if they are alive, they can't come back."

Tom frowned. "Why not?"

She looked reluctant to explain. "When you're in the Twilight, going to sleep doesn't bring you back here if you're not with the anchor—with me. I need to be there to guide your consciousness back and forth. Adrenaline bypasses that requirement, but they don't have any. Dylan used the last of it on you... and me." She spoke the last two words so quietly, her voice so choked with emotion, that Tom could barely hear her.

Tom raised an eyebrow. "That might have been nice to know before now."

Sara threw up her hands in frustration. "There are tons of things it would be nice to tell you, but we're usually short on time and more worried about not dying. I didn't think this particular issue would come up."

"So, if they are alive, then they're stuck in the Twilight." Sara didn't answer. Tom took her silence as confirmation. "Then why the fuck are we still sitting around here? Let's go get them."

"Tom, that's—" Ethan started to object, but Tom raised a hand and cut him off.

"What's the fastest anyone has ever finished the Pilgrimage?"

Ethan frowned. "What's that got to do with anything?"

"Just answer the question."

Ethan sighed. "Four days and two hours."

"As of right now," Tom said, checking his watch, "we still have almost four and a half days. Give us eight hours to go find Alex and Dylan. If they're dead, or we can't find them, I'll get Sara to the end of this thing myself. If we're not back in eight hours, that means we're dead, and you send in the next team."

Ethan crossed his arms. "With four days to finish a Pilgrimage that takes six, on average. The next team would have to break the record."

"We can do this," Tom said.

"There are bigger things at stake here than your pride, Tom," Ethan said gently.

"That's not what this is about," Tom insisted.

"Then enlighten us."

"Isn't the whole point of this insane Pilgrimage to prove that people are still willing to do the right thing? To shoulder terrible burdens so others don't have to? To place the safety and well-being of everyone else above our own?"

Ethan's eyes narrowed. He felt a vague impression of a noose tightening. "That's right," he said.

"You said it yourself," Tom went on. He pushed himself to his feet, wobbling unsteadily for a moment, then found his balance. "Sara is first in line for a reason. She's the most qualified, and you think the people you chose to protect her are the most qualified. We've already covered a good amount of ground. We're doing okay on time." He looked to Sara for confirmation, and she nodded. "Even with just the two of us, we've got a better chance of finishing this thing than a new team does. And there's one more reason," Tom said.

"Do tell," Ethan said flatly.

"You've already placed this horrible burden on your daughter's shoulders. Spare some other father that agony."

The silence that filled the room stretched on for an eternity. Sara looked back and forth between Tom and her father, waiting to see which way the scales would tip.

Finally, Ethan spoke. "What if you suddenly drop dead from the snake bite?"

"Then I'm dead, and there's nothing more to be done for me," Tom said. "Sara takes her adrenaline, comes back home safe and sound, and you send in the next team."

"And if the venom takes longer than eight hours to kill you?"

"Over the next eight hours, I'll either start feeling better, or I'll start feeling worse. If I start going downhill, that's a pretty good sign that I'm not gonna make it, and we'll abort." Tom wasn't entirely sure that was true. He glanced at Dr. Atwood. She raised an eyebrow but said nothing.

"Dad, we can do this," Sara said. "If there's any chance Alex and Dylan could be alive, I won't leave them behind."

Ethan sighed. "Eight hours," he said.

* * *

Sara and Tom, both resupplied and clad in fresh armor, stood in front of the dilapidated hospital. "Why'd you haul my ass up to the third floor, anyway?" Tom asked. Breathing, talking, and walking all hurt, but he'd had worse. He could push through it. Dr. Atwood had shot him full of non-narcotic painkillers to take the edge off.

"You'll see," Sara said cryptically. She looked at him pointedly. "By the way, Dylan carried you."

Tom smiled to himself. "I suppose he fought off the snake, too."

"No, I did."

"Would that have anything to do with why my grenade launcher was empty?"

Sara shrugged. "The thing was huge, and it was covered in chains. Bullets weren't cutting it."

Tom shook his head. "Not bad, kid."

"Call me a kid one more time, and I'll show you how dangerous I can be," she growled.

"Alright, Bonnie Parker, let's move it. Clock is ticking." Tom stepped up to the door and pushed it open slowly, ready for trouble.

Ten paces ahead, a flayed skin was stretched across the hallway, blocking further passage.

"I see what you mean about taking the stairs," Tom said quietly.

"The second floor is like that, too," Sara said, averting her eyes.

Tom turned to face her. "That's a 'keep out' sign if I've ever seen one. Why didn't you run? You should have kept running."

Sara stared back at him coolly. "And leave you to die? Alex needed medical supplies beyond what she had on her. We weren't going to just dump you outside and carry on."

Rather than argue, Tom headed for the stairs.

* * *

Sara swallowed hard at seeing the exam room again, fighting back tears. The lockers had been hurled across the room with tremendous force, reduced to vaguely rectangular hunks of twisted metal. Other than the buzz of fluorescent lights, the room was eerily silent.

Tom walked to the middle of the room and retrieved something from the floor. When Sara saw what it was, she gasped. It was an H&K USP .45.

Dylan's sidearm.

The slide was locked back empty. Flecks of dried blood were spattered all over the weapon.

"Sara, look," Tom said gently, holding the gun out to her. "Tell me what you see."

She was losing the battle against her tears. "I see my best friend's gun, with his blood on it. What the hell kind of question is that?"

Tom shook his head and released the slide. "The blood is black, not red. I don't think it's Dylan's, or Alex's. I'm not trying to torture you, I promise. Look closer."

Reluctantly, she took the gun and started turning it over in her hands. "What am I looking for?"

"Look where the blood is—and where it isn't."

She saw that the sides and back of the grip were clean. "There's no blood here."

"Where Dylan's hand would have been."

Comprehension flashed in Sara's eyes. "He was holding it when the blood got on it." She looked up hopefully. "He was alive? He made it out of this room?"

Tom kept his expression neutral. "Maybe. We can't say for sure based on this alone, but it's a good sign."

Sara's heart lifted just a little. "Let's keep looking."

She handed Dylan's gun back to Tom, and he stashed it in his pack. They split up and examined the room, inspecting everything carefully. Shell casings littered the floor. Sara hadn't realized how many rounds they'd fired.

Suddenly, she stopped. "Where are the bodies?"

"What bodies?"

"The monsters we killed. They were the same things that attacked us in the village, during the first trial. We killed at least a dozen of them. There's black blood all over the place, but the bodies are gone. Where did they go?"

"I don't know," Tom said. "It is a little unnerving."

Sara took a deep breath and tried to stay calm. It was too early to jump to conclusions. She walked over to the window, pointing at it. "This is the only other way out of this room. Dylan tried to find something to climb down with, but he couldn't."

Tom and Sara both leaned out the window and looked down. Sara frowned. "That's new," she said. There were pieces of broken wood in the alley below—and more large, dark stains on the ground. From this high up, and in the pale moonlight, it was hard to discern much detail.

Tom was looking at the building across the alley. "I don't think they could have jumped across, it's too far," he said. Sara hated to admit it, but he was right. Even with a running start and no window to dive through, it would be a nearly Olympic-level long jump.

"Let's go take a closer look," Sara said, leading the way.

Down in the alley, Sara clutched an unlit torch, her hands trembling. In the moonlight, she couldn't tell what color the blood on the ground was. She needed more light, but she was afraid of what it might reveal.

She lit the torch and it flared to life. Sara stared at the bloodstains for a long moment, then sank to her knees amid the splintered fragments of wood.

The blood was unmistakably dark red, not black.

A crimson trail started directly below the exam room window and ran all the way to the end of the alley. There, tattered remnants of Alex's bright orange medic bag flapped in the wind. It was torn to shreds.

Sara dropped the torch, put her face in her hands, and let the tears come. Tom picked up the torch, walked to the orange bag, and looked around the corner. There were bloody footprints made by bare feet everywhere, and signs that something heavy had been dragged away. *Scratch that*, Tom thought as he inspected the markings in the dirt. *Two heavy things.* He'd done enough hunting to know what he was looking at.

He returned to Sara, knelt beside her, and put an arm around her, feeling helpless. "Do any of the monsters in the Twilight have red blood?"

Sara shook her head, barely able to speak through her tears. "No, never. I've read all the reports. It's always some other color. If the blood is red, it's human."

Tom felt his flame of hope dwindle. He didn't know what to say.

CHAPTER SIXTEEN
Denial

Sara dried her eyes and took a moment to steady her voice before she spoke. "I've decided not to believe it."

Tom frowned. "Believe what?"

"That Dylan and Alex are dead."

Tom hesitated, carefully choosing his words and regulating his tone. "Sara, I don't think—"

She cut him off. "What *exactly* do we see here, and what do we not see?"

"Human blood, and signs that... two people were dragged away. Sara, the four of us are the only sources of human blood in the Twilight—"

"That we know of," she cut in. "Daniela survived here for a long time. Maybe another Warden or Maiden did, too."

"Someone who just happened to show up at this exact spot and get killed right after the four of us got separated?"

Sara glared at him. "Anything is possible. Or maybe nobody died at all. Maybe the blood did come from Alex or Dylan, but they could still be alive."

Tom conceded the first point but didn't say so. He felt compelled to challenge the second point. "Sara, look around. Look how much blood there is. It's not possible to survive losing that much blood, that quickly."

Sara stared right back at him, undeterred. "It's not *probable*."

Tom sighed, trying to force her to face the facts without being a jerk about it. "Alright, maybe you could survive it if you were bleeding out right outside a hospital, but it would have to be a hospital with doctors in it, not monsters. Alex was the only doctor around."

Tom expected Sara to break down crying again, but she held his gaze with dry eyes. "My best friend and my mentor are probably dead, I know that. But 'probably' is not 'definitely.' I won't believe it unless I see undeniable evidence."

Tom thought the evidence in front of them was undeniable, but again, he didn't say so. "Alright," he said instead. He shook his head, half in amazement, half in frustration. On one hand, he admired her optimism, her refusal to accept defeat even in the face of a catastrophic loss. He'd known any number of grown men who wouldn't have been able to hold it together half as well as she was. He could see how much Sara cared for Alex, and especially for Dylan. She had to be hurting fiercely.

But on the other hand, her refusal to accept the reality of the situation might get the remaining half of the team killed, too.

Sara stood up. "Let's go," she said.

"Where are we going?"

"We're going to follow the trail. You take point, you're the better tracker."

Tom held back a sigh. He rose to his feet and returned to the end of the alley without comment. He knelt in the dirt, looking for clues he may have missed the first time while Sara kept an eye out for threats. Slowly, carefully, he picked his way along, following footprints and tiny droplets of red blood that became increasingly rare and hard to spot. He grimaced in pain every time he shifted in a way that aggravated the fresh puncture wounds in his chest and stomach. He was surprised to find that, other than the pain of the wounds themselves, he felt mostly alright. Perhaps the venom really had worked its way out of his system.

Their progress was agonizingly slow. Several times, Tom lost the trail and had to double back to the last place he was sure he'd seen something. Sara ignored her grief for the time being and forced herself to stay focused on pulling guard duty so Tom could concentrate.

Tom stopped in front of a short, squat building about a hundred meters down the main road. He tapped Sara on the shoulder and pointed, trying to show her something. She looked and saw a few drops of dried blood on the ground near the building's door—red blood. Tom pressed his ear to the door, listening. After a moment, he beckoned Sara to come closer so he could whisper to her.

"I hear movement inside," he said.

Sara's heart quickened. "Alex and Dylan?" she whispered back. Hope glimmered in her eyes.

Tom held up a hand, imploring silence. He listened a while longer, then shook his head. "I can't really tell. I'll take a look. You wait here and put out the torch."

"But—"

He cut her off. "This is not up for discussion. I go alone or we don't go at all. I'm here for one reason, and one reason only: to protect you. There's probably something horrible in there, and I'm not gonna let you walk right into it."

Gritting her teeth in frustration, Sara doused the torch with dirt and stepped back, away from the door. She held out her hands as if to say,

"Are you satisfied now?"

Tom tested the doorknob and found it unlocked. Ever so slowly, he turned it and pushed the door open, a hair's breadth at a time. As the gap slowly widened, unfamiliar sounds came to his ears.

Wet sounds.

The building seemed to be a garage or mechanic's shop. Dry-rotted tires and rusted tools lay scattered everywhere. Large holes in the ceiling let in just enough pale moonlight to see by. Nothing was moving. On the far side of the workshop area, he could see a large hole in the floor. Silently, he slipped inside.

Tom walked heel to toe in a low crouch, taking extreme care not to step on anything that would make noise. The sounds grew louder as he approached the hole in the floor. He tightened his grip on his shotgun and flicked off the safety.

He reached the edge of the hole and peered down, ready to leap back if anything came toward him. His mind froze for a moment. He couldn't comprehend what he was seeing. He squinted, trying to discern more detail in the dim light. Something large was moving at the bottom of the hole, about ten feet down, but he couldn't tell what it was.

Suddenly, he understood. His mouth fell open.

Dozens of the deformed, humanoid creatures writhed in a solid mass below, crawling over one another like insects. Ripping and tearing sounds drifted up from the hole, accompanied by wet slaps and occasional growls. They were... *eating*.

Tom's heart stopped, and his blood ran cold when he realized what they were eating: chunks of raw meat. Something small fluoresced in the moonlight at the bottom of the hole, a few feet away from the horrid abominations.

Another scrap of Alex's bright orange medic bag. Next to it was a torn piece of light blue cloth.

The same shade of blue as the shirt Dylan had been wearing.

Tom felt vomit rise from his stomach. He couldn't stop it. As quickly as he dared, he backed away from the hole and scurried for the door, trying to stay silent.

He fell to his knees and threw up as soon as he got outside. Sara's eyes widened in alarm. "Tom, what—"

He frantically gestured at her to be quiet. Thankfully, she complied. The nausea slowly faded, and Tom shakily got to his feet. He moved a goodly distance down the street, waving at Sara to follow. When they were safely away from the garage, he turned to her.

"Tom, what did you see?"

He put his hands on her shoulders, ready to catch her if she fell. He could hardly bring himself to say it. But she needed to know.

"Sara, Alex and Dylan...."

Tears welled up in her eyes. "What about them?"

"They're... they're gone. I'm sorry. There's no doubt."

She swallowed hard, not quite ready to take his word for it. "How do you know? What did you see?"

Tom shook his head, trying in vain to banish the horrific sight from his own mind. "I won't tell you. I won't do that to you. They're gone. Jesus Christ, I wish I weren't sure of it. But I am."

She collapsed against him, sobbing freely now. He held her gently, unsure what else to do.

"So, what do we do now? This is your show," he said quietly, after a time. "Your awful, terrible show. You can quit if you want to. Nobody would blame you. Whatever you want to do, I'll back your play."

Sara looked up at him, her bright green eyes dimmed by the crushing weight of the burden she carried. Tom could almost feel his heart physically breaking for her. "You said it yourself," she said, haltingly through her sobs. "We can't dump this on someone else, especially now that we're this far in. We have to go on. It's what Alex and Dylan would have wanted."

Tom wasn't sure about that last part, but he didn't say so. Instead, he said, "Alright. Let's finish it, then." He felt the weight of his duty even more acutely now that the responsibility of protecting Sara—and by extension, the entire world—rested solely on his shoulders.

They walked in silence along the main road. Near the middle of the town, they passed a clock tower. Tom silently prayed that it wouldn't chime and bring a horde of monsters down on their heads. Thankfully, the clock remained still and silent.

The empty plain stretched out ahead of them as they left the last few buildings behind. "Just follow the moon," Sara had said earlier. The moon appeared to be leading them to the foot of another mountain not far ahead—perhaps the location of the mine that gave rise to the town if the Twilight had that sort of logic to it.

Tom felt like he should say something, but he didn't know what to say. He kept a close eye on Sara as they walked. Occasionally, she sniffled or wiped away a tear, but she never looked back. Once again, he marveled at her willpower, even as he silently railed against the insanity of it all. Tom didn't have much in the way of paternal instinct, but part of him wanted to hug her, to tell her that everything would be alright.

But that would be a lie. Things were pretty fucking far from alright.

He wondered what he would do in her position, whether he would have the strength to push on right after losing two of his closest friends—especially if he had the option to quit anytime, to pass the burden to someone else.

He didn't have an answer.

* * *

"Are you sure about this?" Tom asked.

"No," Sara replied, "but we don't have time to go all the way around the mountain. That could take an extra half a day, or longer."

They stood before a rickety wooden elevator that waited to take them down into the mines. Tom shook his head. "Why doesn't anything in this place make sense?"

Sara frowned. "I don't know that we have time to get into that, either. It's a complicated question."

"I just mean the layout of it. Geographically, it doesn't make any sense. We went through a crazy forest with living trees, then an old house that had its own cable car for some reason, then a living cave, and then an old mining town. There's no logic to these places, no reason they would be arranged this way in relation to one another."

Sara rolled her neck, stretching. "Well, that part of it actually does make sense."

"Do tell."

"Like I said before, this place changes and shifts over time. The Twilight is shaped by the souls and personalities of previous Maidens. That mining town we just passed through probably wasn't always a mining town. Twenty years ago, it might have been a botanical garden, or maybe a big hotel. Twenty years before that, it was something different. I'm guessing it's a mining town now because one of the previous Maidens who came this way was somehow tied to mining. Maybe her family owned a mine, or maybe mining was just a thing she was interested in."

"I guess that does make some sense, then."

"Over time, the influence of Maidens from long ago fades away, and the Twilight shifts to reflect the thoughts, desires, and fears of more recent Maidens."

"So, the creatures we've seen, the things straight out of nightmares... they aren't random. They *did* come from someone's nightmares, literally." Sara nodded. "And the places and things we're seeing now are glimpses into who they were—Maidens from twenty, forty, sixty years ago. And twenty years from now, someone else will see parts of who you are now." Again, Sara nodded. "That's... sad," Tom said.

Sara cocked her head. "Why do you say that?"

"It just seems... profane, somehow. This place shouldn't exist. It's evil. It's scary and dangerous. No one should ever have to come here, girls your age least of all. Once you get to the cathedral and do whatever it is you need to do there, you've paid your dues, as far as I'm concerned. You should get to go home and live the rest of your life, without having to leave a piece of yourself here. It's like putting a beautiful sculpture in a sewer instead of a museum. It's just not right."

Sara rubbed her hands together. "I guess I never thought about it that way."

Tom sighed. "Well, let's get on with it if going around the mountain isn't an option." He press-checked his shotgun.

The elevator system before them looked ancient, like something dug up from the 1800s. Two separate cars shared the same pulley system; as one car moved down, the other came back up.

As Tom and Sara approached the elevator, something heavy slammed into the ground behind them, nearly knocking them over.

They whirled around to see the yellow-skinned abomination from the house—the thing that had ripped Daniela Esperanza in half.

The Stalker.

Its toothy mouth grinned maniacally at them from under its filthy blindfold. Its cold, mocking laughter cut through the chilly air.

I was wondering when you'd show your ugly face again, Tom thought, raising his shotgun. Not giving the beast a chance to close on them, he and Sara both opened fire as they backed away, toward the elevator. As before, the creature blinked out of existence momentarily, reappearing once the projectiles had passed by harmlessly.

With speed belied by its size, it charged forward, walking on its massive arms as its thick tail undulated along the ground for balance. It raised one cinder-block-sized fist high above its head, aiming for Sara. Tom shoved her aside just in time, knocking her sprawling a split second before the gargantuan fist slammed into the ground where she'd been standing. The impact was so powerful that Tom felt the very earth shake beneath his feet.

"Get to the elevator!" he shouted, emptying his shotgun. Again, he hit nothing, but he hadn't been expecting to—he just wanted to drive the Stalker away for a second, to buy them time to run. Tom turned and sprinted for the elevator, reaching it just as Sara did.

Once she saw that he was with her, Sara yanked on the lever that disengaged the brake, and the elevator began to slowly descend. The beast had reappeared and was charging toward them with frightening speed.

Tom saw that Sara was groping at her neck with both hands. At first, he thought she was injured. Then he realized that she was looking for something. He saw that the necklace she always wore was missing—something on a thin silver chain, but he'd never seen the whole thing because it was always tucked under her shirt. The chain must have broken when he'd shoved her to the ground.

Tom didn't have time to worry about a necklace. The Stalker was closing fast. He made a split-second decision, judging the risk to be necessary. He reached back with his right hand and pulled the China Lake around his body on its sling. He raised the weapon and fired, not daring to take any extra time to aim.

Despite being blindfolded, the Stalker seemed to sense the threat and skidded to a halt. The 40mm grenade struck the ground just in front of the creature and detonated, the concussive wave knocking Sara and Tom onto their backs. Tom silently thanked himself for loading standard high-explosive rounds; at this range, fragmentation rounds probably would have killed them both.

He and Sara shook their heads, trying to clear the cloud of dizziness and the ringing in their ears from being so close to the explosion. By the time Tom could see straight again, the elevator had descended about twenty feet down the shaft. He looked up in time to see the beast hurtling through the open air, straight toward them.

Instinctively, he rolled on top of Sara, shielding her with his body. The creature slammed into the roof of the car, rocking it violently from side to side. One of its colossal arms punched through the car's steel mesh roof like it was paper, reaching for prey.

Sara shoved Tom aside and raised her sidearm, unable to easily maneuver her rifle while on her back in the tight space. With lightning speed, she emptied the entire magazine. Tom winced in pain; in the enclosed space, even the small .32-caliber rounds made a lot of noise.

Predictably, Sara hit nothing, but the creature did disappear for a moment. His shotgun still empty, Tom drew his own sidearm, but by the time he rolled over and brought it to bear, the Stalker had jumped away from the elevator car and was climbing back up, using the wooden support beams around the sides of the shaft as a ladder.

"Maybe it's had enough," Sara panted, reloading her Walther.

"Somehow, I doubt it," Tom said, carefully getting to his feet. The car was still swinging crazily from side to side.

The Stalker disappeared from view as Tom pulled Sara to her feet. It was gone for only a few moments—and when it returned, it was dragging an enormous boulder.

"God dammit," Tom and Sara said in unison.

They retreated to opposite corners of the car, flattening themselves against the sides not a moment too soon. The rock punched through the roof and floor of the car with a deafening crash of twisting metal and cracking wood. Sara squeezed her eyes shut as the car once again rocked violently, fully expecting it to crash to the bottom of the shaft.

Somehow, it didn't. The steel support cable held fast. Tom and Sara both fell to their knees as the car slammed into the side of the shaft.

Tom looked up. The Stalker was preparing to jump down again.

"Go!" he shouted.

"Go where?" Sara yelled back.

As the battered car swung back toward the opposite side of the shaft, Tom holstered his sidearm and stepped forward, falling through the hole in the floor.

For a moment, Sara was stunned, thinking Tom had deliberately thrown himself to his death. Then she saw him clinging to a support beam on the other side of the shaft, below the other elevator car that was now ascending.

As the descending car swung back to its original position, the beast leaped.

"Sara!" Tom shouted, reaching a hand toward her. "Jump!"

There was no choice. Raw terror powered Sara's muscles, forcing her to step into open space as the car swung back toward Tom. She was able to do it only because staying put would be worse. Her stomach lurched as she began to fall. If she didn't manage to grab one of the beams, the fall to the bottom of the shaft would surely kill her.

Just as the massive creature would if it landed on her.

She managed to grab the same wooden beam as Tom. She'd only fallen a few feet, but even so, she cried out in pain as her arms felt like they might detach from her shoulders. Tom grabbed the strap on the back of her armor, giving her a moment to secure a better grip on the beam.

She refused to look down. If she looked down, the fear would paralyze her. Because they were now below the ascending elevator car, that meant they were more than halfway down the shaft, but it was still a long way to the bottom.

The Stalker hit the descending car like a meteor, ripping it away from the steel cable. Together, the beast and the car fell away, into the abyss. Even as the Stalker fell, its cruel laughter drifted up toward them.

"Move!" Tom and Sara both shouted at one another, realizing what would now happen to the ascending car. Tom shimmied right and Sara went left, climbing horizontally as fast as they could. The rough wood drove thick splinters deep into their hands.

Sara dared not look up. If the car above was going to hit her, she didn't want to see it coming.

Both felt a blast of wind as the undamaged car rushed past them, now in free fall without the other car acting as a counterweight. It missed them by inches.

The first car smashed into the ground below. The resulting crash multiplied in volume as it echoed off the stone walls. A moment later, the second car hit, and the combined cacophony was deafening.

Sara's arms were beginning to tire. She wasn't half the climber Alex was. She glanced at Tom. He seemed to be doing okay, but he was far stronger. As quickly as she dared, she began to descend. It was an awkward climb. Each five-foot section of the elevator shaft was reinforced by six wooden beams that formed a square with an 'X' connecting the corners. As she descended, either her hands or her feet were always on one of the forty-five-degree cross beams, which were difficult to grab or stand on.

"Oh, just fuck off already," Tom yelled from his position just above her.

Sara looked down, already knowing what she would see. The Stalker was beginning to climb back up the shaft, still cackling to itself.

"Try to get under it!" Tom yelled at her. "We need to get to the bottom to have any chance!"

"Okay!" Sara yelled back, with far more confidence than she felt.

The creature climbed with terrifying swiftness, leaping from one side of the shaft to the other. By the time it reached Sara, they were still only two-thirds of the way down.

The Stalker jumped for Sara, as though it intended to fall back to the bottom and take her with it. Gasping in fright, she flung herself to the left, flailing wildly for something to grab on the adjacent wall. She managed to grab another support beam, but her forehead slammed into it as well—she'd underestimated her momentum. Her vision dimmed, and she saw stars. Somehow, she managed to stay attached to the beam as the beast crashed into the wall where she'd just been.

"Sara! Hang on!" Tom shouted, descending as quickly as he could. Sara looked to her right and saw the abomination reaching an enormous hand for her.

It was so close. Too close to evade.

A deafening *bang* reverberated through the shaft as Tom awkwardly fired his .460 with one hand as he hung by the other from a support beam. The massive Magnum was not designed to be fired one-handed, and Tom just barely managed to keep hold of it. The powerful bullet tore a chunk out of one of the wooden beams, but he'd forced the Stalker to vanish again. It immediately reappeared, reaching for Sara once more. Tom fired again, and this time, the recoil was too much. The heavy revolver bucked out of his hand and clattered down the shaft, disappearing into the darkness. As before, the Stalker disappeared.

"Sara! Keep going!" Tom shouted, repositioning himself on the beam. "Don't worry about me!"

The dizziness only partly abated, Sara resumed her descent, her arm muscles burning with exertion. She tried to climb more by feel than by sight, not yet trusting her vision. It was even slower going than before. She hadn't gotten far when the Stalker reappeared just above her.

His perception of time slowed by adrenaline, Tom realized, in a sudden moment of clarity, that Sara would have to finish the journey without him. There was no way they could safely descend another forty feet with this thing hounding them the whole way.

Tom could see only two options: Either they both died, or only he did. The Stalker could dodge bullets, but maybe it couldn't dodge him. After all, it seemed to prefer using its hands to kill its targets, and it couldn't do that while it was dematerialized. Maybe the reverse was also true—maybe it couldn't phase out if someone was already touching it.

It was worth a shot.

His mind made up, he felt strangely calm. With cool precision, he released his grip on the beam, using his legs to push himself to the left as he began to fall. With his right hand, he pulled his knife free from the sheath on his belt. As he fell onto the Stalker's back, he hooked his left arm around its tree trunk of a neck and wrapped his legs around its chest—as far as they would go, anyway.

He slammed the knife into the right side of the Stalker's neck and ripped it forward with all his strength, sawing the sharp blade through its throat.

At least, that had been the plan. He didn't get that far.

With a scream of primal hatred that seemed even louder than the gunshots—the first sound they'd heard it make other than the insane laughter—it reached back with both hands to grab its attacker. They both fell away from the wall, into the darkness.

Sara, I'm sorry, he thought.

"Tom!" Sara shouted, powerless to do anything but watch him fall.

For some reason, Tom expected the fall to happen in slow motion, as falls always did in movies. He expected his life to flash before his eyes. He expected to have all the time in the world to contemplate his sins and achievements.

Instead, the crash came a few heartbeats later. He and the Stalker had rotated in midair, and the beast hit the ground first. Its muscular body absorbed some of the impact, but Tom was still hurled away violently. His back hit something hard, cracking the rear ceramic plate in his armor. He continued to bounce and roll like a marble being shaken in a tin can. Against all odds, his skull remained intact despite at least two more hard hits, the second of which finally, mercifully knocked him unconscious.

Her sore muscles pushed past their limits by fear and worry for Tom, Sara scrambled the rest of the way down the shaft. There was no sign of the Stalker. Tom lay face down, next to a heavy steel door. He wasn't moving.

When Sara's feet finally touched solid ground, her arms were shaking from the grueling climb. She nearly fell, her sore legs unwilling to support her. She stumbled over to Tom, shaking him. "Tom! Get up!" she shouted. He didn't move, but he groaned—that was a good sign.

Something moved behind her. She turned to see the Stalker advancing on her slowly, cackling maniacally.

Sara felt something tighten in her chest as her fear gave way to rage. "Okay, asshole," she said, the steadiness of her own voice surprising her. She drew her Walther and started tapping the trigger about once per second, just quickly enough to stop the Stalker from advancing toward her. With her other hand, she dragged Tom toward the steel door by his armor, straining mightily. She never would have been able to move him if not for her temporary, adrenaline-fueled strength.

Grunting with effort, she began to turn the rusted locking wheel. For some reason, the Stalker wasn't moving in to kill her. It just stood there, near the wrecked elevators, laughing. She remembered what Tom had said: It liked to toy with its prey.

It was mocking her, letting her know that it was choosing not to kill her yet.

"Well, fuck you, too," she snarled at it.

The door creaked open. With the last of her dwindling strength, Sara hauled Tom over the threshold. She spotted his scratched revolver lying nearby, snatched it up, and tucked it behind her belt. She pulled Tom's M67 hand grenades from their pouches on his armor. She pulled the pins free, taking care to keep the safety levers engaged, then tossed the grenades into the shaft, where they rolled to a stop just in front of the Stalker. As quickly as she could, she did the same with her own grenades, then slammed the heavy door shut just as the Stalker looked down at the explosives with its blindfolded eyes, a curious frown on its vaguely reptilian face.

She didn't have time to lock the door. It hit her in the chest like a battering ram, knocking her down as it was blasted open by the unbelievable force of four grenades detonating almost simultaneously. Her armor absorbed most of the force, but even so, she yelped in pain.

Without the armor, the door surely would have caved in her chest.

With a great, low rumble, huge chunks of stone began to fall from above. The elevator shaft, badly damaged by the massive explosion, was collapsing. The Stalker chuckled at her one last time before disappearing again, just before a rock the size of a pickup truck would have crushed it. Within another few seconds, the bottom part of the shaft was filled with rock. A thick cloud of stone dust billowed into the passageway beyond the door, causing Sara to cough and choke.

Moaning in pain, she grabbed the edge of the door and slammed it closed. She dragged herself to her feet and turned the wheel, locking the door once more. She pressed her ear to the door and listened. She heard nothing on the other side. It seemed the Stalker was gone.

For now.

Sara cracked a glow stick so she could see. "That may have been excessive," Tom wheezed from behind her.

"Tom! You're okay!" Sara said as she turned to face him. She hugged him, causing him to cry out in pain.

"'Okay' is an overstatement, I think," Tom coughed. "Give me a minute to test everything." She waited anxiously as he gingerly moved each limb. "Everything hurts like hell. Might have broken a rib or two, I'm not sure. Vegas money's on a concussion, at the very least." He stopped abruptly, as though he'd been about to say something else.

"I wish Alex were here, too," Sara said softly.

"Just... let me rest for a few minutes," Tom said, changing the subject. "You know, you're lucky you didn't collapse this tunnel, too. Four grenades were probably overkill."

Sara folded her arms and glared at him, unamused. "What did you tell us the other day about half measures in combat?"

"'When your life is on the line, there's no such thing as overkill. Terrify and overwhelm your enemy with unrestrained violence. Anything less gets you and your friends killed,'" Tom said, quoting himself. "You were listening."

Sara's frown deepened. "Of course, I was listening."

"You could have collapsed the tunnel and killed both of us, but even so, you did the right thing," he said, grunting in pain as he rose unsteadily to his feet. "In a moment of great need and little time to think, you took action. You did what you had to do."

"Desperate times," she said quietly.

"That they are," he agreed.

CHAPTER SEVENTEEN
Flight

Tom and Sara cracked more glow sticks for light, reloaded their weapons, and assessed their injuries. Sara turned around for privacy, removed her armor, and pulled up her shirt, grimacing at what she saw. The door had left a volleyball-sized bruise right in the middle of her abdomen. It was already starting to turn purple, and it hurt like hell.

"You alright?" Tom called from behind her.

"I guess. Moving and breathing both hurt, but I don't think anything is broken. I think you got it worse than I did."

"I hope so," Tom said, gingerly touching the back of his head. "I think I finally stopped bleeding."

Once Sara had carefully put her armor back on, hissing through her teeth at the pain, she turned back around. "Tom," she said, waiting for him to meet her eyes.

"What's up?"

"You... gave your life for me. Or at least, you thought that was what you were doing."

His expression was unreadable. "Isn't that the whole point?"

She offered him a thin smile. Tom was sure she didn't mean it to look unsettling, but paired with her glassy, faraway eyes, it did. "I'm glad you're okay. We've lost enough friends today."

He tried to lighten the mood. "Does this gig come with health care for life?"

"Of course," she said, settling back into her usual businesslike demeanor. "We'll pay for whatever medical care you need when this is all over."

"At this rate, it might be cheaper to just build me a new body." Tom didn't say so, but he felt a small pang of regret at seeing her put her warrior face back on. Throughout the years he'd known her, a smile had been her default expression. Had that all been an act? No, he didn't think so. She hadn't been pretending, not exactly. She'd simply been doing her best to live a normal teenager's life. They had a little more than four days left to finish the Pilgrimage. He intended to see her smile return after that.

Although, with Alex and Dylan gone, that day might be a long way off.

Sara was staring at him with concern. He realized that some trace of his dark thoughts must have been showing on his face. He shook himself out of it. "You know, we both almost died, but it wasn't a total loss. We learned something about the Stalker," he said.

"We did?"

"It can't dodge hand-to-hand contact. Or maybe it can, and it just didn't because it was so surprised that I would try to grab it. Either way, I don't think it can phase out while someone is touching it. If it could, it would have blinked away and let me take the full force of the fall."

Sara nodded slowly, thinking it over. "Makes sense. Whatever the reason, I'm glad it took the worst of the fall and not you."

"Me, too. I also think it can't teleport, not exactly."

Sara thought about that for a second, then nodded. "Every time it disappears, it reappears in the same place. So, it can dodge attacks, but it can't move to a different location while it's phased out."

"That's what I think, but if it shows up again, be ready for anything—our assumptions could be wrong. Shall we continue?"

"I guess," she sighed. She glanced at her watch. "We have about three hours until we need to check in with my dad."

"Maybe we should do that now. Missing that deadline could be pretty bad."

She shook her head. "No, it's fine. If he tries to send in the next team while we're still here, they won't be able to enter the Twilight. Multiple teams of Wardens and Maidens can occupy different versions of the proving ground at the same time, but only one team can be in the Twilight proper. So, if the next team tries to come here, and they can't, my dad will know we're still alive."

"But we were able to come through, and Daniela had been here for sixteen years."

Sara sighed. "She must have voluntarily undone the binding ritual so the next team could take over." She stopped, looking as though there were more, but she didn't want to say it.

Tom took a guess. "Condemning herself and her Wardens to death. They knew they were done for, so they locked themselves in this nightmare to give someone else a chance." Sara nodded, unable to meet his gaze. Tom changed the subject. "I still think we should rest. We're both pretty banged up."

Sara peered down the tunnel. In the faint blue light of the glow sticks, she couldn't see very far. "We don't know what's down here. Maybe it's smarter to get somewhere safer before we rest."

Tom nodded. "Safer is good."

Not far down the tunnel, they came to another steel door that blocked further passage. Next to it, a faded sign read: "DANGER—METHANE GAS. DO NOT PROCEED."

"Well, shit," Tom said.

"So much for torches," Sara sighed.

"That's not all," Tom said. "We can't fire our guns in there, either."

Sara stared at him incredulously. "What?"

"Methane gas is highly flammable. The sparks created when a bullet is fired probably wouldn't ignite the gas, but if the conditions are just right, it could happen. If it does, our little quest comes to a quick and toasty end."

"Perfect," Sara said with intense sarcasm.

"It gets worse."

"Oh, do go on."

"Methane gas displaces oxygen in the bloodstream."

Sara frowned, thinking back to science class. "Meaning... if we breathe it for too long, we suffocate."

Tom nodded. "Just like carbon monoxide poisoning. Let's head back to your place and get some gas masks or respirators from the armory." Before they could act on that plan, faint skittering sounds began to drift toward them from the direction of the collapsed elevator shaft. "Quiet," Tom said, raising his shotgun. "Light, and ears."

Both quickly donned their hearing protection. Sara tossed her glow stick a short distance ahead so they could see what was coming. Tom lifted one side of his earmuffs and strained to hear. There were quiet clicking sounds, and they were gradually getting louder. It sounded like many small, hard things tapping against the stone.

Sara screamed when the first fat, round spider came into view. It was the size of a large dog.

Without hesitation, Tom opened fire. Heavy buckshot tore the grotesque thing apart, splattering the rock walls in thick green goo. Within a heartbeat, a dozen more spiders skittered into the small circle of light cast by the glow stick. Sara raised her rifle and started firing single, carefully aimed shots.

At least these things aren't hard to kill, Tom thought, blasting another into green paste. Were they venomous? Probably. He certainly didn't want to find out. They were starting to move more aggressively, and they were showing up faster than Tom and Sara could gun them down.

"Where did they come from?" Sara shouted.

Tom was about to yell that he didn't know, but then he saw one squeeze into the tunnel through a crack in the ground no wider than a finger, and he understood.

During a brief lull in the wave of advancing spiders, Tom reloaded his shotgun, then reached into one of his armor pouches for his adrenaline syringe. "Let's get out of here!" he yelled.

Sara, seemingly in agreement, fumbled for her adrenaline as well.

Tom stopped when he saw his black plastic case. It was badly bent and crushed. It was reasonably strong, but the forty-foot fall must have been more than it was engineered to handle. Fearing the worst, he pried it open.

The syringe inside was cracked, the liquid medication long since absorbed into the case's fabric lining.

"We have a problem," Tom said.

Sara's syringe was intact, and she was about to inject herself. She stopped when she saw Tom's face.

Sara's mind raced. She couldn't give her adrenaline to Tom. He could get more from her basement, but even with sedatives, he wouldn't be able to come directly back to her. Without her to guide him, he would have no control over where he reentered the Twilight.

"Go," Tom said, as if he'd read her thoughts on her face. "I'll wait here. Come back with more."

There were too many spiders for either of them to hold off alone, and they both knew it.

Sara made her choice, putting the syringe back in its case. "I lost two friends today because I left them behind. I will not lose a third."

Tom could see in her face that she meant it. He wouldn't be able to talk her out of it before more spiders arrived, which sounded like it would be sometime in the next five seconds.

Out of options and low on ammo, Tom shoved open the heavy door behind them, swearing the entire time. "Run, but try to hold your breath!" he shouted, grabbing Sara's arm to pull her forward, deeper into the tunnel. He realized how stupid that sounded right after he said it.

Once they were both through the door, Tom slammed it shut. He pulled two more glow sticks from his shirt pocket, cracked both, and handed one to Sara before they started running again. They hadn't made it a dozen steps down the tunnel when he realized that the door wouldn't stop the dog-sized spiders. More began appearing behind and ahead of them as they ran, squishing their bulbous, hairy bodies impossibly flat and using their spindly legs to pull themselves into the tunnel from cracks and crevices that seemed far too small.

Tom and Sara did their best to avoid inhaling as they sprinted, but it was impossible. Both realized that trying to run without breathing would probably cause their bodies to demand more oxygen than would otherwise be necessary, and they gave up the pointless attempt.

The arachnids were fast. Those that got close enough lunged at Tom or Sara, their cartilaginous fangs dripping wetly. Tom reached for his knife, his fingers grasping only the empty sheath. Then he remembered—his knife was buried at the bottom of the elevator shaft, under a hundred tons of rock. It had bounced away when he'd hit the ground.

Fortunately, Sara still had hers. She slashed as one of the spiders jumped at her, cutting open its engorged body. As the creature fell to the ground, mortally wounded, its abdomen ruptured with a wet tearing sound.

Thousands of tiny spiders surged forth from the deflating sac, joining the chase.

Sara nearly vomited, but terror and adrenaline kept her focused and kept her legs moving. She glanced back to make sure Tom was still with her. He'd fallen behind by a few steps to cover their retreat and was using his shotgun as a club, batting away any spider that got too close.

I guess one of Sara's predecessors really hated spiders, Tom thought as he punted one back down the tunnel before it could bite him. "You guys should pick girls who are only afraid of kittens and rainbows, it would make this whole process a lot easier," he shouted.

"I'll put it in the suggestion box," Sara yelled back. Tom could hear that she was panting heavily and regretted making her use more oxygen by talking. He couldn't smell or taste anything unusual in the air, but that wasn't comforting—methane gas was odorless and tasteless.

They were struggling badly. Their fresh injuries were becoming increasingly taxing, and it was getting harder to ignore the pain. Both had taken hard impacts to the chest, and both were finding it difficult to draw full breaths. Had they been uninjured and fully rested, they probably could have outrun the spiders with ease, but as it was, they weren't able to sprint for more than a few steps at a time.

The gas was beginning to have an effect, too. Sara, being smaller, felt it first. Her head was starting to spin. She felt dizzy and nauseous. Running in a straight line was rapidly becoming more difficult.

Suddenly, a split in the tunnel loomed before them. The glow sticks gave off so little light that Sara nearly ran headlong into the wall. One tunnel veered to the left, another to the right. "Which way?" Sara shouted, gasping for air. She was acutely aware that each ragged breath drew more of the deadly gas into her lungs.

"Left!" Tom shouted, clubbing a spider with the buttstock of his shotgun hard enough to crack its exoskeleton and rupture one of its many eyes.

"Are you sure?" she hollered back.

"Yes!" Tom shouted. *No*, he thought.

Sara darted left and Tom followed. "Look!" she said, pointing at the ground. Tom looked down and saw that they were running alongside mine cart tracks. "Maybe these lead out!"

Ten steps after she voiced that hope, it was dashed. Tom and Sara skidded to a halt in front of a rock wall.

It was a dead end.

An ancient steel mine cart sat on the tracks, mockingly useless.

Tom turned back to face the way they'd come, panting. The pursuing spiders hadn't yet entered the light, but by the sound of it, there were hundreds of them.

They'd never get past such an army.

"Tom! What do we do!" Sara cried, her voice trembling. She threw her arms around his waist, burying her face in his side as her precocious strength and willpower began to fade.

He briefly considered opening fire. As he'd said before, gunshots *probably* wouldn't ignite the gas. Even so, there were simply too many targets. Any second now, he and Sara would be crushed under the sheer weight of their numbers.

"I have an idea," Tom said.

"A good one, I hope," Sara said, looking up at him with moist eyes.

"Let's not get ahead of ourselves," he muttered, reaching into a pouch on his plate carrier. He pulled out his last grenade. Stenciled on it were the letters "WP."

They stood for white phosphorus.

In one smooth motion, Tom pulled the pin and tossed the grenade down the tunnel. The metal grenade body made a pleasant tinkling sound against the stone.

Just as the first wave of spiders shambled into the dim light of the glow sticks, Tom turned and kicked the top edge of the mine cart as hard as he could. As it began to tip over, he pulled Sara into a tight embrace and forced her to the ground. With his other hand, he pulled the cart on top of them, creating a protective turtle shell.

Their faces inches apart, Tom and Sara stared at one another in the blue-white light.

A second later, the precisely mixed chemicals in the grenade combusted as the fuse expired. A tsunami of fire filled every inch of the tunnel as the methane gas ignited. Hundreds of spiders chittered in pain for a brief instant before they were incinerated, leaving behind smoking heaps of charcoal.

The force of the explosion rocked the heavy mine cart and instantly heated the metal. Careful not to touch it with his hands, Tom flipped onto his back and used his feet to heave the cart aside.

"I can't tell if that was the smartest or dumbest idea of all time," Sara wheezed.

"A little of both, I think," Tom said. "There will be more. We need to move." He stood and helped Sara to her feet.

"I don't feel any better," she said. "I think I feel worse." She was badly short of breath.

"The fire burned off all the gas, and the oxygen with it," Tom said, also panting. "Try not to talk. The oxygen will come back soon—but so will the gas."

More chittering and clicking sounds drifted toward them from farther down the tunnel.

Tom used hand signals to indicate that he wanted Sara to help him flip the mine cart back over. The metal was still hot, but they could touch it for a few seconds at a time. Working together, they managed to right the cart and set the wheels back on the tracks.

Tom hoisted Sara like she was a toddler and deposited her in the cart. He got behind it and began to push, building up speed as he went. Heat from the still-burning white phosphorus grenade washed over them like a blast furnace as they rolled past it. "Hold on, and pray there are no sharp turns," Tom said. He was gasping badly now. Slowly but surely, oxygen was filling the tunnel again, but it would be a bit longer before breathing was comfortable again.

By the time they passed the junction, the cart was moving at a good clip —and more spiders were closing in from the main passage. Tom hopped into the cart, afraid that it would leave him behind if it sped up more.

Not far down the right-hand tunnel, the downward slope became steeper, and the cart began to feel like a roller coaster. The wind whipped Sara's hair into her face. More spiders flashed by in the darkness as the tunnel widened. Some tried to leap into the cart. Most missed, but on a few occasions, one managed to snag the cart with its front legs. In each case, a fist or boot to its ugly face dislodged it.

Tom and Sara could finally breathe a little easier, at the price of feeling increasingly lightheaded and nauseous as more methane gas filled the tunnel along with the oxygen. Neither spoke, trying to get the most out of every breath. They kept their heads down as the cart raced along, lest they be taken off by a low-hanging obstacle.

With no warning, the cart slammed into something, ejecting both of its occupants with the force of a low-speed car crash. They tried to protect their heads as they skidded painfully across the stone floor, leaving behind strips of skin. Sara finally rolled to a stop with her head inches from a large rock. Tom hadn't gone quite as far. Both panted and swore, so wracked with pain and dizziness that it was difficult to move.

Sara tried to push herself up. Her left wrist buckled unnaturally, and she screamed in agony as broken bones ground against one another.

Sara's scream sent a fresh pulse of adrenaline into Tom's bloodstream. Pushing through the pain, he scrambled to his feet. "Sara! What's wrong!" He reached into his pocket and brought out another glow stick so he could see.

"I'm fine," she lied. Her voice shook with pain and anger. "Well, not fine, but I'll live."

Tom looked behind them. A large wooden beam lay across the tracks. The cart must have hit it and derailed. It had come to a rest against the far wall of the tunnel, its mangled wheels spinning uselessly.

He looked the other way. It was faint, but there was light at the end of the tunnel. Moonlight? Maybe.

Again came the clicking and skittering. More spiders.

"Sara, can you run? We're almost out." Tom pulled her to her feet. She was holding her left hand against her chest. Tom winced when he saw it. Her broken wrist was badly deformed.

"Come on," she panted, taking the lead. They both limped down the tunnel, pushing as hard as their injuries would allow. They were moving so slowly, but neither could wring any more speed out of their battered bodies.

The spiders were closing in.

With agonizing slowness, the light grew brighter and larger. It was a hundred meters away now, ninety, eighty. Sara's heart lifted. It was definitely moonlight. They were almost outside. Just a little farther.

By the time they reached fresh air, the spiders were almost on them. Neither Tom nor Sara could run anymore. Their legs simply refused. Both fell to their knees, rolling onto their sides. Sara drew her Walther with her right hand and aimed it at the tunnel exit, fighting back tears as lightning bolts of pain shot through her left wrist. Tom, on his back, awkwardly raised his shotgun.

The onslaught didn't come. A lone spider raced out to pounce on them, but as soon as it skittered into the moonlight, it hissed in pain, a shrill, piercing sound. Smoke rose from its exoskeleton, as though it were burning. The spider darted back into the tunnel.

The others, denied their meal, chittered furiously. No more ventured outside.

Finally, the hisses and clicks receded into the darkness, and all was quiet.

Tom and Sara dropped their weapons and lay on the ground, panting.

Neither said anything about their inexplicable good fortune, as though putting words to it would make the spiders realize that they had no reason to fear moonlight.

"I hate this," Tom finally said.

"I can't imagine why," Sara replied, sobbing quietly as she clutched her broken wrist.

CHAPTER EIGHTEEN
Introspection

"Here, bite this," Tom said, handing Sara a stick he'd cleaned off as best he could. "I won't lie to you, this is gonna hurt."

Without comment, Sara bit down on the stick and held out her broken wrist.

"On three," Tom said. "One...."

Holding her left elbow in place, he pulled hard on her injured hand, setting the broken bones more or less back in their original positions. Her scream of anguish echoed far into the night; Tom hoped that nothing had heard it.

"You... bastard," Sara panted. "You said three."

"Sorry, but I knew you were gonna tense up on three, which would have made it worse. Hold still, let me wrap it." As gently as he could, he applied an elastic bandage, then used an entire roll of medical tape to fashion a makeshift cast.

Neither of them said, "Alex would do a better job," but they were both thinking it.

Once Sara's wrist was stabilized, they helped one another treat their road rash, cuts, and other lesser injuries. By the time they'd disinfected and bandaged the worst of it, both of their medical kits were nearly depleted.

"If we have to shoot anything, try to use your sidearm if possible," Tom said. "You can use that busted hand to fire your rifle if absolutely necessary, but let's call that a last resort."

"No argument there. We really need to get back and check in."

"Agreed. Let's see if we can find somewhere relatively safe to sleep."

They were still just outside the mine, in a clearing that was mostly dirt and rocks. A small, weed-choked footpath led out of the clearing and around a high rock wall, in the direction of the moon. The path sloped down as it went, winding its way along a grassy hill dotted with white lilies like the ones they'd seen at the house with the cable car. At the bottom of the hill, the ocean met the shore in a large bay, many miles across. A dense, ghostly fog rose from the water. On the far side of the bay, an intermittent flash of light penetrated the fog every few seconds.

"I guess we've been sticking pretty close to the coast this whole time," Tom said.

"Is that a lighthouse?" Sara asked.

"That would be my guess. This is actually a nice view. Or it would be, if not for the weird green ocean water and the constant threat of agonizing death."

"Look there," Sara said, pointing with her good hand. Just below them, at the bottom of the hill, a large wooden boat was moored to a dock, bobbing gently in the waves.

"I'm not a boat expert, but that looks like an old Spanish clipper," Tom said. "It should have interior cabins with doors that we can lock or at least barricade. It's probably the safest resting place we're going to find."

Sara scanned the landscape, looking for other options. She saw no other structures, nothing but open, unprotected space. "That boat creeps me out. I don't like it, but you're probably right," she said.

Before long, they reached the dock. Now that they were closer, they could see another, smaller boat moored on the far side, opposite the clipper. It looked like a speedboat. "That one looks like it might have a motor," Tom said. "Let's check it out."

Sara fidgeted nervously. "Are you sure? We really need to get back home."

"I just want to take a quick look. Walking all the way around the bay would take way too long. We're gonna need a vehicle of some kind if we want to make good time when we come back."

"It didn't look like walking would be that much of a detour."

"Distance can be deceiving, especially when water is involved. At sea, things usually look a lot closer than they really are. The lighthouse is probably about twenty miles away. The bay is almost a perfect half circle, so we can use a formula to estimate the circle's circumference if we know its diameter. If the lighthouse is twenty miles away, going around the bay is about thirty miles of walking. That could easily take a whole day. With a decently fast boat, we can cut that to an hour or two."

Sara made a face. "Did you have to bring math into it?"

"Isn't that what you pay me for, to get you to the cathedral quickly and safely? Oh, right. You don't pay me."

Sara rolled her eyes as they reached the speedboat. Tom hopped in and began checking it over. "Looks like it's in reasonably good shape," he said. He yanked on the rip cord to test the engine. Nothing happened, even after several more tries.

"Can you fix it?" Sara asked.

"Maybe, but I would need tools, parts, and time."

Sara almost said, "Dylan can do it," but she caught herself. Making an effort to keep her voice steady, she said, "Maybe we should walk, then."

Tom sighed. "Well, one thing at a time. For now, let's get some rest and check in with your dad. We can decide about this later."

* * *

"This should work," Tom said, dropping his pack on the floor of the captain's cabin. He was bone-tired and in serious pain. "You take the bed, I'll take the floor."

"Are you sure?" Sara said.

"The only alternative is for me to take a bed in another room, and there's no way I'm leaving you alone."

"I guess."

"I dunno about you, but I expect I'll be out in minutes. I don't think I've ever been so tired."

"Me neither."

Several hours later, both were still awake, lying on their backs, staring up at the rafters. Moonlight filtered in through a small, warped glass window, illuminating the interior of the modest cabin just enough that they could make out vague shapes and shadows.

"Are you still awake?" Tom whispered.

"Yeah," Sara replied. "I'm so tired, but I just can't fall asleep. You need to fall asleep first anyway, so you don't get stuck here."

A long silence stretched between them. "I'm sorry about Alex and Dylan," he said.

"There's nothing to be sorry about. They're still alive." There was a hint of irritation in her voice, and it sounded more like a plea than a statement.

Tom changed the subject. "Maybe we could each take half of your adrenaline and return that way."

"I thought of that, but I'm pretty sure it won't work. It wouldn't be a high enough dose for either of us."

Another uncomfortable silence stretched between them. It was quiet for so long that Tom thought Sara had fallen asleep and left the Twilight, but when he rolled over, he could still see her silhouette on the bed.

He stood up, careful not to trip on anything in the darkness. "I'm going to get some air for a minute, maybe that will help me fall asleep. Don't leave without me."

"I won't, I promise," Sara said.

Tom left the cabin and headed for the main deck. The hallway wasn't very long; he would be able to hear Sara if she called for him.

As soon as he stepped outside, he realized that they had a problem.

The ship was moving.

He rushed to the side and looked over. Somehow, the ship was gliding along the surface of the water, but it seemed unaffected by the waves. It wasn't sailing—it was hovering. That would explain why neither of them had felt it moving.

Tom leaned over the side as far as he dared. He couldn't see anything but fog in any direction.

Below, a dozen shark fins cut silently through the water, escorting the ship to its unknown destination.

"This place is starting to piss me off," he muttered to himself.

* * *

Tom had left the cabin door open. Sara considered getting up to shut it, then decided that it didn't matter.

She sat up. She was beyond exhausted, but she couldn't risk falling asleep before Tom; that would trap him in the Twilight, alone, until she came back. She rubbed her eyes and stretched, trying not to come fully awake. Hopefully, Tom would return in a few minutes and be able to sleep. Then, she could follow.

A young boy with short, dark hair and bright blue eyes appeared in the doorway, smiling at her. A heartbeat later, he moved on. Sara distinctly heard footsteps receding down the hallway.

Her heart leaped into her throat, and her pulse doubled. Like it or not, she was fully awake now. Before she even realized what she was doing, she'd bolted to the doorway. She saw nothing in the direction the boy had gone, only an open door leading lower into the ship.

Her mind raced. She tried not to think about Daniela Esperanza's brutal death, but the harder she tried to suppress the memory, the more vividly it played in her head. She wouldn't let that happen to anyone else, especially not a kid. She darted to the open door. It was so dark that she could hardly see anything. A narrow flight of stairs descended to the next deck, but she couldn't see more than a few steps down.

This is stupid, she thought. *I'm being stupid.* The boy needed help, but she shouldn't be going anywhere alone. She'd go get Tom, and they could look for the boy together.

Wait a minute. There can't possibly be any kids in the Twilight.

The door slammed shut, hitting her in the back and knocking her off balance. She spun her arms, trying to recover.

It was too late. She was already falling.

Sara yelped as she tumbled down the stairs, her recent injuries flaring with fresh pain. She covered her head with her right arm as best she could while keeping her broken left hand tucked into her stomach.

Miraculously, she rolled to a stop on the rough wooden floor at the base of the stairs with no new wounds, although her whole body was aching again. She blinked. Suddenly, she could see, plain as day. Light, so bright that she had to shield her eyes, was coming from somewhere.

She reached down with her right hand to push herself up. She felt not rough wood but green grass. She was... outside? And it was daytime?

Too stunned to speak, she looked around.

Inexplicably, she was in her own backyard. Adults and children were everywhere, talking and laughing. She recognized some of them. Some were people she knew but hadn't seen in years.

Birds sang merrily in the trees nearby. Brightly colored koi fish darted to and fro in the pond, enjoying the exercise. Honeybees danced a summer jig in the flower garden, visiting the roses, tulips, and hibiscus in turn. The air was warm, and a cool breeze ruffled her hair. She reached up to remove her hat, but it wasn't there.

Everything looked too big. She recognized the wooden picnic table to her left, but she was barely taller than it was. She looked down at herself.

Her armor and weapons were all gone. Instead, she wore a white cotton sundress with smiling yellow ducks on it. She had white sandals on her feet, and each of her toenails was painted a different color.

Beginning to understand, she pulled the neck of her dress out and looked down at her flat chest.

I'm... a kid?

"Sara!" someone called. Startled, she looked around. There he was—the boy she'd seen earlier. His eyes were the same shade of blue as the clear sky above. He was smiling at her, his head cocked to one side. He was missing two teeth.

Sara gasped when she recognized him.

"Come over here," Dylan called, waving at her. He disappeared into the birch trees.

Against her will, she felt her feet moving. Her mind felt disconnected from her body. She tried to stop walking—she needed time to figure out what was happening. Whatever it was, it couldn't be good. She needed to get back to Tom.

But her body wouldn't listen to her mind. It carried her forward no matter how desperately she willed it to turn around. It felt like she was watching a home video through her own eyes, trapped in a body that felt strangely unfamiliar even though it was hers.

She felt herself running through the trees, heard herself giggling in a voice that sounded too high-pitched. Vivid memories started to come rushing back. Hide-and-seek in the forest used to be one of their favorite games to play. Dylan never was a very good hider—he always gave himself away in one way or another.

She heard muffled giggling somewhere off to her right. No longer trying to fight it, Sara simply went along for the ride inside her own head. She kicked off her sandals so she could walk more quietly. Silent as a field mouse, she crept between the trees. The wispy grass tickled her bare feet.

She saw a white sneaker sticking out from behind a tree. Grinning triumphantly, she approached stealthily from the back and grabbed Dylan around the waist. "Got you!" she cackled. He squealed in surprise and fell to the ground, dragging her with him. He knew her weakness—he went right for her ribs, tickling her furiously, and she rolled away to put an end to it.

"I got you something," Dylan said, sitting up. He stuck a hand in his pocket.

"Dylan, you didn't have to do that," Sara heard herself say.

He frowned. "Of course, I did. It's your birthday." He pulled out his hand, his fist closed tightly around something small. "Close your eyes and turn around." She obeyed. She felt him move her hair out of the way and hang something around her neck. "Okay, you can look now," he said.

She opened her eyes and looked down. A beautiful silver rose hung on a fine silver chain. It was so detailed that she could see each individual petal. In the center of the flower, a tiny ruby sparkled in the sunlight.

Sara gasped. "Dylan... it's so beautiful." She turned and hugged him, careful not to squash the flower between their chests. "Did your dad give you the money?"

He gently pushed her away and huffed, genuinely offended. "No way. I've been saving for a long time, mowing lawns and stuff. Mrs. Miller even gave me twenty dollars to fix her toaster."

She smiled and wiped away a tear. "It must have been expensive.... You shouldn't spend all your money on me."

He put his hands on his hips and frowned at her like a scientist studying some kind of alien. "You're my best friend. What else would I spend money on?"

Sara leaned forward and planted a kiss on his cheek. She knew that would make him turn red as a tomato, and it did. "Thanks, Dylan. Let's go get some cake."

* * *

Tom ran back to the cabin. "Sara, we—"

He stopped. The cabin was empty.

"Sara!" he yelled at the top of his lungs. There was no reply. Had she fallen asleep? No, that didn't seem likely. She would take great care not to strand him here.

Tom ran back into the hallway and looked in the cabin next door. It, too, was empty, as was the next, and the next.

There was only one door left in the hallway. He shouldered it open and charged inside.

He nearly ran straight into the opposite wall. The room was smaller than he'd been expecting, and it was lit so brightly. He shielded his eyes.

Turning back to the door, he blinked in surprise. He was... somewhere else. Water dripped from the tap of a dirty white sink. There was a toilet without a seat and in desperate need of cleaning. Tom's jaw dropped when he saw his reflection in the scratched mirror above the sink.

It was him but younger, and clean-shaven. He patted his chest. His armor and weapons were gone, as were his recent injuries. Instead, he wore a forest-green button-down shirt, jeans, and sneakers.

Muted music, laughter, and voices rose in volume on the other side of the door. He yanked it open. A bar? Wait... not just some random bar. He knew this place. It was Willy's Roadhouse, just off I-95 outside of Bangor.

But he hadn't been there in more than twenty years.

"Tom!" someone shouted from across the bar. "Come on, man, your beer's getting warm."

Holy shit, Tom thought when he saw who it was. *Manny?*

Despite having no intention of moving, he found himself walking across the bar toward his best friend. He tried to fight it, tried to turn back and look for Sara, but it was no use. He slid into a seat next to Manny and across the table from his parents, Manuel Sr. and Leticia. Manny's father drained his beer and spoke, raising his voice over the music.

"It's getting late, and I'm sure you boys want to celebrate the rest of Manny's birthday without us old farts hanging around. But first, Tom, step outside with me."

"Uh-oh, you're in trouble," Manny snickered, finishing off his own beer —the first one he'd ever bought legally.

"Shut your dumb face," Tom said, without meaning to say it. *I guess I can't control what I say either,* he thought.

Tom stood and followed Manuel Sr. out to the parking lot, where they could hear one another. He shivered, rubbing his bare arms. There was snow on the ground. That made sense—Manny's birthday was in January.

Manuel shrugged into his denim jacket, adjusting the shoulders. "Tom, all kidding aside, I want you to know that Leticia and I are both as proud of you as we are of Manny. She'll never say it; I have to give the speeches in our family." His expression turned serious. "You're almost as much of a son to us as he is. You'll take care of him over there, won't you?"

In Kuwait, Tom remembered. Pieces of the long-buried memory were starting to come back to him. It was January 1996. He and Manny had both signed up for basic training and were due to ship out next month.

"Yes, sir, you know I will," he said.

Manuel put a fatherly hand on his shoulder. "Your old man would be proud of you too, you know." Tom said nothing. Manuel studied his eyes as though searching for the answer to some ancient riddle. Apparently not finding it, he went on. "I just want to ask you one question. No bullshit, this is serious."

"Of course, sir."

"This army business—is it really what you want? I mean, is it what *you* want? Not just what your daddy wanted?"

No, Tom thought. *That was my old man's dream for me, not mine.*

"Yes, sir," he said. "Been dreaming about it ever since I was a kid."

Bullshit, Tom thought. Had he really said that? Thinking back on it, he realized that he probably had. *I never wanted to be in the military, I just felt like I had to do it because it was my duty. Dad never would've let me hear the end of it if I didn't sign up. I guess I was too young and dumb back then to be honest with myself.*

Manuel raised a finger to emphasize his next point. His normally jovial tone turned deadly serious. "I'm asking you this because Manny is everything to me, and to his mother. He's all we've got. He signed up because you did, not because he wanted to. You know that, right?" Tom swallowed but didn't answer. He felt his knees trembling. "You're a good kid, Tom. I shouldn't say kid—you're a man now. Part of being a man is taking responsibility for your choices and for your friends. Manny is your friend, isn't he?"

"He's my best friend, sir."

"Then I expect you to look out for him. He's following you to parts of the world that Leticia and I would prefer him never to see. We want him back safe and sound, you hear me?"

"Loud and clear, sir."

"Good. Now, enough of that, come here." Manuel put an arm around Tom's shoulder and drew him into a tight hug. When he backed away, he looked Tom dead in the eye. "Now give me your word on it. Protect my son." He extended his hand, waiting.

Tom watched himself extend his own hand and shake Manuel's firmly.

You stupid son of a bitch, Tom thought to his younger self.

The front door of the bar creaked open, briefly letting out the loud music. Manny joined them as it swung shut again. "What are you guys doing out here?"

Manuel smiled. "Just having a little man-to-man talk. I'll go get Leticia, and we'll get out of here. You enjoy the rest of your birthday, son. And remember—"

Manny cut him off. "I know, I know. I won't drive, and I'll call you if I need a ride."

Manuel clapped his son on the shoulder. "Right. You boys have fun." With that, he went back inside to retrieve his wife.

"My dad isn't busting your balls too hard, I hope," Manny said.

"Nah, just normal dad stuff," Tom said vaguely. "Come here. I got something for you." Tom led Manny over to his car, a beat-up old Pontiac. He put a hand on the trunk but didn't open it, pausing for dramatic effect. "If you're serious about being a Ranger sharpshooter, you'll need a serious rifle." Tom popped the trunk and stepped back so Manny could see what was inside.

"No. Fucking. Way," Manny said, his eyes wide. "You serious?"

"Happy twenty-one, bro."

Manny knew better than to take the rifle out of the trunk in the parking lot of a bar. Instead, he leaned over it, running his hands lightly over the weapon. "What is it? I don't recognize it."

"It's brand new. It's called the Accuracy International AWM, some guys in the UK just rolled it out."

"What caliber?"

".338 Lapua, with a variable 6–24 by 50mm Trijicon scope. I already zeroed it in to five hundred meters for you. Five-round magazine, integrated flash hider, 27-inch barrel, 1:11 right-hand twist. Apparently, all the hot shit spec-ops snipers love the .338 round because it stays straight and level out to a thousand meters, or farther with the right loads. I reworked the bolt so it's smooth as butter."

Manny stared at him. "This could not have been cheap."

"You bought me so many illegal beers over the years, I guess we're square now."

Manny pulled Tom into a tight hug. "This is awesome man, thank you. But you know I can't take it with me to Ranger school, right?"

"No shit. But you can practice with it until then, and it'll be here waiting for you when we come home."

* * *

Without warning, Sara was once again on the old clipper ship, standing at the top of the stairs. The sudden transition back to her normal body was jarring, and she felt dizzy for a moment. A brief inspection revealed that all her gear was back where it belonged—and all of her injuries had returned as well. She sighed. She had enjoyed not being in pain for a little while.

Tom, she thought. She raced down the hall, shouting his name. He'd said he was going outside to get some fresh air. Maybe he was still on the deck. She opened the door that led outside, rushed through it—and stopped.

God dammit, she thought. Instead of being on the deck of the ship, she was back home, in the dining room this time.

"Oh, it's you," said a low, accusatory voice behind her. She whirled around.

"Dylan!" He looked just as he had at dinner a few nights ago, but his face was… different. Hard. Angry. "What's going on? Is this real?" she asked.

"Is what real? Your unbelievable arrogance? Seems real enough to me."

She took a step back, noting that she could control her own movement this time. "What? Dylan, are you okay? Are you in the Twilight? Where are you? Are you hurt?"

"What do you care?" He crossed his arms. He was looking at her in a way he had never looked at her before—like he hated her.

"What's that supposed to mean? Of course, I care. I've been worried sick about you."

Abruptly, he disappeared. Sara turned around. Somehow, he'd gotten behind her. Now he was leaning back in one of the dining room chairs, his feet kicked up on the table.

"Dylan—"

He cut her off, speaking in a dull, bored voice as he inspected his fingernails. "You know what your problem is, Sara? You don't care about anything or anyone except your goddamned Pilgrimage. You certainly don't care about me—you don't even care about yourself. The ends justify the means, right?"

She could hardly believe her ears. "What? How could you say that?"

"How can you deny it?" Sara jumped. He'd spoken the words from directly behind her, his lips almost touching her ear. She again turned to face him. "Look around at all the blood and death and pain. This place is worse than hell. You brought me here against my will—that's bad enough —but you chose to put *yourself* in this nightmare." He raised an eyebrow and leaned in, his face uncomfortably close to hers. "That's even worse than what you did to me."

"Dylan, why are you saying this?"

"Tell me I'm wrong," he said.

"You're wrong," Sara said. But why did her voice crack when she said it?

"Did I ever mean anything to you? Or were you lying to me, manipulating me, grooming me to be your meat shield even when we were kids?"

Tears streamed freely down her face. Her hands were balled so tightly into fists that she could feel her nails cutting into her palms. "You don't mean that," she whispered.

He laughed, cruelly. She'd never heard such a demeaning sound come out of his mouth. "I'm glad I'm dead. At least I don't have to follow you around like a whipped dog anymore. For the first time, I'm free, and I'm happy—because I'm away from you." He turned on his heel and walked away.

"Dylan! Wait!" Sara reached out for him, sobbing. Her hand went right through his arm, as though he were made of fog. His words had cut her like knives. She chased after him. "Dylan! It's not like that! Come back!"

In a blink, her house disappeared. There was no solid ground under her feet. She was falling, with nothing to grab onto.

Dark green water reached up in waves, eager to welcome her.

The sharks were hungry.

* * *

Tom blinked, closing his eyes only for a fraction of a second. When he opened them again, the parking lot of the bar was gone. He was back on the deck of the ship.

"You know, it's probably a good thing you don't have any kids. You'd be a shitty dad," said a drawling female voice behind him.

Tom turned, instinctively reaching for his shotgun. "Alex!" he cried, stunned. He lowered the shotgun when he saw her.

She held her arms out to the sides and took an exaggerated bow. "In the flesh."

Tom frowned. "No, I don't think you are. I think you're dead, and this ship is fucking with my head. Where's Sara?"

Alex cocked her head, a puzzled frown on her face. "Why do you care?"

"What kind of question is that?"

"A serious one."

Tom folded his arms, his expression darkening. "I've already put my life on the line for her half a dozen times and damn near lost it once. Who the hell are you to ask me that?"

"No, Tom, the real question is, who the hell are *you*?" Either the specter of Alex had moved impossibly fast or it had teleported. She was right in front of him, wearing a condescending grin, lightly smacking the sides of his face like she was patting a toddler's cheeks. He raised a hand to swat her away, and she disappeared again.

"I don't have much patience for games," Tom said. "Where's Sara? I won't ask again."

"You're not in much of a position to make threats, I think. You can't shoot your way out of this one." Alex had reappeared and was now sitting atop a barrel, resting her chin in one hand. "Do you even know how to solve problems any other way? Or are you just a dumb grunt?"

"I'm not big on rhetoric, either."

The ghost of Alex laughed. "Ooh, 'rhetoric.' Very good, Tom. That is a big word for a trench monkey."

"If you have something to say, say it. I'm guessing you won't let me find Sara until you feel like you've made a point, whatever you are."

"There you go prattling on about Sara again. Your concern is touching, or rather, it would be if it were sincere."

Tom took a deep breath, trying to keep his temper in check. "I've already proven myself to her."

"So, you're her caring and responsible guardian, then. So caring and responsible that you don't care if she lives or dies."

"You're not making any sense."

"You really are thick, aren't you? Fine, I'll spell it out for you. If you had any shred of decency left in you—if you really cared about protecting her —you would have taken her away from this hellhole at the first opportunity."

"And go where? If we run, everyone dies, including her. How does that count as protecting her? I'm not happy about any of this, but she's right about one thing: We have a duty to the rest of mankind."

"Ah, yes, duty. The oldest excuse in the book."

Tom felt his anger heating. "Sara is in danger no matter what, I can't change that. All I have to do—all I *can* do—is protect her long enough to get her to the end of this path she's on. That's the only way I can protect everyone else, too."

Abruptly, Alex was right in front of him, looking at him like he was a bug in a jar. "You don't sound too sure about that. Like I said, I'm glad you don't have kids. Only bad parents rationalize their kids' bad choices."

Tom's anger exploded. "What the fuck are you talking about? Whoever, whatever you are?" He forced his anger down and shook his head, muttering to himself. "I'm arguing with a damned figment of my own imagination."

"You don't sound too sure about that, either."

Tom turned away and marched to the side of the ship, looking over the railing. He still couldn't see anything but green water and fog. "We're done here."

"Not quite. You have one more question to answer."

He sighed and turned back around. "Out with it, then."

"Have you learned anything yet?"

He grunted. "Yeah, I've learned that you're a pain in the ass."

Alex's face contorted into a mask of hate and fury. "Wrong answer."

She lunged at him so quickly that he reflexively jumped back. The backs of his legs hit the railing and he began to tip over. He struggled to right himself, but he was a fraction of a second too late to reverse his momentum. He let out a strangled yell as he went over the side, flipping head over heels. He reached out with both hands, grabbing for the railing.

He missed.

Up in the crow's nest, one of four dark silhouettes let out a ghostly sigh. *I was wrong, sisters*, it said in a voice like rustling autumn leaves.

Perhaps. Perhaps not. There is still time, said another that spoke with the timbre and cadence of wind chimes.

* * *

Within a few seconds, the clipper ship was gone, sailing away faster than seemed possible. The fog parted like a curtain permitting its passage, then swirled closed behind it.

Sara flailed her arms, struggling to keep her head above water. Her gear was heavy. It was dragging her down.

"Sara!" Tom called as he swam toward her, looming up out of the fog. He had even more gear and was barely managing to tread water.

"Tom! What the hell—"

"I don't know. I think the ship evicted us."

"Tom, my gear is too heavy, I can't stay afloat."

He growled in frustration. "We can't get rid of it."

"It's not gonna help us if we drown! Dead is dead, it doesn't matter how!"

She was right. Bellowing in frustration, Tom removed his shotgun and grenade launcher, letting them sink. Sara did the same with her rifle.

"We're still too heavy, we have to lose our packs and armor, too," Tom said, spitting out a mouthful of water. He helped Sara remove hers, then she returned the favor. The last of their gear rapidly sank out of sight, swallowed by the dark sea.

Finally, they could tread water more easily.

"Now what?" Sara said, trying to stay calm.

"I'm thinking," Tom said. "We have to just pick a direction and swim. Maybe there's land nearby."

"Oh, no," she said, looking over his shoulder. He turned to see what had caught her attention.

Half a dozen gray dorsal fins were slicing through the water toward them.

"Oh, fuck me," Tom said. "Go!"

They started to swim as fast as they could. Even without their heavy gear, their clothing and boots were still weighing them down—not that it would make a difference. They couldn't hope to outrun sharks in the water in any case, and they both knew it.

The fins were closing in rapidly.

They both stopped swimming. It was over. There was no chance.

Sara buried her face in Tom's shoulder, weeping. She couldn't think of anything to say.

Tom wrapped one arm around her in a futile gesture of protection. "I'm so sorry," he said, his voice choked with emotion. "Close your eyes. Don't open them."

He drew his Magnum and held it in one hand above the water, waiting for a target. He thumbed back the hammer. If he was exceptionally quick—and lucky—he might be able to take out one or two of the sharks.

He knew better than to think he could get all of them.

A dull roaring sound became audible, rapidly getting louder. At first, Tom thought it was the sharks, but it didn't sound like a noise that any living thing would make. He couldn't see anything through the thick fog.

Suddenly, he and Sara were both jerked up and out of the water. They punched and kicked, fighting back instinctively. Something grabbed Tom's revolver and wrenched it away.

"Guys! Relax! We've got you!" said a familiar voice.

Tom blinked. Sara swiped water out of her eyes.

Alex and Dylan stared back at them.

"What the hell," Tom said.

"Hang on!" Dylan yelled from the driver's seat of the speedboat. He gunned the throttle. The boat lurched and roared away, its engine crescendoing powerfully.

A massive shark lunged at them, its deadly maw open wide. It snapped its powerful jaws shut, missing the side of the boat by inches. A moment later, they were away, the gray fins circling angrily behind them.

"Dylan! You're okay!" Sara yelled. She threw her arms around him from behind.

"Agh! I'm driving!" he cried. The boat veered crazily to the left, then to the right, nearly tipping over.

"Sorry!" Sara said, releasing him.

"Alex. I'll be damned," Tom said, shaking his head as he smiled at her.

"Nice to see you, too," she said.

"Is this another illusion?"

She frowned at him. "Huh?"

"Never mind."

Once they had left the sharks far behind, Dylan slowed the boat to a comfortable cruising speed. Sara was crying openly, but for once, they were tears of joy. "I knew you guys weren't dead. I knew it."

Tom thought it would be inappropriate to say that he'd been sure of the opposite, so he kept his mouth shut.

"I'm glad to see that you're alive, too," Alex said to Tom. "I wasn't sure you'd survive that massive dose of adrenaline."

"I feel fine now. Well, not fine—I've been beaten all to hell today. But I think the snake venom is gone, at least."

Dylan chimed in. "Remember how Sara said nothing that originated in the Twilight could come back to our world? So, we can bring guns and equipment here, but we can't take anything back except whatever we brought with us?"

"I remember," Tom said.

"I figured that included snake venom, too. The snake is from here, so no part of it can exist in our world. If I could get enough adrenaline into your system to send you back, then you wouldn't need antivenom."

"I'll be damned," Tom said.

"Instant detox," Alex said. "Dylan had a great idea."

Tom carefully maneuvered himself into the unoccupied passenger seat next to Dylan and put a hand on his shoulder. "Thanks, Dylan. That was some quick and clever thinking. I owe you one."

Dylan blushed furiously. "If the Ouroboros comes back, try not to let it bite you. I'm not sure the same idea would work again. It was kind of a long shot."

"Oro-what?" Tom asked.

"Ouroboros," Dylan said. "The snake that eats its own tail. Dates all the way back to ancient Egypt, but the myth shows up in other cultures, too. Some versions say it was big enough to wrap all the way around the whole world."

"I like the myth better than the real thing," Tom grumbled.

"How did you guys find us?" Sara said.

"We found your tracks in the mud, and they led directly to the dock, so we knew you'd taken a ship of some kind," Alex said. "We also saw the lighthouse light, and the moon was directly above it, so we guessed you'd gone that way."

"But how did you find us in all this fog?" Tom asked.

"It seemed safe to assume that you would head straight toward the lighthouse, using the light to guide you through the fog, so we did the same. I fixed up this boat as fast as I could, and we followed," Dylan said. "We got here just in time to see Tom go overboard."

"Dylan's on a roll today," Sara said, smiling at him. Tom didn't think Dylan could turn an even brighter shade of red, but apparently, he could.

"What happened on that ship, anyway? Are you guys okay?" Alex asked.

"Maybe we should just start at the beginning and bring each other up to speed," Tom said. "It's been a busy day."

"Oh, I almost forgot. Here," Dylan said, reaching back toward Sara. She held out her hand and he dropped her necklace into it.

Sara looked at him, stunned. He looked over his shoulder long enough to flash her a quick grin. "We found it outside the mine. It's a little dirty, and it needs a new chain, but other than that, it's fine."

Only Alex was looking at Sara when Dylan handed the necklace back to her. For the briefest moment, intense pain darkened Sara's face when she touched the silver rose. The expression vanished as quickly as it had appeared, but Alex was positive she'd seen it.

"Start at the beginning," Tom said as Sara carefully tucked the necklace into her pocket. "Tell us what happened at the hospital."

CHAPTER NINETEEN
Salvation

Alex and Sara were beginning to lose the struggle. They were becoming fatigued, and the wave of creatures crashing into the lockers over and over was relentless.

Suddenly, with perfect clarity, Dylan knew what he had to do.

Detached and numb, as though watching his own body from far away, he grabbed Sara from behind, wrapping one arm around her neck in a clumsy choke hold.

"Dylan! What the hell are you doing!" Alex screamed, nearly fainting in disbelief.

He didn't answer. There was no time. Sara hadn't reacted yet, undoubtedly because she was still processing what had happened, but she would start elbowing him in the ribs any second. With his free hand, Dylan reached into the pouch on her armor, withdrew the plastic case, and popped it open. Just as Sara was beginning to fight back, he flicked the safety cap off the adrenaline injector and rammed it into the side of her leg.

"You're the one who needs to survive," he whispered into her ear.

A heartbeat later, she was gone.

Dylan took her place, throwing all his weight against the lockers. Alex, finally understanding what he'd done, gave him a single, grim nod. Even though Dylan was stronger than Sara, it wouldn't be enough of a difference. The lockers were slowly but surely being pushed out of the doorway, farther back into the room. Blue-gray hands covered with cuts and bruises were reaching through the gap, grabbing wildly for prey. The feral howls were so close and so loud.

So hungry.

"I think this is it," Dylan said, his voice choked with heartbreak.

"You were very brave," Alex said. "I'm proud of you."

"Hey! Over here!" an unfamiliar voice shouted in a Scottish accent.

Alex and Dylan looked to the window. Across the alley, an old man with gray hair and a dirty beard was waving at them from the opposite building. Stunned to see another seemingly normal person, they both stared in shock for a moment. The old man picked up a long board and began feeding it through the open window, creating a bridge between the two buildings. "Hold on just another minute!" he yelled as he began doing the same with another three boards.

Dylan and Alex redoubled their efforts, shoving against the lockers with all their remaining strength. They gained a few inches but immediately lost them again. More blue-gray hands were reaching through the gap.

"Okay, c'moan! Keep yer heads down!" the old man hollered. He was now holding an ancient lever-action rifle.

"Alex, go!" Dylan yelled. "I'm stronger, I'll hold it!"

"No, you first!" she protested. The floor was covered in fresh blood, and her feet were slipping. She didn't have much stamina left.

Dylan remembered Tom shoving him, yelling at him, forcing him to act. He understood now. Tom wasn't being a hard-ass for no reason; he was thinking of the team as a whole—doing what had to be done to get everyone out alive.

Dylan was physically stronger than Alex, there was no question of that. He could hold the lockers longer. "Go!" he shouted again, more forcefully. He let go of the lockers just long enough to push Alex toward the window, then threw himself against the barricade once again. She stumbled a few steps in that direction, then turned back toward him. For a moment, Dylan thought she was going to come back, but then she ran for the window.

The old man had extended four long, thick boards across the alley, side by side to make a bridge. "Spread yer weight across all the boards or they'll break!" he hollered. Alex carefully hoisted herself onto the bridge, distributing her weight as best she could.

Dylan slipped when the barricade rattled with an especially violent impact. It slid forward nearly two feet. Instantly, two creatures squeezed through the gap. "No!" he shouted, hurling his weight against the lockers once again. He managed to wedge them back into the door frame, but the two monsters were already in the room.

Running straight for Alex.

A sharp *crack* echoed across the alley. The old man knew how to use his rifle; the first creature went down, the top third of its head blown away. He worked the action and fired again, but the second shot missed. He was having a difficult time aiming around Alex.

The creature leaped onto the bridge. Alex was nearly halfway across, but there was no way she could make it the rest of the way in time. The monster lunged, latching onto her back like a tick. She let out a strangled cry and reached back, trying to fight off her assailant. She wobbled on her knees, and the boards buckled under her.

Alex realized that the creature was mostly attached to her pack. Struggling to keep its teeth away from her neck, she pulled her arms out of the straps and lunged forward, kicking out blindly with her left leg as she went. Her foot caught the creature in the side with just enough force to knock it off balance. It fell to the ground, taking her pack with it.

Dylan couldn't hold out any longer. He was beyond exhausted. He was afraid that if he taxed his muscles any further, he wouldn't have any strength left to run. It was now or never. With one final shove, he wedged the lockers into the door frame as tightly as he could, then abandoned them and sprinted for the window.

He had hardly any lead at all. He hadn't made it two steps when the lockers flew across the room with a deafening *bang*, crashing into the far wall. Dylan turned and started to raise his UMP, then remembered that it was still empty—he'd never gotten a chance to reload it after the last wave. He let it drop and drew his sidearm, firing blindly behind him as he ran. He dived through the window, landing on his stomach atop the boards. They rattled and swayed under the sudden impact, threatening to hurl him to the ground.

He could hear several creatures right behind him.

Trying to buy another few seconds, he turned onto his left side, aiming with his right hand, and emptied the pistol as fast as he could. A few of the rounds hit true, dropping one abomination and stunning another. A third lunged for him, ripped the empty USP out of his hands, and tossed it aside. With amazing speed, it crawled on top of him, grabbing his belt to pull itself up his body.

"No!" Dylan cried, raising his hands in front of his face.

But it didn't go for his face. Instead, it bit him in the side, right in the gap between the front and rear plates of his armor. Its sharp teeth sank deep into him and tore away a chunk of his flesh, along with pieces of his shirt.

His strangled scream of agony ripped through the night air.

Another loud *bang* echoed in the alley, and the monster on top of him tumbled away.

"Dylan! Hurry!" Alex yelled. She'd made it to the other building and was reaching toward him, beckoning him onward.

Dylan rolled back onto his stomach and crawled as fast as he dared, refusing to look down. Dark red blood ran steadily down his side and dripped to the ground far below. Adrenaline blunted the pain and drove him onward.

He reached the opposite window. Alex grabbed his hands and pulled him inside, into an interior stairwell, and they fell to the floor in a tangled heap. Dylan screamed again when his injured side twisted painfully.

"Sorry, folks; bridge is closed!" the old man cried. Dropping his rifle to the floor, he picked up a sledgehammer that was leaning against the wall. He held it outside the window, raised it high in both hands, and brought it down on the boards just in front of the advancing monstrosities. One board snapped in two. The old man brought the hammer down again and again, breaking another board each time.

With a final *crack*, the last board fell, along with three creatures that had been a little more than halfway across. They screeched in fury, clawing at one another as they dropped away.

Dylan and Alex regained their feet and looked outside just in time to see the creatures hit the ground. Two of them landed head-first and went limp instantly. The third, seemingly unfazed by the fall, immediately leaped to its feet, spinning in circles as it searched for prey.

Howling in rage, the surviving creature grabbed Alex's medic bag and tore it open, scattering medical supplies everywhere. From within the bag, it pulled out an insulated lunchbox and sniffed at it, as though it smelled something tasty inside. It dropped the medic bag and tore into the lunchbox, pulling out two bags of O-negative blood Alex had packed for emergency transfusions. It ripped into the blood bags with wild fury, slurping hungrily.

Most of the blood splashed to the ground, quickly spreading into a large pool.

Seemingly dissatisfied with the snack, the creature grabbed its two fallen brethren by their necks, one in each hand, and began to drag them down the alley, through the human blood, creating a smeared trail.

It would have something to eat, one way or another.

"Show's over. Let's go," the old man said as he retrieved his rifle. "Those other bastards'll find their way up here soon." He charged ahead, up the stairs. As he ran past Dylan and Alex, they saw that his eyes had the same glassy, far-away look as theirs.

He was a Warden.

Holding their questions for later, they followed.

By the time they reached the roof, Dylan was limping, unable to move without clutching his injured side and gasping in pain. Blood leaked steadily through his fingers and left a clear trail. Alex did her best to stay calm so that he might draw strength from her. "Come on, honey, just a little farther," she said, helping him along as best she could. She had no idea where they were going, how much farther it was, or whether they could trust this strange man who had showed up at a suspiciously convenient time.

But she did know that the two of them stood no chance on their own, not with Dylan wounded and dozens of those things chasing them.

"This way," the old man said, carefully picking his way across another board laid between two adjacent rooftops. Looking around, Alex saw a number of makeshift bridges and ladders on other roofs nearby. *He must live here,* she thought.

Once they were clear, the old man pulled the board across to their side. "Ah think we should be alright now, ah dinnae think they can jump that far," he said. "But let's keep movin' just in case."

They crossed two more rooftops before the pursuing creatures began to swarm onto the roof of the building across from the hospital. Without hesitation, they leaped across the first gap as they reached it. Some came up short and fell five stories to the pavement below, but others cleared the jump.

"Or nae," the old man muttered. "Right then, over here." He led them across several more rickety bridges to a homemade elevator that looked like it had once been a scaffold like the ones used to wash windows on the outsides of skyscrapers. Once they were all aboard, he pushed a big yellow button.

Nothing happened.

"Bugger it, nae now," he shouted. He slammed the button again. Still, the elevator didn't move. He dropped his rifle and ripped open a junction box underneath the button. The wires and parts inside looked like they had seen better days.

"Please hurry," Alex begged. The creatures were only two buildings away.

"Ah'm workin' on it, lass," he muttered. He didn't look confident in what he was doing.

"Move," Dylan wheezed. He shoved the old man aside, taking care not to bleed on him. Trying to ignore the stabbing pain in his side, Dylan fished around in his pack for a screwdriver and went to work on the junction box. Alex and the old man turned their attention to the creatures, taking potshots at any that got too close.

"Dylan, hurry!" Alex shouted.

"Got it!" he replied. He slapped the button. Not a moment too soon, the elevator began to move. One of the deformed creatures flung itself wildly at them but didn't quite manage to grab the platform.

Alex and the old man both sighed in relief once they were well above the advancing horde. She looked up to see where the elevator was taking them.

"A clock tower?" she said aloud.

"Safest place within a day's walk. It's all barricaded up inside, those bastards cannae get in. This here lift's the only way up," the old man said.

"Name's Jacob, by the by."

"I'm Alex, and this is Dylan. He's hurt. He needs medical attention, but I lost most of my supplies."

"Ah've got some basic bandages and such," Jacob said, patting Dylan's shoulder reassuringly. "We'll get ye patched up, lad."

* * *

Alex wiped her forehead again. She couldn't stop sweating. Jacob had provided some reasonably clean needles and thread, which she had used to stitch Dylan's wound as best she could, but it had taken a while and been horrendously painful for him. He sat on the floor at the top of the bell tower with his back against the stone wall, shirtless, his chest and side wrapped in bandages.

His eyes were closed, and he was softly snoring.

"That's not good," Alex said.

"Nae, ye won't be able ta return without yer Maiden," Jacob agreed.

Alex didn't have a bead on him yet. She didn't think the old man was an enemy, but as far as she was concerned, everything in the Twilight wanted them dead until proven otherwise. "Thank you for your help," she finally said. "I have to admit, your timing was a bit... convenient."

Jacob raised an eyebrow. "Ye think ah mean ye harm?"

Alex carefully controlled her tone. "The thought had crossed my mind."

She was worried that he might get offended, or angry. Instead, he shrugged. "Ye seem like a smart lass. Ah dinnae think that ye think ah'm yer enemy."

She considered it carefully. She was still wary, but even so, she was inclined to take him at his word. After all, if he wanted to hurt them, he'd had a dozen chances already.

"No, I don't think you are our enemy," Alex said. She forced a smile, trying to lighten the mood. "Dylan and I are still just shaken up. We're lucky that you showed up when you did."

"Gey jammy," Jacob agreed.

"I'd not like to count on that sort of luck again."

"Nor would ah, but sometimes, even the best and smartest of us cannae get by any other way. Sometimes it takes a bit of luck ta remind us that we're mortal and fragile. Keeps us humble. Helps us develop healthy respect fer the dangers we face."

"That it does," Alex said. After an awkward silence, she said, "I guess you've been here a long time."

"Aye, far too long."

"Can we take you back home somehow? When we find Sara, I mean. Our Maiden."

"Ah doubt it, lass. Far as ah ken, only mah Maiden could take me home, and she's long gone. But ah suppose there's somethin' ta be said fer hope."

"I'm sorry," Alex said softly. "I thought a week sounded like a lifetime to be stuck in this place. I can't imagine what it's like being here for... as long as you have."

Jacob, whittling at a piece of wood with a dull knife, cackled. "It's alright, lass. Ye say ah'm old, ah ken it."

"Did you come here during the previous cycle?"

"Nae, the one afore that, nearly forty years ago now."

A long silence filled the small room, punctuated only by Dylan's breathing and the quiet strokes of Jacob's knife. Unable to stand it any longer, Alex asked the question that had been rattling around in the back of her mind for some time. "What happens when the Maidens get to the end of the path? To the cathedral?"

"Ah dinnae ken, lass." Alex expected him to say more, but he fell silent.

"It's okay if you don't want to talk about it."

"Ah dinnae."

Not knowing what else to say, Alex stepped over to the filthy stained-glass window of the clock face and looked out over the small mining town, thinking. After a time, she looked down at Dylan, her chest tightening with guilt.

"It's my fault," she said, almost to herself.

"Eh?"

"Dylan's hurt, and it's my fault. I should have made him go first. He got hurt because I went first. He could have died. He still might—god knows what sort of awful infection is incubating in him right now. He needs antibiotics, and soon. But we can't leave this place, can't get him the treatment he needs unless we find Sara. If he dies before then, it's my fault. I will have killed him."

When she turned back to face Jacob, he twirled his knife around and pointed it at her like a nun shaking a ruler. "Now, ye listen here. What's done is done. That lad needs ye, and ye cannae be there fer him if yer too busy feelin' sorry fer yerself."

Alex harrumphed but said nothing. Abruptly, she yawned. Exhaustion was quickly smothering her like a heavy blanket.

"How will ye find her? Yer Maiden," Jacob asked, inspecting the crude dog he'd managed to carve.

Alex thought for a moment. "It's best to wait here. We got separated not far from here. One of her other Wardens needs medical attention... but

Sara will come back, with or without him. She has to." Her voice quavered when she said "without him."

Jacob nodded slowly. "Likely best ta wait fer them, then."

"You should come with us. You must know more about this place than anyone. We could really use your help."

"That… would nae be a good idea."

"Why not?"

He looked up at her with sudden anger smoldering in his eyes. "It just would nae. Take mah word fer it."

She swallowed, her hackles rising. "Alright."

He softened his tone. "Ye and the lad need kip. Rest, now. Ah'll keep an eye out fer yer Maiden, and ah'll wake ye when ah see her, ah can do that much. It's a small town with only the one road. Ah'll spot her afore she gets far."

Alex could already feel her eyelids drooping. "Thank you, Jacob. You won't fall asleep and miss her, will you?"

"Nae, lass. Dinnae worry. Ah'll bade awake and keep edge."

Alex curled up on the floor near Dylan and was asleep within moments. True to his word, Jacob took up a perch near the window where he could see the main road while he whittled.

Before long, his age caught up to him, and he dozed off.

CHAPTER TWENTY
Burdens

December 28, 2021
Day Four

The speedboat broke through a wall of fog, into an open stretch of dark green water. Just ahead, an imposing lighthouse of white stone rose into the sky like a mighty torch.

"As it turns out, Jacob did fall asleep," Alex said. "I guess I can't blame him, he is pretty old. You guys must have come back to the Twilight and hoofed it out of town while we were all snoozing. When we woke up, we went down to the street, found tracks that had to be yours, and followed them. We couldn't have been more than a few hours behind you. We made it to the mine, and Dylan found Sara's necklace in the mud outside the elevator, so we knew you'd gone that way. We couldn't follow because the elevator shaft was collapsed, so we had to take the long way around the mountain."

"Yeah, guess who you can thank for the busted elevator," Tom grunted, jerking a thumb in Sara's direction.

She folded her arms. "I didn't hear you complaining while I was saving your ass," she said.

Dylan glanced over his shoulder at Sara. "Did you know Jacob was stuck here?"

She shook her head. "No. I didn't know Daniela was still alive, either. As far as we knew, all the Maidens and Wardens from previous cycles had returned home after their Pilgrimages... or they were dead."

Tom said something, but Sara didn't hear him. Ever since Alex had described the terrible injury that Dylan had suffered, Sara had been watching him closely. He did look unusually pale and sweaty. At first, she'd thought the moisture on his face was just sea spray, but now she suspected that he probably had a fever.

Sara felt a pang of guilt in her chest. She couldn't look at Dylan without hearing what he had said to her on the ship. Even if it wasn't really him—even if it had been a ghost or something, trying to mess with her head—its words had carried the painful sting of truth. How could he not resent her for this? She deserved to be resented—and far worse—for forcing this hell on him. He would certainly hate her forever after it was over if he somehow didn't already.

She dragged herself out of her dark thoughts just as Tom finished recounting the tale of their harried flight through the mines and their experience on the ghost ship. He left out the part about encountering a doppelganger of Alex, not wanting to upset her without good reason. Sara didn't mention her distressing conversation with the specter of Dylan, either.

"Sara, let me see your wrist," Alex said. Sara extended her left arm and Alex performed a gentle exam, poking and prodding lightly to assess the damage. Sara gritted her teeth and forced herself not to cry out with each fresh stab of pain.

"It's definitely broken," Alex said with a heavy sigh. "Hopefully, there's a safe place to rest in that lighthouse, or somewhere nearby. This needs a proper cast."

"Some painkillers wouldn't hurt either," Sara griped.

"Eyes up, we're here," Tom said quietly. Dylan slowed the speedboat to a crawl and clumsily brought it alongside the dock, bumping it several times.

"Sorry," he said sheepishly. "I can barely drive a car."

Alex patted his arm as Tom hopped out and began to tie off the boat. "You did fine, sweetie."

Dylan looked back at Sara, grinning, like he expected her to say something. When he saw the pained expression on her face, his smile faltered. "What's wrong?" he asked.

Sara forced a smile and a lie. "Nothing, I'm just tired and worried about you. You look like you're not feeling well."

Dylan scratched his head. "Ah, yeah, but I'll get some medicine soon. I'm sure I'll be okay. I'm just glad you're still in one piece. I was really worried about you, too."

Sara couldn't bring herself to reply to that. She knew with certainty that if she tried, she would break down in tears.

Tom saved her from the awkward silence by reaching his hand down to help her out of the boat. She walked a few steps down the dock so that Dylan would be behind her, and she wouldn't have to look him in the eye.

"Tom, Sara, where is your gear?" Alex asked with sudden concern. "Has it been missing this whole time? I guess I didn't notice because we were so relieved that we found you."

"Yeah, we had to ditch most of it after that damned ship booted us overboard," Tom said with a heavy sigh. "I feel naked now."

"The *ship* booted you overboard?" Dylan said incredulously as he clambered out of the speedboat. "What does that mean?"

Tom waved a hand as if it didn't really matter. "Another long story for another time. Sara and I still have our sidearms, that will have to do for now. Let's get somewhere safe."

With that reminder, the four of them readied their weapons and began to move slowly down the dock. The dark green seawater crested into small waves that turned into white foam as they met the rocky shore. Just past the end of the dock, the ground sloped gently upward, leveling out once it reached the lighthouse. Beyond that, a number of rusted, dilapidated buildings were visible. Many were little more than sheet metal nailed to simple wooden frames, but they were too far away to see in more detail.

As usual, Tom was in the lead, with Sara behind him. As they stepped off the dock and onto rocky soil, he stopped, holding up a fist. "Wait," he said. "Something's not right."

"That is correct," said an unfamiliar voice from farther up the hill. Tom raised his Magnum and thumbed back the hammer. A split second later, the others followed suit.

"Show yourself," Tom called.

"You are in no position to make demands, my friend, but I will grant you this one," the voice answered. A tall, burly, tanned man stepped out from behind a large rock. He spoke in perfect English that was almost too clean, as though it were a second language he'd practiced extensively. He was holding something in his hand. "The ground all around you is littered with a variety of explosives, some of which are pressure sensitive. I would suggest staying right where you are."

Tom didn't lower his weapon. He was staring intently at the object clutched tightly in the stranger's hand. "And I'm guessing that's a dead man's switch," he said, clearly not pleased about it.

"Also correct," the man responded. "I had you pegged for a military man. American? Bomb technician?"

"Combat engineer," Tom replied, keeping his voice even and his tone neutral.

"What's a dead man's switch?" Alex whispered.

"He's holding down a button on a detonator. If we kill him, or if he lets go of that button for any other reason, we all die," Tom whispered back.

"Let's... let's not upset him, then," Dylan stammered, swallowing hard.

"If you were a combat engineer, then you know exactly how much chance you have of making it up this hill alive—none, provided what I have just told you is true. And I think we both know that it is," the stranger said.

"What do you want?" Tom said, neither challenging nor cowing to the threat.

"No, sir, that is my question to ask. What do *you* want? Why are you here?"

Sara started to step forward, but Tom quickly thrust an arm in front of her. "Don't move," he growled. She suddenly remembered that they were surrounded by land mines and felt a little stupid.

She stayed put and raised her voice to be heard over the wind, trying to sound more authoritative than she felt. "You know who we are and why we're here. There's only one reason people come to the Twilight. You'll gain nothing by killing us except ensuring the annihilation of humanity."

"Humanity is not here, señorita. I care little for a world I will never see again, the very world that saw fit to dump me here like yesterday's garbage."

He called me señorita, Sara thought.

She knew who he was.

"You're Roland Alvarez," Sara called up to the man, in a gentler voice. He said nothing. His dark eyes, glassy and distant, bored into hers. "We... met Daniela not too long ago."

Still, he said nothing. Tom, Alex, and Dylan waited in silence. Sara seemed to have some leverage in this negotiation, and none of them wanted to sabotage it.

"She was brave, strong, and beautiful," Sara said. The sharp wind rising from the sea should have carried her words away, so quiet was her voice. Somehow, everyone heard her clearly. "I wish I could have known her."

The silence stretched on. No one moved. Tom couldn't tell if this man called Roland was contemplating blowing them all to bits or simply lost in his own thoughts.

Finally, he flipped several switches on the detonator in his hand, then dropped it into the pocket of his long leather coat. "The explosives are disarmed. Come inside," he said, heading for the lighthouse door.

* * *

Roland took off his battered, wide-brimmed hat and hung it on a broken coat rack just inside the lighthouse door as the others filed inside. "You could be lying about Daniela, but for some reason, I do not think you are." His tone was gentler now, his accent somewhat more prominent.

"We found her not long after we left the village," Sara said, her voice choked with emotion. "She was alive but badly hurt. We tried to help her, I give you my word on that. But....” She couldn't go on.

“I thought Daniela died a long time ago,” Roland said, sinking onto a ripped couch. “She survived all this time....” He looked up, searching their faces. “How did she die?”

Sara opened her mouth to reply, but Alex put a hand gently on her shoulder, silencing her. “Bravely,” Alex said.

Roland nodded, his eyes moist. “Thank you for not telling me. A moment ago, I thought I wanted to know the details. I now realize that I do not.”

“We're sorry to impose, but do you think we could rest here, just for a little while?” Alex asked.

Roland, on the verge of tears moments ago, suddenly turned gruff. “No. You need to move on,” he said, standing up and waving them toward the door.

Alex stared openly, taken aback. She had assumed that he would agree, given that he was once a Warden himself and knew what they were going through.

“But... why?” Sara asked.

“You bring trouble, whether or not you mean to. The only way I survive is by avoiding the notice of the things that roam around here. They will be drawn to you, and I do not want you in my house when they find you.”

“Roland, please. We're injured. The kids are both hurt badly. They need medical attention, and soon. We don't have any adrenaline, the only way we can return home is by sleeping. And we lost some of our weapons, we can't go back out there under-equipped,” Tom said, surprising the others with his diplomacy.

Sara bristled at being called a “kid” again, but she supposed Tom was trying to appeal to Roland's emotions.

“I am sorry, but that is not my problem,” Roland said, with more iron in his voice than before. He pointed to the door again. “Now go.”

Alex took a deep breath and mentally prepared herself. *This is what I'm here for*, she thought. Being turned out of the lighthouse was simply not an option, for all the reasons Tom had given and more. Fighting this man was also not an option. She needed to convince him to allow them to stay, just for a little while.

Based on the impression she'd formed of him so far, she decided to start hard, then soften up.

“Stop being a coward,” Alex said, carefully controlling the level of aggression in her voice.

Roland blinked in surprise, then turned to face her. “Excuse me?” he said. Tom, Dylan, and Sara all gave Alex startled looks as well.

"I get it. You have reasons to be angry and upset—more reasons and better reasons than almost anyone. The Circle took much from you, and then this horrible place took everything you had left. But none of that gives you the right to send children to their deaths, and deep down, you know that's exactly what you're doing if you kick us out."

Roland stared at her, shocked that a stranger whose life he had spared only a few minutes ago would speak to him so brazenly. Before he could recover, Alex pressed the attack.

"Not just these children, either. You'd be killing billions of other children, and their parents, and their siblings, friends, and neighbors. Sara is the only hope they've got, and she needs a place to sleep."

Roland's hands curled into fists at his sides, and he started to tremble with rage. "You have five seconds to get out—"

Alex took a step toward him and changed her tactics to throw him off balance. "You loved her, didn't you? Daniela. What would she say, if she were here now?"

Everyone in the room froze. Alex's heart hammered in her chest. She had made a risky gamble. Roland might do a bit of soul-searching in response to Daniela's memory being leveraged against him—or he might fly into a rage. Alex held her breath and waited to see which way the scales would tip.

Finally, all the tension seemed to leave Roland's body. He hung his head, and his shoulders slumped. No one said anything. Alex waited. She didn't want to give him the answer, she wanted him to say it.

After another long moment, he did. "Daniela would say, 'Roland Alvarez, you give this girl a place to rest right now, or I will break my foot off in your ass.'"

Tom was visibly struggling not to laugh. Fortunately, Roland wasn't looking at him.

"I usually sleep upstairs. I will go there now. Take as long as you need," Roland said quietly. With that, he began to climb the spiral staircase.

No one said anything until they were sure he was out of earshot. "How did you know he loved her?" Dylan asked.

"I didn't. I took a guess," Alex said.

"Is that what being an adult means? Acting like you know what you're doing when you really have no idea?" Sara asked, a clear tone of disapproval in her voice.

"That's about half of it," Tom said as he dropped heavily onto the couch. "Bedtime."

* * *

"That should do it," Alex said, pulling off her nitrile gloves.

Dylan, panting and sweating, took a gulp of water. "Are you done hurting me now?"

"I'm sorry, Dylan," Alex said. Dr. Atwood was glaring disapprovingly at her from across the room. Alex suspected that she was offended that Dylan had asked for Alex to properly disinfect and restitch his bite wound. She had suggested that perhaps Dr. Atwood was more qualified. That was probably true—Alex was a rehab specialist, not an ER doc—but he had insisted.

"Alex, Dylan. I can't tell you how relieved I am that you're both alright," Ethan said as he stepped into the small treatment area. "I was out picking up some supplies, I came as soon as Dr. Atwood called to tell me you'd all returned safely."

"'Safely' might be an overstatement, but we're alive, at least," Alex said.

"Yes, well. I'm glad for that. When Sara told us how you got separated, we feared the worst. She's already filled me in on the events of the past eight hours, so I'll leave you to rest for now," he said as he excused himself.

A few minutes later, Sara came around the privacy curtain as Alex was putting fresh bandages on Dylan's injury. "Hey, Dylan, feeling better?" she said. He yelped, instantly turned beet red, and pulled up the sheet to cover his bare chest. "Uh, sorry," Sara said, also blushing. "Just... come outside when you're ready, to the backyard." She reversed course and hastily left the basement.

"What are you smirking at?" Dylan grunted.

Alex shook her head. "Was I? A thousand apologies." He squinted at her, clearly not as amused as she was.

Dr. Atwood bustled over. "Dylan, I really must have a look at you now. You may be injured in ways that Dr. Warner isn't qualified to treat. No offense."

Alex shrugged. "None taken." She looked back at Dylan. "I'm going to shower, but I won't leave the house. I'm here if you need me." She patted his leg as she stood up to go.

Once Alex had showered and changed into fresh clothes, she found Tom waiting for her in the living room. "Got a minute?" he said.

"For you, I have two," she said.

"I heard you with Dylan, downstairs. Don't you think it's a little much?"

Alex looked up at him as she dried her hair with a towel. "What do you mean?"

"He's sixteen, but sometimes you talk to him like he's eight."

"You think I'm infantilizing him?"

Tom leaned against the back of a chair. "Aren't you?"

Alex frowned. "I think everyone around him is a hard-ass. You certainly are—not that I blame you. His relationship with Sara is... atypical, she's definitely the dominant one. I'm just trying to be a soft, reassuring, feminine presence—something he's had precious little of."

Tom looked like he was debating whether to say what he was thinking. Finally, he did. "Do you think now is the best time to be the mom he never had?"

Alex kept her tone assertive but not confrontational. "I think he's never needed one more. I'm not trying to replace his mother, but if I can help him feel calm and safe when his world is collapsing around him, that's not nothing, and it helps the team, too."

Tom nodded. "Fair enough."

They both stopped talking when they heard Dylan's familiar footsteps clomping up the basement stairs. When he came into the living room, he was walking so quickly that he nearly ran into Alex.

"Oh, uh, Dr. Atwood wants to talk to you," he said to her. Before Alex could respond, he slipped out the patio door and vanished into the backyard, his shoes crunching through the snow.

Alex found Dr. Atwood at her usual station in the doom room. "Ah, Dr. Warner. Is Dylan...?"

"He went outside. He's not eavesdropping."

"Good. I need to talk to you about his recent injury."

Alex felt her heart speed up. "What's wrong?"

"When Wardens come back from the Twilight with bites, cuts, or other injuries that break the skin, we generally administer a custom blend of antibiotics. We've gotten pretty good at it over the years, so these wounds rarely become infected."

Alex raised an eyebrow. "Are you sure that's why?"

"What do you mean?"

"Do you really think wounds sustained in the Twilight don't get infected because you're just that good at mixing antibiotics?"

"Do you have some other explanation?"

"I do, actually, and I'm not even the one who figured it out—Dylan did. How's Tom doing?"

"Dr. Shin checked him out a little while ago. His recent injuries will need time to heal, but there seem to be no lingering effects from the snake venom."

"Why do you think that is? Surely not because of your antibiotics."

"Of course not."

"Dylan saved Tom's life. Nothing that originates in the Twilight can come back here—including snake venom." Alex fell silent and let Dr. Atwood work out the rest for herself.

"Interesting.... Yes, I see. If that's true, then any pathogens that originate in the Twilight would also disappear when Wardens carrying them cross back over. Of course, it's a one-way street—fresh wounds can still be infected by microorganisms from our world."

"You guys have been doing this for five thousand years and never figured that out?"

"Germ theory is barely a few centuries old, Dr. Warner."

"What did you want to tell me about Dylan?"

Dr. Atwood sighed, took off her glasses, and rubbed the bridge of her nose. "Usually, when Wardens are injured in the Twilight, they return here shortly thereafter and receive immediate medical treatment. But according to what you told us, Dylan suffered that bite nearly a full day ago."

"That's right."

"Whatever bit him must have been nasty. The wound is showing signs of localized necrosis."

Alex's heart rate accelerated again, and when she spoke, her mouth felt dry. "Tissue death?"

"I suspect that, even if all harmful microorganisms were removed from his body when he came back, the damage may already have been done. I just finished some blood tests. His white count is up, but there's no sign of an active infection."

"You think it's an autoimmune response."

Dr. Atwood nodded. "Exactly. I suspect his body is attacking the dying tissue, and the healthy tissue around it as well. His immune system may not realize that the original bacteria—or whatever it was—is gone. If the damaged tissue is necrotic, and if the necrosis spreads...."

"It will kill him, unless his own immune system kills him first," Alex said, her heart sinking. "What can we do?"

"For now, I recommend aggressive antibiotics to ward off regular infections, and observation. Perhaps it's nothing, and it will eventually heal like any other wound."

"And if it doesn't?"

"Then we'll need to surgically remove the necrotic tissue and perform a skin graft."

"That would put him out of commission for days."

"But there's another reason we can't do it, not yet. Skin grafts that extensive can't be done under local anesthesia." Dr. Atwood paused, waiting to see if Alex would extrapolate.

Alex closed her eyes, trying to stay calm. "General anesthesia would send him back to the Twilight."

"Precisely. So, to summarize, if the tissue is necrotic, he can't have surgery to fix it until Sara finishes her Pilgrimage... but the necrosis, or his own immune system, might kill him before then."

Alex's voice cracked. "Did you tell him this?"

"I told him what he needed to know."

"What does that mean?"

Dr. Atwood gave her a hard look. "It means that more lives than Dylan's are on the line here. A great many more."

Alex stared right back at her. "I see. So, you'll continue to use him as your pawn and worry about his life once the game is over—if he lasts that long."

Dr. Atwood sighed. "I take no pleasure in any of this, Dr. Warner."

"You don't have to like it for it to be an asshole thing to do."

"What would you have me do? Burden his already fragile psyche with news that could very well distract him in a way that gets Sara killed? Need I remind you that we are already past the point of no return? A second team has no chance of success if you fail."

"Dylan could sit out the rest of it. Maybe you can't do the surgery yet, but he can get supportive care in the meantime."

"That would require artificially keeping him awake for three days or longer. In his condition, that alone could kill him. Sara cannot undo the binding ritual selectively, for only a single Warden—it's everyone or no one. Besides, could you finish the rest of the Pilgrimage without him?"

Alex thought about all the times they had been able to progress only because Dylan had noticed something or repaired something.

She thought about the time he'd saved her life in the house.

"No, probably not," she admitted. "Without him, we'd likely all be dead already. I know Tom and I both would be."

"It's settled, then," Dr. Atwood said. Alex was getting the impression that this woman was not used to others arguing with her once she'd made up her mind. "You're a doctor; you're more than capable of keeping an eye on him as the Pilgrimage continues. If he worsens, we can reevaluate our options at that time." She pulled a bottle of pills from the pocket of her lab coat and handed it over. "Ensure that he takes one of these, twice a day. If nothing else, they should ward off normal infections."

"Other than that, I just have to lie to him," Alex said.

"If necessary, yes. And at least for now, it's necessary."

CHAPTER TWENTY-ONE
Confession

Dylan rubbed his arms, shivering. He thought about going back for his heavy coat but decided against it; he was already out here. His hoodie would be good enough for now. He pulled the hood up to cover his ears.

"Sara?" he called. There was no sign of her. "Sara?" he yelled, louder this time.

Silence.

The forest was pretty big. Maybe she was farther out there, for some reason. He started winding his way through the trees, kicking up puffs of snow. When he thought he was more or less in the center of the twenty-acre forest, he stopped and tried again. "Sara?"

No answer.

"Sara, come on, if you're out here, say something. You're starting to w—"

Something grabbed him around the waist. Instinctively, he reached for his UMP, then remembered that he was unarmed.

"Got you," Sara said behind him. She'd taken care to grab him gently, mindful of his injuries.

Dylan turned around to face her. "What are you doing out here?"

She cocked her head. "What were you going to say?"

"Huh?"

"Just now, you were going to say something."

"Oh, uh, nothing."

Sara's breath formed a big cloud as she sighed. "Come on, tell me."

Dylan averted his eyes. "I was just going to say... that you were starting to worry me. I've been doing a lot of that lately—worrying about you." He scratched his arm self-consciously.

Sara sat down on the stump of a tree her father had chopped down for firewood earlier that winter. "I know."

Dylan sat beside her. For a time, they said nothing. They simply shared one another's company, watching their breath make clouds in the air. Dylan's leg brushed against hers, and he quickly pulled away.

Sara looked at him. "Do you remember when we were kids, how we used to play hide-and-seek out here?"

He shrugged. "Sure."

She stood up and held her right hand out to him. Dylan noticed that she had a proper cast on her left wrist now. "Play with me," she said.

He blinked. "What?"

"Come on. You hide first."

He frowned at her. "Are you serious?"

"Why not?"

She dropped her hand to her side when he stood up without taking it. "Don't you think we have more important things to be doing right now?" he said.

"At this exact moment? No, not really. Rest is important, too. We need to spend some time here and recover before we go back to the Twilight." Dylan sighed but didn't say anything. Sara put on an exaggerated pouty face, trying to make him laugh. It didn't work. "Just play a game with me," she pleaded, more quietly this time.

"No!" he snapped, suddenly angry. Surprised, Sara took a step back.

"Okay. Sorry," she said.

"No, I'm sorry," he said, more gently. "I didn't mean to snap at you, I just don't understand why you want to play hide-and-seek, all of a sudden. We're not little kids anymore."

Sara waited for him to look at her. When he did, she said, "Because...." Her voice cracked, and she cut herself off. She tried again. "This... might be our last chance."

Dylan said nothing for a long time, avoiding her gaze again. When he finally spoke, his voice was as unsteady as hers. "I know. That's why I don't want to."

Sara nodded, trying not to cry. "Okay. Let's just... go back inside then."

She turned toward the house and started trudging through the snow. He watched her go, thinking. After a moment, he closed his eyes and sighed.

Eventually, Sara realized that Dylan wasn't beside her. She turned around. There was no sign of him, except for footprints leading away from where she'd last seen him, deeper into the trees. She smiled and gave chase.

The footprints stopped at a fallen log. Sara nodded approvingly. In winter, the seeker had a distinct advantage. If he didn't want her to follow his footprints, he had to avoid creating any by leaping between logs, rocks, and snow-free patches of grass, or by swinging between low branches.

Neither was in any condition to be swinging by their arms, though. At least it leveled the playing field.

Sara spied an overturned rock and headed in that direction, crouched low, moving quietly. She wound her way through the trees, following clues as she found them, never quite sure what was a real trail and what was a fake sign meant to throw her off.

Then, she saw it—a small patch of black against the white snow. She crept closer to get a better look. It was definitely part of Dylan's hoodie, sticking out from behind a tree. Like a panther, she slunk low, taking her time, until she was right on the other side of the tree.

She jumped around it, grabbing him. "Got you!" she shouted triumphantly.

Only, she didn't have him. She had a fistful of his empty hoodie, hung over a branch.

Something moved to her right. She turned her head just in time to catch a snowball in the face. "Ugh!" she cried, sputtering as she wiped frigid snow out of her eyes.

Dylan's mocking laughter drifted away from her. By the time she could see again, he was gone.

"So, it's like that, is it?" she yelled.

"Just remember, you started this," he hollered back, from somewhere behind her.

Clearly, he had improved since her ninth birthday. Still, she knew her woods better than he did. It was time to change her tactics.

It was time for guerrilla warfare.

* * *

Dylan was getting cold. There hadn't been any sign of Sara for a long time. He'd found a hiding spot with good visibility in all directions, so he should have been able to see her if she was anywhere nearby.

After what felt like an hour, he couldn't take it any longer. He started walking back toward the house. "Sara?" he called. "Did you give up? I win if you don't catch me, you know."

No reply.

Dylan shrugged and kept walking. He could see the house through the trees now. He was a little disappointed, but a victory by default was still a victory.

Suddenly, the ground exploded beneath his feet. He yelled and tried to jump away, but he was too slow. Something grabbed his legs and pulled him to the ground. He twisted as he fell, trying not to land on his injured side.

Sara's cackling face loomed before him. "What the hell?" Dylan said, dumbfounded. Then he understood. She'd found a tarp somewhere, piled mud and snow on top of it, smoothed it all over to blend into the surrounding terrain, and wormed herself under it to wait. "What are you, a damned Moray eel?" he griped.

"Spoken like a sore loser," Sara said. "You took long enough, I was freezing my butt off under there."

"Thirty," Dylan said, staring at her with a deadly serious expression.

She frowned at him. "Thirty?"

"Twenty-nine."

"Oh!" Sara said. She giggled, scrambled to her feet, and sprinted away as Dylan counted down. When her time was up, he rose to his feet.

The prey had become the hunter.

From the back porch of the house, Ethan sipped at a mug of hot tea and listened to the laughter in the trees. He smiled to himself, glad that Sara had found a sliver of time to forget her worries.

An hour later, Dylan and Sara were sprawled on their backs in a patch of frozen grass, panting. "That last one was kind of cheating," Dylan said.

"Can't be cheating if there are no rules; we're in the big leagues now. You know, the extreme, hardcore, illegal, underground... hide-and-seek circuit."

They both collapsed into laughter again, Dylan wincing in pain as the fresh bite wound on his side flared up again. When they'd finally recovered their breath and their senses, they lay in silence for a while, watching the muted white orb of the sun climb slowly toward its zenith behind a thick blanket of gray clouds.

"How's your hand?" Dylan asked.

"It hurts, but it's tolerable now. How's your side?"

"It hurts like hell when I move wrong, but otherwise, it's not too bad."

After another long silence, Sara sat up. "Dylan, I need to tell you something." He looked over at her but stayed on his back, waiting for her to go on. She seemed to lose her nerve and picked at her cast with a fingernail.

"What is it?" Dylan said, sitting up.

Sara took a deep breath and let it out slowly. "It's about... what happened on that old clipper ship, just before you and Alex rescued us. Thanks for that, by the way." She smiled at him, but it felt weak and forced, so she let it drop.

"That's why I'm here, right?" he said.

She had to tell him. She couldn't drag him back to the Twilight again, back to that twisted hellscape of blood and pain, without telling him. She forced the words out. "I... saw you on that ship. It wasn't really you, obviously. It must have been a ghost or something, or another monster that looked like you. But it could talk, and it sounded like you. And... it said things." She trailed off, unsure how to put it.

"Sara," Dylan said softly. He put a hand on her knee and left it there for a moment. All of a sudden, he seemed to realize what he'd done and pulled it away. "You don't have to tell me this, it's obviously not something you want to talk about."

"No, I do have to tell you. I don't want to, but I have to."

He nodded. "Okay."

"You said—or rather, it said—that you were glad to be dead, so you didn't have to be around me anymore. Because only someone really evil would do what I did to you." She left out the other part.

He didn't say anything for a long time. He looked away, plucked two blades of frozen grass out of the dirt, and started idly weaving them together. Finally, he said, "I could never hate you, Sara."

"You should."

"That's ridiculous. I don't understand why you're so upset about this. That thing, whatever it was, it wasn't me, and it said whatever it said because it was trying to upset you, that's all. It was wrong."

"No, it wasn't," she said. She was surprised to find that she wasn't crying. Instead, she felt numb but not from the cold. She felt like she was outside of herself, watching the conversation from somewhere else. "The more I thought about it, the more I realized... that I don't deserve you."

"Sara—" She raised a hand to cut him off.

"I've always thought of you as my best friend, and for what it's worth, I always meant it. But now I see that my intentions didn't matter. If you really care about someone, you have to show it with your actions; thoughts and words alone don't mean much. There's a certain way that friends have to treat one another, or else they aren't really friends. What I've done to you —no one does that to a friend. The things I've put you through, the danger I've put you in—those are things you do to your worst enemy, not your best friend." She sniffled. The tears were starting to flow now.

Dylan turned to face her. "Sara, you said it yourself. You didn't have a choice, not really. If we don't do this, a lot of innocent people die."

"We always have choices, I see that now. I'm just sorry that I was too dumb to figure it out before I did this to you. It didn't have to be you. I could have picked someone else. I just selfishly wanted you with me. I never considered your safety or what you might want, not really. Deep down, I knew that I couldn't allow myself to think about it because the answer was obvious. No one would sign up for this. No one would choose this life, this terrible burden. I was born into it. The moment I was born, it was already too late for me. But this was never your life or your burden.

"When I thought you and Alex were dead, I... I thought about killing myself right then. I'd never felt so guilty in my life. Until then, I'd been telling myself this lie that I could somehow guarantee your safety, that after this was over, everything could go back to normal. But I've known all along that that was never a possibility. If you somehow don't hate me, you should. I deserve it. I would give anything to undo it, to choose someone else and leave you out of it. I'm so sorry." Sara put her face in her hands and wept quietly.

Dylan absorbed it all with an unreadable expression. When it finally seemed that Sara had no more to say, he put a hand on her back. "Sara, you said what you needed to say. Now I need to tell you something." She wiped away tears and snot with the neck of her shirt and looked toward him but not at him; she couldn't bear to meet his eyes. "If you had told me about all this ahead of time, and if you were somehow able to convince me that it was true... I would have volunteered anyway. There's nothing more important to me than knowing you're safe. I still think another copy of Tom would be a lot better at keeping you safe than I am, but even so... I'd still have been your Warden. In fact, you wouldn't have been able to stop me."

Sara stared at him in shock for a moment, then broke down in tears again. This time, she fell into his arms, unable to resist even as she berated herself for having the audacity to seek comfort from the very person she'd betrayed.

Dylan said nothing. He simply held her, and he would hold her for as long as it took for her to feel better.

That was a Warden's job, after all, as he'd come to understand it.

* * *

Once Sara and Dylan had cleaned themselves up and changed clothes, they found Tom, Alex, and Ethan in the armory. Tom was browsing the available shotguns, looking for something to replace his lost Benelli. He turned to the door when the teens entered. "Ready to get back to it?" he asked.

"Ready as anyone could be," Sara sighed. "I need a new rifle, too."

Tom picked up a solid steel shotgun that looked like it weighed twenty pounds. "Is this what I think it is?"

"If you think it's a heavily modified version of a Pancor Jackhammer, then, yes," Ethan said.

"Only a handful of these were ever built," Tom said.

"Of the original Jackhammer design, yes. There are a few master gunsmiths in Circle families around the world. When needed, they design and build weapons suited for the… unique challenges one might encounter in the Twilight."

"Give me the rundown," Tom said, studying the weapon's odd features.

"It's a bullpup 12-gauge design, so it loads from the rear. The original Jackhammer utilized preloaded cylinders, which are far too wide and bulky to carry around comfortably, so this version uses twelve-round box magazines that will fit into the pouches on your armor." Ethan pointed to various levers and switches on the gun as he discussed their functions.

"This looks like a standard magazine tube," Tom said, pointing to a long, metal cylinder affixed to the bottom of the barrel. "Why does it have two separate feed systems?"

"Are you familiar with the Keltec KSG?"

"Yeah, it has two magazine tubes. You can load two different types of ammo and switch between them freely."

"So, it is here. Because the barrel is short, the tube only holds five shells, but with twelve in the magazine and one in the chamber, that's eighteen total. Use this lever here to switch between the magazine and tube as needed. And of course, it features semiautomatic and fully automatic fire modes."

Tom rummaged around in one of the nearby ammo cans and came out with a handful of bright orange shotgun shells. "And are these also what I think they are?"

"Incendiary shells, yes. Magnesium shards that burn somewhere around four thousand degrees Fahrenheit—more than hot enough to ignite almost anything remotely flammable within about twenty meters. However, they don't produce enough recoil energy to cycle the action, so you'll have to work the bolt manually between each shot."

"I can live with that," Tom said, loading five of the orange shells into the Jackhammer's magazine tube and slotting another dozen into the shotshell holders on his new plate carrier. After that, he began loading additional magazines for the Jackhammer, some with buckshot, some with slugs.

While Tom got to know his new weapon, Sara chose a Barrett REC7 rifle similar to the one she'd lost. This one was chambered in 6.8mm SPC —superior to the 5.56 in terms of stopping power but more difficult to control and somewhat less accurate. Because some of the creatures they'd encountered had been astonishingly difficult to kill, she judged the trade-off to be a good one. For the same reason, she traded her .32 Walther for a .45-caliber STI Edge, the biggest caliber she could fire one-handed.

"Alex, Dylan, are you both comfortable with your gear? Do you want to make any changes?" Tom asked as he carefully placed plastic explosives, nonelectric detonators, and other supplies in a new backpack.

"It's probably best if I stick with the one I've gotten to know. I'm afraid that if I switch to something else, having to learn a new gun will get one of us killed," Alex said.

"Same," Dylan agreed.

"I think that's wise," Tom said. "Try these, though." He picked up a heavy ammo can and brought it over to Alex and Dylan. "These are called +P rounds. They have more gunpowder in them, so they fly faster and hit harder. That means more recoil, but you guys have had enough practice now that I think you should be able to handle it. Sara, I see you've swapped to a .45 sidearm. You should grab some of these, too."

"Alright, if you think that's best," Dylan said. He, Alex, and Sara got to work unloading their magazines and reloading them with the new ammunition. As they did so, Tom selected a Milkor MGL six-shot 40mm grenade launcher to replace his lost China Lake.

"Okay, final check. Let's make sure we aren't forgetting anything," Tom said.

"Ready," Sara said, putting her game face back on.

"Ready," Dylan said with much less confidence.

"I've got my new medic bag, freshly restocked, weapons good to go. Given the problems we had last time, I thought it would be wise to have more adrenaline on hand, so I added two more injectors to each of our kits—and one more sedative, just in case," Alex said.

"Good call," Tom said.

"How are we doing on time?" Alex asked.

Sara checked her watch before answering. "I'd say we're about on schedule, but there's no way to know exactly how much ground we have left to cover. As long as we keep up the same pace as before, we should be okay."

Ethan gave Sara a quick hug. "I love you; be careful," he said. He then leaned in closer and whispered so that only she could hear him. "I would give anything not to have to ask this of you." Sara kept her face carefully composed, showing no outward reaction.

Ethan spoke to the rest of the group. "And everyone else as well, be careful. Hopefully the worst of the Pilgrimage is behind you, and it will be less taxing from here."

"Somehow, I doubt it," Tom said.

CHAPTER TWENTY-TWO
Connection

Sara pushed open the rusted steel door leading out to the gallery deck of the lighthouse. "There you are," she said when she spotted Dylan leaning over the railing, gazing out at the dark sea. She joined him. "It's kind of pretty, if you can forget where we are," she said.

"Yeah," Dylan replied. His voice was flat and quiet.

Sara was surprised to see that the old clipper that she and Tom had boarded was moored at the dock. It hadn't been there when they'd arrived in the speedboat. Following Dylan's gaze, she saw that he was staring at it.

"That's the ship Tom and I came in on," she said. "Or tried to, before it threw us overboard."

"Mmhmm," Dylan mumbled.

"Roland said he'll lead us out of this area. He's set traps everywhere, and we'll run into them unless he shows us where they are. But after that, he doesn't want to see us again. I guess I can't blame him. I'm amazed that he let us stay here at all."

Dylan didn't say anything or look at her. He just kept staring out at the ocean.

"What's wrong?" Sara asked. She noticed that he looked pale and clammy.

He sighed. "Nothing. We should go." Before Sara could press him for more information, he pushed away from the railing and went back inside. She stayed and watched the sea a moment longer, then followed.

Everyone else was waiting for her outside the lighthouse's main door. Sara watched Dylan carefully. Over the past day or so, he had grown more confident, but now, he seemed more like he had at the beginning of the Pilgrimage—more distracted, fidgety, and inattentive.

"Everyone stay close to me, and do not open any doors or touch anything unless I tell you to," Roland said. He was carrying an old Ithaca pump-action shotgun, and he wore a long-barreled Colt Single Action Army in a belt holster under his long coat. "If you wander off and get cut in half or blown up by one of my traps, it will not be my fault."

"Understood," Tom said. "Ready when you are."

"Out of curiosity, where did that old ship come from? The one that wasn't here when we arrived yesterday," Sara said.

Roland grunted. "It comes and goes on its own schedule, whether or not anyone is aboard. Many of the vehicles around here do that."

"Good to know," Alex said.

Roland led them farther inland, through a place that reminded Sara of a waterfront industrial area. Many of the run-down buildings resembled warehouses, factories, and fish hatcheries. *A previous Maiden must have had ties to a place like this,* she thought. She wondered who that girl or woman was and what her life had been like. Had she had siblings? A crush? What had she done for fun?

What dreams and joys had she given up so that the rest of humanity might enjoy their own, blissfully ignorant of her sacrifice?

Sara shook herself out of it. There was no point thinking about such things. They passed a patch of dirt with white lilies growing in it, like those they had seen a few times already. She couldn't help but smile at the sight of something vibrant and beautiful, so rare in this twisted land of waking nightmares.

"Roland," Alex said quietly. "Do you know a man named Jacob? He's another Warden... trapped here."

Roland shook his head. "I have never seen anyone else here, until you. I rarely leave this area. There is no reason to; it is mostly safe."

"What do you do all day?" Sara said, then winced when she realized how it sounded. "Sorry, I didn't mean it like that. I was just curious."

Roland grunted. "Being alone is not so bad, I suppose. Some days I write or play an old guitar I found. Lately, I have been trying to teach myself to paint. It is... not going well. But it is something to do."

Alex smiled sadly. "Well, if you ever do run into Jacob, please don't kill him. He's a nice man, and he saved our lives once already."

"I will bear it in mind," Roland said in a low voice. He waved a hand, beckoning the rest of them to huddle around him. "Be careful. We need to cut through this alley, but it is heavily trapped. Stay close behind me and step *exactly* where I step, nowhere else."

As Sara's group fell in behind their guide, a light rain began to fall, creating pinpricks of cold on her skin. At some point while she had been lost in her thoughts, thick clouds had moved in, blanketing most of the sky. She could barely see the dirt beneath her feet darkening as the rain fell. Without the moon, there wasn't much light to see by.

At least the rain wasn't upside-down this time. That had been unnerving.

Sara rummaged around in her pocket for a glow stick, cracked it, and handed it to Roland. He accepted it with a nod of thanks. Tom and Dylan produced glow sticks of their own, brightening the small halo of soft, blue-white light around the party.

Carefully, they picked their way through the alley, taking great care to place their feet exactly where Roland showed them. A few of the traps were visible in the dim light, but most were masterfully concealed, invisible even to Tom's eye until Roland pointed them out. He hadn't been exaggerating—the alley was a deathtrap.

At the far end of the alley, they saw the results of one of the traps that had been triggered. One of the creatures with damaged faces had been cut nearly in half by an incredibly powerful spring-loaded blade. The creature's lifeless eyes stared up into the rain. Black blood had soaked deep into the dirt all around.

Roland heaved a heavy sigh at the sight and shook his head. He whispered something to himself, but the others couldn't make it out. He seemed strangely upset by the dead creature, especially in contrast to the hard, kill-or-be-killed attitude he'd displayed earlier.

"Up here," Roland said quietly. He turned the corner at the end of the alley and ducked into the building next door, a three-story warehouse with large crates piled everywhere. He ascended a rusted metal staircase in the corner, up to the top floor. Sara and her Wardens followed, weapons raised, ready for trouble.

High above the warehouse floor, a catwalk crisscrossed back and forth. Roland led them along it to the far side of the building, where there was a large opening in the wall. A heavy-duty pulley system hung from a rafter just outside the opening, the frayed rope now soaked by the rain. Sara guessed that it must be used for hauling large items to the upper floors—or that's what such a system would be used for in the normal world, anyway.

On the ground outside, dozens more of the disfigured monsters roamed around. Some walked upright, hunched over, clicking and screeching to themselves. Others loped about on all fours, reminding Sara of an unsettling documentary she'd seen about feral children. All of them had horribly damaged and disfigured faces, just like the others she'd seen so far.

Roland beckoned them to follow as he moved away from the opening. He went behind a large crate and sat on the floor, indicating with a gesture that they should do the same. "Best to wait them out," he said. "Cutters usually do not stay in one place for long. I would rather not try to sneak past them, they should move on soon."

For several minutes, no one said anything. Sara picked at her cast while Alex moved things around in her medic bag. Tom inspected his weapons. Dylan stared off into space.

Finally, Alex could stand the silence no longer. "Why did you call them

Cutters?" she asked.

Roland shrugged. "I have been here for nearly half of my life now; I had to come up with something to call them."

"But why 'Cutters?' Does it mean something?" Alex was already pretty sure that it did mean something; Roland struck her as the kind of man who had reasons for everything he did.

He gazed at her for a long moment. She thought he wasn't going to answer, but he finally did. "You said you met Daniela, so you must have seen the scars on her face."

The horrible memory once again flashed through Alex's mind. She could see on Sara's and Tom's faces that they, too, were reliving that poor woman's agonizing death. Dylan wasn't listening. "No, I didn't notice any scars," Alex said carefully.

Roland frowned suspiciously. "They are hard to miss."

Alex had done him a kindness earlier by not telling him how his love had died. She still didn't want to tell him. She realized that, if Daniela had scars on her face, they must have been obscured by the blood.

There had been so much blood.

Alex came up with a lie. "It was very dark. We couldn't see her face well."

Roland grunted, seemingly satisfied by the answer. "A few years before Daniela's Pilgrimage, she was involved in a nasty car accident. A drunk driver hit her. She barely survived. She needed extensive surgery to reconstruct her face. The surgeons did their best, but her face was so badly damaged that a perfect repair was impossible. She was very self-conscious about her scars. Of course, in my eyes, they did nothing to diminish her beauty."

Roland abruptly stopped talking. Alex could tell that he was having trouble composing himself.

After a long silence, Sara chimed in, her voice low. "She thought she was ugly. She wasn't, but she couldn't shake that perception of herself. The surgery saved her life and repaired much of the damage, but she couldn't accept her new face. These monsters—they're her monsters, born of her thoughts and fears. You called them 'Cutters' because it's a slang term for people who obsessively undergo plastic surgery. That would also explain why there were so many of them at the hospital. They're mad with rage, attacking anything on sight... just as Daniela must have been driven mad by what happened to her."

Roland gave a single nod. "You are a smart girl."

Sara laid her rifle aside and waddled over to him on her knees. Before he could react, she wrapped her arms around him. "I'm so sorry," she whispered. "Please believe that we tried our best to help her."

Alex saw the dam break behind Roland's eyes. He collapsed into tears. Haltingly, awkwardly, he returned Sara's embrace. Alex realized that he'd had no human contact for nearly two decades. The unexpected sensation of being hugged must have been overwhelming.

The others watched in silence. Even Dylan had come out of his gloom and was overcome with empathy for Roland.

Finally, Roland gently pushed Sara away. "I am sorry," he said, wiping tears from his face. "I thought she died sixteen years ago. To learn that she survived on her own all this time, and that I might have been reunited with her if only I had known to look for her.... And now I must endure her death a second time."

"You, of all people, have no need to apologize to us," Alex said, rubbing his arm gently. "I don't understand, though. These 'Cutters' are 'her' monsters—Daniela's monsters? What does that mean?"

"Oh, that's right," Sara said. "You and Dylan weren't around when Tom and I talked about this." She told them how the Twilight shifted over time to reflect the thoughts, memories, and fears of previous Maidens.

"Tell us about Daniela," Tom said, breaking his long silence.

Roland blinked in surprise. "I... do not think I can do that just now," he said.

Tom set his shotgun aside and leaned against the wall behind him. "Give it a try," he said. "I... know what it's like to lose people. I was in the army. I lost more than one friend. Sometimes, talking about the good times makes it hurt just a little bit less."

Alex had the impression that, under normal circumstances, Roland would have preferred to isolate himself and combat his grief privately. He reminded her of Tom in that way—strong and self-reliant, preferring not to involve others in his problems. But she could read some of his thoughts on his face. It was clear to her that, after sixteen years of being trapped alone in this hellish place, the comfort of other people was a balm he desperately needed.

The others listened attentively, respectfully, as Roland began to speak. "Daniela and I are from the city of Córdoba, in Argentina. We met at a football game—you Americans call it soccer, yes? In much of South America, football is life, and Argentina is no different. My brother played for one team, and her brother played for the other. I found myself sitting next to her, in the seats reserved for close friends and family of the players. If you know anything about football in South America, you know that the fans can get... passionate.

"All around us, those who knew the players were yelling at one another, divided by fierce loyalty to their respective teams. There was even a fistfight, which is not uncommon. Daniela and I both loved football, and we were supportive of our brothers, but by the end of the game, I was her Romeo, and she was my Juliet—star-crossed lovers from opposing teams whose families would never allow us to be together."

Alex couldn't help but smile at the comparison.

"Only… I never told her," Roland said, his voice breaking.

"Never told her what?" Dylan asked.

"How I felt about her. She probably knew—not much got past her—but I never put words to it."

"Why not?" Sara asked.

"For the same reason that any man fails to confess his love to a woman: simple cowardice. I thought she loved me, but I was not sure. I suppose that I feared being wrong more than I wanted to be right, so, in my youthful stupidity, I said nothing. We spent a lot of time together, as friends, and I will always be grateful for every moment I was able to share with her. After her accident, I visited her in the hospital every day until she was fully recovered, trying to reassure her that her scars meant nothing to me and that she should not be bothered by them, either.

"But fate, it seems, has a cruel sense of humor. One day, about two years after the accident, I finally worked up the courage to confess my love. I had tried many times before, but this time, I felt different—more sure of myself. I knew that this time, I would be able to tell her."

Roland fell silent for a long time, trying to get his emotions back under control. The rain drummed on the tin roof overhead, leaking through holes in places. Finally, Tom prompted him gently. "What happened?"

"I never got the chance," Roland said, his voice barely a whisper. "That night, she took us into the Twilight, and her Pilgrimage began."

Talk about horrible timing, Alex thought, her heart heavy.

"Once I got over the initial shock, and once I realized that all of this was indeed real, I decided to wait. It would do neither of us any good to be thinking about love here, in this place." Roland gestured vaguely around himself. "Such distractions would only place Daniela's life in even greater danger, and that I could not allow. Once it was over—once we were back home, safe and sound—I would tell her then. We were still young; we would have the rest of our lives together."

Once again, Roland fell silent. He buried his face in his hands. The others knew the rest of the story without needing to hear it. Somehow, Daniela had been separated from her Wardens. Somehow, the situation had seemed so dire that she'd had no choice but to reverse the binding ritual so that the next team could replace them. The details didn't seem to matter—certainly not enough for any of them to ask Roland to speak of such a horrible day. Surely, he was already reliving it in his mind.

After another long silence, Roland got up and walked back to the opening in the wall. A moment later, he returned. "They are gone," he said. "We should go."

* * *

Slowly, carefully, Roland led them around and between the buildings. It seemed to be taking forever. Tom realized that they were doing a lot of backtracking and taking many circuitous routes, undoubtedly to avoid traps altogether when possible. Along the way, they saw several more dead monsters, blown apart or viciously bisected by Roland's defenses.

"You must spend a lot of time checking and setting traps," Sara said.

"Whatever it takes to keep them away from the lighthouse. It is not like I have much else to do around here," Roland grunted.

"How much farther?" Tom asked, keeping his voice quiet.

"Not too far," Roland said. "Maybe twenty minutes, but this last area is the most dangerous of all. It is the most heavily protected. The Cutters wander into town from that way, in huge numbers." He pointed in the direction of the moon. "I put extra traps around the edges of town to stop them from getting inside the perimeter. It works, mostly. A few make it past the traps from time to time, but most of them seem to sense the danger and stay out."

The group approached another alleyway, this one a little wider than the others had been. Roland raised a hand, ordering a halt. "I call this 'death row.' You will see why," he said. "I would take you a safer way if there were one, but this close to the edge of town, there is not. This is the safest way out for a large group because it is wide, easier to maneuver. Same as before, be very careful and follow my steps exactly."

Progress through the alley was agonizingly slow. Several times along the way, Roland made them wait while he carefully disarmed a tripwire or pressure plate, then made them wait again once they'd passed it so he could rearm the device. Dylan looked to be scared and impressed in equal measure by the engineering ingenuity of the lethal traps.

About halfway through the alley, everyone stopped when they heard Tom mutter, "Ah, shit."

The others followed his gaze. He was looking up, at the roof of the building on the left. A single Cutter was perched on the edge of the roof, squatting, and chewing on something clutched in its filthy hands.

Everyone held perfectly still. There was nowhere to hide. All they could do was hope that it left before it saw them.

The seconds ticked by. All of them breathed as quietly as they could. Slowly, silently, they donned their hearing protection, just in case things got loud. Finally, after several long minutes, the creature finished its meal and rose to its feet, wiping dark liquid from what remained of its face. The people below tensed their muscles, silently willing it to turn to its left, away from them.

It turned to the right.

It was looking directly at them. It blinked once, twice. It seemed surprised, if indeed it was capable of emotion. Then, with an ear-splitting howl of fury, it hurled itself off the roof, dropping twenty feet to the ground.

Tom and Roland were in front, closest to the creature. They raised their weapons, but before either could fire, it took a single step toward them—directly into a tripwire.

A massive explosion sent a shockwave down the alley that blew the windows out of the buildings on either side. Chunks of the Cutter's putrid flesh spattered all over Tom and Roland. The concussive force of the explosion knocked most of them to the ground; only Tom managed to stay standing. Fortunately, there didn't seem to be any shrapnel in the bomb, only gunpowder or some other explosive compound. Their ears rang painfully, even though their earmuffs had dampened the noise somewhat.

"God dammit. Anyone hurt?" Tom growled, turning to check on the others.

"Nothing serious, I don't think," Alex said, quickly scanning Dylan and Sara. They seemed frightened and stunned but unharmed. She helped them get to their feet.

"We are about to have company," Roland said, groaning in pain as he pushed himself up. "We need to move fast, but do not panic, stay behind me. I still need to guide you past the rest of the traps."

As if to affirm Roland's prediction, a chorus of feral screams rose into the night.

They sounded very close.

Moving as quickly as he dared, Roland resumed disarming traps, not sparing the time to rearm them afterward. Where possible, he showed them how to step around or slide under a trap so he wouldn't have to spend precious seconds disarming it.

They were still about ten meters from the exit when the first wave of Cutters showed up at the far end of the alley, the side from which Sara's group had entered. Unaware of the danger—or perhaps heedless of it—they charged ahead, salivating and screaming.

The first one's head was taken off by a lawnmower blade rigged to a heavy spring. A few steps later, the next one stepped on a pressure plate and was brutally impaled by a rusted section of chain-link fence to which Roland had welded hundreds of long nails. A third Cutter ran into a tripwire, and the resulting explosion vaporized it.

Roland finally reached the last trap and carefully stepped over the tripwire, showing the others where it was and helping them clear it safely. Tom fired round after round of buckshot down the alley, cutting down the creatures that managed to evade the traps. Once Sara and the others were clear, he jumped over the tripwire and resumed the lead. "Which way?" he shouted at Roland, taking the opportunity to reload his Jackhammer.

"Here," Roland replied as he took off running to the left, toward a small, dilapidated building that looked like it had once been a textile workshop. He led them through it, weaving around collapsed rafters and broken furniture. Another explosion rumbled through the ground and shattered more windows as a Cutter triggered the last tripwire in the alley.

More of the disfigured creatures were assaulting the building from all sides, forcing themselves through gaps in the bent sheet-metal siding and dropping through holes in the ceiling. Underneath his controlled panic, Tom noted with satisfaction that Dylan, Alex, and Sara were doing a reasonably good job of staying cool and focused, firing only at targets that got too close or blocked their path.

"Empty!" Alex shouted, dropping a spent mag from her MPX.

"Got you covered!" Sara hollered back, shifting her aim to fire at a Cutter that was getting dangerously close to Alex. The older woman fumbled the new magazine and nearly dropped it, but after taking a deep breath to steady her nerves, she managed to load it correctly and closed the bolt, chambering a fresh round.

Just before they exited the building, a large group of Cutters dropped from the ceiling, nearly landing on Sara. In the resulting chaos, her group was scattered and separated, each fighting fiercely to carve a path through the crowd. Afraid of shooting one another, they resorted to shoving, kicking, and stabbing whenever possible.

A Cutter leaped onto Tom's back, knocking him sprawling. He'd unslung his shotgun to use it as a melee weapon, and the gun clattered away, out of his reach. He covered his neck with his hands and tried to roll onto his back, doing his best to avoid the jagged teeth gnashing at him from behind.

Eventually, Tom managed to get onto his back, but just like the Cutter he'd fought hand to hand in the village, this one was impossibly strong. He struggled to draw his sidearm, but he couldn't reach it; the creature had him pinned. Instead, he seized its throat in both hands and struggled to shove it away, at least far enough that he could reach his Magnum, or even his knife.

"Help!" someone shouted. Tom risked a glance to his right and saw that Roland had one of the creatures up against a wall, the barrel of his shotgun shoved into its chest. It was fighting fiercely, and Roland was using all his strength to keep it pinned down. Tom could see that his shotgun's action was open, and the chamber was empty. It seemed that Roland didn't want to risk trying to draw his Colt for fear that the creature would overpower him first.

"Roland! Catch!" Tom shouted. Holding his attacker at bay with his left hand, he grabbed a shell with his right and tossed it. Roland snatched it out of the air, and only then did Tom see that it was bright orange.

"Oops," Tom sighed.

In one smooth motion, Roland slapped the orange shell into the open chamber, slammed the pump forward, and squeezed the trigger.

An inferno roared out of the Ithaca's barrel, instantly setting the Cutter aflame. "Mierda!" Roland screamed as he was driven back by the heat of the unexpected conflagration. The ignited Cutter roared and began to stumble around blindly, waving its clawed hands in a vain attempt to extinguish itself. A blackened crater was growing in its chest as the white-hot magnesium shards burned away the surrounding tissue.

Roland's coat had also caught fire. He pitched to the ground and rolled around in the dirt, but the flames were tenacious. Realizing that stop, drop, and roll wasn't working, Roland wormed his way out of the coat and left it behind, escaping with only minor burns.

Finally, Tom managed to gain enough control over his assailant to reach his sidearm. He pulled it free with his right hand and thumbed back the hammer as he placed the barrel directly under the Cutter's deformed jaw. The incredibly powerful Magnum cartridge blew away half of its skull. Because he was used to the recoil, he managed to stop the gun from clocking him in the forehead but just barely. He shoved the dead creature aside and leaped to his feet, looking around to assess the situation.

Alex and Sara were nowhere to be seen. Hopefully, that meant they'd escaped the building. Dylan was backed into a corner, firing his USP wildly, without aiming. His UMP hung on its sling against his chest, the bolt locked open. Half a dozen Cutters were advancing on him, temporarily driven back by the hail of .45 slugs, but Dylan's sidearm would run empty any second now.

"Dylan! Shut your eyes!" Tom shouted as loudly as he could. Hopefully, Dylan had heard him, but Tom didn't dare wait to be sure. He yanked a flashbang from his armor, pulled the pin, and tossed it directly into the pack of Cutters.

Thankfully, Dylan squeezed his eyes shut just before the grenade detonated. A teeth-rattling *bang* shook the small building, accompanied by an intense flash of blinding white light. Even with his hearing protection, Dylan would surely be disoriented, so Tom needed to move quickly. He retrieved his shotgun and charged into the mass of Cutters, kicking them aside as they flailed about, temporarily blinded and deafened.

"Time to go!" Tom shouted. He grabbed Dylan's hand and pulled him back through the creatures. Dylan was stumbling, barely able to walk. Even though he'd closed his eyes, his vision was still somewhat impaired, and the assault on his eardrums had probably affected his equilibrium as well. Across the room, Roland had found a moment to reload his shotgun and was doing his best to thin the herd.

A moment later, Tom, Dylan, and Roland managed to force their way out of the building, back into the cold rain. Slowly but surely, Dylan's vision and hearing were returning to normal, and he was able to let go of Tom's hand. They ran on, following Roland, trusting that he knew the best path to safety.

"Dylan, where's your sidearm?" Tom shouted.

Dylan's right hand went instinctively to the holster on his thigh, finding it empty. "I... must have dropped it," he said.

Tom bit back a reprimand. Before he could tell Dylan to reload his UMP, an ear-splitting scream rang out from somewhere up ahead.

"That sounded like—" Tom said.

"Sara!" Dylan shouted. He broke into a sprint, overtaking Roland within a heartbeat, headed for the next building.

Tom glanced back and quickly weighed his options. There were still dozens of Cutters right behind them. If Sara was in trouble, she would be in even more trouble if they brought this horde right to her.

"Go!" Tom shouted to Roland, his mind made up. "I'll handle these!"

Without waiting to see if Roland would comply, Tom turned to face the advancing horde. He flicked the selector switch on the Jackhammer to full auto and shouldered the weapon, bracing for the immense recoil. He depressed the trigger and held it, the heavy shotgun bucking hard against his shoulder. The steel frame helped to dampen the recoil somewhat, but firing the weapon on full auto was still unpleasant, and it was difficult to control. Even so, it was necessary—he had many targets and little time.

Within the span of two heartbeats, the twelve-round magazine was empty, and half of the Cutters were down. He dropped the empty mag, letting it fall into the mud as he grabbed a fresh one and slammed it home. In a blink, the second mag was empty. He quickly counted—five targets were still up, but they were close. He didn't have time to reload again, and he dared not use the grenade launcher or the incendiary rounds at this range.

Tom dropped the Jackhammer, letting the sling catch it. He drew his revolver and, realizing that he couldn't spare the time to cock the hammer, committed to the heavy, double-action trigger pull. The .460-caliber bullet, nearly as thick as a Chapstick tube, demolished a Cutter's face, and it dropped like a sack of bricks, a burst of gore and bone fragments spraying high into the air. He fired three more times, emptying the Magnum as quickly as he could.

Each shot hit true, but that still left one target standing, and it was about to be right in his face.

Tom tossed the revolver aside, snatched his new knife from its sheath, and rammed it upward, hard, in a tightly controlled thrust. The heavy blade slammed through the Cutter's throat just as it reached for him.

The blade must have been long enough to pierce the creature's brain because it went limp instantly. Tom wrenched his knife free as the dead weight fell to the side. Panting with exertion and fear, he wasted no time. He sheathed his knife, retrieved his Magnum, and quickly reloaded both guns. For the moment, the path behind was clear.

Tom ran to the building where Dylan had gone. He wasn't sure if he had heard any more screams or gunfire; he'd been too focused on his own fight.

He rounded the corner of the building and nearly ran into Roland, who was standing just outside the open door, staring inside, his mouth halfway open. In the dim moonlight filtering in through the building's windows, Tom saw a scene unfolding that took a moment to understand.

A Cutter had Sara by the throat, with her back pressed against the wall. Sara had her knife in her right hand, but the creature had one hand clamped over her wrist, stopping her from using the weapon. Sara's other hand was desperately trying to shove away the monster, but it was far stronger, and she was quickly losing the struggle. Within moments, its razor-sharp teeth would find her throat.

Dylan, already halfway across the room, dived forward and hit the Cutter from the side like a truck. They tumbled across the floor, with Dylan coming out on top. Screaming in primal fury that shocked even Tom, he brought his UMP up to the creature's face and squeezed the trigger.

Nothing happened. He'd never reloaded it.

Tom had never thought he would see Dylan so pissed. Even from all the way across the room, he could see how red Dylan's face was, and he could see the veins bulging in his neck. Dylan furiously hurled the empty gun aside and began pummeling the Cutter's face with his fists, screaming incoherently. Tom could see that Dylan's knife was still in its sheath on his belt, but he didn't bother drawing it. He was lost in his rage.

Roland took a step forward, but Tom reached out to stop him. "I've seen this before," Tom said. "Just... let it play out. You don't want to be in Dylan's way right now." Roland looked unconvinced, but Tom gave him a nod of reassurance. He glanced around the building and back outside; he could see no other threats.

Dylan wasn't especially big or strong, but adrenaline and rage were powerful steroids, and he had plenty of both. Red and black blood flew from Dylan's knuckles and spattered the wall behind him as he laid into the Cutter over and over. The creature that had attacked Sara was still alive, but its movements were slowing, becoming jerkier.

Finally, it went still, but Dylan wasn't done. He kept punching, smashing its face to mush with his bare hands, his chest heaving. "Fucking die, you fuck! Stay away from Sara! Die!" he screamed, his voice hoarse.

Sara was frozen, her eyes wide, her mouth open. Her knife fell from her hand and clattered to the floor. She seemed even more stunned than Tom was.

Finally, Dylan rose to his feet, his arms and legs visibly shaking. His hands, face, and chest were coated in blood, some of it his. He aimed a final kick at the Cutter's liquefied skull, missed, and collapsed to the floor, exhausted.

"What in the hell...," said a voice behind Tom and Roland. They turned to see Alex. She must have witnessed the last part of Dylan's rampage.

"Alex, are you okay?" Tom asked, looking her up and down for injuries.

"A few scrapes, nothing major," she said distractedly, trying to look over Tom's shoulder at Sara and Dylan. "A pack of them were chasing me, but I lost them." Gently but firmly, she shoved her way past Tom to check on the teens.

"Dylan...," Sara said. She seemed at a loss for words. She'd fallen to her knees beside him, and she was holding his head in her lap. He was panting heavily, too drained to move. Sara glanced up as Alex approached. "Dylan, you're hurt. Let Alex take a look at you."

He said nothing, nor did he resist when Alex gently pushed Sara aside so she could examine Dylan's injuries. Tom came up beside her, slowly, so as not to startle Dylan.

Alex glanced up at Tom. "I think he's okay, physically, anyway. Lots of cuts and bruises, maybe a broken finger, but nothing immediately life-threatening. What happened?"

"That thing... it had Sara," Tom said quietly, pointing to the barely recognizable remains of the Cutter.

"Oh... I see," Alex said.

With a groan, Dylan sat up, blinking rapidly. He looked like he was waking up from a bad dream. Sara was still on her knees a few paces away, watching him. "Dylan, are you okay?" she said, her voice trembling.

At the sound of her voice, Dylan seemed to come more fully awake. He scrambled over to Sara and threw his arms around her, hugging her tightly. Her rifle was mashed into his chest; it must have been uncomfortable, but he didn't seem to care.

Dylan was sobbing freely. Sara looked like a deer in the headlights. After a delay, she wrapped her arms around him. "It's okay," she said. "I'm okay."

Dylan said nothing. He only continued to cry, his face buried in her shoulder. Tom and Alex looked at one another, sharing a wordless mixture of emotions.

Roland spoke softly from his position in the doorway. "I understand that this is... a difficult time, but we should get going. It is still not safe here."

"You're right," Alex said quietly. "Dylan, honey, we need to go. Come on, Sara and I will help you."

Tom turned to face Roland. The question he'd been about to ask evaporated from his mind when he saw the enormous black shape filling the doorway behind their guide.

"Roland!" Tom shouted, instinctively reaching out a hand. Seeing the fear in Tom's eyes, Roland turned to see what was behind him.

He never had a chance.

A featureless, amorphous mass folded around him, like thick oil. Within seconds, Roland was completely engulfed. The massive blob squirmed its way into the room, sliding across the floor, picking up bits of debris as it went. Those, too, disappeared inside it. A moment later, it stopped and began to shake itself violently.

Roland's skull, picked clean of all flesh and muscle, emerged from the ooze and clattered to the floor, along with several more bones.

"Holy fucking god," Alex whispered.

Sara and Dylan could only stare in shock.

"Run," Tom said.

CHAPTER TWENTY-THREE
Manifestation

Dylan crashed through the window at the far end of the large room, glass shards flying everywhere. He yelped as the sharp edges cut his arms and face. He slammed into the ground on his injured side, screaming in agony when the pain flared anew. The frigid rain had intensified to a downpour, soaking his clothes almost instantly.

He'd barely evaded the blob thing. It slammed into the window frame a fraction of a second too late to catch him, absorbing glass shards and splintered wood into itself. Without slowing, it began to ooze itself up and over the bottom edge of the window, single-minded in its pursuit of prey.

Dylan had never been so badly injured in his life. He mentally shoved the pain aside and forced himself to get up. Blood ran down his forehead and into his eyes. He had to keep running. He'd seen what the blob had done to Roland.

From somewhere behind him, he heard the rapid *boom* of Tom's automatic shotgun. Glancing back over his shoulder, he could see small bits of black ooze spraying in all directions. Tom's shots were hitting the thing, but they were having no effect. It simply absorbed the lead pellets just as it had absorbed everything else it touched.

Suddenly, the blob burst into flames. Tom must have fired one of his incendiary rounds. The magnesium shards were more than hot enough to burn in the rain, but even so, the flames sputtered and went out mere seconds later as folds of black goo smothered them.

Nothing seemed to be working.

"Hey! Over here!" Alex shouted. Dylan looked to his right as he ran with everything he had left. Alex was sprinting toward him, but she was shouting at the blob. Dylan realized that she was trying to get it to target her instead of him. He tried to yell at her, to tell her not to put herself in danger, but he was so exhausted and out of breath that he couldn't make any words come out. He knew that he wouldn't be able to run from this thing for very long.

At least it wasn't going after Sara.

That thought gave him a small but desperately needed burst of fresh stamina. He reached for his UMP, intending to pepper the blob with .45 slugs in case it needed extra encouragement to stay focused on him.

His UMP wasn't there. In a flash of cold panic, he remembered that he'd hurled it aside to beat the Cutter to death, and he hadn't retrieved it. He still had his knife and a few grenades, but other than that, he was unarmed.

If the ball of black ooze somehow didn't kill him, Tom would.

Dylan ignored the burning pain in his chest that commanded him to stop running. He cut between buildings at random, changing directions as often as possible, hoping to lose his pursuer in the labyrinth of alleyways. At some point, he lost sight of Alex—the blob had gotten between them and cut her off.

At the last possible instant, he saw a glimmer of moonlight reflecting off something metallic in front of him, at knee height.

A tripwire.

He couldn't stop in time. Instead, he flung himself forward, diving awkwardly over the tripwire, once again slamming into the ground hard. The bite wound in his side once again roared with red-hot pain. Dimly, he wondered if the stitches were still intact. He didn't see how they could be.

He wondered how much blood he was losing.

He was shocked to see the blob closing fast. It was less than twenty paces behind him.

It was going to hit the tripwire.

Scrambling to his feet, Dylan took off, heedless of further traps. There was no time to look for them. He needed to get clear of the explosion.

He succeeded—mostly. He'd only made it ten steps when the trap went off behind him. The shockwave once again threw him to the ground. His head slammed into the dirt, and a wave of nausea roiled through him as his vision dimmed. He struggled not to throw up.

For the briefest instant, he considered giving up. He could just lay there, and in a few seconds, the ooze would roll over him and digest him—or whatever it had done to Roland. Even if it hurt, it would be over in a few seconds.

No. Then it would go after Sara.

With a groan, he rolled onto his back and looked down the alley. He was surprised to see that the explosion had destroyed the blob. Small orbs of black ooze were splattered across the ground and the walls of the surrounding buildings. Those stuck to vertical surfaces slid downward slowly, like milk leaving trails on the side of a glass.

Dylan panted, trying to catch his breath. Ever so slowly, the nausea faded, and his vision returned to normal. His head still throbbed painfully.

At first, he thought he was imagining it. He stared hard at the black ooze, watching. No, he hadn't imagined it. The pieces were pulling themselves back together.

"Motherfucking shit," Dylan wheezed, once again struggling to get to his feet. He had to grab a nearby dumpster to pull himself up.

Somewhere off to his left, he heard automatic gunfire. Multiple people were shooting—Alex and Sara for sure, maybe Tom, too. Whatever they were shooting at, it wasn't the blob. The shots were too far away, and buildings were in between.

That meant something else was trying to hurt Sara.

One thing at a time, Tom's voice said in his head. *Be aware of secondary threats, but don't let them distract you. Deal with the threat that's right in front of you first.*

Dylan turned and limped away, no longer able to run. He wasn't sure how long it would take for the blob to reform itself. Probably not long. The alley ran straight for another fifty paces, then turned sharply to the left. Dylan stopped when he rounded the corner, fresh panic constricting his chest.

A ten-foot fence blocked further passage. The gate was wrapped in a heavy chain, locked by a thick padlock. The fence was topped with razor wire.

Dylan quickly considered his options. He figured he had ten, maybe twenty seconds to do something. There was no way through the gate. That left climbing. If he had time to be careful, he could probably get over the fence with only minor cuts, but he didn't have time, and he'd already lost a lot of blood. If he tried to climb the fence quickly enough to get away from the blob, he'd surely cut himself to ribbons and bleed out within minutes.

The only way out was back down the alley, the way he'd come. He limped back around the corner, hoping that the relentless ooze hadn't yet reformed itself.

That hope was dashed immediately. The blob was whole, and it was rolling right toward him. There was no way past it—it filled nearly the entire width of the alley. Dodging around it would be impossible.

Dylan gritted his teeth in pain and frustration, then hobbled back to the fence. His heart felt like it was hammering at two hundred beats per minute. He put his back against the fence and pulled out his two fragmentation grenades, holding one in each hand.

"Come on, you son of a bitch," he growled.

* * *

"What in the holy hell is that?" Alex stammered, temporarily frozen in shock.

"A threat," Tom replied coolly. "Put it down." He and Sara had caught up to Alex in the maze of buildings just after she'd lost sight of Dylan—and just in time to see yet another walking nightmare.

At a glance, it didn't look like much of a threat. It resembled a petite, emaciated, filthy woman with tangled black hair and empty eye sockets. It was naked, and its spine was horribly deformed, forcing it to walk with its torso nearly parallel to the ground. Its wrists were bound by heavy iron shackles linked by a short chain. The rivets in the shackles were mushroomed out, locking the restraints permanently in place.

Although it looked like a small, harmless woman, Tom, Alex, and Sara knew better. It radiated an unmistakable aura of malice.

Tom fired, emptying an entire magazine of buckshot into the creature in the blink of an eye. Nearly all the pellets struck flesh, the incredible force hammering the monstrosity to the ground. Its right arm was torn clean off, spraying bright blue blood and bits of diseased flesh everywhere.

"Shit, I'm out of buckshot," Tom said. He didn't sound too worried, seemingly convinced that his target was down for the count.

But in a flash, it was on its feet, shrieking in rage. Within the span of two heartbeats, a new, shriveled arm erupted from the damaged socket, fully formed. With the new arm, the creature grabbed its old one, now dangling from the shackles, and pulled with tremendous force, ripping it free. The severed hand fell to the ground.

The creature shoved the shattered end of its own forearm bone deep into its torso and let out another piercing scream. Along with the scream came a shockwave of light, heat, and pressure so strong that Tom, Alex, and Sara all had to take a step back or be knocked over. Even at twenty paces, the heat was significant, like having one's face too close to an open oven.

The monster ripped the bone back out of its chest, now with something long and misshapen affixed to the end of it. It took the others a moment to understand what it was.

Somehow, the creature had generated enough heat within its own body to melt Tom's buckshot into a solid, elongated mass, which was now welded to the broken bone, forming a misshapen but nonetheless razor-sharp blade.

In less than five seconds, it had made a sword, using its own arm bones as the hilt.

"Fire and fall back!" Tom yelled. "Aim for the head!"

Alex and Sara complied, walking backward to get some distance as they fired short, controlled bursts. Tom joined in with his Magnum, letting the empty Jackhammer hang on its sling.

The creature's head snapped back over and over from the repeated impacts, but still, it charged forward with frightening speed. In short order, half of its head was blown away. Halting its advance briefly, it rammed a fist into the gaping wound, and another burst of light and heat flooded the alleyway. With a bloodcurdling howl, it ripped a tennis-ball-sized lump of red-hot lead from its skull and hurled it straight at Alex.

She tried to step aside, but she wasn't fast enough. The heavy mass struck her in the neck. It only made contact for a fraction of a second, but even that was long enough to burn her. She let out a choked scream and dropped her MPX, both hands flying to her throat. She coughed and gasped, struggling to breathe. Another inch to the left, and it probably would have crushed her trachea.

"Alex!" Sara cried, reaching out toward her, wanting to help but unsure what to do.

"Get her out of here and find Dylan," Tom said. "I'll handle this."

The creature was already sprinting toward them again, its macabre sword held low at its side. Tom holstered his Magnum and spun the MGL around on its sling, assuming a firing stance. The weapon held six 40mm high-explosive grenades in a large cylinder, and it could be fired as quickly as one could pull the trigger.

Tom emptied the launcher in less than two seconds.

A hail of grenades impacted the ground just in front of the creature. Two struck it directly in the chest. The resulting chain of explosions was catastrophically loud. A rush of hot wind blew past Tom, but he was far enough away not to be in any real danger.

Wasting no time, he opened the weapon's cylinder and started pulling out the empty casings, tossing them aside. He then gave the empty cylinder a hard spin to rewind the spring and rapidly loaded six fresh rounds. By the time he reshouldered the weapon, once again ready to fire, the smoke had mostly cleared.

His jaw dropped at what he saw. He'd been expecting—or maybe just hoping—that nothing would remain of the creature but blue paste and a handful of chunks. Instead, all four of its limbs had been blown off and were already replaced by fresh ones. Each of its dismembered limbs lay on the ground, the exposed ends of long bones blasted into sharp spears. Moving with unbelievable speed, the creature began scooping its limbs off the ground and hurling them like javelins.

Tom barely managed to drop to the ground in time. Two razor-sharp femurs slammed into a dumpster behind him with enough force to pierce the metal. A third spear shattered a nearby window, and the last sailed far down the alleyway. Thankfully, Alex and Sara were already gone.

This is not going well, Tom thought. He'd only brought twelve 40mm rounds; six were gone, and they'd accomplished nothing. There was no point wasting the remaining six, especially because he was also running low on everything else. He decided to run.

Before he could get up, the monster screamed again, bent its legs, and reached the roof of a nearby building in a single jump. Tom blinked in surprise. It was a two-story building—easily a twenty-foot standing vertical jump. It sprinted away, leaping between rooftops.

Tom scrambled to his feet and took off, following Alex and Sara's tracks in the mud. Somewhere to his right, off in the distance, he heard one explosion, then another a few seconds later. They sounded like frag grenades, not Roland's traps.

It was too much, and it was all happening too fast. Most of the creatures they'd encountered so far had at least been easy to kill or easy to avoid, but some—the Ouroboros, the Stalker, and now the black ooze and the indestructible woman—were much, much tougher and more dangerous. It seemed like the more progress they made, the more the Twilight threw at them.

Tom wasn't sure they would make it if the stakes got much higher.

He silently reprimanded himself as he ran, following the tracks in the mud. Hundreds of people throughout history had pulled this off, and most hadn't even had the benefit of guns. He couldn't imagine trying to do this with swords and plate armor. He tried to focus on the advantages they had rather than waste energy wishing that the Pilgrimage were easier.

One thing at a time, though. Even if the four of them were together, they could fight neither the blob nor the indestructible woman—certainly not both at the same time. They needed to regroup, escape their pursuers, leave the area, and make a new plan.

Tom rounded another corner, finally leaving the maze of buildings and emerging into a larger, more open area. His stamina was flagging, and his knees were threatening to give out. Once again, he wished he were twenty years younger. About fifty meters ahead, he saw a single, large building, with nothing beyond it but steep hills and the rocky walls of a canyon. This must be the edge of town, roughly where Roland had been leading them.

Sara, Alex, and Dylan were at the building's front door. Alex was struggling to pry it open with a crowbar. Dylan didn't look good; he was sitting on the ground with his back propped against the wall, and Sara was pressing a rain-soaked bandage against his thigh. Even at this distance, Tom could see that Dylan was covered in blood.

Just as Tom reached them, Alex gave a strangled cry of rage and threw all her weight against the crowbar. With a screech of protest, the rusted latch bolt snapped, and the door scraped open a few inches. Tom helped her force it open enough for everyone to squeeze inside. He went last and pulled the door closed behind them. He locked the deadbolt, hoping it would hold if something tried to get in.

They all panted in silence for several minutes, beyond exhausted. They'd been sprinting or fighting nonstop since that first Cutter had spotted them in the alleyway. That had to have been half an hour ago.

"Dylan," Alex finally managed to say. "Are you hanging in there?"

"Yeah," he croaked back. "Somehow. Everything hurts so bad, and I feel weak and dizzy."

Tom moved to a small, dirty window close to the door and looked outside. The rain was coming down in sheets, but he saw no sign of either the blob or the woman. "I don't want to jinx it, but I think we're okay for now," he said. "I don't see or hear anything."

He took a moment to look around more carefully. They were in some kind of reception area. The dirty linoleum floor was covered in trash and broken furniture. There was a long desk with several typewriters and old rotary phones. A double door led farther back into the building.

"Dylan needs a lot of patching up. A blood transfusion wouldn't hurt, either. He should be okay, but I need time," Alex said, keeping her voice calm so as not to worry him further.

Tom nodded. "Do it," he said. "Sara and I will keep watch."

CHAPTER TWENTY-FOUR
Revelation

Alex shook her head and sighed. There was no doubt about it: Dylan's bite wound was getting worse. It had grown from the size of a tennis ball to the size of a softball. The tissue was black in a half-inch border all around the edges, and Dylan showed no reaction when she pinched it, confirming her suspicion that the nerves in that area were dead.

She recalled from her medical school textbooks that one in five people with necrotizing fasciitis died, even with treatment. Death rates were much higher among those who weren't treated promptly. Dylan didn't have necrotizing fasciitis, but dead tissue was never a good thing, especially when it was spreading.

"How's it look?" Dylan asked. He was lying on his left side, facing away from her. Alex was glad for that because she wasn't a very good liar. Her face usually gave her away.

"It's... hard to tell," she said, choosing her words carefully.

Dylan looked over his shoulder at her. "Will I be okay?"

She turned away from him and started rummaging through her bag, looking for an excuse to avoid eye contact. "I'm sure you'll be fine, honey. You're on some good drugs, they just need time to work."

She was not at all sure of that.

Alex busied herself applying fresh bandages to Dylan's injuries. Once she'd finished, she helped him put his shirt and armor back on. Sara, who had been keeping watch out the front window, walked over to them. "How's he doing?" she asked, kneeling beside Dylan. His eyes were closed, but he wasn't asleep—if he were, he would have left the Twilight.

"Better, but I've had to give him low-dose stimulants to keep him awake," Alex said, wiping sweat from her forehead. It had taken several hours to treat all his wounds and transfuse two units of blood. "What he needs now is real sleep, and lots of it. Of course, that's not an option."

Sara placed her hand gently on Dylan's forearm. His eyes fluttered open. His face, neck, and arms were covered in cuts and bruises, a few of which had needed stitches. His right cheek was badly swollen. He looked awful— except for the smile that he showed only to her. "Hey," he said, his voice cracking.

"Dylan, it's time for your pills," Alex said, producing the bottle Dr. Atwood had given her. "Take one now, then you hang onto the bottle. Remember to take one every twelve hours. I'm especially worried about infections, because... well." She gestured around at the filthy lobby. "I took extra care to keep everything sterile, but this is hardly an ideal setting for invasive medical procedures."

Dylan sat up, shook one pill into his hand, and choked it down.

"How are you feeling?" Sara asked.

"About 30 percent less awful," he said with a weak smile. He turned to Alex. "Thanks for fixing me up."

She smiled back, positive that Dylan would see right through her and realize that she was lying to him. He didn't. "Anytime," Alex said. She rose to her feet and began repacking her medic bag.

Tom came around the corner and sat down next to them. "Feeling better?" he asked. Dylan nodded and wiggled his hand in a "more or less" gesture. "Good," Tom said. "Alex, how about you? That burn on your neck looked nasty."

"It's not as bad as it looks," she said. "I put some burn cream on it. It'll heal up eventually. I'm just glad I didn't get my throat crushed."

"Me, too," Tom said. "How are the little ones?"

"Sara has some new cuts and bruises, nothing too serious. Dylan is in rough shape, but he should be okay to carry on now, as long as he takes it easy."

Tom scratched his beard. "Not sure that will be an option."

"What were those two things, anyway?" Dylan asked. He'd briefly glimpsed the shriveled creature as it fled across the rooftops but hadn't gotten a good look at it.

"I think we should talk about that before we move on," Tom said. "I know we're always on a time limit, but intel is important. We should know as much as possible about the things that are trying to kill us."

"How are we supposed to learn about them? It's not like we can send spies into their camp, or whatever you military guys do," Alex said, sitting down next to Dylan after finding a relatively clean spot on the floor.

Tom grunted something resembling a laugh. "No, but I've learned something important from Sara these last few days—something I think past Maidens and Wardens may have overlooked." Sara waited to see what Tom would say, her expression unreadable. Dylan slowly shifted into a new position, wincing in pain with every movement.

Tom went on. "While Alex was fixing up Dylan, I was doing some thinking about everything we've seen and done since we first came here. At first, I thought this place didn't make any sense, that everything was just random chaos and evil, with no rhyme or reason. But I don't think that anymore."

Alex raised an eyebrow. "You're saying that this nightmare world... makes sense?"

Tom nodded. "In a way, yeah. I think this place does have natural laws and rules. We may not know what all of them are, and they may not be the same as the laws and rules of our world, but they exist. Some of what I've been thinking about isn't directly related to the monsters, and I know we're on a time limit, so I'll get to the point. Broadly speaking, the monsters we've encountered fall into one of two types or categories. Has anyone else noticed that?"

The others thought it over for a minute. Finally, Dylan said, "Well, some of them are unique, and much, much more dangerous than the others. I guess you could think of the two types as 'regular' and 'super' monsters."

Tom gave Dylan a brief round of applause. "Exactly."

"Okay, but how does that help us?" Sara said.

"Where do the monsters come from?" Tom prompted.

"They manifest here based on the perceptions and fears of past Maidens, we've established that already," Alex said.

"All of them?" Tom asked.

Alex made a face. "Yes?" she said, after some hesitation.

Tom shook his head. "I don't think so."

"You could just tell us what you're thinking instead of dragging it out," Sara said.

"I could, but I want you to work this out on your own. I want to know if you come to the same conclusion I did, without me telling you the answer ahead of time. If you do, that would more strongly support my theory."

"Well, I'm trying to think about which monsters we've seen most often. That would definitely be the Cutters," Dylan said. Tom nodded his agreement.

"And according to Roland, they're manifestations of Daniela's distorted image of herself," Alex said.

"Which means the Cutters didn't exist before she came here," Sara added.

Again, Tom nodded, and again, he offered a gentle prompt. "What about other monsters we've seen, those that are less common? Excluding the super monsters, for now."

"Well, there were the spiders in the mines, we only saw them there," Sara said. She bit her lip, thinking. "Plus, the living trees in the forest, and the...

tongues, in the mountain."

Alex snapped her fingers. "Sara, you said that, over time, certain places in the Twilight fade away and are replaced by places related to Maidens who have been here more recently. So, it stands to reason that the same would be true of the creatures. The tongues, spiders, and tree-things only appeared once each because they're born from the fears of Maidens who came here long ago—before Daniela."

"Right, those Maidens' influence on the Twilight is fading as time passes," Dylan said, poking the inside of his cheek with his tongue as he worked it all out.

Tom smiled grimly. "Now, let me add another question to the pile: What if Maidens aren't the only ones who can influence the Twilight?"

Alex blinked in surprise. Sara frowned, and Dylan rubbed his chin. Tom could see the wheels turning in each of their heads, especially Dylan's. *He does love to figure things out*, Tom thought.

Alex stood up and started pacing, hands clasped loosely behind her back. She muttered to herself, too quietly for the others to hear. Finally, she turned back to them and said, "The Maidens have the greatest influence on the Twilight because they're closely connected to it. They spend their whole lives preparing to come here. They learn some of its rules, they learn rituals to bind Wardens and cross the veil, who knows what else. But they aren't the only ones who influence the Twilight."

"Wardens come here, too," Dylan said softly.

"Therefore...," Tom prompted.

"Some of the monsters could be connected to Wardens," Sara said.

Dylan shot to his feet, surprising the others. In his condition, it must have hurt him to stand up so quickly, but he showed no pain on his face, only the shock of sudden comprehension. "*We* created the strongest monsters, the super monsters. If a person's influence on the Twilight fades with time, what could be stronger than the influence of people who are here now?"

A stunned silence filled the room.

"I think we're all on the same page now," Tom said. He didn't sound pleased about being right.

Alex shook her head in disbelief. "It sounds like it makes sense, but if this cycle has been repeating for five thousand years, surely someone would have figured this out before now." She cast a pointed glance at Sara as though awaiting confirmation.

Sara was silent for a long time. No one rushed her; she looked deep in thought. Finally, she said, "Maybe. I don't know. Most of what I learned about the Twilight was very broad and general. I did study written accounts of past Wardens, but I always thought their words seemed...

edited, like chunks of text were missing or changed. I asked my father about it once, and he said there's far too much information for any one person to take in, so the Circle leaders periodically abridge material, leaving only the most important parts. If Tom's right about where the monsters come from, and if we're not the first ones to figure it out, the Circle leaders must have thought it wasn't important enough to tell us about."

Tom frowned, suspicion darkening his face. "It seems pretty important to me. Learning what these creatures are and where they come from can only help us kill or avoid them more effectively. The more effective we are, the better your odds of finishing the Pilgrimage."

Sara shrugged. "I would agree. Like I said, I don't know what I wasn't told, or why."

"Speaking of where the super monsters come from—I think we should talk about that, too," Alex said. Tom said nothing, but the expression on his face suggested that he had a theory of his own. He rolled his hand, inviting Alex to continue. "The first super monster we ran into was the Stalker, in the house in the forest. Then the giant snake outside the mining town, the Ouroboros. After that, Tom and Sara ran into the Stalker again outside the mine."

"And just now, with the black slime and the naked woman, at the same time," Sara finished.

Dylan's eyes went wide when he heard Sara say "naked woman."

"Did all of those incidents have anything in common?" Tom said.

After another long silence, Alex sighed and spoke so softly that the others could barely hear her. "Strong negative emotions."

Sara looked at her. "Huh?"

"None of us are having a good time here, obviously," Alex said. "But in that house, when we entered that dark room, I could tell something was very wrong. And when the lights came up, and we saw what had happened to Daniela...."

"That was a pretty shitty feeling for all of us, I imagine," Tom agreed.

"Especially me," Sara said, picking at her cast again. "I didn't say anything because... because I'm supposed to be in charge of this whole thing. I'm supposed to know what I'm doing. Outside the house, when Tom was so mad at Dylan for pulling him into that mud pit—for just a second, I thought Tom might kill my best friend, or at least hurt him. That was the first time I really started to doubt myself, to feel like I was in a situation far beyond my ability to control. I might have looked calm on the outside, but I wasn't. I was positive that I was about to get all of you killed."

"So... what? That thing, the Stalker—it's *your* monster? Your negative emotions created it, or summoned it?" Dylan said, scratching his head.

"Maybe," Sara said, shrugging.

"Think about the second time we saw it," Tom said, keeping his voice gentle.

"Outside the mine... when I was hating myself and wanting to die because I thought I'd gotten Alex and Dylan killed," Sara said. A single tear trailed slowly down her face, tracing a clean path through the grime.

Tom laid a hand on her shoulder. "I think the giant snake is on me," he said.

"At Sara's house, the first night, when you and I stepped outside to discuss Ethan's offer, you told me you hated snakes," Alex said.

"That's right," Tom said. "But I think there's more to it than that. I don't think my fear of snakes, by itself, is strong enough to create a monster that dangerous."

"So, you were feeling some other intense negative emotion at the time?"

Tom sighed. "I was thinking about how much I don't want to be here. I was wishing I was at home, with my dog, having a beer and watching a movie, or reading a book, or something. I was resenting Sara for dragging me into this."

"I don't blame you," Sara whispered, her voice trembling slightly.

"But then I realized that the fact that I don't want to be here doesn't matter. I have to be here. Whether I agreed to it or not, this is my duty. Sara needs me—all of humanity needs me. I can't turn my back on that responsibility."

"That naked woman—the 'Prisoner,' if we have to call it something—I think that one might be my fault," Alex said. "When that black slime thing killed Roland, all I could think about was how his death was my fault. I talked him into letting us stay at the lighthouse. I talked him into guiding us out of town. If not for me, he wouldn't have been out here, and he'd still be alive."

No one asked where the black ooze had come from. Only one of them hadn't yet claimed a monster of their own.

"Dylan, you've been distracted since we left the lighthouse. What's on your mind?" Alex asked.

"We need to know. It could end up being the difference between life and death for one of us, or all of us," Tom added.

Dylan heaved a sigh. "I was just thinking about my mom. She loved the water. She loved to sail, water-ski, and jet-ski, even though she wasn't very good at any of it. We were on the ocean so long, I couldn't help but start thinking about her. And... how I was never able to find out what happened to her. No matter how hard I tried, I was never good enough."

Dylan hung his head in shame, unable to go on. Sara gently rubbed his back, offering some small comfort.

* * *

After a brief trip back to Sara's house to refill ammunition and replace Dylan's lost gear, they were getting ready to move out. "Dylan, how did you get away from the slime thing?" Sara asked.

"Yeah, that would be good to know," Tom said.

Dylan shrugged self-consciously. "It cornered me in an alley that was blocked off by a big fence, and the gate was locked. I didn't have anything except two grenades, so I used one to blow up the slime thing and the other to blast open the gate."

"Good thinking," Sara said.

"I'm pretty sure that slime thing is indestructible, though. It got blown up twice, but both times it just pulled itself back together. Still, it bought me enough time to get through the gate. I got away while it was still reforming, so I guess it gave up," Dylan said.

"For now, maybe," Tom said. "We've seen the Stalker twice already. I expect we'll see its friends again, too."

While Alex and Sara were checking over their gear, Dylan gently pulled Tom aside, speaking in a low whisper so the others couldn't hear him. "There was, uh… something about a naked woman?" He looked around like a toddler expecting to get caught with his hand in the cookie jar.

Tom grinned, unable to resist the opportunity to make Dylan uncomfortable. "Why, are you interested?"

Dylan instantly turned bright red. "No! What is wrong with you?"

Tom cleared his throat and spoke loudly, so everyone could hear. "Sure, Dylan, I'll tell you about the naked woman."

Alex and Sara both looked over with expressions of mixed amusement and discomfort. Dylan leaned in so that only Tom could hear him. "I will end you," he whispered furiously.

Tom clapped him on the shoulder. "Not on your best day, but I like your confidence," he said.

"Well, Dylan didn't see it, he does need to know about it," Alex said as she joined them. "I guess we're calling it the 'Prisoner' because it was shackled."

Tom nodded. "The bad news is that it seems to be basically unkillable, like the slime thing."

"The Glutton?" Dylan said, shrugging.

"Huh?"

"These things need names, right? I dunno. 'Glutton' seems to fit the slime because it eats everything in its path."

"Good a name as any, I suppose," Tom said. "Anyway, the Prisoner, we shot it to hell, and I blew it up with half a dozen grenades, but none of it mattered. It can regenerate somehow, and really fast. It was regrowing brand-new arms and legs in a matter of seconds."

"And it can make weapons from its own body parts," Alex added. "It somehow generated intense heat within itself, which seemed to melt the bullets in its body. It formed the bullets into a blade and attacked us with it. That's also how I got this burn, it threw a ball of hot lead at me." She gently rubbed the fresh bandage on her neck.

"And it threw spears at me," Tom said. "Spears made from its own bones."

Dylan stared in bewilderment. "It's like something out of a comic book," he said.

"I was thinking, if these super monsters are created or summoned by our negative emotions, maybe we can stop them from showing up," Sara said.

Alex frowned. "How? By just not feeling negative emotions? That seems easier said than done, especially in this place."

Sara shrugged. "Yeah, but it's worth a try. Maybe if we stay calm and keep our emotions in check, they won't bother us."

"I agree that it's worth a try, but we still need to be ready for them," Tom said. "Clearly, killing these things is not an option. They're all immune to physical damage in some way. If they show up, we need to run. Don't waste ammo on them unless absolutely necessary. We need to be careful not to get split up again, too."

Sara glanced at her watch. "We need to get moving. It took a long time to get through this area and even longer to rest and resupply."

"Where are we going?" Alex asked.

Tom glanced out the window. "It's still raining, but it seems to be letting up. We're following the moon, right? It's right over that canyon, so I guess we go through it."

A loud *bang* echoed from somewhere farther back in the building, behind the double doors. It was followed by sounds of a struggle and a voice screaming for help—a male voice, with a Scottish accent. A moment later, the ruckus faded away.

"That sounds like Jacob," Alex said, shock and worry evident on her face.

"The old guy who rescued you at the hospital?" Tom asked. Dylan nodded in confirmation.

"He's on his own," Sara said, her voice uncharacteristically cold. "We need to get moving."

Alex stared at her in disbelief.

"I'm surprised to hear Sara say that, but she's right," Tom said. "We have an objective, and this Jacob guy isn't it. If we get killed trying to help him, the world ends, remember? It sucks, and I hate to say it, but we can't afford unnecessary risks."

"He already saved our lives—all of our lives, not just mine and Dylan's," Alex said. "Because after Jacob saved us, Dylan saved Sara. If he hadn't been around to do that, game over."

"True, but not relevant to our mission," Tom said. "Everyone on Earth owes him a debt, but we can't take this risk."

"We're leaving," Sara said, starting for the front door.

"The hell we are," Alex said, taking up her MPX. "Dylan?"

Dylan blinked in surprise. "Huh?" he said dumbly.

"Are you with me?" Alex said.

"Maybe... maybe Sara's right." His voice was squeaky and mouse-like again. He'd shown remarkable courage fighting off the Glutton a few hours earlier, but he'd been cornered at the time, with no option but to fight. Running headlong into danger when a convenient escape was available—that was something altogether different.

Alex sighed. "Fine. I'm going. You guys can follow, or you can let me die." Before anyone could stop her, she sprinted through the double doors.

"What did I just say about splitting up?" Tom yelled after her. Sara's mouth hung open in astonishment. "Come on. Don't leave my side," Tom growled.

Together, they barreled through the doors, Dylan trailing far behind.

CHAPTER TWENTY-FIVE
Misgivings

Unlike most of the other buildings they'd seen so far, this one had power. Ancient, bare lightbulbs hung from cords in the ceiling at random intervals along the hallway. The bulbs were so covered with grime that their pale-yellow light was hue-shifted to a dingy, burnt-orange color.

We shouldn't be doing this, Tom thought. He vividly remembered what had happened the last time he'd decided to prioritize a stranger's life over a friend's life.

He forced down the thought. It was too late to change course now.

Sounds of a commotion grew louder as Tom, Sara, and Dylan ran down the hall. They paused at each door, listening, trying to figure out where the noises were coming from. The source of the sound turned out to be behind the very last door, a heavy one caked in rust. The noise died down and faded out just as they reached the door.

"Me first," Tom said. Sara nodded and fell in behind him. Dylan swallowed hard, trying to stop his hands from shaking.

Surprisingly, the door offered only a single quiet squeal of protest when Tom pushed it open. He peeked around the corner, exposing his head only long enough to take a quick look around the room.

He didn't know what he'd been expecting, but it wasn't a 1950s slaughterhouse. He saw a gigantic concrete room with a high ceiling and dozens of drains in the floor. Metal tables covered in dried blood were littered with filthy cleavers and bits of unidentifiable carcasses. Conveyor belts and suspended lines crisscrossed all over the room, but none held recognizable animals.

Instead, they bore dozens of Cutters in various states of dismemberment and decomposition. Some were still alive, thrashing uselessly against their restraints. In the far corner, a bearded old man was suspended by his wrists from an overhead conveyor line. He looked to be unconscious, or close to it. *That must be Jacob*, Tom realized.

"Brace yourself," Tom said to the others. "It's not a pretty sight."

Taking another quick look, he spied Alex kneeling behind a pile of boxes not far from the door. After confirming that there were no visible threats,

Tom sprinted over to her, followed by Sara and Dylan a moment later.

Tom shook a finger at Alex. "We're gonna talk about this later," he said.

"Fine," she replied. "After we get Jacob out of here."

With a loud cacophony of grinding clanks, the machinery around the room began to whir to life. The conveyor lines moved in fits and starts, the carcasses dangling from them swaying back and forth. After a moment, they stopped.

"Wh—what the hell is that," Dylan stammered, pointing.

Something had entered through a door on the far side of the room, near Jacob. At first, Tom thought he was looking at an enormous pink and white ball. A moment later, he realized that it was human—or rather, human-ish.

Standing more than seven feet tall, it walked on two legs and wore clothes—a tattered pair of bloodstained brown pants, a filthy white shirt, and an equally unsanitary apron. It was enormous, easily five hundred pounds or more. Pink skin was stretched tight over its bald head, but the skin loosened toward the middle of the face, falling in folds over two tiny black eyes and a mouth full of broken, green teeth.

It carried a huge meat cleaver in one gorilla-like hand.

"Something tells me that's another super monster," Sara whispered.

"Quiet," Tom said. "No talking."

It didn't seem to have heard them. Tom was seriously considering grabbing Alex and dragging her out of the room. They shouldn't be here. Sara, not Jacob, was their responsibility. As much as Tom's heart broke for the old man, the stakes were far too high to permit a rescue mission unrelated to the Pilgrimage.

Tom's emergency evacuation plan fell to pieces when the butcher-like creature pulled a large lever on the wall next to the door it had used. Gates made of wrist-thick iron bars slammed shut on both sides of the room, blocking both exits. The creature then locked the lever in place with a heavy padlock.

God fucking dammit, Tom thought, grinding his teeth in frustration.

"It doesn't want its live prey getting away," Dylan whispered. Tom smacked him on the leg, not hard, just as a reminder that they were in mortal danger and needed to be quiet.

Sara tapped Tom on the shoulder and pointed. He followed the line of her arm to see what she was looking at.

The Butcher had a large ring of keys hooked through one of its belt loops.

Alex suddenly unslung her MPX and shoved it into Tom's hands. Before he could react, she sprinted out of cover and slid under one of the nearby conveyor belts.

Dylan started to go after her. Tom snatched the collar of his shirt and yanked him back. "Absolutely not," he growled, keeping his voice as low as possible.

"She's lost her mind," Sara whispered. Tom could see her knuckles turning white from gripping her rifle so tightly.

Tom was inclined to agree. "Sara," he said, "when that thing isn't looking at us, run to that big machine on the left and get behind it. Dylan, you go right and hide behind the dumpster. I'll stay here for now. I don't know what Alex is planning. Just be ready to provide support or draw its attention away from her as needed."

A moment later, they got their opening. Dylan and Sara ran to their new positions, staying low and quiet. The Butcher waddled over to a wriggling Cutter suspended by its wrists from an overhead line, grabbed it by the throat, and pulled hard. One arm ripped free at the elbow, the other at the shoulder. Black blood sprayed from the grievous wounds. The Cutter's piercing wails of rage and pain echoed throughout the cavernous room.

Jesus Christ, Tom thought. *That thing can rip limbs clean off. Alex is done for if it gets ahold of her.*

The Butcher slammed the Cutter onto one of the metal tables, one massive, bulbous hand still locked around its throat. With the other hand, the Butcher raised its cleaver and brought it down, hacking off the Cutter's left leg just above the knee. The miserable creature shrieked even louder.

Across the room, Sara struggled mightily not to throw up. Her heart was pounding with fear. She tried not to visualize what that thing would do if it caught her—or any of the others. She took several deep breaths, trying to steady her nerves and her trembling hands.

Alex was making slow but steady progress toward Jacob, crawling under conveyor belts and tables, moving only when the Butcher's back was to her. She held her breath, trying not to gag as her hands and knees squelched through the cold, jellified viscera coating the floor. She was closer to Jacob than the others were, close enough to see his face. His eyes were closed, and he wasn't moving. She felt naked with only her sidearm.

Abruptly, the Butcher turned toward her and snatched another Cutter from the line not far from where she was hiding. Alex's heart jumped into her throat; she thought it might have seen her. As quietly as she could, she scrambled behind a large machine that looked something like a woodchipper. She tried not to think about what it was used for.

The Butcher bellowed and took a step toward her hiding place, sending tremors through the floor. Alex slapped a hand over her mouth, trying to remain absolutely silent.

The floor rumbled again, then once more. It was getting closer. She could hear wet, choked, snuffling sounds, as though it were sniffing the air, searching for her. It bellowed again. Alex thought she heard a note of suspicion in the animalistic sound.

Slowly, she drew her Glock and held it tightly against her chest, her finger resting on the side of the trigger. Cold sweat dripped down her face. A panicked whine rose in her chest. She choked it off.

She saw the monster's shadow on the floor to her right, rapidly growing larger as it approached. Keeping her back pressed against the cold steel, she shuffled to her left, rounding the corner just as the Butcher poked its head around the far side of the machine.

She could hear it sniffing again. Could it smell her?

Suddenly, Alex heard a metallic *clink* on the other side of the room, near the door. The Butcher whirled around and roared before charging off to investigate, creating a minor earthquake as it went. It was unbelievably fast for its size.

Alex glanced over at Sara, who was giving her a thumbs up. Alex understood—Sara had thrown something to distract the creature. Alex nodded her thanks, holstered her pistol, and ran toward Jacob, crouched low, careful to stay out of the Butcher's sight line. She saw Tom leaning out of cover, holding his grenade launcher at the low ready. Apparently, he had no intention of screwing around if they had to fight.

That was probably wise.

Alex reached Jacob and stood on her tiptoes, trying to undo the iron manacles around his wrists. She gasped when she saw that they were cutting into his flesh. Blood ran down his arms and dripped to the floor. The chain connecting the two shackles was draped over a hook, but she couldn't simply lift him off it. He was heavy, and she wasn't strong enough.

She swore quietly when she saw that the shackles were permanently locked with rivets. She had assumed that there would be a lock she could open once she had the keys.

Jacob's eyes suddenly fluttered open. When he saw her, he blinked in surprise, then opened his mouth to say something. She slapped a hand over his mouth and crossed her lips with a finger, commanding silence. His eyes darted around the room, processing the situation. After a moment, he looked at her and nodded his understanding. Alex took her hand away and ducked behind a large bin filled with offal, trying not to gag from the smell. Jacob pretended to be unconscious again.

A moment later, the Butcher came back to the center of the room, stomping and snorting its displeasure. Dylan was now closest to it. Alex waved to get his attention, then mimed turning a key in a lock. She pointed at the exit door, then at the ring of keys hanging from the Butcher's side. Even if the keys couldn't unlock Jacob's restraints, they were probably the only way to open the padlock barring the exit.

Alex knew Dylan understood when she saw his eyes widen in fear.

For the time being, she was trapped. The Butcher had gone back to chopping up Cutters, but it was facing the bin she was hiding behind. There was no way to move without it seeing her.

Across the room, Dylan was trying to work up the courage to sneak up on a creature that could probably kill him just by slapping him, without even having to use its giant meat cleaver.

There was no way out of this room without getting those keys. Tom, Alex, and Sara couldn't move without being seen. Only he could approach the Butcher from the rear. Everyone else was depending on him.

It was time to man up.

Against every instinct of self-preservation, Dylan darted out of hiding, taking up a new position under a conveyor belt. He crawled along as quickly as he dared, taking a roundabout approach to minimize the time he spent out in the open. With one hand, he held his replacement UMP firmly against his chest so it wouldn't clack and rattle against the rest of his gear.

Suddenly, almost unexpectedly, he was within arm's reach of the Butcher. It was still bisecting and quartering Cutters, some of which were alive when it got started. It was still facing the same direction, making it impossible for anyone else to leave their hiding places. Dylan could see that the keys were clipped through one of its belt loops with a carabiner. Unclipping it to remove the keys was out of the question; he was no trained pickpocket, and it would surely feel him fumbling around.

That left cutting the belt loop.

Dylan drew his knife, his hand trembling badly. He glanced toward Tom, who had switched back to his shotgun. Tom gave him a single, grim nod, indicating that he was ready to act if Dylan needed help. Dylan couldn't see Alex or Sara from his position. He hoped they were ready.

Ever so slowly, he crept forward. Every fiber of his being ached to retreat, to scramble back to the relative safety of his hiding place.

But Sara already thought he was a coward. He had to be brave for her. Besides, Jacob had risked his life to save Dylan's. The least he could do was return the favor.

The Butcher was rapidly raising its meat cleaver and slamming it back down, causing its whole body to jiggle with each movement. The keys jangled and bounced unpredictably. How was he supposed to cut the belt loop without getting caught?

Suddenly, he had his opening. The Butcher paused for a moment, just long enough to wipe sweat from its bald head. Trying not to visualize the consequences of failure, Dylan slipped the knife blade through the belt loop and pulled back gently, trying to balance speed and caution. Fortunately, the blade was razor sharp, and it cut easily through the dry-rotted fabric. Dylan quickly grabbed the keys with his other hand, holding them in a tight fist so they wouldn't rattle.

Underneath his terror, Dylan felt a small surge of elation. He had the keys. The Butcher had gone back to chopping; it hadn't noticed him. Grinning triumphantly, he turned around to move back to his previous hiding spot.

When he turned, his UMP bounced on its sling, clacking loudly against the spare magazines on his armor.

Roaring in fury, the Butcher whipped around and spotted him. Before he could scramble away, it brought its cleaver down in a powerful overhand chop. Dylan screamed and rolled to the side. The thick blade made sparks as it rebounded off the stone floor.

It was so goddamn *fast*. Before Dylan could move again, it reached down and seized him by the neck, hauling him up as if he weighed no more than a few pounds. Dylan tried to yell for help, but no sound came out. Its powerful fingers were crushing his throat. He kicked his legs uselessly. The Butcher pulled its cleaver arm back, preparing to slam the deadly weapon into his forehead.

A thunderous *boom* echoed around the room. The Butcher's head snapped to the side and hot, purple blood splattered Dylan's face. It dropped him, and he fell onto his back, sliding through the gore on the floor. Tom had fired a 12-gauge slug right through the side of the Butcher's head, creating a hole the size of a golf ball.

The Butcher didn't seem especially concerned about the injury. It reached down once again. Dylan shuffled backward, then realized that it wasn't reaching for him.

The keys. He'd dropped them.

"Open fire! Don't hit Dylan!" Tom shouted. A deafening chatter of gunfire erupted, peppering the Butcher with shotgun and pistol rounds from all directions.

The Butcher snatched the keys, raised them high above its bulbous head, and dropped them into its gaping maw, even as it was being pelted with lead. With a gurgling, choking swallow, they were gone.

Dylan scrambled away on his hands and knees, panting in ragged fear, too terrified to worry about the fact that escaping the room was impossible without those keys. Once he'd gained some distance, he got to his feet and started firing his UMP in long bursts, joining the others in trying to hammer down the Butcher with gunfire.

It wasn't working. The abomination didn't seem to regenerate like the Prisoner or the Glutton had; it just seemed unaffected by its wounds. Even Tom's slugs weren't slowing it down.

The Butcher made a sound they hadn't heard before, a sort of malevolent croaking. It took Dylan a moment to identify it as a laugh. With one meaty hand, it slammed a green button on the side of one of the nearby machines.

With a jerk, the conveyors started moving again. Jacob began to kick and thrash, trying in vain to free himself as the conveyor line pulled him up a steep incline, higher into the air. Alex was doing her best to push his legs up, to give him enough support that he could slip his bound wrists up and over the tip of the hook, but she simply wasn't strong enough. A moment later, his feet were nearly ten feet above the floor, and she could no longer reach him.

The Butcher turned away from Dylan and headed for Tom. He immediately began falling back, trying to keep his distance. The room was large, but there was a lot of furniture and machinery strewn about, making it difficult to maneuver. Tom loaded a fresh magazine of buckshot, switched to full auto, and emptied twelve rounds into the Butcher, all of which hit it in the abdomen, neck, and face.

It didn't even slow down. It punched at Tom with its left hand with enough force to knock over a brick wall. Tom twisted to the side, barely avoiding the blow. The Butcher immediately followed up by swinging its cleaver while Tom was off balance, displaying an unexpected degree of intelligence.

Tom cried out in pain as the heavy blade slammed squarely into the center of his chest.

"Tom!" Alex screamed, horrified. Tom had fallen to the floor, and she could no longer see him. She advanced on the Butcher, hammering the trigger on her Glock, stitching the beast up the side with 9mm +P rounds, trying to get its attention. She wasn't yet used to the more powerful ammunition; the increased recoil was making the pistol difficult to control.

Sara and Dylan weren't watching. Both had just noticed that the Cutters in front of Jacob on the conveyor line were being dropped one by one into the hopper of a large machine. Inside it, heavy steel drums covered in sharp projections ground against one another, smashing the carcasses into meaty paste.

Jacob began to shriek in terror when he saw where he was headed.

Dylan ran to the control panel the Butcher had used to start the conveyor line and pushed the red emergency stop button over and over.

Nothing happened. He pressed it several more times, praying that the contacts were simply corroded and needed another chance to break the circuit.

The conveyor line kept advancing. Growling in frustration, Dylan reached into his backpack, rummaging around for a screwdriver. Maybe if he could pop off the panel, he could fix the button without electrocuting himself. He glanced at Jacob, trying to estimate how long he had until the old man was fed into the machine.

Not long.

From behind him, Alex leaped onto one of the metal tables and nearly slipped in the gore, barely managing to keep her footing. Carefully, she started hopping between the conveyor belts, toward Jacob.

Trusting that Alex had a plan, Sara drew her STI and ran toward Tom. He was still on his back, stunned. She noted with relief that his armor seemed to have stopped the blade. "Hey, ugly!" she shouted. When the Butcher turned toward her, she raised her STI and hammered the trigger as fast as she could, trying to ride the recoil as Tom had shown her. Most of the rounds went where she wanted them to. The slide locked back empty as the Butcher began to advance on her. Surprised at how steady her hands were, she dropped the empty mag and reached for another one.

Then she remembered that her left hand was broken. She could reload, but not quickly.

The Butcher was suddenly right in her face, reaching for her. How was it so fast? She vaulted over a steel table to her right, hit the ground, and rolled away, silently thanking her father for making her take gymnastics for four years. The Butcher's huge fists closed around empty air.

Tom took advantage of the distraction, shaking his head to snap himself out of it. He wrenched the cleaver out of his armor and tossed it aside. Sara holstered her empty STI, raised her rifle, and started lobbing 6.8mm rounds at the Butcher, awkwardly using her cast to support the barrel.

Jacob was hyperventilating, drowning in panic. The Cutter directly in front of him jerked to a halt over the open hopper. The hook it was hanging from rotated backward, allowing the chain to slide off. The dead creature dropped into the machine, between the grinding drums. Within seconds, it was obliterated, smashed into pulpy chunks. Jacob furiously swung his feet back and forth, trying to generate enough momentum to lift his arms up and over the top of the hook. It wasn't working.

The conveyor line clanked forward again, grinding to a halt directly above the gore-covered steel drums. Jacob's heart felt like it was trying to tear its way out of his chest. Shivering violently in fear, he watched helplessly as the hook that held him suspended began to rotate backward.

With a metallic *clunk*, it locked into position. The chain binding his wrists slipped down and over the tip. He shut his eyes and screamed in wild terror as he fell.

Suddenly, he jerked to a halt. He opened his eyes and looked down. He was floating in midair, the drums gnashing hungrily just below his feet. Confused, he looked up.

"Gotcha," Alex said. She was hanging from the top of the conveyor track with one hand. With the other, she'd grabbed the chain between Jacob's wrists. "Come on, swing your feet," Alex said, her face turning red with the effort. "I can't hold you for long."

Beginning to understand the plan, Jacob kicked his feet, trying to match Alex's timing, building momentum. "Hurry," she choked out.

Just as the chain slipped through Alex's fingers, Jacob reached the apex of his swing and kicked out as hard as he could. The back of his head banged painfully against the lip of the hopper, but he cleared it. He hit the ground on his back, howling in pain.

Still, it was a lot better than the alternative.

Finally able to use both hands, Alex shimmied away from the machine until she could safely drop to the floor, panting heavily. She reached down and pulled Jacob to his feet.

Across the room, Tom and Sara had reached the lever that controlled the gates blocking the exit doors. The Butcher was chasing Dylan, who was diving across tables and under conveyor belts, trying to stay ahead of it. He shrieked as some of the stitches in his side tore, causing the bite wound to flare with hot, nauseating pain.

"Time to go! Everyone on me!" Tom shouted.

"But we don't have the keys!" Sara cried.

"Don't need 'em," Tom said, giving her a confident wink. He press-checked his Jackhammer, ensuring that he had slugs loaded and not buckshot. He placed the barrel directly against the padlock at a slight angle. "Turn your face away," he said to Sara, then he did the same.

The 12-gauge slug blasted the lock into scrap metal, leaving the hasp hanging loose. Tom pulled it free and yanked upward on the lever, returning it to its original position. The iron gates squealed open, finally granting access to the exit.

Dylan and Jacob hit the door at the same time, bursting out into the night. Alex was only a few steps behind. Tom shoved Sara out the door ahead of him, then slammed the lever down again and rapid-fired three more slugs, destroying the mechanism entirely. He rolled under the security gate just before it closed again and kicked the door shut behind him.

The Butcher slammed its bulk against the door over and over, but the iron gate held fast. Without waiting to see if it would be able to smash its way through with brute strength, they ran for the canyon.

* * *

By the time they reached the mouth of the canyon, there was still no sign of anything chasing them. They stopped to catch their breath but kept looking back, not yet convinced that it was over.

"Thanks fer yer help," Jacob finally said. He looked well over sixty, and he was pretty beat up from his encounter with the Butcher. Tom was amazed that he'd been able to keep up with them. The iron manacles were still locked around Jacob's wrists. Dried blood covered his forearms from where the metal had torn into his skin.

"You saved Dylan and me earlier; the least we could do is return the favor," Alex said.

"Aye, lass, that was quite the acrobatic rescue," Jacob said, clapping her on the shoulder.

"Quiet," Sara said. "We don't know what's out here. Let's find somewhere safe to rest."

Tom's eyes narrowed, his suspicion flaring again. In all the time he'd known Sara, he'd never seen her act this way. She was often businesslike and matter of fact, especially when they were in the Twilight, but he'd never seen her act downright cold. She seemed indifferent to Jacob's plight, even mildly hostile toward him.

For now, Tom decided to listen and observe. He would force Sara to explain if necessary, but he may be able to learn more by letting this play out.

They walked on in silence for a time, maintaining a brisk pace to ward off the cold. Tom noted that it was quite a bit colder than it had been at the village just a few days ago. Would the temperature continue to drop the closer they got to the cathedral? He made a mental note to remind everyone to dress warmly the next time they came back.

Dylan was whimpering quietly and limping, his left hand clutching his right side. "Let me see, honey," Alex said, gently pulling his hand away. Dylan hissed in pain as she lifted his shirt enough to inspect the wound. "It's not too bad, just some torn stitches. Nothing we can't fix. Hang on just a little longer, we'll find somewhere to rest and get you patched up again." Dylan nodded his appreciation.

Gradually, the sound of their footsteps changed as they moved farther into the canyon. Hard-packed dirt gave way to softer sand. Small rocks littered the ground, growing in both size and number as the group walked on. Before long, great boulders began coming into view here and there, perhaps remnants of a major rockslide. The five travelers kept a wary eye on the canyon rim, high above.

About an hour's walk from the slaughterhouse, the canyon curved gently to the left. "Should be a train yard up ahead," Jacob said. A little farther on, past the bend, they found it, just as Jacob had said. Disused tracks began next to a raised wooden platform and wound their way deeper into the canyon, although there was no train in sight. Thick weeds and brambles clawed their way up from the soil amid patches of tall, brown grass, covering the rotting ties almost entirely. Piles of broken machinery and scrap metal lay everywhere, some stacked taller than a man.

"Stay close to me, let's check it out," Tom said quietly. He raised his shotgun and took the lead, moving slowly, checking behind the piles of scrap and under the train platform. There was no sign of anything living.

"Maybe we can find something here to get these chains off Jacob," Alex said.

"That would be much appreciated," the old man agreed.

Tom nodded. "Alright, two teams. Sara, with me. Dylan, Alex, and Jacob, you guys check over there," he said, pointing to an area a little farther away. "Stay close to each other and stay within sight of Sara and me. Don't go too far."

Tom and Sara began to pick through piles of scrap as the others moved away to search elsewhere. Tom kept one eye on Sara, watching her face and body language carefully. As he'd expected, she seemed even more agitated once Jacob was far enough away that she could no longer hear him. She kept glancing over at the other group, not really paying attention to what she was doing.

A few minutes later, Jacob's group returned. Dylan was holding a rusted pair of bolt cutters. "Will these work?" he asked.

"Maybe, if they don't break first," Tom said. He took the bolt cutters from Dylan and gestured for Jacob to hold out his arms. Slowly and carefully, so as not to cut him, Tom worked the cutters under the heavy manacle on the older man's right wrist. Once they were in place, he gently pushed the handles together, increasing the pressure steadily. The long handles provided good leverage, but the iron was thick and difficult to cut. Finally, after several minutes, the manacle split with a loud *crack*, emitting a small shower of orange sparks. While Tom worked on the other one, Alex cleaned and restitched Dylan's wound. By the time Jacob was free of his restraints, Tom was sweating, and his arms were shaking from the sustained effort.

Jacob rubbed his sore wrists. "Cheers, again," he said.

Alex gently took his hands in hers, inspecting his injuries. "Come over to the platform, and let me see what I can do," she said. "Some of these cuts are deep. They need to be properly cleaned and bandaged so you don't get a nasty infection."

While Alex rummaged through her medic bag for the supplies she needed, Tom and Dylan sat nearby on the platform, taking the opportunity to rest for a few minutes. Sara leaned against it instead, trying to act disinterested.

"Jacob, what were you doing out here?" Dylan asked.

The old man sighed heavily. "Lookin' fer a new home, ah'm afraid."

Alex looked up. "Did something happen to the bell tower?"

"Aye, shortly after ah parted ways with ye last time. Overrun by the same bastards from the hospital. They figured out how ta work the lift, maybe by accident. Suppose the 'how' does nae matter. All mah supplies, gone, and the lift damaged. Could nae fix it, nae with them crawlin' all over the place."

Alex was staring off into space. Tom could tell from her eyes that she was beating herself up about something; he'd learned to recognize the look. He realized that she must be thinking that Jacob had lost his home—such as it was—because he'd chosen to help her and Dylan.

"Alex," Tom said softly. "Remember what we talked about a little while ago."

"Hmm?" she said, meeting his eyes. She frowned in confusion, not sure what he meant. Tom nodded toward Dylan, who looked like he'd been run over by a truck. Then he touched his neck, in the same place where Alex had a fresh bandage on hers. She finally understood. Trying to push her negative thoughts aside, she went back to work on Jacob's wounds. The older man raised an eyebrow in curiosity, but he said nothing.

"I'm glad you're okay, but I'm sorry you have to move," Dylan said.

Jacob shrugged. "It's alright, lad. Nae the first time ah've been involuntarily relocated." He winced in pain when Alex poured disinfectant over an especially deep cut.

"I can't imagine how you've survived so long in this place," Tom said. "If you're from two cycles ago, then I was just a kid when you first came here."

"Ye get used ta it after a while. The trick is stayin' unnoticed. Most of the time ah just stay hunkered down in a good hidin' spot, maybe scratch out a bit of bad poetry here and there."

Why not just kill yourself? What's the point of living here? Tom thought, then reprimanded himself. He stole a glance at Sara. She was trying far too hard to act casual, leaning against the waist-high platform as though she were only half-listening. But her right hand was gripping her rifle so tightly that her knuckles were white as snow.

Tom returned his attention to Jacob. "Now that we're here, is there some way we can take you home? Back to our world?"

The old man shook his head. "Ah dinnae think so."

"Sara?" Tom said.

She finally looked over at them. After a moment of silence, she shook her head. "No. I'm sorry. Once the Maiden who brought you here undoes the binding ritual, dies, or leaves the Twilight, there's no way for her Wardens to return."

No one said anything else for a long time. If Jacob was upset by this confirmation, he didn't show it. Tom supposed that if he'd spent two-thirds of his life here, he too would have fashioned his own armor of grim acceptance long ago. Alex finished cleaning, stitching, and bandaging one of Jacob's arms, then started on the other.

"Will you tell us what happened with your group?" Dylan said, finally breaking the silence. "Your experience might help us protect Sara."

Jacob heaved a sigh. "What happened ta us will nae be much help ta ye, lad."

"Then maybe you can join us, help us get to the cathedral and wrap this thing up," Tom said. "I know that's a lot to ask, but you know what's at stake here. You've been here for almost forty years. You've got to know more about this place than anyone."

Alex shot Tom a surreptitious look that suggested he'd said the wrong thing. *Too late now*, he thought.

"Ah dinnae ken much fer sure, anymore. But ah do ken that ah'd be no help ta ye," Jacob said, his voice breaking slightly.

Alex looked up from her work, meeting Jacob's eyes. "Your Maiden... something happened to her. Something bad. That's why you won't come with us. You think you failed her, and you think you'd fail Sara, too."

Jacob said nothing. He stared straight ahead, out over the scrap yard, as though he hadn't heard her. But he had, and his silence all but confirmed Alex's theory.

"We got separated," he finally said. "About four days into our Pilgrimage. Nae far from this very spot, in fact, although there was a river runnin' through this canyon at the time, instead of train tracks. We were crossin' a bridge over the river when that damned thing showed up, that bastard ye saved me from—the Butcher, ah call it. We tried ta fight it off, but it destroyed the bridge. Only ah'd made it all the way across. The others... they were lost ta the river. It was a terrible long way down, and the current was mighty. Ah dinnae see how they could have survived. Ever since, that cunt of a Butcher shows up from time ta time, ta hunt me down, ta finish what it started. Ah always managed ta steer clear of it until today."

He again fell silent for a time. No one else said anything. They simply waited for him to continue at his own pace. Sara was watching him like an owl eyeballing a field mouse.

After taking a moment to compose himself, Jacob went on. "Her name was Lily, mah Maiden. She looked much like ye, lass, though she was a bit older, her hair a bit longer," he said, nodding toward Sara. "Very quiet, she was. Soft-spoken, and kind. She dinnae belong in a place like this. Although, ah suppose that's why those sorts of girls come here. It takes the kindest of hearts ta walk right into hell of yer own free will, head held high, so that everyone else might never have ta ken that evil such as this is real, always fightin' against its leash ta get at them."

Jacob lifted one arm and pointed. The others looked and saw a single white lily rising defiantly from a tangle of dead weeds alongside the train tracks. Its petals shone brilliantly in the moonlight.

"Lily was nae her birth name," Jacob said quietly, letting his arm drop. "But she preferred ta go by it, she loved 'em so much. She used to grow 'em, ye ken. Thousands of 'em, far as the eye could see behind her home in Shetland, way up north. Time was, ye'd see lilies all over here, in the Twilight. Ah always thought it was some miracle ta see that bright part of her soul here, somethin' bonny and pure, little patches of light in this damned forever darkness. But as time went on, those pieces of her started to fade away. There's hardly any lilies left here, now.

"Anyway, ye dinnae want me followin' ye. Ah could nae protect Lily, ah cannae protect anyone. Ah dinnae ken how come ah kept on livin', ta be honest. Too much of a coward ta off myself, ah suppose. Ah dinnae ken how the next team made it ta the cathedral in three days, but they must've."

"Jacob," Sara said. It was the first time she'd addressed him by name. "There was no second team. Lily made it. She finished her Pilgrimage."

Jacob stared at her in disbelief. "Are ye pullin' one over on me, lass?"

Sara shook her head. She seemed more relaxed, more like her usual self, although she was clearly touched by Jacob's story and close to tears herself. "You didn't fail her. You helped her do what she needed to do. You got her this far."

Jacob shook his head in disbelief. "Is she... she's still alive, then?"

Sara sighed. "I'm sorry. She died about ten years ago. Cancer. I never met her, but I read a bit about her. I think she had a good life. I'm sure she never forgot you."

Jacob could only nod. He looked too overcome by emotion to speak. Alex deduced the question he wanted to ask and voiced it on his behalf.

"What about her other Wardens?"

Sara shook her head again. A single tear rolled down her face and fell to the ground. "Lily... was the only one who came back."

There was no sound other than the whisper of a gentle breeze through the tall grass. Alex finished treating Jacob's injuries and began to repack her bag. He nodded his thanks to her.

"It's been a long day," Tom said. "Let's head back home and get some rest."

CHAPTER TWENTY-SIX
Recollection

December 29, 2021
Day Five

"Sara, can I use your phone?" Dylan asked. His hair was still dripping wet. Showering around all his injuries had been a slow and painful experience. He'd tried not to look at the bite wound, which was now a mixture of angry red and midnight black.

"Hmm?" she said. "Oh, you want to call your dad?"

"Yeah. I can't go home looking like I just crawled out of a ten-car pileup."

Sara gave him her phone, along with a tight, worried smile. Dylan stepped into an empty guest bedroom for privacy and dialed Richard's number. The phone rang once, twice, three times. Just when he was about to hang up, there was a soft *click* as the call connected.

"Hello?" Richard sounded like he'd just woken up. Wincing, Dylan realized that he probably had—it was after midnight. His sense of time was all screwed up.

"Hey, Dad. It's me. Sorry to call so late."

"Dylan? Where are you? What's wrong?"

"I'm still at Sara's. Nothing's wrong."

"You've been there an awfully long time. I called Ethan yesterday to check on you, he said you and Sara went to a movie."

"Yeah." Dylan paused, unsure what else to say. What *could* he say? "Hey, Dad, just so you know, this might be the last time we ever talk because I could die horribly soon, and if that happens, you'll probably die, too."

"I don't mind you staying over at Sara's for a couple days at a time, but I think it's time to come home now," Richard said, sounding a little more awake.

"I... can't. Not yet."

"Why not?"

Again, Dylan didn't know what to say. "I just can't. I'll be home in a few more days, I promise." He struggled to keep his voice steady. He wasn't at all sure that he'd be able to keep that promise.

There was another long silence before Richard responded. "It's time to come home, Dylan. I'll pick you up in the morning, after breakfast, if you need a ride."

Dylan's heartbeat quickened. It was rare for Richard to put his foot down and make a firm parental declaration. He needed to think fast. He conjured and discarded half a dozen lies over the next few seconds. Unable to come up with a good one, he said, "I can't see you right now."

Another long pause. "I see," Richard said, his voice flat and quiet. Dylan realized that his father had heard something other than what he'd meant to say. He'd meant, "I can't see you right now because you'll want to know why I look like a reanimated corpse," but Richard had heard, "I'm tired of being around you, tired of having to parent myself because you won't do it."

"Take as long as you need," Richard said quietly, then hung up. Dylan stared at the phone in his hand, dumbfounded. That hadn't been what he'd meant.

Or had it?

He leaned back against the wall and slid down until he was sitting on the floor, trying to ignore the stabbing pain all over. He nearly hurled the phone across the room in frustration, then remembered that it was Sara's and set it gently on the floor.

Dylan felt hot tears starting to well up. With a clipped growl of anger, he fought them back. *God dammit, I'm sixteen, not six*, he thought. *I feel like I've cried a hundred times in the last few days. Enough crying already. It's time to grow up.*

He was so tired of thinking about death, pain, and danger all the time. They were only on day five of the Pilgrimage, but he felt like he'd been living in a nightmare for months. The constant adrenaline and fear were exhausting. He needed to think about something else for a bit, something not horrible.

Unconsciously, his gaze roamed over Sara's phone on the floor next to him. He picked it up and typed in the password, unlocking it. He opened the photo app and scrolled down to the pictures they'd taken at Wonder World a few weeks earlier. Sara wouldn't mind him looking through her phone; they had no secrets from one another.

He stopped. Sara had kept at least one secret from him—a pretty damn big one.

Dylan sighed, pushed the thought aside, and returned his attention to the photos.

* * *

Richard tightened the belt on his bathrobe.

Drip, drip, drip. The fresh coffee slowly trickled into the pot, filling the small kitchen with a pleasant aroma.

He glanced at the clock on the stove: 3:20 a.m.—that magical time of night when it was both absurdly late and absurdly early to be awake. After the short conversation he'd had with Dylan, his mind had been too cluttered with thoughts to go back to sleep.

Richard yawned as he cracked open the refrigerator and pulled out a container of half-and-half. He paused, shaking it.

Empty.

With a sigh, he tossed it in the trash and went back to the fridge to look for more. There was none. There was hardly anything in the fridge—only a few rotten vegetables, a single can of beer, and four eggs.

Richard hated coffee without cream, but the coffee was already made. He poured some into a cracked mug and added extra sugar to compensate. He sipped at it, grimacing. He left the mug on the counter and shuffled over to the fireplace to build a fire. It was chilly, and he couldn't afford to turn on the heat.

Once the fire was going strong, he retrieved his coffee and flopped onto the couch. He stared straight ahead, his mind wandering. Every time he felt his thoughts start to drift toward Dylan, he snatched them back irritably. There was no point thinking about any of that now. Maybe later.

The clock on the mantle ticked relentlessly. The sound was starting to grate on his nerves. He picked up the remote and turned on the TV to drown it out. A newscaster flickered into view, a young woman talking about an oil spill somewhere in the Gulf of Mexico. Dimly, Richard noticed that most of the buttons on the remote were faded with age.

Except the channel button. He rarely used that one.

As he set the remote back down, a stack of unopened mail on the coffee table caught his eye. Most of the envelopes had angry red stamps on them reading "FINAL NOTICE" or "URGENT RESPONSE REQUIRED." He swept them aside, onto the floor. He sipped his coffee again.

Bitter, even with the sugar. Without cream, the flavor was too harsh. He thunked the mug down on the table. A bit of coffee sloshed over the side, onto the old, pitted wood.

Richard stared at the spilled liquid, thinking.

He didn't like coffee without cream. He didn't like the sound the clock made. He didn't like thinking about the overdue bills. He didn't like his work anymore. He didn't like Dylan spending days and days at Sara's house with hardly a phone call.

He *especially* didn't like not knowing where his wife had been for the last sixteen years.

Richard frowned. What if....

No. He shoved the thought aside and stood up. He walked back to the kitchen, sprayed some bleach on the counter, and started cleaning. He needed something to do, something to keep his pointless thoughts at bay.

But no matter how hard he scrubbed, the thought he kept pushing aside kept creeping back, as if *it* had a mind of its own and had declared that it would not be ignored any longer.

Finally, he gave up. He hurled the sponge into the sink and leaned over the half-clean counter, hanging his head. Reluctantly, he opened the gates in his mind and let the thought come racing in.

The bad coffee. The clock. The bills. Gradually, over the years, he'd started to think of everything in terms of what he wanted, liked, or preferred.

He wanted nothing more than to find out what had happened to Marie. Her disappearance didn't make any sense. There *had* to be answers out there somewhere. She was everything to him. He wouldn't let her fade away, wouldn't let her become nothing more than a painful memory—not without finding out what had happened to her, at the very least.

But what if....

What if it *didn't fucking matter* what he wanted or didn't want, liked or didn't like?

What was the point of it all? He couldn't remember anymore. Marie was dead. She had to be. No one went missing for sixteen years and then turned up all of a sudden, alive and well. He supposed it did happen— there had been that Canadian woman on the news—but that was a million to one, a *billion* to one.

He supposed that, if he were Dylan, he'd run off to a friend's house for days at a time, too.

Richard turned around and leaned his back against the counter. He closed his eyes and forced himself to listen to the clock. It irritated him. He tried to pretend that it didn't. His mind flashed back to one of the last times he'd seen his son, several days ago. Dylan had made spaghetti, but he'd gone to bed without eating any. Why? Richard struggled to remember, forcing his exhausted brain to work.

Yes, of course. Dylan had gotten angry with him for bringing up Marie again. What was it Dylan had said?

Can you just... be my dad? Please? I could use at least one parent.

Richard heaved a deep sigh. Whatever had happened to Marie, he knew one thing for sure: She loved her son more than life itself. She loved him, too, of course—she always had. But Dylan was her child, her first and only. Richard had seen a light in her eyes when she looked at Dylan not quite like anything he'd ever seen before. She would have given anything for him, including her life, without hesitation.

What would Marie think if she could see Richard now? Would she approve of the job he was doing raising their son?

Richard shut his eyes.

He knew the answer.

* * *

Tom and Alex sat on lawn chairs next to the backyard fire pit, holding their hands over the flames for warmth. Tom cleared his throat.

Alex glanced sidelong at him. "Well, out with it," she said.

He didn't look at her. "Out with what?"

"Don't play dumb. You've been waiting for a chance to chew me out for running off by myself to help Jacob."

Tom nodded slowly. "Yeah, I was."

"I'd do the same thing again."

"I know you would."

"Aren't you going to lecture me about endangering the whole world for one person?"

Tom scratched his beard. "No."

Alex blinked, taken aback. "No?"

"I can if you really want me to."

She frowned. "What's up with you?"

"'You must understand that there is more than one path to the top of the mountain,'" Tom said absently.

"I don't recognize it, but I feel like that's another Musashi quote."

"It is."

Alex crossed her arms. "Enlighten me, sensei."

Tom leaned back in his chair and finally looked at her. "At the time, I thought you were doing the wrong thing. After thinking about it some more, I've changed my mind. But the fact that you were right doesn't mean I was wrong."

She raised an eyebrow. "How can two people who disagree both be right?"

He gazed calmly at her. "Why did you decide to go after Jacob? By yourself, if you had to?"

"Because life matters—it's *the* thing that matters. It's why we're doing this insane Pilgrimage, isn't it? To protect and preserve human life?"

"Should we save one life even if it ends up costing billions of others?"

"Humanity is not some hivemind. The human race is made up of individual people, individual lives. You can't claim to value billions of lives if you won't act to preserve one."

Tom smiled at her. "I couldn't agree more. And yet, in war, the rules change. In war, a soldier who fights to protect innocent life must eventually weigh some innocent lives against others. The fact that his enemy forced that choice on him doesn't change its consequences."

Alex nodded slowly, mulling that over. They looked up when they heard footsteps crunching through the snow, coming toward them. Dylan trudged into the ring of firelight.

"Hey," he said. He looked and sounded exhausted. "Mind if I join you?"

Alex gave him the special, comforting smile she seemed to have created just for him. "Not at all." Tom said nothing but held out a hand, inviting Dylan to sit between them.

Dylan settled himself in the empty third chair. "I guess you figured I'd turn up sooner or later." Tom closed his eyes and smiled.

The three of them sat together in silence for a time, listening to the fresh wood snap and pop as it burned. Somewhere off in the trees, an owl hooted softly. Dylan held his hands over the fire, appreciating the oddly comforting contrast between the freezing air on his cheeks and the warmth slowly soaking into the rest of his body. Dimly, he noted the assortment of fresh and semi-healed cuts all over the backs of his hands. He turned them over to look at his palms instead.

Alex leaned back in her chair, gazing up at the night sky. Dawn was still a long way off. The stars twinkled like a handful of silver glitter strewn across a black carpet. The moon was nowhere to be seen, hiding behind a cloud somewhere. She closed her eyes and soaked in the fire's heat for a while.

Feeling a vague need to say something, Dylan asked, "Has anyone seen Sara? Or Mr. Holcomb?"

"They're strategizing, or whatever it is they do between our... excursions," Tom said.

"They locked themselves in Ethan's office and said they would be a few hours," Alex added.

Her heart skipped a beat when her eyes met Dylan's. When he looked at her, she was suddenly reminded of the terrible secret she was keeping from him. She forced herself to maintain eye contact and offer him a smile, forced herself not to look at his right side, at the wound that was slowly killing him.

The antibiotics weren't working. Every time she changed his bandage, the wound looked worse. Even in the orange glow of the firelight, he looked terribly pale. All four of them were tired, but Dylan seemed to be on the verge of passing out. A few hours ago, he'd had to take some caffeine pills so he wouldn't drift off and end up in the Twilight by himself. He coughed, covering his mouth with the back of one hand. He'd been coughing more lately. She didn't think he'd taken much notice of it yet.

She had.

Almost before she realized what was happening, she bit back the words that had been about to come tumbling out of her mouth. "Dylan, you're dying," she'd nearly said. Her conscience was begging her—no, *ordering* her —to come clean.

Then again, maybe Dr. Atwood was right. Maybe this wasn't the time or the place to tell him. Maybe he would take the news in stride and keep it together well enough to see Sara safely to the end of her path—or maybe he wouldn't.

But if Dr. Atwood was right, why did following her advice feel so shitty?

Alex mentally shook herself out of it. Tom and Dylan were staring at her. She realized that some trace of her thoughts must have been showing on her face.

"What's wrong?" Dylan asked.

"Nothing," she said. "I...."

"You what?" Tom said.

She said nothing. Daggers of guilt were stabbing into her heart, over and over.

"You look like something's bothering you," Dylan said, fidgeting nervously.

"Something you need to get off your chest?" Tom prompted.

Internally, Alex started to panic. She must have been doing a piss-poor job of hiding her thoughts. She forced a smile. It wasn't fooling anyone, and she knew it.

"No, everything's fine," she said.

"Bullshit," Tom grunted. "Something's bugging you, and it could get all of us killed if it distracts you in the Twilight—or if it creates another super monster."

Alex picked up a stick and poked at the fire, rearranging the logs. A small plume of sparks shot up into the air and drifted away on a cold breeze.

"Alex," Dylan said. He coughed again. "Something's been bothering you for a while now—at least since the cable car."

She frowned. What was he talking about? The cable car ride had been well before Dylan was bitten.

"That's right," Tom said. "Sara said something about you 'making amends' to your patients. I didn't say anything out of respect for your privacy, but privacy is a luxury I don't think we can afford any longer. Whatever's eating at you, it's gonna get worse and keep distracting you. We need to know what's going on."

Suddenly, Alex understood. They thought she was feeling guilty about something unrelated to Dylan. That was true—there was usually at least one thing gnawing at her conscience at any given time—but her concern for Dylan had pushed her usual guilt aside for the time being.

Tom clearly wasn't ready to let this go. His face was a hard mask of determination. Even Dylan looked ready to claw it out of her if necessary, although his face suggested that he was more concerned about her than the mission.

Alex sighed—and took the opportunity to keep her worry for Dylan disguised a little longer.

"You're right," she said. "The reason I'm here, the reason Sara chose me for this... mission... there's more to it than you know."

"That much is obvious," Tom said. Dylan shot him a disapproving look.

Alex tossed her makeshift fire poker into the flames. "Sara chose me for this duty for the same reason I became a doctor in the first place, almost fifteen years ago now." She looked at Dylan, then at Tom. They both waited patiently for her to continue.

"Both of my parents were doctors," she said.

"Family business?" Dylan guessed.

Alex shook her head. "Not exactly."

"Wait, you said 'were,'" Dylan said. "Are your parents... dead?" Alex nodded. "I'm sorry," he said. "You don't look that old."

Despite herself, Alex laughed. "That's just what every woman wants to hear, Dylan—that she 'doesn't look that old.'"

"I'm sorry!" he said. His face was turning red again. Tom was trying not to laugh. "I didn't mean—"

"It's alright." Alex cut him off with a gentle wave of her hand. "My parents didn't die of old age. It was a car accident, a long time ago. I was... in prison at the time."

Tom looked up at her. "Say again?" Dylan just blinked in surprise.

Alex sighed. The cat was partway out of the bag now; there was no putting it back in. "My father was a surgeon, and my mother was an obstetrician who specialized in difficult births. They both made a lot of money. We were quite well off, but I didn't appreciate it—or them.

"I started doing heroin when I was only a little older than you," she said, nodding at Dylan.

He gasped in shock. "Really?" he said.

"Your chosen profession is starting to make more sense," Tom mused. "Go on."

"But why would you do drugs?" Dylan said. He was wringing his hands like he didn't want to believe what he was hearing.

Alex shrugged. "Why does any spoiled rich girl do anything? Sometimes to spite her parents, sometimes because she's chosen her friends poorly, sometimes just because teenagers are stupid. In my case, it was all three." Dylan sank back in his chair, looking hurt. Alex patted his knee. "I didn't mean you, honey. You're a lot smarter than most."

Even though she was confessing her dark past primarily to avoid having to confess what was really bothering her, talking about it *was* making her feel better. When that thought crossed her mind, she immediately felt like a jerk again. She shoved the guilt aside and made herself keep talking.

"My parents were hardly ever home; they worked such long hours. I went to an expensive private school with other spoiled rich girls who hardly ever saw their parents, either. At that age, peer pressure is the worst drug of all. When you have a group of teens with low self-esteem and even less parental guidance, it only takes one druggie in your circle of friends to get everyone else to start using, too.

"At first, it didn't really seem like a big deal. I didn't want to be the only one not shooting up, so I gave it a try. As soon as I stuck that needle in my arm, everything about my life changed for the worse—I just didn't know it yet. With a drug like heroin, the first time you get high—it's not something I can explain to you. It's euphoria beyond anything you can imagine. It feels so incredible that, once you come down, you can't think about anything except getting high again.

"That's the bitch about drugs. No high is ever as good as the first one, but that doesn't stop you from trying to recapture that feeling."

Tom and Dylan were staring at her with rapt attention now. Neither said anything. They could tell that she was on the verge of revealing something about herself that very few other people knew.

Alex paused for a moment to dredge up more willpower. Talking about her past was not easy, especially when she was using it to cover up another lie. "It only took a few months for my parents to figure out I was using. They were beside themselves when they found out. When they yelled at me, I expected to hear, 'These drugs are going to kill you. You're our daughter, and we won't let that happen.'

"But that's not what they said. Instead, they said, 'How are you going to get into medical school if you're high all the time?"'

"Jesus," Tom whispered.

"Hearing them say that… hearing that they were worried about the family legacy and not about *me* was more than I could handle. They yelled at me for another hour or two, but I didn't hear any of it. I tuned it out. I was just waiting for it to be over so I could call my dealer.

"My parents made me go to rehab. It didn't work, partly because I didn't want it to work. To their credit, they did try to get me clean, even if not for my sake. For two years, they tried. Eventually, when nothing worked and I just kept spiraling down into hell, they cut me off financially —stopped my allowance and canceled my credit cards.

"Addicts aren't evil, at least not at first. For a while, they're just sick. But if you want to push an addict over that line, if you want to see real evil, just take away their money so they can't get high anymore.

"After almost two days without heroin, I couldn't take it any longer. I broke into someone's house, an old lady who lived a few streets over. I didn't know her, I just picked the house at random. It was in the same upper-class neighborhood; she must have had money.

"It was the middle of the night, and I was hardly an experienced thief. When I couldn't find any cash, I started to get angry. I found some silverware that looked like it might have been worth something and started dumping it into a pillowcase. The racket must have woken her up because the next thing I knew, there she was, standing at the top of the stairs, staring right at me.

"I panicked. I ran past her—or at least, that was the plan. My brain was so scrambled from withdrawal that I couldn't even walk straight. I ran right into her and knocked her down the stairs. She hit her head and died instantly."

"Alex…," Dylan whispered. He was covering his mouth with his hands. At first, she thought he was looking at her in horror and revulsion, disgusted by what she'd done. But after a moment, she realized that his eyes were filled with empathy, not contempt.

Tom said nothing, his face impassive. He waited patiently for her to go on when she was ready. Alex felt a tear winding its way down her face, a tiny crystal of frigid cold in the night air. She wiped it away.

"The police came to my house the next day. Like I said, I was a shitty burglar. I must have left plenty of evidence and made myself easy to find. I pleaded guilty to manslaughter and did eight years in prison. Once I'd been clean for a few months and my brain was slowly starting to piece itself back together, I made up my mind to spend the rest of my life atoning for the one I'd taken. I applied to every correspondence program in the country until I finally found one willing to accept a convicted murderer, a bottom-of-the-barrel state college in Utah. I got my biology and psychology undergrad degrees by mail." Alex looked up to make sure that Dylan and Tom were both looking at her. "Guess how I paid for them."

They both shrugged. Alex paused a moment longer, for dramatic effect. "I got a scholarship from Jumpstart International."

Dylan's jaw dropped. "Mr. Holcomb's charity?"

Alex nodded. "It was new at the time; Ethan couldn't have been much older than I was, but he had money already, and he was using it to better the world. One of the charity's scholarship programs was for inmates sincerely committed to turning over a new leaf. It was a hell of an application process, but I was serious about making up for my past, and Ethan could tell."

Tom shook his head, amazed. "It's like a daytime soap opera," he said. When Alex squinted at him, he added, "With better writing."

Alex took a deep breath before continuing. "When I got out of prison, it was even harder to find a medical school that would take a convicted felon, even one with a perfect GPA and an origin story straight out of Hollywood. Finally, I found one. Prestigious, it was not, but it got me the medical degree. With Ethan's endorsement, I signed on with New Horizons shortly after I graduated; unlike everyone else, they were only too happy to have me. Who could be better at building rapport with addicts than a doctor who was once an addict herself?"

"That's one hell of a story," Tom said.

"Sara knew this all along," Dylan said.

"Not exactly," Alex said. "When Sara was born, I asked Ethan not to tell her about my past. I would tell her myself when the time was right. I was never sure how I would know when the time was right, but Ethan honored my request."

"Then how did Sara know?" Dylan asked.

"She found out when she was spying on our dreams," Tom guessed.

Alex nodded. "I have no doubt that she saw exactly what I was having nightmares about." She was struggling mightily to keep her voice steady. "I never got a chance to apologize to my parents, or to show them how serious I was about trying to turn my life around. The car crash.... They died a year before I got out of prison."

Without saying a word, Dylan stood up and walked over to her, his shoes crunching quietly through the snow. He hugged her, as she'd done so often to him in his darkest moments. She returned the embrace, grateful for the display of affection and understanding.

"I get it now," Tom said softly. He seemed to be making a deliberate effort to take the usual hard edge out of his voice. "I get the whole 'making amends' thing. You became a rehab doctor to stop other young people from taking the path you took, but it's bigger than that. You don't only want to save addicts, you want to save everyone. You feel like you *have* to save everyone to make up for what you did so long ago. Sara's Pilgrimage, being her Warden... that's how you can save everyone—including Jacob."

Alex broke down in tears, burying her face in Dylan's shoulder.

CHAPTER TWENTY-SEVEN
Unrest

The sun was just beginning to peek over the horizon as Tom fumbled around in the glovebox of his truck, looking for his phone. He blew on his hands and rubbed them together while he waited for the phone to start up. When it did, he blinked in surprise as missed call notifications started popping up one after another—more than a dozen in total. Why were so many people trying to call him? All calls were supposed to go to Teddy or Greg whenever Tom was out, and everyone in the office knew that.

He scrolled through the call log and noticed that most of the missed calls were from Deanna, one of the HR ladies. There was also a voicemail from her. He played it.

"Tom, it's Deanna. I know you're dealing with a family emergency, but I need you to call me back right away. It's important."

Tom sighed as he pressed the return call button. The line began to ring. What was so important that Teddy couldn't deal with it? He racked his brain for ideas, but he had none. Teddy knew almost as much about the company's inner workings as Tom did; he should be able to handle anything that came up.

The line clicked as Deanna answered. "Tom, thank god. How is everything? Are you okay?"

Absolutely not, he thought. "Yes, I'm fine. What's up?"

"I'm afraid I have some bad news. It was too important to leave a message. I think you should sit down."

Tom frowned. "Come on, it can't be that bad."

"I really think you should sit down."

Tom's heartbeat quickened as he dropped into the passenger seat of his truck. Deanna had never spoken this way before. He was beginning to worry. "Okay, tell me."

"It's about Teddy. He… he's dead. I'm so sorry."

Tom suddenly felt far away from himself. He sat in numb silence, holding the phone to his ear. Surely, he'd misheard, or Deanna had misspoken.

"Tom?"

"I'm here."

"I'm so sorry."

"You said... Teddy is dead? There must be some mistake."

"I wish there were."

"What... what happened?" Tom swallowed hard, fighting to keep his voice steady.

"It was the night before last. You remember Gavin, right?"

The ungrateful punk Tom had kept out of jail by lying for him. "I remember."

"He broke into the office late at night. The police said he was looking for something valuable to steal. They found some cash in his pockets, and the coffee fund jar was empty, he must have taken it from there. He must not have known that Teddy was working late in his office. Teddy heard the noise and came out to investigate. He surprised Gavin in the break room and... Gavin hit him with a wrench, in the head. Teddy hung on for a few hours, but he died in the hospital."

Tom's mind refused to accept what he was hearing. He felt tightness low in his chest, as though he knew on some level that it was true but couldn't yet allow himself to acknowledge it by feeling shock or pain. He stared blankly toward the Holcombs' mailbox at the end of the driveway, not really seeing it, his eyes unfocused.

"I don't...." Tom trailed off. He felt like he'd had something to say, but the words kept evaporating in his mind.

"Tom, I'm so sorry. I know how close you and Teddy were. The police caught Gavin; they have him in custody."

"Yes, thank you." His voice was flat and toneless.

"There's a... memorial service tomorrow, at 2. This whole thing is so horrible, but I'm glad I was able to get ahold of you today. I knew you would want to go."

Tom glanced at his watch. The clock was running down on Sara's Pilgrimage, with less than three days to go. None of them knew how much ground they had left to cover. They could be ten miles from the cathedral, or a hundred. There was no way to tell.

"Tom?"

"Thank you for telling me, Deanna. I... don't think I can make it to the memorial." Saying those words out loud finally cracked the temporary dam in his heart. Tom rubbed his eyes, struggling to hold back tears.

It was Deanna's turn to sit in stunned silence. She knew that Tom and Teddy had been close friends for more than twenty years. She knew that they had served in the Rangers together, killed for one another, and saved each other's lives. She also knew that, in the past, Tom had dropped everything to attend an employee's funeral—and no employee meant more to Tom than Teddy did.

Deanna cleared her throat and tried to be helpful. "Is it a money problem? I know changing flights at the last minute can be expensive, but I'm sure we can call it a business expense. There are also plenty of points on the company travel card if that helps."

Tom felt his muscles tighten as he summoned all his willpower to keep his voice steady. "No, it's not a money issue. I have a… commitment that I can't back out of."

What commitment could be more important than Teddy's funeral? Deanna didn't say it, but Tom could hear her thinking it. Instead, she said, "I understand."

She didn't understand. Tom wasn't sure he did, either.

He needed to end the conversation and think for a minute. "Thank you for telling me. Please work with Greg to keep things running until I get back and ask him to stop by my house and check on Riley twice a day. I'll pay him. I'll come home as soon as I can." He ended the call.

Tom closed the truck door and leaned his head back against the headrest. He needed to be alone for a while.

* * *

The Twilight moon shone brightly on the single white lily near the train tracks, making the petals seem to glow. The flower and the clumps of weeds around it swayed in a cold breeze. The eternal night was eerily quiet.

"Do you think Jacob is okay?" Sara asked. There was no sign of him.

"I hope so," Alex said. "I'm sure he's fine. He's survived here almost as long as Tom and I have been alive."

"You and I have different definitions of the word 'fine,'" Tom said, press-checking his Jackhammer.

Dylan pointed at the empty train platform. "Roland said that there are vehicles that come and go on their own. Maybe the train will show up if we wait a bit. It would be a lot faster than walking."

Alex closed her eyes at the mention of Roland's name. Vivid memories of his death flashed through her mind, and her heart grew heavy with guilt. Sara touched her arm gently in solidarity.

"I'm not sure we can spare the time to wait for a train that may or may not show up," Tom said. "Besides, the last time Sara and I took a boat, it didn't go so well." Alex thought that Tom seemed distracted, as if something were bothering him.

"I agree," Sara said. "We should start walking. I have a vague sense that we're doing okay on time, but I can't be sure of that. We need to keep covering ground."

They set out deeper into the canyon, following the train tracks. Loose gravel crunched beneath their feet. After a while, the monotonous sound, in the absence of any other noise, became lightly maddening. Unable to stand it any longer, Tom decided to get some answers to his nagging questions.

"Sara, I think it's time you told us why you were being so weird around Jacob."

Tom was walking beside her. He watched her face closely as he spoke. Her eyes darted sideways to glance at him, but otherwise, she showed no reaction to the question. Alex and Dylan watched the exchange. Their expressions suggested to Tom that they had noticed Sara's odd behavior, too.

"I don't know what you mean," Sara said, her voice entirely too casual.

"You're a bad liar," Tom said. "You know exactly what I mean."

"I just wasn't sure if I could trust him at first. He's been here for thirty-six years. The Twilight could have twisted him into a serial killer, for all we know."

"Bullshit. Your reaction to Roland was completely different, and your reaction when we heard Jacob yelling for help in the slaughterhouse was way out of character for you. You're one of the kindest people I know—shit, look at where we are, at what you've taken on to help everyone else. But you weren't even conflicted about helping Jacob, you were ready to cut and run with no hesitation. I've heard a lot of stories that don't add up in my time. You can't fool me. In life-or-death situations, secrets get people killed. We need to know whatever you're not telling us."

Sara glanced to her other side, at Alex and Dylan. Their faces were softer than Tom's, but they, too, wanted answers. She felt a sudden chill and rubbed her arms. "It's getting colder," she said.

Tom had also noticed the sudden drop in temperature but didn't say so. "Don't change the subject," he said.

Sara heaved a deep sigh. Stalling for time, she fished a hair tie out of her pocket and pulled her hair back into a short ponytail, muttering about the wind blowing it in her face. Finally, she spoke. "I lied to Jacob when I said I had read 'a little' about Lily's Pilgrimage. In fact, I read a lot about it—everything there was to read."

"Why?" Alex asked.

"It was a... unique case. According to the reports, Lily was extremely upset when she came back after completing her Pilgrimage. She said that 'everyone' had died, meaning, all three of her Wardens. She was so upset that it was really hard to get much detail out of her. Eventually, she refused to talk about it altogether. I guess I don't blame her. All we know for sure is that all her Wardens died somewhere near the cathedral—or we *thought* we knew that for sure, until today."

"So, you thought Jacob was dead and were surprised to see him alive? That doesn't explain why you were so weird about it," Tom said.

Sara shook her head. "There's more to it than that. I need to tell you something. I didn't want to tell you this, but I guess there's no avoiding it."

Tom sighed. "This is starting to become a pattern, you not telling us things. I don't like it."

"I had a reason for not wanting to tell you this. It's bad. It's upsetting. There's nothing we can do about it, so if I told you, it would just give you another thing to worry about, and we already have enough of those."

Tom sighed again, trying to keep his rising anger in check. "Go on."

Sara wrung her hands, clearly nervous about what she had to say. "The cathedral is in a place called the Hollow. I mentioned it when we first came here. The Hollow is... I guess you can think of it as the heart of the Twilight. It's the worst place there is. It's more dangerous than anything else we've seen."

Dylan blinked. "More dangerous?"

Alex cut in. "How so?"

Sara paused, choosing her words carefully. "It's bad in a few ways. For one thing, something... happens if you die there." She stopped again, looking increasingly reluctant to go on.

"Sara, look at me," Tom said. When she did, he went on. "What happens if you die in the Hollow? No more lies, even if you think you're protecting us. We need to know what we're walking into."

Sara closed her eyes for a long moment, gathering her composure. "Wardens and Maidens who die in the Hollow—they don't just die. The Twilight breaks down their bodies and turns them into something else. It turns them into the super monsters we've seen. We—the Circle—have a name for them. We call them Eidolons. The same thing happens to anyone killed *by* an Eidolon, whether in the Hollow or elsewhere."

Tom, Alex, and Dylan all stopped walking. They were staring at Sara incredulously. She walked on for another few steps before realizing they had stopped. She turned to face them, her eyes cast toward the ground.

"You knew about those things? You knew about them all along? And then you played dumb back there in the slaughterhouse when we were all trying to figure out where they came from?" Alex's face was heating, as was her voice.

"What possible reason could you have for keeping that from us?" Tom said. "Is this whole thing a fucking game to you? Do you not realize that you're playing with real people's lives here? What else do you know that might have helped us stay alive?" His hands were balled into fists at his sides, and his jaw was clenched so tightly that his teeth began to ache.

Sara raised her hands defensively. "Just hear me out, please. I can explain. For one thing, the Circle has strict policies about what we tell Wardens."

Tom leaned toward her, struggling not to yell in her face. "Ask me if I give one single shit about your goddamned policies."

Sara hurried to explain. "Most things about the Twilight are on a 'need to know' basis. We tell Wardens as much as they need to know, based on what happens or seems likely to happen during any given Pilgrimage. We can't tell you everything—for one thing, there just isn't enough time—it took me more than a decade to learn what I know. Imagine what would happen if we tried to tell Wardens about all the ways the Twilight is dangerous or horrible. You'd be so worried and distracted you wouldn't be able to function. Some Wardens would refuse the Pilgrimage altogether—and if too many refuse, then there won't be anyone left to undertake a Pilgrimage, and the world ends."

Tom crossed his arms. "I don't approve of the Circle's position on informed consent."

Alex stepped between Tom and Sara to defuse the tension. "Sara, let's pretend, for the sake of argument, that we accept the need for that policy. It doesn't explain why you wouldn't tell us about the super monsters—the Eidolons. They appear often, don't they? Shouldn't you tell us about them so we know what to expect? That can only help us protect you better."

"It's not the existence of the Eidolons we don't want you to know about," Sara said. "It's just that we didn't want to burden you with the knowledge of what they are and where they come from. We thought it best to avoid the subject altogether, as much as possible. The more we talk about it, the more likely it becomes that Wardens will ask questions that are best left unanswered."

"That's not your call to make," Tom said.

Sara shook her head, looking more resolute now. "I'm sorry, but it is. Billions of lives are in my hands. I have to do whatever it takes to save them. You guys are barely keeping it together as it is. That's not a criticism —you've all been wonderfully brave, and I'm so lucky to have you with me, even though I will never forgive myself for dragging you into this nightmare. I just can't take the risk of telling you any more than absolutely necessary. How am I to know which bit of horrible knowledge will be the final straw that causes one of you to quit the Pilgrimage or to become distracted at the wrong time? All of us have narrowly avoided death several times already. The margin for error here is slim. If keeping certain things from you betters our chances of survival by even a tiny bit, then I will keep them from you."

Tom rose to his full height, towering over Sara. "That's horse shit. You have no right to dance us around like puppets, deciding what we need to know. You're seventeen. You might know all there is to know about this insane hell we're standing in, but you know fuck-all about life, leadership, or how people are supposed to treat their friends."

Alex and Dylan expected Sara to cower before Tom. Instead, she met his eyes with iron in hers. "You mean to tell me that, in your military career, you never led men into battle without telling them everything they were up against? You never hid things from them to protect them? Not even once?"

Tom felt his shoulders tensing up again. "That's different."

Sara stared back at him coolly. "How?"

"For one thing, you're a child. You don't have the training or experience to make decisions that could get someone killed. In war, sometimes it's necessary. A squad of soldiers is not a democracy. In war, sometimes the leader has to make a hard decision, and everyone else just needs to fall in line, whether they agree or not—whether they know all the facts or not."

Sara spread her arms as if to say that Tom had just proven her point. "Are we not at war right now? Are we not standing in a war zone at this very moment? Does this war not have higher stakes than any war ever fought before? I may be a child—to you, anyway—but who among us is more qualified than I am to know what's best here, in this place? I haven't lived as long as you, but I've spent most of my life preparing for this. You know more than any of us when it comes to weapons and tactics, and we let you call the shots in those areas, but you don't know the Twilight like I do. You'd have nightmares for the rest of your life if you did—if you even made it to the cathedral, which is a big 'if.'"

Tom turned away from her. It wasn't as simple as she was making it out to be.

Alex stepped in to redirect Sara's attention and to give Tom a minute to cool off. "Sara, you said that the Eidolons are created when a Maiden or Warden dies in the Hollow, or when an Eidolon kills someone. So, everything we thought we had figured out about them is wrong?"

Sara shook her head. "No, not everything. You got a lot right, actually. I hadn't considered the part about the Eidolons being attracted to strong negative emotions; that may be a new discovery. We do know that each Eidolon is unique and is somehow tied to a living Warden—Tom and the Ouroboros, me and the Stalker, you and the Prisoner, Dylan and the Glutton. But those specific Eidolons weren't created until sometime after we came to the Twilight for the first time.

"When Wardens or Maidens die in the Hollow, or get killed by an

Eidolon, their life force—if you want to call it that—collects in the Hollow, in a sort of mist. The whole place is covered in a fog of pure hate and pain—it's a living energy. When new people come here, the Twilight begins to learn about their fears and weaknesses. Before too long, a new Eidolon is born from the mist, in the image of the person whose thoughts created it —and it goes hunting for them."

Dylan chimed in. "I don't understand the connections, though. The only ones that seem to make any sense are the Ouroboros—Tom admitted he's afraid of snakes—and the Prisoner, Alex accidentally killed an old woman. But what does that Stalker thing have to do with Sara? What does a blob of black ooze have to do with me?"

Sara shrugged. "I don't know, but I don't think it matters. Only one thing matters: getting to the cathedral."

Tom turned back around. He still looked angry, but his temper had cooled somewhat. "How are we supposed to do that if we can't trust you?"

Sara's shoulders slumped, and she shook her head sadly. "I'm sorry I lied to you, but I did what I had to do, and I would make the same choice again. I'm sorry if I've broken your trust in doing so. Please believe that I never meant to hurt any of you. I was only trying to protect you—and everyone else on Earth."

Alex raised her hand to interject. "I think we got a little off track. What does any of this have to do with Jacob?"

Sara nodded her thanks for the reminder. "Like I said, Lily said that 'everyone' had died. We thought she meant that all her Wardens died near the cathedral—in the Hollow. That would mean that Jacob couldn't possibly be alive, so I was suspicious to hear that he saved you at the hospital. Still, he was long gone by the time the four of us met up, and I figured we'd never see him again. I was worried that the person you met wasn't Jacob at all—I thought it might have been an Eidolon—some horrid monster born in the Hollow that only looked like Jacob. So, I was surprised to hear that he—or 'it'—helped you and then let you go. I wasn't sure what to think, but I saw no point in bringing any of this up.

"When we heard the screaming in the slaughterhouse, and when you said it was Jacob, I got worried again. I didn't think it could be the real Jacob, and I wasn't sure it meant us harm, but I didn't want to take the chance if it did. Alex ran off without us, so we didn't have much choice except to follow."

"Is that why you were so suspicious of him at the train station?" Dylan asked. Sara nodded.

"You were gripping your rifle like you were ready to shoot him," Tom observed.

Again, Sara nodded. "I was ready to shoot him, if he said or did anything threatening."

"But then, all of a sudden, your attitude changed," Alex said. "After Jacob told us what happened to Lily, you relaxed, like you didn't seem to consider him a threat anymore."

"That was when I finally put it all together. Jacob said he got separated from Lily and her other Wardens here, in this canyon. If that were true, that would mean he never made it to the cathedral, which would mean he couldn't have died in the Hollow. Still, if it wasn't Jacob—if the thing we were talking to was an Eidolon—it could have been lying about that part. But then I remembered the Butcher."

"What about it?" Alex asked.

"Every Eidolon is tied to a Warden or Maiden—a *living* one. When a Warden or Maiden dies, so does the Eidolon tied to them, and in the two cases we talked about, the now-dead person *becomes* an Eidolon. It's a horrible cycle. Roland was already dead, and every other Maiden and Warden from the last two cycles was also confirmed dead—except for Jacob. So, the Butcher must have been Jacob's Eidolon. If he himself were an Eidolon, the Butcher couldn't exist."

"What makes you so sure the Butcher was an Eidolon? What if it was just another monster?" Dylan asked.

"I don't think so," Sara said. "Eidolons are so difficult to kill that they might as well be invincible. Sometimes you can hurt them enough to slow them down, but that's usually all you can manage. We've had a few rare reports of someone killing an Eidolon, but we were never able to confirm those. If the Butcher were just another monster, Tom alone would have killed it ten times over, not to mention all the damage the rest of us were doing to it."

"So, putting those pieces together finally convinced you that Jacob really was Jacob, not another monster waiting to kill us," Alex said. Sara nodded.

"I don't want to die and... become something that kills someone else," Dylan said, clearly struggling to maintain his composure. Sara put a comforting arm around him.

Tom sighed, clearly still exasperated. "Sara, what you say makes sense, but keeping all this from us wasn't the right way to handle it."

"I guess we'll have to agree to disagree," she said.

Tom adjusted his armor and started walking, unwilling to argue anymore. The others followed, glad to be moving again, if only because the freezing wind was starting to make their teeth chatter.

"Jacob said he got separated from Lily in this canyon, and it sounds like she finished her Pilgrimage soon after that, without leaving the Twilight in between," Alex said.

"That's what I gathered from the report I read," Sara said.

"That must mean we're close to the cathedral," Dylan said, picking up on Alex's reasoning.

Sara shrugged. "Maybe. I hope so, but we can't be sure. Remember, the Twilight shifts and changes over time. The path we're walking now isn't exactly the same one that Lily took."

Another blast of frigid wind howled through the canyon. The temperature seemed to be dropping rapidly. Alex and Sara were shivering violently; Tom and Dylan weren't much better off.

"S-should we b-be worried about how c-cold it's getting? It feels like it's b-below f-freezing," Alex stammered.

"Everything about this place should worry you," Tom said dryly.

"*That* definitely worries me," Dylan said, swallowing hard. The others looked to where he was pointing.

High above, at the canyon's rim, four dark silhouettes looked down on them, human-shaped patches of blackness blotting out the stars above.

Tom raised his shotgun and flicked off the safety. "Be ready. Keep your eyes open in all directions—don't get tunnel vision."

Another gust of wind kicked up, carrying with it a sound like wind chimes. It was so cold that all four of them could barely move.

"H-hypothermia," Alex stuttered. "We c-can't stand c-cold like this f-for long."

"Are they causing it?" Tom said. He tried to fire at the silhouettes above, but his trigger finger wouldn't move. Grunting, he fell to his knees as his numb feet tripped over rocks.

"It's the... the w-witches...," Sara muttered, so faintly that the others barely heard her.

The witches? What did that mean? Tom was having trouble making his brain work.

"It's g-getting so cold, so f-fast," Dylan gasped. He, too, fell to his knees, struggling to move against the icy gale. Another sound came with the wind this time, like tinkling shards of glass.

"Sara?" Alex whispered, her voice low and hoarse. Sara was on the ground, face down, not moving. "Sara!" Alex tried to crawl over to her. She couldn't make much progress. A moment later, her muscles stopped working altogether, and she fell onto her side. Her face was so cold that she couldn't even make her eyes blink.

"God dammit," Tom growled. With a mighty effort, he looked back, toward the others.

All three of them were lying down, motionless.

Before Tom could think of a way to get them to safety, the cold took hold deep within his bones, and his vision faded. Faintly, as though he were far away from himself, he felt his body fall sideways onto the frigid ground.

CHAPTER TWENTY-EIGHT
Guilt

Tap. Tap. Tap.

The noise was getting annoying. It was quiet, yet somehow loud and grating at the same time.

Tap. Tap. Tap.

Cold. Still so cold, especially on her back.

Tap. Tap. Tap.

Slowly, Alex began to remember who she was. Her brain felt heavy and tired, her thoughts sluggish, like a car reluctant to start in cold weather.

Why was everything so dark? She blinked rapidly. There, she could see a little better now. Her eyes felt crusty and dry, like she'd been asleep for a long time. Her body felt odd, like she was in an unnatural position. She wasn't sitting or kneeling, but she wasn't quite standing up, either. There was pressure on her chest.

She tried to move. A metallic sound came to her ears. She could move her arms a little, but not much. Something was holding them in place, out to her sides.

Finally, as her eyes began to focus in the dim light, and her thoughts became clearer, she understood. The things holding her up were chains.

She was chained to a stone wall, completely immobilized.

Her chest immediately tightened with panic. She began to hyperventilate. She struggled against the chains with all her might, but it was no use.

Where were the others? Where was Sara? Were they nearby? Everyone on Earth was depending on Sara, and Sara was depending on Alex. She needed to find Sara, which meant she needed to free herself—which meant she needed to calm down.

Alex closed her eyes and remembered her first arrival in the Twilight, when she'd been trapped in the mausoleum and then in that infernal drainage pipe. She'd been convinced that she was going to die then, but she'd pulled through, with Tom's help. She remembered what he'd said to her, how he'd kept his voice calm and appealed to her reason. Above all else, she must not give in to her fear. If she did that, she would definitely be done for.

She closed her eyes and took a deep breath, then another, and a third, willing her heart to slow. Gradually, it did. She opened her eyes and looked around. Step one was figuring out where she was.

It was dim, but not as dark as she'd first thought; her eyes had simply needed time to adjust. The walls were rough stone, cold against her back. The air had a stale, musty quality to it, as though she were deep underground. Yellow-orange light danced across the wall to her right, suggesting firelight somewhere nearby, perhaps around a corner.

The *tap, tap, tap* sound was dripping water. The ceiling was low enough that she could see long-calcified stalactites that reminded her of the time her parents had taken her to Carlsbad Caverns when she was a girl. Water was collecting on some of the stalactites and falling rhythmically to the ground.

Alex looked down at herself. Her pack, armor, and weapons were gone. She had only her clothes. Ever since she'd realized that she was underground, her claustrophobia had been on a low simmer in the pit of her stomach; it flared back into full-blown terror when she saw that she was unarmed. She couldn't see any tools or objects nearby that might help her escape—not that she could reach them if there were any. She forced the fear down again. She didn't try to deny it. Instead, she acknowledged it and then ignored it, as Tom had shown her.

A sudden whisper of air moved through the cave. It wasn't much, but she definitely felt a light breeze. An odd sound came with it, like leaves rustling across wet grass. Embedded deep within the sound was... not a voice, more like a suggestion of words. As she listened, she felt a sense of intent behind the sensation, as though something were trying to communicate.

Suddenly, a single word crystallized in Alex's mind, as though someone had implanted it. It was an invasive, alien feeling, but not exactly hostile.

Think.

Alex had seen too many living nightmares this week to feel anything more than mild surprise at the notion of actual telepathy. She frowned. Who or what was commanding her to think, and why? That wasn't very helpful. Of course, she had to think. She knew that much.

Do you?

That time, Alex jerked, rattling her chains. Apparently, this line of communication ran in both directions. The presence, whatever it was, could hear her thoughts. Out of habit, she responded aloud.

"Who are you? Or what are you?"

Again, the faint sound of rustling foliage brought foreign words into her mind.

Your proctor.

A proctor? Of what? Alex decided to ask a more practical question. "Did you bring me here and chain me up?"

Yes.

"So, you're my enemy."

Not necessarily.

Alex sighed, fighting to keep her cool. "Where's Sara?"

Do not worry about her just now. Worry about yourself. Think. Your mind is your greatest weapon. Think or die.

"I don't have time for this. We have to get Sara to the cathedral, or *everyone* dies. We're running out of time. Let me go!"

Silence. The voice-that-wasn't-a-voice was gone. Frustrated, Alex thrashed against her bindings. They didn't budge. She raged uselessly for a minute or two, then gave up. There was no sense wasting her strength; she couldn't force her way out of the chains. She tried to think creatively, but she couldn't come up with any good ideas. How was she supposed to escape without any tools?

Another sound came to her ears, different than before. This was a sound of something heavy scraping against stone. It was around the corner, behind her, where she couldn't see what was making it. But it was getting louder.

It was coming closer.

The panic rose again in Alex's chest. Her breathing quickened, and her heart hammered against her ribs. She didn't want to turn her head, didn't want to see what was coming for her.

When it finally came into view, she screamed. Her shrieks of terror echoed around the stone chamber, but no one was there to hear them—no one to come help her.

It was the Prisoner.

Alex screamed again as it came closer. Its filthy, shriveled flesh hung loosely from its bones. Its spine was so deformed that its torso was nearly parallel to the ground. Heavy iron manacles bound its wrists together, a short length of chain between them allowing limited independent movement of each mummified hand.

One hand was dragging a crude sword made of several femurs fused together by extreme heat. The bone scraping along the ground was splintered—and razor sharp.

Alex struggled with all her might, her muscles enhanced by adrenaline, trying to somehow free an arm or pull the chains away from the iron spikes driven deep into the stone. It was useless. She couldn't move. Tom was far stronger than she, but even he would be powerless to free himself by strength alone.

Her breath came in ragged gasps as the Prisoner inched closer, moaning to itself. Its guttural murmurs sounded more animal than human, yet they carried unmistakable shades of profound grief and suffering. Alex pushed herself backward, against the stone, trying in vain to retreat.

With a wail of anguish, the Prisoner lashed out with its weapon, swinging the bone blade with ferocious speed and power. Excruciating agony flared in Alex's left leg. Her scream of pain would have shattered glass, had there been any nearby. Afraid of what she would see, she forced herself to look down and assess the damage.

Her mind violently rejected the grim reality of what her eyes saw. Her leg was severed at mid-thigh, lying several feet away. Bright red, arterial blood sprayed from the stump in time with her racing heart, creating a rapidly spreading pool on the ground. The shock of having her leg cut off created a temporary wall in her mind that blunted the searing pain, but a moment later, the wall collapsed, and she screamed again.

Before Alex could have any more thoughts, the Prisoner struck again, severing her right arm at the shoulder. It hurt, but not as much as her leg did. Dimly, in the back of her mind, Alex knew that the pain gating mechanism in her brain was working. The human body could only experience so much pain at one time; there simply weren't enough nerves to carry any more pain signals beyond a certain threshold.

The knowledge was hardly comforting.

She could already feel her consciousness fading, and her vision was getting darker. Missing two limbs, she would bleed out in a minute, at most. She struggled to think. The voice had commanded her to think. But think about what? How was thinking supposed to help if she couldn't move?

Alex felt intense pressure in her right leg, another spike of dull pain. Blinking rapidly, she struggled to see. Both of her legs were gone now. Her terror had receded to the back of her mind, with confusion taking its place. Where was Sara? Was she okay? There was no way to know.

Fresh, white-hot agony temporarily revived her. With only one limb, there was nothing left for the chains to hold, and she had slipped free. The raw stumps of her missing legs had slammed onto the ground, and the all-consuming pain focused her mind again.

I'm... I'm just a torso. It can't end like this. We made it so far. Not like this.

Acting on pure survival instinct, Alex struggled to pull herself along the ground with her remaining arm. Her fingers slipped in her own blood, already cooling as it spread across the stone. Her heart felt like it was racing at three hundred beats per minute, and yet she felt so tired.

So very tired.

Something hit her in the ribs, flipping her over onto her back—the Prisoner had kicked her. She could hardly see anything, but she could just make it out, standing above her, its grotesque weapon raised high.

Her executioner rammed the sharp bone through her stomach with enough force to pierce the stone below, pinning her in place like a bug. She barely felt it. Idly, she thought that that shouldn't be possible—bone couldn't pierce rock. But then she remembered photos she'd seen of plastic straws driven all the way through telephone poles by terrible hurricanes. Maybe it was something like that.

As the last of Alex's blood trickled out of her veins and her brain began to die, the Prisoner stood above her and howled, in fury and in victory.

* * *

Alex inhaled so sharply that she choked herself. Coughing violently, she covered her mouth with her hands.

Wait. Hands?

She sat up and looked herself over. Her limbs were where they belonged, although they ached with dull, phantom pain. She lifted her shirt to examine her stomach. There was no evidence of a puncture wound. She looked around. There was no blood on the ground.

But the chains that had held her against the wall were still there. What had happened? Was it a dream? No, it couldn't be—no dream was that vivid, that horrifying, that physically painful. Besides, she was in the Twilight—she was already in a nightmare. She couldn't explain her recent death.

Alex placed two fingers against her opposite wrist. Her pulse felt nice and strong, and because she could feel it in her wrist, she knew her blood pressure was normal.

Her lingering panic began to fade, ever so slowly. There was no sign of the Prisoner, or of any other living thing besides herself.

Think.

She jumped. The not-voice was back in her head, its return heralded by another breeze. Its quality reminded her of fat raindrops falling on the leaves of thick jungle plants.

Alex got to her feet, somewhat unsteadily. "Enough!" she shouted. "I know I need to think! I'm thinking about how to get out of here, how to find Sara, how to put this nightmare behind us. What do you want?"

We want you to think.

We? Who was "we?" Was there more than one voice? Alex decided that it didn't really matter. "If you insist on wasting our very valuable time with games—with this sadistic *torture*—then you're no different from any of the other monsters here."

We are not your enemy.

"Your actions prove otherwise."

It comes. Think. Run.

Alex felt her eyes widen. "It" comes? The Prisoner?

The wailing moans that drifted toward her a moment later were her answer.

"God dammit," Alex said. Remembering Tom's advice, she did her best to channel her fear into anger, to turn it into something useful. She still didn't have her gear, but she was free now. She could move.

She could escape.

Wasting no time, she darted down a side passage, away from her pursuer. A few steps down the tunnel, she found the source of light: a torch on the wall, in an iron sconce. She snatched it up and continued running, forcing herself to slow down enough to see what was in front of her.

The passage behind her echoed with the Prisoner's wails, alternately sorrowful and furious. Memories of her recent execution flashed through Alex's mind, causing her to stumble and fall. The panic was doing its best to lock her muscles. She fought it off and kept running. Whenever she came to a fork, she chose a direction randomly. For now, all she wanted to do was gain some distance on the thing chasing her.

No matter how fast she ran or how many random turns she took, she couldn't seem to get farther ahead of it. Somehow, it was always close behind. Its howling reminded her of hunting dogs nipping at her heels. She was getting tired, but she pushed on. The tunnels had to end or change somewhere. Eventually, she'd find something useful.

No, that was a passive approach—the wrong approach. She couldn't just wait for some random stroke of luck. If there was no apparent escape, she needed to *make* one. But how? *Think*, the disembodied voice had kept telling her. Alex gritted her teeth in frustration. She *was* thinking. She was trying her best. What was she supposed to think of? What brilliant idea could make use of rock walls and a torch? She still hadn't seen anything else, no tools, weapons, or changing scenery.

Suddenly, she realized that the tunnels had fallen silent. She'd thought that she was scared before, but now she was terrified. The Prisoner's moans and wails, horrible as they were, at least let her know where it was. Not knowing its location was much worse.

Alex ran on, hoping against hope that she'd finally gained a strong lead. She went left, right, left again at the next three forks. The only sounds were the pounding of her own footsteps, her ragged panting, and the torch's flickering flame.

When she rounded the next corner, the Prisoner stabbed her in the neck.

Her feet flew out from under her, and she slammed onto her back. The torch clattered away, and her hands flew to her throat. She felt terrible damage. Blood was gushing over her hands and filling her trachea. She coughed violently, already drowning in it. She rolled onto her side, away from the Prisoner. It was holding the same bone sword, and her blood was dripping from its point.

Before her mind could fully register what had happened, before she could even feel the next wave of rising terror, the Prisoner tossed its weapon aside and fell to its knees beside her. Its shriveled, impossibly strong hands shoved hers out of the way as it seized her by the neck. Weakly, Alex tried to fight it off, pounding her fists against its skeletal body.

Empty, soulless sockets stared down at her.

She knew that her struggle was pointless. Tom had said he'd blasted this thing with six grenades, and it had just shrugged them off. It probably didn't even feel her pathetic punches.

With a final, deranged scream, the Prisoner wrenched violently, snapping Alex's neck like a twig. It tossed her lifeless body aside, reclaimed its weapon, and retreated back down the tunnel, dissolving into the shadows beyond the dying flame of the discarded torch.

* * *

Alex's eyes snapped open.

Think.

"Fuck you!" she managed to scream into the darkness. Or at least, she tried to scream. It came out more like a strangled whisper. Instinctively, she felt her neck.

It was fine. There was no blood.

This can't be real, she thought. *It must be some kind of illusion.*

But illusions couldn't produce pain or fear anything like what she was going through. Or could they? She was beginning to question her own sanity. What if *none* of this was real? What if there was no Twilight, no Pilgrimage, no sleeping god to mollify? What if she was unconscious in a psych ward somewhere, loaded up with Haldol?

It is real, the voice said. *As real as the consequences of your beliefs and choices.*

"For your sake, I hope you don't have a body. I hope you're just a voice. Because if you have an ass, I swear to god I'm going to kick it six ways to Sunday," Alex choked out, struggling to rise to her knees.

She realized that, in her condition, her threats were probably not very threatening.

As she fumbled in the darkness, her fingers closed around the cold torch. She picked it up as she stood, not sure what she was planning to do with it. Maybe it would be useful somehow.

Everything was pitch black. She held up her hand, right in front of her face, but she couldn't see it. She reached out carefully, felt a cool rock wall, and began to follow it.

Perhaps we were wrong about you. Perhaps you are not ready.

Alex considered not answering. Then she decided that, if she could keep the voice talking, she might be able to learn something useful from it. She sighed.

"Ready for what?"

To think. To see the truth.

"If I wanted empty bromides, I would go read my notes from freshman philosophy class."

We cannot give you the answer. For the answer to have meaning, to have power, you must discover it yourself.

Alex sighed again as she stumbled slowly down the dark passage. "You keep saying 'we.' Who or what are you? Just give me a straight answer."

I told you. I am your proctor.

"A proctor of what?" Alex suddenly felt lightheaded as a terrible realization dawned on her. "If there's more than one of you... are you torturing Tom, Sara, and Dylan like you're torturing me?"

We are not doing this to you. You are doing it to yourself. You started it. Only you can stop it. We merely observe.

Alex was trying to figure out what that was supposed to mean when she had an idea. A bad idea, but it was better than no idea. She stopped walking and examined the torch with her hands, feeling every inch of it. She unwound the wick and tossed it aside. The handle of the torch was wood, with a metal band under the wick. It felt like heavy, solid wood. Near the bottom, it tapered into a thinner, rounded edge.

Carefully, she put the thinner end of the torch on the ground and held the thicker end up at an angle, about thirty degrees. As best she could in the dark, she stamped down on the torch with her right foot, hard. It took a few dozen awkward kicks and stomps, but finally, the wood cracked, then snapped, then broke. Panting with exertion, she examined the broken edge by touch. It was sharp but irregular. Feeling more confident, she placed the jagged point against the stone wall and scraped it back and forth to sharpen it. Wood and stone were hardly ideal materials for the task at hand, but after some effort and time, she had a reasonably sharp stake.

She had a weapon.

"You're not going to comment on how this won't help me?" she said aloud. The voice didn't respond. It was gone again.

Her wooden knife probably wouldn't help her. Tom had blown the Prisoner to bits, and it had regenerated in a matter of seconds. What good would a pointy stick be?

Alex tried not to think about it. She tried not to think about how many times the Prisoner would murder her and then revive her, just to do it all again. She tried not to think about how painful and terrifying her next death would be.

Not thinking about such things was easier said than done.

She continued fumbling her way down the tunnel. At first, she chose paths at random whenever the passage forked, but then she remembered the old maze trick: You could escape any labyrinth by following the same wall at every juncture. It didn't matter if you went left or right, as long as you picked a direction and stuck with it. She decided to take only right turns from then on. Eventually, she would find her way out.

Assuming the Prisoner didn't kill her again first.

Alex stumbled around in the dark for what felt like hours, always trailing her hand along the wall to her right. Her watch was gone, so she wouldn't be able to check the time even if she could see. She hoped that the others were okay. She hoped that they would all reunite soon, escape the underground torture chamber, and finish this goddamned Pilgrimage.

Hope is not a strategy, Tom said in her head. She told him to shut up.

For the briefest instant, Alex found herself wondering if the human race even deserved to go on. The Pilgrimage was a hell worse than any she could have dreamed up a week ago. Hundreds of good people had given their lives just to buy humanity a little time until the bill came due again. Was there no end to it? Even if she and the others survived, they would be broken for the rest of their lives—maybe even shipped off to an asylum. Did people, in general, deserve to be the beneficiaries of such sacrifice?

Alex reprimanded herself. Most people had no idea what was happening, didn't know the terrors others were enduring on their behalf. They couldn't be blamed for something that they had no knowledge of and weren't responsible for.

A subtle change in the light drew her attention away from her morbid thoughts. At first, she thought she was imagining it, but after a minute, she was positive. Slowly but surely, the tunnel was getting brighter. Finally, she rounded a corner and found the light source—another torch. She nearly cried aloud in relief, then remembered that the Prisoner was still out there somewhere, hunting her. She celebrated silently for a moment, then snatched up the torch and continued on.

Now that she could see, her progress quickened tenfold. She continued following the right-hand wall, hopeful that she would find her way out before running into the Prisoner again. She was tempted to call out for the others but decided that the risk of drawing unwanted attention was too great. If they were down here, she'd find them. She wouldn't leave without them. If she found the exit first, she'd figure out a way to leave a trail or make a map so that she could find it again, once they were all together.

Her thoughts of escape ground to a halt as she rounded another corner and saw the Prisoner staring right at her with its empty eye sockets, waiting for her, several paces ahead.

Her fear kicked into overdrive again. Instinctively, she retreated the way she'd come, into a wider section of the passage where she could maneuver more easily. Her heart pounded against her ribs, and her mind showed her visions of all the different ways the Prisoner might kill her this time.

Not helpful, she told herself. She knew that she stood little chance of besting the creature in a fight, but what alternative was there? Just lie down and die? She refused to consider it.

Alex heard the Prisoner's rapid footsteps coming for her. She heard its horrible sword scraping against the stone. She heard its ragged breathing, its pained, insane mumbling.

She did her best to remember what Tom had taught her about fighting in tight spaces. The Prisoner would likely try a thrusting attack—the tunnel was too narrow for a wide swing—so she turned her body slightly, ready to dodge to the side. If she got an opening to counterattack, she needed to take it right away. *Go for the vital areas. Hit hard and fast*, Tom's voice said.

Except that this monstrosity had no vital areas. It could seemingly regenerate any damage.

Alex pushed the thought down and lowered her stance. She had to try.

The Prisoner came around the corner faster than she would have thought possible, already thrusting its weapon toward her. She was able to hop to the side and avoid the fatal attack only because she'd been anticipating it.

There—its torso is wide open.

With all her strength, Alex thrust her stake upward, under the creature's ribs. She felt it pierce the leathery skin and make solid contact with something inside—what would have been the liver in a person. The Prisoner showed no reaction to the attack, but it was already drawing its sword arm back, preparing to impale her again.

Time slowed to a crawl as more adrenaline flooded her body. In the next elongated second, an idea came to her.

She had a torch. Maybe fire would work better than stabbing or guns. It was worth a try.

Alex let loose a scream of feral rage, releasing all her pent-up fear and frustration. With her other hand, she slammed the torch into the Prisoner's chest and held it there, willing the dried-out flesh to ignite.

Surprisingly, it did. The flames caught and spread quickly. The shriveled breasts blackened and split as the fire climbed up the creature's body, toward its face. It dropped its weapon and howled in fury, the haunting sound deafening in the tunnels. Alex took a step back, giddy with excitement. She'd done it. She'd actually found a way to hurt the goddamned thing.

But there was no way to know how quickly it would recover. She turned and started to run.

Strong hands grabbed her shoulders and pulled her back. Alex let out a strangled yelp as she started to fall over.

But the Prisoner had no intention of letting her fall. Slowly, almost tenderly, it pulled her close, wrapping her in its arms, holding her tight against its burning body.

Alex shrieked as the flames seared her skin. She struggled to pull away, to escape the blistering inferno, but it was no use. Her screams became louder as her skin turned deep red, then brown, then black, all in a matter of seconds. Superheated air scorched her throat and lungs every time she inhaled. She was out of her mind with fear and pain, unable to form thoughts or words.

Distantly, as though she were far away from herself, she noticed that she heard something bubbling and popping. A moment later, even more distantly, she realized what it was.

Her fat.

A pleasant aroma of roasting meat came to her nose. It was Alex's last sensation before her brain shut down in response to the overwhelming trauma being inflicted on her body. The Prisoner continued to hold her, almost lovingly. Several long minutes later, when Alex's body was nothing but charred remains, it finally released its prey and shuffled away, back into the dark tunnels, its scorched flesh already healing.

* * *

Alex opened her eyes. Her mind felt sluggish again, reluctant to process sensory data or form thoughts. What was the point?

She noticed that she was crying. Her tears felt frigid on her cheeks. She wiped them away and felt that the skin on her face was smooth, unburned, normal.

For a long time, she lay on the cold stone floor and wept, partly out of fear for herself, but more so in frustration at her inability to stop this madness. She felt like she'd been trapped in these endless tunnels for days. Even if, by some miracle, she found the others and they all escaped within the next hour, they were probably already out of time. Ardu would wake up soon, discover the ritual uncompleted, and punish all of mankind for Alex's failure.

The crushing weight of guilt on her shoulders had never felt heavier.

Suddenly, she noticed that she'd been able to see all along, ever since she woke up again. She sat up and looked around. A soft, white light filled the small room, emanating from a source she couldn't identify. Someone—or something—had moved her. She was no longer in the tunnel she last remembered.

A small altar sat against the stone wall in front of her. Various items lay atop it: a tarnished silver necklace, a small model of a sailboat exquisitely carved from wood, a dried and preserved pink flower, and a handful of other things. For some reason, Alex felt a quiet aura of serenity radiating from the objects. On their own, they looked like little more than trinkets— even trash, in some cases—and yet they were arranged on the altar with obvious reverence. She was taken aback by the sight of something so ordinary and nonthreatening—so *human*—in the Twilight.

For what it is worth, we regret your suffering.

Alex jumped as the ethereal voice filled her mind again. She spun around and saw something that would have made her fall over, had she not already been sitting down. A young woman stood—no, *hovered* in front of her, floating a few inches above the ground. An aura of white light shone from her, soft and comforting, yet paradoxically bright enough to make the details of her body indistinguishable. Alex couldn't *see* that she was naked, but somehow, she *felt* that she was.

Only the woman's face was clearly visible. Her lips bore a wistful smile, with youthful dimples at the corners of her mouth. Her hair was dark, short, and wavy, a bit shorter than Sara's but thick and full, reinforcing Alex's estimate that she was in her late teens or early twenties.

Her eyes were a deep, rich brown, the color of fertile soil.

Alex saw a heavy black cloak hanging on the wall behind her. Next to it, on a separate peg, hung an intricate porcelain mask with strange symbols etched into it.

Suddenly, Alex understood. She rose to her feet, slowly. "You're the voice that's been talking to me."

I am. Her mouth didn't move, and yet the words filled Alex's ears and mind as though she had spoken. A gentle breeze ruffled Alex's hair, and she heard, quietly, the sound of leaves blowing in the wind.

"Why are you doing this to me?"

I told you before, we are not doing this. You are doing it to yourself.

"That doesn't make any sense." Alex noticed that she'd instinctively assumed a fighting stance, her legs bent, her hands held out in front of her defensively.

I assure you that it does. Whether you come to agree, in time, will be up to you.

"Let me go. I need to find Sara, and the other Wardens."

I will let you go soon; you have my word. We need to talk first.

"I don't find that very reassuring." Despite Alex's hostile tone, she found it difficult to *feel* threatened by this woman. For reasons she didn't understand and couldn't explain, she felt inclined to trust her—or at least, to hear her out.

We are not your enemies.

"I'll ask again: Who's 'we?' What are you? How many of you are there?" A sudden memory flashed into Alex's mind. "Wait a minute…. In the canyon, when it got so cold that we all passed out, there were four figures up at the top of the cliff, watching us. That was you, but you were wearing those cloaks." Alex gestured to the garment hanging on the wall. "You knocked us out with the cold and brought us here."

The woman's smile changed subtly, becoming sadder. *Correct.*

"Just before I passed out, I heard Sara say something. She called you… 'the witches.'"

As good a name as any. Call us witches if you wish.

"She knows what you are."

I very much doubt it.

"She must know something about you if she has a name for you."

The glowing woman paused as if considering something. *She believes that she knows what we are. She is mistaken.*

"Then what are you?"

Proctors. We watch, listen, and wait.

"For what?"

The right ones.

"The right ones? You mean a Maiden and Wardens who can reach the cathedral and put Ardu back to sleep?"

The path you walk is darker and more dangerous than you realize. We are here to shine a light for you so that you might see and understand.

"By kidnapping us and torturing us? Forgive me if I fail to see how that helps us."

The woman sighed, a ghostly, mournful sound like falling rain. *You are partly right, in a sense, but you do not understand.*

Alex felt her face harden into a frown. "Then help me understand. If you truly intend to let me go, as you said, then let's get on with it. We're running out of time."

The floating woman swayed slightly from side to side. She fell silent for a long moment. Finally, she seemed to decide on what to say.

This creature that hunts you—you call it "the Prisoner." It is real. It is you. It is out there, beyond these stone walls. She gestured around, indicating the vast network of tunnels. *It cannot get in here. For the moment, it cannot reach you.*

"Bullshit. It's been up my ass the whole time. It's killed me three times—very painfully, I might add." Alex noticed with mild surprise how much she sounded like Tom. She supposed his gruff, no-nonsense personality had been rubbing off on her.

The woman shook her head. *No. The creature in these tunnels is not your Prisoner. It is merely a… mirror image. An approximation.*

"An illusion?"

"Illusion" is… not quite the right word. An illusion is unreal, a fake—an imitation. We can make and unmake things, within limits.

"Was I actually dead?"

No. Not even we can reverse death. Should your Prisoner catch you out there, beyond these walls, you will be dead; make no mistake.

"Then how did you do what you did? And more importantly, why?"

The "how" is beyond your understanding for now. We have been here a long time. We have learned to do things here that anyone might learn, given enough time in the Twilight. As for the "why," as I said, we are here to illuminate the path you have chosen to walk.

"What does that mean? You're not making any sense. Speak plainly."

The woman heaved a deep, melancholic sigh and closed her eyes briefly. When she opened them again, they blazed with renewed determination. *If you continue on this path, your life will be forfeit. This is not merely a possibility; it is certain.*

Alex's mouth suddenly felt bone dry. "You… you mean that if I help Sara finish her Pilgrimage, I'll die?"

It pains us to do what we have done here, in these tunnels. But you need to understand the magnitude of the suffering that awaits you if you continue on this path.

Alex swallowed hard. "You… tortured me and killed me to make me understand what will happen if I help Sara finish her Pilgrimage?"

Yes.

Alex let out a frustrated sigh. "How do you know that? I don't think I believe you. I don't believe you can see the future."

It has always been up to you to decide what you believe.

"How could you possibly see the future?"

The woman drifted slowly around Alex in a circle. Alex turned in place to hold her gaze as she moved. *We do not see the future. We only understand cause and effect. Your current path has only one possible end, much like a rock always falls to the ground no matter how many times it is dropped.*

"You still haven't told me what you are."

You may learn that in time.

"Are you going to tell me anything useful?"

Everything we have shown you and told you is useful. You will decide to make use of it or you will not.

Alex shut her eyes, thinking. None of what she was hearing made sense. She tried a different tactic. "Let's assume, for the sake of argument, that I believe you can somehow know what the future holds. You're saying that... that if I help Sara finish her Pilgrimage, I'll die."

Perhaps not right away. But your life will be forfeit; and until your death, your suffering will be immense.

Alex shut her eyes again, trying to steady her nerves. "But Sara will finish her Pilgrimage, if I help her."

Most likely.

"What about Tom, Sara, and Dylan? Are you saying they'll die, too?"

I do not know where their paths end. My sisters are speaking with them as I am speaking with you. It has fallen to me to illuminate your path and yours alone. You will have to ask your friends what they learned when you see them.

"So, you created this image of the Prisoner to torture me, to kill me, to test my resolve. You're saying that I need to know what I'm in for if I continue to help Sara."

Precisely.

"I don't believe that you know that. Not for sure." Even as she said it, Alex felt a nagging doubt in the back of her mind, small but persistent.

As I said, you will choose what you believe. We all choose our beliefs. I can only show you the path. You will then choose to walk it or not.

"Even if you're telling the truth, and even if you're right... I don't have a choice. I have to do this. What am I supposed to do? Let everyone on Earth die?"

You always have choices.

Alex was becoming increasingly aware of the clock running down on Sara's Pilgrimage. "Is there something else you want to tell me? We're running out of time."

You are free to leave whenever you wish. But know that, once you leave this place, our protection ends. The very real dangers of the Twilight will once again hunt you.

Alex had some choice words about what this mysterious glowing woman thought of as "protection," but she held them back. "I need to go and find the others. Where are they?"

You have made your decision? You understand what awaits you at the end of this path, and you wish to press on nonetheless?

Alex hung her head. She wasn't sure what to think or what she believed about any of this. But she knew that letting billions of people die simply wasn't an option. She would never be able to live with herself if she backed out now.

If she even lived at all once Ardu was turned loose on the world. That seemed like a big "if."

She thought of all the pain and death she'd already caused. She thought of the old woman she'd killed all those years ago—saw her lifeless eyes staring up at her from the landing, her neck twisted so unnaturally. She thought of Daniela—relived her brutal death over and over in her mind, a death she'd suffered because Alex had been too slow to free her. She thought of Roland—watched his bones clattering to the floor after she'd convinced him to endanger himself.

She thought of Dylan—pictured the ugly, festering wound that would kill him in a matter of days, if not sooner.

The chains of guilt around her heart felt like an anchor dragging her down to the bottom of the ocean. She had to redeem herself. The only way she knew to do that was to save everyone—even if it cost her life.

"I have to go," she said quietly. "I have to find Sara and help her finish her Pilgrimage."

So be it. Your things are there, in that chest. The woman pointed to a wooden box on the other side of the room. *Take that passage, there, and follow it to the end. You will find the exit and your friends.*

Alex hurriedly retrieved her gear, suddenly unsure what to say to the strange woman. As she was putting her armor on, she turned back, feeling as though she had to say something.

The room was empty. The woman was gone.

CHAPTER TWENTY-NINE
Duty

"How are those steaks coming?" Teddy asked, handing Tom a cold beer.

Tom accepted it gratefully and took a sip. He gently prodded the sizzling meat with his tongs. Fat dripped into the flames below, causing them to leap and flare. "Just about done," he said. "Two minutes or so." Teddy settled himself in one of the patio chairs, turned it to face the setting sun, and cracked open a beer for himself.

May was Tom's favorite month in Maine. Most days, the sky was clear, and the sun shone down with just enough warmth to take the chill edge out of the wind. Today, it was cool but not cold—perfect weather to grill outdoors.

As Tom nursed his beer, keeping one eye on the steaks, Riley sauntered lazily around the corner and sat next to him. The aging golden retriever, who still thought he was a puppy, nudged Tom's leg with his nose. Tom looked down to see that Riley had a ball in his mouth. Tom grinned and took it when it was offered, then threw it across the yard. Riley jogged after it, not in a hurry.

The glass patio door slid open just as Tom was plating the steaks. "Hey, you made it," he said.

"Of course, I made it. Not like I have other friends to hang out with, much as I wish I did," Manny said, shutting the door behind him.

"Perfect timing, as usual," Teddy said. "Too late to help with the prep, just in time to eat."

"That just means you're on dish duty," Tom said to Manny, setting the plate of steaks on the table.

"Deal. Good to see you, bro," Manny said, pulling Tom into a tight hug once his hands were free.

"How long were you gone? Three months?" Teddy asked Manny. He rummaged around in the ice chest for a beer and handed it over, along with a bottle opener. Manny took both, opened the beer, and drained half of it.

"Almost four. It was a big job, but it's finally done. Good news is, I shouldn't be traveling anymore for at least six months."

Tom removed the foil from a plate of baked potatoes he'd taken out of the oven earlier while Teddy started filling salad bowls and passing them around. "Remind me what it is you do again? I can't seem to get my head around it. Some dumb computer shit, right?" Tom said.

Manny punched him on the shoulder. "Hey, man, green isn't your color. You're just mad because I make triple what you do."

"Right, yeah," Tom said, clicking his grill tongs thoughtfully. "And you'll have your student loans paid off in about... twenty years? Must suck, having student loans. I wouldn't know."

Teddy found the medium rare steak and passed it to Manny. "I think what Tom meant to say was something along the lines of, 'Tell us about this big, important job you finished, because we're your friends, and we care about your life.'"

Tom tipped his beer in Teddy's direction. "Sure, yeah. What he said."

Manny sat down and cut into his steak. "Right, so, this tech company, ProTech Systems, they're our biggest client ever. They make proprietary cybersecurity software for all the big oil and fintech companies in Europe. The problem everyone's trying to solve nowadays is that criminals are getting better at hacking just as fast as the good guys can develop more secure systems.

"So ProTech hired us to create custom servers using all new hardware that's not even available on the civilian market. It's mostly DoD stuff, real cutting-edge shit. I wasn't sure we could do it, but we did it. I was all over Europe for the last four months, showing all these billion-dollar companies how to use the hardware we made. I had a ProTech guy with me showing them the software side. To be honest, I was nervous as hell, but for the most part, it went off without a hitch. ProTech's clients are happy, so ProTech is happy, so my boss is happy. I've got a fat bonus coming and a hell of a reference on my resumé."

"That's awesome, man," Tom said, raising his beer in a toast. Teddy and Manny clinked their bottles against his. "There's one thing I don't understand, though."

"There are *many* things you don't understand," Manny said. Teddy chuckled.

Tom ignored them. "How's a wetback like you get a computer job, anyway? Does your dad know? I bet he's disappointed. Y'all ain't good for much except digging ditches."

Manny shot to his feet and assumed a boxing stance, throwing jabs in Tom's direction. "Hey, asshole, the only ditch I'll be digging is your grave."

Tom rose to the challenge, and they traded punches for a minute, lightly, never intending to hurt one another. Tom laughed when Manny ducked under a punch and managed to get him in a choke hold. Teddy rolled his eyes and ate his steak without comment.

Their roughhousing finished, Tom and Manny returned to their food with renewed appetites. "You know I'm just fucking with you, man," Tom said. "All kidding aside, I'm proud of you. I know you worked your ass off to get this job and worked even harder to climb the ladder. You did it —you slayed the dragon. If your boss doesn't promote you after this, he's an idiot."

"I'll drink to that," Teddy chimed in, raising his beer again for another toast.

"Enough about my bullshit," Manny said. "How have you guys been? How's the construction business doing?"

"Really good," Tom said. "We just landed a contract to build part of the new hydro dam going up in Southampton. It's good money, but we've got another job lined up after the dam that's even better. I can't tell you what it is—NDAs and all that shit—but trust me, it's a big fish." Tom glanced at Teddy, his construction manager. "Teddy, you want to tell him?"

Teddy cleared his throat. Manny looked over at him, waiting for the announcement of something obviously important. "Tom made me a conditional offer—full partner, assuming the next two jobs go well."

"I'm sure they will," Tom said, clapping Teddy on the shoulder. "You're a good friend and a hell of an engineer. You've outgrown your usefulness as a manager, I know you'll do right by me and the company." He turned to Manny. "Teddy's taking the lead on the next two projects, just like I normally would. With a few exceptions, he'll be doing my job, and I'll be watching to see how he does it. It's just a formality, really. I have every confidence he'll knock it out of the park."

"Well, shit," Manny said. He finished his beer and reached for another. "Cause for celebration all around."

"Enough about work, though," Teddy said. He paused long enough to spear some grilled onions along with his next bite of steak. "I worked seventy hours this week. I'm ready to talk about literally anything other than work this weekend."

"Fair enough," Tom said. They ate in silence for a few minutes, enjoying one another's company as the sun slowly dipped behind the hills to the west. A sensor clicked, turning on the automatic patio light. Riley napped contentedly nearby, his favorite ball tucked protectively under one paw. The air was getting colder; it would be time to head inside soon.

Tom noticed that Manny had a faraway look on his face, like he was thinking about something. "What's up?" he prompted.

Manny's eyes snapped back into focus as he met Tom's gaze. "Hmm?

Oh, nothing, really. I was just wondering something."

"Anything interesting?"

"This might seem like it's coming out of nowhere, but I've been thinking about it lately. Do you… regret not joining the army?"

Tom frowned, taken aback by the unexpected question. "No. I did for a while, back in the day, but that was my old man's dream for me, not mine. What brought that up?"

Manny scratched his head and leaned back in his chair. "I was just thinking about where my life has ended up. It's not a life I ever expected to have. That's not a bad thing; I like where I'm at and what I'm doing. For a while, though, I thought you were gonna do it—join the army. I'm glad you didn't, because back then, I would have followed you. I didn't have the balls to go off and do my own thing—I didn't even *have* my own thing yet. Now, though, I'm fully capable of telling you to go fuck yourself," Manny said.

Tom was only half-listening. Something was nagging at him, deep in his mind. He couldn't quite put his finger on what it was. He just had a vague feeling that something was wrong.

"It's getting cold," Teddy said, snapping Tom out of his thoughts. "Wanna head inside?"

"Yeah, sure," Tom said. He stood up and started collecting dishes. Manny was as good as his word—he washed them without complaint. Tom got to work cleaning the grill and putting it back in the shed for storage. As he scrubbed and scraped, the nagging feeling returned. He chewed it in his mind, like a dog chewing a piece of gristle. He wanted to figure out what was bothering him, and why.

Suddenly, it clicked. When Manny brought up Tom's decision not to join the army—more than twenty years ago—it got Tom thinking about all the years he'd known his best friend. They'd met in fifth grade and remained fast friends all through middle and high school. They'd drifted apart slightly in their thirties, while they were both working hard to build their careers, but they always kept in touch and made it a point to meet for dinner at least every few weeks.

He remembered most of his life with Manny clearly. But for some reason, he couldn't remember when or where he'd met Teddy.

"You look like you're thinking about work again," Teddy said, coming up behind him to help lift the grill over an uneven bump in the concrete. "It's the weekend. Let it be the weekend."

Tom shook his head. "No, it's not work. Teddy, I have a weird question."

"My favorite kind. Shoot."

"How did you and I meet? All of a sudden I can't remember."

Teddy frowned. "You serious?"

"Yeah."

"You're not getting that early-onset Alzheimer's, are you?" Teddy asked, referencing the terrible disease that had killed Tom's father.

Tom huffed. "No. I'm just... having a brain fart, I guess."

They got the grill into the shed, and Teddy shut the doors. He turned back to Tom, scratching his head. "Come on, man. You hired me right after you started the company. I was your first employee. You're kidding, right?"

Tom racked his brain. Was that right? It must be. Still, it felt... wrong. Why couldn't he remember?

"I'm sure it's nothing," Teddy said, waving a hand dismissively. "We all have random brain failure sometimes."

Tom stared at him. "I think forgetting how you met one of your best friends qualifies as more than random brain failure."

Teddy shrugged. "Weird shit happens, it's no big deal. You'll remember tomorrow, I'm sure."

Tom wasn't so sure. Alzheimer's had killed his father in his mid-fifties. Tom occasionally worried that the disease would come for him someday. He made a mental note to make an appointment with a neurologist.

Teddy studied his face for a long moment. "You good?"

Tom forced a smile. "You're probably right. I'm fine."

Teddy nodded, seemingly satisfied by the answer. "Let's head inside, it's cold out here. I wanna try that new pool table you got."

* * *

Three weeks later, the doctor called with the results of Tom's tests. The doctor had previously explained that there was no definitive diagnostic test for Alzheimer's. Rather, diagnoses were made largely by eliminating other possible conditions. Tom had had an MRI and a comprehensive panel of neurological tests; all of it came back normal. The doctor's opinion was that an isolated instance of memory loss related to one event was odd but not medically significant on its own. In short, there was no evidence of Alzheimer's, but given Tom's family history, it would be prudent to schedule yearly rechecks.

Tom felt better after he hung up the phone... mostly. He was certainly glad that his brain was healthy, but it still bothered him that he couldn't recall, in detail, how he'd met Teddy.

He was shaken out of his thoughts when a car horn beeped in the driveway. Leaning over to look out the kitchen window, he saw a red van parked outside. Ethan waved at him from the driver's seat. Tom grabbed the beach bag he'd packed the night before, checked Riley's food and water, and made sure the dog door was unlocked. He gave the retriever a farewell head scratch before heading out.

Tom slid open the van door and looked for an empty seat. "Mom, scoot over," Dylan said. Marie moved to the far side of the rear bench seat, making room for Tom. He hopped in and tossed his bag into the back, then buckled his seat belt.

"Hey, good to see you," Alex said, turning around to offer him a warm smile. She was on the bench seat in front of his, with Sara and Dylan. Tom returned the smile and the greeting.

"Everyone ready?" Ethan called back from the driver's seat.

"Check. Let's go," Sara replied.

"Ocean City, here we come," Ethan said, carefully backing out of Tom's driveway.

From the front passenger seat, Claire passed a bottle of sunscreen back to Sara. "Honey, you should put some on now. It's a long drive, and it'll be sunny. You don't want to burn before we even get to the beach."

"Mom, I'm fine," Sara said, blushing slightly. Dylan glanced back and forth between Sara and her mother.

"I swear, you get embarrassed about the silliest things," Claire said. "It's just sunscreen. Dylan's almost as white as you are; he could use some, too. You don't want to get skin cancer, do you?"

Now it was Dylan's turn to blush. Alex glanced back at Tom; she was smirking to herself. Tom shook his head and chuckled silently along with her.

Richard rummaged around in his pack and produced a bag of trail mix, offering some to the others. Tom accepted and chewed some honey-roasted peanuts as Ethan merged onto the freeway. "It's about a ten-hour drive," Ethan said, loudly enough for everyone to hear. "I figure most of us will go straight to bed when we get there so we can have a fresh start tomorrow."

"It'll be like, eight o'clock," Dylan whined. "I've never gone to bed that early."

"Stay up if you want, we're on vacation," Marie said. "Just don't cry about it if you're tired all day tomorrow."

"We've got ten hours of boring freeway ahead," Sara said, elbowing Dylan gently in the ribs. "Take a nap now if you want to stay up late."

"I don't need a nap," Dylan griped.

Half an hour later, he was asleep, snoring quietly, his head on Sara's shoulder. She rolled her eyes and put on her headphones.

Marie leaned forward so she could see past Richard and get Tom's attention. "Tom, Richard and I wanted to thank you again for the internship, Dylan is super excited." She kept her voice low so as not to wake her son.

"You're very welcome," Tom said. "He's a prodigy, and I'm not just saying that. If he gets a few summers of real work experience under his belt now, he'll be unstoppable by the time he finishes high school. College will just be a formality at that point."

Richard and Marie beamed with pride for their son. "We thought we'd talk with you now, since we're all here," Richard said. "We just wanted to make absolutely sure he'll be safe. A dam under construction can be a dangerous place."

Tom nodded, taking their concerns seriously. "It can be, yes, but Dylan won't be near any of the dangerous stuff. He'll be with me or Teddy at all times. Teddy is my construction manager, and he knows the dam project even better than I do. Most of the hands-on stuff Dylan will be doing is in the control rooms or the spillway. On the electrical side, it's all low-voltage equipment—the same kind of stuff he already messes with at home, in his room. I won't put him near anything dangerous, I promise."

Marie and Richard both nodded in relief. "That's good to know," Marie said.

The rest of the drive was uneventful, and they made good time, pulling into the hotel parking lot just a few minutes after eight. Contrary to Dylan's earlier prediction, he was out by nine, as was everyone else.

* * *

The next morning, after a late breakfast on the boardwalk, the eight of them headed to the beach. The weather was perfect—warm, but not hot, with a gentle breeze and clear skies. Several other families had organized a series of water volleyball games just offshore, with several nets so that multiple games could be played simultaneously. Dylan, Tom, Claire, and Marie beat Sara, Alex, Richard, and Ethan by a single point, but it was a hard-won victory.

After the volleyball game, the adults set up lounge chairs on the beach while Dylan and Sara went to explore a nearby rock jetty. "Be careful," Claire hollered after them. "Those rocks are sharp, don't fall and bust your heads." The teens waved back to indicate that they had heard.

"Time to reapply," Alex said, handing a bottle of sunscreen to Tom after taking some for herself.

"Thanks," Tom said as he squirted some into his hand.

"This is nice," Ethan said. "Oh, honey, did we bring the ice chest?"

"Yes, it's in the car, I'll get it." Claire retrieved the car keys from Ethan's bag and left, her flip-flops kicking up puffs of white sand.

"Thanks again for inviting us," Tom said to Ethan.

"Anytime," Ethan said. "I think all of us work too much. We should make it a point to take longer vacations, and more of them."

"Speaking of work," Marie said, a hint of good-natured disapproval in her voice. She tilted her head toward Richard, who had his camera out and was taking wide shots of the shoreline.

"I'm not working, I promise. These are just for the family photo album," Richard said. "See?" He pointed to where he'd been shooting.

"Aw, that's sweet," Alex said. Sara and Dylan were far away, about halfway down the jetty. They were with a younger boy none of them knew, maybe seven or eight. Sara was holding his hand while Dylan, a few steps ahead, beckoned him onward, encouraging the boy to take another step. The boy seemed unsure of himself, even though the waves were small and gentle. He took a step toward Dylan, then another, then several more. Sara kept a tight hold on his hand and walked with him. When they reached the end, the boy suddenly broke into a wide grin. Sara and Dylan clapped and cheered for him. The adults were too far away to hear, but the sight was heartwarming, nonetheless.

"Should they be taking someone else's kid that far out?" Marie said.

"I think those are his parents, there," Richard said, pointing. "They're watching, and they look fine with it."

"Sara is a great swimmer," Ethan said. "The boy is in good hands as long as she's nearby."

"I can't believe she even taught Dylan to swim," Marie said. "He's been terrified of water his whole life. It took her years to talk him into letting her teach him, but she did it. Now he's almost as good as she is."

A moment later, Claire returned, carrying the small ice chest. She opened it and passed beer and wine coolers around, according to each person's preference.

"So, Alex, are you and Tom dating?" Marie asked.

Alex chuckled, not unkindly. "No, we're just friends."

"How did you meet?"

Tom didn't hear Alex's answer. He was frowning, lost in thought. How *did* he know Alex? He knew that she'd been something of a mentor to Sara for years and that she worked at a rehab place over on Lakeview—one that his company had built about a decade ago. Tom and Ethan were both Chamber of Commerce and Rotary Club members, so they crossed paths often. But how had he and Alex come to be friends? They'd had short conversations here and there, but the more he thought about it, the odder it seemed that they were on vacation together.

"Tom?" Claire said. He snapped out of it and looked up at her. She was holding an ice-cold beer out to him. He accepted it with a smile that felt slightly forced.

He realized that everyone was staring at him. "Did I miss something? Sorry, I zoned out for a minute."

Marie smiled. "Alex was just telling us how the two of you met in college, how you were in the same study group when you were undergrads."

He blinked, taken aback. College? He'd gone to the University of Maine, just down the road from his parents' house, but Alex had gone to some place in Utah—he'd seen the diploma on the wall in her office.

Something was wrong. The thing with Teddy was weird, but now his memory of his relationship with Alex was also conflicting with what other people were telling him.

Am I going crazy?

"Tom, you look a little pale. You okay?" Ethan asked, leaning forward.

"Yeah, I'm... fine," he said. He sat up in his chair, intending to take a short walk and think for a minute. Instead, he fell to one knee as he tried to stand up, overcome by a brief bout of dizziness.

Richard was nearby and caught him under one arm. "Hey, Tom, what's the matter? Maybe Alex should take a look at you." He guided Tom back to his chair.

Alex came over and knelt in front of him, just as Dylan and Sara returned. "What's wrong?" Sara asked, drying her hair with a towel.

"Tom, take a few deep breaths," Alex said, shifting into her calming doctor voice. "What's wrong? Do you feel sick?"

"No, I...." He trailed off and looked around. His vision was a little blurry; he blinked rapidly to clear it. "Something's wrong."

"Tell me. I can help," Alex said.

Tom met her gaze. Her smile was as warm as ever, her dark eyes attentive and kind. "I don't think it's a... physical issue," he said slowly.

"What's up? You're starting to worry us," Ethan said.

"We're your friends; you can tell us," Claire added. Marie and Richard nodded in confirmation. Dylan and Sara knelt in the sand nearby, watching him with obvious concern.

They *were* his friends—his good friends. Other than Manny and Teddy, they were the best friends he had. Sara and Dylan were almost like his niece and nephew. He'd been looking forward to this vacation for months—

there was nowhere else he'd rather be.

So why did he feel so reluctant to confide in them?

Suddenly, a strong breeze kicked up. It carried an odd sound with it, a sound that seemed out of place at the beach—something like icicles or glass shards clinking together. *Probably just the ice in someone's drink*, he thought.

"Tom, help me out here," Alex said. "Help me, help you. What's going on?"

He heaved a sigh. He was being silly. He could tell them. They were good people, and he trusted all of them.

"A few weeks ago, I had a… strange problem. You know my construction manager, Teddy Jackson?" Everyone nodded. Some knew Teddy better than others, but they all had met him at least once or twice. "All of a sudden, I couldn't remember when or how I'd met him. It was the weirdest thing. I've known him for more than twenty years, and I just up and forgot how we met. Even after he reminded me, I still couldn't remember it."

"That doesn't sound so weird," Alex said. "We all have random brain failure sometimes."

Tom frowned at her. "Why would you say it like that?"

She returned the frown. "Like what?"

"'Random brain failure.' That's exactly what Teddy called it, verbatim."

"Tom, Alex is a doctor, after all," Ethan said, trying to sound reassuring. "If she says it's nothing to worry about, I'm sure she's right. Have you been working too much? Maybe you just need a good night's rest."

Tom shook his head. "The more I think about it, the more I feel like something is definitely wrong. I saw a neurologist a few weeks ago, and he ran some tests."

"And?" Alex prompted.

"Everything came back normal, but—"

"Well, there you go," Alex said, cutting him off gently. She raised her hands in a "mystery solved" gesture.

"I agree with Alex," Sara said. "She's a good doctor. If she's not worried, I don't think you should be, either."

Tom took a deep breath and let it out slowly. "Maybe you're right," he said. "I'm getting older, pushing fifty now. Maybe this is just how old people start to forget things. But there's more to it. Just now, the same thing happened again—with Alex. I know we met in college, she just said so. But for the life of me, I can't remember it."

Alex patted his leg. For some reason, the gesture struck Tom as vaguely condescending. It seemed like the sort of thing she might do to a child who was being unreasonable. "Tom, of course we met in college. Where else would it have been? Sit back down and finish your beer," she said. "I'm sure you'll feel better in no time."

Almost without realizing it, Tom found himself complying. He lay back in the chair, shifting until it was comfortable. He took a sip of beer. It was cold and delicious.

Something lurched in his mind, like two tectonic plates grinding past one another.

He wasn't crazy or imagining things. Whatever was going on, it wasn't just weird. It was *wrong*.

"Wait a goddamned minute," Tom said. He shot to his feet, feeling steadier now. "What the hell is going on?"

Alex stood up with him and put her concerned doctor face back on. "What do you mean? We're just having a good time at the beach."

Tom took two steps back, away from her. He suddenly felt like he was in danger. The woman in front of him seemed... not like the Alex he knew—or *thought* he knew.

"This doesn't make any sense," Tom said, anger rising in his voice. "I just told you that I've had not one but two major episodes of memory loss. You're a doctor, and a damn good one—I've seen you with your patients. You take them seriously and treat them with dignity and respect, even when they say shit that's downright stupid. But now you're gonna blow me off when I tell you I'm losing entire years from my memory? I don't buy it. Who are you? Who are *any* of you? What's really going on here?"

Alex's frown darkened into a scowl. "What do you mean, 'who are we?' We're your friends. What's gotten into you?"

Tom snapped his fingers and pointed at her. "You fucked up again. The Alex I know wouldn't be annoyed and offended if I said that to her. She'd be hurt and confused. She'd be really worried about me."

Abruptly, the mood shifted. Tom realized that all the faces around him were no longer looking at him but at one another. Sara, Dylan, Alex, Marie, Richard, Ethan, and Claire—they were nodding at each other, trading knowing looks—no, *conspiratorial* looks.

The silent debate apparently settled, Alex sighed and shook her head, her shoulders slumping. "Tom," she said, her voice barely a whisper, "why couldn't you just leave it alone?"

Tom noticed that there was no longer anyone else on the beach. All the other people had simply vanished. The waves breaking on the sand seemed taller than they had a few minutes ago. Thick clouds had appeared and moved in front of the sun. The warm breeze suddenly turned biting cold.

"It's not too late," Marie said. She held out her hands toward him, palms up, in a pleading gesture.

Tom took another step back. "Not too late for what?"

Sara stepped forward. "You can still stay with us."

Dylan came closer as well. "It doesn't have to end," he added.

"You have such wonderful friends, Tom," Ethan said. "Not just us, but Manny and Teddy, too. We all know how much you care for them."

"You're so good at your job, and your company is growing so fast. Who knows how much more success you could enjoy?" Richard mused.

"The sky's the limit," Claire agreed.

"But only if you stay with us," Alex said.

Tom noticed that, at some point, he'd bent his legs and assumed a defensive stance, as though he were expecting to be attacked. "Stay with you?" he repeated. "What... what are you talking about? What's happening?" He had a vague but increasingly persistent feeling that he was supposed to be somewhere else, *doing* something else—something very important.

"All you have to do is stay here, and the life you always wanted is yours," Sara said. Her voice sounded deeper than usual—warped and discordant.

"Stay... where?" Tom stammered.

"Wherever you like," Alex said softly. Her voice, barely a whisper, was also unnaturally deep and distorted. "We can take you anywhere. Just tell us where. You've carried such terrible burdens for so long. You've done your duty. It's time to rest."

Duty.

The veil in his mind shattered. In an instant, the curtain was drawn back, and he remembered everything.

Sara—the real Sara—needed him.

"End this, now," he hissed through gritted teeth. "Whatever this is—stop it. Whoever—*whatever* you are, I'll fight you to the death if I have to. Let me go or kill me. Those are your two choices."

The specter of Alex hung its head. "As you wish," it whispered.

* * *

Tom was briefly blinded by an intense flash of white light. Even before it had faded, he was fumbling for his shotgun. There, he found it, on its sling, resting against his chest, where it belonged. He raised it, seated the buttstock firmly in his shoulder, and flicked the selector to full auto, blinking rapidly to clear his vision.

When he could see again, he was in a small room with roughly carved stone walls. The air was cold, damp, and heavy. He suspected that he was underground.

Something in front of him was still giving off white light, though not as bright as before. He detected a vaguely humanoid shape, and a face—a young woman? Somehow, her entire body was glowing so brightly as to make its contours and details indistinguishable, but her face was visible. Raven-black hair fell well below her shoulders, and her eyes were so blue that they were almost violet. She was looking at him with an odd expression, a mixture of a wistful smile and a pitying frown.

Instinctively, he started to squeeze the Jackhammer's trigger. Four pounds into the five-pound trigger pull, he stopped. For some reason he couldn't quite put his finger on, the oddly glowing woman in front of him didn't feel like a threat—not exactly. She—or it—seemed to emit an antagonistic aura, but Tom didn't think she was his enemy.

The thought was enough to stay his trigger finger but not enough to convince him to lower his weapon.

Despite appearances, I am not your enemy.

Tom flinched at hearing a soft, feminine voice inside his head. Her lips hadn't moved. As the words echoed in his mind, a sound like running water came to his ears, quiet but unmistakable.

A dozen questions began to pile up in Tom's mind. He started with the most important one. "Where's Sara?"

Nearby.

"Is she safe?"

As safe as one can be in the Twilight.

"Why should I believe you?"

What you believe is up to you.

Tom frowned. Whatever had just happened, it had an oddly familiar quality. "That... vision, or hallucination, whatever it was. You did something similar to Sara and me on that ship, the other day."

Yes.

"Why?"

To see how you would react.

Tom very nearly shot her. "Is this a fucking game to you?"

Quite the opposite. This is a gravely serious matter—that is why we must learn about you.

"Who is 'we?'"

My sisters and I.

"Sara called you 'witches.'"

Think of us that way if you wish. It makes no difference what you call us.

Tom was torn by two conflicting desires. On one hand, he desperately wanted to find the others and get moving—if they were still alive. And yet, he found himself wrestling with an equally strong desire to understand the cryptic, ghostly woman.

He lowered his shotgun a tiny bit. "What did you do to me?"

I showed you your life as it could have been and might still be.

"My two best friends are dead. You expect me to believe you can change that?"

The woman heaved a deep sigh that sounded like raindrops pattering on glass. *No. Please believe that I would return your friends to you were it in my power.*

Despite his simmering rage, Tom found himself struggling to hold back tears. His initial instinct to kill something was fading, being replaced by an aching sense of loss. Whatever this strange woman had done to him, it had felt so deeply and completely *real*. He hadn't had time to even begin to process Teddy's death, but Manny had died twenty years ago. Tom thought about him at least once a day, every single day. He'd made new friends in the intervening years, but they were merely buddies, not brothers.

The three weeks he'd spent with Manny and Teddy just now had felt so... *right*. So normal. It had felt like the life he was meant to have.

A single tear fell to the ground. The cave was so still and quiet that he heard it splash against the stone.

You can be with them. You can have the life you wanted.

Angered and embarrassed, Tom refused to reply until he was sure he could keep his voice steady. "What are you saying?"

I can give you a life with your friends and anything else you desire. Love, money, travel. You have earned it.

Tom meant to say that Sara needed him. Instead, different words came out, words he hadn't planned to say. "You just said that you can't resurrect the dead."

I cannot. But I can make it feel real—so real that you will never know the difference.

He was so damn *tired*. The offer was sorely tempting; he couldn't deny it. Again, he found himself speaking almost involuntarily, saying things he didn't mean to say. "So, you just... put me to sleep in some cave, and I dream whatever I want to dream until the world ends?"

The world need not end. It was here long before you were born, and it will go on long after you die.

"Not if Sara doesn't finish her Pilgrimage."

Come here. I want to show you something. The woman floated away, toward a nearby passageway. Tom blinked in surprise at the realization that she was *hovering*, not walking. Had she been doing that the whole time? He wasn't sure.

Almost against his will, Tom felt himself following. He still had his finger on the Jackhammer's trigger, but he held the weapon at the low ready, no longer pointing it at her. He had no trouble seeing where he was going—

the woman's body glowed softly, illuminating the tunnel for several meters ahead and behind.

After a time, Tom felt a cool breeze, and the air felt lighter, crisper, as he breathed it in. They were nearing the outside.

The woman stopped at a large opening in the right-hand wall. As Tom halted beside her, he saw that it was almost like a window. He was surprised to see that he was high in the mountains, not underground as he'd first thought. Barren plains stretched out below, bathed in the ghostly light of the ever-present Twilight moon. Beyond the plains, the terrain looked different—lusher with foliage.

She raised an arm and pointed to a towering structure in the distance. It rose from the earth like a spear, high into the night sky, as if in open challenge to the moon directly above it.

"Is that what I think it is?"

The cathedral.

"Are we really that close?"

This is no illusion; I give you my word.

Tom suddenly realized that he had no idea how much time had passed while he was in the waking dream. He glanced at his watch and balked.

"I've been here almost a full day?"

Perhaps. It is hard for us to measure time.

His anger flared momentarily, then cooled. "But... if we're really this close, then we should have plenty of time."

Yes. If you choose to go that way.

He turned to face her. "You mean... instead of staying here."

The life we create for you will be long. Out here, it may last only days, but to you, it will feel like decades.

"You mean it might last only days because, without me, Sara might not make it to the cathedral... and it's already way too late for another team to take over."

It is possible that she will fail. But we believe she will succeed. The cathedral is close, and she has two other Wardens.

Tom felt a stab of guilt deep in his chest. Was he actually considering the offer of a fake life, away from all the death and fear? He realized that he was. What did it matter what was real if the fantasy were indistinguishable from reality?

Hadn't he paid his dues in the army? By losing both of his closest friends? And here, in this nightmare world? Hadn't he earned some rest and real happiness?

Tom swallowed hard. His voice trembled slightly with his next question. "But it wasn't perfect. I could tell that something was wrong. Isn't that why you dropped the act? Because I figured out it wasn't real?"

The ghostly woman's gentle smile broadened. Tenderly, she touched his cheek. He expected her touch to be cold, but it was warm and comforting. *It was... a first effort. Given more time, we can create a life for you that is truly complete, with no holes or mismatched memories.*

Tom folded his arms and turned away from her. He chose his next words carefully. "I appreciate the offer. I really do. I can't tell you how badly I want to say 'yes.' But I can't."

Why not?

He turned back around. His eyes were dry again, his jaw set in hardened resolve. "I can't turn my back on Sara, or the rest of the world, no matter how close we are. I have to get her across the finish line. It doesn't matter what I want. What kind of person would I be if I backed out now? Even if there's a good chance that Sara could make it to the cathedral without me, it's a chance I can't take."

I see.

"Besides, even if...." His voice cracked. He started over. "Even if I can live a dream that feels real, it's still just a dream."

Does it matter?

Tom sighed. "I have a responsibility to Sara and to everyone else. I can't turn my back on them."

The woman's smile turned wistful again. *You have a duty.*

Tom nodded. "I do."

Very well.

"I have to go."

You may.

"Where are the others?"

She pointed. *Keep following this tunnel. You will find them.*

Tom pulled a torch from his pack, lit it, and took several steps in the direction she'd indicated. He felt more determined now. He felt better, but only a little—not as much as he'd expected to feel.

Abruptly, he stopped. He turned back to the strange woman. He felt the need to thank her for her kindness, even if her offer was misguided.

The words died on his lips. She was nowhere to be seen.

CHAPTER THIRTY
Doubt

Dylan grimaced. The bite wound was getting worse.

Much worse.

He poked it gingerly. It was bigger than a grapefruit now. Most of the stitches were torn out again. The inner part was an angry red, covered in a thick layer of dried blood and pus, and it flared with hot pain when he touched it or moved. The outer edges of the wound, though, were black, and those areas didn't hurt. He had no sensation at all there.

That worried him.

He felt hot, and he was sweating like crazy. He dug around in his pocket, searching for the plastic bottle of pills. It was gone, like all the rest of his gear except for a few glow sticks. He supposed it didn't matter; he didn't think the pills were helping anyway. He couldn't even raise his right arm over his head anymore. He felt tired and short of breath, nauseous and dizzy, even though he was sitting down, not doing anything.

Slowly, carefully, he stood up. His vision swam. He swayed on his feet a moment.

As near as he could tell in the dim blue-white light of a glow stick, he was in some kind of underground cavern, at the edge of a small lake. The water was deathly still—and rancid, by the smell of it. He couldn't remember how he'd gotten here. He just remembered being cold, and....

The witches. That was what Sara had said, "It's the witches." What did that mean?

More importantly, where was Sara now? Was she okay?

That thought brought him out of his funk a bit. He tried to ignore how terrible he felt. He needed to find Sara—and Tom and Alex.

But the only way forward was through the water. There was nothing behind him except a fifty-foot tunnel that ended at a rock wall.

He hated water. His first near-death experience in the Twilight had been water related. Once was enough.

Dylan closed his eyes and took a deep breath. He pictured Sara's face in his mind. Every second he screwed around, waiting for a solution to appear magically in front of him, she could be in mortal danger—or already dead.

No one else was going to solve this problem. No one else *could* solve it.

He took two steps forward. Frigid, slimy water immediately seeped into his shoes. His instincts screamed at him to turn back. He ignored them and took another two steps, then two more. He was up to his knees now.

He was surprised to find that each step forward, into the inky depths, was a little easier than the last. A tiny flame of courage flickered in his mind. Mentally, he cupped his hands around it, protecting it from the winds of fear. He took several more steps into the water, picturing himself adding kindling to the small flame.

The water was up to his chest now. His heart was pounding. He wasn't sure if he could willingly submerge his head, but for now, it wasn't necessary. The bottom seemed to have leveled out.

Holding the glow stick high, he slogged forward. His wet clothes were heavy, and the cold was starting to seep into his bones. His teeth began to chatter. Every time he passed a particularly large patch of rancid algae, the smell made him gag.

Sara, I'm coming, he thought.

Abruptly, he had nowhere else to go. A rock wall loomed in front of him, jutting out of the water. He shuffled to the left, trailing his hand along the wall, feeling for an opening. After several minutes, he found himself back where he'd started, near the shore. He doubled back and went the other way. Again, he circled around to the shore. The lake wasn't as big as it had seemed.

There was no way out.

Unless....

Dylan shook his head. He didn't want to think about it.

He reprimanded himself. It didn't matter whether he wanted to think about it or not. He needed to face reality, no matter how difficult or terrifying it was. Before he could talk himself out of it, he took a deep breath and bent his knees until the water covered his head. It was shockingly cold on his face. It felt slimy and dirty.

If he survived this, he would need several showers, back-to-back.

He forced his eyes open. He blinked once, twice. The water stung a bit, mostly because it was so cold, but it wasn't too bad. The real problem was the darkness. The water was murky, almost opaque. He held the glow stick out, inspecting the rock wall that blocked further passage. Even with the light, it was hard to see.

There. About ten feet to the right, near the bottom—a hole about three feet wide and two feet tall. He stuck the glow stick inside, trying to see how far back it went. He couldn't tell, but it was definitely a passage of some kind.

No way, he thought. He stood up, breaking the surface. He wiped gooey pond scum out of his eyes and hair.

I can't do this. That hole is way too small. There's no telling how far it goes, or if it goes anywhere at all. There's no room to turn around. If it's a dead end, I'll drown.

He was starting to hyperventilate. Sara was going to die, and he couldn't do anything to stop it. Walking around in chest-high water was one thing, but swimming through a pitch-black tunnel barely wider than his shoulders? He'd rather sit here, on the shore, and wait to starve to death.

Except... he didn't need to eat or drink in the Twilight. He would just sit here forever.

He slapped himself, hard. The stinging pain focused his mind a bit.

All his life, he'd let fear and doubt be his guides, let them goad him into choosing the path of least resistance. Where had that gotten him? He could barely look at himself in the mirror because every time he did, he saw a sniveling coward. He still wasn't sure why Sara had ever thought he was strong enough, smart enough, or brave enough to be her protector.

And yet... maybe she had seen something in him that he was too blind to see himself. He thought about everything that had happened over the previous week. There were times when he'd been paralyzed with fear, or so wracked with self-doubt that he ended up creating new problems for the team or making existing problems worse.

But at other times he'd surprised himself. He'd saved Alex's life in the house by tackling her just before the Stalker could rip her apart. He'd fixed the cable car, the speedboat, and the elevator to Jacob's hideout. He'd come up with a clever way to save Tom from the Ouroboros's venom, and then, just a few minutes after that, he'd saved Sara by giving her the last of their adrenaline. In that moment, he'd been ready to die for her.

It was more than that—he hadn't just been *ready* to die. He'd actually traded his life for hers, or at least, it had seemed that way at the time. Had Sara died there, in the hospital, the Pilgrimage would have been over—and very likely, by extension, the world.

And then, when that Cutter had almost killed her, and he'd been overtaken by rage.... He shook his head. It wasn't a pleasant memory.

He'd thought of himself as useless and powerless for so long that self-doubt had become a comforting cloak, one he wore day and night until it had become part of him.

But he wasn't useless. He had saved his friends' lives multiple times. Without him, *all* of them would be dead. The Pilgrimage wasn't finished yet, but nor had it failed, in part because of him.

Useless people couldn't do such things.

"I can do this," he said aloud to himself. "I *will* do this."

The small flame grew a little bigger, a little brighter. The fear and doubt were still there, still nagging at him, still telling him to turn back and wait for someone braver and more capable to fix everything.

He ignored them.

Dylan drew the deepest breath he could manage and dived. He found the hole and went in head-first, his arms stretched out in front. The hole was far too small to swim through, which, in a way, was a good thing—he didn't know how to swim. He would have to use his hands to pull himself forward.

At first, it wasn't too bad. He crawled along at a measured pace, trying to use his air efficiently. The tunnel curved gently to the right. Other holes and passages far too small for him branched off to the sides.

What sorts of creatures used them?

The unexpected thought triggered a brief spike of panic. He gasped, and a large air bubble escaped. He scolded himself for wasting it. For the moment, he still felt okay. It had only been twenty seconds or so. As long as the passage wasn't too much longer, he would be alright.

He focused on the light given off by the glow stick. It was his one tangible source of comfort and reassurance. He could see where he was going. That made him feel a little better, made it a little easier to keep the fear at bay.

Something moved suddenly, a few feet ahead. Dylan stopped and tried to raise his hands defensively, but he could hardly move in the confined space. He was so startled that he dropped the glow stick. In its small radius of light, he saw what had scared him—some kind of eel. His heart rate doubled. Was it going to attack him?

No—it was swimming away, down one of the smaller holes off to the side. Internally, he breathed a sigh of relief.

As quickly as his panic had started to fade, it spiked again.

The glow stick was drifting down, into one of those small holes.

He lunged out, trying to grab it. He missed. Instead of closing his fingers around it, he bumped it with his knuckles. Desperately, he jammed his fingers into the hole, trying to grab the glow stick before it sank out of reach.

He couldn't feel it.

The tiny halo of light sank down, steadily shrinking. A moment later, it was gone.

The panic seized his heart in a death grip. He let out an involuntary scream, losing more air. He managed to choke it off, but his chest was starting to hurt, and not only from the fear. His lungs were burning, and he couldn't see.

Darkness swallowed him. He had more glow sticks in his pocket, but he couldn't reach them—the tunnel was too narrow to bring his arms down to his sides.

No longer trying to move slowly, Dylan pulled himself along as fast as he could, fumbling blindly in the darkness. His hands bumped and scraped on the rough stone, and the cuts burned in the cold, dirty water. A few feet later, he slammed his head—hard—into an outcrop he hadn't been able to see.

He almost blacked out. He felt dizzy and nauseous, even more than he already had. He tried his best to ignore the pain and kept dragging himself along. His chest felt like it was about to explode. His lungs screamed for air.

Suddenly, his hands moved more freely. He swung his arms out to the sides, feeling for some tactile clue. He still couldn't see anything, but he seemed to be in open water again. The oppressive silence blocked any sound that might guide him to the surface. Pressure was building behind his eyes. He felt like he was going to pass out any second. He flailed his arms and kicked his legs wildly.

Once again, he found himself wishing he'd gotten over his fear of water and learned how to swim.

It was getting harder to move his muscles. His brain was telling them to work, but they just wouldn't. His chest was on fire. His head was pounding. The water was so cold, and his clothes were so heavy. His shoes were dragging him down. His last thought echoed in his mind.

Sara... I'm sorry.

Something yanked hard on his arm. A flurry of sensations followed, but he was too close to unconsciousness to identify any of them. He felt only a vague impression of movement and pressure.

Something hit him in the chest. It hurt. He woke up, partially. He coughed and choked, felt water leaving his lungs. He blinked, trying to see something. He couldn't tell if he was blind or if there was simply nothing to see.

There—a faint sliver of light. He blinked again. Something was giving off white light nearby.

He felt himself rolling onto his side, not by his own choice. Something hit him in the back once, twice, three times. He coughed up more water. A little more of his vision returned. For a moment, he slipped closer to unconsciousness again, then came more fully awake.

His head was pounding fiercely, his chest hurt, and the bite wound in his side was pulsing with raw agony, but he could think and see.

Mostly.

He sat up. He was on a shoreline similar to the one where he'd started, but this one was different—the rock was a darker color, and it felt smoother. He was somewhere else.

The source of white light was behind him. He turned around. For a long moment, his mind refused to accept what his eyes were telling him. His mouth moved, but he couldn't make the word come out. He swallowed and tried again.

"Mom?"

* * *

Marie smiled.

I knew you could do it.

Her voice filled his mind, but her mouth didn't move. It was her voice, there was no doubt about it—he'd watched all the home videos so many times that every frame was burned into his memory. A different, quietly musical sound came to his ears when she spoke, like wind chimes.

She was... *glowing.* The light was so bright that he couldn't see her body, but he could see her face clearly. She looked just as she did in the photos and videos, like she hadn't aged a day.

Dylan crawled forward and collapsed into her arms. Not for a moment did he worry that this might be some kind of trick or trap. Somehow, for some reason he couldn't put words to, he didn't think it was. He just didn't believe that a place as evil as the Twilight could create something so pure and beautiful.

Marie wrapped her arms around her son as he cried into her shoulder. *It is alright. You are so very brave, and I am proud of you.*

He looked up at her. "How... are you here? And how are you talking like that, into my head?"

She smiled again. *There is not much time. Let us not worry about such things now.*

"What happened to you? Where have you been all this time?"

Her smile turned wistful. *Later, my love. There is something more important that you must do now.*

He pulled away from her just a bit, surprised. "What could be more important?"

I think you know.

Dylan closed his eyes. "Sara."

She needs you.

"Can't we talk, just for a few minutes? Is time really that short?"

It is. I am sorry.

"When will I see you again?"

Suddenly, Marie looked away, behind him. Her expression changed from comforting to concerned. He followed her gaze but couldn't see anything.

"What is it?"

It comes.

"What comes?"

He listened. He couldn't hear anything except dripping water. *Tap. Tap. Tap.*

Marie stood up and pulled him to his feet. *Be ready.*

He didn't understand. "Be ready for what? Why? What's coming?"

He turned around again, trying to see what had her so worried. Abruptly, the white light winked out and was gone. He turned back around.

"Mom?"

She was nowhere to be seen.

Dylan heaved a deep sigh. He felt as if his heart were breaking. He didn't think it had really been his mom, but he wanted to believe it was. Why had she disappeared so suddenly? If something dangerous was coming, wouldn't she want to help him?

Tap. Tap. Tap. Tap. Tap.

The water sounded like it was dripping faster now. He fished around in his soggy pocket for another glow stick, cracked it, and shook it to mix the chemicals inside. He could hear the water dripping, but he still couldn't see it. He took a few steps toward the sound. What was so dangerous about water, anyway?

Then he saw it. At first, because it was so dark, he thought it was the same murky, cloudy water he'd been swimming in.

Then he realized it wasn't water. It was far too thick. It was dripping from a crack in the ceiling and pooling on the stone below, spreading into an oily, black puddle.

A very large puddle.

Dylan gasped and took a step back when the black ooze started to move. With a loud, wet *slap*, the rest of the Glutton fell through the hole in the ceiling, splashing caustic goo everywhere. It was pulling itself up, into a more or less humanoid form.

He turned and ran. The glow stick didn't provide enough light to see more than about five feet in front of him, so he was forced to slow down. Knocking himself out by running head-first into a wall wouldn't help.

The rocky ground sloped upward at a steep angle, so steep that he had to use his hands to steady himself. Every time he moved his arms, the festering wound in his right side flared with fresh pain. He risked a glance back over his shoulder, and his eyes widened at what he saw. The Glutton was rolling up the hill, smoothly and easily. It picked up rocks as it went along, even a small frog that was too slow to hop out of its path. The poor creature squeaked in agony before disappearing into the ooze.

It was so close that he could see it in the faint light of the glow stick. It would be on him in seconds if he didn't speed up.

Dylan crested the hill and sprinted onward, no longer worried about running into something. He stumbled along, half blind, the rock walls on either side whipping by too fast to see in detail. He felt so violently ill that it took all his remaining willpower to keep running. He was lightheaded and covered in sweat, already feeling hot despite having taken a swim in frigid water only a few minutes ago.

The narrow passageway suddenly widened into a vast cavern, which he felt more than saw. The air felt lighter, thinner, and his footsteps echoed off something high above. He couldn't see his pursuer, but he could hear it, rolling and squelching relentlessly along.

Something whacked his shin painfully, and he tumbled forward. He cried out when he hit the ground on his injured side. He swore and looked back —he'd run into a large rock.

The Glutton loomed into view on the other side of the rock, rising above him like a mighty tidal wave about to crash down. Dylan screamed and rolled to his left. The blob slapped to the ground just beside him, smaller tendrils of goo already reaching toward him hungrily from the main body. He scrambled to his feet and kept running.

Moving in a straight line was becoming increasingly difficult. He was so dizzy that he felt like he'd been spinning in circles for five minutes straight. He couldn't remember ever being so sick before, not even when he was eight and had been hospitalized with a fever that had nearly killed him.

By now, it was clear that the bite wound on his side wouldn't stop at "nearly" killing him. Before much longer, it would take his life, if the Glutton didn't get him first.

His foot kicked something as he ran. He stumbled but managed to keep his footing. In the brief light of the glow stick as he passed, he saw that it was a tool with a long wooden handle—a pickax, maybe? For a brief instant, he considered going back for it, then discarded the idea. The Glutton was close behind, and he wasn't sure how a pickax would help.

It did tell him something, though. Maybe there were other tools in the area, and one of them would be more useful.

As far as he could tell, he was still in some kind of massive cavern. He couldn't see anything to his sides or above, just more rough stone underfoot. He ran on, panting raggedly, acutely aware that his lungs would give out soon. He doubted that the Glutton was limited by a cardiovascular system. He needed to think of something, and soon. He kept running, trying to think. It wasn't easy in his condition, and the wet, hungry sounds of the Glutton close behind weren't helping.

Dylan skidded to a halt when a wall loomed out of the darkness before him. Wasting no time, he bolted to the left, following the wall. It seemed to go on forever. It was hard to tell how long he followed it; as tired as he was, minutes felt like hours.

He came to a narrow crevice in the wall, barely big enough to squeeze into sideways. He stopped, just for a second, rapidly considering his options.

Something ahead and slightly to the left caught his eye—something white, high up in the air. After squinting at it for a moment, he realized it was light —bright light, but it was far away.

He had a handful of seconds to think. The narrow passage could prove to be an advantage. If it split off into other tunnels, maybe he could lose the Glutton.

Or it could be a dead end, and the Glutton would simply suck him out of the crevice at its leisure.

Light meant there was a way out. Maybe. He couldn't be sure, but light seemed more promising than going deeper into the caves. He cut left and kept running.

The light above grew brighter and larger with agonizing slowness. Distance was deceiving in the dark, especially in such a large space. For several agonizing minutes, he forced his exhausted body to keep moving, running on raw willpower.

Finally, he stood below the light, his chest heaving with fear and exertion. It was *very* high up. A heavy iron chain, connected to a massive block of stone nearby, ran straight up toward the ceiling, into the halo of light. Up there, near the ceiling, he could see another large object on the other end of the chain, maybe some kind of counterweight.

Was this a quarry? He didn't have time to entertain his curiosity. The Glutton was coming.

But there was no way he could climb that chain. It must have been a hundred feet long, at least. He couldn't climb that even if he were uninjured and fully rested.

Based on the ghastly sounds coming toward him out of the darkness, he had about ten seconds to figure something out.

Dylan shut his eyes and tried to block out all distractions. *Think, dammit,* he commanded himself. *You're an engineer; you're supposed to be good at solving problems.*

An idea came to him. He was far from sure that it would work, but he had no time to come up with a better one.

Dylan tucked the glow stick into the waistband of his pants and wrapped both hands around the chain, as high as he could reach. He grimaced at the pain in his side. He bent his legs slightly and waited.

"I'm right here, you sack of shit!" he shouted. "Fresh meat—come and get it!"

The Glutton seemed more than happy to rise to the challenge. It entered the circle of light like a bullet train, lunging right for him. Dylan yelped and jumped as high as he could, using his hands to pull himself up the chain. He drew his legs up, trying to keep them out of the Glutton's reach.

The abomination rolled up onto the stone block and rushed past like a polluted river, inches below his shoes. The chain passed right through it, doing nothing to slow its advance. His heart lifted a little—that had been exactly what he was hoping for.

The Glutton rolled to the far side of the stone block and turned around with shocking agility. It started moving back toward him, reaching, as though it intended to pull itself up the chain to reach its prey. Dylan had no doubt that it could.

He looked down at the length of chain below him. Small orbs of black goo were stuck to it. Steam rose from the iron links as the corrosive substance rapidly ate away at them.

Dylan screamed and shut his eyes as the Glutton reached for him.

It missed his foot by a hair's breadth as one of the chain links snapped and fell away. Dylan's arms were nearly ripped out of their sockets as the chain rocketed upward, now free of the stone block. He felt a rush of air as the counterweight whizzed by, inches from his face.

It suddenly occurred to him that he should probably look where he was going. He glanced up, squinting into the bright light.

As he rose through the hole in the ceiling, the section of chain he was clinging to was rapidly approaching a giant pulley system. Dylan's heart jumped into his throat. In about a second, he would be yanked through the pulley wheels and pulverized.

He had no time to think about how stupid this plan was. Acting mostly on instinct and reflexes, he let go of the chain but kept his arms over his head. He continued to ascend, rapidly losing momentum.

He hit the pulley's wooden support beam harder than he'd wanted to. His right shoulder took most of the impact, forcing another pained cry out of him. He flailed wildly and managed to catch the wooden beam with his left hand.

The broken end of the chain whizzed through the pulley and whipped him in the leg as it came out the other side, opening a long gash that immediately started to bleed steadily. Dylan screamed again, then growled in frustration. "Can I get a fucking break?" he mumbled to no one.

He reached up with his right hand to get a better grip on the beam. When he did, the last few stitches in his side tore. He was already in so much pain that he barely felt it, but he did feel warm blood trickling down his side.

"Guess not," he griped in response to his own question.

He looked down. Thankfully, the wooden beam extended past the edge of the hole below. He shimmied over, his strength rapidly dwindling. He wanted to make it all the way to the end of the beam, but he could tell that he wouldn't be able to. His arm muscles burned fiercely, and he was running on fumes. He pushed on as long as he could, but his arms finally gave out and refused to cooperate. He fell ten feet to the stone floor below, his freshly injured leg taking most of the impact. He rolled onto his side. He'd cleared the hole, but just barely. He was too tired and hurt to care.

Finally, all was silent, except for his own labored breathing.

If the Glutton could get up here, it deserved him.

* * *

Even though Dylan wanted nothing more than to lie motionless and rest for a minute, he still had pressing problems to solve. He could feel blood pooling under his right leg. He sat up to inspect the new injury, trying to remember the basic first aid crash course that Alex had given. The cut was long, running from just above his knee nearly to his ankle. It was deep, and painful, but the blood oozing from it was dark red, not bright. That was a good sign, or at least, as good as he could hope for under the circumstances—it meant he hadn't severed an artery.

Here, your things. You need them.

He jumped when the voice came into his head again, accompanied by the sound of tinkling wind chimes. He looked over his shoulder and saw his mother smiling at him. She gestured to a pile of stuff on the ground nearby—his gear.

"Where am I? What's going on, and where's Sara?" he asked, still out of breath.

Questions come later. You are hurt.

She was right. Dylan crawled over to his things and found his trauma kit. Marie watched him with a small, sad smile on her face.

He rolled up his pant leg as far as he could, then found a bottle of disinfectant. He gritted his teeth. This was going to hurt like a bitch.

His scream echoed over and over in the stone room. An inferno seared his leg, like a thousand fire ants biting him. Thankfully, the pain faded to a tolerable level within a few seconds.

"One more," he panted. He found a packet of QuikClot in the first aid kit and ripped it open with his teeth. Alex had told him not to use it unless he was bleeding severely or he had no other way to bandage the injury. The cut on his leg wasn't quite severe, but it was far too large for a pressure dressing, and the bleeding would become problematic soon if he didn't stop it. He didn't see any other choice.

Before he could lose his nerve, he sprinkled the powder over the entire length of the wound, then screamed a while longer. The hemostatic agent hurt roughly a billion times worse than the alcohol had. It rapidly forced the blood to clot, creating a self-sealing dressing of sorts. Within thirty seconds, the bleeding completely stopped.

When the pain finally tapered off, he wrapped a roll of gauze around his leg and taped it in place. It would have to do for now.

Better?

Dylan turned to face her. "You're not really my mother, are you?"

In answer, the woman closed her eyes. The light emanating from her body slowly grew brighter, until Dylan finally had to look away. A moment later, it dimmed, and he looked back.

A different woman stood—no, *hovered* before him. He was only mildly surprised to see her levitating; he'd seen far weirder things lately. She was beautiful. Red hair fell well past her shoulders, and her eyes were a bright, sparkling green—almost as bright as Sara's.

Dylan thought that she looked remarkably like Sara might look in five years or so, if she let her hair grow out.

He thought that he should feel threatened, but he didn't. "Why would you make yourself look like my mother?"

Did it sadden you? The voice in his head had changed. It no longer resembled his mother's voice. It was younger, a little higher.

"Of course."

Is that all?

"What do you mean?"

Did you feel only sadness? Nothing else?

Dylan sighed. "No. It was... nice of you to do that for me. It was nice to see her, even if it wasn't really her, even if it hurt at the same time. But still, why did you do it?"

To give you what you needed.

Comfort and courage, he thought.

"Thank you," he whispered. The strange, glowing woman smiled warmly at him. "Who are you?"

A watcher.

A fragment of a memory came to him. "That was you watching us in the canyon." She nodded. "Why?"

To learn about you.

"Learn what? Who are you? What do you want?"

She cocked her head slightly. *It falls to you to discover those answers on your own —if you can.*

"What is that thing that keeps chasing me? The black ooze."

It is you.

"It's me? What does that mean?"

Another answer I cannot give.

"You mean you know the answer but you just won't tell me."

Yes.

He sighed. "Can you at least tell me if my friends are safe?"

They are, for now. They are nearby.

"Did you bring me here? Take my things and leave me down there, where I almost drowned?"

Yes.

Dylan's features hardened into a frown. "That was much less kind than appearing as my mother."

It was kinder.

He was starting to get irritated. "How do you figure?"

Instead of answering his question, she posed one of her own. *Why are you here?*

"You know that already."

If I knew, I would not ask.

"To protect Sara, obviously."

Why?

He folded his arms. "What do you mean, 'Why?' So she can finish her Pilgrimage."

Why?

"So the world doesn't end!"

Is that the only reason?

The question caught him off guard. "Well... no, not the only reason. She's my friend. I want her to be safe."

And you are qualified to protect her?

He very nearly said "no," out of habit. He paused, thinking. She waited patiently.

"Yes, I am," he finally said. With great effort, he rose to his feet. He tested his injured leg, putting weight on it gingerly. It hurt, but not as bad as he'd feared it might. "I'm not a fighter like Tom, or a healer like Alex. But… I can help Sara in my own way. I know that I have a lot to learn and a long way to go. But I'm done running and hiding. I'm done giving up before I've even tried."

Her smile returned. *You believe that she needs you?*

He realized that he was looking down at the ground—again, out of habit. He lifted his head and met her eyes. "I do. But…." He trailed off. It took him a moment to work up the courage to say something deeply personal. "It's not just that Sara needs me. I need her, too."

To what end?

"I… want to be with her. After this is all over, I mean. For a while, I was really mad at her for dragging me into this. I still don't think it was right for her to do that, but I understand why she did it, and I think she knows, now, that it was wrong. I think she learned something important about herself, so I owe it to her—and to myself—to do the same. I need to be the person she thinks I am. Not for her sake—for mine."

The glowing woman regarded him with an expression of intense curiosity. *Even now, with the fate of the world resting on your shoulders, you think of your own dreams? Your own happiness?*

Almost against his will, Dylan felt his hands tighten into fists at his sides. "When you… made yourself look like my mom, I realized something. I just didn't have time to really think about it until now."

Oh?

"Seeing her—or, thinking it was her—it made me wonder what she would think of me. If she would be proud of me. The way I've been for years now, crushed by doubt, feeling sorry for myself all the time… she wouldn't be proud of me for that. It would break her heart. If something about my life sucks, she would want me to get off my ass and do something about it. So, I will. Again, not for her—for me. I've only got one life. I need to start living it instead of letting it happen to me."

A long silence stretched between them. *What of your wound?* The glowing woman lifted an arm and pointed at his right side.

He glanced down at it, his attention suddenly drawn back to how sick he felt. "I… don't know."

It will kill you soon.

"I know."

It is easy to be courageous when inevitable death draws near.

"That's not what this is about!" Dylan spoke more loudly than he'd meant to, his voice heated with anger.

No?

"I don't intend to die anytime soon."

Your intentions may not be enough.

He let out a frustrated sigh. "I know I can't just wish it away. Believe me, I know—I've spent my whole life trying to solve problems by wishing them away. I don't know how to fix this infection, or whatever it is that's killing me, but I'll figure it out. That's what engineers do—they figure things out. And I'm a damn good engineer."

You speak with confidence. Or is it bravado?

Dylan pointed behind him, down the hole he'd just come from. "I just flew up here on a chain. Before that, I managed to swim through a hole barely bigger than I am. Normally, I can't even bring myself to go in the kiddie pool at the water park. In the past few days, I saved Sara, Tom, and Alex—all of them. I saved Sara more than once. I didn't have a plan for any of that, but I figured it out. I may not have a plan for how to fix this bite, but I'll figure that out, too. I've done it before, and I'll do it again."

The glowing woman's smile returned in full force. She lifted her arms out to her sides and slowly, gently, her bare feet settled on the ground.

Your friends are waiting.

"I can go?"

I could not stop you even if I wanted to.

CHAPTER THIRTY-ONE
Progression

December 30, 2021
Day Six

Dylan felt like the passageway went on forever. How long had he been walking since leaving the glowing woman's chamber? An hour? Two?

He still felt like garbage. He tried not to think about it. For now, all he had to do was put one foot in front of the other. One step at a time.

Finally, he emerged into a larger cavern. In the center of the space, he saw someone sitting on the ground, in the flickering orange light of a torch.

"Sara!" he cried. He ran toward her, ignoring how much running hurt. He fell to his knees beside her.

"Dylan! I'm so glad you're okay." She hugged him tightly but quickly withdrew when he yelped in pain. "Sorry! I forgot. You look terrible." Her face was etched with obvious concern.

"Thanks," he wheezed.

They heard footsteps coming from one of the other passageways. "Friendly coming in, don't shoot me," came Tom's voice.

"Ditto," Alex yelled from yet another tunnel. A minute later, they had all convened around Sara. In the combined light of several torches and glow sticks, they could see one another clearly.

"Dylan, honey," Alex said. She looked like she was going to say something else, but she changed her mind. Instead, she touched his forehead. "You're burning up."

"I know," he said. "I really don't feel good."

Alex sighed. "Dylan, I need to tell you something."

"That I'm dying? I figured that out already." Sara's eyes opened wide in alarm at hearing that. Alex saw her expression and put a comforting hand on her arm, imploring patience.

"Dr. Atwood convinced me not to tell you," Alex said. She was looking at the floor. She sounded deeply ashamed.

"Let me guess," Tom said. "She didn't want to risk Dylan freaking out and getting us all killed if he was worried about dying." Alex nodded.

"That bitch," Sara snarled. The others stared at her, surprised to hear her use such language.

"Dylan, there's hope," Alex said. "Really. We can do surgery to remove the dead tissue. We just... can't do it until the Pilgrimage is over."

Dylan closed his eyes. "Because sedation would send me right back here."

Alex smiled warmly at him. "I still think you're the smartest one here," she said.

"How much farther?"

"Well, there's a bit of good news," Tom said, rubbing his chin. "Not too long ago, I saw the cathedral. Hard to say how far away it was—fifty miles, maybe farther. But I could see it. We're close."

"In Dylan's condition, fifty miles isn't close," Alex said. She was trying to keep her voice calm and reassuring for his sake. She was only partly succeeding.

Tom nodded. "I know. We'll figure it out. Maybe we can catch the train or find another vehicle." He laid a hand on Dylan's shoulder. "Don't worry, Dylan. We'll finish this thing and get you fixed up. We've lost almost a whole day, so we need to hurry."

"A whole day?" Alex cried. She looked at her watch. "Oh, no... I was so focused on finding you guys that I didn't look at the time."

"Me neither," Dylan groaned. The timer on his watch said the same thing: They had just over forty-two hours to reach the cathedral.

Sara hadn't said anything for a while, and she didn't seem especially surprised by the looming deadline. She was sitting next to Dylan, resting a hand on his knee. He put his hand on top of hers, and she gave him a small smile. *Good*, Alex thought. *He needs all the positive energy he can get.*

"Alright, we need to haul ass. Let's walk and talk," Tom said, rising to his feet. He helped the others up. "Which way?"

"Look," Alex said, pointing. "There are five tunnels. I came from that one. Which ones did you guys come from?" The others pointed. "Then that must be the way out," she said, indicating the passageway none of them had used.

They started down that tunnel, two by two, with Tom and Alex in front. "Alright, question. What the fuck just happened to all of us?" Tom said.

"I take it we all had... encounters with glowing women," Alex muttered. Dylan nodded his agreement. The three of them looked at Sara, waiting for an explanation.

She sighed. "They must have been the witches. I don't know much about them."

"You know they're called 'witches,'" Tom said.

Sara shrugged. "Someone gave them that name a long time ago, and it stuck. I really don't know much—I would tell you if I did. Most teams never see them. They only reveal themselves to a few Maidens or Wardens, here and there. The last confirmed sighting was over a hundred years ago. Most of that team died, and the survivors told vague stories about being 'tested.'"

"And you never mentioned it because you didn't think we'd see them," Tom said, a note of suspicion in his voice. When she nodded, he added, "We've heard that from you a lot lately."

Sara let out a frustrated sigh. "I know I've kept things from you. I'm sorry. Maybe, in some cases, it was the wrong call. If I could go back and make a different decision, maybe I would. I'm not perfect. I'm just trying to get us across the finish line so we can all go back to our lives."

Tom wasn't sure he believed her. He didn't completely buy her story about why she'd acted weird around Jacob, either. It sounded plausible, and he couldn't find any obvious holes in it.

Still.

Sara went on. "I really don't know anything else about the witches. Apparently, they 'test' Wardens and Maidens according to some standard or pattern that only they understand."

"Maybe they were testing us to see if we have what it takes to finish the Pilgrimage," Alex offered.

"Maybe," Dylan said. "But if so, why wait until now, when we're almost at the end?"

"I don't think they did wait until now," Tom said.

"The ship," Sara said. "You think that was them."

He nodded. "They may have been watching us before that, too."

"But still, I don't get it," Dylan insisted. "If they were testing us to see if we have what it takes to reach the cathedral, wouldn't they test every team, not just a few?" He sounded out of breath.

"I would think so," Alex said.

"Let's get our cards on the table," Tom said. "Maybe once we all share what happened to us, the pieces will fit better." He recounted the grand illusion he'd lived through, doing his best to remember every detail, as well as his conversation with the strange hovering woman afterward.

"Let me get this straight," Alex said. "In your perfect world, we're still your friends, and we go on beach vacations together?" Tom glowered at her but said nothing. She grinned back and patted his shoulder. "I think it's sweet. Maybe someday soon."

Alex went next, omitting no detail—except the part about the witch saying that her life would be forfeit if she helped Sara finish her Pilgrimage. She shed a few tears, clearly upset by having to recount her own death multiple times. Sara touched her hand reassuringly, and Dylan gave her a side hug when it seemed appropriate.

"I'm sorry you had to go through that," Tom whispered when she'd finished.

Alex offered him a tight smile. Clearly, she was eager for someone else to speak. "Dylan?" Silence. She looked back.

Dylan wasn't there. Sara seemed to suddenly realize that he wasn't beside her and looked back down the tunnel.

All they could see was his glow stick, ten paces behind.

"Dylan!" Alex cried. She shoved past Sara to get to him. The others followed, anxious at what they might find.

Alex knelt beside Dylan. He was on his back, and his eyes were closed. "What happened?" Sara asked, her voice trembling. She was wringing her hands.

"He's unconscious, or close to it," Alex said. She pressed two fingers to the side of his neck. "His pulse is irregular, and he feels like an oven. The infection, or whatever it is... it's...." She stopped, her voice choked with emotion.

"It's killing him," Sara cried. She knelt beside Dylan and cupped a hand gently to his face. Tears fell from her eyes onto the stone below, creating dark patches in the dust.

"Not yet, it isn't," Tom said. He gently pushed Sara aside, removed Dylan's UMP, and handed it to Alex. "Help me get him up. I'll carry him." Once Tom had Dylan securely on his back, he set off again at a light jog.

"He's not gonna make it," Alex sobbed. "I did this. I killed him. I should have told him sooner."

"He's not dead yet, and he won't be. Not for a long time," Tom said. He sounded surer than Alex or Sara felt. "We're gonna finish this, get him home, and he'll be fine. We all need to stay calm and focused to make that happen."

"Right," Sara said, her voice a little steadier. "He'll make it. We'll make it."

They fell silent as they jogged on, conserving their stamina. Running gave them something to do, something to focus on besides Dylan's sickness.

A few minutes later, the air began to feel a little warmer. "I think we're almost outside," Tom said. He was right—after the next bend in the tunnel, they emerged into fresh air. They stopped to catch their breath and to look around.

"Where's the cathedral? I can't see it," Sara panted.

"Look, there. The train," Alex said, pointing. They were at the top of a rise, at the edge of a canyon—the same one they'd traveled through after rescuing Jacob. She was pointing at the same train platform where they'd rested the previous day. This time, a steam locomotive was waiting there.

"We're all the way back here?" Sara yelled. Her clenched fists trembled at her sides. Tom hadn't seen her this upset in a long time.

Of course, she's upset—her best friend is dying, Tom thought. He knew all too well how scared and angry she was.

"But this time we have a train," Alex said. "Let's get on before it leaves. The tracks head that way, toward the moon—toward the cathedral. I can do more for Dylan on the train, and we'll be moving at the same time."

Afraid that the train would leave without them, they made their way along a winding footpath that snaked down from the canyon's rim. When they finally reached the platform half an hour later, they all shared a sigh of relief—the train was still there. Wasting no time, they climbed the platform and boarded through an open door in the second-to-last car.

As soon as they were inside, the door hissed closed quietly, and the train began to move.

Tom gently laid Dylan on his back in one of the long bench seats. "Alex, see what you can do," he said. "Sara, with me. Let's do a sweep up and down the train to make sure we're alone."

"Okay," Sara said. She was clearly still upset, but she seemed a little more collected. Another tear trailed down her cheek. She wiped it away angrily and readied her STI.

* * *

"How is he?" Sara asked a few hours later. Sitting in silence for that long had been agonizing, but Alex had insisted that she needed time to look Dylan over and figure out what to do. Finally, she looked to be done for the time being.

Alex sighed as Sara approached. She pulled Dylan's shirt back down before Sara could see the bite wound. "He's alright for now. I gave him acetaminophen to bring down the fever and amiodarone to stabilize his heart rhythm. He's still unconscious, but the drugs are helping."

"Maybe we should give him adrenaline, to send him back. Maybe the doctors at home can do more for him," Sara said. She squeezed Dylan's hand. He was covered in sweat and mumbling quietly to himself. They couldn't make out the words.

Alex shook her head. "Way too risky. His heart isn't working normally. Even a low dose of adrenaline might kill him."

"Does he have... permanent heart damage?" Sara asked, her voice cracking.

Alex pulled her into a gentle hug. "I don't know. That's the honest answer. I won't lie to you guys anymore, I learned my lesson. All we can do is finish this as quickly as possible."

"It's not your fault," Sara whispered. She was holding Dylan's hand tightly. Her eyes were squeezed shut, and she was crying again. "It's mine. You wouldn't have had to lie to him if I hadn't dragged him into this in the first place. He should be safe at home right now, working on one of his inventions. I never should have brought him here."

"Sara, honey." Alex stopped. She didn't know what else to say.

Tom was lost in thought, still sitting by himself a few rows away, staring out the window. He couldn't stop thinking about the strange conversation he'd had with the glowing woman—the witch. Much of what she'd said hadn't made sense. Did she really think he would abandon Sara and risk the lives of everyone on the planet to live in a dream world where everything was perfect?

And yet, he almost had.

He shook his head. He supposed it didn't matter. If she was testing him, he must have passed. After all, she'd let him go with no further trouble.

Still. Based on what Alex had said about her "test," it had seemed far less benevolent than the one he'd been subjected to. What did it all mean?

A second later, a violent impact rocked the carriage, sending all four of them hurtling into the aisle.

"Motherfucker!" Tom shouted. The impact was so hard that he was amazed the train hadn't tipped over.

"What was that?" Alex yelled.

"Dylan!" Sara screamed. He'd fallen onto the floor and rolled onto his stomach. She rushed to his side to check on him.

"Stay here!" Tom yelled, leaping over Sara and Dylan. He sprinted toward the last car, where the impact had come from. The gangway door clattered shut behind him.

A moment later, it banged open again. Tom was sprinting back toward them. "Don't stay here! Run!" he shouted.

Before Alex or Sara could move, an enormous, reptilian maw smashed through the gangway connecting the two cars. Meter-long fangs gleamed in the moonlight.

The Ouroboros.

Shards of twisted metal and broken glass flew in all directions. Alex flung herself protectively over Dylan to shield him from the dangerous debris. Tom halted next to the others and raised his shotgun. The Jackhammer roared, pelting the snake with twelve rounds of double-aught buckshot in less than two seconds. None of them had had time to put on hearing protection; the gunshots were painfully loud, even with part of the train car missing.

Most of the projectiles pinged harmlessly off the thick chains wrapped around the snake's entire body. A few pellets made it into the behemoth's mouth, but they didn't seem to do any significant damage. "Go!" Tom yelled. "Move Dylan!"

Sara and Alex each grabbed one of Dylan's arms and started dragging him down the aisle. Tom dropped his empty mag and slammed a new one home, this one loaded with lead slugs. Maybe they would do more to damage or dislodge the chains.

With speed that seemed impossible for its size, the Ouroboros lunged forward, smashing train seats into splintered toothpicks under its massive bulk. It barely fit in the car. Tom hopped back, away from the deadly fangs. He squeezed the trigger and held it down, emptying another magazine. He screamed in frustration when the heavy slugs failed to cause any significant damage.

Not bothering to reload, he instead flicked the selector switch behind the Jackhammer's magazine tube and worked the action manually, chambering an incendiary round.

The snake rushed him with terrifying speed, its maw wide. Jerking back in fear, Tom panic fired. Magnesium shards sprayed into its mouth and ignited, burning the soft tissue. The Ouroboros snapped its jaws shut, hissing furiously.

It was the only thing that saved Tom from being swallowed whole. He fired again, and again, emptying the magazine tube and covering the snake in a blanket of fire.

He risked a glance back over his shoulder. Alex and Sara had made it to the next car, dragging Dylan as fast as they dared.

"Alright, dickhead," Tom said to the snake as it thrashed its head back and forth, trying to extinguish the flames. "See how you like this." From his plate carrier, he took two frag grenades, one in each hand. He pulled the pins and lobbed the explosives, then dived for cover behind a seat. He took the opportunity to pull his earmuffs up over his ears.

The simultaneous explosions enraged the snake further, but it still wasn't taking much visible damage. Growling in frustration, Tom slipped off his backpack and reached into the main pocket for a two-pound block of Semtex. He had no time to shape it or carefully consider where to place it. He shoved a Nonel detonator into the block and tossed it toward the writhing beast. He then sprinted through the gangway door into the next car, following Sara and Alex.

He looked back just in time to see the Ouroboros slithering toward him. It had extinguished itself and was almost at the door he'd just passed through. *Jesus Christ, it's so fucking fast*, he thought. He had been hoping to get more distance before blowing the Semtex.

No such luck. He depressed the detonator.

Tom, Alex, and Sara were thrown hard to the ground by the shockwave. The plastic explosive demolished the floor of the previous car, along with the axles underneath. The car derailed and flipped onto its side, pulling the enormous snake along with it. The creature hissed in fury as it tumbled away.

Tom hadn't been entirely sure that the explosion wouldn't derail their car as well. He hoped to not have to roll the dice like that again.

"How's Dylan?" Tom shouted over the ringing in his ears.

"Alright for now," Alex yelled back. "Is it gone?"

As if in answer to her question, the huge snake righted itself and violently whipped its body back and forth, hurling away the shells of train cars that had been wrapped around it. It began slithering down the tracks, gaining rapidly on the train.

"Alex, here," Tom said, unslinging his MGL. He passed it over to her. "Just pull the trigger. Fire the whole cylinder." He picked up Dylan, trying not to jostle him any more than necessary. "Sara, with me. Cover Alex."

Alex felt strangely calm as she shouldered the heavy weapon. She wasn't sure it would do much beyond buying them a few seconds, but it felt reassuring to have high explosives at her disposal.

She waited for the snake to come closer.

When she'd let it get as close as she dared, she fired, working the trigger as quickly as she could. A hail of grenades flew downrange. Three scored direct hits on the snake's face, and the other three detonated on the ground just under its jaw.

"Eat that!" Alex yelled. She lowered the empty launcher, anxiously waiting for the dust and smoke to clear. For a long moment, nothing happened.

Then, out of the debris cloud, four massive white fangs lunged at her. She screamed and jumped back, falling over. The fangs snapped at her feet. She scooted back, stood up, and ran.

Tom, carrying Dylan, was almost to the next car. Sara was using the top of a seat as a rest for her rifle and was firing past Alex, trying to cover her retreat. Alex heard 6.8mm rounds ricocheting off the chains.

"Get to the front of the train!" Sara yelled. When Alex passed her, she fell in behind, and they ran to catch up with Tom. The Ouroboros was slowed somewhat by having to smash through rows of seats every few feet.

But there was only so much train left.

"There's a bridge coming up!" Tom yelled from somewhere up ahead.

Alex and Sara paused to lean out the windows and take a look. Sure enough, the train had exited the canyon and was heading for a ravine spanned by a truss bridge. They couldn't see into the ravine yet, but it looked deep.

Tom had gone as far as he could, up to the gangway door leading to the locomotive. Dylan was lying on the floor, still unconscious.

Sara recognized the look on Tom's face. "Tell me you're not gonna do what I think you're gonna do," she said.

"Wait here," he said, and took off, back down the train, toward the advancing serpent.

"He's gonna blow up the whole train, isn't he," Alex said.

"I believe he is," Sara replied. She reloaded her rifle and took a knee in front of Dylan.

If the snake wanted him, it would have to go through her first.

Tom moved back one car and pulled the rest of the Semtex out of his pack. He had two blocks left, at two pounds each. He hoped it would be enough.

The Ouroboros was two cars back, squeezing its massive body along. The train cars acted like compression sleeves, making it difficult for the creature to slither quickly. Tom figured he had about thirty seconds. He got to work, splitting the plastic explosives into thirds. He rolled the sections between his hands, working them into long snakes.

"Ha. Snakes," he chuckled to himself.

Once he had enough, he worked the pieces into a continuous line on the floor, running from one wall of the train to the other. He wanted the explosive force focused downward as much as possible, across the entire width of the track. He tried to ignore the sound of shattering glass and splintering wood coming closer to him.

He looked up. The snake was twenty feet away. His heart was hammering. His hands were sweaty, and he fumbled the detonator cord, dropping it. He snatched it back up and crammed the blasting cap into the putty-like explosive compound.

Tom scrambled to his feet and sprinted back into the gangway. The snake was almost on top of the explosives. He couldn't risk it crawling over them, knocking them out of place. He leaned over the railing to see where the train was. He couldn't detonate until they were on the bridge, preferably halfway over the ravine. If he did, the whole plan would be for nothing—and the snake would have them.

The locomotive was just starting to cross the bridge. It had slowed down considerably. It wouldn't reach the halfway point for about twenty seconds.

That was too long.

"Open fire!" he shouted. He set the detonator on the floor and raised his shotgun. "Hit it with everything! Drive it back!"

He heard Alex's MPX and Sara's REC7 open up on full auto behind him. He joined in with the Jackhammer, all thoughts of ammo conservation thrown to the wind.

As usual, the hail of lead did little to damage the snake, but the sheer weight and velocity of all the rounds did halt its forward progress for a bit. Sparks flew everywhere as metal smashed against metal. Someone hit it in the eye, probably by accident, causing the snake to jerk backward and hiss loudly, its forked tongue lashing out like a whip.

"Aim for the eyes!" Tom yelled back over his shoulder, adjusting his own point of aim. He was crouching, and leaning as far to the left as he could. Bullets whizzed through the air above him, some so close that he could hear small *cracks*. He hoped Alex or Sara wouldn't shoot him in the back.

Or the head.

Tom loaded his last magazine of buckshot and slammed the bolt release, chambering a fresh round. He aimed carefully, waiting for an opening. Buckshot would be much more likely to hit a small target.

The Ouroboros lunged, shrugging off the incoming pistol and rifle rounds. It was almost on top of the Semtex again. There—it turned its head to the side, just slightly. Tom slammed the trigger and held it down, sending a volley of 108 lead pellets downrange.

At least one must have hit home. The snake snapped its head back again and thrashed, furious that its prey kept hurting it. Tom could see pale-yellow fluid leaking from its right eye.

That was it—he was empty. No more buckshot. He had only slugs left, a handful of incendiary shells, and his sidearm. He stood up and leaned over the railing to check the train's position.

The car with the snake in it wasn't quite yet at the halfway point.

They couldn't wait any longer. He hoped it was close enough.

Tom scooped up the Nonel detonator and hammered the ignition button.

A catastrophic explosion ripped the following car in half. Tom was positive that, had he not been wearing his ear pros, he would have gone permanently deaf. He'd been hunkered down behind the lower part of the car's outer wall, but even so, the concussive force knocked him over.

The bridge buckled as steel girders twisted unnaturally. Rivets popped out of place like bullets. Tom shot to his feet and tried to run toward the others, toward the front of the train.

He would have made it, had the Ouroboros not violently thrashed its whole body, in a final, defiant attempt to ensnare its prey.

The remains of the destroyed car began to fall. The mangled bridge supports might have been able to hold its weight if it were empty, but not with a ten-ton snake inside. Tom lost his footing and tumbled backward, right toward the snake's open maw.

He reached out with both hands and snatched a seat that was still mostly bolted to the floor. The Ouroboros snapped its jaws, trying to reach him. It almost succeeded.

"Tom!" Sara shouted. She was running toward him.

"Stay back!" he ordered.

The destroyed car was rapidly sliding away into the ravine, along with all the cars behind it and the middle portion of the bridge. Tom felt his stomach lurch as his center of gravity shifted wildly.

He had to get to the next car.

He jumped as hard as he could. The last remnants of the destroyed car tore free and fell away, taking the Ouroboros with it. The gargantuan snake hissed wildly as it tumbled into the ravine.

Tom managed to grab the gangway door frame. The next car was rocking from side to side, but miraculously, it was still on the track. The gangway door slammed shut on his knuckles, and he let loose a string of creative profanity.

The car leveled out. Thankfully, the bridge hadn't been completely destroyed. Tom pulled himself along the damaged floor, struggling with all the extra weight of his gear. His feet were nearly dragging on the tracks. Alex and Sara rushed over to help pull him into the gangway. Once he could stand, they retreated into the car behind the locomotive—the only one left.

"Do you always have to solve problems by blowing things up?" Alex said. She was panting, and her hands were shaking. The bolt on her MPX was locked open.

"Sometimes the simple solutions work best," he retorted. He checked himself over. He had new cuts and bruises, but nothing too serious.

The shortened train cleared the bridge and began to speed up again.

"We're lucky the whole bridge didn't collapse," Sara said.

"No one was sharing any good plans, so I had to go with a bad one," Tom griped.

"Do you think it's dead? Or gone, at least?" Alex said.

Tom shook his head. "I doubt it. That thing shrugged off explosions that would have blown a five-ton truck into confetti. I don't think a little tumble will hurt it much, but it's off our asses for now, at least." He dusted his hands on his pants. "Is Dylan okay?"

"As okay as he can be, or he was, before that thing showed up," Alex said. "Let's go check on him."

CHAPTER THIRTY-TWO
Confrontation

Hours later, the train slowed down, then gently came to a stop. The car door slid open on its own, beckoning the passengers to exit. Tom cautiously leaned out and looked around. "There's another platform here, and the tracks don't go any farther. Looks like we're walking. Good news —I can see the cathedral," he said.

"Finally," Alex groaned.

Tom gently picked up Dylan and stepped out onto the platform. Alex and Sara disembarked and stood beside him. "Hey, Sara," Tom said.

"Hmm?"

"I need to tell you something."

"Yes?"

"You smell like a horse."

She smacked his armor with the back of her hand. "Ow. You don't smell so great yourself," she griped.

"A proper bath sounds lovely," Alex added.

"Soon," Tom said. "Don't get lazy just because we're almost there. Anything can happen, and we're not done until we're done. Stay focused and alert."

None of them mentioned the need to hurry for Dylan's sake. They were all acutely aware that his time was running out.

They descended the platform stairs. Ahead was a field of green grass, and beyond it, a lush grove of cherry trees stretched as far as they could see. The trees were in full bloom, their pink and white blossoms swaying in a gentle breeze. It was the least threatening place they'd seen in the Twilight.

"It's beautiful," Alex said as they started walking.

"I don't trust it," Tom said.

"Look," Sara said, pointing. Beyond the cherry trees, an imposing structure jutted into the night sky. From so far away, it was hard to see much detail, but its angles were sharp and irregular.

"That's the cathedral?" Alex said.

"That's it," Sara confirmed. "Let's hurry."

They set off toward the cherry trees at a jog. Dylan was still unresponsive on Tom's back. Occasionally, he muttered something that none of them could understand. Every time Alex checked his temperature, he felt hotter.

The grove welcomed them with a pleached alley. The branches of trees to either side arched high overhead and intertwined with one another, forming a protective tunnel. Millions of blossoms had fallen to the ground, creating a soft, fragrant carpet. The only sound was the quiet rustling of branches in the wind.

"Remember that creepy forest when we first came here? The trees there did the same thing," Tom said.

"Except these are much more welcoming," Alex said.

"I know it doesn't mean we're safe, but I don't feel threatened here, like I did in the forest," Sara said.

"Maybe this is… kind of a reward, or something," Alex said. "A little breather before the end."

"That raises the question: What do we need to be prepared for?" Tom asked.

No one could come up with a comforting answer to that.

About halfway through the grove, they stopped for a short rest. Tom, in particular, was getting tired from having to carry Dylan. Sara wandered among the nearby trees and began picking fresh blossoms.

"Almost there," Alex said. Tom gently laid Dylan on the ground, and Alex took a seat next to him so she could check him over.

"I still don't quite believe it," Tom said. "I think we've all gotten used to the insanity and horror over the past week, but… this is real, right?"

Alex offered a humorless smile. "The longest recorded dream was only three hours. We've been here a lot longer than that."

"How's he doing?" Tom asked, gesturing at Dylan.

Alex shook her head and sighed. "A little worse. I can control some of his symptoms with drugs, but only for so long." She rummaged around in her bag, found a vial and a syringe, and began drawing up more medication.

Tom glanced at Sara to make sure she was out of earshot. "Is he gonna make it?"

"I'll make sure he does. I did this to him. It's my responsibility to fix it."

They rested a few more minutes until Sara came back. "Look, Dylan," she said softly, kneeling beside him. "Cherry blossoms—your favorite. I brought the prettiest ones I could find." She opened her hands to show him the flowers she'd collected. She gently opened his left hand, placed a few flowers into it, and curled his fingers around them. "Dylan… please wake up," she whispered.

He didn't respond. His breathing was rapid and shallow, his skin deathly pale.

A tear fell from Sara's face onto his. She carefully placed a few flowers into one of his empty armor pouches, then picked the one with the longest stem and threaded it into her hair, behind her left ear.

"The best thing we can do is keep moving," Alex said, rubbing Sara's back. "Tom, have you rested enough?"

He nodded. "I'm alright now. Let's head out."

They crossed the second half of the grove in silence.

* * *

"What in the blue fuck is that?" Tom said.

The three of them stood at the edge of the cherry tree grove, looking up a short but steep hill. Atop it was an enormous stone building, its only visible entryway blocked by a massive iron gate. Skulls ten feet tall, carved into the stone on either side, were leering down at them. Each of the skulls' four eye sockets had an iron brazier in it, but none of them were lit.

Endless rivers of dark red blood poured from the skulls' mouths, through iron grates below.

"All of the vegetation between here and there is dead," Alex said. Tom and Sara noticed that she was right. "I take it that's not a good sign."

"Probably a safe bet," Tom said.

"And going around is out," Alex added. "Those same thorny black trees from the forest outside the village—they're all over the place."

The ominous wall of thorns stretched as far as they could see in both directions. It also covered the walls and roof of the structure, preventing climbing. Getting through it would take weeks, even with flamethrowers and chainsaws.

The way forward was clear. Passage was permitted only through the gate.

"Let's take a closer look," Tom said. He didn't really want to get any closer, but he could feel Dylan's shallow, irregular breath on the back of his neck. He didn't have much time. Tom wanted to push on quickly, for his sake.

"This is the Hollow I mentioned earlier," Sara said as they carefully picked their way up the hill. "This is the most dangerous place in the Twilight. See the mist?"

At first, Tom and Alex didn't. They looked closer. There it was—thin tendrils of greenish-gray fog wafting through the bars of the gate and up through the iron grates that served as drains for the macabre waterfalls of blood. Behind the gate and below the grates, the mist was much thicker.

Sara went on. "That mist... it's the souls of Maidens and Wardens who were killed here or by an Eidolon. Maybe not 'souls' in the way we normally use the word, no one is really sure. But that mist definitely has some kind of energy—bad energy. It's raw evil."

"And you have trouble getting people to sign up for this job? I never would have guessed," Tom said.

"If we die here, in that mist... we become part of the Twilight. We become Eidolons that will hunt and kill the next people who come here," Alex whispered.

"Yes," Sara said. Her voice was even quieter. "And once we go in there, we can't leave by sleeping. Not even adrenaline will wake us up."

"So, what you're saying is, once we go into the Hollow, there's no turning back. No breaks or do-overs. It's the final push, and one way or another, it'll be over soon," Tom said.

"That's right."

"Then maybe we should head back and resupply now, if it's our last chance."

"Normally, I would agree, but...," Alex said, gesturing at Dylan.

"We can't leave him here. We need to hurry," Sara said. Tom could tell from her face that it was a mighty effort for her to keep her voice steady.

"Maybe I can go back with Sara, just one quick trip. Just long enough to grab some ammo and medical supplies. Alex can stay here and keep an eye on Dylan," Tom said.

"I don't know," Sara said. She circled around Tom and rested a hand on Dylan's arm, studying his face.

"What's your medical opinion, doc?" Tom said.

Alex sighed. "We have plenty of time to reach the cathedral, but Dylan doesn't. I think we need to push on. He needs help as soon as possible."

Tom nodded. "Alright, I trust your judgment. Let's get this done and get Dylan fixed up."

"How do we get in?" Alex said, turning back to face the gate.

"You're not gonna like it," Sara said. She walked over to the left side of the gate and let her rifle hang on its sling.

"Well, I've loved everything else about this trip so far, I suppose I can handle one little letdown," Tom said dryly.

Sara pointed with both hands, at two small alcoves carved into the stone on the left side of the gate about waist high. At first, Tom and Alex had assumed they were decorative.

"This place... it's basically the outer courtyard of the cathedral, kind of like how the ancient Egyptians used to build a bunch of smaller temples around the main temple. It's called the Vile Abbey," Sara said.

"I can see why," Tom said.

"To get into the Vile Abbey, you must offer a sacrifice. Of blood," Sara said, clearly not expecting this revelation to go over well.

"Again, I can see why," Alex said, staring pointedly at the blood cascading from the mouth of the ten-foot skull to her right.

"What kind of blood sacrifice are we talking about here?" Tom asked.

"Four altars. Four hands," Sara said, pointing again to the two alcoves on the left of the gate, and another two on the right.

Alex stared at her. "You're kidding."

"Like a horror movie? We put our hands in there and… what? Get them cut off?" Tom said.

"Nothing quite that bad. It's just a minor bloodletting."

Alex closed her eyes. "There's no other way?"

Sara shook her head. "None."

"Then we do what we have to do," Alex said. Tom was impressed by her determination, even if it was largely on Dylan's behalf.

"Can I do it twice? So Dylan doesn't have to?" Tom said.

Sara shook her head again, clearly upset by the question. "No. I wish. Each of us must offer blood. The Abbey knows if one of us doesn't, and the gate won't open."

"But in Dylan's condition…." Alex trailed off.

"I know," Sara whispered. "But he has to. This is the only way we can help him… by hurting him first."

"Let's get on with it, then," Tom said. "Every second we screw around is a second Dylan may not have." He stepped over to the alcoves on the right. "Sara, Alex, you go left."

Alex's heart was pounding. Against every instinct, she forced herself to place her left hand into the alcove, flat against the stone.

It was a small price to pay to make up for what she'd done to Dylan.

A spring-loaded, razor-sharp blade fired out of the stone, out of a crevice she hadn't even seen. Nearly a foot long, it cut right through her hand, between her third and fourth finger bones. By the time she felt the pain, the blade had already retracted.

But feel the pain she did. She let out a strangled scream and a string of profanity.

"Keep your hand there," Sara said. "Let the blood run down."

As Alex watched, panting, her hand on fire, the blood trickled down through a small channel cut into the stone, into a reservoir the size of an egg. Once it was full, one of the four braziers in the skulls' eyes burst into flame.

"This is horrible, I'm not saying it isn't, but you have to admit that's kind of cool. It's like the greatest metal album cover of all time," Tom said, trying to lighten the mood.

"I don't have to admit shit," Alex grumbled. "Hurry up. Your turn."

Tom made his sacrifice and swore even more than Alex had. A moment later, Sara did the same, her scream piercing the night air. Three of the four braziers were now lit.

"Now for the hard part," Alex sighed, walking over to Tom. "Let me help with Dylan. I'll patch us all up after we get inside."

Sara turned away. She couldn't bear to watch.

Tom crouched so that Alex could maneuver Dylan's left hand into the alcove. She squeezed her eyes shut. Doing this to Dylan felt much worse than doing it to herself.

When the blade pierced his hand, his eyes shot open, and he let out a hoarse, guttural scream.

"Uh, I think he's awake," Tom said.

"Dylan!" Alex tried to comfort him. "It's me! It's us. We're here."

He was staring at his bleeding hand in shock and disbelief. His mouth moved, but no words came out.

The fourth brazier sparked into flame, and with a low rumble, the gate began to move, raised by some unseen mechanism.

"Let's get inside," Alex said. "It's okay, Dylan. We're almost home."

* * *

The heavy gate slammed closed as soon as they'd all passed under it.

"We're committed now," Tom said.

"Dylan, relax, it's okay. Let me see your hand," Alex said. She gestured for Tom to help Dylan sit on the floor while she fetched bandages from her bag. She cleaned and dressed his wound first. He was so disoriented that he didn't even seem to feel the burning disinfectant.

"Sara? Where's Sara?" he mumbled.

"Here. I'm right here," she said, kneeling next to him. She gripped his other hand tightly.

Dylan smiled weakly at her. "Did we do it?"

She smiled back. "Almost. Just a little farther. We're very close."

"Good." His eyelids drooped.

"Dylan, honey, try to stay awake," Alex said. She paused when she noticed Dylan's eyes—they were even more glassy and glazed over than usual, and his irises, normally bright blue, had faded to a much lighter shade. Alex looked at Tom and Sara; their eyes, too, had changed. She assumed that hers had as well.

"What's up with our eyes?" she asked.

"We're in the Hollow now," Sara said. "It's another layer of the Twilight that's even farther removed from our world. Different regions of the Twilight are analogous to different stages of sleep. If the rest of the Twilight is like the first stage, light sleep, then the Hollow is the second stage—deep sleep. As far as we understand it, that's why adrenaline won't work here. We're too far removed from our world to come back directly."

"I see," Alex said. She finished wrapping Dylan's hand and moved on to her own, so she could then treat Tom and Sara more efficiently.

Dylan opened his eyes again, with effort. "So tired," he sighed.

"I know, but you gotta stay awake. Maybe an hour or so. We're almost there, then we'll go home, and you can get the surgery, and then you'll have plenty of time to rest," Sara said. Tears were trickling down her face again.

He mumbled something that none of them could understand. By the time Alex had cleaned and wrapped everyone's hands, Dylan was mostly unconscious again.

"Let's move," Tom said, picking him up.

It was impossible to avoid breathing in the thick, greenish mist. It had a sour taste, like expired milk. The entire area radiated a palpable aura of malice.

A narrow stone bridge stretched out before them, disappearing into the dark interior of the Vile Abbey. Torches flickered in iron sconces mounted on the walls at regular intervals. The bridge was supported by pillars, but something about them looked odd. Tom had to squint for a long moment before he realized what the pillars were.

Each one was made of hundreds of human spines, woven together like grotesque thread.

More skulls were carved into the walls, between the torches. Continual rivers of blood ran from their mouths. Alex gagged. The coppery, pungent smell of blood was overpowering. "There must be swimming pools of blood down there," she said.

"Alex, take point," Tom said. "Sara, get behind me. I'm starting to get tired, and I have to carry Dylan across the bridge. It looks pretty long, and I want someone on either side of me in case I need help with him."

The bridge was only a few feet wide. The cascading blood on both sides fell away into darkness, pooling somewhere too far below to see. Alex lit a torch and began to make her way across the bridge. The others followed single file, slowly, carefully. Dylan was awake, just barely. His eyes were closed, and he babbled nonsense whenever Tom shifted his weight or moved unexpectedly.

The stench of blood was becoming nauseating by the time they reached the far side of the bridge. The walkway broadened into a wide platform made of stone, suspended in midair by heavy chains that must have been anchored in a ceiling high overhead. This area had brighter torches and more of them. They stood upright in iron cages that sat on the platform itself instead of being mounted on the walls. The open flames burned away the mist in a small radius.

"Sara, grab another torch," Alex said.

"Good call," Tom said.

Sara picked up a torch, then met Alex in the center of the platform. Their lights illuminated a circular stone well about three feet tall and five feet wide. It was filled with a thick, black liquid.

"Is that oil?" Sara asked.

"Maybe. Don't get the torch too close in case it's flammable," Alex said.

"Let's keep moving," Tom said.

They pressed on. At the far end of the platform, another bridge extended into the darkness, this one even narrower than the last. Tom sighed. He'd been carrying Dylan for hours and was nearing exhaustion.

He mentally shook himself. He would carry Dylan another twenty miles if that was what it took. That was all there was to it.

"This place freaks me out," Sara said as they started to pick their way across the second bridge.

"I'd be concerned if it didn't freak you out," Alex said.

"Yeah, but I think it's messing with my head. I'm starting to hear things."

"You're hearing things?" Tom said.

"Yeah, like a... a squishy, liquid sound."

"Hang on," Alex said. She stopped walking. She cocked her head, listening.

Tom stopped as well and listened. "I hear it, too," he said.

They turned back toward the platform.

A gelatinous black mass was oozing up and over the stone wall, rising to its full height.

"Fuck me, not now," Tom said.

"Go!" Alex shouted.

They ran across the bridge as fast as they dared, the mist parting before them and swirling closed like curtains behind them. It was a little easier now that they had more torchlight to see by, but the bridge was so narrow that even walking was tricky. Tom, in particular, was having a hard time keeping his balance with Dylan on his back. With every step, his heart beat faster. One slip, and he would fall to some horrible place he couldn't begin to imagine—and he would take Dylan with him.

The Glutton rolled along behind them, having no such difficulty.

"Alex, flashbang," Tom wheezed. She pulled hers and removed the pin. She held it for a count of two, then tossed it. It was a good throw—the grenade detonated in midair just before it struck the Glutton. The resulting *bang* was muted in the large, open space, but the flash of bright light appeared to have some effect. The Glutton paused momentarily. Dozens of gooey projections shot out of its body like spring-loaded spikes before retracting a moment later. It remained motionless, vibrating and jiggling. It appeared to be trying to shake itself out of it.

"That did something," Alex called to the others. "Give me your flashbangs. I'll keep tossing them whenever it gets close to us."

Tom and Sara stopped long enough to pass theirs back to Alex, along with Dylan's. They only carried one each.

Hopefully, it would be enough.

Alex threw the second flashbang about twenty seconds later, and the third about fifteen seconds after that. The Glutton seemed to recover more quickly and to increase its speed each time.

"Any ideas? Last grenade," Alex yelled. Her hands and voice were trembling. If it caught them before they reached the other side of the bridge, she would be its first meal.

"I can see the end! Almost there!" Sara shouted back from the front of the line.

Tom and Sara heard another loud *bang*—the last grenade. They resisted the temptation to look back, trying to stay focused on keeping their balance on the narrow bridge.

The Glutton was barely ten feet behind Alex when Sara reached the far side. In the light of her torch, stone steps rose into the darkness. She took them two at a time.

"Slow down!" Tom yelled at her. "I can't go that fast!"

Sara doubled back and tried to help Tom climb the stairs faster. It was no use; with Dylan on his back, and as tired as he was, he simply had to take them slowly. Sara gave up trying to help him along and stayed beside him, holding out the torch so that he could see. Alex caught up to them.

"It's having a little trouble climbing the stairs. It's not as fast as it was a second ago," she reported, trying to catch her breath. "But I'm not sure how long that will last."

"Slow and steady," Tom grunted. He took the stairs one at a time, placing each foot down carefully. If he fell, it was all over. His thigh and calf muscles were on fire. His back ached fiercely. Dylan was so terribly heavy.

"I see more torches. I think there's a landing ahead, not too much farther," Sara said.

The squelching sounds below were getting louder. The Glutton had figured out the stairs and was gaining on them.

"Dylan said explosives slowed this thing down," Tom said, panting heavily. "Who has grenades left?"

Before anyone could answer, he tripped.

His right leg buckled, and his foot didn't quite go high enough. The toe of his boot clipped the top edge of a step and he pitched to the right. Reflexively, he threw out his hand to steady himself—and let go of Dylan.

To Sara, the next few seconds seemed to pass in slow motion. She saw Tom grimace in pain as he cracked his knee on one of the stairs. She saw Dylan begin to slide off Tom's back. She saw Alex's face begin to contort in horror as she realized what was happening.

Dylan crashed onto his right side—his injured side. That brought him fully awake again; his pained scream left no doubt about it. Alex dropped her torch and reached out for Dylan, trying to catch him.

She missed.

Dylan rolled down the stairs, picking up speed. Alex's discarded torch clattered down after him.

Finally, Dylan managed to throw his arms out and slow himself. He rolled down a few more stairs and finally came to a stop on his right side, facing upward, toward the others.

Alex's torch rolled to a stop a few stairs above Dylan, still burning.

In its flickering light, the Glutton loomed out of the shadows behind him.

"Dylan!" Sara screamed. She dropped her torch and snapped her rifle to her shoulder, taking aim. She felt so terribly slow. Tom and Alex screamed Dylan's name also, bringing their weapons to bear. It was so close to him. They couldn't fire without hitting him.

Dylan was looking down at something—something small, clutched in his right hand. His fever-addled brain struggled to remember what it was called.

Cherry blossom. That was it.

He frowned. Why did he have one? Where had it come from? Maybe that nice woman had given it to him—the one who had made herself look like Marie. That had been so very kind of her. Dylan smiled at the memory.

He saw that one of the pouches on his armor had come open. There was another cherry blossom inside it.

Voices were calling his name, quietly. They must have been very far away. He looked up, toward the sound.

"Sara?" he whispered. He could barely talk. His throat was so dry. He needed water.

Sara was reaching toward him, her face frozen in terror. She was looking at something over his shoulder, behind him. What was she so worried about? Whatever it was, it couldn't be that big of a deal.

Twenty steps up, Sara was screaming incoherently. She couldn't make herself fire her rifle. The Glutton was too close to Dylan.

Dylan was moving so slowly, so casually, like he had all the time in the world. What was wrong with him? Did he not realize that the horrid monstrosity that had killed Roland was right behind him?

Finally, he looked back. He must have seen the Glutton; it was only an arm's length away, still rolling up the stairs toward him.

He looked back at Sara. She expected to see terror on his face that mirrored her own.

Instead, he was smiling.

He winked at her—and rolled backward, down the stairs, directly into the pulsing mass of black ooze.

Within two heartbeats, it swallowed him.

"No!" Sara screamed. Neither Alex nor Tom could move. Neither had ever heard a more heartbreaking cry.

Sara fell back onto the stairs. Her eyes were fixed and distant, staring straight ahead at nothing. Her mouth hung open.

Tom's combat training kicked in, and his muscles unlocked. He mentally shoved his sorrow and revulsion aside. They would mourn Dylan later. If they didn't move fast, there would be no "later" for any of them. He could tell that Sara wasn't going to move on her own. He didn't bother yelling at her—he just picked her up.

"Alex! Move!" he shouted.

Thankfully, she heard him and responded. Her face was drained of all color. She moved haltingly, in fits and starts, but at least she was moving. She snatched up the torch that Sara had dropped.

The Glutton kept coming.

Tom and Alex reached the top of the stairs. Ten paces ahead was another iron gate, this one smaller than the first. It, too, was closed. Tom put Sara down and started running his hands over the gate, looking for a way to open it.

"Alex, find a switch, a lever—something," he said.

"O—okay," she stammered. Holding the torch in one hand, she started searching.

Tom knelt down and grabbed the lowermost crossbar, near the bottom of the gate. He flexed his legs and pulled with all his might. The gate moved about an inch, then slammed back down. He was badly out of breath, and his muscles were fatigued. Maybe he could move it on his own if he were rested.

He had a feeling he wouldn't get the chance.

Tom and Alex turned back to face the stairs just as the Glutton advanced into the ring of torchlight. They raised their weapons, ready to fire, both knowing it would do no good.

Sara remained frozen on the ground, staring straight ahead.

"This might be it," Tom said.

"You're a good man, Tom," Alex replied. "Thank you for everything."

CHAPTER THIRTY-THREE
Enlightenment

"Hang on," Tom said. He lowered his shotgun. "Look."

The Glutton had suddenly stopped. It was quivering, almost vibrating, but it wasn't coming toward them anymore. It seemed... thicker than before, a little less liquid, a little more solid.

As they watched, the oozing mass began to harden. Small black flakes chipped off and fell away. Cracks began to form, first two, then three, then —a dozen. Slivers of white light shone through the openings. As more and larger chunks fell away, the light became brighter, until it was so bright that Tom and Alex had to shield their eyes.

With a loud *crack* and a final, blinding flash, the Glutton exploded. A thousand pieces of chalky black residue spun away into the darkness.

Dylan fell to his knees in front of them, then onto his stomach.

"What...," Alex said.

"The hell," Tom finished.

"Dylan?" Sara whispered. She'd snapped out of her trance. Tentatively, she crawled toward him.

"Sara, be careful," Tom warned.

She ignored him. She gripped Dylan's shoulder and rolled him onto his back, fearing the worst.

He grinned up at her. "Hey," he said.

Sara gasped and covered her mouth with her hands. "Dylan! You're...."

"Fine," he said.

Alex rushed over and knelt down, inspecting her patient. "Tom... you're not gonna believe this," she said a moment later.

"Consider my credulity strained," he said.

Dylan sat up and spun around. Even in the dim firelight, Tom could see that he looked... great. All his visible wounds were gone. He was no longer sweating, and his skin had regained its normal color. Alex snatched his wrist and checked his pulse. He let her, still grinning, obviously pleased with himself.

"Dylan... how...?" Sara couldn't even form the question.

"Check this out," he said. He unbuckled his armor and shrugged out of it, then pulled up his shirt. The skin on his right side was smooth and clean. There was no sign of the ugly, festering bite wound.

"What is this *X-Files* shit?" Tom said.

Before Dylan could respond, Sara threw her arms around him. She buried her face in his shoulder, crying freely. He returned the embrace and patted her back reassuringly. "I'm alright, really. Better than ever, actually," he said, mostly to Sara. "No tricks. I promise."

She pulled away and looked up at him, her filthy face tear stained. "But how?"

He reached up and gently pulled the cherry blossom out of her hair. "I'm an engineer. Engineers solve problems," he said cryptically.

"Boy, you'd better start talking sense," Tom growled. "I'm itching to beat something."

"It was the witches—one in particular," Dylan said. "She helped me figure it out. I was going to tell you. I guess I passed out before I got the chance."

Alex sank to the floor, mesmerized. Dylan offered the borrowed flower back to Sara. She took it and held it in her hands, waiting intently to hear the story. He recounted his time with the witch, starting with waking up on the shore of the underground lake.

When he finished, Sara cut in. "But how—"

Dylan raised a hand gently, imploring patience. "I finally figured out what the Glutton was. Actually, I didn't really figure it out. The witch told me that part, I just didn't know what she meant at the time.

"The Glutton was me—the worst part of me. My self-doubt and self-pity, given physical form. It was its MO that gave it away."

"Its MO?" Alex asked, tilting her head.

"What do self-doubt and self-pity do to you, if you let them fester long enough?" Dylan asked.

"They… smother you. Eat you alive," Alex said, starting to catch on. She'd seen it in her patients hundreds of times.

"Just like the Glutton crushed and absorbed everything in its path," Dylan confirmed.

"But how did it not kill you? You fell right into it. We saw what it did to Roland," Tom said.

Dylan heaved a sigh and shook his head. When he spoke, his voice was laden with sorrow. "I feel so bad about Roland. He was just in the wrong place at the wrong time. Only I could have killed the Glutton—and only by turning the tables."

"How?" Sara asked.

"This journey has helped me realize something: I'm not useless. My whole life, ever since I can remember, I've felt like I could never accomplish anything important or difficult. When most kids turn six, they have birthday parties at a laser tag place. I spent my sixth birthday looking through newspapers with my dad, trying to figure out what had happened to my mom.

"We never figured it out. Every dead end, every cold trail made me feel worse. It was a terrible feeling, loving my mom as much as I did without having any memories of her. I only knew her from photos and videos. But I saw how badly my dad wanted to find her and… I guess I just absorbed his sadness. I wanted to find my mom, not just for myself, but to help my dad, too.

"Self-pity and self-doubt are funny things. They can blind you to the very evidence that can destroy them, if you let that happen. I've never been useless. I *can* do things. I'm good at building and fixing stuff if nothing else. I've even won a few awards for things I've designed. And yet, somehow, I kept convincing myself that I was powerless to do anything meaningful. I ignored the evidence that proved otherwise, evidence that was right in front of me all along. It was easier to just… believe that the future was out of my hands. It was easier to tell myself that the only way to stop bad things from happening is to not try. If you don't try, you can't fail."

Dylan turned to face Sara. "Sara, you're my best friend," he said. "I would do anything to keep you safe. I know that now, but I didn't *know* it before. Not really, not fully. When I was trapped down there in those caves, alone, with no way out except underwater…. For the first time in my life, there was nothing I could do but face the facts. There was nobody to come rescue me, nobody who would do the hard thing if I didn't. My only two choices were to face my fear, to do something terrible and terrifying and difficult, something I was totally unprepared for, by myself, with no help… or to sit around being scared and doubting myself and let Sara die. I made my choice.

"At first, I thought the witch was torturing me. But she wasn't. She was giving me a chance to see the truth. What I did just now, I could have done it back there, in those tunnels, but I wasn't quite ready yet. I hadn't figured it all out yet. There was still a piece missing.

"The flowers you picked for me were that missing piece. Cherry blossoms are my favorite flower… because they were my mom's favorite. But I can't keep living in the past. I can't build a life for myself using only the pieces she left behind. I'll always have the photos and the videos, but she would want me to move on and start living my own life. *I* want to have my own life. I want to do things that make me happy. I want to be with my best friend… and I guess you guys are okay, too." He smiled at

Tom and Alex. They smiled back. Even Tom was getting a little choked up.

Dylan turned back to Sara, who was watching him with rapt attention. "When I looked down at the flower in my hand, I saw my past. When I looked up at you, I saw my future. In that moment, I knew what I had to do. I knew how to kill the Glutton. It wanted to swallow me and reduce me to nothing, smother me with my own self-doubt and self-pity. I realized that there was only one weapon against that: real confidence, and real hope for my own future. I realized that if I stood up to the Glutton, if I showed no fear, if I faced it with absolute certainty about my own power and potential, then it could pose no threat to me. Instead of it absorbing me, I absorbed it, in a way. I confronted and accepted that part of me—and then killed it.

"I had to be certain, and I was. Any shred of doubt would have left me wide open. I know I'm not perfect—far from it. I know I have a lot to learn. I'm gonna make more mistakes, I'm gonna fail, and I'm gonna make a fool of myself. I don't care. None of that matters. What matters is that I have my whole life ahead of me, and starting today, I'm gonna live it.

"When the Glutton swallowed me, and it felt that certainty—it couldn't tolerate it. It was like an unstoppable force meeting an immovable object. That can't happen in reality; something's got to give. I knew it wouldn't be me. So here I am, newly reborn—in more ways than one." To emphasize his point, he unwound his fresh bandage and showed them both sides of his hands. Even the nasty cut he'd suffered only minutes ago was gone.

Tom took two steps forward and extended his hand. When Dylan took it, Tom pulled him to his feet. "I owe you an apology," Tom said.

Dylan frowned. "For what?"

"For calling you a 'boy' a little while ago. You're a man now—one of the best I've met."

* * *

Together, Tom and Dylan lifted the gate easily. When it slammed back down behind them, the resulting *boom* echoed in the cavernous space beyond.

The malevolent mist was especially thick here. The ceiling, high above, was made of interlocking iron bars that allowed a clear view of the night sky. The moon, directly overhead, bathed the Vile Abbey in white light tinted greenish yellow by the mist.

The room itself was massive, easily five hundred meters long. Structurally, it was similar to the previous room, from the bridge to the wall-mounted skulls vomiting blood into some hellish pit far below. Here, though, the bridge was much wider. Spanning its entire length were two rows of statues, one on either side. The statues were spaced at even intervals, but each one was different. Some were small, only four or five feet tall. Others towered twenty, even thirty feet.

Each depicted some vile abomination, poised to kill.

"The Hall of Eidolons," Sara said, her voice tinged with disgust.

Tom took a few steps forward, scanning for threats. Seeing none, he turned back to Sara. "These statues...."

"One for every Eidolon that has ever existed," Alex said.

"One for every person who died here or was killed by another Eidolon," Dylan said.

"There must be hundreds of statues here," Tom said.

Sara nodded, confirming that all of them were correct.

"What a horrible place," Alex said. "It's like a shrine to depravity and suffering."

"That's why we're here," Sara said softly. "To make sure the suffering stays here and doesn't come to our world. We have enough suffering already."

Dylan turned to Sara and offered his hand. With a small smile, she took it. "Let's get it over with, then," he said. "I don't know about you guys, but I'm ready to go home."

They started across the bridge. Tom and Alex took the lead, brandishing the two torches to burn off some of the foul mist. They tried not to look at the hideous statues. It was easier said than done.

"I can see something up ahead," Tom said, keeping his voice low. "Looks like a giant door, or another gate. In this light, it's hard to be sure, and it's still pretty far away."

"Is that the cathedral?" Alex asked.

"Just beyond that door is a courtyard. That's where the cathedral is," Sara said.

"We made it," Dylan said.

"Not yet," Tom countered. "The job's not done until it's done. Stay frosty."

"Uh, guys," Alex said. The others turned around. She had stopped a few paces back and was looking up at one of the statues.

"Come on, let's go, we're so close," Dylan said.

Alex ignored him. "Look." She pointed to the statue she was looking at.

Dylan's jaw dropped.

Alex was pointing at a life-sized sculpture of the Stalker. To its left, the Prisoner reached out toward them with gnarled, stone hands. On its other side, an enormous serpent reared its head toward the sky.

To the right of the snake was an empty pedestal. It held nothing but a few fragments of broken stone.

"Our Eidolons," Sara whispered.

"Does this mean something?" Alex said.

"It means we're wasting time," Tom said. "There's a statue here for every one of those monsters. It makes sense that ours would be here, too."

"I don't like it," Dylan said.

"Me neither," Alex agreed. "Tom's right. Let's go."

"Wait... what's that?" Dylan said. He pointed.

Something was changing about the mist at the base of the three statues. Throughout the Vile Abbey, the mist had drifted lazily through the air, barely moving at all. Here, it was swirling around more quickly and picking up speed. A thicker cloud was beginning to form, pulling in more mist from nearby, condensing it.

Sara, Tom, Alex, and Dylan slowly backed away.

A black void flashed within the mist, like inverse lightning. With a loud *crack*, a large shape burst forth, lunging toward Sara.

"Stalker!" Tom shouted.

Sara screamed and ducked, narrowly avoiding the Stalker's wide swing. Another two loud *cracks* came forth in quick succession, a little farther down the bridge.

The Prisoner.

The Ouroboros.

"Run!" Dylan shouted. He shoved Sara toward Tom, toward the cathedral gate. She needed no encouragement; she was already moving.

"Get in front of me! Go! I'll cover us!" Tom shouted. He moved to the side and waved the others past.

Before Sara could reach him, the Stalker leaped forward, covering an incredible distance in the blink of an eye. It landed just behind Sara with an impact that reverberated through the bridge like a small earthquake.

It wrapped one enormous hand around her midsection and snatched her up.

"Drop her, shitbag!" Dylan yelled. He snapped his UMP to his shoulder and squeezed the trigger, rattling off a long burst of .45 slugs. The Stalker blinked out of view and Sara fell back to the bridge, rolling onto her side. Dylan ran back to help her.

The Prisoner shrieked wildly and the Ouroboros hissed. They were racing toward Dylan and Sara, almost on them.

Tom allowed himself a fraction of a second to weigh his options. The targets were too close to Dylan and Sara to use grenades; the explosion would kill them for sure. The Prisoner could be temporarily hammered down with gunfire, but doing so would provide it with metal that it could use to make another deadly weapon.

None of their weapons could do much against the Ouroboros.

Unless....

Tom unslung his Jackhammer and shoved it into Alex's hands, slapping her MPX away. "Prisoner!" he shouted.

Alex didn't argue. She grunted as she raised the shotgun; it was massively heavy, and she wasn't used to the weight. Tom took up his MGL and lined up the front sight on the snake's head. He waited. It opened its massive jaws wide and reared up, preparing to strike.

Dylan had just pulled Sara to her feet. They wouldn't be able to make it on their own—the enemies were too close and too fast.

Alex depressed the Jackhammer's trigger and held it down, aiming for the Prisoner's chest. Five slugs flew downrange before the incredible recoil knocked her back a step, forcing her to stop firing. Three of the slugs hit, tearing golf ball-sized holes through the Prisoner's ribcage, halting its advance momentarily. Bright blue blood painted the bridge behind it.

Tom lowered his aim a fraction of an inch to account for the grenade's arc. There—it was now or never.

He heard the distinctive *chunk* of the MGL firing. A single 40mm grenade sailed through the air, toward its target.

The Ouroboros lunged toward Dylan. The grenade flew directly into its open mouth, impacting the back of its throat at 250 feet per second.

Tom had been hoping the massive snake had a gag reflex.

It did.

The massive jaws snapped shut in response to the unexpected projectile entering its mouth. A tenth of a second later, the grenade detonated.

The snake hissed and writhed in fury. Black smoke belched from its mouth. Tom wasn't sure how much damage he'd done, but he and Alex had bought Sara and Dylan a few seconds to move. The Stalker reappeared, laughing sadistically.

The teens sprinted past Tom as Alex handed his shotgun back to him. The Prisoner and the Ouroboros had already recovered and were charging toward them. Tom pushed Alex ahead so he could cover their retreat.

"Whoever has grenades, use 'em!" Tom shouted. "Use everything we've got! Slow them down!"

The others each had two frag grenades left. Dylan pulled the pin on one of his and tossed it backward, over Tom's head. It bounced on the bridge, once, twice, then rolled to a stop just as the Stalker reached it. The explosion forced the Stalker to dematerialize again but had little effect on the other two Eidolons. A moment later, Dylan tossed his second grenade, then Sara threw both of hers, with a slight delay in between. Alex did the same.

The grenades blasted sizable craters in the bridge and reduced several statues to rubble but delayed the Eidolons by only a second or two. Alex and Sara laid down suppressing fire, taking care not to hit Tom or Dylan. Tom turned around and ran backward as he toggled the ammo selector switch on his Jackhammer and laid down a carpet of flames behind them. He fired his last two incendiary shells, one at the Prisoner and one at the serpent, setting both aflame.

The Stalker reappeared and used its powerful arms to launch itself, clearing the fire like an Olympic long jumper. It landed almost right on top of Tom and knocked him over. He rolled to the side to avoid being crushed, nearly falling off the bridge.

But the Stalker wasn't after him. It wanted Sara.

Dylan's UMP ran dry a split second before he saw the Stalker coming. He switched to his sidearm and hammered the trigger, forcing the Stalker to dodge the heavy slugs. Sara turned around and joined in with her STI, unable to use her rifle with a broken hand while running.

But the Stalker was learning. It seemed to recognize that there was a predictable rhythm to the gunshots. Every time Dylan or Sara fired, it blinked away just long enough to evade, then reappeared immediately, advanced a few feet, and dematerialized in time to dodge the next attack.

The slides on both of their sidearms locked open. A heartbeat later, the Stalker reappeared, right in front of them, leering down at Sara with its hateful grin. Even though it was blindfolded, it seemed to be staring right at her.

Alex screamed and dropped to the ground as a deadly javelin made of fused arm bones and molten lead sailed over her head.

The Stalker cackled as it reached for Sara. Tom was busy evading the Ouroboros's deadly fangs. He could do nothing to help.

Dylan pulled his knife as he stepped in front of Sara. With a scream of rage, he slashed at the Stalker. It disappeared, reappeared, and punched him in the chest. Dylan tumbled away and landed on his stomach. The Stalker brushed past Sara and advanced on him. Apparently, he had angered it enough to warrant death.

As the Stalker reached for Dylan, Sara threw herself on top of him, shielding him with her body. Undeterred, the monstrosity went for her instead. It lifted her up as if she weighed no more than a feather. Its smile widened as it wrapped its other hand around her legs.

Sara struggled as hard as she could, but it was no use. Horrific images of Daniela's death flashed in her mind. She screamed. It was going to do the same thing to her.

It was going to tear her in half.

Alex, still on the ground, drew her Glock and fired three quick shots at the Stalker. It disappeared, a wicked laugh echoing in the air. Once again, Sara fell to the ground and tumbled onto her back. Dylan had recovered enough to stand and to help Sara up.

Tom fired two more grenades, one at the snake, one at the Prisoner, to buy himself a second or two. He sprinted back to the others and quickly pulled Alex to her feet. Together, they ran.

The enormous door, nearly twenty feet tall, loomed before them. It appeared to open outward.

"That had better be unlocked," Alex yelled.

"Get the door! I'll cover you!" Tom shouted. He turned back to face their pursuers as Alex, Sara, and Dylan all threw themselves against the door. Working together, they pushed as hard as they could. Slowly, it began to open, groaning loudly on rusted hinges.

The Stalker had reappeared once again. All three Eidolons were moving together, as a pack. They were thirty paces away and closing fast.

Tom fired his last three 40mm grenades, pausing for half a second between each shot. The rapid chain of explosions knocked the Prisoner down, caused the Ouroboros to recoil in pain, and forced the Stalker to evade.

Tom was out of grenades, and his shotgun was empty. He snatched his Magnum from its holster and thumbed back the hammer. Before he could fire, the Prisoner hit him in the chest like a linebacker.

The force of the impact was incredible. He heard and felt the ceramic plate in his armor crack. He was launched through the air, into Alex, Sara, and Dylan. All four of them tumbled through the half-open door, landing in a tangled pile. Tom rolled away, onto his back, and readied his Magnum. The others raised their weapons as well. Four trembling guns were aimed at the door.

All three Eidolons had stopped just on the other side of the threshold. One hissed, one screamed, and one laughed.

All three vanished in a swirling eddy of mist.

"Where'd they go?" Dylan panted.

"We made it," Sara said, equally out of breath. "They can't enter the cathedral courtyard. We're here. It's over."

One by one, they all stood up and turned around. They reloaded their weapons, then holstered or slung them.

The courtyard was barren and foreboding. Roughly rectangular in shape, it was enclosed by stone walls covered in the black thorns. Here and there, dead husks of unrecognizable plants dotted the hard-packed soil.

Black stone pavers led straight ahead to the ancient cathedral. The imposing monolith towered overhead as if struggling to pierce the moon. Great spires of polished black stone jutted from the structure at odd angles. Pairs of small, yellow lights dotted the exterior, placed seemingly at random.

Some of the lights winked out briefly, then came back on. A moment later, others did the same.

"What are those lights?" Tom asked.

"Those aren't lights...," Dylan said. He sounded worried.

"They're eyes," Alex gasped.

Half a dozen black shapes clung to the cathedral, perched atop its peaked roofs and crenellations. Camouflaged as they were against the black stone and the night sky, it was impossible to tell what they were—but they were definitely alive.

"Hostiles?" Tom said.

"No," Sara said. "They won't attack. The Pilgrimage is over—the dangerous part, anyway. We've proven ourselves. We've suffered enough." She started walking toward the cathedral.

"Now what?" Tom said. "You said there was some kind of ritual?"

Sara glanced back over her shoulder. "Yes, it'll be quick. We need to get up to the top floor. Once we're there, I just have to draw some symbols and say some weird words in a dead language. Ten minutes, tops."

"Then what?" Dylan asked.

"Then we go home," Sara said. "We go back to our normal lives, as much as that's possible after something like this."

"I doubt I'll ever sleep without having nightmares again," Alex said, shaking her head.

"Same," Dylan said.

Sara stopped walking and turned around to face them. Her lower lip was quivering. "I... just have to say this again. I'm sorry for doing this to all of you. Everything we've been through... everything I put you through. The danger I put you in, over and over. The pain and the injuries, not just to your bodies, but the damage to your hearts and minds...." Her voice broke, and she trailed off.

No one said anything for a long moment. It was Alex who finally spoke. "I'm still not fully on board with your recruitment process, but I understand why you did what you did. This is important. Someone has to do it. This nightmare we've all lived through for a week now... it's broken something in me, I won't deny it, but it's brought me a measure of peace, too. Tomorrow night, when I go to sleep in my own bed, I'll be dreading the dreams to come. But I'll also know that every man, woman, and child on Earth is safe because of us. That's not a bad consolation prize."

Tom nodded his agreement. Dylan took Sara's hand in his and gave it a reassuring squeeze. "Let's get it done," he said.

Sara smiled and wiped away a tear. "Let's get it done," she agreed.

CHAPTER THIRTY-FOUR
Refutation

Sara climbed the three steps leading to the cathedral's only entrance. She placed her hands flat against the door. The wood was rough and uneven against her palms.

She closed her eyes, took a deep breath, and pushed.

The door swung open silently, easily, as if it had been expecting her. The interior was lit by thousands of candles in chandeliers and sconces. Another thousand sat in bunches of twenty or thirty on the floor, bleeding white rivers of wax across the carefully fitted stones. Straight ahead, seven rows of pews faced a pulpit on a dais. The pews were black as pitch, possibly carved from the thorned trees. On the wall behind the pulpit hung a cast-iron emblem—two large, concentric circles. Seven short lines, evenly spaced around the perimeter, connected the two circles.

Every pew was filled with monsters.

About half were Cutters, their blue-gray skin and matted hair unmistakable, even from behind. Humanoid creatures that Sara didn't recognize sat in some of the other seats. Even a few of the living trees from the forest, sitting like people, were facing forward attentively. Half a dozen large, fat spiders clung to the walls and ceiling. A thick layer of mist hovered just above the floor, swirling around the candle flames.

As the door swung open, every monster turned to face Sara. None left their seats. They just sat there, staring.

Waiting.

Tom tightened his grip on his shotgun. He had only one magazine left. "Is this gonna be a problem?" He kept his voice low.

Sara shook her head without looking back. "No. Stay close to me. Don't shoot anything."

She strode down the aisle between the pews, purposefully, her head held high. She projected an air of relaxed authority, as though she belonged here and would brook no challenge to her station. Every monstrous head tracked her movement.

As they drew near the dais, a faint, rhythmic sound filled the air.

Da-thum. Da-thum. Da-thum.

"What is that?" Dylan whispered.

"It sounds like... a heartbeat?" Alex whispered back.

Sara led them around the dais, into an area that, in a normal church, would have been reserved for employees and volunteers. "Ardu's heartbeat," Sara said, keeping her voice low. "He's sleeping. Up there." A rickety wooden staircase spiraled upward, so high that it appeared to converge on itself.

Da-thum. Da-thum. Da-thum.

"What happens if he wakes up?" Tom said.

Sara shook her head. "He won't. That's why we're here, to make sure he stays asleep. Relax. We got here early." She tapped her watch.

"He's never woken up early? Not even to get a midnight snack?" Dylan chuckled nervously at his lame joke. No one else did.

"Never," Sara said. "Don't worry." She mounted the stairs and began to climb. "Pace yourselves on the stairs, it's a long way up."

The heartbeat grew louder as they ascended, reverberating between the stone walls.

Da-THUM. Da-THUM. Da-THUM.

Dylan stayed right beside Sara, one hand protectively on her lower back. Alex gripped her MPX hard enough to make her knuckles turn white. Tom continually scanned above and below, alert for threats. The ancient wooden stairs creaked and groaned underfoot. Once, a dog-sized spider descended on a thick strand of webbing from somewhere above. It paid them no mind and continued its leisurely journey to the bottom.

The stairs terminated at a heavy iron gate. Sara tugged on the latch. It was unlocked but heavily rusted; it wouldn't budge. She unslung her rifle and used the buttstock to strike the latch several times. Flakes of rust fell away. Eventually, the latch moved a bit, then a little more, until she was able to disengage it. It took several tries to shove the gate open. It, too, was badly rusted.

Tom, Alex, and Dylan were expecting to find a small room behind the gate, perhaps an attic or belfry. Instead, a large, open space stretched out before them. Long cracks ran through a mosaic tile floor. Large sections of the floor were missing entirely, exposing dangerous pitfalls.

Some of the stone walls were badly damaged. Others were missing entirely, as was the ceiling. Almost the entire area was open to the sky. At some point since they'd entered the cathedral, black clouds had arrived to block the stars. Only the moon remained uncovered, bathing the profane structure below in paradoxically angelic light.

"Hang on a second," Tom said. He frowned, consulting the mental map of the cathedral that he'd been constructing as they moved through it.

"This room… can't exist."

Dylan wrung his hands nervously. "I was thinking that, too," he said. "We didn't see it from the courtyard—because it wasn't there."

Alex gasped when she realized that they were right. The cathedral's tallest tower had been nothing more than that—a tower. There had been no room attached to it, certainly not one this large.

"Welcome to the Twilight," Sara whispered.

Dozens of human skeletons littered the broken tile floor of the room that couldn't exist. Some were propped against the walls in seated positions. Others lay on their backs, their empty eye sockets staring up at the sky. Still others lay prone, arms outstretched as if reaching for help.

Straight ahead, near the back of the area, stood a small mausoleum of polished white marble. It sat only a few paces away from the farthest edge of the broken tile. The tower must have been at least a hundred meters tall. A fall from such a height would undoubtedly be fatal.

DA-THUM. DA-THUM. DA-THUM.

The heartbeat was so loud that Alex had to raise her voice to be heard. "Don't tell me you're going in there," she said.

In response, Sara walked toward the mausoleum.

Her Wardens stepped gingerly, afraid that the damaged tile might collapse at any time. They avoided stepping on bones whenever possible.

It wasn't always possible.

"Who are all these people?" Dylan asked. No one answered. Maybe they hadn't heard him over the incessant heartbeat.

DA-THUM. DA-THUM. DA-THUM.

Sara halted five paces from the mausoleum door. The heartbeat stopped when she did.

An eerie silence blanketed the room. A cold breeze whispered past, ruffling their hair and clothing.

"This is it," Sara said. Her voice was barely audible. She turned to face the others. "Only I can go in there. Wait here. As long as you stay here, on this side of the gate, we'll return home automatically as soon as I finish the ritual. *Don't go back through the gate.* If you do, you'll be stuck in the Twilight forever. Once the ritual is finished, I can't come back to get you if you're still here."

Tom raised an eyebrow. "Look around. There are a hundred dead people here. I'm not letting you go in there alone."

She met his gaze. Her face was impassive. "You have to. Only Maidens can enter the ritual chamber."

"What killed all these people?" Alex insisted.

Sara didn't answer. She had already pulled open the mausoleum door and slipped inside. Silently it swung shut behind her.

* * *

Two torches illuminated the small space. Sara stood near the door and looked around. Living roots covered the floor and walls. The roots pulsed rhythmically, first black, then crimson, then black again. In the silence, Sara could faintly hear liquid rushing through them.

Were they roots... or veins?

A heavily pregnant woman was nailed to the far wall. More of the pulsing veins crisscrossed over her body, holding her tightly against the white marble.

Sara took a step forward. "I'm here," she said softly.

The crucified woman stirred ever so slightly. She wore a simple robe that, once upon a time, had been white. Now, it was covered almost entirely in dried blood. Her face was covered by an ivory mask etched with strange symbols, her hair concealed by a bloodstained habit.

With great effort, the woman lifted her head. The mask's painted eyes bored into Sara's.

"It is time?" The voice was hoarse and deep, barely human.

Sara went to her knees in the center of the room. "It's time."

The woman collapsed into a violent coughing fit. Blood dripped from under the mask and spattered on the floor. When the coughing finally subsided, she spoke again. "Recite the oath."

Sara bent forward until her forehead touched the floor. She shut her eyes. Her hands were shaking. Her heart was pounding. She could hear her blood rushing in her ears.

She began to speak in the long-dead language. The cadence of the words was stiff and irregular; the dialect required it. As before, when she had invoked the binding ritual six days earlier, a single mistake in pronunciation or inflection would snuff out her life.

She recited the oath flawlessly.

She opened her eyes and stood. The pregnant woman succumbed to another coughing fit. Sara waited patiently until she recovered.

Faintly, Sara heard a baby crying.

"I pass this burden to you, of my own free will, so that men may one day find salvation in suffering," the woman croaked.

"I accept it, of my own free will, so that I might show the way by grace," Sara whispered.

She took another step forward and reached for the mask.

* * *

Tom checked his watch. "How long did Sara say this would take?"

"About ten minutes," Dylan said.

"It's been eleven."

"Tom, Dylan. Come look at this," Alex called. She was on the other side of the room, kneeling next to one of the skeletons. She'd been wandering around, inspecting the remains ever since Sara had gone into the mausoleum. Tom and Dylan carefully picked their way over to her.

"What's up?" Dylan said.

"Did Sara say who these people were?" Alex asked. She was frowning.

"No, I don't think so," Tom said. "They're Wardens, right? Who else would they be?"

"And Wardens can be young, middle-aged, old? Men or women?" Alex said.

"That's what Sara said," Dylan replied. "Look at us, we're pretty diverse."

"Look here, at the pelvis," Alex said. She pointed to the skeleton, but Tom and Dylan didn't know what they were looking at.

"What about the pelvis?" Dylan said, scratching his head.

"This was a young woman," Alex said, looking up at them.

"So?" Tom said.

Alex swallowed hard. Her eyes left no doubt about her meaning. "*All* of these skeletons are young women."

Comprehension hit Tom like an avalanche. Sara's evasiveness and half truths. Her sudden stoicism ever since entering the cathedral. Her insistence on being alone in the mausoleum.

"She's going to kill herself," he said.

* * *

Gently, Sara worked her fingers under the ivory mask, at the jawline. She lifted it slowly, revealing the face underneath. The woman's eyes were closed, her head sagging forward. Her face was filthy and wracked with torment.

Sara turned the mask over in her hands. She took a deep breath and let it out slowly. Tears fell from her eyes onto the pulsing veins at her feet. Her hands were shaking so badly that she nearly dropped the mask.

She lifted it to her face.

She heard the sound of stone grating against stone. Before she could turn around, something heavy hit her in the middle, knocking her to the floor. The mask flew from her hands and clattered away.

Tom was on top of her, his face red with rage. "What the fuck is wrong with you!" he shouted in her face.

The crucified woman let out a piercing shriek. She thrashed against the nails driven through her wrists and feet, spraying fresh blood on the walls and floor. The scream rising in her throat didn't sound human.

"Sacrilege!"

"Tom! You—"

He jumped to his feet and yanked her up by the strap on her armor, then grabbed her legs and picked her up in a fireman's carry. A second later, he was out the door. Sara screamed incoherently, kicking her legs and beating his back with her fists. He ignored her.

"Run! Get out!" Tom shouted. He waved Dylan and Alex toward the gate and sprinted after them. Sara fought with all her might, but physically, she was no match for him.

Another ghastly shriek came from the mausoleum. The cracked floor began to rumble, gently at first, then more violently. Chunks of tile began to fall away. Dylan yelped and jumped over a new hole just in time. Alex dodged around another gap that opened in her path. She reached the gate first and held it open, waving Tom and Dylan through. Dylan leaped over another hole and cleared the gate. Tom was still ten paces away.

He felt the floor shift under his boots. He tried to jump to the side, but with Sara on his back, he was too heavy and too slow.

The tile shattered like glass. Tom's stomach lurched as he dropped into the abyss. Sara screamed when he involuntarily let go of her.

"Tom!" Alex shouted, reaching down toward him.

"Sara!" Dylan screamed. He, too, reached out, trying to catch one or both of them.

It was too late.

Tom's back slammed hard into the slanted roof of a lower floor. Sara landed a few feet away, bounced, and began to roll downward. He tumbled after her. Sara screamed again as she rolled over the edge, unable to stop herself. She threw her hands out, flailing for something to hold onto. There was nothing.

Tom snatched her wrist just before she plummeted to the ground. He slammed the toes of his boots into the clay roof tiles and threw his left arm out, trying to slow himself down. He slid to a halt with his chest hanging over the edge. His vision swam as an intense bout of vertigo took hold. The ground was so far away. If they fell, they would be little more than red stains in the dirt.

"Tom! Pull me up!" Sara shouted. She was hyperventilating, staring down at the ground in wide-eyed fear.

He pulled as hard as he could, but the angle was too strange, his balance too precarious. If he slid down the roof any farther or let go with his left hand, they would both fall.

"I'm not strong enough!" he yelled.

Sara mentally shoved her fear down and forced herself to think. "Window! There's a window!"

"Can you get to it?"

"Hang on!"

He was holding her right wrist. Awkwardly, she fumbled with her rifle, using her left hand—her broken hand. The weapon was hanging at her right side, instead of against her chest, where it belonged.

"I'm slipping!" Tom yelled.

"Almost got it!" Sara managed to grab the rifle and raise it. She yelped as the broken bones in her wrist flexed. Pushing through the pain, she aimed the rifle at the window and squeezed the trigger three times.

Three bullet holes appeared in the glass, in a rough triangular pattern. "Swing me!" she yelled.

Tom was too winded and weak to question her plan. He swung her away from the window, then back toward it as best he could. His strength was fading rapidly. "Hurry!"

Sara kicked her feet out and hit the window hard. The weakened glass shattered, and she tumbled through the opening. She cried out in pain as razor-sharp glass shards sliced her arms and face.

Tom's aching shoulder sagged in relief. He flipped around, carefully dropped his feet off the roof, and swung himself through the window behind Sara. She was lying on the floor, weeping. Tom gasped—her face was bleeding badly. He pulled her up to take a closer look, gently turning her head to the left, then to the right.

"You'll have some scars, but it's not too bad," he said.

She slapped his hands away. "You ruined everything!" The blood dripping from her face and the fury in her eyes made her look like a wild animal.

Tom's anger flared hot in the pit of his stomach. "Ruined what? You killing yourself? You're welcome!"

"You had no right! I have to finish the ritual!"

"I had *every* right! I'm here to protect you!"

"You did protect me—you got me here. Your job is done, but mine isn't. I'm going back."

"The hell you are." Sara darted away, but Tom was ready. He snatched her arm and dragged her back. She tried to punch him. He blocked it, then spun her around and put her in a headlock. He applied just enough pressure to stop her from getting away but not enough to hurt her.

A cacophony of inhuman screams echoed from somewhere below. Long bursts of gunfire followed.

"Alex and Dylan," Sara said. For the moment, she'd stopped struggling. Tom let go of her and rushed to a nearby railing. They were still high above the ground floor but in a different part of the building. This must be the bell tower—it was tall and narrow, with another wooden staircase winding downward.

Tom glanced up. Sure enough, an enormous bell was suspended overhead.

Somewhere below, a door banged open. A horde of Cutters and tree monsters rushed in and began climbing the stairs, their bloodthirsty howls deafening in the enclosed space. "We have company," Tom said.

Sara looked over the railing. "There are so many," she said.

Tom quickly did the math. He and Sara were both low on ammo and out of grenades. Fighting their way down the stairs would be impossible.

He looked up again. The bell had a long, frayed rope attached to it. As far as he could tell, the rope went all the way to the ground floor.

Sara saw where he was looking. "No," she said.

He looked at her. "You have ten seconds to come up with a better idea."

The monsters were coming. They packed every inch of the staircase from wall to railing. There must have been a hundred of them, at least. Sara racked her brain.

"Time's up. Motion passes by default," Tom muttered. He took several steps toward the window, turned back, and sprinted. He jumped, planted his boot on top of the railing, and pushed off, sailing into open space.

He grabbed the rope and swung wildly across the tower, almost hitting the opposite wall. The bell clanged, deep and loud. As he swung back toward Sara, he wrapped his legs around the rope and held one hand out toward her.

"Come on! I'll catch you," he yelled.

"Are you nuts?"

"I'm not the one who was about to kill myself! Jump!"

The monsters were almost at the top. One floor to go.

Sara growled in frustration. She took five steps back, ran, and jumped. She screamed in terror as she sailed over the railing. A Cutter lunged for her, missing her boot by inches. It tumbled over the railing and plummeted down the tower. Partway down, its face smashed into the side of the staircase. Tom heard the sickening crunch of bone, even over the other monsters' enraged howling.

Tom snatched Sara's right wrist. "Gotcha! Grab the rope!"

As best she could with a broken hand, Sara secured her grip on the rope just below Tom and began to slide down. Tom followed, wincing in pain as the rope ripped skin from his palms, but he dared not slow down. Sara at least had her cast for some protection.

The bell clanged wildly overhead. The horde of creatures began to spill back down the stairs. Tom and Sara reached the ground floor and made for the door the monsters had come through, now smashed to splinters and dangling by a single hinge. Thick mist billowed through the opening.

"How are they so goddamn fast," Tom growled. A lone Cutter, already at the bottom of the stairs, lunged for him. He drew his Magnum and shot it in the face.

Sara and Tom ran down a short passage and through another door, into the main room of the cathedral. They were in the back, near the dais.

"Tom! Sara! Let's get out of here!" Dylan shouted and waved from the other side of the room. Alex was next to him, reloading her MPX. Tom assumed that the pile of monster corpses in the middle of the room was their doing.

The four of them sprinted for the front door—until living trees began to pour in from outside.

"They hate fire! Burn them!" Alex shouted. Dylan and Sara began picking up candles and lobbing them like grenades, fistfuls at a time. A few tree-things caught flame and wailed in agony, but most of the candles bounced away harmlessly.

"Need an exit! Now!" Tom shouted. He was firing his shotgun down the hallway they'd come from. Each heavy slug blasted through several creatures, but there were simply too many to kill all of them.

"Back here! I saw another door!" Dylan said. He took off running, and the others followed, firing at any creature that got too close. Dylan found the door and hauled it open. A narrow staircase descended into darkness.

Alex reached it first. There was no time to hesitate, no other exit. She practically flew down the stairs. Dylan held the door until Tom and Sara went through, then followed, slamming the door behind him.

Dylan and Sara were each holding a candle. There was just enough light to see the stairs. Tom was impressed at their foresight in the heat of battle.

The door rattled in its frame with a tremendous *bang*. Alex reached the bottom and kept running across an empty, open space. She charged through another door in the opposite wall just as the first door was smashed into kindling. Feral screams filled the basement as waves of monsters threw themselves down the stairs.

Tom was the last through the second door. He slammed it closed. "This one's pretty heavy; maybe it will stop them," he panted. He noticed a heavy iron bolt on the door and shoved it into place.

A tidal wave of rotten flesh and living wood slammed into the door. It rattled as dozens of fists, branches, and claws pounded on it. They watched and waited, weapons raised. The door was nearly six inches thick and seemed to be holding.

"Come on," Tom said. "Let's get out of here." They jogged down the passageway, through the swirling mist.

CHAPTER THIRTY-FIVE
Dissonance

The catacombs under the cathedral were vast and confusing. Dylan and Alex lit torches to supplement the meager candlelight. The mist was thicker here than anywhere else, so thick that they could barely see through it. Every few feet along both walls, deep alcoves held skeletons yellowed with age, some still wrapped in decomposing burial shrouds.

None of the skeletons looked human.

"Here," Tom said quietly. He waved the others down a side passage and pointed to a small door. He pushed it open slowly, shotgun at the ready. Once he was satisfied that the room was empty, he ushered the others inside.

There was nothing in the room except a stack of heavy wooden crates. Tom and Dylan shoved two of them in front of the door to barricade it. Sara watched, scowling, her arms folded.

"Alright, Sara. Explain yourself," Tom said. He parked himself in front of the door and leaned against the crates. He had no intention of letting any of them leave until he was satisfied.

Sara unfolded her arms. "No, *you* explain yourself," she countered. "You might have just doomed the entire planet." She glanced at her watch. "Fortunately, I still have time to get back up there."

"Yeah, that's not gonna happen," Tom said, scratching his stubble.

Dylan stepped in front of Sara. "Were you... really gonna kill yourself? That's what this whole thing has been about? You knew all along?"

Sara closed her eyes but said nothing. She couldn't bear to look at him.

"Sara...." Dylan trailed off. He threw his arms around her and held her tightly. She gently pushed him away.

Alex and Tom could see in his eyes how difficult it was for him to keep it together. He retreated to a corner of the room and slumped to the floor.

"This 'ritual' to put Ardu back to sleep—it's a goddamned human sacrifice. It always has been. You knew, Ethan knew, everyone else in your death cult knew. Everyone except us. You played us for fools," Tom said.

"Your father... knowingly sent his daughter to her death," Alex whispered. Her face was drained of all color. She looked like she might faint.

"It's for the greater good," Sara whispered.

"The greater good," Tom repeated flatly.

"This is the real reason you were so mistrustful of Jacob," Alex said. "When we first met him, you didn't know whether he'd made it this far, all the way to the cathedral. If he had, then he would have known that Maidens kill themselves. He would have told us, and your plan would have been ruined. Once you were sure he had never been here, you no longer considered him a threat."

Sara looked down at the floor. Again, she said nothing.

"I'll take that as confirmation that Alex is right," Tom said.

Sara looked up, her green eyes blazing with anger. "Tom, you of all people should understand that this is the only way," she said. "I chose you because you were a soldier. You understand the importance of duty. The most important duty of all time has been entrusted to the four of us. We have no right to reject it, not when all of humanity is depending on us—on me—to do what needs to be done."

Tom unslung his Jackhammer and leaned it against the wall before taking a seat on top of a crate. "I'll tell you what I've learned about duty these last few days, and especially in the last half hour," he said. "Twenty years ago, when I turned my back on my best friend to save a little boy instead, I did my duty. I turned my back on someone I loved to help someone I didn't know and would never see again after that day. Everyone praised me and told me I did the right thing. I'll tell you what: It sure as shit didn't feel like the right thing when I handed Manny's parents a crisply folded flag.

"Obviously, I'm not saying that little boy deserved to die. He didn't belong there. He was just an innocent kid, caught in the wrong place at the wrong time. If he had died that day, instead of Manny, it would have been a fucking tragedy, no one's disputing that. But I didn't put him in that situation. The same brand of cockroach that blew up the World Trade Center put him there. My 'duty' required me to take responsibility for evil done by others, to fix a problem I didn't create—at the cost of my best friend's life. No matter how you slice it, that's some majorly fucked up shit.

"Duty is someone else telling you what should be most important to you. Actually, it's worse than that—it's someone else *dictating* what *is* most important to you, whether or not you agree. In the military, your duty determines your every move. The mission comes first. Protecting civilians comes second. *Then* you protect your friends, if they're still alive after you've done all that other shit.

"Of course, that's not officially mandated. You won't find it in the army handbook, and they don't say it out loud during training. But that's the culture and the expectation. Guys who save their friends' lives get a medal and a handshake. Protecting your friends, doing everything you can to make sure they go home to their wives and parents—that's alright, it's fine, it's a nice thing to do. But it's not the stuff real heroes are made of.

"Guys who save the peasant woman in the village—they're the real heroes. They make the headlines and get buildings named after them. Bonus points if you get your legs blown off shielding her from the bomb. That's who everyone wants to be. Or rather, that's who the military says you *should* want to be. Putting yourself in danger for your friends—that's respectable, but in terms of karma, it's not worth a whole lot. Putting yourself in danger for someone you've never met, or even someone you hate—*that's* virtue, or so we're told. That's what duty really means. It means that the people and things that are most important to you go to the bottom of the list *because* they're important to you.

"But duty is even more sinister than that; when you accept the idea that strangers' lives are more important than your life and the lives of your loved ones, you willingly give your enemy control of the battlefield. The Taliban sure as shit knew that we were unofficially required to protect anyone and everyone except ourselves, and they used that against us. Every day, they manipulated us and distracted us from killing them by deliberately putting civilians in danger—even kids, sometimes. And we fell for it over and over—I certainly did. If we'd had the balls to actually *fight* the war, we would have won it in six months instead of losing it in twenty years. How many more innocent people died in the end because of our obsession with duty over victory?

"Manny and I never should have been in Afghanistan—never should have been in the military in the first place. I never wanted to be a soldier. I signed up because my dad was a soldier, and he expected me to follow in his footsteps. I had a duty to my father and to my country. The very fact that I didn't want to join the army *made* it the right thing to do—supposedly. Manny wanted to be an army man even less than I did, but I convinced him that he had a duty, same as I did. I sold him on an idea I didn't even understand, and it got him killed.

"Over and over throughout my life, I chose to accept someone else's judgment about who and what should be most important to me instead of making those decisions for myself. Every time I chose to follow my duty instead of what *I* judged to be true and good and right, I brought my best friend one step closer to Afghanistan—one step closer to his death. There isn't a day that goes by that I don't regret every single one of those choices with every fiber of my being. Everyone tells you that sacrifice is the ultimate act of nobility and virtue, that giving up what you love most somehow makes the world a better place. But that's horse shit—a sacrifice is a loss, not a gain. It's death and destruction for no good reason.

"I guess I've never been very good at learning lessons, because right up until today, I was still letting duty ruin my life and the lives of the people I love. I got a phone call yesterday, just before we ran into the witches. My second best friend, Teddy Jackson, my construction manager, my brother.... He was murdered on Monday night. And his death, like Manny's, is on me."

Alex gasped. "Tom, I'm so sorry. What happened?"

"I happened. I did it. I killed Teddy—by doing my duty. His skull was beaten in by an ex-con who worked for me, a guy named Gavin—a guy I kept out of jail by lying for him. I never liked him. His work sucked, and his attitude was worse. I should have fired him and kicked him back to his parole officer a long time ago, but I didn't. It was my duty to be the guy who gave him a second chance, and a third, and a fourth, when no one else would. It was my duty to cut him slack *because* he didn't deserve it. Most of us are raised from birth with that idea, the idea that we all have some kind of automatic duty to people who haven't earned any of our time or love or money—*because* they haven't earned it. I'm just now starting to realize how fucked up that idea is."

Tom leveled a hard gaze at Sara. "You're asking me to make the same mistake again, to sacrifice someone I care about—you—in the name of duty. Why, because some asshole said so? The Circle is doing the same thing to you that the Taliban did to me: keeping you distracted from the real problem by telling you that you have a 'duty' to protect everyone except yourself. And what will you achieve by fulfilling that duty? Continued suffering with no end in sight, so that someone else has to lose his wife or daughter or sister a few years from now, and then on into the future after that, forever and ever? It took me twenty years, but I've finally learned my lesson. I'm done with duty, and I'm done making sacrifices. You can order me around all you want—I don't give a shit. I'm not taking your orders anymore, not if you're ordering me to let you throw your life away for nothing."

* * *

Slowly, Sara sank to her knees, moving as if she were underwater. A single tear trailed down her face. "Tom... I can't believe you would say that. This must come as a shock, and it must feel like a huge betrayal of your trust. You're upset, and you have a right to be. But listen to what you're saying. This last week, you've taught me to use my head, to not be ruled by my emotions, to stay cool and think clearly when the stakes are high. You have to do the same."

Tom shook his head. "For the first time in my life, I *am* thinking clearly about duty—about what it really means, and all the lives it destroys."

"You're not. By the time you calm down and realize what you've done, it will be too late. You will be guilty of sentencing the whole world to death."

Alex sat down on the floor and rested one arm on her knee. "Guilt.... I know a thing or two about guilt," she mused. "More than most, I think. Sara, what is the purpose of your Pilgrimage?"

Sara sighed. "To stop Ardu from killing billions of people. We really don't have time to go over this again."

Alex ignored the protest. "And why does Ardu want to do that?"

Sara threw up her hands. "He doesn't *want* to, not really."

"So then, why would he do it?"

"To punish us. Humanity."

"Punish us for what?"

"For our collective moral failure."

"Failure to do what?"

"To be properly selfless and compassionate toward one another."

Alex leaned back and nodded slowly, as though she were deep in thought. After a moment, she said, "So the Pilgrimage is the mother of all guilt trips."

Sara blinked. "What?"

"Is it not? To guilt trip someone is to weaponize the guilt they feel because of their sins, real or imagined, as a way of trying to make them do what *you* think they should do. It's bad enough to do that to someone who's done something wrong, but it's a *really* horrible thing to do to someone who hasn't."

Sara frowned. "What's your point?"

"Humanity doesn't have anything to atone for—and neither do you. There's no such thing as collective responsibility. I'm responsible for my actions, and you're responsible for yours—period. Most of us are raised from birth with the idea that being a good person means putting everyone else's wants and needs ahead of your own, but where did that idea come from? Who decided that selflessly sacrificing yourself makes you a good person? The more I think about it, the more I realize that it doesn't make any sense.

"Just now, up in the cathedral, when we realized that you were going to kill yourself, that's when it really hit me. Your plan was to offer up your life, the most precious thing you have, in a desperate plea for forgiveness on behalf of all mankind—but we don't need forgiveness, certainly not from the likes of Ardu or the Circle. They don't get to declare that some people have to give up their happiness, their freedom, or their lives for others and then kill us if we don't want to play along.

"For the first time in my life, I finally understand something critically important: the difference between earned and unearned guilt. Back when I was a dumb kid strung out on heroin, and I accidentally killed that woman... I should have felt tremendously guilty for that, and I did. I still do. I wronged someone, gravely. I wronged her friends and family, who had to go on without her. I alone bear responsibility for that terrible, stupid choice I made. Once I'd detoxed and I could think straight again, I decided to spend the rest of my life doing whatever I could to make up for the worst mistake I'd ever made.

"But now I see that I didn't actually want forgiveness, because forgiveness has to be earned, and I thought that I could never earn it—not for taking an innocent person's life. I became a doctor to help others avoid the mistakes I'd made... only, that wasn't the real reason, either.

"I finally understand, now, that the real reason I became a doctor was to punish myself. Somewhere, on some deep, subconscious level, I'd decided that I could never earn the right to be at peace with myself, no matter how many addicts I saved. I see now, finally, that I've had the wrong mind-set all along. I can never erase or undo what I did, but the way to make up for it —to the extent that that's possible—isn't to flog myself with guilt every day for the rest of my life. The way to make up for it is to learn from my mistakes—to really, truly learn from them—and to spend the rest of my life running toward something good and important instead of running away from myself. I finally understand the right way to deal with the guilt that we deserve.

"But guilt that we *don't* deserve—that's a whole different story. The only way to deal with unearned guilt is to *reject* it, and to reject those who try to use it as a weapon against us. I'm guilty of the wrongs *I've* done to myself and to others, nothing more. Same goes for you, Tom, Dylan, and everyone else. You're not going to kill yourself to appease some pissant god who claims that you should pay the price for other people's failures, real or imagined. I won't let it happen."

Sara closed her eyes and remained still for a long time. When she opened them again, she seemed to have regained some of her composure. "Maybe you're right, about some of it at least. It's not like I want to die, but it doesn't really matter what any of us think about it. The facts are what they are. We either complete the Pilgrimage, or Ardu wipes out most of humanity, the good along with the bad. It's my one life against eight billion others. There's no choice to be made here."

Alex moved closer to Sara and put a hand on her arm. "Sara, don't you see? Look at all this pain, death, blood, and torture around us. The blame for *all* of this lies with Ardu, even more with those who have enabled and appeased him for five thousand years. You, Sara, are not one of those people—not yet. But if you kill yourself to keep this cycle going, you will join the ranks of those responsible for this living nightmare. For five thousand years, the so-called Circle of Mercy has achieved nothing but endless death and pain—false security for all of humanity, built on a lie. They aren't the solution to this problem—they *are* the problem. I'm with Tom. I won't help you anymore, not if you insist on feeding the innocent into a nightmare machine created by the guilty."

Sara shot to her feet, her tightly clenched fists trembling at her sides. "What the hell are we supposed to do? Just let the world end? How does that fix anyone's suffering? How is that justice for the good people?"

"That's not what we're suggesting," Tom cut in. His voice was surprisingly gentle. "We'll help you find some other solution, but like Alex said, we won't help you feed the nightmare machine." Alex nodded her agreement.

Sara stamped her foot. "There *is* no other way, and it's pointless to waste what little time we have left looking for one!"

Quick as a snake, Tom darted toward Sara. Before she could react, he'd taken her rifle, sidearm, and knife. He unloaded the guns and tossed all the weapons aside. "What the hell are you doing?" she shrieked.

"Relieving you of command," Tom said. "You're not in your right mind. Alex, give me a hand." Without comment, she complied.

Sara stared incredulously at Alex. "You're really helping him take all my weapons? Here? Not just in the Twilight, but in the Hollow? The most dangerous place of all?"

Alex sighed. "Things have changed. We can't trust you, not until you come to your senses."

Sara's mouth fell open. "You really think I would... try to hurt you?"

"No, I don't think so," Tom said. He patted her down to make sure he hadn't missed any weapons or tools. "But we can't take that chance. You're talking crazy, and crazy people don't get to carry weapons." He pulled three zip ties from his pocket, fashioned a pair of handcuffs, and secured Sara's hands in front of her. "Take a seat. Relax for a bit."

Alex crossed the room to where Dylan was sitting in the corner, watching the mutiny in stunned silence. She knelt next to him. "See if you can talk some sense into her. She won't listen to Tom or me, but if anyone can get through to her, you can."

Dylan nodded. "I'll try."

* * *

Dylan sat down next to Sara. He could hardly see her face in the flickering torchlight. "Hey," he said.

She didn't answer. Her head was lowered. Her bound hands rested in her lap.

Dylan glanced over his shoulder. Tom and Alex had retreated to the far side of the room to give them some privacy.

"Sara, I… I agree with everything Tom and Alex said. This is insane. You can't possibly think we would let you… kill yourself." His voice cracked a bit, but she didn't respond or look at him. He cleared his throat and went on. "I think you're making another kind of mistake, one that I've been repeating my whole life. I didn't realize how much it was hurting me until today, until I managed to kill the Glutton."

Sara raised her head just enough to meet his eyes, but still, she said nothing.

"Growing up not knowing what happened to my mom… it broke me. My earliest memories are of helping my dad try to figure it out—and failing. When I was just a little kid, I tried this massive, impossible thing, and I failed. It made me terrified to try anything difficult or scary ever again. The more challenges I shied away from, the more I came to believe that I was powerless to shape my own world—much less the entire world.

"I always admired your confidence and determination, two things I definitely didn't have. Whenever someone told you something couldn't be done, you ignored them, and you did it anyway. It seemed like you always knew what you wanted and would do whatever it took to achieve it. It's no secret that you've always been the leader, and I was the follower. You blazed your own trail, no matter what anyone else thought about it.

"But now, for the first time, I finally get it. Your whole life, you've been training and preparing for this… quest. Every important thing you ever did was somehow related to this. You weren't blazing your own trail; you were just clearing obstacles from a path that your dad and the rest of the Circle had already chosen for you. I thought you always knew exactly what you wanted out of life, but you had no idea, and you still don't. You never thought it was important. What's the point in wanting anything for yourself when you know you're going to die soon?"

Dylan paused and heaved a deep sigh. Sara was watching his face intently. He went on. "I know two things for sure. One, the path of least resistance never leads anywhere good. I know better than almost anyone how easy it is to look at a big, impossible problem and feel powerless to solve it. It's easy to think, 'I can't do this, but someone else can, someone who's smarter and stronger than me.' The Circle thinks they have this problem figured out, and they've convinced you that they have it figured out, but they don't. Like Alex said, they're not solving the problem, they're making it worse and worse.

"I know now that I'm not powerless—I can do a lot, if I look for new solutions, try my best, and keep trying if I fail the first time. If I don't like any of the roads in front of me, I can make a new one, and I don't have to care what anyone else thinks about it. This road your dad put you on isn't the only one. You can be the trailblazer I always thought you were. You can step off this shitty path and make a new one, and I'll help you.

"The second thing I know for sure is...." He trailed off, suddenly looking less sure of himself.

"What's the other thing, Dylan?" Sara's voice was hardly louder than a whisper.

She thought he wasn't going to answer. He just sat there, looking down at the ground, picking at a crack in the stone with a fingernail. Finally, he looked up at her with renewed confidence in his eyes. "The second thing I know for sure is a simple thing. If you love someone, you don't let her kill herself."

A long silence stretched between them. They stared at one another, neither blinking. It was Sara who finally broke eye contact and dropped her gaze back to the ground.

"Sara...." Dylan scooted closer and put his hand on her leg. She didn't react or look up at him. "I'm ready to be someone worth loving—for my sake, not yours. When we started this journey, I wanted to help and protect you, at the cost of my own life, if necessary. Now I see that I had the wrong idea. I don't want to die, and I don't plan to. I want to live, I want to have a life worth living, and I want to share it with you. I want to walk beside you, not behind you—on a path that we choose for ourselves."

Still, she didn't look at him. Still, she said nothing.

Dylan shut his eyes, trying to hold back tears. Without another word, he removed his hand, stood up, and walked away.

CHAPTER THIRTY-SIX
Suppression

"Here's what's gonna happen," Tom said, taking a seat next to Sara. "We're gonna find a way out of the Hollow, and you're gonna take us back home until we can figure out our next move." Sara glanced sideways at him but remained silent. "But we're not going to your house, you're taking us to the dam. From there, I'll take us to an undisclosed location— somewhere safe. No one will find us there, not even your cult, no matter how hard they look."

Tom held up a finger to emphasize his next point. "Don't take us back to your house. I don't want to hurt Ethan, or anyone else there, but I will if you put us in that position."

Sara heaved a heavy sigh and nodded.

"Everyone ready?" Tom said. He handed Sara's rifle to Dylan, who slung it over his back. Tom stored the rest of her weapons in his pack.

"You're really taking me out there, into the Hollow, with my hands tied?" Sara asked.

Tom frowned at her. "What's the matter? I thought you wanted to die."

Alex glared at Tom. "Not helping," she said.

Tom scratched his head. "You're right. Sorry. Let's move. Huddle up around Sara so nothing can get to her without going through us."

"This is insane," Sara muttered. She glanced at her watch. "Twenty-seven hours to go, and you're holding me prisoner."

Tom ignored her. He press-checked his Jackhammer, then put his hand on the door. "Ready?" he said.

"No, but let's go," Alex said.

"I'm ready," Dylan said.

Tom paused, his hand still on the door. He turned back to Sara. "There's one more thing I need to know." Sara sighed and shrugged in a "get on with it" gesture. "This... ritual. Obviously, you have to kill yourself up there, in the cathedral, in some specific way. If you die down here, or somewhere else, it doesn't count."

"Yes," Sara said tersely.

"What is the ritual? What were you going to do?"

Sara glanced at Alex, then Dylan. "Does it matter?"

"It might. We won't know until you tell us. There was... someone, or something else in there with you, in that mausoleum. Alex, Dylan, did you see it?" They both shook their heads. "I could have sworn it was... a pregnant woman, nailed to the wall. Crucified. But she was alive."

"That's awful," Dylan whispered.

Sara said nothing. Tom, Alex, and Dylan stood still, waiting. Finally, Tom said, "We're not going anywhere or doing anything until you tell us, and you're the one who's so worried about the schedule, so waste as much time as you want."

Sara closed her eyes. It was obviously not something she wanted to share, but she was even less enthusiastic about sitting around doing nothing. "You're right. It was a woman—the Maiden from the previous cycle."

Alex and Dylan gasped. Tom's eyes went wide. "Are you serious?" he asked.

Sara nodded reluctantly. "When a Maiden completes the final ritual and thus her Pilgrimage, she is no longer referred to as a Maiden. She becomes a Matron."

"But... shouldn't she be dead? If the ritual requires the Maiden to sacrifice herself?" Alex asked.

"She would have died shortly after I completed the ritual. Tom stopped me, just moments before I could finish."

"All those skeletons... they're all the other Maidens," Dylan said, shaking his head in disbelief.

"Who is she?" Alex said.

"Her name is Anna Foss, from Denmark. Her team went in when Daniela's team disappeared, and she completed her Pilgrimage."

"How does Ardu fit into all this?" Dylan said.

"You remember the loud heartbeat we heard all throughout the cathedral? How it got louder as we went higher? Ardu was there, at the top. In the mausoleum."

Tom frowned. "No one else was in there. It was a small space—I saw everything."

Sara closed her eyes again. Her voice was so quiet that they could barely hear her. "He was there. Inside Anna."

"Inside? What does that—" Alex cut herself off and covered her mouth with both hands, an expression of shocked understanding dawning on her face.

"Ardu is... a fetus?" Tom said.

"I wasn't exactly lying when I said he was asleep. I was just... being metaphorical," Sara said.

"What were you going to do, Sara?" Tom pressed.

"A cycle ends when the Matron's body can no longer tolerate Ardu's presence inside her. It's worse than hell. It's extraordinarily painful, beyond anything you can imagine. When a new Maiden completes the final ritual, she relieves the Matron of her burden and takes her place. She… takes on the duty of incubating Ardu, of keeping him unborn and undeveloped, so that he leaves our world alone."

"This woman Anna has been up there, in indescribable pain—for sixteen years?" Alex asked. Sara nodded.

Alex suddenly looked pale. She retreated to a corner of the room and vomited.

Tom and Dylan were both staring at Sara in shock and horror. It was Tom who spoke. "You were going to take an evil god fetus into your body."

"Yes," Sara whispered.

"How?"

Her shoulders slumped, and she looked down at the floor. "I'm not going to tell you that. I don't care how long you make us sit here. I won't add to the lifelong nightmares I've already given you."

Dylan turned away from her, struggling to compose himself.

* * *

The catacombs were eerily silent. The mist was thicker than ever, almost an opaque white cloud, swirling about in lazy circles. Sara carried a torch so the others could keep both hands on their weapons.

"Which way?" Dylan whispered.

Alex pointed. "This way. Just take left turns whenever possible. If we always go left, and only go straight or right when left isn't an option, we'll eventually find a way out. It's an old trick for solving mazes."

Tom took point and led them along, hugging the left-hand wall. The only sound was their boots scraping through the dirt, occasionally crunching on small bone fragments. They walked on, slowly, quietly, for what felt like several hours. They said nothing, afraid to draw the attention of whatever things might be lurking in the dark.

Finally, Tom held up a fist, signaling the others to stop. "This can't be right," he whispered. "I swear we've passed this exact spot three times already. Look: This skull has teeth missing in a really weird pattern. Unless there are three more skulls down here exactly like this one, sitting in that exact position, we're going in circles."

"That shouldn't be possible," Alex whispered. "The maze trick always works. Any two-dimensional maze is just one continuous line, and if you follow a line in the same direction long enough, you always reach the end."

"It always works back home, where the laws of nature don't change," Dylan corrected.

"Dylan's right," Tom said. "This place is fucking with us. It doesn't want to let us out."

"Hang on a second," Dylan said. He pointed ahead, seemingly at nothing. "Look."

Alex and Tom both stared, unsure what they were looking for. Sara refused to participate in the discussion.

"What are we supposed to be seeing?" Alex said.

"The mist—look how it's moving. It's not just swirling around randomly. Watch it for a bit. It's slow, but it's flowing, like there's an air current."

After watching for a minute, they realized that he was right. "The mist is flowing that way," Tom said, pointing. "If there is an air current, then maybe there's a way out."

"Worth a try," Alex said.

They followed the mist, stopping at every juncture to see which way it was going. Progress was slow, but after a while, Tom, Dylan, and Alex began to feel more hopeful. They were no longer going in circles, as far as they could tell.

"Here." Tom stopped and held out his hand. "Torch." Sara passed it over without comment.

Tom held up the torch to inspect a tall, narrow crack in the stone wall. It was barely a foot wide. Careful not to drop the torch, he stuck it inside, trying to see how far back the opening went.

"It widens up a bit farther in," he reported. "The mist is going that way. This might be our exit."

"Extremely tight spaces. My favorite," Alex said dryly.

"I'm the biggest, so I'll go first," Tom said. "If I can fit, then you guys can, too. Dylan, you bring up the rear."

"Alright," Dylan said.

Tom removed all his gear and stuffed as much as he could into his pack. He took a deep breath and shuffled into the crack sideways, grunting with effort, awkwardly dragging his equipment behind. Once he'd made some progress, Sara followed, then Alex, and finally Dylan.

The passage was narrower than it had looked. Tom was compressed so tightly between the stone walls that he couldn't draw a full breath. He forced himself to remain calm and pressed on, slowly, carefully, a few inches at a time.

"Alex, are you doing okay? This must be really tough for you," Dylan wheezed from the back of the line.

Alex smiled at him, even though he couldn't see her in the darkness. "I'm alright, honey. I wouldn't say I'm having a good time, but we have each other. We've already accomplished so much together. We can handle a little tight squeeze."

Tom thought that they were no longer a team—he, Alex, and Dylan were prison guards, and Sara was their prisoner.

We're real Wardens now, he thought. He chuckled humorlessly at the double meaning.

"How much farther?" Alex called. Tom could hear that she was having trouble breathing.

"Almost there, I think," he yelled back. "I can breathe a little easier. It feels like it's opening up more."

A few minutes later, the passage did indeed widen enough to allow faster progress and easier breathing. Not long after that, they emerged from the crevice into fresh air. They were outside. Stars twinkled overhead, but the moon remained hidden behind a thick barrier of black clouds.

"There's no more mist," Tom said. "We're out of the Hollow?" Sara nodded in confirmation. She didn't look happy about it.

"Where's the cathedral?" Dylan asked.

"That way." Tom pointed toward the faint silhouette of the Vile Abbey in the distance. "We covered more ground than I thought." He checked his watch. "Twenty-five hours to go. We have one day to come up with a genius plan that no one else managed to think of in five thousand years."

"Maybe the problem wasn't that they couldn't think of anything else— they just didn't try to," Dylan said. "We'll figure something out." He sounded surprisingly confident.

Tom took out two of his adrenaline injectors. "Sara, take us to the dam. I'll inject you and me at the same time. Don't fight me—you'll lose. Alex and Dylan, you go first."

* * *

Tom was relieved to see the familiar stairs leading up to the dam's main control room. He hadn't been sure Sara would cooperate. He turned around to verify that the others were with him.

"Everyone good?"

"We will be once the adrenaline wears off," Alex said. All of them were flushed and sweating. "I have mild sedatives ready if we need them."

Tom led them to one of his company trucks parked near the stairs. He knelt by the front left tire and felt around in the wheel well until he found the magnetic box containing the spare key. "Everyone in. Alex, you drive. Dylan, you ride shotgun. I'm in the back with Sara. Turn off your phones in case Ethan can track us that way." He'd already searched Sara and verified that she didn't have her phone.

It felt good to be somewhere familiar and nonthreatening, even though the doomsday clock was still counting down. The truck hummed quietly along the highway, its powerful headlights illuminating an undisturbed blanket of fresh snow on the road. They rode in silence, each lost in his own thoughts, except when Tom spoke up to tell Alex where to turn.

Half an hour from the dam, they left the highway and turned down a dirt road so overgrown and little used that Alex never would have seen it had Tom not pointed it out to her. Tom continued giving directions, guiding them deeper and deeper into the frozen woods.

A little before midnight, Alex pulled the truck into a clearing and shut off the engine. The headlights illuminated a small wooden cabin, little more than a shack.

"Where are we?" Dylan asked.

"My uncle's hunting cabin," Tom said. "It's completely off the grid, and I'm the only other person who knows it exists. It's got gas-powered generators and enough bottled water to last until judgment day." He glanced at his watch and grunted. "Which might be tomorrow."

"That's not funny," Sara said.

"It's a little funny," Dylan said.

Tom opened the door and got out. "The point is, there's no record that this place exists. It's not connected to any utility lines, and it's not on any map. We're safe here for now."

"Safe for a day. Then we die with everyone else on Earth," Sara snapped.

Tom turned and leaned back into the truck to retrieve his gear. "Don't be so negative, you'll get wrinkles," he said.

CHAPTER THIRTY-SEVEN
Reflection

December 31, 2021
Day Seven

Tom came back into the cabin and stomped snow off his boots. His cheeks were red from the cold. "I got the generator started," he said. "There's plenty of gas. I'll turn on the space heaters—it'll get warm soon."

The cabin had only two rooms, a bathroom that was little more than an indoor outhouse and a combined kitchen/bedroom stocked with canned food, ammunition, and two folding cots. A single, bare bulb provided enough light to see by. The gas generator rumbled loudly outside, under a small awning.

Sara was zip-tied to a chair, quietly seething. She refused to look at or talk to any of the others. Alex and Dylan watched her closely while Tom adjusted the heaters and did a quick check around the property. When he came back, he stared at Sara for a long moment, deep in thought.

"What now?" Dylan said.

Tom pinched the bridge of his nose and sighed. He turned to Alex. "What do you think?"

She blinked, bewildered. "I think I'm flattered that you think I have an answer to this problem. Obviously, we're not letting Sara kill herself. Beyond that, I don't know what to do."

Tom paced back and forth. "Let's pretend, for the moment, that this is just any other problem. A big one, but not end-of-the-world big. What would you tell a patient or client who didn't know what to do?"

Alex thought for a minute. "Sometimes, getting some distance from the problem is the best thing. I know we don't have much time, but even so, stepping back and collecting ourselves for a few hours might make it easier to see other options."

"You mean... taking some time alone?" Dylan said.

Alex nodded. "Apart from each other, at least. We've been together basically every minute for a whole week, and we've spent a good chunk of that time fighting for our lives. Our minds are exhausted, just like our bodies are. Seeking out people or places that are important to us might help clarify our thoughts."

Tom frowned. "You think it's worth spending two or three of our remaining twenty-four hours to just... meditate? Or hang out with someone?"

"If you have a better idea, I'm all ears."

No one said anything.

"We can't leave Sara here alone," Tom said.

"I'll watch her," Alex said. "I'm a single woman with no close family. Dylan, go see your dad. Tom... I'm sure you have people you want to see, too."

Tom picked up his Jackhammer and handed it to her. "I loaded it with beanbag rounds. If Sara tries anything fishy, shoot her—just not in the head. It'll knock her down and hurt like a bitch, and it'll leave a hell of a bruise, but it won't kill her."

Dylan swallowed hard. Sara stared at Tom with simmering rage in her eyes. He stared right back with cold steel in his.

Tom picked up his keys. "Dylan, let's take a drive."

* * *

Dylan waited to go inside until Tom's truck had pulled away. He'd left his gear in the truck, except for his backpack, and he was wearing his normal clothes. He allowed himself a small smile; now that all his injuries were healed, he could see his dad without having to worry about questions he couldn't answer.

Well, there were still some questions he couldn't answer.

Dylan unlocked the door and pushed it open gently. Richard was in the kitchen, pouring a cup of coffee.

"Hey, Dad," Dylan said.

"Dylan! It's the middle of the night. You've been at Sara's almost a week. Are you okay?"

Dylan didn't answer right away. Instead, he crossed the kitchen and gave his father a tight hug. Richard stood frozen in surprise for a moment, then returned the hug, somewhat awkwardly. It had been a long time since Dylan had hugged him.

Dylan looked up. "I'm alright, Dad. Really."

Richard pushed aside his coffee cup and scratched his beard, nodding slowly. "Do you, uh... want something to eat? Are you hungry?"

Dylan realized that he was. "Starving, actually."

Richard opened the refrigerator. "We don't have much, but I did go to that Chinese place you like yesterday. There's some leftover chow mein and Mongolian chicken."

Dylan smiled. "Sounds great."

Richard pointed to a cell phone on the kitchen counter. "I got your phone replaced; there's your new one. It's all charged up."

"Thanks." Dylan slipped the phone into his pocket. Richard put the leftover food in the microwave and pressed a button. While it was heating, Dylan went upstairs to his room. Everything looked just as he'd left it. He took the box of photo albums out of his closet and put the top album, his favorite one, into his backpack.

He wasn't sure that he or anyone else would live through the next day. If the worst came to pass, he wanted to be able to look at the photos one last time.

He took a quick shower and put on fresh clothes, hoping that his dad hadn't noticed how bad he smelled. Back downstairs, Dylan took a seat on the couch and looked around as though he were seeing the tiny, dingy apartment—really seeing it—for the first time in years. Richard brought the hot food to him, then sat in the recliner opposite the couch.

"Thanks, Dad." Dylan forced himself to eat slowly, even though he was famished.

Richard frowned. "You seem different."

Dylan paused. "Do I?"

"What's going on? I know I haven't been the most attentive father, but even I can tell something's up with you."

Dylan swallowed a bite of chicken and chose his words carefully. "I've been doing a lot of thinking. Sara has helped me see some things more clearly."

"Oh?"

"Dad, I… I'm not ready to come home yet. I'm just stopping by for an hour or so. I'll be home the day after tomorrow, I promise."

He was not at all sure that he would be able to keep that promise.

Richard shook his head. "Dylan, enough. The secrets, the coming and going in the middle of the night—it has to stop. Tell me what's going on."

Dylan didn't respond right away. He set the half-eaten container of food on the coffee table. In the past, a great many fights between them had started just like this.

Well, not quite like this. Something was different this time. Usually, it started with Richard forgetting that Dylan existed because he couldn't be bothered to pause his pointless hunt for clues about Marie. Dylan would get angry about having to be his own parent, whether he was forging his father's signature on a permission slip, searching the apartment for cash to buy groceries, or making his own doctor appointments. They would argue, and then they wouldn't speak to each other for a few days, and then the cycle would start all over again.

It was time to break the cycle.

"Break the cycle," Dylan muttered to himself.

"What?" When Dylan looked up, Richard was frowning at him, confused.

"Dad... you know I love you, right?"

"Of course. I love you, too. I guess I'm not the best at showing it."

"And we both love Mom." This time, Richard couldn't bring himself to agree out loud. He nodded instead. "I have to go back to Sara's house one more time. I'll be there for one more day. I have to do something important—something more important than anything else I've ever done."

"What do you mean? College stuff? Are you filling out applications?" Richard furrowed his brow in thought. A moment later, his expression changed to one of hope and excitement. "Did Ethan give you one of his scholarships?"

Dylan shook his head. "No, it's more important than college. But I'll only be gone for one more day. After that, when I come back home... it has to be different."

Richard looked down at the floor. A long silence stretched between them. Finally, he said, "You're going to ask me to stop looking for her."

"Dad, you know I would give anything to find out what happened to Mom. I want to know just as much as you do. But Mom's not here with you—I am. And I need you. Not just for the next year and a half, while I'm finishing high school and need a place to live. I don't want to grow up only talking to you on the phone for ten minutes on holidays."

Richard looked up and met his son's eyes. "I was right about one thing, at least," he said softly. "You are different. But I have a feeling you won't tell me why or how."

Dylan got up and sat on the edge of the recliner, next to his father. "We have to face the fact that Mom is gone. It's a terrible, horrible fact, I know. But we can face it together. Mom wouldn't want us to do this to ourselves or each other. She wouldn't want you sitting around playing detective all day while the bills pile up, and she wouldn't want me moving out the day I turn eighteen because I can't stand watching you waste away."

Richard regarded him with an unreadable expression. "Why do you need to go back to Sara's house right now, in the middle of the night?"

Dylan sighed. "I can't tell you that. I'm sorry, but it's really important, and it's something only I can do. You have to trust me."

"Trust you to do what?"

"I'm... not sure yet."

"You're not sure what you have to do? Then how do you know it's important?"

Dylan couldn't answer that, so he ignored it. "Promise me that you'll give it up. All of it. We have to look forward, not back. I need a dad like the one who took thousands and thousands of wonderful pictures—pictures of a life worth living and a world worth living in."

Richard shook his head. A single tear trailed slowly down his face. "Dylan... what you're asking me to do—I can't. I'm sorry. I can't give up on her."

Dylan closed his eyes. He didn't know what else to say. His own words replayed in his mind as he tried to think of a different way to put it, a way that his father might understand.

A life worth living. A world worth living in.

I have to do something important—something that only I can do.

Break the cycle.

It hit him like a bolt of lightning. He gasped and shot to his feet. Richard stood up as well, looking concerned. "What is it? Dylan, tell me."

Dylan snatched up his pack and ran for the door. "I have to go. I'll be home tomorrow."

The door slammed behind him before Richard could move or say anything. He heaved a sigh. The conversation they'd just had was all too familiar, as was the ending. He sat down on the couch and looked around. His gaze fell on the half-eaten food. He considered finishing it, so it wouldn't go to waste, then decided against it. He wasn't hungry.

He picked up the papers he'd been looking at before Dylan had come back. It was a report that a private investigator had put together almost fifteen years ago. There wasn't much to read in the report because there hadn't been much evidence to find, but maybe Richard had missed something. Perhaps something helpful was buried in the report, hiding in plain sight—some clue that would give him a new trail to follow, something that might eventually explain where Marie had gone.

He stopped reading. A thought had suddenly occurred to him. He'd picked up the report purely out of habit, not because he'd actually wanted to read it.

He thought about the time Dylan had called to check in a few days ago. He had sounded different then, too. Tonight, he seemed... bolder. More confident. But on the phone, he had sounded upset—more upset than he'd been in a long time.

Richard thought about what he'd done after that phone call. In a rare moment of unfiltered introspection, he'd considered whether he might have been the reason Dylan was so upset. Dylan had said, "I can't see you right now." At the time, he'd pushed aside the thought and ignored it until it sank below the surface of his memory and disappeared.

Tonight, Dylan had said that Marie wouldn't want her husband or son to be so consumed by grief that they stopped living their lives. It was far from the first time Richard had heard that—he'd thought it himself after Dylan had called a few days ago, and he'd thought it many times before that.

Only... he hadn't thought about it. Not really. He hadn't *engaged* with the idea, hadn't forced himself to confront the reality of what his relentless search for Marie was doing to his relationship with Dylan. He'd simply swept the thought aside and waited for it to go away, much like he was doing now.

Dylan had mumbled something to himself while he was eating. Richard didn't think it was directed at him—it had seemed more like Dylan was talking to himself. What had he said?

"Break the cycle."

Richard closed his eyes and leaned his head back against the top of the couch. He sat motionless for a long time, forcing himself to think, forcing himself to grapple with ideas he'd suppressed and ignored day in and day out for sixteen years.

When he finally opened his eyes again, the sky outside the window was still dark, but in the east, it was just a touch lighter. Dawn wasn't far away.

Exhaustion hit him like a ton of bricks. He yawned. When had he last had a real, full, good night's sleep? He couldn't remember.

He needed more time to think and a clearer head to do it with. He stood up and made his way to his bedroom. He was asleep within moments after his head hit the pillow.

Most nights, he dreamed of Marie. Tonight, Richard dreamed of his son.

* * *

Dylan shut the truck door behind him. He shivered and rubbed his arms. His cheeks were bright red from the cold. "Thanks for coming to pick me up so quickly," he said.

Tom nodded. "No problem. I was nearby, and I was done anyway."

"Tom?"

"Yeah?"

"Where did you go?"

Tom sat still, staring out the windshield. He drummed his fingers on the steering wheel. Dylan thought he wasn't going to answer.

"I went to see Manny's parents," Tom finally said.

"Manny... your friend who died in the war."

Tom nodded. "Best friend I've ever had."

"How did it go?"

Tom allowed himself a small smile. "At first, I thought they weren't going to let me in. I don't blame them. It's the middle of the night, and I haven't spoken to them since the funeral—since before you were born."

Dylan sat in silence for a moment, thinking. "They blamed you for Manny's death."

"Rightly so. It was my fault."

Dylan shook his head. "No, it wasn't."

Tom looked over at him, frowning. "What?"

"I was just thinking about what Alex said about guilt. She was right. Maybe you should have made a different decision, I don't know. I wasn't there, and I didn't see your dreams like Sara did. I've just put together an idea of what happened based on what I've heard you say. But I do know that even if you didn't help your friend when you should have, that doesn't mean his death was your fault. The people who killed him—they were terrorists, right? They killed a bunch of other innocent people?" Tom nodded slowly. "They're the guilty ones, not you. Maybe you and Manny never should have been there in the first place, like you said. But that's a separate issue, and it doesn't mean you killed him—the bad guys did."

Again, Tom nodded slowly. "Manny's parents said almost the same thing. I didn't go there tonight expecting them to forgive me. But they did, after I explained that I finally understood that I joined the army for the wrong reasons and that I shouldn't have encouraged Manny to follow me. You're only partly right, though."

Dylan frowned. "How so?"

"Manny's death was the bad guys' fault—mostly. But I do bear some responsibility. My blind allegiance to my so-called duty—to other people's ideas about what Manny and I should have been doing with our lives—put both of us in harm's way, and Manny paid the price. I told his parents the same thing. I think they'd been waiting twenty years for me to figure it out."

Dylan offered Tom a small, sad smile. "But you learned something, and you know better now, right? You'll never make that mistake again."

Tom nodded solemnly. "I sure as shit will not, and I won't let Sara make it either."

Dylan's smile widened. "I'm sorry about your friend, but I'm glad he's still helping you, even now. You're a great guy, Tom. You're brave, smart, and strong. I hope I can be more like you one day. Manny would be proud of you."

"Alright, alright," Tom grunted irritably. "Just because the girls aren't here doesn't mean you have to provide all the estrogen."

Dylan laughed. "You want more testosterone, huh? Well, I had an idea a little while ago—one that might be right up your alley. I might know a way to stop Ardu."

Tom glanced over at him. "You don't say? I had an idea myself. I wonder if we're thinking the same thing."

Dylan studied Tom's face for a moment. "I bet we are."

"Then let's get back to the cabin and share with the rest of the class."

Dylan noticed a long, black case in the back seat. "What's that?"

"A gift. From Manny's parents."

"Something that will help us fix this mess?"

Tom put the truck in gear and started to drive. "I think it will."

CHAPTER THIRTY-EIGHT
Evasion

Alex glanced at her watch. Twenty-one hours to go.

"I need to pee," Sara said.

"That sucks," Alex said dryly.

Sara scowled. "You're really gonna sit there and let me pee my pants?"

"I'm considering it."

"The bathroom is right there, and it only has one door. You have the shotgun, and my hands are tied."

"A compelling case. You'd make a good lawyer."

Sara sighed and shook her head. "I don't have any of my gear, and I don't have any sedatives. What do you think I'm gonna do? Fall asleep on the toilet and go back to the Twilight by myself, unarmed, with my hands tied, right into the army of monsters guarding the cathedral?"

Alex leaned forward. Her eyes blazed with conviction, and her voice was dangerously low. "You're so far off the reservation that nothing you tried would surprise me."

Sara closed her eyes. "I'm sorry that you have such a low opinion of me."

"I have a very high opinion of you, actually—that's why we're here. Apparently, I think more of you than you think of yourself. You're a smart, brave, beautiful girl, but sometimes smart girls do stupid things—I know that firsthand. We're gonna sit right here, nice and cozy, until we figure out how to fix this without throwing you to the wolves."

"I just want to go to the bathroom."

Alex sighed. "Okay. But the door stays open."

Sara's eyes widened. "You're kidding."

"I'm a woman, too—and a doctor. You don't have anything I haven't seen a million times before. Final offer; take it or leave it."

Sara shook her head. "Fine. Whatever."

Alex used her knife to cut the zip ties securing Sara's arms to the chair but left her hands bound together. She took several steps back and kept the shotgun at the low ready, not quite aimed at Sara, but not pointed away from her, either. "After you," she said.

Sara shuffled to the bathroom, grumbling the whole way. She found the light and flicked it on. She turned back to Alex. "Can I at least close the door halfway?"

Alex didn't answer right away. Bright light washed over her face—the headlights of Tom's truck shining through the cabin's single window. For the briefest instant, Alex's eyes darted reflexively in that direction.

Sara seized the opportunity. Quick as a fox, she lunged forward and slammed into Alex with all the force she could manage. They both crashed to the floor. Alex yelped and tried to raise the shotgun, but it was long and heavy, and Sara was grappling her.

Remembering her years of martial arts classes, Sara rolled to one side and managed to get Alex in a choke hold. She wasn't strong, but she didn't need to be—she just needed to be a little stronger than Alex, and only for a few seconds.

Squeezing as hard as she could, Sara compressed the arteries on either side of Alex's neck, cutting off the flow of blood to her brain. Within seconds, her movements started to slow, and her wild, backward punches got weaker. A few seconds later, she went limp.

Sara quickly released the hold so as not to risk seriously harming her friend and mentor. Alex wouldn't be out long—fifteen seconds, maybe thirty at most. Sara scrambled to her feet and looked around. Her gear and weapons were in Tom's truck; he'd known better than to leave them in the cabin, where she had even a small chance to recover them.

She looked down. Tom's shotgun was far too heavy for her to use with one hand, and it was loaded with nonlethal beanbag rounds. It wouldn't do much good in the Twilight. Alex did have her sidearm, though. Sara snatched it up and pulled the slide back to verify that there was a round in the chamber. It was difficult with her hands tied together, doubly so with one of them in a cast.

She heard voices outside. "There's plenty of canned food. I could go for some beef stew," Tom was saying.

Sara growled in frustration. There was no *time*. She tucked Alex's Glock into the waistband of her pants, ran to the front door, and pressed herself against the wall behind it.

A second later, the door swung open. "We're back," Dylan called into the room. "Tom and I...." He trailed off when he saw Alex lying unconscious on the floor.

Sara saw that Dylan was holding his pack in one hand. She would need supplies—whatever he had would have to do. She darted from her hiding place and sprinted out the door, snatching Dylan's backpack as she went.

"What the hell!" Dylan's shout echoed in the small space. "Tom, Sara's getting away!"

Tom was already running for her. He was big, but she was agile. She faked left, then cut right at the last second. He tried to turn back around and grab her, but she was already gone.

Sara ran as hard and fast as she could. Everything and everyone was depending on her. If Tom or Dylan caught her, it was over. She could already hear them gaining on her.

She reached the tree line and careened headlong into the forest. She passed beyond the reach of the cabin's exterior floodlight and into nearly total darkness. She was afraid of running face-first into a tree, but she dared not slow down. If she did, they would catch her, and everything would end.

She risked a glance back and gasped in fright—Dylan was right behind her. He jumped, trying to tackle her around the waist. She leaped aside, and he crashed into the snow, swearing. Tom was a little farther behind, but he was catching up.

Sara started weaving chaotically between the trees as they grew thicker and closer together. Her only hope was to break line of sight, then lose them in the darkness. They would still be able to follow her footprints in the snow, but slowing down to track her that way would give her a chance to increase her lead.

Tree branches whipped her in the face as she ran, tearing open the fresh cuts she'd gotten from crashing through the cathedral window. She felt hot blood running down her forehead, cheeks, and nose.

Daniela and I have something in common now, she thought grimly. By this time tomorrow, they would have two things in common.

They would both be dead—or as good as dead, in Sara's case.

Tears streamed down her face as she ran, mingling with the blood. She amended her previous thought when she realized that she would have a third thing in common with Daniela.

She, too, would leave behind a young man who loved her.

Abruptly, the ground beneath her feet disappeared. She let out a short, clipped scream as she fell into nothingness. A moment later, she crashed painfully onto her side, then her back, then her chest. She rolled over and over down a steep hill, slamming into logs and rocks. An especially violent collision knocked the wind out of her. At some point, Alex's Glock flew away into the darkness.

When Sara finally rolled to a halt on level ground, she could barely move. Everything hurt. Gingerly, she moved her arms and legs, testing for newly broken bones. Miraculously, there didn't seem to be any, but she felt like the victim of a severe beating.

She heard shouting at the top of the hill. She didn't think Tom and Dylan knew where she'd gone, but they'd figure it out any second. Digging deep into her dwindling reserves of willpower, she forced herself to sit up, then to stand, gritting her teeth against the pain. She saw a dark shape nearby—Dylan's backpack—and snatched it up. There, a few steps away, another dark shape—Alex's Glock. She grabbed that, too, and kept running.

Her eyes had adjusted somewhat to the night. In the dim light of an almost-new moon, she could see patches of grass beneath her feet that weren't covered by snow. The tree branches overhead were so thick that some of the snow hadn't made it to the ground. She began searching for snow-free patches and ran across them whenever possible. Tom and Dylan wouldn't be able to follow her footprints if she didn't leave any.

Sara ran on for what felt like an hour, pushing far past the limits of her endurance. She stopped only when her lungs forced her to. She lay on her back in the frozen grass, panting, listening intently for any sound of pursuers.

She heard nothing other than her own ragged breathing.

What was her next move? She couldn't reenter the Twilight at the cathedral. It was in the Hollow; direct entry and direct exit were both impossible. She suspected that Tom, Alex, and Dylan would soon reenter the Twilight to wait for her, to try to stop her. She had told them that returning to a specific location in the Twilight without her guidance was impossible, but that wasn't entirely true, and they were smart enough to figure that out sooner or later. They had heard her recite the ancient chant enough times that one of them had surely memorized it by now. As long as they got the words right, all they had to do was concentrate on a mental image of the place in the Twilight where they wanted to return. She couldn't undo the binding ritual to lock them out—that would lock her out, too.

They would come after her. She had no doubt about it.

They also would realize that she couldn't get into the Vile Abbey without their blood, so they would guard the secret exit they'd found in the catacombs. But she did have their blood—in the lab refrigerator, back at her house. Dr. Atwood had drawn a few extra vials from each of them to hold in reserve for medical reasons, but Sara, Ethan, and the Circle doctors were the only ones who knew that.

As for fighting her way back to the cathedral once she was inside the Vile Abbey, one person in the Twilight could help her do that.

Slowly, Sara began to feel calmer, if not better. She had a plan. It would work.

It had to work.

She allowed herself a few minutes to cry. She would never see Dylan again. She didn't want to die. She desperately wanted to live, to see what kind of life they might have together. But that had never been on the table. She had done her best to cherish every minute with him, knowing that in all likelihood, she wouldn't make it to her twentieth birthday. She felt as though she had already spent a lifetime with him, but at the same time, now that it was over, it felt like the years had passed in the blink of an eye.

She thought about everything the others had said after they'd stopped her from completing the ritual. They'd said things about duty, guilt, and self-doubt that Sara had never considered before, and much of it seemed to make sense. Maybe they had a point.

She sighed. Even if they were right, it didn't change what she had to do. The way was the way, and crying about it wouldn't help anyone. There wasn't much time left. All she could do for her friends now was save their lives. If her own life was the price, then so be it.

Sara choked off her tears, sat up, and opened Dylan's bag to see what was inside. She found a glow stick and cracked it so she could see better. She then found a utility knife and used it to cut the zip ties binding her hands. She stretched her wrists and flexed her fingers, sighing with relief as the feeling began to return.

There was something large and heavy in the main pocket of Dylan's backpack. She pulled it out. A book? Why would he have a book?

She opened the cover. It was a photo album. On the first page was a spread of six photos that Richard presumably had taken many years ago, before Dylan was born. There were beautiful sunsets, smiling families, and soot-covered men working on large machines. She flipped a few more pages. A sad smile touched her lips as she looked at the pictures, each taken with great skill and care.

She stopped on a page that caught her attention. Frowning, she brought the glow stick closer so she could see.

Her heart leaped into her throat.

"Oh, my god," she whispered.

* * *

Sara parked the stolen car a quarter mile away and left the keys inside. *Add grand theft auto and assault with a deadly weapon to my rap sheet*, she thought grimly, adjusting her shirt to conceal the gun she'd used to commit her first carjacking. She walked the long way, around the side of her family's lot until she found a hidden spot in the trees not far from the front of the house. She could see movement inside. Tom's truck and Alex's car were still parked in the driveway. A few other cars she didn't recognize were parked in the street, probably owned by other Circle members brought in to resolve the emergency.

The sky overhead was just beginning to turn pink in the east. She checked her watch. Eighteen hours to go.

Sara was furious with her father. How could he lie to her about something so important?

She closed her eyes and shook her head. She supposed she could understand it. She had lied to her friends for the same reason. The Pilgrimage was too important. If lies were necessary to see it through, so be it.

After nearly forty-eight hours with no word from his daughter, Ethan was undoubtedly preparing to execute the contingency plan, the emergency ritual that was only when all else had failed. She couldn't allow that to happen. She had her own plan, but it didn't involve Ethan or anyone else. She had to get inside, get what she needed, and get back out undetected. If anyone saw her, they would rope her into the contingency plan, by force if necessary.

Sara could still make everything right, without having to invoke the emergency ritual, but she had to do it her way.

Alone.

She had to move now, while she still had the cover of darkness. Staying low, she darted across the street and slid into cover behind Tom's truck. A second later, the house's front door opened, and her father's voice drifted out.

"Tell the other Maidens to be ready within six hours. We have to find Sara before then. If she's alive, the contingency won't work without her. All other considerations are secondary."

"Understood. We'll do our part." The second voice belonged to a man named Otto Bauer, the patriarch of a Circle family from Germany. *They got here fast*, Sara thought.

Before the door closed, she heard her father's voice again. "God forgive me. I would give anything not to have to do this."

She heard footsteps approaching—by the sound of it, Otto was alone. He was coming right toward her; his car was parked on the other side of Tom's truck.

Holding her breath, Sara ducked and rolled under the truck, flattening herself on the driveway. The ice-covered concrete was shockingly cold on her stomach, and her T-shirt provided no protection. She waited until she saw Otto's feet, then rolled out from under the truck, on the opposite side.

She took cover at the corner of the garage and watched the front door for a moment. She saw no one through the window. Quickly, she hopped across the front yard, taking care to step in the fresh footprints Otto had made so as not to leave evidence of her infiltration. She cleared the front yard and ducked behind the heat pumps on the north side of the house.

She needed to get to the basement, but there was only one way: through the living room. The shortest path to the living room was through the kitchen, but surely people would be in there. She'd never be able to go that way without being seen.

That left the hallway connected to Ethan's office, on the west side of the house. The office probably would be empty; he used it mostly for work, not so much for Circle business.

Sara pressed her back against the house and stepped sideways, staying in the narrow patch of grass that the roof had shielded from snow. Each time she passed a window, she ducked under it. She could hear many voices inside, faint mumbles through the glass.

She reached the office window without incident. It was closed but unlocked—the lock had been broken for ages. Glancing in both directions to make sure no one was approaching, she rummaged in Dylan's pack for the utility knife and carefully wedged the thin blade between the window and the wooden sill. Gently, she wiggled the knife up and down until the window slid open about an inch.

She paused when she saw her reflection in the glass. Involuntarily, she touched her face. Some of the cuts were deep, the skin around them sore and inflamed. Dried blood on her cheeks looked like it had come from her eyes in the form of macabre tears. She remembered the heartbreaking story Roland had shared about Daniela and her scars. She understood, now, what the other Maiden had been worried about.

Would Dylan think she was ugly?

Sara felt a sudden ache in her chest when she remembered that it wouldn't matter. She had seen him for the last time, and she'd been running away from him. She hadn't gotten a chance to say good-bye, or to tell him....

She steeled herself and wiped away the fresh tears that were forming in her eyes. She couldn't let such thoughts distract her now. She wedged her fingers into the gap, opened the window the rest of the way, climbed inside, and quietly shut it behind her.

Voices drifted into the office from the hallway. Taking cover behind the door, Sara peeked around the corner just long enough to observe the situation. She swore quietly—two women were in the hallway, talking to one another, and at least four people were milling around in the living room, talking on phones or writing on notepads.

The women in the hallway were blocking passage to the living room, and they didn't look like they would move anytime soon. She didn't recognize them, but they had surely seen pictures of her and would be on the lookout. She couldn't just wait until they moved; every second she remained in the house increased her chances of being discovered.

Think, dammit. She looked around the office for something useful. There —Ethan's winter hat and long coat, hanging on the back of the door. He was taller than she, but only by six inches or so. She put on the hat and coat, taking extra care to hide her red hair. She found his winter gloves in the coat pocket and put those on, too—her cover would surely be blown if someone saw her small, feminine hands or the cast on her left wrist.

All the clothing was too big. Still, if she kept her head down and moved quickly.... It might work, but not without a distraction. She needed a way to make everyone look away from the office door, just for a second or two.

Her roaming gaze fell on Ethan's computer, and an idea came to her. She tapped the keyboard to wake it up, then opened the VOIP calling app and typed in her home phone number. She paused with the mouse cursor over the call button and took a deep breath. She closed her eyes and leveraged the meditation techniques she used when she was stressed out. She stilled her breathing and did her best to clear her mind of distractions. She visualized the outcome she wanted in her mind, watched it unfold like a movie, pictured her plan working perfectly.

She would get one chance at this. If she messed it up, all was lost. She had to be fast and confident. Her timing had to be precise. She had to acknowledge her fear, then shove it aside and get the job done.

Sara opened her eyes, clicked the call button, and darted back to the door. A second later, the phone in the kitchen began to ring. As she'd hoped, every eye darted toward it reflexively in response to the unexpected sound.

Now.

She lowered her head, stuffed her hands in the coat's pockets, and strode quickly down the hall. The two women were looking toward the kitchen, their conversation momentarily forgotten. She brushed past them quickly but not rudely, keeping her eyes on the floor.

One of the women called after her. "Oh, Ethan! I didn't know you were in your office. I need—"

Sara didn't slow down or turn around. She raised her right hand over her shoulder, as if to say, "Not now, I'm in a hurry."

A man in the kitchen picked up the phone. "Hello?" The others watched him curiously, wondering if it was an important call related to their mission.

Sara cut left at the end of the hall and headed straight for the basement door on the far side of the living room. "Hello? Who's there?" the man said again.

Sara reached the basement door, which, fortunately, stood open. She started down the stairs. Her heart was racing. A burst of excitement supplanted her terror. She'd made it. No one yelled after her or tried to follow her.

A moment later, her elation faded, again replaced by trepidation. She was going into the basement blind. She had no way to know who was down there or where they might be.

She heard footsteps coming up the stairs, toward her. Her stomach dropped. The stairs paused at a landing halfway down, turned ninety degrees, and continued to the basement. Whoever was coming up was still around the corner. They couldn't see her yet, but in about two seconds, they would walk right into her.

Sara remembered something she'd seen in a movie once. It was an incredibly stupid idea, but she had no time to come up with a better one.

She'd taken gymnastics for four years. It might work.

As quietly as she could, she kicked one foot up on the wall to her left, pushed off, and kicked out toward the opposite wall with her other foot. Using her hands for balance, she wedged herself between the staircase walls with both feet off the floor. Spiderlike, she scrambled higher, toward the ceiling, as though climbing a chimney.

The person reached the landing and turned the corner.

It was her father.

He was looking down at his phone and mumbling to himself. If he looked up, even a little bit, he would see her.

Sara held her breath. Ethan continued his ascent, taking the stairs with agonizing slowness. He stopped directly under her, still staring at his phone. He was talking to himself, but she couldn't make out the words. He sounded upset.

Dad, move! she thought. Her arms and legs were beginning to ache and tremble. He was just standing there, reading a text message or an email, taking his time.

Finally, blessedly, he put away his phone and continued up the stairs. The second he reached the basement door and stepped out of view, she dropped. She was light, and she aimed her landing well, making little noise on the carpeted stairs. Again, she thanked her father for the gymnastics lessons that had helped her avoid him—lessons that would ultimately help save everyone on Earth.

Her legs trembling from the exertion, she crept the rest of the way down the stairs. The den was empty. She tiptoed to the open secret door leading to the doom room. Dr. Atwood and a few others were inside, bent over their workstations. Silent as a mouse, Sara darted to the armory, punched in the access code, and slipped inside.

She breathed a sigh of relief when the heavy door softly *clunked* shut behind her. Wasting no time, she tossed Ethan's clothes aside and put Alex's Glock on an empty shelf, then found new armor, strapped it on, and filled the pouches with spare magazines and grenades. She grabbed a new pack and filled it with anything that might come in handy—rope, medical supplies, flares.

When she removed Dylan's pack to put on her new one, she paused. She found herself staring at his pack, running her hands over it. It was the last thing of his she would ever touch.

She shook herself out of it. There was no time to think about her own selfish desires. She kissed the tip of her finger and touched Dylan's pack one last time before laying it gently on a shelf.

She grabbed a combat knife, a new 6.8mm Barrett rifle with a foregrip that would better accommodate her broken hand, and a Springfield Lightweight Operator .45 sidearm, along with several extended ten-round magazines. She paused briefly, considering what else she might need, then selected a Serbu Super Shorty 12-gauge shotgun. The weapon was just sixteen inches long and would fit in a thigh holster on her left leg, opposite her sidearm. She had no room for extra shells, but the four in the gun might come in handy.

Finally, Sara lifted an M72 LAW antitank rifle from its resting place on a wire rack. It was surprisingly light, even when loaded with a 66mm high-explosive rocket. She couldn't carry any extra ammunition, but she just might have a need to blow something up.

Her idiotic plan required all the firepower she could get her hands on.

She slung the launcher over her back and wedged it under her pack. She felt heavy and slow, carrying so many weapons, but she had a feeling that she would soon shed a lot of weight in the form of empty casings and magazines. When she was as ready as she could be, she carefully, quietly pushed open the armory door.

Ethan was staring right at her.

He blinked. Sara felt her heart rate triple.

"Sara, what—"

She lowered her shoulder and charged into him, knocking him aside. She managed it only because she took him by surprise and because she was fifty pounds heavier than normal. Ethan went sprawling, and his phone clattered across the floor.

He recovered quickly and shouted. "Guards! Sara's here! Stop her!"

She needed the vials of Tom, Alex, and Dylan's blood. They were in a small refrigerator on the other side of the room, next to Dr. Atwood. She took off in that direction, willing her legs to move faster. With all her extra gear, she felt like she was running through molasses. She could hear heavy footsteps stomping down the stairs. The guards were coming.

Dr. Atwood turned when she heard the commotion. Her eyes widened behind her glasses when she saw Sara charging toward her like an enraged commando. Sara's pulse was pounding in her ears. Adrenaline flooded her bloodstream and made everything appear to move in slow motion.

Finally, she reached the refrigerator. She stretched out her hands toward the handle.

One of Ethan's bodyguards tackled her from the side. They both rolled away. He was far stronger and came out on top, holding her down with one massive hand. She could hardly breathe under his weight. She glanced to the side. Four more guards were halfway across the room and closing. If they all got to her, it was over.

Sara bucked her hips to the left, reached behind her back, and pulled her knife. The guard's eyes widened when he saw it, and he reached for the weapon, intending to disarm her. She slashed awkwardly, inflicting a deep cut on his forearm. He cried out and recoiled, just enough to take most of his weight off her. She kneed him hard in the groin, and he rolled away.

The other guards were almost on her. She snatched a flashbang from her vest, pulled the pin, and tossed it. She rolled over onto her stomach, squeezed her eyes shut, and clapped her hands over her ears.

When the grenade detonated, the floor vibrated, and glass shattered all around the room. Even though Sara was covering her ears, the sound was painfully loud. Dimly, through her muted hearing, she heard cries of pain and shock.

Time. There was no time. She scrambled to her feet, trying to shake off the dizziness. She stumbled to the refrigerator, yanked it open, and groped around blindly inside. There—the vials. She brought them up to her face, squinting, trying to read the labels. It would do no good to return to the Twilight only to find that she had the wrong blood.

The guards were starting to recover. Sara ran over to the closest medical crash cart and yanked open the top drawer. She pulled out items and tossed them aside. Oxygen masks, suture kits, cardiac drugs—none of it was what she needed.

There, a syringe with a blue label. She grabbed it, popped off the safety cap, and rammed the autoinjector into the side of her leg. Another guard tackled her, knocking her to the ground again.

It was too late. A heartbeat later, she was gone.

CHAPTER THIRTY-NINE
Clarity

Sara lit a torch and knelt in the sand to look for clues. She was back in the canyon, near the train platform. The single white lily by the tracks had finally withered and died, no longer able to resist the Twilight's malevolence. She let out a quiet, mournful sigh.

So much vibrant beauty lost to this nightmare.

She found what she was looking for: their footprints from two days ago. The soft sand had preserved them well. She swept her torch slowly back and forth, looking for other footprints in the flickering light.

There—Jacob's tracks, leading away in a different direction. She followed them at a light jog, back through the canyon, toward the slaughterhouse. Some distance later, the tracks veered to the right, toward the base of the canyon wall, and stopped there. Sara looked up. Jacob must have climbed the wall to get out of the canyon. She could see why he'd chosen this spot. In most places, the canyon walls were almost perfectly vertical, but here, they were not quite as steep. The stone was rough, with plenty of holes and outcrops to serve as handholds.

Sara doused her torch and stretched for a minute. She wasn't half the climber Alex was, especially with a busted left hand. But if a tired old man could get up this wall, so could she.

Slowly, carefully, she picked her way upward. It wasn't as daunting a climb as she'd feared. She slipped once but caught herself before she tumbled back down. The whole way up, she doggedly refused to look down. Before too long, she was at the top, out of breath but no worse for wear.

The soil at the rim wasn't as soft. She could see Jacob's tracks after relighting her torch, but they were harder to make out. She continued to follow them, jogging whenever possible. She had no way to know how far he'd gone. All she knew was that she had to find him soon. The Vile Abbey was a long way away, easily twelve hours on foot. Jacob was old. She hoped he was up for such a grueling trek—she needed his help to get back to the cathedral.

A vast, empty desert stretched out before her. Scraggly, thorny bushes defiantly rose here and there from the parched dirt. Every so often, a tumbleweed rolled past, pushed along by a frigid gust of wind. Sara kept up a sustainable pace, following the old man's tracks.

A surprisingly short distance later, the tracks ended at a large rock. Confused, Sara looked around for a minute. No footprints led away from the rock, but a single, continuous line did, about three inches wide. Another, similar line approached and ended at the rock from a different direction. Sara gasped when she realized what the lines were.

Motorcycle tracks. That was how Jacob had gotten to the canyon just a day and a half after saving Alex and Dylan at the hospital. He must have parked his bike here while looking for a new hideout, then been captured by the Butcher and taken to the slaughterhouse.

Her heart quickened. A motorcycle would get her back to the Vile Abbey with time to spare. Sara took off at a fast run, following the tire tracks that headed away from the rock, no longer worried about conserving her stamina.

About an hour later, a tall structure came into view over the horizon. Sara was winded and sweaty but feeling alright. She silently thanked herself for all the time she'd spent on the treadmill.

As she drew closer to the structure, she saw that it was a water tower. It stood at the edge of a tiny frontier town—barely a handful of buildings lined up along a single dirt road that led nowhere. It reminded her of Tombstone, Arizona, where she'd been on vacation once with her father years ago.

She'd bought Dylan a leather wallet in a gift shop. He still used it.

He kept a picture of her in it.

Sara pushed aside her thoughts of Dylan as she drew to a halt at the base of the water tower. She bent over, hands on her knees, trying to catch her breath. When she'd recovered, she cupped her hands around her mouth and shouted up at the tower.

"Jacob! It's me, Sara! I need your help!"

Silence. She looked around. He must be here somewhere—a beat-up old motorcycle was parked nearby. The water tank was made of thick steel and would be reasonably soundproof. Maybe he couldn't hear her if he was in there. She raised her rifle and fired three quick shots into the sky.

A metal door slammed open high above. A moment later, Jacob's grizzled face was peering down at her. "Lass? What are ye doin' here?"

"Jacob! Lower the ladder, please. Time is short. I need your help."

"Ye dinnae want mah help, lass. It's nae good." He stared at her in silence for a moment. "Where are yer Wardens?"

Sara was surprised to realize that she hadn't anticipated that question. She didn't know how to answer it. Telling him the truth was out—he'd never help her if he knew that completing the final ritual would bring her a few decades of constant, hellish torment as the surrogate mother of a wrathful god, followed by a grisly death.

She found herself thinking of Tom, Alex, and Dylan. Memories of all they'd been through together flashed by in her mind. They had all grown so much throughout their journey. She was so proud of all of them. Why did it have to end like this? Why couldn't they understand that this had to happen, that there was no other way?

She closed her eyes. At least her new plan would bring some small measure of comfort after she was gone.

Suddenly, she was weeping silently. Her tears stung the fresh cuts on her face.

"Come on up, lass," Jacob called softly. He began to lower the ladder. Once Sara had climbed up, he gave her a gentle hug, as if she were made of porcelain and he was afraid she might break. She suddenly realized that he thought she was crying because her Wardens were dead.

If a lie by omission got her back to the cathedral in time, so be it. What was one more lie?

"Jacob, please," she said. "You're my only hope—the world's only hope. I can finish this, I can save everyone, but I can't do it alone. I know it's horribly unfair to ask you to help me, to endanger yourself after all the pain and loneliness you've endured in this place. But I have to ask it."

Jacob scratched his beard thoughtfully. "Sounds dangerous."

Sara nodded. "Extremely."

"There's a good chance we both die."

"A very good chance."

He reached into his pocket and took out a battered old wallet. He flipped it open, pulled something out, and handed it to her. It was a faded, wrinkled picture of Lily. Gorgeous red hair fell halfway down her back, cascading over her white dress like a waterfall. She was bathed in a golden shaft of sunlight that made her hair sparkle like rubies. Her eyes were closed, but Sara knew they were green, like hers.

"She was beautiful," Sara said. She handed back the photo.

"When ah first saw ye, ah thought ye looked so much like her," he said. He stared at the photo for a moment, then tucked it back into his wallet. He sighed, then leaned his elbows on the railing and looked out over the empty desert below.

Sara took up a similar position next to him and waited patiently. He was clearly deep in thought, and she didn't want to interrupt him. A light breeze ruffled her hair and his beard.

Finally, he spoke. "Do ye ken why ah live here, lass?"

She looked at him. "You mean in this water tower?"

He shook his head. "Nae. Ah mean, do ye ken why ah go on livin' here, in the Twilight, when there's nothin' fer me here and no hope of goin' home."

She had wondered the same thing more than once. "Honestly? No."

He gave her a small smile. "Neither do ah. Suppose ah'm just afraid ta end it."

"I would take you home if I could."

"Ah ken, lass, but that's nae on the table. Ah often wonder what Lily would tell me ta do. Ah hope she had a good long life after she left this hellhole."

Sara felt another pang of guilt in her chest. She knew that Lily hadn't lived a long life. She'd never left the Twilight. She'd reached the cathedral, completed her Pilgrimage, suffered horribly for twenty years and seventeen days, and then died in agony.

"She did," Sara lied.

Jacob nodded slowly. "She finished her journey, ah suppose it's time ta finish mine. 'Tis the whole reason ah was brought here in the first place, ta escort a Maiden ta the cathedral. Maybe if ah finish the job ah've been puttin' off fer thirty-six years, ah can die with some bit of peace and dignity."

"Thank you," Sara whispered.

* * *

Jacob whistled as he looked up at the massive gate, the leering skulls, and the waterfalls of blood. "Nae what ah was expectin'."

Sara turned to face him. "What were you expecting?"

He shrugged. "Ah dinnae ken, but nae that." He dismounted the motorcycle and stood beside her.

"Jacob," she said. "This place is evil. It's the most evil place anyone's ever been to. There are hordes of monsters in there, a foul mist that blackens your very soul, and god knows what else."

"Yer sayin' ah dinnae want ta buy a timeshare."

She chuckled despite her dark mood. "I suppose not."

"Hordes of monsters, ye say. How are two of us supposed ta fight through 'em?" He had his prehistoric .45-70 rifle and a battered old .44 Blackhawk revolver, but even with all the hardware Sara had brought, they'd run out of ammo long before making a dent in the army that awaited them.

Sara amended that thought. They wouldn't run out of ammo—they'd be torn to pieces long before then.

She glanced at the motorcycle. "What if we don't fight through them?"

He followed her gaze and grinned when he caught on. "We *ride* through 'em."

"There are lots of stairs. And... a few narrow bridges."

"How narrow?"

"Very."

Jacob shrugged. "Ah've ridden most of mah life."

"You're sure you can do it?"

"What happens if we dinnae make it? 'Tis nae the end of the world."

"That's not funny."

"Ah disagree, lass. Seems ta me a sense of humor is about all the two of us've got left."

Sara grunted but didn't argue. "How will we see where we're going?"

Jacob flicked a switch on the motorcycle and a bright headlight flared into life. "Much better than fire," he said.

Sara had read his file in the Circle archives. "You were a mechanic, right?"

"Aye, and ah've had plenty of time here ta build things and tear 'em apart. Put this old bike together from about ten others ah found layin' around."

She smiled wistfully. "You and Dylan would have gotten along."

Jacob laid a hand on her shoulder, then changed the subject. "How do we get in?"

Sara reached into her pocket and pulled out two of the blood vials. "See those two alcoves there? Pour one of these into each of them. Don't spill it on the ground, I don't have any more." She wasn't positive this would work and was unwilling to think about what she would do if it didn't.

Jacob raised an eyebrow but said nothing. He took the vials and stepped over to the alcoves on the left side of the gate, ready to follow her lead. On the other side, Sara removed the stopper from the third vial and poured it into the reservoir. Jacob did the same with his two. Three of the four braziers in the skulls' eye sockets ignited.

Sara had an idea. Instead of placing her already-injured hand in the other alcove to be painfully impaled a second time, she drew her knife and pulled the blade lightly across her forearm, then dripped the blood into the fourth reservoir. It hurt, but not nearly as bad as being stabbed through the hand.

The fourth brazier burst into flame, and the gate began to rumble open. Tendrils of malevolent mist rolled out to greet them. Sara sighed. She felt silly for not thinking to try that the first time. She wrapped some gauze around her arm and settled on the back of Jacob's bike. He sat in the driver's seat and started the engine.

He looked over his shoulder at her. "Ready?"

"No."

"We goin' anyway?"

"Yes." She toggled her rifle to full auto and held onto Jacob with her broken left hand. She was not looking forward to firing and reloading the weapon one-handed while trying not to fall off a moving vehicle.

Somewhere inside the Vile Abbey, a chorus of unearthly howls rose into the night.

"Punch it," she said.

* * *

Alex checked her watch. "Thirteen hours to go," she said. "Are we sure Sara will come this way?"

Tom nodded. "It's the only way she can get back to the cathedral by herself."

"The only way we know of," Dylan added. "She might know some other way. It wouldn't be the first time she's kept secrets from us."

"True," Tom said. "But we can't guard an entrance we don't know about. All we can do is wait here."

They had stationed themselves in the catacombs, within sight of the narrow crevice. If Sara came this way, she would have to squeeze through that crack, and they would see her coming. They would be able to subdue her easily.

"Here," Tom said. He unslung his MGL and handed it to Dylan, along with a bandolier holding an additional twelve 40mm grenades he'd found in his uncle's extralegal arms stash at the cabin.

Dylan frowned. "You're giving this to me?"

Tom clapped him on the shoulder. "You're all grown up now, you can handle it. Just don't explode me or Alex."

"Or Sara," Dylan said, looking concerned.

Tom nodded. "Or Sara." He showed Dylan how to unload, reload, and prime the launcher.

Alex gestured at the long, black case Tom had brought along. "I'm guessing you have another new toy for yourself."

Tom unlatched the case and opened it. "I bought this for Manny before we shipped out for the army. He was a sniper, and a damn good one. Last night, I went to see his parents for the first time since his funeral. We had a good chat, and they gave me this, said Manny would want me to have it. I think they were right. He'd get a kick out of knowing that this rifle helped save the world."

Tom pulled out the Accuracy International AWM and looked it over. He retracted the bolt and inspected the chamber, then loaded a magazine holding five match-grade .338 Lapua Magnum rounds.

"Those bullets are huge," Dylan said.

"We have big things to make dead," Tom said with a conspiratorial wink. Satisfied with his inspection of the sniper rifle, he slung it over his back, took several more magazines from the case, and stored them in his armor pouches.

Somewhere far away, muffled gunfire echoed through the catacombs. A moment later, a different sound followed.

"Was that an engine?" Dylan said, his eyes wide in alarm.

"Sara?" Alex asked, also alarmed.

"Who else would it be?" Tom said.

"How did she get back here?"

"Doesn't matter. Let's go get her."

Each of them lit a torch from their packs and started running toward the gunfire. They followed the mist upstream, toward its source, pausing briefly at each junction to see where the current would lead them. Gradually, the gunfire and engine sounds grew louder.

"Is that a... car?" Alex asked.

"Sounds like a smaller engine. Maybe a motorcycle," Tom said.

"Where would she have gotten a working motorcycle?"

"We can ask her once we have her tied up again," Dylan growled.

"Looking forward to getting Sara tied up, are you?" Tom joked.

"Not funny!" Dylan protested.

"I thought it was funny," Alex said.

The rock wall ahead of them exploded. Tom managed to dodge to the side and stay on his feet, but Alex and Dylan were knocked to the ground by flying chunks of stone. Their armor saved them from broken ribs—or worse.

"Ouroboros!" Tom shouted.

The warning was unnecessary, the massive serpent's gleaming fangs and glowing eyes already having announced its arrival. It lunged for Tom, snapping its jaws hungrily. Tom fired an incendiary shell into its open mouth, buying a few seconds. He helped Alex to her feet and together, they retreated farther down the tunnel.

They were separated from Dylan—the snake filled the entire passage, and he was on the other side of it. "Dylan!" Alex yelled. "Go stop Sara!"

"We're counting on you!" Tom added. He drew his Magnum and

thumbed back the hammer, unable to use his shotgun as long as he was holding a torch. "Alright, shithead," he said to the Ouroboros as it violently slammed its head against the wall, trying to extinguish the flames. "You're between us and Sara."

"And that's the last place you want to be," Alex said, drawing a .45-caliber Glock 41 Tom had given her from his personal armory.

"Don't die!" Dylan yelled as he darted down another passage, following the mist.

"Do you have a plan?" Alex said to Tom.

"You know, I think I do. Do you trust me?"

She smiled at him in the flickering torchlight. "Completely."

He grinned back. "Get it to chase you. Just don't let it eat you."

She nodded. "Can do."

They bolted in opposite directions just as the Ouroboros recovered its senses. It hissed furiously and slithered after Tom, its rusted chain armor scraping against the stone. He ran, choosing turns at random, trying to stay far ahead of it. He didn't fire his weapon. He wanted Alex to get its attention, preferably by making it mad.

"Hey! Over here!" Alex yelled from somewhere around a corner. Loud *bangs* echoed through the tunnel as she fired her .45. The heavy slugs pinged harmlessly off the chains in small showers of orange sparks. The Ouroboros ignored the pointless attacks. Tom was its prey.

Tom had another bad idea. "Alex!" he shouted. "Yell so I know where you are!"

"Over here!" she called back. She was close.

"Keep making noise!" Tom yelled. He dived to the side as the Ouroboros lunged, barely missing him. He got to his feet and kept running, careful not to damage the rifle on his back or its delicate scope.

"This way!" Alex shouted. Tom ran toward her voice, turning right, then left, then right again.

There she was, straight ahead, waving her torch. Tom ran toward her. He could tell by the look on her face that the Ouroboros was right behind him.

"Shoot it in the mouth!" Tom yelled, then pitched forward, onto his stomach. He covered his head with his hands and held his breath. His heart pounded. His instincts screamed at him to get up and run from the threat or fight it. He ignored them and lay still.

The Ouroboros opened its jaws wide. It didn't know why its prey had suddenly given up, and it didn't care. It drew its head back, preparing to strike.

Alex fired her heavy pistol as quickly as she could pull the trigger.

Powerful .45 +P slugs ripped apart the soft tissue inside the snake's mouth. Pale-yellow blood spattered the walls and ceiling. The snake thrashed its head back and forth, enraged by the pain.

Tom scrambled to his feet. "Go!" he said. "Do a lap, lead it back here, and get it to stop at the torch!" He dropped his torch on the ground and darted left, cracking a glow stick as he went.

Alex ejected her empty magazine, slapped in a fresh one, and released the slide. "Come with me, ugly!" she shouted, then ran down another tunnel, to the right. The Ouroboros followed her, slithering its bulk along with frightening speed. The first part of Tom's plan had worked—Alex had hurt it enough to piss it off, enough to get it to chase her.

She hoped the rest of his plan would work, whatever it was.

Farther down the main artery of the tunnel system, Tom turned back around and unslung his AWM. He removed his pack, tossed it on the ground, and dropped prone beside it. He unfolded the rifle's attached bipod and took a moment to adjust his grip on the weapon. He put his right eye behind the scope but kept his left eye open, waiting for his target to reveal itself.

Making the shot he needed to make would not be easy in the dark. Easy or not, he would have to pull it off. Failure was not an option.

The rifle was zeroed to five hundred meters. He adjusted the scope's elevation turret to fifty meters, counting the clicks carefully. He rested his finger along the side of the trigger and waited.

Alex was having trouble making a mental map of the tunnels in her head while running for her life. She could do one or the other well enough, but doing both simultaneously was quite a bit more challenging. She went left, left again, straight, right, then left. Every few steps she turned back to fire at the snake. In the open, she never would have been able to outrun it, but it couldn't maneuver easily in the cramped catacombs. Bones flew in all directions every time the snake's massive body slammed into a wall or upended an ancient coffin.

She screamed in frustration when she turned another corner and found that she wasn't where she thought she should be. She was getting tired, and the Ouroboros was steadily gaining on her. She needed to buy time.

Alex holstered her sidearm and tossed a flashbang behind her. The concussion was deafening. Her ears rang painfully. She didn't stop to look back and see if the snake had been disoriented.

There, finally—an orange dot in the distance, Tom's torch. Alex dug deep for a final burst of stamina and sprinted toward it. Stone dust fell from the ceiling and made her cough as the Ouroboros crashed violently into walls behind her, struggling to reach its prey.

By the time she reached the torch on the ground, she was badly winded. She spun around, dropped her own torch, and raised her MPX.

The serpent was terrifyingly close. It opened its mouth, baring its swordlike fangs.

She depressed the trigger and held it, emptying an entire magazine of 9mm +P rounds into the creature's open maw.

As before, the snake thrashed and writhed in fury. For a brief instant, it halted its advance. It recovered quickly from the minor injuries, but for the span of a single heartbeat, its enormous head went still.

Tom held his breath and stroked the trigger. The immensely powerful . 338 Lapua round exploded from the rifle's barrel traveling faster than half a mile per second. The AWM kicked hard against his shoulder. The round struck true, directly in the center of the snake's right eye, delivering five thousand foot-pounds of energy—enough to carry it through four inches of concrete like a hot knife through butter.

The Ouroboros's furious bellow was drowned out by the astonishingly loud *crack* of the powerful rifle in the enclosed space. The snake rolled over onto its back, stunned by the concentrated violence of the attack, its liquefied right eye dribbling yellow fluid onto the stone.

Tom worked the bolt and lined up another shot on the left eye. He fired —and missed. Sparks flew as the heavy bullet shattered against the thick chains. He worked the bolt, fired again—missed again.

Stay cool, he thought to himself. He chambered another round. The snake's movements were sluggish and jerky, but it was already starting to recover. Tom inhaled, exhaled, and held his breath. He lay perfectly still and watched through the scope.

Don't rush the shot. Wait.

He waited.

There. He saw the eye in his scope, reflecting the flickering light of the torches as the snake began to rise again.

He fired.

The left eye exploded, spraying more pus and jelly in all directions. Again, the Ouroboros flopped to the ground, writhing weakly. Tom set aside the rifle, snatched up his pack, and sprinted toward the snake.

"What should I do?" Alex hollered.

"Get clear!" Tom yelled back. He was reaching into his backpack. Alex understood and backed away, down one of the side passages.

Tom skidded to a halt and fell to his knees beside the gargantuan head. He pulled two large blocks of Semtex from his pack, both already shaped and fitted with Nonel detonators. He forced the putty-like explosives under the chains covering the snake's body, directly against its glistening scales. It took a few seconds to smash most of the Semtex into the narrow gap.

The Ouroboros started moving more rapidly, pulling itself back to an upright position, ready to continue the chase despite its blindness.

"Too slow, asshole," Tom said. He ducked around the corner and depressed the detonator.

A catastrophic shockwave rocked the tunnels. Several smaller passages collapsed entirely. Tom wasted no time. He immediately returned to the snake and saw exactly what he'd been hoping to see. The focused explosion had dislodged the chains just behind the snake's head, and a heavily damaged section of its body was now exposed. The Ouroboros thrashed, but its movements were weak. Its forked tongue hung limply from the side of its mouth.

Tom pressed the attack. He raised his Jackhammer and emptied an entire magazine of slugs into the snake's damaged neck, blasting away more soft tissue in a cloud of gore. He reloaded and dumped another magazine into the same area. Patches of white bone were showing through. He loaded his last magazine of slugs and emptied it. Thirty-six 12-gauge slugs had almost decapitated the fearsome serpent.

For Tom, "almost" wasn't good enough.

He unslung his shotgun and tossed it aside. With a scream of primal rage, he seized the exposed spine in both hands, braced his right foot against the cave wall, and pulled with all his might.

The vertebra, already badly damaged, began to crack and splinter. The body spasmed and jerked, trying in vain to fight back. Veins bulged in Tom's neck and arms as he strained his muscles to their limit. The weakened spine cracked again, and again. Fist-sized scales sloughed away, tendons snapped, and muscle tissue tore.

With a final, furious roar, Tom ripped the head free. It rolled a few feet away as the body continued to twitch, more slowly now.

A moment later, it was done. The snake went still. The catacombs were silent except for Tom's labored breathing. His arms, chest, and face were covered in yellow blood, dislodged scales, and bits of wet tissue.

Alex came up beside him and picked up one of the torches. "Remind me never to piss you off," she said slowly.

"Only the wicked have anything to fear from me," Tom said.

The dead snake began to shimmer, as though it were a mirage. A moment later, the head and body both dissolved into white mist, which swirled and folded into the rest.

"And so another Eidolon dies," Alex said quietly.

"About damn time," Tom grunted.

She turned to face him. "How did you know what to do?"

Tom wiped a chunk of snake gore out of his eyes and flicked it aside. "Dylan."

"What about him?"

"He killed his Eidolon first. How did he do it?"

Alex thought back to what Dylan had said about how the Glutton was a physical manifestation of his self-doubt and self-pity. For the Glutton to die, Dylan had to first kill that part of himself. "His suffocating self-doubt was holding him back," Alex mused, beginning to understand.

"Just like the chains of duty were holding me back," Tom said, nodding. "I had to cast off the chains. My passive acceptance of obligations I never chose and never wanted made the Ouroboros invincible. My critical weakness became its armor."

"Cast off the chains," Alex repeated softly.

A tortured scream echoed through the catacombs. It was close—and familiar.

"Tell me that's not what I think it is," Tom said.

As if in answer to his challenge, the Prisoner shambled into the ring of torchlight.

Tom snatched up his Jackhammer and slammed in a fresh magazine of buckshot. He raised the weapon and lined up the front sight on the abomination's forehead. His finger found the trigger.

To his shock, Alex stepped directly in front of him, exposing her back to the Prisoner. "Alex, move!" he shouted.

She didn't move. She stared right at him. The Prisoner took another step toward her, scraping its bone blade along the ground.

"I trusted you," Alex said. "Do you trust me?"

"Alex, get out—"

She cut him off. "Do you trust me?" she asked again. The Prisoner took another step. It was almost within striking distance. Still, Alex didn't turn around.

Tom's instincts commanded him to fight. His mind commanded him to trust his friend.

He lowered the shotgun. Alex gave him a confident smile and turned around to face the Prisoner. She didn't raise her weapon. She didn't assume a defensive stance. She didn't move at all. She just stood there with her hands at her sides, letting it close on her.

The Prisoner let loose an ear-splitting wail and swung its weapon directly at Alex's neck. The strike was so fast and so powerful that the crude blade whistled through the air.

"Alex!" Tom shouted. He reached out a hand to help her. He could already tell that he would be far too slow.

The bone sword stopped an inch from Alex's throat, instantaneously, as though it had slammed into an invisible wall. She didn't even blink. She stared calmly into the Prisoner's empty eye sockets. It screamed again, pulled back the sword, and slashed once more. Again, the blade failed to make contact, halting in midair a hand's breadth from Alex's heart.

The twisted abomination leaned forward, its grotesque face nearly touching Alex's face. "Fiiiiiiggghhttt," it moaned. "Strrruuuggggglllleee."

Tom was shocked. He hadn't thought it could speak.

"No," Alex said.

The Prisoner flew into a blind rage. It slashed over and over and over, trying to cut Alex into pieces. Each time, the blade failed to make contact. Its bloodcurdling screams made Tom wince.

Alex just stood there, watching, waiting. The Prisoner fell to its knees, still trying to attack her, but more slowly, as though it were getting tired. Its hateful screams became quieter and less shrill.

It fell onto its side and curled into a fetal position. The dry, mummified skin began to crack. The stringy black hair receded into the deformed skull and disappeared. Chunks of skin fell away, revealing a twisted skeleton. Dimly, Tom recalled a documentary he'd seen that had shown time-lapse footage of a dead deer decomposing.

With a final, ghostlike sigh, the Prisoner's bones collapsed into mist, along with its cursed blade. Alex turned back to Tom, a peaceful smile on her face.

He crossed his arms. "Let's catch up with Dylan. You can explain how that worked on the way," he said.

Tom started to run, and Alex fell in beside him. "I used to think heroin was a hell of a drug," she said. "It is—don't get me wrong. But guilt— that's the worst drug of all. Some of us get addicted to it—we get addicted to punishing ourselves. We tell ourselves that we have to seek redemption, we have to do penance, we have to atone. But then you start to think: If I atone, if I forgive myself and start enjoying my life again, that means I'm not really sorry for what I did. I have to suffer forever to prove my sincerity.

"Ever since I killed that woman, I've been punishing myself for it. But guilt is a hungry monster. If you feed it, it just gets bigger and hungrier. There's no end to it. Eventually, the only thing left for it to eat is you."

"So, the solution is to stop feeding the guilt, stop fighting it," Tom said. He was beginning to understand. He paused at a junction to see which way the mist was coming from, then followed it. "If you wrong someone, do your best to make amends. It's natural and normal to feel guilty for a while, but you can't become a prisoner to your own guilt, serving a self-inflicted life sentence."

Alex nodded. "And if you *haven't* wronged someone, then guilt has no place in your heart. As poisonous as earned guilt can be to your soul, unearned guilt is infinitely worse. I felt guilty when I couldn't save Daniela. I felt guilty when I couldn't save you from the snake venom. I felt guilty when Dylan got injured because I thought it should have been me instead. I felt guilty when Roland was killed because I convinced him to guide us, to expose himself to danger. But I had nothing to feel guilty about—except when I lied to Dylan about his injury. He had a right to know what was happening to him; I had no right to keep him in the dark.

"In those other cases, I should have felt *shitty*, yes, because good people were getting hurt, and I couldn't protect them. But feeling shitty when bad things happen to good people isn't the same thing as feeling guilty for crimes you didn't commit. I didn't start any of this. I didn't send anyone here, to this blood-soaked horror show. I didn't decide to sacrifice innocent girls. The blame for all this pain and evil—every last shred of it—is on the people who kept the cycle of death going for five thousand years. I won't be one of them."

"Speaking of guilt, I owe you an apology," Tom said.

"For what?"

"Do you remember what I said to you on the first day, to convince you to sign up for this madness?"

She thought for a moment. "You said that I could back out, but if I did, I would pass this burden on to some other girl and the people she'd drafted to protect her. You asked if I could live with that, and you knew I couldn't." Alex paused again. "You guilt tripped me."

"I'm sorry. That was a shitty thing to do." They slowed to a halt in front of the door leading to the cathedral's basement. "Forgive me?"

She smiled at him. "Done. Just give me your word you won't do it again."

"Done. Now, let's shut down the nightmare machine—together." He held out his hand, and Alex grasped it firmly.

"Together," she said.

* * *

Dylan closed the iron gate behind him and latched it. He was badly winded from running up so many stairs. The unnerving heartbeat was louder than ever.

DA-THUM. DA-THUM. DA-THUM.

He looked around. There was no sign that Sara had been here yet. The top floor of the cathedral—the room that couldn't exist—was just as they'd left it eighteen hours earlier. The mosaic tile floor had many new holes in it, but there was still enough solid ground to walk on. Fifty paces away, the mausoleum door stood open a few inches. Dim, reddish light shone from within.

As he watched, the heavy stone door began to move, scraping along the tile. A pulsating, tendril-like vein snaked through the opening, then several more. One by one, they wrapped themselves around the mausoleum door, dragging it open. Dylan gasped and ducked behind a nearby barrel. He knew he should stay hidden, but he couldn't resist the temptation to peek out.

When he saw what was coming out of the mausoleum, he slapped both hands over his mouth, afraid that he might involuntarily cry out in terror.

At first, he thought it was a giant spider because of all the legs. But they weren't legs—they were more of those fleshy veins that rapidly swelled and deflated as blood flowed through them. Each moved independently but in coordination with the others. Each was connected to a woman's body, and together, they held her suspended several feet above the floor.

She was heavily pregnant, seemingly ready to give birth at any moment. Her arms and legs hung limply, as though they were vestigial limbs long supplanted by the prehensile veins. She wore a tattered full-length dress that appeared brown, but when Dylan looked more closely, he realized that it had been white once upon a time and was now covered in dried blood. A bloodstained habit covered her hair, and an ivory mask etched with arcane symbols hid her face.

That must be Anna, the Matron, Dylan thought. Sara had mentioned her earlier. His heart broke for her. He couldn't begin to fathom the agony this woman had endured for years, with a hateful god growing inside her. Undoubtedly, the unborn Ardu was largely or completely controlling her movement.

A thought came to him. He suddenly knew what the significance of the mask was: to erase her individuality. The entire point of the Pilgrimage was to further reinforce the already widespread idea that an individual's wants and needs—even her very life—were subordinate to those of "the group," whoever or whatever that may be.

The more he thought about it, the more the notion sickened him. He wouldn't let Sara sacrifice herself on the altar of such vile ideals.

Once the pitiable creature was in the open, the infernal heartbeat rose in volume, nearly deafening. Dylan could feel the floor vibrating in time with each contraction.

DA-THUM. DA-THUM. DA-THUM.

In between heartbeats, he heard wood creaking—footsteps on the stairs, on the other side of the gate.

Sara was coming.

Dylan shifted his position behind the barrel so that he would be hidden from both Sara and the Matron. Quietly, he retracted the bolt on his UMP and verified that there was a round in the chamber.

In a burst of panic, he realized that he didn't know exactly what he was going to do. Should he tackle Sara as soon as she opened the gate and try to drag her back down the stairs? That seemed dangerous in the extreme. Undoubtedly, Anna, the person, was long gone, driven beyond madness by the evil gestating inside her. He had no idea what the unholy fusion of Ardu and Anna was capable of. It might kill them both in the blink of an eye, especially if Sara put up a fight when Dylan tried to drag her away, which she surely would.

The gate creaked open. *Shit*, he thought. He had hoped that Alex and Tom would have caught up by now; he would feel a lot better with their support. He hoped that they were okay and that they would arrive soon. The three of them had come up with a plan to stop Ardu, but it wouldn't work unless Sara could be convinced to cooperate. For now, he would have to stay hidden and wait for an opening.

Sara came through the gate and strode confidently across the broken floor. Dylan closed his eyes and shook his head when he saw her fresh cuts and bruises. She didn't flinch or recoil at the sight of the monstrosity that awaited her. She walked toward it resolutely, purposefully, her head held high.

She halted ten paces away and waited. The pounding heartbeat became quieter. The corrupted Matron emitted a series of rasping coughs. It took Dylan a moment to realize that it was speaking. He was hearing what must have been Ardu's voice coming from Anna's mouth, in a deep, quavering register.

"wHerE aRe youR WarDens?"

"Not here. I couldn't trust them. I came alone," Sara said. Her voice was clear and steady.

"tHEiR ActiONs, tAnTAMounT tO BlASpheMY."

"That's why I came back without them. I didn't know they would interrupt the ritual."

"yoU aRe READy To COMpLetE thE sACRIfiCE?"

"I am. But I have a condition."

Dylan tightened his grip on his UMP and flicked off the safety.

"MaIDenS DO NOT neGotiATe."

"This one does. If you want my life, you'll offer me a small concession in return. It's easily within your power."

Quick as lightning, the Matron lashed out with a fleshy, tendril-like vein. It smashed through the mausoleum with a thunderous *boom*. Chunks of white stone flew everywhere. The entire top third of the structure had been demolished.

"SPEak."

"The current Matron—the one whose body you're in now. Release her. Heal her body and her mind. Let her leave the Twilight and go home."

Dylan frowned. He wasn't sure he'd heard correctly.

"DeNIeD."

Sara crossed her arms and stood her ground. "Then you get nothing from me."

Again, the Matron slammed a thick vein through the remains of the mausoleum, sending more stone projectiles spinning in all directions.

Dylan's eyes widened when he saw a fifty-pound rock hurtling directly toward him. He reacted on instinct. He dived to the side, out of his hiding place. A heartbeat later, the stone missile smashed into the barrel, reducing it to splinters.

The Matron's eerie mask was looking right at him.

The creature screamed, an unearthly, feral vow of rage and hate. Before Dylan could even try to get up, it lashed out with an impossibly long vein. The pulsing appendage ripped through the air so fast that it cracked like a whip. Dylan cried out as it wrapped around his chest and yanked him forward, pinning his arms to his sides. The Matron pulled again, drawing him closer, bringing him between itself and Sara.

All the color drained from her face when she saw him.

"LIES. YOu bRiNG tHe SaME treACHerOuS wArdEN. yoU wILL cOMpLETe tHE SACRifiCe nOw, oR tHIS oNe wIll sCReAm foR CeNTurIEs."

The bloody vein was squeezing Dylan so tightly that he couldn't speak. He could hardly breathe. He fought with all his strength, trying to slip free. It was no use.

At the sight of Dylan in mortal danger, Sara's adrenal gland kicked into overdrive, flooding her body with a nearly superhuman surge of adrenaline. Time slowed to a crawl in her eyes. She could see individual drops of sweat on Dylan's forehead. She felt as though she could count the hairs on his head. She saw the veins in his neck pulsing in slow motion, in time with his heartbeat.

Every moment of the previous seven days flashed through her mind. Most of the memories rushed by in an incomprehensible blur that left only vague impressions of emotions. A few stood out with crystal clarity.

She recalled what Tom had said about sacrifice, that it was a net loss—the surrender of something precious in exchange for something worth less, or nothing at all. He'd said that to accept a duty—an unchosen obligation—was to surrender one's judgment of right and wrong to the judgment of others. He'd said that to accept a duty like the Pilgrimage was to eagerly desecrate one's soul in service to an endless cycle of death.

She recalled what Alex had said about unearned guilt, that to lock oneself in a prison of eternal penance for one's own crimes was to abdicate the future—but to accept responsibility for evil done by others was the ultimate betrayal of everything that made life worth living. She'd said that the blame for this waking nightmare rested solely on the shoulders of everyone who embraced the notion that a group's wants or needs outweighed an individual's right to his own life—and that Sara would join the ranks of the guilty if she willingly threw herself upon a sacrificial altar.

She recalled what Dylan had said, that she didn't have to believe that there was no other path merely because others said so. He'd said that to blindly trust their judgment over her own was to doubt the efficacy of her own mind and to concede that her life was not hers to live but theirs to dispose of. He'd said that the antidote to self-doubt was not obedience but courage—the courage to rebel, to forge a new path when the well-traveled road led only to the lowest circle of hell.

He'd said that he loved her and that he wanted to be worthy of her love—for his own sake and happiness, not only for hers.

To let him die now or to break his mind and spirit forever by forcing him to watch her give up her own life.... Wouldn't either choice be a complete and total surrender of good to evil?

Sara closed her eyes and made an effort to slow her breathing. "I'm ready," she whispered.

The Matron drew closer. *"yOU hAvE chOSeN WIseIY."*

She opened her eyes. "You're goddamn right I have."

Sara drew her Operator and shot the Matron in the face.

The ivory mask shattered. Razor-sharp pieces spun away into the night, along with thick strings of dark-red blood. The Matron's howl of malicious contempt shook the cathedral's very foundation. The loathsome veins contracted, then relaxed as the ungainly creature staggered to one side. Dylan screamed as he fell to the floor, landed hard on his back—and rolled over the edge of the broken tile into open space.

Sara dived toward him. She landed on her stomach and slid a few feet, both hands outstretched, flailing wildly for his arm, shirt, pack—anything to grab onto.

Her momentum carried her to the edge of the broken floor, and she nearly went over as well. The crushing vise of fear around her heart relaxed when she saw Dylan hanging by one hand, then tightened again when she saw the ground a hundred meters below. Closer to the entrance to this room, other rooftops were below the floor, but not here.

Sara grabbed Dylan's forearm. "I've got you," she said.

Dylan tried to pull himself up. Sara pulled with all her might, but even together, they weren't strong enough. His armor alone weighed twenty pounds, not to mention all his other gear. They were both losing stamina rapidly.

"Dylan, you're too heavy," Sara panted. He was trying to remove his armor with his free hand, to make himself lighter, but it was no use. He needed both hands to take it off.

His right hand, the hand that Sara was holding onto, slipped a little. She screamed and tightened her grip.

"Sara...," Dylan said. He was looking up at her, directly into her eyes. "You have to let go."

"Like hell I do," she growled.

Dylan closed his eyes briefly. "I'm already dead. There's no way I'm taking you with me."

"Shut up, Dylan."

He shook his head. His hand slipped a little more. "You have to let go." His voice was calm and steady.

"Never," she said. "I love you—I have for years. I'm sorry I was too stupid to say it. If we die, we die together, but I'll be fucked if I'll let go of you now."

Dylan's eyes widened in shock. "Sara!"

She risked a glance back. Her breath caught in her throat. The Matron's face, smeared with dark blood, loomed inches away.

"ALL oF maNkInD wILL BeAR thE cOST oF YouR hUBrIs."

The pulsing veins contracted, preparing to strike. Sara screamed.

"Sara, let go! Get out of here!" Dylan shouted.

"No!" she yelled back.

Sara felt hot gore splash her face. A deep *boom* and a loud *crack* came with it. The Matron shrieked and fell back, its cursed veins thrashing the air. Reddish-black blood pumped from a ragged, gaping hole in Anna's chest. The Matron thrashed in impotent rage, then fell still.

Tom fired his Magnum four more times, emptying the cylinder into the body that had belonged to Anna. Alex rushed forward and knelt beside Sara. Together, they hauled Dylan back up. He collapsed onto his back, panting. Sara lay beside him, equally out of breath.

Tom leaned over her. "Are you done being a fucking idiot?"

She nodded. "I am."

"Good." He held out his hand. She took it, and he pulled her to her feet. Alex helped Dylan stand. Sara threw her arms around him with tears in her eyes. He returned the embrace.

The Matron twitched. One of the veins curled, then uncurled. A low, guttural moan echoed in the creature's throat.

Tom flicked open the Magnum's cylinder and dumped the smoking casings. "Alright, Sara. What do we do now? You're the plan maker, right? The one in charge? What's the play?"

She gave Dylan a small, private smile as she gently pushed him away. Turning to face the wounded Matron, she removed the magazine from her rifle, verified that it was full, then replaced it. She flicked the selector switch to full auto. "Now we break the cycle," she said.

Alex gave her a sidelong glance. "And how do you intend to do that?"

The Matron began to pull itself up. The blood pumping from Anna's chest slowed to a trickle, then stopped. The gaping wounds rapidly stitched themselves shut.

Sara glanced at her watch. "We still have twelve hours until the deadline —twelve hours until Ardu becomes invincible, leaves the Twilight, and lays waste to Earth."

Tom loaded five new Magnum rounds and snapped the cylinder closed. "Sounds to me like you're saying that for the next eleven hours and change, he's decidedly fucking *vincible*."

"That sounds like plenty of time to me," Alex said. She press-checked her MPX and flicked off the safety.

"Tom and I had the same thought last night," Dylan said. He raised his UMP and rested it on his shoulder. "I'm glad we're all on the same page now."

The Matron towered over them, Anna's limp body borne helplessly aloft by the throbbing veins. *"inSECts. MAN'S FATE iS sEAlEd. tHE deATh wARRaNt oF EVERY wReTCHEd SOuL is SiGNeD iN tHe ink oF YouR aRRoGanCE."*

"Shove your death warrant up your ass," Sara said. "You can't imagine what we've been through together, all the impossible odds we've already overcome—by working together and, more importantly, by thinking for ourselves. You're the same kind of cockroach we've been squashing all week, just bigger. The only difference between them and you is that it'll take a little longer to scrape you off my shoes."

The Matron raised its lashing veins and slammed them down, smashing more holes in the tile. Its piercing wail crescendoed into a deep, rumbling battle cry.

"No turning back now," Dylan said.

Sara grinned. "Good. I'm done looking back. Starting now, we go forward."

CHAPTER FORTY
Resolve

Sara ducked, narrowly dodging a vicious swing, then rolled to the side to avoid a second attack. Tom and Alex opened up on full auto, hammering the Matron with a relentless hail of lead. Bullets and buckshot tore away great chunks of flesh and drove it back several feet. In response to the assault, thick layers of scarred flesh erupted from Anna's back, quickly wrapping her entire body in a protective cocoon.

Dylan emptied the MGL, briefly pausing between each shot to adjust his aim. The first two grenades missed, sailing out into empty space to detonate harmlessly on the ground far below, but the other four hit center mass, shredding away the fleshy armor in a cloud of reddish-black gore. The cocoon instantly regenerated. The Matron lunged forward, knocking Tom to the ground as it went for Dylan. It wrapped two veins around him and pulled hard in opposite directions. Dylan cried out in pain, but Alex and Sara were nearby and ready. Sara drew her knife and slashed twice, severing one of the veins in a pressurized burst of dark blood. A second later, Alex followed suit, and Dylan was free. He shook off the severed veins and retreated to reload the grenade launcher.

Tom, now behind the Matron, rolled into a kneeling position and rapid-fired five incendiary shells into the creature's body. As the abomination burned and shrieked, he dropped the empty mag from his Jackhammer and slapped in a fresh one. In response to the attack, the Matron whipped a vein toward Tom, wrapping it around his shotgun. It pulled hard, trying to yank away the weapon. Tom, still attached to it by a sling, was jerked forward several steps. He pulled his knife and severed the vein, reclaiming his weapon. He darted left, jumped over a hole in the floor, and sprinted away, gaining some distance before thumbing more incendiary shells into the Jackhammer's magazine tube.

The Matron reached toward the moon and shrieked into the night air. A moment later, far below, hundreds of lesser monsters answered.

"She's calling for backup!" Sara yelled. She shouldered her rifle and dumped thirty rounds of powerful 6.8mm hollow points into the Matron's body, trying to interrupt the cry for aid.

"Dylan! Go block the stairs!" Tom yelled in between volleys of slugs.

"On it!" he shouted back. Dylan took off toward the gate. By the time he reached the top of the rickety wooden staircase, the first wave of the horde was nearly there. The stairs groaned and rocked violently under so much weight, ready to collapse at any moment. Dylan couldn't understand how they hadn't already.

"Stairs closed for maintenance," he muttered to himself. He aimed and fired two grenades, blasting the landing below into flying splinters. Several monsters caught in the explosion were reduced to gory mist, and several more tumbled into open space, screeching as they fell. He ducked for cover behind the open gate, narrowly dodging a flying spear of wood.

The living tree creatures near the front of the pack tried to jump across the gap in the stairs, but they were far too heavy. They missed by a wide margin and hurtled back to the ground. The Cutters, though, were more agile. Some cleared the gap and charged straight for Dylan. He snapped his UMP to his shoulder and fired several long bursts, cutting them down one by one. When his sub-gun ran dry, he let it drop and drew his sidearm, taking slow, deliberate shots as Tom had shown him. Four more Cutters dropped.

The slide on his USP locked back empty, but there was a small break in the assault wave, at least. He would have to be quick to take advantage of it. He reloaded his USP, holstered it, and took up the MGL again.

When in doubt, use excessive force, Tom said in his head.

Dylan fired all four of the remaining grenades at the already damaged staircase below, demolishing another twenty-foot section and another dozen monsters. Those behind roared in impotent fury, unable to reach their prey. "Let's see you jump that!" He pumped his fist in the air, pleased with his victory.

As if in answer to his challenge, something large and black rose up from below, directly in front of him, large wings beating powerfully. Bright yellow, predatory eyes glared at him. Thick saliva dripped in long ribbons from a canine maw.

"Ah, shit," Dylan said. The silhouetted creatures they'd seen clinging to the outside of the cathedral earlier.

He'd forgotten about those.

The wolf-gargoyle dived toward him, claws outstretched. Dylan flung himself to the right and rolled to his feet. The creature doubled back with unbelievable speed and seized him by the shoulders, razor-sharp claws biting deep into his flesh. He screamed in pain as he felt himself being lifted off the ground. It carried him through the gate, back toward the Matron, gaining height as it went.

Tom, Sara, and Alex were busy dumping rounds into the Matron and dodging its vicious attacks; they hadn't seen him yet. Dylan's heart dropped when he realized where the gargoyle-thing was taking him—past the boundary of the upper floor, into open air. It could kill him just by dropping him or cart him off somewhere else to dine on his flesh at its leisure.

He had to make it let go.

His UMP was empty, and he couldn't reach his sidearm—but he could reach his knife. He snatched it from its sheath, and with a furious yell, hacked violently at the backs of the creature's arms. It shrieked in pain and dropped him. He hit the tile floor dangerously close to a large hole and rolled away, spraining an ankle in the process. Tom saw the wounded wolf-gargoyle, took careful aim, and blasted it out of the sky with three well-placed slugs.

Thirty paces away, Alex was pelting the Matron with long bursts from her MPX while Sara rolled a grenade under the mass of scarred flesh in the center of the lashing veins. When the grenade detonated, it took a large chunk of the damaged floor with it and knocked the Matron off balance. Sara immediately followed up with another grenade, with similar results.

"Alex! Sara!" Tom shouted. While the Matron was recovering, they risked a glance at where Tom was pointing—another half dozen gargoyles were coming, streaking out of the sky like black comets. Sara and Alex turned their attention to the new threats while Tom and Dylan moved in on the Matron.

Tom pressed the advantage that Sara had created, dumping round after round of buckshot into Ardu's host. Dylan loaded a new 25-round stick mag into his UMP, slapped the charging handle to release the bolt, and shouldered the weapon, preparing to fire. He stopped with his finger on the trigger. The floor underneath the Matron's spiderlike body was badly damaged. Smaller pieces of tile and masonry were still breaking off and falling away.

An idea came to him. "Tom! Keep it busy!" he yelled. Dylan dropped his UMP onto its sling and took up the MGL, opened the cylinder, and started removing the empty 40mm casings. He'd only loaded two rounds when Tom's shotgun ran empty. The Matron immediately began to advance on him, its fresh wounds already healing.

Two rounds would have to do.

"Tom! Get clear!"

Tom glanced at Dylan, saw him brandishing the grenade launcher, and broke into a sprint without hesitation. Dylan waited as long as he dared, letting Tom get as far away as possible before he fired. He could hear the sharp *cracks* of Sara's rifle and Alex's submachine gun behind him. He would have to trust that they had the gargoyle-things under control for the moment.

He couldn't wait any longer—the Matron was moving away from the broken edge of the floor. He fired both rounds in quick succession. The dual explosions obliterated the floor underneath the creature, sending sharp bits of tile rocketing away in all directions. Dylan cried out in pain when one hit him in the neck, leaving a deep cut.

When the dust began to settle, the Matron was nowhere to be seen. Cautiously, Dylan took a few steps forward. Tom fell into step beside him, his shotgun ready. Looking over the edge, they saw the roof of the bell tower that Tom and Sara had fallen onto earlier. It wasn't far below, maybe fifteen feet at most. At the closer end of the roof, a short, pointed spire rose skyward.

The Matron was clinging to the broken edge of the floor, pulling itself back up. It shrieked hatefully at them.

The pointed spire was almost directly under it.

Tom and Dylan looked at one another, an unspoken agreement passing between them. Together, they charged forward. Tom dropped his Jackhammer onto its sling and grabbed one of the long veins in both hands. On the creature's other side, Dylan did the same. Each of them took a deep breath—and jumped.

The Matron was freakishly strong, but its grip on the broken floor was tenuous. It wailed in fury, trying to pull itself back up to the top floor. Tom landed on his feet, on the lower roof's flat peak, just to the left of the spire. At the same time, Dylan landed on the right side. The impacts were jarring and painful, forcing them to roll awkwardly as their momentum carried them forward, but they held fast to their respective veins. If either of them let go, the abomination would turn its attention to Alex and Sara, leaving Tom and Dylan stranded below and powerless to help them.

In unison, they turned around and began pulling on the veins with all their combined strength. The Matron was still holding on to the broken floor above with three of its other veins. It added a fourth, then a fifth, reinforcing its grip. Tom and Dylan were shocked at how strong it was. They were being dragged along the roof, toward the edge, where the drop was eighty meters or farther to the ground.

Above, Alex and Sara combined their firepower, focusing on the last gargoyle. It was fast and agile, twisting back and forth in random patterns as it flew toward them, making it exceedingly difficult to hit. The bolt on Alex's MPX locked back. "Empty!" she shouted.

"Me, too!" Sara replied.

The gargoyle folded its wings and plummeted toward Alex, picking up an amazing amount of speed. It hit her like a cannonball before she could draw her sidearm. Both went tumbling across the damaged floor, coming to a halt barely a foot from a large hole. Alex was on her stomach, with the beast straddling her back. It was so heavy. She couldn't flip over, couldn't draw a full breath. She couldn't reach any of her weapons. The gargoyle reached its clawed hands toward her neck. It knew where the vulnerable arteries were.

Sara pressed the barrel of her Operator against the side of the beast's lupine head and squeezed the trigger. Bits of bone and dark green blood sprayed from the opposite side of its head as the powerful .45 slug tunneled through its skull.

"Dodge that," Sara muttered. She kicked the corpse aside and helped Alex get to her feet.

"Thanks," Alex panted. "I think the boys need help." She pointed with a trembling finger.

She was right. The Matron had nearly pulled itself back up to the top floor. Two of its elongated veins were stretched taut, extending downward, toward the roof of the bell tower below. Tom and Dylan must have been trying to pull the creature down, but they weren't strong enough.

Sara and Alex reloaded their primary weapons, empty magazines clattering to the floor. Both opened up on full auto as they walked toward their target. Small bits of rotten flesh tore away in bursts of dark blood, but new scar tissue covered the wounds immediately.

"Aim for the veins!" Alex shouted. She pulled her last MPX magazine from her vest and slapped it in. Sara, also on her last magazine, reloaded as well. They shifted their aim down and continued to fire in long bursts, shredding the veins that were gripping the floor. The bullets raked long trenches in the surrounding tile. Several more veins were severed by the relentless hail of lead, but two remained when Alex and Sara ran out of ammo.

Below, Tom and Dylan were nearing exhaustion—and the edge of the roof. Suddenly, they felt the force pulling against them lessen a bit. Looking up, they saw that Sara and Alex had blasted off several of the Matron's veins, weakening its hold on the floor. Tom and Dylan redoubled their efforts, pulling back with all their dwindling strength. Slowly, they regained some of the ground they'd lost, an inch at a time.

Sara and Alex saw the pointed spire below and understood the plan. They both drew their knives and went to work on the two remaining veins. The Matron roared and thrashed, enraged that it had no way to attack its targets. Sara's knife cut through the last bit of tough flesh connecting the vein to Anna's cocooned body. A moment later, Alex finished her task as well.

Tom and Dylan suddenly lurched backward, all resistance gone. Above, the monstrous body began to fall toward them. In unison, they pulled as hard as they could, screaming twin battle cries.

The mass of flesh enveloping Anna slammed directly onto the spire. The pointed peak impaled the creature's core and erupted out the other side in a geyser of dark fluid. The Matron's bellow of pain and fury rattled the brass bell, causing it to vibrate strongly enough to emit a deep, eerie tone. Tom, Dylan, Alex, and Sara all screamed and clapped their hands over their ears, so painful was the sound.

Sara and Alex felt the floor lurch beneath their feet. Small chunks of tile near the edge began to fall away, then bigger ones. They looked back toward the gate. Existing holes in the floor were getting larger. The top floor rumbled again, more violently this time. It had sustained too much damage; it was coming down.

"Time to go," Alex said. She and Sara leaped down to the roof below. It was a long drop, far enough to break bones if they landed badly, but the prospect of falling twenty times farther was a powerful motivator.

They crashed to the rooftop on the left side of the spire, near Tom. Alex cried out in pain. Tom rushed over to help her while Dylan checked on Sara.

"You good? Anything broken?" Tom said.

Alex gingerly flexed her ankle. "No, I don't think so. It hurts, but I'll be alright."

The Matron, terribly wounded, used its remaining veins to drag itself up and over the spire. Its fleshy bulk tumbled to one side, onto the flat peak of the bell tower roof. Ragged, inhuman snarls and gasps came from Anna's mouth, somewhere inside the central mass. Already, the grievous wound was closing, but it seemed to be healing more slowly than previous injuries had. One vein regenerated in a burst of blood. The others didn't.

"What the hell is that?" Dylan said. He was pointing to the top of the spire, where a small, pulsing mass of bright red flesh was still impaled.

"Are those... arms and legs?" Tom said.

"Holy shit, it's a... *fetus*," Alex said, her eyes wide with shock.

"Ardu," Sara growled.

"Let's finish it," Tom said. He raised his shotgun and took aim.

With surprising speed, the fetus ripped itself away from the spire. Tom fired two quick shots but missed. The aborted god rolled down the spire, bouncing with wet *slaps*. All four of them opened fire, but the target was small, and it was moving erratically. None of the shots made contact.

The infant Ardu rolled off the roof and plummeted toward the ground, far below.

"Will that fall finish him off?" Tom asked.

Sara shook her head. "I doubt it. Like I said at the beginning of the Pilgrimage, Ardu has been born a few times when Maidens failed to reach the cathedral in time. Once he's born, he grows very quickly. He'll attain a mature adult form at midnight on the eighth day. When that happens, he'll be completely indestructible, and he'll be able to kill people by the tens of thousands—hundreds of thousands."

"If he gets to our world, which he won't," Tom said.

"We need to find him and finish him off," Alex agreed.

"We will, but don't underestimate him. Even as a toddler or child, he'll be tougher and more dangerous by far than anything we've seen," Sara said.

"Guys... come here," Dylan said softly. He was several paces away, looking at the withering mass of flesh that Ardu had been controlling from within. It was still writhing, but its movements were growing slower and weaker. As they watched, the cocoon of tissue began to slough away, in small pieces at first, then in large chunks. Each piece of flesh dissolved into whitish-brown liquid as it fell away from the main body, then dissipated into mist.

The last of the scar tissue was gone. A naked woman lay on her side, turned away from them. Her blonde hair was matted with blood and dirt. Her body was covered in dark bruises and deep cuts.

"She's breathing," Alex said, rushing to the woman's side. "She's still alive. Dylan, come help me." Dylan obediently approached and knelt next to Alex, ready to offer whatever help he could. He couldn't begin to imagine what this poor woman had endured these past sixteen years.

Gently, Alex rolled the woman onto her back. When Dylan saw her face, his heart stopped.

* * *

"Mom?" Dylan said. His voice was so choked with shock and disbelief that the word came out a strangled whisper.

"What?" Tom said.

Alex furrowed her brow in confusion. She looked at Dylan's face, then back to the woman's. Comprehension flashed in her eyes. "It can't be...."

Sara knelt beside Dylan and put a hand gently on his back. "Dylan... I'm sorry," she said.

Dylan took Marie's hand in his. "Mom... is it really you?" Tears streamed freely from his eyes.

Marie smiled up at him, weakly. She could hardly keep her eyes open. "Dylan, it's me," she said. "I'm here." With great effort, she raised her other hand to touch his face.

"But how?" Dylan stammered. Alex pulled a thin blanket from her bag and draped it over Marie, for light warmth and modesty. She set about assessing Marie's injuries, trying to stay out of the way as much as possible.

Marie coughed violently. Blood trickled from her mouth. With a trembling hand, she wiped it away. "Dylan," she said, after she'd recovered her breath. "I love you so much. I hoped you would never come here, to this awful place. But... you did it. I'm so proud of you."

"Did what? What did I do?"

"You broke the cycle."

Dylan nodded. Hard resolve burned in his blue eyes, even as tears ran from them. "Not yet. But I will."

Marie turned her head, looking at Sara, Tom, and Alex. "Thank you... all of you. For protecting my son and helping him." She lifted a trembling hand toward Sara. "Who's this?"

Sara took Marie's hand gently. "My name is Sara Holcomb," she said. "Ex-Maiden. This is Alex, and that's Tom, my Wardens—we're all Wardens now, true Wardens, protectors of humanity instead of its destroyers. Dylan is incredible. I was blindly following the path, like all the rest, but he helped me see. He helped me understand."

Marie closed her eyes and nodded. A single tear escaped and trickled down her cheek. "Sara Holcomb... Ethan's little girl."

"Mom, hang on," Dylan said. "Alex is a doctor. She can help." He looked up at Alex hopefully.

"Dylan, I...." Alex trailed off.

"You can help her," Dylan said. His lower lip trembled. "You can fix her." It was a statement, not a question.

Alex laid a hand on Dylan's forearm. "Dylan, honey... I'm sorry. There's nothing I can do." Now she, too, was crying. Tom watched and listened from a respectful distance.

Marie coughed again. More blood came up. "Richard.... How is Richard?"

Dylan squeezed her hand tightly in both of his. "He's alright, Mom. He never stopped looking for you. He loves you and misses you so much. I'll take care of him, I promise."

"Dylan...." Marie's voice trailed off. Gently, she pulled her left hand free of his. With her right, she removed her wedding ring and pressed it into his hand. She looked like she wanted to say something else, but she was having great difficulty speaking.

He closed his fingers around the ring. "Mom, I love you. I missed you so much."

Marie smiled up at him. She could barely keep her eyes open. "I love you, too, kiddo. Finish it. Break the cycle. Sara, Alex, Tom... help my son. Look out for him and be good to him."

"We will," Sara said. She was trying to be strong for Dylan, but she could no longer hold back her tears.

"Always," Alex agreed.

"On my word," Tom said with a solemn nod.

Marie's eyes were fully closed now. She gripped Dylan's hand tightly and sang to him, so softly that none of the others could hear.

Slumber time is drawing near,
Night is gath'ring round us.
Stars will all be bright and clear,
When the sandman has found us.
Dream sweet dreams the long night through,
Mother will be near to you.
Go to sleep, my dear one.

"Mom... hold on," Dylan whispered. "Hold on."

Marie didn't answer. Her chest was still. Her hand went limp in his.

Dylan collapsed on top of her, sobbing.

CHAPTER FORTY-ONE
Evolution

A steady rain had begun to fall—or rather, to rise from the ground into the sky, as it had the first time they'd entered the Twilight, nearly seven days earlier. Sara, Dylan, Alex, and Tom stood at the edge of the cherry tree field, watching a gigantic plume of dust rise high into the air. After Marie died, her body had dissipated into mist, and a few minutes later, the cathedral and the Vile Abbey had begun to collapse. Their escape through the catacombs had been harrowing as they'd dodged falling stones the size of cars, but only a few monsters had chased them. The rest had been crushed.

It seemed that the temple of sacrifice could no longer stand with Ardu and the Matron both gone.

"Sara," Dylan said. His voice was hard and low. He turned to face her. "Did you know?"

She heaved a deep sigh. "At first, no. I swear on my life, and for the first time, I actually value my life enough to swear by it. I really did think the Matron was Anna Foss. That's what my father told me, and she's listed as the current Matron in the Circle archives—or at least, in the records we have at my house. It's pretty obvious now that our copies have been altered."

"You said, 'at first.' When did you find out?"

"Last night, when I escaped from the cabin. I took your backpack and found the photo album inside. That's when I recognized Marie. I'd seen her face for the first time earlier that day, when I nearly completed the final ritual."

Alex frowned at Sara. "You'd never seen pictures of Dylan's mom before?"

Dylan shook his head. "No, she hadn't. I was... very private about the photos and home movies. I didn't want to share her with anyone else, except my dad."

Tom nodded. "I guess I can understand that."

Dylan took Sara's hand and gently squeezed it. "I understand what your plan was now. When I overheard you talking to Ardu, when he was controlling my mom's body...." He stopped and closed his eyes, taking a moment to compose himself. When he was ready, he went on. "You said you would complete the ritual and sacrifice yourself, but only if Ardu healed the Matron and sent her home. You had just found out that the Matron was Marie, not Anna. You were trying to give my mom back to me before you... died."

Sara nodded. A tear ran down her face, mixing with the rain. "But then, when I saw you in danger, when I thought Ardu was going to kill you... that's when I finally, fully saw the truth. In the back of my mind, I'd always known that I would be... leaving you behind. But I thought there was no other way. I thought that as long as you got to go home and you had your mom back, everything would be okay. I rationalized my decision by convincing myself that I was committing suicide for your benefit—saving the rest of the world was just a bonus. If one of us had to die, I wanted it to be me, not you.

"But then, when Ardu grabbed you, everything I'd been ignoring and evading was suddenly right in my face. I couldn't deny it any longer. All along I'd been telling myself that the end of this journey was written in stone, unchangeable and unavoidable. I told myself that accepting my death was the courageous thing to do, but in reality it was the ultimate act of cowardice. I finally realized, in that moment, that neither one of us had to die. All my life, I'd been fed a false alternative, and I bought it. I chose to believe that there was no other path because I was too much of a coward to make one. But I found my courage—because of you, Dylan. For the first time in my life, I knew what I wanted, and more importantly, I knew that I had a *right* to want things, a right to live my own life. I want to be with you, and I know you want to be with me. Who the hell has a right to tell either of us that we can't make that choice? Who has a right to tell any of us that our lives aren't ours to live?"

Dylan's eyes were tired, but his smile was warm. "No one," he said.

"Hear, hear," Alex agreed.

Tom jerked a thumb in Dylan's direction. "What he said."

Dylan closed his eyes and took a deep breath. "I don't understand how my mom got here, though," he said. "She was raised in this cult? Just like you were?"

Sara nodded. "She must have been."

Dylan's eyes bored into hers. "Your dad knew. He must have."

"I'm sure he did. I expect that's why, at first, he tried to talk me out of choosing you. I'm sure he thought that if he overruled my choice, I would then pick a less suitable Warden, someone with whom I shared a weaker bond. That could jeopardize my Pilgrimage and, by extension, the whole world. He wouldn't take that risk."

"But my dad doesn't know about any of this. My mom never told him?"

"In the Circle, marriages are arranged, in a sense. Once Circle women turn thirty, they're exempted from future Pilgrimages and allowed to marry, as long as they choose a husband who was also raised in the Circle. That's how the Circle survives across generations—imagine falling in love with an outsider, having a daughter with that person, and then trying to convince your partner to send your daughter to her death. Most people wouldn't be very receptive to that idea—and they would think you'd gone crazy. Dylan's dad wasn't raised in the Circle. Marie broke the rules by marrying him."

Dylan smiled sadly and shut his eyes. "And she would have told them to cram their rules up their asses."

Sara returned the smile. It faded once she started talking again. "Outsider or not, Maidens aren't supposed to fall in love or have families until we turn thirty or otherwise become exempt from the Pilgrimage. What would be the point? Any Maiden under thirty could be chosen to undertake a Pilgrimage of her own...." She trailed off.

"And if she does, she dies, one way or another," Tom finished.

"Even though Marie wanted her own family, she must still have believed in the Pilgrimage to some extent, because she kept up her training and chose her own Wardens. Maybe her strategy was simply to hope that she wouldn't be called. After all, the odds were in her favor—dozens of Maidens are trained for every cycle, and usually, the first one in line completes her Pilgrimage. Daniela Esperanza was the first Maiden in line during the last cycle, but she disappeared, and Marie's name came up to replace her. I'd guess that Marie was farther down the list and was called only because several other Maidens and Wardens refused the Pilgrimage— or didn't survive the proving ground. She had the audacity to start her own family before she turned thirty, and with an outsider, no less—the audacity to place her own desires above her so-called duty to others. In the Circle's eyes, she wouldn't have been selfless enough to be at the top of the list, but she could be considered a tertiary backup plan.

"However it happened, the Circle called on her to undertake the Pilgrimage... right after Dylan was born. Years later, when Dylan and I started to become friends, my father must have realized that I would eventually choose him to be one of my Wardens. So, he convinced the other Circle families to let him alter our copies of the records—to erase all traces of Marie."

Dylan hung his head. "My mom was so kind and compassionate. I'm sure that once she met my dad and had me, she wanted to leave the Circle.

She probably did, at least unofficially. But if she got that call, and if she really believed that all the other options had failed... if she really believed that the world would end unless she gave up her life... she would have done it. But to her, that would have been a secondary reason. Above all else, she would have done it to protect me and my dad." Dylan could no longer contain his emotions and began to weep quietly.

"That's why sacrifice is so evil. I understand it now," Alex said. She pulled Dylan into a gentle embrace and let him rest his head on her shoulder. "A call to sacrifice appeals to some of the best traits within people—kindness, generosity, benevolence—and twists them toward evil ends. Marie had other people's safety and happiness in mind when she agreed to the Pilgrimage; nobody is questioning her motives. The Circle knew that she wanted to protect people, wanted to save her own family and other families from the fate she would suffer—and they used that against her. They used her kindness to perpetuate the very cycle she wanted no part of."

"Dylan... I'm so sorry for what we did to your family," Sara said. She, too, was crying. She wrapped her arms around him, begging his forgiveness.

For a moment, Tom and Alex weren't sure if he would return her embrace. Then, his expression softened, and he did. "It's alright," he said to Sara. "What happened to my mom... it's not your fault. Like Alex said—if you had killed yourself, if you had given your life to keep this madness going, then you would have joined the ranks of the guilty. But you didn't. You used your head and saw reason. You decided to stand and fight, to find a real solution to this problem." Sara pulled away and looked up at him. His eyes were red, and he looked exhausted, but the smile he gave her was genuine. "It bothers me that my mom became part of the problem, but she realized her mistake before the end, and knowing that makes me feel better. Her death is on the people who raised her in a cult and sent her here, not on you. Now that you've seen the truth and decided to fight to end the cycle, you're no longer on the wrong side of history. I have to blame those who are actually responsible and hold them accountable, not let them deflect their guilt onto others. Alex helped me understand that."

Alex smiled at Dylan. "Happy to help," she said.

Dylan wiped his eyes. "I just don't understand why my mom would disappear without saying anything. She must have known what that would do to my dad and, later, to me."

Alex laid a comforting hand on his shoulder. "What could she have said? No explanation she could have given would have made sense, and she knew that. It's obvious that your mom and dad really loved each other. I'm sure she agonized over that decision, whether to feed him a lie she knew he wouldn't believe or simply vanish without saying anything. No matter what she said or didn't say, her disappearance would have torn him apart."

"It did," Dylan said.

"She must have decided, for whatever reason, that this way would be a little less horrible," Alex said. "Maybe she was right, maybe not. Who can say?"

Dylan sighed. "Looking back on it now, it seems so obvious. There are little pieces of her all over the Twilight. The house where we found Daniela —that was our house, where we lived when I was a baby. That's why I thought it looked familiar when we went there; I just couldn't place it because I'd only seen it in a few photos. The boat Tom and Sara used to cross the bay—it's just like the ones Mom used to build models of. We still have a few of her models around the apartment. And right here, cherry blossoms—her favorite flower." He gestured at the nearby cherry trees. "But there's one thing I don't understand. The Twilight is supposed to manifest places and creatures based on the thoughts and fears of the people who come here, but we never saw any monsters that have any obvious connection to my mom."

Tom scratched his beard. "I think I know why." When the others looked at him expectantly, he went on. "Marie was a unique case. When she accepted the call to come here, she already had a son. Sara explained one reason Maidens aren't supposed to have children of their own. This is another reason."

Alex frowned. "I don't follow."

Tom raised an eyebrow. "Marie's greatest fear *did* manifest here, in the Twilight."

Sara gasped. "Her greatest fear was that her son would come here as a Warden."

Tom nodded. "And he did."

A stunned silence fell over the small group. Thunder rumbled from the night sky, long and low.

"I know one thing for sure," Dylan finally said. He looked at Sara, Alex, and Tom in turn, with iron in his eyes. "I'm not letting the Twilight have her. When she died, she turned into that goddamned mist. I won't let that stand. Whatever might be left of her, I won't let it be part of this evil place."

"What are you going to do about it?" Tom said. His tone made it clear that he believed it was a problem Dylan could solve.

"I'm gonna destroy it," Dylan said. "This whole place, so it never hurts anyone again. By myself, if I have to."

"You don't have to do it alone. I'm in," Tom said with a grin.

"Well, we've come this far. We still have to kill a god, but I suppose we can find time to destroy the Twilight, too," Alex said, as if she were discussing her lunch plans.

Sara took Dylan's hand. "You're not going anywhere without me," she said.

* * *

"What's that?" Tom said. He was pointing toward the train station, away from the Vile Abbey. At first, the others didn't see anything.

"I see it," Sara said. "Something's moving. Looks like it's coming this way."

A small dot on the plains slowly grew bigger. They stood and watched it, gripping their weapons anxiously. A low, droning sound became audible.

"Sounds like a motor," Tom said.

"Jacob!" Sara cried. "It has to be."

A few minutes later, the old man rode up to them and slowed his bike to a halt. "Ah knew ye was trouble, lass," he said, tilting his head toward the plume of dust where the cathedral had once stood. Lightning flashed from the dark clouds covering the moon, followed by a deep rumble of thunder.

Sara threw her arms around him. "I'm so glad you're okay," she said.

He grunted. "Ah dinnae ken about 'okay,' but ah'm alive." Alex, Dylan, and Tom exchanged smiles and greetings with him. "What happened? Far as ah ken, no Pilgrimage has ended with a controlled demolition before."

Tom snorted. "It wasn't exactly controlled."

Sara wiped rain from her eyes. "It's getting cold. We'll freeze if we stay out here in the rain. Let's find somewhere dry." Together, they circled back around to the low hill that concealed the secret entrance to the catacombs. Near the crevice they found a rock overhang that provided some shelter. It seemed that, in some respects, the upside-down rain functioned like normal rain; if there was no clear path from the ground to the sky, no rain fell—or rather, rose—in that area.

Sara wrung water out of her hair while Jacob covered his bike with a ragged tarp. "Jacob, I have to ask for your help one last time," she said.

Jacob barked a laugh. "What more's there fer me ta help with? What haven't ye blown up yet?" He looked around, grinning, as if he were expecting someone else to follow up with another joke. His grin faded when he saw their faces.

"Jacob... there will never be another Pilgrimage. Ever again," Sara said.

He frowned. "Oh?"

"Before I tell you what happened, there's something else I need to tell you. I lied to you before, and I have to come clean." Jacob waited for her to go on, his expression unreadable. It took Sara a long moment to work up the courage to tell him. "Lily finished her Pilgrimage; that much is true. But she didn't go home afterward. No Maiden ever has."

Jacob swallowed hard. "What are ye sayin', lass?"

Sara looked down at the ground, unable to meet his eyes. "The final ritual that keeps Ardu dormant, keeps him away from our world... it requires the Maiden to sacrifice her life."

A deep silence fell over the group. Tom turned away from Jacob slightly to conceal the fact that his right hand was on his holstered sidearm. He was ready to protect Sara if the old man lashed out. Slowly, he thumbed back the hammer, using his palm to muffle the quiet *click*. Jacob's eyes were unfocused and distant, even more than was usual for Wardens in the Twilight. He didn't move. He just sat there with his hands in his lap, looking not at Sara but through her.

Finally, he spoke. His voice was so quiet that the others had to listen closely to hear him over the noise of the storm. "Ah should've figured it out sooner. The lilies... they kept growin'. Fer thirty years, they kept growin'. Ah suppose ah should've stopped seein' 'em a long time ago, if she had left this cursed place."

He reached under his tattered jacket and drew his Blackhawk. Tom snapped his .460 out of its holster and leveled it at Jacob's head. Jacob looked at Tom with an odd, remorseful smile. "Dinnae worry," the old man said. "Ah'd nae try ta hurt any of ye."

He cocked the Blackhawk's hammer and placed the barrel against his temple.

"Jacob!" Sara cried. Alex gasped. Dylan jerked forward, wanting to interfere, then stopped, afraid of making things worse.

"All mah life, ah've cocked things up," Jacob whispered. He shut his eyes. "But ne'er this bad. Ah delivered Lily ta her death."

"You didn't know," Tom said. His voice was gentle and sympathetic. Cautiously, he lowered his weapon but didn't holster it.

"That hardly makes a difference," Jacob said.

"It makes all the difference in the world," Dylan said.

Jacob opened his eyes but said nothing.

Alex pressed the advantage. "Lily didn't kill herself. She was murdered— murdered by Ardu, but even he doesn't carry the largest share of the blame. He's just a symptom of a deeper disease—a disease rooted in dangerous ideas. Lily was murdered by people who preach that an individual's life means nothing. They preach that only the group matters, and that innocent individuals must be sacrificed to the group whenever they deem it necessary."

"Jacob," Sara said softly. She raised her hands in a disarming gesture, begging him to hear her out. His wet eyes focused on hers, but he kept the barrel of his gun pressed against his temple. "Every Maiden was a victim, including Lily. She was trying to help people. She was a good person who was trying to do the right thing—we all know that. But she was deceived. The Circle used her as a tool. They brainwashed her into believing that her life didn't matter, that it was her duty to pay for everyone else's so-called mistakes. She gave her life in service of evil, but she didn't know that that's what she was doing. What we do matters, but *why* we do it, and whether we understand the full context of the choices we make—those things matter even more.

"Like Dylan said, you now know something you didn't know before. You can't be held responsible for what you did as a result of others lying to you, and you can't be blamed for not having knowledge you couldn't possibly have had. The Circle, and everyone else who believes as they do, that individual lives are dispensable—they're the guilty ones here, not you. They *knowingly* feed the nightmare machine. Don't let them get away with it. Don't you dare take their guilt onto your own shoulders. Together, we can stop them. With your help, we can dismantle the machine and make sure it never claims another innocent life. That's how you honor Lily's memory."

Jacob stared at Sara for a long moment. Everyone else held perfectly still, afraid to tip the scales.

Finally, slowly, he tilted the barrel of his Blackhawk away from his head and decocked the hammer. "How old are ye, lass?" His voice quavered with emotion. A single tear ran down the weathered creases of his face.

"I'm seventeen," Sara said. "And a half."

Jacob smiled. "Wise beyond yer years. Like Lily. Ah... just wish that the cycle could have stopped with her. Nae only fer her sake, but so ye and yer friends never had ta live this nightmare."

The others visibly relaxed when Jacob holstered his Blackhawk. Alex breathed an audible sigh of relief.

"There's a whole story here ah'm not gettin'," Jacob said. "How exactly is it that ah looked over mah shoulder ta see the cathedral comin' down in a cloud of smoke?"

Sara recounted the tale, beginning with their first arrival at the cathedral. She told Jacob how Alex had figured out that Maidens always died and how Tom had interrupted the ritual. She told him everything that had transpired after that. The others jumped in to correct her memory or add missing details as needed. He sat still, nodding occasionally, absorbing the tale. A few times, he asked questions or added small epiphanies of his own.

"Jacob, I'm sorry I lied to you," Sara said. "I'm sorry I asked you to help me... kill myself."

He heaved a sigh. "What's done is done, lass. Ah ask only fer yer word that ye've learned yer lesson and will nae try anythin' so daft again."

Sara smiled. "I promise."

"What's yer plan now, then?" Jacob asked.

"We kill Ardu and destroy the Twilight," Tom said matter-of-factly.

Jacob blinked. "Oh, is that all?"

"Simple plans are usually the best ones."

"We may have different ideas as ta the meanin' of 'simple.'"

"I said simple, not easy."

Jacob grunted, conceding the point.

"We're committed now, anyway," Sara said. "Ardu has entered our world a few times before, when past Maidens failed to reach the cathedral before midnight on the eighth day. Every time it's happened, he's caused death and destruction on a massive scale. The Circle has a... backup plan that they've used in those cases, but that option is closed to us now—even if we were willing to consider it."

Alex narrowed her eyes. "What is this 'backup plan,' anyway? You mentioned it before, after we came here for the first time, but you didn't say what it was."

Sara looked down and picked at her cast, reluctant to answer. Finally, she heaved a sigh. "Every Maiden in the world must kill herself, except one."

Alex, Dylan, and Jacob balked. Tom shook his head. "I guess I shouldn't be surprised," he said.

"In Ardu's eyes, a mass sacrifice proves that although humanity is still weak and corrupt, some are still willing to pay the price for others' sins, so he returns to the Twilight, reverts to his infant form, and... inhabits the last remaining Maiden. And so the cycle continues."

"Jesus," Jacob said, shaking his head.

"But like I said, even if we were to consider that option—which we won't—Ardu would certainly refuse the mass sacrifice and kill everyone on the planet. I'm sure that, to him, my act of arrogant selfishness puts all of humanity beyond redemption."

"Yes, how dare you assert your right to your own life," Alex muttered. Dylan patted Sara's hand reassuringly.

"We're wasting time. Let's go ice him," Tom said.

"How long do we have?" Jacob asked.

Sara checked her watch. "Just under eleven hours. Tom's right—we should get moving. We needed a short rest after the fight we just had, but I think we're good to go now."

"Sara, you said Ardu can't leave the Twilight until midnight tonight," Tom said. "Where would he go in the meantime?"

She didn't have to think about it for long. "The Deep Nothing," she said.

"The what?" Alex said, frowning.

"You remember how I said that the Hollow is the worst and most dangerous place in the Twilight?" The others nodded, except for Jacob, who seemed to be picking up the gist of the conversation through context clues. "It is, but that's not the full story. There's a part of the Hollow called the Deep Nothing that's even worse. A few Wardens have seen the entrance, but no one's ever gone inside. There's no reason to—it's not on the path to the cathedral. According to ancient records, it's where the mist comes from, and it's where all the monsters in the Twilight come into being, including the Eidolons. Some say it's also where Ardu came from, but no one knows for sure."

"The source of all the evil in the Twilight," Dylan said. He looked worried.

"You could say that," Sara said, nodding.

"Sounds dangerous," Tom said.

"Very."

"Can we really do this? And survive?" Alex said.

"Yes, we can," Tom said.

"Ye sound confident," Jacob said.

"With good reason. Sara, do you remember, a week ago, after we passed the trial at the village and came back to your house? You said you had reasons for choosing us as your Wardens."

Sara nodded. "I remember. What about it?"

"You were wrong about what you saw in us. You saw that I was motivated by duty; Alex by guilt; Dylan by his strong desire to protect you, even though he didn't think he could. You saw weakness in each of us and mistook it for strength, because the Circle brainwashed you into thinking that vice is virtue. But you didn't only see our vices. You also saw something in each of us that, on some level, you recognized as real and good, even if you didn't know it consciously. So, in the end, you were right, just not in the way you first thought—you did pick a hell of a team. We can do this."

"No one's ever gone so far off the path before," Jacob mused.

Sara looked at him with steel in her eyes. "That's why it's going to work," she said.

* * *

"There's another problem," Sara said.

"Of course, there is. Why should it get easy now?" Tom grumbled.

"I don't know exactly where the entrance to the Deep Nothing is, but according to the Circle records, it's under the basement of the cathedral."

"Which is now buried under about a thousand tons of rock and dirt."

"Then how do we get in?" Dylan asked.

"I'm not sure," Sara admitted. "But there must be a way. We have to find a way. If we don't figure it out… well, we know the stakes."

A silence fell over the group as they thought about it.

"While we're trying to work this out, let's see how much ammo we've got left," Tom said, removing shells and magazines from his plate carrier. "We used most of it in that last fight."

Alex and Sara were both completely out of ammo for their primary weapons and had only one magazine each for their sidearms. Tom was down to half a magazine of buckshot, no slugs, ten incendiary shells, and ten Magnum rounds. Dylan had the most ammo left; he gave some of it to Sara and Alex because both of their sidearms were chambered in .45, the same caliber as both of his weapons. He was left with forty rounds for his guns, plus six in the MGL. Jacob had a handful of cartridges for his old .45-70 rifle and six .44 Magnum rounds for his Blackhawk. Dylan had a single M67 fragmentation grenade, which he gave to Sara. He still had the launcher.

"This isn't much," Tom said, shaking his head once they'd laid out all their remaining ammunition. "We're supposed to kill a god with this? I've burned through more ammo in ten minutes at the range."

"Maybe we should head back and resupply," Dylan said. "Obviously, we can't go back to Sara's house, but Tom has plenty of ammo at the cabin."

Sara shook her head. "We can't."

"Why not?" Alex said.

"Humans can only cross the veil between our world and the Twilight under certain conditions, and Ardu can exert conscious control over the veil when he's awake or in the process of waking up. He can decide who comes and goes, but he can't cross the veil himself until he attains his mature adult form, which happens at midnight on the eighth day. If we leave the Twilight now, he'll know, and he'll lock the door, so to speak. We won't be able to come back."

The other four stared at her. "You're saying that no matter how this shakes out, we're stuck here until it's over," Tom said. Sara nodded.

Tom turned to Jacob. "Do you have any other ammunition or weapons stashed away somewhere? Other supplies? Anything at all that might help us?"

The old man shook his head sadly. "Nae, what ye see here is what ye get. Ah've been rationin' mah ammo fer almost forty years, mostly by stayin' hidden and avoidin' trouble as much as possible. Ah'm amazed ah've got any left at all."

"There's one more problem," Sara said. She winced as she said it, clearly not happy about divulging yet another roadblock.

Tom threw up his hands. "Fuck's sake," he muttered.

Dylan laid a hand on Tom's shoulder. He looked surprisingly calm. "Whatever it is, we'll figure it out," he said. "We've come this far. We'll finish it."

"The Deep Nothing is… dark. And I mean *dark*. Pitch black. No light whatsoever. Same goes for the lowest levels of the Vile Abbey and the cathedral, where the entrance to the Deep Nothing is," Sara said.

"We're supposed to fight a god in the place where the super monsters are born, in the dark, with nothing but torches, glow sticks, and a few dozen rounds of ammo." Tom shook his head. "This is suicide. I know I've said that before, but I really mean it this time."

Dylan scratched his head. "I think we can solve at least one of those problems."

"How?"

"Electronics from our world don't work here, but electronics *from* the Twilight do, right?"

Sara nodded. "Right."

"I've been thinking for a while now, trying to figure out why that is. It must have something to do with the power supply."

"What makes you think that?" Tom said.

"A few things, but explaining my theory would take longer than testing it."

"Alright," Alex said. The others still weren't quite sure what he was getting at.

Dylan turned to Tom. "On the first day, you had flashlights for all of us. You put them in your belt pouch when Sara said they wouldn't work. Are they still there?" Tom nodded and dug the four SureFire tactical lights out of the pouch, plus the handheld flashlight he always carried. Dylan took them and turned to Jacob. "Your bike has a working headlight. What's the power supply?"

Jacob stroked his beard thoughtfully. He was beginning to understand what Dylan was thinking. "Well, when the engine's runnin', the light gets power from there, just like any other bike or car. But ah did put together a battery backup system. Primitive batteries are nae hard ta build, once ye ken how they work, and ah've had nothin' but time ta experiment."

"How many cells?" Dylan asked.

"Sixteen. Dry cells, one-point-two volts each."

Dylan grinned. "Perfect."

Tom, Dylan, and Jacob huddled together around the motorcycle, discussing voltage and wiring requirements. Dylan took various tools and parts from his pack and passed them around. They seemed to have forgotten about Alex and Sara.

"I guess they're doing boy stuff," Alex said.

"In the meantime, we can work on figuring out how to get into the Deep Nothing," Sara said.

"I might have an idea. Do you remember how we got out of the catacombs the first time? How it was super confusing, but we eventually found the exit?"

Sara thought back on it. "The mist had a current to it, almost like a river. We followed it 'downstream' to the exit."

Alex nodded. "When Dylan, Tom, and I came back to stop you from doing the ritual the second time, that's how we found our way back to the cathedral, by following the mist 'upstream.'"

Sara furrowed her brow, thinking. "If the Deep Nothing is the source of the mist...."

"Then we should be able to find it by following the mist upstream. You said earlier that the entrance was somewhere under the cathedral basement. That fits with what we already know—the mist seemed to be coming from somewhere in that area."

"But the basement is completely collapsed. We'll never get back in there."

"No, we won't. But I think there's another way into the area *below* the basement."

"Where?"

Alex raised an eyebrow. "Where else did we see the mist moving with an obvious current to it?"

Sara thought hard, mentally reliving every step of their journey through the Hollow. A minute later, all the color drained from her face. "Oh, shit," she said.

Alex sighed and nodded. "Oh shit, indeed."

Sara tilted her head toward Tom, Dylan, and Jacob, who were bent over the bike, disconnecting wires and talking among themselves. "They're not gonna like it."

"*I* don't like it. If you can think of another way, I'm all ears."

Sara glanced at her watch. "We need more time," she growled in frustration.

"Agreed, but we don't have more time. At the moment, we have exactly one plan."

"This is going to be a nightmare."

"Yes, it is," Alex said quietly. "For Ardu. If he's never felt fear before, he will now. We'll make sure of that."

Dylan, Tom, and Jacob finished what they were doing and rejoined the others. Dylan was holding one of Tom's SureFire tactical lights. He unscrewed the cap, removed the battery, and inserted a larger one that looked as if it had been Frankensteined together from scrap metal and plastic. It was slightly wider than the standard battery; Dylan had to ram it in with the heel of his hand to make it fit. He screwed the cap back on.

"Moment of truth," Tom said. He crossed his fingers. Dylan took a deep breath and let it out slowly. Jacob watched, fidgeting anxiously.

Dylan clicked the power switch. A brilliant, bright beam of light flared to life, illuminating a large section of the rock wall behind them. The light was almost blinding in comparison to the dim moonlight they'd all become accustomed to.

"Yes!" Dylan shouted. He pumped a fist in the air. Tom and Jacob celebrated as well, clapping Dylan and each other on the shoulders. The three of them immediately got to work modifying the other flashlights.

Sara smiled despite her dark mood. "Like I've always said, he can fix anything."

Alex's lips curled into a playful smirk. "Even foolish girls."

Sara shut her eyes and chuckled. "Even foolish girls."

CHAPTER FORTY-TWO
Assault

Tom folded his arms. "You're shitting me, right? You're completely and utterly shitting me?"

Sara glanced sideways at him. "No, but I'll say 'yes' if it'll make you feel better."

Dylan winced, an expression of mixed horror and revulsion on his face. "We have to go… down there?"

They were back at the entrance to the Vile Abbey—what was left of it. The front wall and gate were still standing, but everything beyond had been reduced to rubble. The blood-spewing skulls carved into the stone leered down at them.

Thick mist rose from the iron grates that served as drains for the blood.

Alex cracked her knuckles. "We have to get to the Deep Nothing, but we don't know exactly where it is. All we know with any degree of certainty is that it's down there, somewhere. We know that it's the source of the mist, so it stands to reason that we can find it by following the mist. And as far as we know, this is the only possible way to access the area under the cathedral. If anyone has a better idea, any alternative at all, let's hear it."

Silence.

"Alright, then," Tom sighed. "We're running out of time. Let's do it."

"Ah cannae believe we're doin' this," Jacob said.

"You can bail. None of us would blame you," Tom said.

"Ah would," Jacob replied. "How do we get the grate off?"

The thick iron bars were embedded deep into the stone below their feet. There was no hatch, no sign that the grate could be opened or removed.

Tom was staring at Jacob's bike. "How much torque can you get out of that thing?"

Jacob nodded as he picked up Tom's reasoning. "Probably nae enough, but we can try it."

Tom, Alex, Dylan, and Sara each had a fifty-foot length of rope in their packs. They unraveled all four and wove them together, creating a thicker, stronger rope. Alex used her knowledge of climbing knots to secure one end to the grate and the other to the bike's chassis. Jacob kept the bike in low gear and drove down the hill until the rope snapped taut, then kept revving the engine, trying to pull the grate free.

It was no use. The bike simply couldn't generate enough power, nor did it have enough traction. The wheels just kept spinning in the mud.

Tom sighed. "I didn't think that would work, but I don't know what else to try."

Alex was staring at one of the blood waterfalls with a resigned expression on her face. "I do," she said. The others watched her, waiting. She scratched her head. "That blood… it's coming from somewhere. Presumably, it's coming from the place we're trying to get to."

Dylan balked. "Oh, hell no," he said.

Tom blinked. "You, the doctor, the medical professional, are suggesting that we swim down a pipe full of blood. How many bloodborne diseases are there, anyway? Let's have a contest and see who can get all of them first."

Alex shrugged. "That part won't matter. We'll either get instant dialysis when we leave the Twilight or we'll get killed before then."

"You're a better doctor than a motivational speaker," Sara muttered.

Tom sighed. "I'll go."

Sara frowned. "Alone?"

"We have to go one at a time anyway. If someone's alone on the other side for any length of time, it should be me; I have the most combat experience. Plus, I'm the biggest, so if I can fit through the pipe, you guys can, too."

"I don't like it, but it makes sense," Alex said.

She separated the four ropes and tied them together, creating a single piece two hundred feet long. "Take one end with you," she said to Tom. "We'll tie this end to the grate. When you get through, tie your end to something and give the rope a tug, that'll be our signal that you made it. The rest of us will have a guide rope to pull ourselves along."

"Can I just point out how terrifying this is?" Dylan said.

"And disgusting," Sara added.

"And necessary," Jacob said.

No one could argue any of it.

"Jacob," Tom said. "Can I convince you to give up the tarp you use to cover your bike?"

"Aye, take it if ye need it."

Tom unslung his AWM and removed the sling. He laid the rifle carefully in the center of the tarp and wrapped it tightly. "Dylan, you got any tape?"

"What kind?"

"Any kind, I just need lots of it."

Dylan rummaged in his pack and found a roll of duct tape. He handed it over with a grin. "An engineer's most essential tool," he said.

Tom wrapped the entire tarp in duct tape, creating a sealed bundle. He then attached the sling with several more layers of tape and slung the whole, awkward package over his back.

"Are we ready?" Tom said.

"No," everyone else said, in unison.

Tom allowed himself a humorless chuckle. "Are we going anyway?"

"Damn right we are," Sara said.

Tom took one end of the rope and climbed up into the mouth of the right-hand skull, using the stone teeth for support. "I'm gonna puke," he mumbled.

"Do it now, before you get... submerged," Alex said.

"Tom?" Sara said. He looked back at her. "Don't die."

He grinned. "I won't. Not today."

Before he could lose his nerve, he took a deep breath and forced himself headfirst into the fountain of hot, sticky blood.

* * *

Jacob was the last to emerge from the far end of the pipe. As soon as his head broke the surface, he released the deep breath he'd been holding, then vomited.

Tom put a hand on his shoulder. "It's alright, you're fine. You're not the first." Only Alex had been able to keep her stomach.

In a vast cavern under the Vile Abbey was a lake of blood, stretching in all directions, seemingly without end. Enormous chunks of stone lay everywhere, shaken loose by the violent collapse of the structures above. The five of them stood waist-deep in the blood, covered head to toe in it. The smell was nauseating. They did their best to wipe it out of their eyes and hair, but there was just too much.

Alex and Sara had attached their lights to their sidearms and were sweeping the bright beams around, trying to get a feel for their surroundings. Dylan had attached his light to his UMP. Tom and Jacob's weapons lacked rail systems, so Tom used copious amounts of tape to secure his light to the right shoulder strap of his armor. Jacob did the same with the strap on the shoulder of his long coat. It would have to do. The powerful beams cut through the thick mist, allowing limited visibility. Sara had been right; without the lights, it would have been pitch black. In such a large and open space, torches and glow sticks simply wouldn't have cut it.

Sara screamed. The others whirled around to check on her.

A skull caked in dried blood had floated past her. Other bones rose to the surface with sickening, wet sounds. "Sorry," Sara said. "Just startled me."

"From here on out, no talking unless absolutely necessary," Tom whispered. "Maximum noise discipline."

"Where do we go?" Alex whispered back. She gagged and coughed, unable to stop herself. Blood was in her hair, her eyes, her mouth. Nausea roiled in her stomach.

"Quiet," Jacob whispered. "Everyone listen."

All five of them held their breath and stopped moving. They listened, straining to hear. At first, the only sound was the rushing torrent of blood behind them. Then, faintly, another sound came to their ears, from somewhere far away.

da-thum. da-thum. da-thum.

"He's here," Sara whispered.

Tom waded forward, taking the lead, his Jackhammer at the high ready. The others stayed close behind, back-to-back, ready to meet an attack from any direction.

Slowly, they wove around and between fallen stones, some as big as small houses. Occasionally, smaller rocks tumbled down from somewhere high above, splashing into the sanguine sea. Once, Jacob yanked Alex out of the way just before a fist-sized rock struck her in the head. She nodded her thanks and took a deep breath to steady her trembling hands.

They got lost several times. The fallen stones were so numerous and close together that they were forced to turn and double back frequently. Maintaining a consistent heading was impossible, and the heartbeat was so faint that it was hard to tell where it was coming from. The blood they were covered in from the waist up began to dry, forming a macabre second skin on each of them.

"We're not getting anywhere," Alex whispered. "We need a new strategy."

"I'm so tired, and my head is starting to hurt," Dylan complained.

With no warning, Sara let out a clipped yelp and disappeared below the surface. Tom, Alex, and Dylan yelled her name in unison. There was no reply. A single bubble rose to the surface where she'd been standing, then popped.

"Find her!" Tom said. Before he could take a step, something rushed toward him, creating ripples in the blood. Tom was knocked off his feet and vanished below the surface.

Dylan caught movement out of the corner of his eye. He whirled around and fired a short burst into the blood. A moment later, he was knocked sprawling. He slammed into Alex, and they both went under.

Jacob was the last one standing. He held his .45-70 tight against his shoulder, waiting for a target. He dared not move. He held his breath, listening. His own heartbeat was so loud in his ears that he could hardly hear anything else.

A geyser of blood erupted to his left. A large beast with yellow-gray skin leaped onto a nearby foundation stone that had fallen at an angle, creating a ramp of sorts. A ragged blindfold covered its eyes, and it was holding Sara tight against its body with one of its massive, muscular arms. She was coughing and choking on blood. It had a long, serpentine tail instead of legs, and it used it to slither rapidly up toward the top of the stone block.

Malevolent laughter echoed around the chamber of horrors.

Jacob lowered his aim and fired, afraid of hitting Sara if he went for a headshot. The heavy bullet missed, sending up a puff of stone dust just behind the monstrosity. He worked the lever, but it moved stiffly, reluctant to chamber another round. He swore; the blood was gunking up the action. He tried again, ramming the lever forward, hard, then slamming it back. Chunks of coagulated blood flew from the chamber. Finally, he got the next round to feed properly.

He fired again. To his amazement, the creature simply blinked out of existence. Sara yelled and fell onto her side, near the top of the stone block. Tom breached the surface a few steps away, followed by Dylan and Alex a moment later. All three of them were blinded, struggling to wipe hot, sticky blood out of their eyes.

The grinning creature reappeared in the same place Jacob had last seen it. He worked the action and fired but missed. Before he could try again, the creature scooped up Sara, tucked her tight against its chest, and retreated into the shadows.

"No!" Jacob yelled. He waded forward until he could leap onto the stone block. He ran to the top as fast as his legs would carry him. By the time he reached the place he'd last seen the creature, it was gone. "Sara!" He shouted.

Silence.

"What happened? What was it?" Tom yelled from below. When Jacob described the creature, the others gasped.

"The Stalker," Alex said.

"Ye've seen it before, then," Jacob said.

Dylan nodded. "It's tried to get Sara a few times already." His voice cracked a bit. He was desperately trying to stay calm, to think of what to do next, to not let his fear and worry for Sara consume him.

Jacob slowly sank to his knees atop the large stone, his eyes closed. "It got her this time," he whispered. "Ah... could nae protect her."

Alex started making her way toward the base of the stone block. "Jacob, it's alright. You said it didn't kill her? It took her away?"

"Aye."

"Then it wants her alive for some reason, or maybe Ardu does. Maybe he sent it. Either way, it didn't kill her. That's good. We'll get her back," Tom said.

Jacob hung his head and began to weep softly. Alex reached him and knelt beside him, trying to think of something comforting to say.

"It's alright," Alex said. "Like Tom said, we'll get her back."

"Nae, it's no alright. Ah brought Lily ta her death, whether ah meant it or nae. Then ah did the same with Sara—brought her right ta the cathedral's front door, so she could kill herself. And just now, when ah finally thought ah had it figured out, when ah finally thought ah could do some good—ah fucked it up again. That thing took her god knows where."

The thick mist hovering just above the surface of the blood lake began to swirl in a circular pattern.

"Oh, shit," Tom said.

Dylan raised his UMP, not sure what to expect. "What is it? What's happening?"

Tom shouldered his shotgun and flicked off the safety. "What's another word for someone who does things badly?"

Alex's breath caught in her throat. "A butcher," she whispered.

With a thunderous *boom* and a brief flash of total blackness, like inverted lightning, the Butcher burst forth from the mist, already charging full-tilt toward the base of the angled stone—toward Jacob. Great waves of blood sloshed in its wake, knocking Tom and Dylan off balance.

"Run!" Tom shouted. "We don't have time or ammo for this!"

The massive stone shook beneath Alex and Jacob's feet as the behemoth sprinted toward them. Jacob shoved Alex hard, sending her over the side to splash back into the blood lake. He then jumped after her, dodging the Butcher's cleaver by a hair's breadth. It raised its bulbous head and roared in frustration.

As soon as Jacob got back on his feet, Dylan grabbed his shirt and shook him. "Jacob! The Butcher—it's related to your perception of yourself!"

Jacob spit out mouthfuls of blood and rubbed his eyes. "What?"

The Butcher started making its way back down the stone. Dylan tried to talk fast. "It's a super monster, it's called an Eidolon. It's a physical manifestation of your worst vice. You said you mess everything up—you 'butcher' everything. You can kill it, but you have to change your thinking first."

"What are ye goin' on about, lad?"

Tom fired a short volley of buckshot at the Butcher's ankles, slowing it down momentarily. The beast tripped and rolled into the blood on the far side of the stone with a heavy splash. "Dylan's right," he shouted. "Alex, Dylan, and I all had Eidolons of our own. We fixed the flaws in our thinking—we corrected the problems in ourselves that brought the Eidolons to life in the first place. Once we did that, we were able to kill them."

Jacob frowned, then nodded. "Ah'll try," he said. "Ye three—go and get Sara."

The ground rumbled beneath their feet as the Butcher resumed its pursuit. They couldn't see it yet, but it would round the corner and be on them any moment.

"We're not leaving you here alone with that thing," Alex said.

"Sara's short on time," Jacob said. "Every second that thing's got her, she's in terrible danger. Go and get her. Dinnae waste yer time here." He pointed in the direction the Stalker had gone.

Tom grabbed Alex's arm and started to pull her along. "Jacob's right. Sara needs us." Alex resisted for a moment, then relented. Sara was in grave danger, especially if the Stalker was taking her to Ardu. What could he want with her?

Nothing good.

"Jacob, here!" Dylan unslung the MGL and tossed it. Jacob caught it. "It's full. Six rounds. Just pull the trigger."

Jacob slung his rifle and tucked the launcher into his shoulder as the Butcher rounded the near side of the stone, brandishing its filthy cleaver. "Go on, now," he said. His voice was quiet and steady. "Ah'll get it right this time. Dinnae let her down."

Tom, Alex, and Dylan slogged forward, wading through the blood as fast as they could. Behind them, they heard an explosion, then another. Tremors rocked the ground beneath their feet. Then came shouting, an animalistic roar, and several loud *cracks*—Jacob's old rifle. They pushed on, resisting the temptation to turn back. As much as they wanted to help, Sara needed them more than Jacob did. Only he stood a chance of killing the Butcher, anyway—it was his demon.

The sounds of battle dragged on, growing fainter as they gained more distance. Finally, several more explosions echoed in the darkness. After the last one faded away, all was quiet.

* * *

No matter how much Sara struggled, it was no use. The Stalker had dragged her down through a whirlpool in the blood lake, which had been horrifying enough on its own. It had then carried her a short distance farther—it was hard to see much with all the blood in her eyes—and chained her to a bed with thick iron manacles locked around her wrists and ankles.

It could hardly be called a bed. The mattress was little more than a burlap sack stuffed with straw. It smelled foul, and it was covered in ancient, dark stains.

She tried not to think about what the stains were.

She willed herself to stop fighting. She needed to conserve her strength and think of something else. She closed her eyes and stilled her breathing. Her heart was pounding, and she was sweating badly from the anxiety of not knowing what was about to happen to her. She still had her weapons and gear, but she couldn't reach any of it.

Sara opened her eyes and looked around. The Deep Nothing was... not what she had expected. She had expected something akin to the blood lake, with skulls, gore, and pitch blackness. The cursed mist was so thick that she couldn't see more than a few feet in any direction. To her left and right, she could just barely make out two more beds, also covered in dark stains. They were empty.

She squinted, trying to see through the mist. Each bed had two long, thin objects attached to the iron frame, near the bottom. She couldn't tell what the objects were. She looked down at her own feet, trying to see if the bed she was on had the same things attached to it.

It did. When she realized what they were, her heart started hammering even faster, and bile rose in her throat.

Stirrups.

"Mom's awake."

She jumped, startled by the unexpected voice. It had come from somewhere behind the head of the bed, where she couldn't see. It was deep. It sounded familiar. She'd heard it before.

Coming from Marie's mouth, before they'd freed her from Ardu's control.

Her blood ran cold.

A small boy appeared to her left, the mist parting before him. He looked to be about five years old, and he was naked. He looked ethnically ambiguous, with a vaguely olive complexion and short, dark hair, as though he were a genetic average of people from all over the world. His eyes were closed, and his lips bore the slightest ghost of a smile.

Sara wasn't fooled for an instant by his facade of purity and vulnerability. He opened his eyes, revealing them to be completely white and opaque, with no visible irises or pupils. His smile widened.

Sara struggled to keep her terror in check, to look and sound more confident than she felt. "I suppose you're going to kill me now," she said.

He stuck out his bottom lip, making an eerily childlike pouty face. *"Kill you? Heavens, no."*

Her heart was pounding so loudly; surely, he could hear it. She could hear his, faintly.

da-thum. da-thum. da-thum.

"What happens next, then?"

He leaned forward and folded his arms, laying them flat on the edge of the mattress. He let out a tired sigh and rested his chin on his arms. His face was uncomfortably close to hers.

"Death is much too simple, much too good for you, after what you've done."

Sara didn't know what to do, other than to stall for time and hope the others found her soon. "What I've done? I've done nothing but realize that my life is mine, and mine alone. Same goes for everyone else."

Ardu snorted and shook his head. *"Your' life is not yours at all. No man's life belongs to him; it belongs to those who most need it. For five millennia, I have waited patiently for men to learn this basic moral truth. It seems I have wasted my time."*

"I finally understand why the Twilight is the way it is, why it's a land of living nightmares, a place of blood and pain and death."

Ardu frowned. *"The Twilight is merely a blank canvas—it always has been. When the first men came here, there was nothing, but the desires of their hearts began to give it shape. For all human history, men's hearts have harbored the same grave sin: selfishness. If men would only repent and reform, if men would only accept their duty to selflessly love and care for one another, with no thought of praise or reward, the Twilight would change accordingly. It would become a true paradise—a living garden of Eden."*

Sara shook her head. "Wrong. The Twilight is a hellscape because most people *have* learned the lesson you wanted them to learn. I'm here because *I* was raised with that lesson, and everyone else was, too. I was raised to believe that everyone else's lives and happiness matter but mine don't. I was taught that I exist to serve others—to die for them, if necessary. The moral code of sacrifice is alive and well in our world. The only difference between me and most other people is that I was ready to take it all the way. The Twilight looks exactly as it should: vile, corrupt, and evil, just like the idea that my life belongs to anyone other than me."

Ardu's frown continually deepened as Sara talked. He didn't say anything. Instead, he climbed up onto the bed and knelt next to her. Gently, he placed his hands flat on her stomach. *"Other Maidens suffered for decades, but their suffering did eventually end, once they had proven their willingness to atone, proven that all hope for humanity was not yet lost. Through their selflessness, they earned peace in death. Your suffering will be endless. After I tear apart every last man, woman, and child, after I devour every last wretched soul, I will have nothing more to do but sleep. Here, in you.*" He rubbed her stomach tenderly. "*For all time. For endless millennia, you will pray for the release of death. You will never have it.*"

Sara thrashed and bucked her hips, trying in vain to push him away. The shackles around her wrists and ankles bit into her skin, drawing blood. Terror gripped her heart like a vise. He smiled at her and gently pulled her shirt up a few inches, baring her abdomen. "*Starting now.*"

Ardu stiffened his fingers and rammed his hand into her midsection, breaking the skin and ripping through the muscles underneath. Blood welled up, staining her clothes and his hands. White-hot pain lanced through her like lightning. He began to shrink, gradually reverting to a fetal form.

The Deep Nothing had no walls to echo her screams.

* * *

"Now what?" Alex said. "We're running out of time."

DA-THUM. DA-THUM. DA-THUM.

The heartbeat was almost painfully loud. They'd found its source, they were sure of that, but there was nothing to see—just more blood and darkness in all directions. They'd even resorted to crawling around on their hands and knees, fully submerged in the blood, searching for passages or trap doors hidden in the ground beneath their feet. There was nothing.

Tom glanced at his watch. "Fuck," he muttered. "Alright, think. Get creative. What haven't we tried?"

Dylan and Alex paced back and forth, racking their brains. Ardu was in the Deep Nothing, and the Stalker had gotten in with Sara, too. There had to be a way.

"Think of the solution, not the problem," Alex muttered, half to herself.

Dylan snapped his fingers. "I've got it. The Twilight is like the first layer of sleep, right? And the Hollow is a deeper level of sleep?"

"That's what Sara said," Tom agreed.

"And the Deep Nothing is an even deeper level of sleep."

"Right," Alex said. "So what?"

"Remember what Dr. Atwood said the first day, about adrenaline and sedatives?"

"Vaguely," Tom said. He rolled his hand impatiently, imploring Dylan to get on with it.

"She said to never, ever take sedatives while we're in the Twilight because they'll deepen our sleep and make it harder to wake up again."

Alex's eyes widened. "She did say that."

Dylan pulled out his syringe case and retrieved the injector with the blue label. He stared at it in his hand, hesitating.

"Are you sure about this?" Tom said.

"Mostly."

"What happens if you take that and it doesn't work?" Alex said. Or at least, that was what she'd intended to say. She didn't get the chance; Dylan had already injected himself.

A heartbeat later, he vanished.

"Well, presumably, he didn't leave the Twilight," Tom said.

"I think it worked," Alex said. "He went down to the next level of sleep."

"He's a smart kid. Let's do it. But first, let's make sure we leave the door unlocked for Jacob. Got a pen?"

"I think so." She dug around in her pack and found one. Tom scribbled Jacob's name on one of his two sedative injectors, then laid it atop a nearby rock.

That done, Tom and Alex took deep breaths and injected themselves.

For a moment, nothing happened. Then, the air rippled around them, as though their vision were distorted by intense heat. Out of nowhere, a gigantic whirlpool of blood shimmered into existence fifty paces ahead. Four enormous statues of young women stood around it, facing inward, each at least thirty feet tall. Each had her hands clasped in prayer or supplication, and each roughly carved face bore an expression of dire agony. Blood trickled from the statues' eyes and dripped slowly into the vortex below.

A thick column of mist rose from the center of the whirlpool like smoke from a chimney, spreading outward to settle over the sanguine lake.

Dylan turned around to face them. Alex gasped. "Dylan, your eyes!"

In the same moment, he noticed hers. They were completely white, her irises and pupils invisible—or gone. Tom's looked the same.

"Our eyes changed when we entered the Hollow, too," Dylan said. "This must be the Deep Nothing. We're really far from home now."

"That definitely looks like the entrance to a place called the Deep Nothing," Tom said, sweeping his flashlight beam over the rushing whirlpool. He didn't sound happy about it.

"It's rather... dramatic," Alex said.

Dylan clenched a fist. "We're wasting time. Let's go get Sara."

He waded forward, sloshing through the waist-deep blood. With no hesitation, he walked right into the rushing current, letting it sweep him off his feet. He held his breath, crossed his arms, and tried to relax.

Easier said than done.

"I guess I can't let a sixteen-year-old with no chest hair show me up," Tom griped. He, too, waded forward.

Alex followed without comment, her heart racing.

Dylan shut his eyes and waited for it to be over. Hot, sticky blood washed over his hair and coated every inch of his gear. He tried not to think about how disgusting it was. He counted his own heartbeats to give his mind something else to focus on. He felt himself being swept around in a spiral that continually got smaller.

Suddenly, he was falling through open space, in the middle of a hollow column of blood, almost like a waterspout. He splashed down into yet more blood, another waist-deep pool, but this one was small, only a few paces across. Coughing and wiping blood out of his eyes, he made for the edge of the pool and climbed out. A moment later, Tom and Alex splashed down behind him.

"Finally, solid ground," Dylan said, relief evident in his voice. He shook himself off like a wet dog and looked around. Hundreds of half-melted, flickering candles circled the small pool. Three stone steps led down to... nothing. A seemingly endless black void stretched out before them. There was nothing to see except a wall of mist in every direction.

"Sara... we're coming," he whispered. Tom and Alex hauled themselves out of the pool and stood beside him, doing their best to wipe off the sticky blood.

"It is now officially impossible to gross me out," Alex said.

"See? Everything has a silver lining," Tom said. He descended the steps and extended his boot gingerly into the void beyond, testing to see whether he would fall. His foot made contact with something solid, and he leaned forward a little more, still being cautious, ready to leap back onto the stairs if necessary.

"Seems alright," he reported. He took another few steps forward, until he was standing completely in the void. All three of them held their breath, afraid that he would suddenly plummet into the blackness. He didn't. The mist swirled around him, caressing him tenderly.

A shape shot out of the mist like a bullet, flashed briefly through the beam of Dylan's light, and slammed directly into Tom, knocking him sprawling before vanishing back into the haze. He rolled to his feet and brought his shotgun to bear, scanning for a target. He glanced down for a fraction of a second, long enough to see a rip in the fabric lining of his plate carrier, right over his heart.

Something had cut him, and only his armor had stopped it.

"On me, back-to-back," he said. Dylan and Alex ran over to join him, their weapons raised. Between the three of them, they could see in all directions, but for the moment, there was nothing to see but more mist.

Out of the corner of her eye, Alex caught movement. She snapped her .45 in that direction and double-tapped the trigger, hitting nothing. Even with their powerful flashlights, it was so hard to see. Without them, the Wardens would be completely blind.

"Watch your ammo, we don't have much," Tom cautioned.

Dylan's eyes darted left and right, scanning for movement. He blinked. When he opened his eyes again, Sara was sprinting out of the mist, right for him. He yelped in surprise and dropped his UMP onto its sling.

Adrenaline slowed his perception of time. Was Sara... pointing her gun at him? She couldn't be.

But she was.

She charged right into him, pushing him back into Tom and Alex. Quick as lightning, she slammed the barrel of her Operator directly against his forehead and squeezed the trigger.

His reflexes enhanced by natural adrenaline, Dylan slapped the gun away just in time. He winced in pain as it went off right next to his ear. The heavy bullet flew past his head and over Alex's.

Fortunately, Tom was quick to respond. He pivoted around, already snatching his knife from its sheath with his right hand. When he saw that it was Sara, he sidestepped around her and snatched her right wrist with his left hand, twisting it back and down to disarm her.

With speed and strength he knew she didn't possess, she spun to her right and slashed with the knife he hadn't seen in her left hand. Somehow, the cast on her wrist was gone, and she was using her left hand normally, as if it were fully healed.

Tom thought that he knew how that had happened. He'd noticed that her stomach, normally flat, was now more rounded and slightly distended.

He snapped his right forearm up and got inside of her swing, stopping her knife hand before the weapon reached his face. She headbutted him in the nose. It hurt like a bitch, and he reflexively released her right wrist. She immediately brought the .45 to bear in a compressed, one-handed stance and fired it twice, directly into his chest. Tom grunted in pain as the powerful slugs mushroomed against his armor plates. That would leave a nice bruise.

He decked her hard in the face with his left hand. She spun around, hit the ground on her back, then nimbly rolled to her feet and retreated into the mist.

"Tom! Don't hurt her!" Dylan shouted. Alex swept her sidearm back and forth, looking less sure about firing it.

"I won't kill her, but not hurting her is probably off the table," Tom said. He touched his nose. It was bleeding, possibly broken. No time to worry about it now.

"Why is she attacking us?" Alex said.

"Because she's not Sara. Not entirely," Tom said. He fell back in with the others, his knife raised defensively.

Mocking laughter drifted toward them from somewhere in the mist. It sounded like two different voices layered on top of and interwoven with one another—Sara's and a much deeper, more sinister voice.

Dylan blanched. "Ardu… he's inside her."

"Controlling her like he was controlling Marie," Alex said, her voice trembling with a heated mixture of sorrow and rage.

"Be careful. Don't hurt me too much. I may decide that fixing her body isn't worth the trouble." The twin voices seemed to be coming from all directions at once.

"Fuck you! I'll kill you!" Dylan screamed. His face was flushed, and his chest heaved with rage.

"Calm down," Tom said to him. "He's trying to piss you off so you'll make a mistake. Use your anger but stay in control of it. Fight with your head, not your heart. We'll get her back."

Sara appeared out of the mist to Alex's left, firing her .45. Alex dropped to her stomach and rolled away, narrowly dodging the gunfire. Dylan rushed Sara from the side and clotheslined her, catching her by surprise and knocking her to the ground. He tried to grapple her, but she was too fast. She kicked him in the jaw, causing him to cry out in pain and stumble back. She brought her .45 to bear and put the front sight post on Dylan's head, but Tom was already there. He kicked away the gun and reached down to grab her.

Her knife flashed, and Tom yelled in pain, clutching the deep cut in his forearm. Sara rolled to her feet and went for Alex, who was still on her back. Sara drew the Serbu 12-gauge from her leg holster and unfolded the foregrip. She aimed the deadly weapon right at Alex's face. At this range, a single round of buckshot would kill her several times over. She'd have no chance.

A loud *bang* echoed from somewhere behind all of them, and the shotgun spun away into the mist. Sara screamed in rage and whirled around, searching for the new threat.

Jacob, covered in fresh blood and kneeling by the stairs leading up to the pool, racked the lever of his .45-70. The empty casing bounced away, still smoking. "Risky shot, that was," he grumbled.

"Jacob!" Alex cried, clearly relieved to see him alive.

Sara threw back her head and screamed in rage, a feral, animalistic sound. Again, she retreated into the mist.

"Group up," Tom called. "She's trying to separate us and pick us off one at a time. Stay close, back-to-back, and work as a team. Try to restrain her."

"And then what?" Dylan asked.

"Still working on that part," Tom muttered.

Jacob fell in with the others, each of them covering a ninety-degree arc.

"Teamwork… that's a good idea," came the sneering dual voice from the mist. *"I have friends I can call, too—friends I believe you've met already."*

Alex, Tom, Jacob, and Dylan all tensed, waiting for a new attack.

Nothing happened.

"Hmm… odd."

Alex cackled as though she'd just realized something amusing. "If you're trying to summon our Eidolons, you're shit out of luck. They're dead."

"And you're next," Dylan yelled.

"You've never fucked with anyone like us before," Tom said.

"And ye never will again. The cycle ends now," Jacob added.

"Insects. I have other ways to exterminate you."

With a roaring howl, the very fabric of the Deep Nothing began to tear. A fierce wind kicked up, forcing the Wardens to shield their eyes. The swirling mist and even the void itself began to crack and peel like old paint, sucked away as if by a tornado.

Suddenly, they were in Roland's shanty town, at the base of the lighthouse. Rain came down in heavy sheets, driven sideways by a hurricane-force gale. Compared to the utter blackness of the Deep Nothing, the pale moonlight was blinding.

Ardu's laughter echoed from somewhere nearby. Mixed with Sara's gentle voice, it sounded especially vile.

"I have other friends, too."

A chorus of hungry screams, not far away, rose into the night.

"Cutters!" Tom shouted. "Conserve your ammo! Make every shot count!"

The four Wardens held their fire as a wave of Cutters came into view, sprinting down the dark road. Once Tom was confident in his aim, he dropped five targets with his last five rounds of buckshot. He swore; the only shotgun ammo he had left were incendiary shells, but he wanted to save them in case they encountered more of the tree things. He switched to his Magnum.

Dylan toggled his UMP to semi and took careful, well-aimed shots, conserving his last magazine as much as possible. Alex and Jacob followed suit.

A deep, metallic groaning sound rose above the howling wind somewhere behind them. Jacob risked a glance back. Ardu, in Sara's body, was hovering twenty feet off the ground. Sara was facing the lighthouse, and her hands were raised, as if she were conducting an orchestra.

Large stones ripped free from the lighthouse's exterior wall and fell away. The entire structure rotated a bit, slowly at first, then faster. The metal railing on the gallery deck bent and snapped. The glass in the lantern pane shattered, the jagged fragments carried away on the roaring wind.

The entire lighthouse was falling.

"Move!" Jacob shouted. He shoved Dylan and Alex to the far side of the road, then grabbed Tom's shoulder and dragged him along. The lighthouse slammed into the ground with a thunderous crash, missing Tom by mere feet. A dozen Cutters and several smaller buildings weren't so lucky. Huge, white stones were hurled in all directions. The four Wardens flattened themselves on the ground, narrowly avoiding the deadly missiles.

Sara hovered above them, looking down with a sinister smirk. *"You don't seem to be having fun here. Let's try something else."*

Again, the ground cracked and began to peel away beneath them, along with the sky above and everything in between. Abruptly, they were on the deck of a ship, pitching and rolling through turbulent waves in the bay—the ship Tom and Sara had taken. Bolts of greenish-white lightning streaked across the sky, and the rain began to come down even harder. Sara hovered well above the deck, laughing maniacally.

A massive, deformed, humanoid arm rose from the sea and grabbed the railing. Putrid black and red tumors pulsed all over it. Another arm appeared and latched onto the ship, then a third, and a fourth.

"Oh, shit," Dylan said.

Sara drew her Operator and began to fire down at the four of them indiscriminately. They scattered and rolled away in different directions, frantically scrambling for cover. The hail of .45 slugs dug deep furrows into the wooden deck.

The incoming fire stopped a moment later; Sara's sidearm had run dry. The empty magazine clattered to the deck as she reached for another—by Tom's count, her last one.

An enormous yellow eye rose over the side of the ship, blinking down at them slowly. The gaping, Lovecraftian maw beneath it opened to reveal flat, dull teeth the size of cinder blocks. The horror from the sea resembled the one Dylan had encountered upon first entering the Twilight, but it was bigger—a lot bigger.

"I kicked your friend's ass, I'll kick yours, too," he yelled, firing a short burst into the giant eye. The leviathan roared and thrashed, nearly capsizing the ship. Dark green fluid sprayed everywhere. The four Wardens struggled to keep their footing as the deck pitched violently.

From her position behind the foremast, Alex fought to keep her fear in check. She looked around, trying to figure out how they were going to get out of this alive. She did a quick ammo count; she had a nearly full magazine in her .45, a single full spare, and that was it. She was out of everything else. She couldn't shoot Sara, and she couldn't do anything useful against the sea monster.

Alex looked up at Sara. She was firing her .45 at Tom, who was trying to stay hidden behind the mainmast. Sara still had an M72 LAW rocket launcher on her back, the one she'd been carrying ever since their fight with the Matron.

It still had a rocket in it.

Sara had Tom pinned down and wasn't paying attention to anyone else. Alex holstered her sidearm and started climbing the foremast netting. The ship lurched, and she was nearly thrown back to the deck. Dylan and Jacob were running back and forth in irregular patterns, dodging the sea creature's attempts to grab them.

Hang on, guys—just a little longer, Alex thought.

She reached the top of the net and clambered out onto the fore gaff. It was slow going; she had to keep her arms and legs wrapped around it and shimmy forward a few inches at a time. The fearsome wind kept threatening to rip her away and toss her into the sea.

Finally, she was more or less directly above Sara. She waited. She had to time this perfectly. The fore gaff swung and jerked back and forth, at the mercy of the storm. Sara, too, was moving, trying to get an angle on Tom. He was doing his best to keep the thick mainmast between the two of them.

Now.

Alex took a deep breath and flung herself into open space. Her stomach dropped as she plummeted toward the deck. Her heart felt like a jackhammer against her ribs.

Sara looked up just in time to see Alex streaking toward her like a meteor. She raised her Operator and got off a single shot. Alex heard the bullet *crack* loudly as it passed her left ear, then she slammed into Sara. They fell to the deck. Sara hit first, on her back. Alex landed on top of her and bounced away, crying out. There was a terrible pain in her chest. Had she broken a rib? It didn't matter. She had to press the attack while Sara was stunned.

Alex scrambled over to Sara and punched her in the face as hard as she could.

Sorry, she thought.

While Sara was reeling from the impact, Alex grabbed her shoulder and spun her around. She snatched the rocket launcher's sling and ripped away the weapon. Tom, finally free of suppressing fire, sprinted over to restrain Sara. The ship lurched again, causing all of them to fall.

Dylan rolled to one side just before the leviathan smashed an arm into the deck where he'd been standing. Splintered wood flew in all directions. Jacob had retreated to the far side of the deck and was trying to line up a shot on the eye, but he was down to his last few rifle rounds and reluctant to waste them. The ship kept tossing and lurching underfoot, making it nearly impossible to aim.

"Dylan!" Alex shouted at the top of her lungs, trying to make him hear her over the storm. Thankfully, he glanced in her direction. She slid the LAW across the deck toward him, then stumbled back to Sara to help Tom restrain her. Dylan scooped up the weapon and rolled away again, narrowly avoiding another of the creature's attacks. He sprinted toward the opposite side of the ship, took a knee, and aimed the rocket launcher carefully. He only had one shot. He couldn't afford to miss.

He had underestimated how long the leviathan's arms were. Before he could fire, it grabbed him around the midsection and jerked him toward its gaping maw. The yellow eye blinked slowly.

Dylan dropped the rocket launcher but managed to grab the sling before the weapon fell beyond his reach. He gasped for breath. The creature was crushing his chest. He could hardly move.

But he could still move his arms. He hauled the launcher up and rested it on his shoulder. The monster's eye was a big target, but it was moving, he was moving, and the ship was moving. He was also finding it difficult to concentrate in light of his imminent fate. Any moment now, he would be pulled into the creature's mouth and devoured, ground into bloody pulp by its blunt teeth. Jacob moved closer and fired the last of his .45-70 rounds in a rapid volley, trying to hurt the beast enough to make it drop Dylan. From farther away, Alex joined in, emptying her sidearm. Most of the shots hit true, causing small bursts of green blood to squirt from the eye, but the leviathan held tight to its prey.

There. For just a fraction of a second, the yellow eye stabilized in Dylan's sights. He pulled the trigger.

The 66mm anti-tank rocket zipped away at five hundred feet per second and struck the eye almost dead center. The warhead pierced the rubbery sclera and detonated. A third of the leviathan's head exploded in a shower of black flesh, green gore, and yellow pus. The iron grip around Dylan's midsection instantly went slack and released him. One by one, the misshapen arms slipped away from the deck, and the dead behemoth disappeared beneath the waves.

Dylan tossed away the empty launcher and got to his feet. Where was Sara?

He turned around just in time to see her throw Alex and Tom clear across the deck. She rose into the air again before Jacob could tackle her.

"What do you hope to accomplish? You can't kill me without killing her, which your pathetic fetish for individual life forbids you to do."

As much as the Wardens hated to admit it, Ardu was right. But there had to be a way.

If not, they would make one.

Sara raised her hands to the sky. As before, the fabric of the Twilight cracked and shifted all around them. The ship and the sea were ripped away into an unseen vortex, only to be replaced by dark, thorned trees all around and hard-packed dirt underfoot.

The forest outside the village. The air was still and cold. Here, there was no rain.

Familiar wails echoed like the tortured cries of damned souls in the trees.

"Those fucking tree things are coming!" Tom shouted.

At the same time, Jacob shouted, "Bound!" Apparently, he'd named the creatures during his long years in the Twilight.

The four of them regrouped, checking their remaining ammo. Jacob had nothing but three .44 rounds in his Blackhawk. Tom's .460 was empty; he had only ten incendiary shells for the Jackhammer and the rifle on his back, still cocooned in a tarp. Alex and Dylan were down to a single magazine each.

"They hate fire," Tom said. He shouldered his Jackhammer and prepared to lay down an inferno at the first sign of a tree doing anything other than staying rooted firmly in the ground. "I'll handle them. You guys figure out how to help Sara."

Alex, in particular, had been thinking about that for a while now. Slowly, pieces of an idea were starting to come together in her head. "Dylan, Jacob," she said. "Hold Sara down and get her armor off. Do whatever it takes."

They both nodded and rushed toward Sara, trusting that Alex had a plan. She removed her medic bag and started digging through it for the items she needed. "Tom, keep them off me," she shouted. "I need a minute."

"Will do," he called back.

Just then, the first of the Bound shambled into the beam of Tom's light.

He held his fire, waiting for more targets. He had ten shells and no way to know how badly outnumbered they were. He wanted to hit multiple targets per shell, if possible.

Tom stroked the trigger when a second Bound appeared just behind the first one. The Jackhammer roared and sprayed a wave of burning magnesium over both targets. They ignited instantly, their death howls crescendoing into the night sky. Tom pivoted and lit up a third cursed tree that had been advancing on Alex from behind.

Sara took to the air before Jacob and Dylan could reach her. She taunted them, hovering well out of their reach as she flitted between the trees. "Tom! Alex! We can't reach her!" Dylan shouted.

"Knock her down!" Tom hollered back. He fired twice more, igniting four more of the Bound.

"How?" Jacob yelled.

It was a good question. Tom thought about it for a second. The Jackhammer ran dry. He locked the action open and reached for one of his last five incendiary shells.

He stopped. What if….

Instead of grabbing the bright orange shells from his plate carrier, he thrust his hand into his pocket. Yes—they were still there. He brought out the two bright blue shotgun shells with the letters "LTL" stenciled on them.

Less than lethal. The beanbag rounds he'd given Alex while she was watching Sara in the cabin.

Tom jumped back as a tree creature swung at him. He slapped one of the beanbag shells into the Jackhammer's open chamber and released the bolt. He thumbed the other shell into the magazine tube and sprinted a short distance away. He just needed the Bound off his back for a few seconds.

Tom snapped the Jackhammer to his shoulder and put the front sight directly on Sara's left side, just above and in front of her kidney. She was facing away from him, dodging rocks that Dylan and Jacob were throwing at her. Her armor protected her front and back but not her sides.

He squeezed the trigger. The lead-filled fabric projectile slammed into her unprotected side like a baseball bat. Sara was thrown into a tree trunk to her right. She was disoriented but still hovering far too high above the ground for Dylan or Jacob to reach her.

Tom chambered the second round and fired again. The beanbag hit Sara in the thigh, spinning her around again. The back of her head hit the tree, and she dropped like a stone. Jacob and Dylan each grabbed one of her arms and started wrestling her out of her armor. She was dazed but conscious, and she was fighting back fiercely.

Tom combat-loaded a single incendiary shell and torched another Bound before it could close on Alex, then loaded his last four rounds. Alex stood up, apparently ready to do whatever it was she had in mind. She clutched a syringe in her right hand. The needle attached to it must have been six inches long.

Alex sprinted toward Sara just as Jacob ripped off her vest. Dylan had her arms pinned behind her back, but she was freakishly strong, and he would lose hold of her any second. Alex dropped to her knees and slid the last few feet.

With her left hand, she lifted Sara's shirt. With her right, she aimed the syringe. She paused, trying to compensate for Sara's wild thrashing. Tom fired the last of his incendiary rounds, igniting another five tree monsters, but a dozen more were already shambling out of the woods. "Whatever you're gonna do, do it now!" he shouted. He had nothing left but his knife. He drew it and dropped into a defensive stance, already knowing that the weapon would be useless.

With a frustrated scream, Alex rammed the needle into Sara's swollen abdomen, just above her waistline, and depressed the plunger. Sara's face contorted and twisted through several expressions—pain, then hate, then fear, and finally, confusion.

She threw back her head and screamed. Abruptly, her stomach contracted, returning to its normal size.

Only Sara screamed. The deeper, sinister edge to her voice was gone.

All the remaining Bound froze in place, then toppled over. They hit the ground as nothing more than irregularly shaped logs. The ones that were already burning began to smolder as the flames died down.

Sara went limp, her head lolling.

"Sara? Sara!" Dylan said, worry taking hold in his voice. He gently shook her. Alex placed two fingers against the side of Sara's neck.

"She's alright," Alex panted. "Just give her a minute."

"What did ye do ta her?" Jacob said. He, too, was badly out of breath.

"I'm also dying to know," Tom said.

Mocking laughter echoed faintly through the trees.

"I leave you with a parting gift." It was Ardu's voice alone, divorced from Sara's.

"Was that Ardu?" Tom asked. "What 'parting gift?'"

Sara's eyes fluttered open. Groggily, she raised her head. She looked at Dylan, managing a weak smile when she recognized him.

When she looked at Alex, her face contorted in raw terror.

Alex frowned. "Sara, what—"

Sara shoved Alex aside, shot to her feet, and took off at a dead sprint.

Tom, Dylan, and Jacob spun around, looking for whatever had spooked her.

The Stalker.

It leaned down and laughed in Sara's face. She planted her feet and straightened her back defiantly, looking up at the sadistic abomination that towered over her.

"Sara! Get away!" Dylan said. He drew his USP, taking aim.

"You want me? Here I am," Sara said to the Stalker. Her voice was rock steady. She spread her arms out to the sides.

"What is she doing?" Alex gasped.

Tom and Jacob ran toward Sara to help. Dylan didn't have a shot; Sara was directly in his line of fire. He started circling to the right, trying to find a better angle.

Before anyone else could intervene, the Stalker accepted Sara's invitation. It picked her up, just as it had several times before. It wrapped one misshapen yellow hand around her chest, the other around her legs. It chuckled, savoring its victory.

Sara reached out, grabbed a fistful of the creature's filthy blindfold—and ripped it away.

"If I can open my eyes, so can you," she said.

The Stalker dropped her and slapped both hands over its atrophied eyes. It shrieked and wailed and pounded its serpentine tail against the ground. Its abhorrent screams rose in pitch and volume until the Wardens were forced to cover their ears.

"Hit it! Finish it off!" Sara screamed. She rolled over onto her stomach and covered her head.

Alex, Dylan, and Jacob needed no further invitation. All three of them brought their sidearms to bear and fired every remaining round into the creature. For the first time, it didn't blink away—it couldn't. Thick yellow blood splattered the ground and trees as the hail of lead ripped apart its flesh.

Dylan's USP locked open, followed by Alex's Glock a moment later. Empty magazines clattered to the ground, but there were no more to replace them. The hammer of Jacob's Blackhawk dropped on an empty chamber.

Sara rolled over and got to her feet. She pulled her knife, took two steps forward, and slammed it into the Stalker's chest. She dragged the blade downward, toward its tail, but the thick flesh was tough. She screamed in frustration and exhaustion, unable to cut more than a few inches.

Suddenly, Tom was beside her. He thrust his own knife into the Stalker's belly. Another geyser of yellow blood sprayed out.

Tom was stronger, and his knife had a thicker, heavier blade. He went to his knees, slashing downward with all his might. His knife caught in the Stalker's flesh for just a moment, then ripped through like he was undoing a zipper.

A five-foot gash opened in the creature's belly. Gray, diseased entrails slopped out onto the dirt. It screamed and thrashed but refused to take its hands away from its eyes. It couldn't—or wouldn't—fight back without its blindfold.

Tom stepped aside, flicking gore off his knife. "All yours," he said to Sara.

She'd already taken the frag grenade from her vest—the last one any of them had. The pin was already out. She darted forward and thrust her arm into the Stalker's abdomen, all the way up to her shoulder.

She opened her hand. She felt the spring-loaded safety lever release and detach from the grenade body. She pulled her arm free, darted to the left, and flung herself to the ground. Tom went right and did the same. The Stalker let out a final, hateful shriek.

The grenade detonated, blowing the abomination almost completely in half. It pitched forward, blood and viscera already soaking into the dirt. Its arms and tail twitched once, twice, then went still.

A moment later, the Stalker dissolved into mist, which was then carried away on a light breeze.

Silence descended on the forest.

"God... damn...," Tom panted.

"For the first time, I'm no longer evading reality," Sara said, wiping mud and blood out of her eyes.

"So, the Stalker can't evade us," Alex said.

"That was... truly somethin'," Jacob said, shaking his head in wonder.

"Yeah, and let's never do it again," Dylan said. He holstered his empty sidearm and went to check on Sara. She reassured him that she was sore, bruised, winded, and thoroughly traumatized but otherwise fine.

"Tom," Sara said.

"Hmm?"

"If you ever shoot me again, I'm calling Child Protective Services."

Tom laughed until his stomach started to hurt.

CHAPTER FORTY-THREE
Risk

The rope they'd used to scale the village gate seven days earlier was still there, just as they'd left it. After using it to return to the relative safety of the village, they sat down near the fountain to rest. They were all wet, filthy, and exhausted. At least the torrential rain had washed away some of the blood. Tom set about unpacking and inspecting Manny's rifle. He still had three magazines for it, but other than that, all of them were out of ammunition.

"We should be safe here, right?" Dylan asked.

Sara nodded. "For now. Monsters have never been seen in the village after the first trial."

"We've definitely upset the normal balance of things, though," Tom said.

"True enough."

Alex laid a hand on Jacob's arm. "Jacob, we're so glad to see you alive. We feared the worst."

He shrugged self-consciously. "So did ah, fer a while. But ye were right. Ah told mahself that the past was the past, and ah could nae change it, but ah could try harder and do better in the future. Once ah started ta believe a little bit—really believe it—ah was able ta hurt the Butcher and eventually, finish it off."

Dylan smiled. "I'm glad. We all are. Not just because you were able to come help us—we couldn't have saved Sara without you—but also just because you're okay." Tom nodded his agreement.

"Speaking of saving me," Sara said, "how did that work?" She turned to Alex. "That was adrenaline you injected me with, right? Or rather, you injected Ardu, inside me."

"That's right," Alex said.

Sara heaved a defeated sigh. "I'm glad I'm not dead, and I'm even more glad that I didn't hurt any of you too badly, but now... Ardu is in our world, and we're stuck here. We can't cross the veil if he's not in the Twilight."

Dylan angrily hurled a small rock into the distance. "That must have been his plan all along, to force our hand. That's why he... put himself inside Sara." He had to close his eyes and take a moment to gather his composure after saying it out loud. "He knew we wouldn't kill her or seriously hurt her. So, either he would force her to kill us or...."

"Or we would use adrenaline to banish him to our world, trapping ourselves here in the process," Alex finished.

"Either way, he wins," Jacob sighed.

"Not yet, he doesn't," Tom said. He loaded the AWM with a fresh magazine and worked the bolt to chamber a round. He checked his watch. "We still have five hours."

"Five hours to do what? We can't cross the veil when Ardu isn't in the Twilight, which means we can't stop him," Sara said. "He handicapped himself by reverting to his infant form, but not by much. He's already growing again, and within a few hours, he'll be big enough to start killing people."

Dylan noticed that Alex was staring blankly into space and put a hand over hers. "Alex, it's okay," he said. "You didn't know."

"Yes, I did," she said.

Tom frowned. "You knew that your plan would send Ardu to our world and make it impossible for us to follow him?"

She nodded. "I was pretty sure. What else could we have done? Kill Sara? That's never been on the table. That's why we're here. We're supposed to be fighting to stop the cycle of sacrifice."

Sara looked like she had mixed feelings about Alex's decision.

Dylan sighed. "Don't get me wrong, I'm glad Alex's plan worked, but I don't understand *why* it worked. It shouldn't have. Ardu's not from our world, so why did adrenaline send him there?"

"But he is from our world. In the most fundamental sense, he has to be," Alex said.

"Alex is right," Sara cut in. "I realized it too, just before he... possessed me." She absently covered her stomach with one hand. "Down there in the Deep Nothing, his eyes were solid white just like ours. He said something weird, and I didn't think much of it at the time, but now it's all starting to come together. He said that the Twilight is a 'blank canvas,' that it reflects the 'core of men's hearts.'"

Alex nodded. "The more I thought about it, the more I realized that that had to be the basic nature of this place. We already knew that the Twilight changes based on the thoughts and fears of those who come here. When people first came to the Twilight thousands of years ago, there was nothing here. Ardu was the first thing to manifest in this place, but he existed long before that—in the form of a very old, very powerful idea."

"The idea that individuals exist only ta serve the tribe, the group, or the 'greater good,' not ta live their own lives," Jacob said, stroking his beard thoughtfully.

"In a sense, Ardu did originate here, in the Twilight, but in a deeper, more fundamental sense, he came from our world," Tom said. He was beginning to follow Alex's train of thought.

She nodded. "Which is why adrenaline sent him back there. He's not native to the Twilight. He just sleeps here, like we do—only he sleeps for generations at a time."

Dylan frowned. "So, it's not really accurate to say that the Twilight reflects 'men's hearts'—it reflects the deepest convictions that people hold in their *minds.*"

"Which explains why the Twilight behaves in such inconsistent, contradictory ways—because everyone who comes here holds inconsistent, contradictory ideas," Sara said.

"But people can choose to change their ideas and their actions. We definitely did," Dylan said.

"Fat lot of good it's done," Jacob grunted. "We came so close ta endin' it, but we failed. We're stuck here now. We cannae do anythin' but sit around while Ardu lays waste to our world."

"You already beat your Eidolon, let's not bring it back," Alex said, keeping her tone gentle.

Jacob nodded. "Yer right, lass. We need ta think of the solution, nae the problem."

"I don't understand what Ardu wants. I get that in his twisted mind, he thinks he's doing us a favor by forcing us to be our brothers' keepers or whatever, but why does he care? What does he get out of this?" Tom asked.

"I think that, now, I finally understand," Sara said. "Ardu doesn't want anything, and he's not pursuing a goal, at least not in the way that people want and pursue things. He's an idea given physical form by the Twilight, right? A manifestation of the idea that selfless sacrifice is noble?"

The others agreed that that made sense.

"So, he's more like a robot than a person—he's just acting on his programming, carrying out the logical consequences of that idea. Same goes for the other creatures in the Twilight—they don't have purposes or goals, they just act in accordance with their nature, which, in turn, was established subconsciously by the person whose thoughts and fears created them. Ardu kills not because he wants to but because widespread death and destruction are the inevitable results of subordinating individuals to groups. There's no other way he *could* act."

"What will he do now, exactly?" Alex asked.

"At midnight, he'll become invincible, but that doesn't mean he's omnipotent. His power, although great, is limited, and he has to use it efficiently. That's why he likes natural disasters, because he can use them to kill tens or hundreds of thousands of people at a time with a relatively minor expenditure of his power. After midnight tonight, it will be almost impossible to stop him—not just because we can't kill him, but because nobody will be able to find him. He'll blend into society and work from the shadows. He knows he can't be killed, but he also knows that somebody could seal him in concrete and drop him to the bottom of the ocean or otherwise permanently contain him, and he won't leave himself open to that risk. He'll vanish for weeks or months at a time, and once he triggers a supervolcano or poisons an entire city's water supply, he'll vanish again, before anyone even realizes what's coming. There will be no way to predict where he'll go or what he'll do next. As long as he's careful and patient, he'll have free rein to wipe us out, a few million people at a time, and we'll never catch up to him."

"Let's try the obvious thing, just to cover all our bases," Tom said. He took out his adrenaline and injected himself. He quickly became flushed and sweaty, but other than that, nothing happened. He sighed. "I didn't think it would work, but it was worth a shot. Now we know for sure. What else can we try? We've gotta figure out how to get back home and end this."

Sara stood up and started pacing back and forth. "I'm thinking, I really am. I just don't have any other ideas."

Alex stood up as well. "Maybe there's a way that you heard about and forgot because it didn't seem important at the time? Something you read in some ancient book? Even just a wild theory?"

Sara shook her head. "No, nothing. You go to sleep or you take a powerful stimulant, like adrenaline. Those are the only two ways to cross the veil that I've ever heard of, and neither works if Ardu isn't in the Twilight."

"Wait a second," Dylan said. "Something doesn't add up. If nobody can cross the veil when Ardu isn't in the Twilight, how did anybody come here before he existed?"

Sara shook her head. "It's a good question, but I don't know." Suddenly, her face lit up. "But people *did* come to the Twilight before Ardu existed, because he was created by people's thoughts once those people were *in* the Twilight. So, it must be possible to cross the veil if he's not here."

"That's right," Alex said. "Sara said that usually, Ardu can't cross over until midnight on the eighth day. He succeeded in forcing us to send him back to Earth ahead of schedule, but he tipped his hand in the process. There is a way to follow him—there must be. We just need to find it."

The five of them brainstormed, debated, and argued. At first, the ideas seemed plausible, if unorthodox. When none of those worked and desperation began to take root, the ideas became increasingly bizarre. At one point, Dylan suggested climbing back to the top of the forty-foot village gate, then jumping off, on the theory that falling in a dream often jarred the dreamer awake.

No one was willing to test it.

"Come on, guys, we have to figure this out," Alex said. "We've come so far and solved so many impossible problems already, we can do this."

"Sara," Tom said, turning toward her, "when Alex banished Ardu back to our world, he was an infant again. Doesn't that reset the twelve-hour clock and buy us more time? You said it took twelve hours for him to fully mature and become invincible."

Sara shook her head. "I wish. It's an absolute deadline, not a twelve-hour clock. Every Pilgrimage is seven days, exactly to the minute. Ardu's power fully matures at midnight on the eighth day if the final ritual hasn't been completed by then." She checked her watch. "We just forced him out of my body about half an hour ago, so right now, with less than five hours to go until midnight, he looks like he's about two years old. He'll grow at a rate of about four years per hour. He's probably hiding in my house somewhere, waiting. In about two more hours, he'll be big enough to start killing people." A moment after saying that, she blanched. "Dad...."

Dylan, who had been pacing and listening quietly, suddenly stopped dead in his tracks. He whirled around and snapped his fingers as his eyes lit up, elated. "The witches!" he exclaimed.

Sara frowned. "What about them?"

Tom, who had been sitting on the ground with his back against the fountain, sat bolt upright, his eyes wide. "Dylan's right. The witches—they were testing us. It makes sense now."

Alex slapped her forehead, suddenly feeling stupid. "Of course! That's what they were testing us for—to see if we could be the ones to break the cycle. We thought we all passed, but only Dylan did. Tom and I failed."

"But now we're ready," Tom said. "If we can convince them, maybe they can help us."

Sara nodded. "It's worth a try."

"But where are they? How do we find them?" Dylan asked.

Tom cupped his hands around his mouth and shouted. "Witches! Are you here? We need your help!"

Silence.

Alex tried. "We understand now! We know what you were testing us for. We weren't ready then, but we are now. Help us!"

Nothing.

Jacob kicked a rock, growling in frustration. Sara pinched the bridge of her nose and tried to think of something else.

"Wait a minute," Dylan said. His brow was furrowed. Clearly, he was deep in thought.

"Dylan? Do you have an idea?" Alex asked.

He looked at her. "I think I know what the witches are. They all looked like young women, right?" Tom, Sara, and Alex nodded. Jacob shrugged; he'd never met one. "Young women who want to break the cycle," Dylan prompted.

Sara gasped. "They're past Maidens."

"Maidens who realized the truth too late to do anything about it—after they became Matrons but before they died," Tom said, rubbing his chin.

"It sounds like it makes sense. That has to be it. Who or what else could they be?" Alex said, a note of hope in her voice.

Dylan looked at each of the others in turn. "There were four of them, right?"

"Right," Sara said.

Dylan fixed his gaze on her. "What if there are five now?"

She frowned. "Five? Where did the fifth...?" Her eyes widened as she trailed off.

Dylan reached into his pocket and pulled out Marie's wedding ring. He closed his fingers around it and shut his eyes. "Mom... if you can hear me, I need your help."

The silence stretched on. The five Wardens held their breath, waiting.

Near the fountain, the air seemed to shimmer and distort back on itself. A faint white light appeared, barely more than a candle flame. Slowly, it grew in size and became brighter until they had to look away from it.

The smile that Marie gave her son was even more radiant than the light had been.

* * *

"Mom!" Dylan shouted. He threw his arms around her and squeezed her tightly. She rested a hand on top of his head. Like the other witches, her body glowed with a warm, quiet light, leaving only her face clearly visible.

"Holy shit," Tom whispered.

"Aye," Jacob agreed.

Sara and Alex could only stare in slack-jawed amazement.

Every time I think I could not be prouder of you, you prove me wrong, Marie said, brushing Dylan's face with the back of her hand. All five of them heard her voice in their heads, although her lips didn't move. Along with the impression of her voice came a sound like a crackling campfire.

The tears coming from Dylan's eyes did nothing to diminish his smile. "Mom, I'm so glad you're... not part of the Hollow, at least. But we're so short on time. The other witches—can you call them?"

Marie nodded. She closed her eyes and bowed her head, as if concentrating intently. A moment later, four more white lights flared into life, one after another.

The witch who had been assigned to Alex spoke first, with an inflection of tree branches swaying in the wind. *You have something you wish to tell us?*

Alex nodded. "We do. But first, please tell us your names. We know that you were once Maidens and that you came to understand that the cycle must end. Please do us the honor of sharing some small part of who you were."

The witch who had been assigned to Alex bowed her head slightly. *I am Ayumi, from Takayama, Japan.*

The one who had tested Tom introduced herself as Irina, from Vladivostok, Russia.

Dylan's witch was Rhosyn, from Swansea, Wales.

The last witch, Sanaa, had been raised in Marrakesh, Morocco.

Alex nodded a polite greeting to each of them. "Thank you for sharing your names. We will never forget them. We finally understand what's really going on here, and why. We know what you were testing us for, and why. We know that Dylan passed, but Tom and I failed. Now, we're ready. We can stop Ardu—for good—but we need your help."

Rhosyn spoke directly into their minds. *What you claim, and what you ask— neither is a small thing.* They heard the soft sound of wind chimes in the distance.

"I failed my test not because of the answer I gave but because of my reasons for giving it," Alex said. "You told me that my life would be forfeit if I helped Sara complete her Pilgrimage. I thought you meant that I would die, but you were talking about something even worse than death. You were trying to tell me that if I changed nothing about myself, if I chose to help Sara as a way of alleviating my own guilt, if I showed myself to be more concerned with the past than the future, I would suffer the worst fate of all. Sara would lose her life to evil, and once I learned the price she'd paid, I would go home to live out the rest of my days with guilt in my heart worse than any I'd ever carried before. That's what you meant when you said that I would 'forfeit my life'—not that I would physically die, but I would condemn myself to a living death, the worst fate of all.

"I'd like to change my answer if it's not too late. I forgive myself for my sins, and I refuse to accept responsibility for the sins of others, real or imagined. There is no defense and no justification for trying to instill guilt in people who haven't done anything to earn it. I want to use what I've learned to help myself and others run toward the future instead of away from the past. I want to help Sara not as a gesture of penance but because life is my highest value."

Tom stepped forward and locked eyes with Irina. "I fucked up my test, too. At the time, I had started to understand what duty really is, but I was still letting other people dictate what I should do with my life. By extension, I was endorsing the idea that Sara's life belonged not to her but to others, and that they could dispose of her as long as they decided it was necessary. You offered me a fantasy life, a dream world where I could have had everything I ever wanted. I thought I passed your test when I rejected the fantasy in favor of my duty to Sara and to the rest of humanity, but all I really did was prove to you that I wasn't yet ready to break the cycle.

"You never wanted me to accept the dream world. That also would have shown you that I wasn't who you were looking for. You weren't testing *whether* I would choose Sara but *why* I would choose her. I also want to change my answer. I want to help and protect Sara because she's important *to me*, not because someone else said that I have a duty to help her. I want to help her protect the world because *I* value human life, not because someone else declared that I should live my life in service to others. You were looking for someone willing to decide who and what matters most to *him*, and to fight hard for *his own* values, no matter what anyone else thinks about it. Only that kind of person would have the courage to reject thousands of years of blood-soaked tradition and find a way to protect the world without throwing away innocent lives. The other day, I wasn't quite ready to be that person, but I am now."

Dylan turned to face the witch who had tested him, Rhosyn. "I should thank you," he said to her. "Down there, in those caves, I thought you were torturing me, but you weren't. You were trying to help me, and you did. You knew that I had started to learn my lesson about doubting and pitying myself all the time, but you weren't sure if I was ready to create a new path that no one had ever even considered before. The only way you could be sure was to put me in a situation where nothing but real, full confidence in my own abilities could save me.

"At first, I pushed myself for Sara's sake, because I was scared of what would happen to her if I wasn't around to protect her. But you helped me see that even though I love Sara and would do anything to keep her safe, I can't live *for* her. I have to live for myself. Sara and I both have to be strong *by* ourselves and *for* ourselves. Only then can we really be good for each other. I'm ready to break the cycle—for her, and for my dad, and for Tom, Alex, and Jacob, and for the sake of everyone else on Earth—but most of all, for me. It doesn't matter that no one else has ever tried to do this. I can do it, and I will—with help from my friends."

Sara heaved a deep sigh and clasped her hands in front of her. Everyone else watched her, waiting to hear what she would say. "Tom, Alex, Dylan…. I was tested too, and I failed—miserably. I won't tell you about the test itself—there's no time, and it doesn't really matter anyway. I was nowhere near ready to break the cycle, which is probably why my test didn't last very long. I really was waiting there, alone in the tunnels, for hours. I must have been a pretty bad student." Sanaa gave her a knowing smile, one that also suggested that she could see how much Sara had grown since then.

Sara raised a fist. "I get it now, thanks to Dylan, Alex, and Tom. They all helped me understand how wrong I'd been. I was ignoring the evidence that my beliefs were flawed, but my eyes are wide open now. I'm ready to finish this, with my friends' help—and yours, if you'll give it."

All eyes turned to Jacob. He blinked, clearly taken aback. "What do ye want me ta say? Ah'm here, aren't ah? Ah dinnae ken about all this testin' business. Ah've had almost forty years ta think about where ah went wrong. But ah suppose that's kinda the point, isn't it? It's time ta stop dwellin' on all mah fuckups. Like the lass said, it's time ta look forward, nae back. Ah can help shut all this down, and ah will. That's how ah go ta mah grave in peace."

No one said anything. Several of the witches frowned at him curiously.

Jacob scowled. "Ah killed the fuckin' Butcher, didn't ah? What more proof do ye want? Ah've learned mah lesson. Let's get on with it."

The witches blinked in surprise. Alex rolled her eyes. Tom and Dylan chuckled to themselves.

Sanaa turned to face Sara. *What would you have us do?*

Sara met her eyes. "Send us back across the veil, to our world, if you can."

What makes you think we can do this?

"If anyone can, you can. You've already shown us that you can do things that are strange and incredible, even in the Twilight. You created a grand illusion for Tom, a perfect clone of the Prisoner for Alex, and took on the form of Dylan's mother. You can take us back."

The witches glanced at one another. Ayumi spoke next. *Perhaps. There is no guarantee. But to make the attempt would incur a great cost.*

"What cost?"

Ourselves.

Dylan's eyes widened in shock. He put an arm protectively around Marie's shoulders. "You mean you would have to… kill yourselves?"

Marie raised a hand to smooth his hair. *We are already dead; we cannot die again. But if we were to attempt to pierce the veil, we would have to carry you to the other side. It is not a path you can navigate on your own.*

Sara slowly sank to her knees, suddenly looking paler than usual. "When you were alive, you were from our world. But now… you're part of the mist, part of the Twilight."

Alex shook her head, her voice tinged with sorrow. "And no part of the Twilight can go to our world."

Irina nodded slowly. *The moment we carried you through the veil, we would cease to be.*

A long silence stretched between them.

"We're asking you to sacrifice yourselves," Alex said. "We're asking you to do the very thing we've been trying to put a stop to."

Ayumi smiled sadly. *Have you learned nothing about sacrifice?*

"It's a terrible thing to ask, but it's not a sacrifice," Sara said. Her voice was low and quiet. "When you make a sacrifice, you give up something more precious and valuable than whatever you get in return. To give what remains of your lives to break the cycle—that's not at all the same thing as me giving up my life to keep the cycle going. They couldn't be more different. The Pilgrimage sacrifices life and hope in service to death and decay. If you were to destroy yourselves to ensure that my Pilgrimage will be the last, it would be in service to the most precious and valuable thing of all: life itself."

Sanaa beamed. *So, you have learned.*

Dylan was crying openly. "What will happen to you if you do that? Where will you go?" He was talking mostly to Marie, and they all knew it.

She gently took his face in her hands. *We will simply no longer be. We are okay with that. There is no life here, in this place. People, living or dead, do not belong in the Twilight.* She lowered one hand and placed it over his heart. *No matter what, I will always be with you.*

Rhosyn stepped forward. *There is more to it than that. You must understand the gravity of what you are asking. If we do this, if we attempt to take you back, there is no guarantee that we will succeed. If we fail, all of us could be forever lost in the empty space between the two worlds. Even we do not know the endless suffering that may entail.*

It could also be that we simply fail in our attempt to return you to your world. You could find yourselves back here, without us, trapped in the Twilight until Ardu finishes raining death on humanity, at which time he will return. He will find you here, he will be invincible, and he will torture you for eternity—unless you take your own lives first. But even that is not the worst of it.

Dylan swallowed hard. "How could it get any worse?"

Ayumi spoke next. *Exterminating humanity entirely would be extremely difficult, even for Ardu. He can incite natural disasters, perhaps even trigger global war, but it is likely that small pockets of humanity will survive, unnoticed by him. After he returns to the Twilight, the planet will gradually heal, and in time, mankind will build new cities and civilizations. It is possible—even probable—that no one will ever discover the Twilight again and that Ardu will sleep here for all time—inside the last Maiden, causing her agony beyond description that may literally never end. It could be that the two worlds will never come in contact again—if you choose not to intervene now.*

Sara's eyes widened in shock. "You mean, if we choose to stay here and let Ardu destroy most of the world? Why would we do that?"

Because of the consequences if you try to stop him and fail. Even if we successfully return you to your world, the veil will be irreparably damaged, that much we know with certainty. If you succeed in killing Ardu before midnight tonight, then all will be well. With Ardu gone and the veil damaged, no human will ever again be able to come to the Twilight. Over time, it will wither, die, and likely fade out of existence. Your world will be safe, at least from this threat.

But if we pierce the veil tonight, and you fail to kill Ardu before midnight, he will become invincible and unstoppable. He will kill the five of you, he will kill most of the rest of humanity—and then he will attempt to return to the Twilight. He will not know that the veil is damaged, and when he attempts to cross it, he will destroy it entirely, creating an open wound between the two worlds. The Twilight's evil will flood endlessly into your world, with no way to seal the breach or stem the tide. Make no mistake. Eventually, the last human on Earth will perish in terror. Some may evade Ardu's wrath, but none will escape the endless wave of death and fear that will cover the world if the veil breaks. In time, mankind will go extinct, as will all other life. One day, when there is no more life to consume, the Twilight will starve, and both worlds will cease to be.

A stunned silence fell over the small group.

Finally, Jacob spoke up. "So, our choices are ta sit here scratchin' our junk while Ardu erases billions of lives, in which case we break the cycle fer whatever future generations may arise in a few hundred years… or we go all in. No mulligans, no second chances. Winner takes all."

Sara closed her eyes for a moment. "No more sacrifices," she said.

Marie gave Sara a comforting smile and brushed her filthy hair out of her face. *It must be unanimous—among all ten of us. If we are to lose ourselves, such as we are, we must do so with full confidence that you will succeed.*

"I vote yes," Tom said. "I won't just kick this can down the road, especially not at the cost of billions of innocent lives. That would make us even worse than the people who started the cycle of nightmares. Every second counts. Let's put this shithole in the rearview mirror."

"Yes," Dylan said.

"Yes," Alex echoed.

"Aye," Jacob said.

"No more sacrifices," Sara whispered, reiterating her original vote.

The five witches traded glances, as though they were speaking to one another on a frequency inaudible to the others. After several long moments, they seemed to come to an agreement.

We will do our best to aid you. We agree that if the cycle can be broken, you are the ones to do it.

Sara looked anxious. "What do we have to do?"

You need only think of where you wish to return. Getting you there is up to us. Your task begins when you arrive. Where do you wish to go?

"My house," Sara said. "We need ammo, and that's where Ardu went, I'm sure of it." She didn't say, "And I need to check on my dad." She didn't have to.

"Agreed," Tom said.

"Uh, slight problem," Jacob said, raising his hand. "Ah dinnae ken yer house, lass, so ah cannae think of it."

Marie smiled. *I do, and I can. The same one you were born in? On Meadowsweet Lane?*

Sara returned the smile. "That's the one."

Marie nodded. *Because I know the place, I can guide all of us there.*

Dylan threw his arms around his mother and held her tightly. "Mom... I love you. We won't let you down. I promise."

She returned her son's embrace and kissed his forehead. *I have never been more certain of anything. Give Richard my love... and tell him what happened here, if you can convince him, and if you judge it the right thing to do.*

The village vanished in a crescendo of pure light.

* * *

Sara, Alex, Tom, Dylan, and Jacob all fell to their knees and vomited. Each had a pounding headache, and their stomachs cramped with intense nausea. The doom room spun crazily around them.

Tom forced himself to stand. "We... made it?"

Sara tried to get to her feet, but a sudden bout of dizziness knocked her back over. "Barely," she said. Whatever the witches had done to pierce the veil, it clearly had had some physical side effects.

Jacob was the first to notice that the room looked like a bomb had gone off. Upended furniture and damaged equipment lay scattered everywhere. Broken glass covered the floor. The air stank of blood.

Dr. Atwood and several Circle bodyguards were in pieces all over the room. The walls and ceiling were covered in gore.

"Holy shit," Dylan whispered when he saw the carnage. "Ardu's definitely been here." Sara, still not quite able to walk, crawled over to Dr. Atwood. It was obvious, even from across the room, that nothing could be done. Everyone was long dead. Sara closed her eyes and sighed, clearly distraught by the sight.

Tom cocked his head, listening carefully. The house was silent. He heard nothing except blood dripping from the ceiling nearby into a coagulated pool below. "Sounds like Ardu's gone, but stay quiet and alert in case he's not," he whispered.

"I don't understand," Sara said. "Ardu shouldn't be able to do this, not yet. It's only been—" She stopped when she looked at her watch. "Oh, no. It feels like we were in the village just a minute ago, but it took almost three hours to get back here. It's 10:40. We're almost out of time."

"Let's haul ass, then," Tom said. He jogged over to the armory door, pulled it open, and ushered everyone inside. "Don't forget to put new batteries in your flashlights, the ones we made from Twilight parts didn't come back with us." They gathered as much ammunition as they could carry. All five of them emptied their packs and filled them with a mix of trauma supplies and extra grenades.

"Ah think we're as ready as we can be," Jacob said.

"Where would Ardu go?" Tom asked, loading a fresh magazine of buckshot into his Jackhammer. "How do we find him?"

"The dam," Sara said without hesitation. "His preferred method of killing people in large numbers is to cause major disasters. Breaking the dam would do it. At least fifty thousand people live downstream."

"Let's go kick his ass, then," Tom said. He led them out of the basement. Blood was spattered all over the stairway. Mutilated corpses littered the living room and kitchen. Sara closed her eyes, trying not to look. Some were people she'd known her whole life. They'd been complicit in appeasing evil by keeping the cycle going, but the carnage nonetheless churned her stomach. She wished she'd had a chance to show them a better way. Perhaps some would have listened.

"Sara," came a hoarse whisper from the hallway leading to Ethan's office. They spun around, weapons raised.

"Dad?" Sara's eyes widened.

Ethan stumbled toward them, a .45-caliber Beretta Px4 held down at his side in his right hand. He was clutching his stomach with his left hand. His shirt and pants had large bloodstains on them, but they were dry. The bleeding seemed to have stopped. "Ardu came through the veil... early," he managed to get out.

"Dad, we're gonna stop him," she said. "We need to go. There's no time."

Ethan coughed. "Stop him? What do you mean, 'stop him'?"

"As in, stop him from breathing and moving. Permanently," Tom said.

Ethan stared at them in wide-eyed shock. "Kill him? You think you can… kill Ardu?"

"Ordinarily, no," Sara said. "But he crossed the veil early. He's not fully grown yet. He's not invincible yet. We have to hurry."

Ethan coughed again. "What happened?"

"Dad, there's no time. We have to go now." She turned to lead them out of the house.

Once they'd moved a few steps toward the door, Ethan spoke from behind them. "I can't let you go."

They turned back to see Ethan aiming his weapon directly at Sara. It trembled in his grip as tears welled up in his eyes. Tom immediately stepped in front of her and snapped his Jackhammer into a firing stance. "Tom, don't shoot him!" Sara shouted.

Dylan had drawn his USP but kept it down at his side. He stared at Ethan in slack-jawed incredulity. "Sending your own daughter to her death isn't bad enough? You'd really murder her with your own hands?" He was nearly shouting, struggling to rein in his anger.

Ethan grimaced but didn't lower his weapon. "You have no idea how much it hurts me to do this. But we have to beg Ardu's forgiveness. We have to enact the mass sacrifice. It won't work without Sara. Every Maiden must offer her life. The others are on standby, waiting for my call. Nothing has changed. Sara is still the only one who can save us."

Tom kept his shotgun trained on Ethan's chest, his finger holding four pounds of pressure on the five-pound trigger. "You're not very good at making threats," he said. "If you need Sara alive to sacrifice her in your sick ritual, then you can't shoot her. We're leaving."

Ethan sighed and lowered his weapon slightly. "You're right. But if I must, I have other ways to force her to do the right thing." He turned the Beretta around and pressed the barrel against his own head.

"Dad, no!" Sara shouted. She started to run toward him, but Tom snatched her arm and dragged her back. Dylan, Alex, and Jacob stood off to the side, wanting to defuse the situation but unsure how.

"You can't kill yourself if the safety's on," Tom said to Ethan, almost casually. Ethan frowned, clearly taken aback. For a fraction of a second, as if he were acting by reflex before he could think about what he was doing, he tilted the barrel away from his head, just enough so that he could see the weapon's safety indicator.

Quick as lightning, Tom snatched a vase from a nearby table and hurled it. It hit Ethan in the collarbone and shattered, sending broken porcelain and water everywhere. Even before the vase made contact, Tom was already moving. He closed the distance to Ethan and slapped away the Beretta. Ethan threw a right hook, but it was sloppy. Tom ducked under it, shot behind him, and applied a blood choke. Within seconds, Ethan's movements became slow, his eyelids drooped, and he went limp. Tom gently lowered him to the floor and released the hold.

Sara rushed over with tears in her eyes. Dylan followed, unwilling to let her out of his sight. "Thanks for not hurting him," Sara said. She sniffled and wiped away the tears. "The other Maidens are waiting on his call to kill themselves. Let's make sure he can't make that call."

Tom dragged Ethan into a guest bedroom across the hall and zip-tied his hands to the heavy iron bed frame. Sara dropped the Beretta's magazine, racked the slide to eject the chambered round, and pocketed it. She tossed the empty weapon down the hallway, then found Ethan's phone in his pocket and took it. "He'll wake up any second," Tom said. "Let's move. We've lost too much time already." Sara stared at her unconscious father for a long moment, a storm of mixed emotions brewing on her face. "Sara, we need to go," Tom repeated. He got to his feet and pulled her along gently. After a brief moment of resistance, she went.

Tom, Alex, Sara, and Jacob darted out the front door. Dylan stayed behind. He stood over Ethan, watching him. Dylan held his USP down at his side.

Ethan groaned, then stirred. His eyes fluttered open. He tried to stand up, then realized that he was firmly immobilized. He looked up at Dylan, blinking several more times to clear his vision.

Without a word, Dylan raised his USP and aimed it at Ethan's forehead. Dylan's face was red. His chest heaved. Ethan stared back impassively. "You were going to kill your own daughter," Dylan said. His voice trembled with rage. "And you killed my mom. You may not have given the order, but you let it happen, and you lied to us about it." With his thumb, Dylan cocked the hammer.

"Do it," Ethan said, quietly. "I deserve it."

Dylan curled his finger around the trigger. A long silence stretched between them.

"Yeah, you do. But Sara doesn't," he said. He lowered the weapon to his side and decocked it. "This is your mess. Clean it up. If there's anything left in you worth saving, you won't make that phone call."

"Dylan! Let's move!" Tom shouted from outside.

Without looking back, Dylan jogged to the front door. As soon as he stepped outside, he saw that they had another problem. Every vehicle in sight had been smashed into twisted lumps of metal. Some were on fire. The closest neighbors were at least a mile away; hopefully, they hadn't been in the path of Ardu's rampage.

"That motherfucker," Tom said, staring at the remains of his truck. "*Now* I'm mad."

"How are we supposed to get to the dam? It's almost fifty miles from here," Sara said, frustration growing in her voice.

A black pickup truck turned the corner at the far end of the road, coming toward them. As it drew closer, Sara squinted at it. "Is that...?"

"Oh, shit," Dylan said, shaking his head.

The truck stopped in front of them, and the door opened. Richard stepped out, his eyes wide at the sight of the five of them in combat armor, carrying guns and explosives.

"Dylan, what the hell? What is all this? I've been calling and texting all day. You didn't answer... I came to check—"

Tom stepped forward and took Richard firmly by the arm. "Sorry, we need to borrow your truck, and we can't leave you here. Trust me, you don't want to be in Sara's house right now, anyway. Hop in the back." Without waiting for an invitation, the others began to pile in. The cab could only hold five, so Jacob climbed into the bed. Dylan slid into the back seat next to his father while Tom got behind the wheel.

"Dylan, why do you have guns? Why are there cars on fire? What is—"

Dylan cut him off as Tom put the truck in gear and headed for the highway. "Dad, nothing I can say is gonna make any sense to you. This is the important thing I said I had to do. Literally, the entire world is in danger. We have to get to the dam now."

Richard blinked. "Have you been taking drugs?"

"Dylan's right, I'm afraid," Alex said from her seat on the other side of Richard.

"All of us will tell you the same thing," Tom added. He sped up, driving as fast as he dared. "Everyone buckle up."

"This is insane. I'm calling the police," Richard said. He dug his phone out of his pocket and started to dial. Dylan rolled down the window, snatched away the phone, and tossed it.

"No cops," Tom said. "Anyone else who gets involved in this will have no idea what they're walking into, and they'll just get killed."

Richard was fuming. "Involved in 'this'? What is 'this'? What have you people roped my son into?"

Sara cut him off. "Tom, turn right here, at the end of the road," she said. "I stole a car this morning. It should still be there at the corner. It's too small for all of us, but Richard can use it to get home."

Richard's eyes got even wider. "Sara stole a car? What the hell is happening?"

Everyone ignored him. Tom turned where Sara had indicated and stopped the truck.

There was no car. Fresh tire tracks in the snow led toward the highway.

"Shit," Sara muttered. "I was afraid of that."

"Don't tell me Ardu took it," Alex said.

Sara sighed. "He was... inside me. He knows everything I know, including how to drive and where I parked that car." She covered her abdomen with one hand, reliving the terrible memory.

"Perfect," Tom said. "Guess Richard's coming with us for now. We'll drop him off somewhere well away from the dam." Tom turned onto the highway and floored it.

"Enough!" Richard roared. Dylan blinked in surprise. He couldn't remember the last time he'd heard his dad yell. "Someone tell me what the fuck is going on, right now!"

Tom glanced back at Alex. "Can you help us out here?"

Alex sighed and rummaged around in one of the pouches on her armor. She came out with a syringe and unceremoniously rammed it into Richard's thigh.

"Ow! What the hell was that?" he yelled.

"Any second now," Sara sighed.

A moment later, Richard's eyelids began to droop. "What... did...?"

He fell sideways, onto Dylan's shoulder. Alex reached over to check his pulse and monitor his reaction to the sedatives. He wasn't unconscious, but he wasn't far from it, either.

"I'm sorry, Dad. You'll be alright," Dylan whispered.

A few minutes later, Tom slowed down and turned into the parking lot of a diner. He parked behind a dumpster, where no one inside would be able to see the truck's license plate. "This is the only shelter between here and the dam," he said. "Get Richard inside and find someone to take care of him. Hurry."

Alex, Jacob, and Dylan carted Richard into the diner and told an employee to call an ambulance. They quickly rushed back to the truck before anyone could start asking questions or taking pictures.

Sara checked her watch as the others piled back into the truck. "Fifty minutes," she reported. "Let's finish it."

The truck roared back onto the highway, tires squealing.

CHAPTER FORTY-FOUR
Vindication

The security guard's name was Jim Greer. Jim was an amateur woodworker who enjoyed hiking and reading mystery novels. He had a wife, a son, and a daughter.

His last thoughts were of them as Ardu wrenched his neck violently to one side and tore off his head. Ardu tossed aside the head as the body fell limply to the ground, crimson blood pumping into the snow. Ardu looked down at his own body; it was coming along nicely. He had finally grown into the suit he'd taken from one of the maggots he'd killed. It looked better on him, anyway.

It was almost time.

Something was coming—something that made a deep, rumbling sound. He turned around.

The truck didn't even slow down. It slammed into him, pinning him to the concrete wall at the base of the stairs leading up to the dam's main control room. Dimly, he felt pain. It was hardly concerning. Mostly, he was angry.

After fighting with the airbags for a second, Tom and Sara kicked open the doors and rolled out into the snow. They both popped to their feet and opened up on Ardu, shredding his flesh with sustained gunfire. Jacob, Alex, and Dylan stumbled out of the backseat, still dazed from the crash.

Ardu's injuries knitted together instantly, wisps of mist escaping from the bullet holes like hot steam. He shoved the truck away hard enough to flip it end over end. Dylan hit the ground on his stomach, and the truck pinwheeled over him, missing his head by inches. "How did you get here?" Ardu hissed. They shouldn't have been able to cross the veil. They should still be trapped in the Twilight.

Instead of answering, Tom fired the last two shells in his magazine, one into each of Ardu's eyes. Fist-sized chunks of his head were blown away, only to be replaced a heartbeat later by fresh bone and muscle. More mist seeped out, evaporating into the frigid night air.

Dylan, Alex, and Jacob opened fire while Tom and Sara reloaded. In the blink of an eye, Ardu was gone. Suddenly, he was behind Jacob, ramming a fist into his back with enough force to break the skin. He closed his fingers around the miserable creature's spine and ripped it out.

At least, that had been the plan. Ardu had underestimated the strength of modern body armor. The rear ceramic plate in Jacob's armor shattered into pieces, and he pitched to the ground, screaming in agony. He felt a deep, terrible pain in his back, so paralyzing that he couldn't move, couldn't draw a breath.

Alex emptied an entire MPX magazine into Ardu's chest, shredding the last tattered remnants of his stolen suit. Again, the wounds healed immediately. He rushed toward her, now aware that the humans' armor was tough. He would go for the throat instead.

Dylan had the same idea, and he was slightly faster. He rammed his knife into the side of Ardu's neck. Hot, black blood spurted everywhere. Ardu reacted with incredible speed, ramming his elbow backward into Dylan's chest. Dylan went flying into a nearby tree, his front and rear armor plates both severely damaged. He hit the ground screaming in pain.

Ardu ripped the knife from his neck and hurled it at Tom, the wound already closing. Reflexively, Tom raised his Jackhammer in front of his face. The knife pinged off the heavy steel frame and ricocheted away into the darkness.

Sara finished reloading her rifle and snapped it to her shoulder. Before she could fire, Ardu bent his knees and leaped, soaring in a single bound to the roof of the control room. Her jaw dropped; it was easily forty feet up.

"I don't have time to play with you," he called down. "You can die with all the rest." He raised one hand to the sky and snapped his fingers. Instantaneously, thick, greenish-black clouds materialized, swirling together like a tornado beginning to form, coalescing into a heavy curtain that covered the entire sky. The moonlight dimmed greatly, leaving the base of the dam in almost total darkness. The five Wardens clicked on their flashlights.

A mighty bolt of lightning flashed from the sky, briefly illuminating the area. When the light faded, Ardu was gone. Alex helped Jacob to his feet and quickly checked him over as he caught his breath. He would have a nasty bruise, but his armor had undoubtedly saved his life.

Frigid rain began to fall in a torrent, mixed with slushy snow and small hailstones. A gust of wind kicked up, so powerful that they had to lean into it to avoid being knocked over. More lightning flashed, and a ferocious *crack* of thunder rolled through the clouds.

"Where'd he go?" Jacob yelled over the wind.

"He's gonna try to break the dam," Sara yelled back. "We have to go after him."

Tom ran to the wrecked truck and retrieved Manny's rifle. Sara knelt by the dead security guard, her heart breaking for the poor man. She snatched the control room keys from his belt and led the charge up the stairway.

There was more fresh carnage inside. Dismembered engineers and security guards were slumped over half-built consoles and flung aside like garbage.

"Fucking evil psychopath," Alex growled through gritted teeth.

The room was pitch black. "Ardu's cut power to the dam," Tom said. "Stay frosty. He could be anywhere." Tom took point, leading the small crew through the door on the opposite side of the room and down the stairs into the generator room, where he'd brought Dylan for a tour just a week earlier. The unnatural storm howled outside, so loud and violent that they could hear it through the thick concrete walls.

A sadistic chuckle echoed from somewhere up ahead. "You look bored. Allow me to invite some friends to entertain you while I'm working."

The Wardens swept their flashlight beams toward the voice, illuminating Ardu as he tore a gaping hole in his own chest. A great cloud of mist billowed out, blanketing the floor. All five of them opened fire, the gunshots deafening in the enclosed space. Ardu darted away faster than seemed possible, leaving them alone with the spreading mist.

Patches of darkness began to appear in the mist, opening and then closing in the blink of an eye, like inverse lightning. A series of thunderous *booms* echoed through the room.

"Cutters!" Dylan yelled.

Dozens of the deformed creatures were rushing them. The Wardens cut them down, firing and reloading as quickly as they could.

"Fall back!" Tom shouted. "That way!" He stopped firing just long enough to wave toward the east side of the room, where other doors led to different areas.

Dylan rammed a new mag into his UMP and slapped the charging handle. "How are there Cutters here? I thought nothing could cross the veil now!"

Sara ducked and rolled away from a Cutter's vicious claws. She came up in a kneeling position and fired three rounds into the back of its head. It went down like a sack of bricks, and her rifle locked open. She dropped the mag and reached for a new one. Realization suddenly hit her. "They didn't cross the veil!" she shouted. "Ardu brought them when he came through!"

"The mist!" Alex cried out. "It's inside him!"

And he was using it to create monsters on the fly.

Working together, they moved toward the nearest door, walking backward and firing into the advancing wave. Jacob hauled open the door and waved the others through. He prepared a frag grenade and tossed it as he followed, shut the door behind them, and locked it. Thick, black blood and chunks of meat splattered against the door's reinforced glass window when the grenade went off on the other side.

Tom slapped a fresh mag of buckshot into his Jackhammer. "I don't think we got all of them," he said. "Let's move. This way." The five of them ran down a long hallway as a wave of Cutters slammed into the door, pounding it with their skeletal fists and screeching in murderous fury.

Tom led them up the next staircase, down another hall, and up another staircase, this one spanning several stories. He charged through a door at the top, back outside, into the raging storm. They were on a maintenance walkway near the top of the dam. The Wardens gasped for air, exhausted from the fight and the long sprint up the stairs.

"There!" Sara shouted, pointing. On the far side of the dam, Ardu was hovering in midair, his hands raised to the sky. In the dark, they could see him only because the driving rain deflected around him to either side, creating an odd, visible distortion in the air.

A low rumble came from the dam, followed by a sound like metal bending.

"He's tearin' the whole damned thing apart," Jacob said.

"You guys start heading that way, I'll catch up," Tom said.

"We have to stop him! He's gonna start ripping holes in the dam any second!" Sara cried.

"I'm on it," Tom said. He dropped the Jackhammer onto its sling, reached over his shoulder, and grabbed Manny's AWM. He laid the barrel over the top rail of the walkway and looked through the scope, estimating the distance. The others, understanding his plan, started sprinting toward Ardu, ready to press the attack as soon as they were in range.

Tom flipped down the rifle scope's night vision overlay and adjusted the elevation and windage turrets, counting the clicks carefully. Give or take, 350 meters. Wind speed... really fast. He put his best guess at seventy miles per hour, given how difficult it was to maintain his footing. He did the math in his head, running through equations he didn't use very often. Tom was a competent rifle shooter, but he was a shotgun man at heart. He tried to remember everything Manny had ever taught him about shooting in high winds with bad visibility.

He found the target in his scope. At least Ardu wasn't moving. Tom steadied the rifle barrel on top of the walkway railing, flicked off the safety, and rested his finger along the side of the trigger. He took a deep breath, let it out halfway, and held it.

The dam rumbled and groaned again. He knew that it was made of many concrete and steel blocks stacked atop one another, all of them covered in a second, continuous layer of concrete. The dam was strong but not indestructible. Ardu was slowly but surely tearing it apart.

The dam groaned again, louder than ever. Tom's instincts screamed at him to fire, that he was running out of time, that the dam would give way any second. For a brief instant, he shut his eyes, forcing himself to focus.

No matter what, don't rush the shot, Manny said in his head. *It doesn't matter how many guys are shooting at you. It doesn't matter how scared you are. You rush the shot, you miss. You miss, you die.*

Tom felt the fat raindrops hammering his face with enough force to cause stinging pain. He stilled himself and felt the wind, letting it speak to him, giving himself a moment to understand its ebb and flow. Once more, the dam groaned. He thought he heard it crack—or maybe it was thunder. Hard to be sure. Didn't matter.

He opened his eyes. Ardu's smug face loomed large in his scope. Tom centered the crosshair on Ardu's right temple. He continued to hold his breath. He waited.

For half a heartbeat, the wind faltered, slowing dramatically.

Tom shifted the crosshair ever so slightly to the left, dropping it "into the pocket," as Manny had called it. He smoothly stroked the trigger.

The immensely powerful .338 Magnum round was halfway to the target in one tenth of a second. Just before impact, the wind kicked up again, pushing the heavy bullet to the right.

Tom had been counting on that.

The match-grade round struck just in front of Ardu's right ear and blasted through his skull like a freight train. Bone fragments and black blood exploded in a cloud that immediately dissipated in the storm. The would-be god went limp and dropped like a stone, plummeting toward the riverbed.

"Thanks, Manny," Tom whispered. "Love you, bro." He put the AWM on safe, slung it over his shoulder, and started running.

* * *

Jacob was aiming his rifle down over the walkway railing, toward the riverbed, when Tom caught up.

Dylan allowed himself a nervous grin. "Nice shot," he said.

Tom nodded his thanks. "Be ready. I doubt we're done here."

The dam bellowed another distressed groan. "Oh, no," Dylan said. "Look." He pointed up toward the sky. In an isolated pocket directly over the reservoir, the rain was coming down impossibly hard, pouring from the clouds like Niagara Falls. Dylan rushed over to a nearby maintenance ladder that led to the top of the dam and started climbing. The others followed.

"That's what I was afraid of," Dylan shouted over the storm. He pointed to the roiling water in the reservoir.

"What's the problem?" Alex yelled.

"The water level's way too high," Tom yelled back. "The main spillway can't drain it fast enough. Whatever Ardu did, it weakened the dam. The more water in the reservoir, the more weight and pressure it exerts on the dam itself."

"If the dam breaks, thousands of people downstream will die," Sara said. "How do we stop it?"

"We've gotta open the auxiliary spillway!" Tom said.

"Where are the controls?" Jacob asked.

Tom consulted his mental map of the dam. "That way, two floors down!" He pointed to the west, opposite the direction they'd come from. An especially violent gust of wind kicked up, nearly blowing Sara into the reservoir. Jacob and Dylan caught her just in time.

Ardu rose up from under the maintenance walkway, levitating before them. He wasted no time with threats or insults; he simply tore open his abdomen and allowed more of the cursed mist to pour onto the walkway. Tom focused his fire on Ardu as giant spiders and Cutters burst out of the mist in waves. The rapidly growing horde separated Jacob and Dylan from the others.

"We'll get the spillway!" Dylan shouted. He sprinted to the west without waiting for a reply. Jacob followed, huffing and puffing, struggling to keep up.

Alex and Sara retreated to the east, tossing grenades into the advancing mob, one after another. Tom stayed close to them, hammering Ardu with a continuous stream of buckshot and slugs. Each grievous wound closed seconds after being inflicted, but the onslaught temporarily forced him to stop spewing mist. Whenever a Cutter or spider got too close to Alex or Sara, Tom shifted his aim just long enough to deal with the threat, then returned his attention to Ardu.

As the three of them approached a heavy door leading back to the interior of the dam, Tom dropped an empty magazine and reached for a new one. During the lull, he noticed something odd—Ardu looked slightly older. Sara had said that at midnight he would reach his full power and become invincible, and at that time, he would appear to be in his late teens or early twenties.

But he already looked older than that. At a glance, Tom would have figured him for a hard thirty. Lines and creases were starting to form in his face. They were subtle, but they were definitely there; Tom could see them clearly in the bright beam of his flashlight. Tom double-fisted two grenades into the horde of monsters before darting through the door that Alex was holding open. She slammed it behind them and engaged the deadbolt.

More empty magazines clattered to the floor as all three of them reloaded. "Did you guys see that?" Alex panted, still struggling to catch her breath.

"You mean Ardu looking like he needs some Botox?" Tom said.

"I saw it. He looks older than he should," Sara said. She checked her watch as the wave of creatures slammed into the door. "Nineteen minutes. How are we supposed to kill him? He just keeps regenerating. We only have so much ammo."

Tom started descending the stairs, keeping his shotgun aimed downward as he went. Alex and Sara followed. "I think the same goes for him," Tom said. "We're limited on bullets; he's limited on mist. It's a finite resource. He needs it to heal himself and to summon monsters."

"So, if we hit him hard enough, he runs out of mist, and he can't regenerate," Alex said.

"It's worth a try if we can do it in the next nineteen minutes," Sara said. "After that, nothing will stop him."

On the other side of the dam, Dylan and Jacob burst through the stairwell door on level eight, where Tom had said the spillway controls should be. A thick cloud of mist rolled out to greet them. A chuckle echoed from the shadows, somewhere unseen.

"Shit," Jacob muttered.

A small army of Bound, Cutters, and spiders were already closing the distance, but they were still far enough away for explosives. Dylan shouldered the MGL and fired all six grenades as quickly as he could pull the trigger. The resulting chain of explosions shredded the Bound into flying splinters and spattered gore all over the walls, some black, some dark green. Desks and chairs went flying. Windows overlooking a pump room below shattered. Jacob took careful aim with his .45-70 and started dropping the remaining Cutters and spiders while Dylan pulled empty casings out of the MGL and rewound it.

"Gonna need yer help here lad, ah cannae do much ta the Bound," the old Warden shouted.

Several living trees had escaped the grenade launcher's explosive fury and were still advancing. One was much closer than the others—far too close for grenades. Dylan fumbled a 40mm round and dropped it, cursing. His heart was pounding. His hands were sweaty and shaking. He snatched up the dropped round and forced himself to slow down. This time, he managed to load it.

Already, the lone Bound was on them. It swung a branch nearly as thick as a telephone pole. Jacob leaped backward while Dylan ducked and rolled under it. He came up in a kneeling position and shouldered the launcher, aiming for the tree creatures that were farther away. He would have to trust that Jacob had his back.

With a loud *chunk*, the grenade was away. It ripped the last, smaller horde to pieces. Dylan pivoted around and switched to his UMP, dumping a full magazine into the surviving Bound once he was sure Jacob was clear. The powerful .45 slugs, devastating to soft tissue, had little effect on solid wood and bone, but they did get the creature's attention. It lunged for Dylan, but he was ready. He hopped to the side, then sprinted toward one of the broken windows. He dropped his UMP and drew his sidearm, firing a few rounds into the Bound to keep it focused on him. It closed on him with frightening speed, exactly as he'd hoped it would. He dived to the side at the last second, out of the way of its furious charge. The tree creature slammed into the wall and sailed out the window, plummeting several stories to the pump room below.

"Nicely done, lad," Jacob panted, thumbing more cartridges into his old rifle.

"Same to you—not bad for an old timer," Dylan replied. He started reloading his weapons.

Jacob scowled. A split second later, his expression morphed into one of horror. He shouldered his rifle and started to shout. "Dylan—!"

Reflexively, Dylan stepped back, unsure where the new threat was coming from. He felt searing pain in his neck, just under his chin. Something flashed past in a blur, moving so fast he could hardly see it. A string of dark blood flew through the air. Dylan's eyes went wide in shock. Was that *his* blood? Instinctively, his hands went to his neck. He felt warmth and wetness. He stumbled back a step, then another.

Ardu doubled back just long enough to hammer the heel of his hand into Dylan's chest. Jacob fired his rifle into the side of Ardu's head, but it was too late.

Dylan tumbled out the window.

* * *

Tom, Alex, and Sara burst through the exterior door, back onto the maintenance walkway just below the top of the dam. There was no sign of

Ardu.

"I hope Dylan and Jacob are okay," Sara shouted over the wind.

"Come on, let's get back up top," Tom said, leading the charge. He scrambled up the nearest ladder. Atop the dam, to the east, the remaining Cutters, spiders, and Bound were still trying to bash their way through the interior access door. The Wardens rolled a handful of grenades in that direction, dispatching the rest of the horde.

The dam groaned loudly enough to be easily audible over the raging storm. Tom looked across the reservoir, squinting, trying to see the auxiliary spillway gate in the darkness. It looked like it was still closed. The water level in the reservoir was rising so quickly that he could see the difference from just five minutes earlier. He didn't know how much longer the weakened dam could hold out, but it couldn't be very long.

"Come on, guys, hurry," he muttered anxiously.

Mist that Ardu had expelled earlier was hovering in a thick layer over the water in the reservoir. Dark shapes flitted and swirled within it. As the three Wardens watched, the mist began to separate itself into three distinct clouds, which then began to rise vertically, coalescing into vague shapes.

"That doesn't look good," Alex said, raising her MPX.

"Be ready for anything," Tom replied.

The Ouroboros burst forth from the mist, darting through the water with impossible speed. It reached the edge of the dam and curled its long body up onto the walkway.

It looked different than before. It was translucent, and it caused the air to shimmer and distort wherever it moved. Tendrils of mist clung to its body, as the chains had before. A moment later, equally ghostlike versions of the Stalker and the Prisoner materialized behind it.

"Here we go again," Sara muttered.

* * *

Bones shattered in Dylan's right leg and ankle when he hit the ground nearly thirty feet below. His scream of agony, loud enough to wake the dead, echoed off the stone walls. His pack stopped his head from slamming into the concrete, which surely would have killed him instantly— the whiplash was bad enough. Dimly, through his own screams, he heard Jacob high above firing his rifle over and over.

Gritting his teeth, he looked down at his leg. His pant leg had ridden up just enough to reveal white bone shards poking through the skin in two places. Blood oozed steadily from the open fractures. The pain was almost totally paralyzing. Frantically, he grabbed at his neck, expecting to feel terrible damage.

His hands came away sticky with blood, but not as much as he'd feared. Carefully, he probed the wound with his fingers, the pain in his leg momentarily forgotten. The gash in his neck was shallow; he didn't think it would be fatal. His shoulders sagged with relief, only to tense again when he moved his right leg slightly, causing a fresh bolt of white-hot anguish.

Something in the back of his mind urged him to pay attention, warning him of nearby danger. He gritted his teeth and forced himself to stop screaming so he could listen. Off to the right, he heard a scraping sound, like wood on stone.

The lone Bound that had hurled itself out the window came shuffling around the far side of a large machine. When it saw him, it screeched, then lunged for its prey.

Short on options, Dylan fumbled for his UMP, raised it, and dumped the entire magazine. Most of the .45 slugs hit, and each one tore away small chunks of wood. A few struck the deformed human skull embedded in the top part of the living tree, sending bone chips flying in all directions. Amber sap dribbled from the bullet holes. The concentrated volley of fire drove the creature back a few steps but did little if any major damage.

Dylan tossed the empty magazine and loaded a new one as quickly as he could. The Bound advanced during the break in fire, then was driven back again by the next magazine. Dylan repeated the process once, twice, and a third time. He was wasting all his ammunition, but he didn't know what else to do. Each time he stopped to reload, the living tree gained a little more ground.

His UMP ran dry, and he had no more magazines. He groped for his USP, brought it up, and hammered the trigger. The pistol had some ability to slow the creature's advance, but it wasn't as effective as the submachine gun had been. Dylan was firing wildly with one hand, snatching spare magazines with his other hand so he would be ready to reload with maximum speed. All the while, he tried to crawl backward, tried to gain some distance, but even the slightest pressure on his right leg brought a fresh jolt of excruciating pain. His USP locked open. He dropped the magazine, slapped in a new one, and kept firing.

When the slide locked open again, he had no more ammo. The air shimmered around the pistol's overheated barrel.

The Bound was chewed into a rough-hewn log, but it was still standing. Still moving.

Still coming closer.

Dylan raised his arms in front of his face and screamed as the abomination descended on him.

Suddenly, it froze. From somewhere behind it, a loud buzzing sound filled the air. A circular saw blade burst through the thick branch that served as the creature's arm, cutting it off cleanly. The Bound roared and spun around to take a swing at its assailant.

Richard ducked under the swing, then brought up the circular saw and sheared off the other arm. Wasting no time, he went to one knee and cut through a twisted leg branch, then the other. The Bound, now limbless, toppled over—but it was still moving, still thrashing around. It was heavy enough to crack Dylan's skull if it landed on him.

"Dad!"

Richard tossed aside the saw. It landed near the workbench he'd taken it from, one that belonged to Tom's company. He bent down and picked up Dylan, grunting with the effort. Dylan shrieked in agony as his broken bones ground against each other. Richard grimaced at seeing his son so badly hurt. "I'm here," he said, panting. "I'm here."

Dylan threw his arms around his father's neck, weeping with relief. Richard quickly stepped away from the thrashing tree monster. "Dad, we're almost out of time," Dylan said between ragged gasps of pain.

Richard didn't know what would happen when time ran out, but Dylan's urgency was all too clear. "Where to?" he said.

Dylan pointed, his arm trembling. "Up the stairs."

Richard climbed the stairs without delay, leaving the thrashing Bound behind. With no limbs, it couldn't come after them. It rolled and slammed into the bottom step, unable to clear it.

"How did you get here?" Dylan said.

"Stole the ambulance you called for me."

Dylan stared at him in shock. "Way to go, Dad. Right at the top of the stairs," he said, gritting his teeth against the pain. He awkwardly holstered his sidearm and aimed his UMP ahead so Richard could see by the bright beam of the SureFire light where he was going. "Follow the signs to the spillway control room."

Dylan suddenly realized that he hadn't heard any gunfire from Jacob in a long time. When they rounded the next corner, he saw why.

The old man was sitting on the floor, his back against one wall. Before their eyes, the nearby corpse of a Cutter dissipated into mist. A dark puddle of blood had pooled under Jacob.

He wasn't moving.

"Dad, stop!" Dylan said. He glanced at his watch. Nine minutes to go. But he had to check on Jacob.

Richard knelt. If he was shocked or sickened at the sight, he didn't show it. Dylan shook Jacob by the shoulder and called his name.

No answer. His eyes were open and fixed.

Dylan put two fingers against the side of Jacob's neck. He couldn't feel a pulse, but he felt more blood. It was cool to the touch.

The old Warden's neck had been savagely bitten.

Dylan shut his eyes as hot tears of sorrow mixed with those caused by the pain in his leg. His lower lip trembled.

Jacob had cleared the path and bought them time. They needed to make good use of it.

"Let's go," Dylan said, his voice barely a whisper. Without a word, Richard got to his feet and continued following the signs.

The spillway control room was farther away than Dylan had thought it would be. He concentrated on taking deep breaths to mitigate the pain, trying not to glance too often at his watch. Finally, the door came into view. Dylan looked at his watch one more time.

Seven minutes.

Inside, Richard gently sat Dylan on the edge of a desk. "What do I do?"

Dylan forced the pain down so that he could speak. "The spillway is controlled by a computer, but the power's out. There's a mechanical override somewhere." He shone his light around. "There!"

Richard ran over to the large, metal lever Dylan had indicated. He gripped it in both hands and pulled hard. With a loud *thunk*, it dropped into position, opening the emergency spillway. Faintly, Dylan could hear rushing water somewhere nearby. He hoped it would be enough to relieve pressure on the dam before it broke.

"Now what?" Richard said, panting from the exertion.

"Back outside, to the top of the dam," Dylan said. He took up the MGL and reloaded it. He had eleven rounds left. "The others need help."

* * *

Alex cried out when the Stalker punched her in the chest. It felt like being hit by a speeding truck. Her armor plate cracked, and the sling holding her MPX in place slipped over her head as she sailed through the air. The weapon clattered across the concrete, bounced into the reservoir, and sank.

She, Sara, and Tom had already dispatched the Prisoner by concentrating their fire, but they'd chewed through most of their ammunition in the process. Fortunately, it seemed that the mist-borne doppelgangers of their Eidolons weren't nigh-invulnerable as the originals had been; once the Prisoner had taken enough damage, it had dissolved into mist with a hateful howl.

The Stalker and the Ouroboros, however, were still causing problems.

Pushing through the pain, Alex fumbled her Glock 41 out of its holster and emptied it into the advancing Stalker. The rounds did some appreciable damage, but the beast was still coming when her weapon ran dry. She dropped the magazine and reached for another—her last one.

Tom entered her field of vision from the side, pelting the Stalker in the head and neck with buckshot. Each shot ripped away large chunks of foggy, translucent flesh. The last few rounds decapitated the monstrosity. The severed head and lifeless body collapsed to the ground, then dissipated a moment later.

"Shit, I'm out," Tom muttered, observing his shotgun's empty chamber. He felt around his plate carrier for another magazine. He had none.

"Tom, look out!" Alex shouted. He reached for his Magnum and started to turn around, but he was too slow. The Ouroboros struck like lightning, closing its mighty fangs around Tom. He screamed in pain; Alex echoed in fear and rage.

Thirty meters away, Sara dumped her last magazine of 6.8mm rifle rounds into the snake's midsection, unwilling to aim for its head for fear of hitting Tom. Alex joined in, emptying her Glock into the same area. When Sara's rifle ran dry, she dropped it and switched to her Operator.

With a vicious hiss, the snake reared its head and flung Tom away like a rocket. He sailed far over the reservoir, finally splashing down nearly fifty meters away. Sara screamed his name while Alex could only stare in stunned silence; she feared that Tom might have broken his neck on impact with the water. The massive snake turned toward Sara and shot forward with predatory speed.

"Sara, drop!" a voice shouted over the storm. Instinctively, she did. Alex looked over to see Dylan aiming his grenade launcher. For some reason, he was sitting down, with his back against the handrail running along the top of the dam. Someone was kneeling next to him.

Alex gasped. Richard?

Dylan lobbed a volley of six grenades in quick succession. One missed and sailed into the reservoir, creating an impressive geyser of water when it detonated. The other five grenades struck the snake or the ground nearby, shredding the beast to ribbons. It hissed in fury, unable to withstand the damage. It collapsed onto its side, then dissolved.

Near the middle of the dam walkway, Dylan breathed a sigh of relief. Alex and Sara were safe for the moment, but he was worried about Tom. He loaded his last five 40mm rounds into the MGL.

"Dylan, I—" Richard started to speak, but he stopped suddenly. Dylan turned to look at him.

Ardu had him by the throat. Richard clawed at the impossibly strong fingers locked around his neck.

Effortlessly, Ardu lifted Richard over the walkway railing and dropped him. He screamed as he fell away. Abruptly, the scream was cut short.

Rage and sorrow exploded in Dylan's chest. "You *fuck!*" he screamed. "I'll fucking kill you!" He reached for his knife. It wasn't there. He'd lost it moments after they'd first arrived at the dam.

Ardu bent down and hauled Dylan up. Lightning lanced through his broken leg, but he was too enraged to care. Ardu cocked his arm to toss Dylan over the side as well.

Black blood splashed Dylan in the face as Ardu's head snapped to the side. Sara advanced on him at a fast walk, firing her Operator rapidly. It was enough of a distraction to make Ardu drop Dylan back onto the walkway. Mist escaped from the bullet wounds as they rapidly closed. Sara could see that Ardu did indeed look older, as if he were pushing forty now.

Her Operator's slide locked back empty. She dropped the magazine and reached for another.

The ammo pouches on her armor were empty.

Ardu charged forward like a freight train, moving so fast that Sara could barely see him. Lightning flashed, briefly disrupting her night vision. Rain pelted her face. She tried to blink it away. She dropped into a defensive stance.

Ardu charged right into her—no, he was *propelled* into her, tumbling through the air like he'd been shot out of a cannon. She heard the explosion and felt the rush of hot air—Dylan had hit Ardu squarely in the back with a 40mm grenade. Sara yelled in pain and surprise as she and Ardu tumbled across the concrete, scraping large strips of skin off her arms. Her Operator flew out of her hand, over the walkway railing, and dropped to the riverbed far below.

Sara managed to get to her feet before Ardu did. At least she hadn't taken a direct hit from a 40mm grenade. She unslung her empty rifle and tossed it aside so she could move more freely. Alex was still struggling to stand, still winded and disoriented from the hard hit to the chest.

"Sara!" Dylan yelled. With all his strength, he threw the MGL overhand. It clattered and rolled across the concrete, coming to a rest near Sara's feet. She snatched it up and sprinted away from Ardu, back toward Dylan, racing to get outside the weapon's kill radius. She turned back to Ardu. He was already getting up, the massive crater in his back filling in with fresh, healthy tissue.

Sara emptied the MGL. The four explosions blasted huge chunks of concrete into dust and reduced Ardu to little more than a skeleton. Once again, with amazing speed, fresh muscles appeared from nowhere, knitting themselves together to cover the exposed bones, followed by layers of fat and skin. A cloud of mist emanated from his body and evaporated in the rain as he expended energy to heal himself. Within seconds, Ardu was whole again but not entirely unaffected. Loose skin drooped from his cheekbones, and his hair, formerly black and thick, had turned gray.

Sara tossed aside the MGL and drew her knife. She dropped to her knees, straddling Ardu before he could get up. "Just. Fucking. Die," she growled. She rammed her knife toward his neck, intending to saw off his head, if that was what it took.

With incredible speed, Ardu snatched her wrist and bent it backward. Bones cracked, jagged fragments separating completely from one another. Sara's scream ripped through the night air, drowning out the howling wind. Ardu caught the knife as it fell from her limp fingers and rammed it into her side, between her armor plates, all the way up to the hilt.

"You first," he whispered.

"Sara!" Alex and Dylan both screamed her name at the same time. Dylan crawled forward, pulling himself along with his arms, trying to reach her. She was so far away. His heartbeat pounded in his ears. Fear and fury drove him onward. Alex finally got to her feet and drew her own knife. She stumbled forward, still disoriented.

Sara couldn't scream. The pain in her side was so intense that it locked her throat shut. She couldn't draw a breath, couldn't move, couldn't even feel her shattered wrist. Ardu shoved her aside and got up. The one called "Alex" was advancing on him. He frowned. Couldn't they see how completely outmatched they were?

Across the reservoir, a football field away, Tom hauled himself out of the water at the far eastern end of the walkway, coughing and choking. Blood oozed from a deep puncture wound in his upper thigh. He was already feeling dizzy from the venom, and his head was pounding.

Come on, he thought to himself. *Job's not done.* His shotgun was empty, and his Magnum was useless at this range, especially in the near-total darkness. He unslung the AWM and flopped onto his stomach, holding his pain and exhaustion at bay with sheer willpower. With trembling hands, he unfolded the bipod. He risked a glance at his watch.

Three minutes to midnight.

The night vision clip-on scope was fried by the water, and the main scope's objective lens was badly cracked. Water had gotten inside the scope through a busted seal and fogged up both lenses. Tom could still see through the scope but just barely. Without the night vision, he could only make out dark silhouettes on the far walkway.

He found Alex in the scope—or at least, he was pretty sure it was her. Someone was walking rapidly toward her.

Ardu. It had to be.

Tom's headache was getting worse by the second. His vision was getting blurry. He felt dizzy and nauseous. He had no time to do math or adjust the scope. He eyeballed the shot and fired.

A chunk of the walkway exploded near Ardu's feet. Tom adjusted his aim and fired again.

Missed. That one went high and right.

He worked the bolt and fired.

The heavy round slammed into Ardu's left side, dropping him to his knees with a grunt. Alex blinked in surprise, then realized that Tom must be the one shooting. She heard the sharp *cracks* of a rifle somewhere off to her right. A moment later, a third of Ardu's head exploded. Black blood, bone fragments, and bits of brain tissue flew everywhere. He fell over, limp, but within a few seconds, he was already getting up again, the damage mending rapidly.

Alex pressed the attack, trying to ignore her worry for Sara long enough to focus on the imminent threat. She slammed her knife into Ardu's chest over and over, trying to inflict as much damage as possible. *Tom, don't shoot me*, she thought. When she estimated that he would be finished reloading, she backed off several steps.

The next five shots came in quick succession, two hits and three misses. Again, Ardu was knocked over, his head nearly blown off. Again, he recovered quickly from the violent attack. Mist escaped from the wounds as they knitted closed. When his face pulled itself back together, Alex was shocked to see how old he looked—she would have guessed seventy or eighty.

With speed she hadn't been expecting, Ardu lunged for her and got his hands around her throat. He slammed her head against the walkway. Pain exploded in her skull, and she saw stars. Her vision narrowed to a tiny point as she fought to remain conscious. Dimly, she heard Ardu's voice, brittle with age.

"Insects. Your time is up."

Alex felt hot blood on her face and heard the whistling *crack* of a rifle bullet passing by barely a foot above her head. Tom fired twice more, blasting Ardu's upper back and skull into meaty ribbons. The damage healed more slowly this time. Alex could hardly see his face, but she could tell that he looked like a withered skeleton, ready to collapse from old age at any moment. His movements were slow and jerky. His arms trembled.

But he was still strong enough to choke the life out of her.

Alex stabbed her knife into his chest over and over, trying to finish him off. The knife wounds just kept closing. He shut his eyes and waited for her to stop moving.

Across the reservoir, Tom's vision went black, and his consciousness slipped away as he succumbed to the venom.

The concrete walkway was slick with blood and rain under Sara's fingers. Her right hand was badly broken, but she could hardly feel it—the blinding pain in her side was much worse. She dared not remove the knife. Alex had told her never to do that. If she did, she risked further damage and would bleed out faster. With her left hand, she slowly pulled herself along, inching toward Alex. She didn't know what she would do when she got there—if she got there. She felt around her vest for ammunition she might have missed. She had nothing. No rifle or pistol magazines. She was unarmed.

Her consciousness slowly fading, Sara felt around in her pockets with her left hand for something, anything that might help.

Her fingers closed around something small and smooth. She brought it out, squinting in the darkness to see what it was.

The single .45 round she'd ejected from Ethan's Beretta.

Too bad she had no gun to fire it with.

Ardu was strangling Alex to death. He looked withered and frail, but he was still stronger than she was. Alex was fighting back weakly. She wouldn't last much longer.

"Sara!" She looked back. Dylan was twenty paces behind her, dragging himself along just like she was. She could see the pain in his eyes, along with fear for her and Alex—and sorrow for his father.

Dylan had something in his right hand. He slid it toward her.

His empty USP. The slide was already locked open.

Sara dug deep for the last of her strength, mentally shutting away her pain and fear. Ignoring the ferocious agony in her side, she forced herself to rise to her knees. She closed the fingers of her left hand around the USP and tucked it under her right arm. Her right hand was useless. The single .45 round in her left hand was covered in blood. She held it carefully in trembling fingers. She tried to drop it into the USP's open chamber.

She missed. The bullet fell to the ground and rolled a few inches away. She snatched it up again.

Alex wasn't moving anymore.

Sara managed to get the round into the chamber. She gripped the gun in her left hand and kept the barrel tilted downward, careful not to let the loose round fall out. She found the slide release with her index finger.

The heavy slide slammed closed.

It felt good to be armed again. She wasn't helpless.

Far from it.

Sara raised the USP in her left hand. It was so dark, and so hard to see through the rain. Her vision was getting dimmer. She was losing a lot of blood. She desperately wanted to help Alex.

Tom's voice, clear as a bell, rang in her head. *Slow is smooth, smooth is fast. I don't care if you only fire once, as long as that one shot hits. Show me accuracy. Speed comes later.*

She waited. The USP's front sight post wavered in her vision. She tried to hold it steady, tried to line it up with Ardu's head. She wasn't left-handed, and she felt so weak. The gun trembled badly.

Ardu looked over his shoulder, toward her. He began to turn his body. He released his grip on Alex's neck, satisfied that he'd finished her off.

The front sight locked into place between his eyes.

Light as a feather, Sara stroked the trigger. The shot sounded so quiet in her muted hearing. She felt it more than heard it.

Ardu fell sideways, a quarter-sized hole in the middle of his forehead.

Sara dropped the USP and fell forward. She couldn't stay on her knees any longer. Her right side hurt so bad. She kept her eyes on Ardu, waiting to see if he would get up again.

He lay motionless in the rain. Alex wasn't moving either. Faintly, Sara heard Dylan calling her name.

With a final, breathless sigh, Ardu's body evaporated into mist. The wind carried it away.

Darkness took her. The last sound she heard was a low, persistent ringing.

Her watch alarm. It was day eight.

New Year's Day.

CHAPTER FORTY-FIVE
Solace

Pain.

Darkness.

Movement.

Her mouth felt so dry, like she'd eaten sand.

More pain, deep and sharp.

A sound. Something high-pitched and repetitive.

She couldn't open her eyes. Or maybe they were already open, and there was just nothing to see.

Where am I? Who am I?

She struggled to remember. Her mind felt heavy and slow, like it was mired in fog.

Sara. I'm Sara.

Her eyes fluttered open.

Light. So bright. Pain.

She shut them again.

Better.

Someone said something nearby, the voice low and muffled. She couldn't make out the words. She heard a steady beeping sound.

Pressure, on her... what was it called?

Hand.

The voice became a little clearer. "She's definitely awake."

A different voice. "Sara, can you hear me?"

She willed her eyes to open. Dark shapes loomed above her, silhouetted against the bright light. She blinked once, twice, three times. Gradually, faces came into focus.

Dylan smiled down at her. "Hey, you," he said. Who was that next to him? She looked familiar. What was her name?

Alex.

Sara tried to talk. No words came out. Her throat was so dry it hurt.

"Here," Alex said. She put a cup of water to Sara's lips and tipped it gently. "Drink slowly. Take it easy."

Relief.

Sara tried again. Her voice was scratchy, but it worked. "Are we dead?"

Alex and Dylan both laughed. "Not even close," Dylan said.

Alex shot him a sideways glance. "Well, it was pretty touch and go for a while."

Sara looked around. The light still hurt her eyes, but it wasn't as bad. She was lying down. An IV bag dripped fluid through a catheter in her arm. Her right wrist was in a cast, and it ached dully. Her lower abdomen was covered in thick bandages; she could feel them under the cotton hospital gown. She moved slightly, and searing agony shot up her side. She grimaced and cried out.

Alex put a hand on her shoulder. "Relax. Try not to move too much. You've got a lot of healing to do." Sara noticed that Dylan had a crutch under each arm. His right leg was in a cast.

Fragmented memories flitted through Sara's mind. Panic spiked in her chest when she remembered. "Tom? Where's Tom?"

"Right here," he said. "You look like hammered shit, by the way."

Dylan hobbled aside so she could see. Tom waved at her from another bed a few feet away. He looked pale and tired but otherwise alright.

Sara blinked. "But... the snake. It bit you."

"Yeah, I remember. Kinda hard to forget," Tom mused, scratching his overgrown beard.

Alex dragged a chair next to Sara's bed and sat in it. "Antibodies," she said.

Sara frowned. Her brain wasn't running at full capacity yet.

"The same snake bit me twice," Tom said. "The way the doctors explained it, the first bite ended up saving my life. Different snake venoms have different effects on the body, but at least in some cases, people can build up immunity if they get bitten multiple times by the same kind of snake."

"Tom had enough resistance to the venom to hold on until we got him here," Alex said. "Then it was just a matter of supportive care. The doctors managed his symptoms, kept him breathing, kept his heart beating until the venom lost its potency and his body could get rid of it."

Doctors. Supportive care. "Where... are we?" Sara asked. Talking still hurt.

Alex heaved a sigh. "How much do you remember?"

Sara shook her head, then winced when the pain in her side flared up. "Not much. The last thing I remember is shooting Ardu in the head. I guess it worked if we're still here."

Dylan patted her hand gently. "You shot him in the head real good. We're all very proud of you."

She smiled weakly. "It was definitely a team effort."

Alex pulled a folded piece of paper out of her pocket and unfolded it. She placed it in Sara's uninjured hand and carefully adjusted her arm so she could read it. "Take your time," Alex said. "We'll give you some space." She and Dylan retreated to the other side of Tom's bed. The three of them whispered among themselves.

Sara frowned. Space for what?

She read the note. She immediately recognized the handwriting.

Sara,

Nothing I can say or do in the future will ever make up for the things I've said and done in the past. I'm a fool, and quite frankly, a terrible person. You are the daughter that every father hopes for but few ever have. I'm sorry that I didn't believe in you. I do now, if that means anything at all. You found a new path—the right path—where no one dared to look before.

Since the day you were born, I haven't known a single night of restful sleep. I told myself that I was doing the right thing, the only thing that anyone could do, and that my guilt was evidence of nothing but my own wicked selfishness. How dare I favor my own daughter's life over the entirety of mankind?

I see now that the truth was much simpler. The guilt that kept me awake every night was my conscience screaming at me, begging me to cast off my blinders and to take my daughter away from this madness.

Whether and to what extent you might ever find it in your heart to forgive me will be up to you. I certainly don't deserve your forgiveness now, but part of me dares to hope that one day, I might be the sort of man who does, if I work hard enough, if I use my abilities and resources to protect and defend life instead of destroying it.

As some small token of penance, I've called in every favor owed to me to ensure that you and your friends receive the best medical care from doctors who know when not to ask questions. The authorities are calling the incident at the dam a "domestic terror attack." Most of the evidence linking you to the scene has been taken care of, and the little that remains isn't enough to prove anything. I've enclosed a business card for a good lawyer— a former Circle patriarch. He knows what really happened and has come to see the truth of it, as I have. Call him if you need him; he was eager to waive his fee. Keep your heads down and deny everything. Eventually, the storm will pass. You and your friends fought so hard for the right of every individual to live his own life. The least I can do is ensure that all of you are left free to live yours.

I won't contact you again—I know that I have no right to. I hope that I will one day have a tenth of your strength and courage. I wish you a life of happiness and peace. No one has earned it more.

Ethan

A single tear dripped onto the page, smudging the ink. Suddenly, Dylan was beside her. He took her left hand in his and squeezed gently. She wiped her eyes, folded the paper, and set it aside.

Thinking about her father made the horrible memory of Richard's death come rushing back to her. "Dylan, I... I'm so sorry about your dad," she whispered. She looked away, unable to hold his gaze.

He squeezed her hand more firmly. "Don't be," he said. "There's nothing to be sorry about."

She looked back up at him. "How can you say that?"

"Because I'm not dead," Richard said. The door swung closed behind him as he backed his wheelchair into the room. His left leg was in a cast, like Dylan's right. Other than that, he had only minor cuts and bruises.

Dylan grinned. "We're twins now."

Sara's jaw dropped. "Mr. Masters!"

He smiled. "It's Richard, please. We're family, aren't we? Or we will be before too long, I imagine."

Sara smacked Dylan in the stomach with the back of her hand. "Was he waiting outside the door until I said he was dead, just so he could come in for the dramatic reveal?"

Richard scratched his beard and chuckled. "No, but to be honest, I did think about it. I figured that would be mean. I just got back from X-ray."

"But how?" Sara said. "He... he dropped you...." She trailed off as the painful memory flashed through her mind again.

"He did, just not as far as he thought," Dylan said.

Sara shook her head when the pieces clicked together in her mind. "The maintenance walkway."

"It was a hell of a drop, as you can see," Richard said, gesturing to his cast. "But I'm okay, really. A couple feet to the right, and it would have been a different story."

Sara closed her eyes. "But... Jacob...." His absence had abruptly dawned on her.

No one said anything. They shared a moment of solemn silence for the fallen Warden.

"He definitely earned the title of 'Warden' in the real and full meaning of the word," Tom said quietly. "He was a true defender of life and freedom."

Sara couldn't stop the tears from coming again. "Lily would be so proud of him. I know I am."

Richard bowed his head in respect and gratitude for the man who had helped and protected his son, and by extension, everyone else on Earth. "It's... a hell of a story," he said softly.

Sara's gaze darted between Tom, Alex, and Dylan. "So, you told him everything, then."

Tom nodded. "We all agreed that it was the right call. Besides, after what he saw at the dam, there wasn't much point in denying it."

Dylan, who was in front of Richard and facing Sara, silently mouthed two words at her. It took her a moment to realize what he'd said: "Almost everything." She understood. Richard didn't know about Marie. It wasn't the time, not yet. She gave Dylan a slight, almost imperceptible nod of confirmation.

Sara looked around for her phone or a calendar but couldn't find either. "How long has it been, anyway?"

"A week," Alex said. "Richard, Dylan, and I were banged up, but we got off easy compared to you and Tom. He just woke up yesterday; we weren't sure he would pull through. We were all really worried about you, too. It took some major surgery to stabilize you. And...." She trailed off.

Sara swallowed, suddenly nervous. "And what?"

Alex sighed. "And... you lost your right kidney. It was too damaged to save."

Sara waved her uninjured hand dismissively. "Is that all? I thought it was something serious. I can live with one kidney."

Alex blinked in bewilderment. Tom, Dylan, and Richard laughed.

"You also have some pins and rods in your right hand. They'll have to stay there for life, but once you heal up, you should have normal function," Alex said.

Sara shrugged. "Whatever. I'm just happy you guys are okay."

"We're better than okay, now that the Twilight is closed forever," Tom said. He paused, then looked directly at Sara. "It is, right?"

She nodded. "That's what the witches said, and I believe them. Even if someone figured out how to cross the veil when Ardu isn't in the Twilight, it's impossible now. The veil is permanently damaged; nobody can go through it."

"What will happen to it now? The Twilight, I mean," Dylan said.

Sara frowned, thinking. "Over time, with no more people going there, the Twilight will have nothing to feed on, no one's fears and thoughts to use as fuel to shape the environment or create living things. Eventually, everything that's there now will fade away, and the Twilight will become... nothing. Just an empty space. It might even cease to exist entirely."

Dylan nodded. "Either way is good enough for me, as long as there's no chance of anyone going there ever again."

Sara shook her head. "None. I'm sure of that much."

Someone knocked softly on the door. Alex opened it and poked her head out. After a moment, she leaned back into the room to look at Sara. "Are you hungry?"

Sara realized that she was. "Starving, actually." She made a face. "But not for hospital food."

Alex said something to the person in the hall, then shut the door. She turned back to Sara with her hands on her hips. "Well, I'm the only one not too messed up to drive, so I guess it's up to me to go get you something."

Sara smiled. "You're such a good friend, Alex."

The older woman shook her head. "What'll it be?"

Sara thought for a moment. "You know, I could really go for a grilled cheese."

EPILOGUE

Awakening

July 10, 2022
Six Months Later

The rain was light and warm, the grass soft and cool under Sara's knees. Her head was bowed, her chin nearly touching her chest. Her breathing was slow and even, her hands clasped in her lap. She had been there, totally still, for some time. An onlooker might have thought she was asleep.

She opened her eyes and placed one hand flat against the polished grave marker. A moment later, she touched the one next to it with equal reverence. The black marble was as smooth as glass and beautifully worked, with light veins of gold running through it.

She took one last look at the brass nameplates, a wistful smile on her lips.

Cara "Lily" Findlay
November 8, 1963—June 15, 2005
Little mourned I for the parted gladness,
For the vacant nest and silent song

Jacob Shaw
August 2, 1961—December 31, 2021
Hope was there, and laughed me out of sadness;
Whispering, "Winter will not linger long"

Dylan approached and knelt beside her. "You picked a good poem," he said. He looked around as if he were searching for something. "What about Roland and Daniela?"

She rested her hand on his leg. "They've had memorial plots in Córdoba for some time already. Lily's family doesn't deserve her, and Jacob had no close family. I think he would have liked to be buried here, next to her, even though… her body is long gone. We can visit them once in a while." She wiped away a lone tear. "How's Marie?"

He smiled. "She's good. We had a nice chat, and I told her all about the plan." He placed his hand on top of hers. "You know, I like your hands better without gunpowder all over them."

She returned the smile. "Me, too." When she saw that Dylan was looking at her curiously, she self-consciously touched the scars on her face. "Don't look at them," she said, turning away.

He rolled his eyes. "I was thinking that your freckles are cute, doofus. I couldn't care less about some dumb old scars. I've got plenty of my own, anyway." He gently untangled a lock of her red hair from the necklace he'd given her nine years ago, now repaired and back around her neck where it belonged.

She turned back to him and smiled. "You're right. It's not important."

Together, they gazed out across the cemetery. The first rays of the rising sun made the cherry blossoms swaying in the breeze look red and orange. They could see Tom atop a gentle slope, sitting on the ground in front of two headstones. Every so often, he gestured or shook his head. They couldn't hear what he was saying. That was as it should be—his conversation with Manny and Teddy was private.

Sara and Dylan watched Alex approach from the other direction. When she reached them, she knelt on Sara's other side and lowered her head, paying silent respect to Jacob and Lily. When she finally opened her eyes, a ghost of a smile passed across her face. "Sara, do you remember what you said to me on the first night of the Pilgrimage to convince me that you could see my dreams?"

Sara thought about it for a moment. "Not exactly, no. I just remember that it was something… Lisa said to you." She faltered a moment, reluctant to bring up the woman Alex had accidentally killed more than two decades ago.

Alex folded her hands in her lap. "She's buried here, you know." Sara suddenly realized where Alex had been before joining them. "I used to see her a lot in my dreams. What she said was, 'I forgive you. You have a lot of healing to do. Better get to it.'"

Sara nodded slowly. "I remember now." She and Dylan waited patiently until Alex was ready to go on.

"I finally know what she meant in my dream. All along, I thought the dream version of her—or my own subconscious, I guess—was telling me to heal others. That was my penance—I had to fix as many people as possible to partly make up for what I'd done.

"But now I see that that was never what those words meant. The one I needed to heal was myself. I needed to fix the thoughts, ideas, and behaviors that led me down that path. Only after healing myself could I even attempt to help anyone else. I didn't know Lisa at all, but in the aftermath of her death, I got to see small glimpses of her through her family. Maybe, just maybe, this is how I can earn her forgiveness: by looking forward instead of back; by never repeating the mistakes that turned me into that ugly, thoughtless, self-destructive version of myself; and by doing my best to help others—without taking the blame for their actions onto my own shoulders."

Sara reached over and touched Alex's arm. "That sounds right to me," she said.

Richard came into view, walking toward them from the direction of Marie's memorial headstone. Her brother had commissioned it long ago, despite Richard's insistence that Marie could still be alive.

Dylan now knew that his uncle had known otherwise.

Tom intercepted Richard, and together, they walked the rest of the way to where the others were kneeling.

"Ready to go?" Tom said. He kept his voice respectfully quiet.

Sara, Alex, and Dylan stood up, brushing grass from their knees. Everyone except Dylan started walking toward the exit. He stayed behind, fidgeting with something in his pocket.

The others turned back when they realized that he wasn't following. "What's up?" Sara said.

Dylan looked at his father. "Dad... before we go, I need to ask you something."

Richard nodded slowly. "Okay."

"What did you say to Mom, when you were alone with her just now?"

Richard was silent for a long time. Alex, Sara, and Tom moved a short distance away, sensing that this was a private family matter.

Finally, Richard took a step closer to his son. "I told her that I was sorry for trying to be a good husband at the expense of being a good father. For some reason I can't explain, I spent your whole life thinking I could only be one or the other; if I gave up my search for her to spend more time with you, it would mean that I didn't love her anymore. Now that I say it out loud, after everything that's happened... I see how silly it is.

"I'm sorry for not being your dad, Dylan. If you give me another chance, I promise to do better this time. I've paid off most of the debts, and I'm slowly building the photo studio back up again. I hope that does something to show you that I'm serious. I won't lie to you. On some level, not knowing what happened to your mom will haunt me for the rest of my life. But I can't—I won't—let that pain *be* my life. Some days will be worse than others, and there will be times when I will need to take a break to mourn her, but I want to look forward, not back. That's what she would want, and it's what I want, too."

Dylan wiped away a tear and took his hand out of his pocket. "I was hoping you'd say that," he said, his voice barely above a whisper. He held out his closed fist. When Richard extended his hand, Dylan dropped Marie's wedding ring into it.

Richard stared at it in silence for a long time. He picked it up with extreme care, as if it were made of delicate crystal. He turned it around in his fingers until he found the inscription on the inside. There could be no mistake. It was Marie's ring.

Richard locked eyes with Dylan, his expression unreadable. "She... was part of all this, from the beginning," he said.

Dylan hugged his father tightly. "I told her how much you loved her."

Richard returned the embrace, haltingly at first, then more naturally. "What happened?"

Dylan looked up with tears in his eyes. "I'll tell you someday, Dad. But not today, okay? It's Sara's birthday. For today, just know that Mom helped us—she helped us end it. We couldn't have done it without her."

Richard said nothing. He carefully put the ring in his pocket.

"Dad? Are you okay?"

Richard took a deep breath and let it out slowly. "Yeah. Surprisingly, but yeah. I'm okay. Really."

Dylan smiled. "Let's go."

As they rejoined the others, the rain lightened to a drizzle. By the time they reached the cemetery gate, it had stopped. The clouds began to move away from the sun. Raindrops sparkled in the grass.

Tom looked up, letting the sunlight warm his face for a moment. He looked back down at Sara. "You sure you don't want something fancier than a beach picnic for your birthday?"

She smiled and shook her head. "Nope. It was your idea, anyway."

* * *

The sun was high overhead in the clear sky, warming the sand beneath their feet. Alex opened the cooler and started passing out drinks and food. She paused in front of Tom and waited until he looked up at her from his chair. She smiled at him and held out a sandwich. "It was very nice of you to look after Sara until she turned eighteen. But don't worry—I won't tell anyone. Wouldn't want to damage your tough guy reputation," she said.

Tom took the sandwich and shrugged. "She's grown on me." Sara and

Dylan were farther down the beach, sitting on a rock, dangling their feet in the water.

"I've been so busy with work, I haven't seen her in a while," Alex said. "How's she doing?"

"Therein lies an announcement, actually," Tom said. He looked over his sunglasses at Richard. "You want to tell her?"

Richard nodded and set his sandwich aside. "Dylan and Sara sat me down last night. They want to take a year off after Dylan finishes high school. After that, he's going to college, and she's going with him."

Alex beamed. "That's wonderful! Where are they going?"

"Nanyang Technological University, in Singapore."

Alex blinked. "Singapore! They're going to the other side of the world? By themselves?"

Richard nodded. "That's where he wants to go. He said they have the program he wants to do."

"Sounds expensive."

Richard smiled. "It won't cost him a penny. When Ethan disappeared, someone else took over his nonprofits, but Dylan's scholarship wasn't affected."

"So, it was a real offer. Dylan should take it; he deserves it. But what's Sara going to do in Singapore?"

"Whatever she wants," Tom said. "She'll work odd jobs until she finds something she likes. I have no doubt that she'll figure it out."

Richard took a bite of his sandwich. "What about you, Alex? What have you been up to?"

She sat back in her chair, gazing out at the ocean. "I've been doing a lot of thinking about what the future holds for me, and I think I have a plan. I want to keep working directly with patients; I know that much for sure. I don't want to be a full-time administrator, but I do want my new treatment protocol to get out there and save lives. It can, and it will. I've decided to write a paper about it, get the paper through the peer review process, and then write a book. Someone will start a clinic with my protocol as the keystone, and when they do, I'll be happy to consult pro bono to help get it off the ground. I have a feeling that, before long, it will take off and grow without me."

Richard smiled. "That's wonderful news."

Tom nodded and raised his beer in a toast. "Knock it out of the park, sister."

Alex turned to Tom. "What about you? What does the future hold for Tom, the warrior?"

He harrumphed. "My warrior days are over. I'm a simple guy. I like beer and building stuff, and I intend to keep doing those things. No need to fix what ain't broken." He paused. "I guess one thing has changed. From here on out, I'll be doing what I want to do, *because* it's what I want to do. It's my life; no one else gets to decide what I do with it. I'm happy to keep hiring ex-cons, but they won't be getting special treatment anymore. They'll be held to the same standard as everyone else. I have no duty to anyone—especially not to losers who are gonna drag down my whole team."

Alex smiled and gave Tom's arm a gentle, reassuring squeeze. "Richard? What about you?"

He scratched his beard. "Slowly but surely, I'm getting new clients. Maybe one day, I'll start doing crazy stuff again, taking pictures of cheetahs in Africa or whatever. But for now, I want to keep it simple—weddings and yearbook photos for the foreseeable future. I've been away from Dylan long enough. For now, I just need to pay the bills and be a dad."

A comfortable silence settled over the small group. They watched Dylan and Sara laughing and playfully shoving one another.

"You know, not to be a rain cloud, but I was thinking… Ardu's not really dead. Not completely," Tom said.

Richard frowned at him. "What do you mean?"

"The idea that started the cycle in the first place—that a man's life isn't his own, that it belongs to others—that idea is still alive and well all over the world. Ardu was just a symptom of a much worse disease. If it happened once, it could happen again."

Alex nodded slowly. "True, but we've done our part. The rest is up to everyone else. All we can do going forward is to try to show others what we've learned, in our own ways, and try to change one mind at a time."

"One life at a time," Richard agreed.

Tom was staring at Dylan and Sara, frowning. They were still sitting on the rock, still playfully pushing and jostling one another. Tom cupped his hands around his mouth and shouted, "Just kiss her already!"

They could all see Dylan turning red. But then, he did kiss her.

Tom nodded slowly, a self-satisfied smile on his face. "I always knew he had it in him."

~ THE END ~

Thank You

From the bottom of my heart, thank you for reading *The Nightmare Machine*. You made it all the way to the end! I hope you enjoyed reading it as much as I loved writing it. If so, please take a minute to leave an honest review on Amazon (or wherever you bought it). More reviews help me write and publish books more quickly :)

Want a free novella and lots of other cool stuff? Join my Readers' Circle mailing list at TimWhiteWriting.com

Acknowledgements

There are two people who inspired and contributed to *The Nightmare Machine* more than anyone else despite having little direct involvement in its creation. The first is my wife, Amy, who shares and reflects my deepest values; who brings irreplaceable joy to my life; who reminds me every day that no darkness, no matter how deep and terrible, can fully extinguish the light of reason; and who works a real job so I can sit around writing stories and designing games all day.

The other person to whom I owe this book's existence is my best friend, Tom Durham, who passed away on April 2, 2017. Tom was more than a friend to me—he was my brother, confidant, business partner, trusted adviser, and the funniest person I've ever known. He lived his life with passion and intensity that I strive to emulate every day, and his death left a hole in my heart that can never be filled. In this book, the character Tom Davis is based heavily on the real-life Tom, but they are not the same person. The fictional Tom's strength, loyalty, intelligence, bravery, work ethic, and sense of humor—these are the pieces of my friend that I wanted to share with the world. The rest of him is reserved for me, his other friends, and his family.

I extend my deepest gratitude to Thomas Walker-Werth, a good friend, a great thinker, and a truly superlative editor, without whom *The Nightmare Machine* would have been 60% worse and finished 200% sooner. If you noticed any instances of British English or incorrectly punctuated conjunctions between dependent and independent clauses, feel free to complain to him directly.

I am also deeply grateful to everyone at Objective Standard Institute (OSI) and The Objective Standard (TOS), particularly Craig and Sarah Biddle, Thomas and Angel Walker-Werth, and Jon Hersey. All of them have tremendously accelerated my growth as a thinker and a nonfiction writer. Many people regard fiction and nonfiction as essentially opposite kinds of writing, but they are, in fact, deeply intertwined with and dependent on one another. In order to create stories that will have deep, positive, and lasting impacts on people's lives, storytellers must learn how to tell compelling stories *about* people—and in order to do that, storytellers must *understand* people, especially themselves. Storytellers must understand what is good and bad for human life and flourishing, and they must be able to point to evidence in the real world and say: "This is how I know it." The knowledge and skills I have gained from OSI and TOS form indispensable parts of the foundation upon which I have built my storytelling career—and my life more broadly.

Many thanks to my launch team, who helped me reach critical mass with regard to the Amazon algorithm and/or provided valuable feedback on the second draft of the manuscript:

Angel Walker-Werth
Audrey Platt
Debbie Goulet
Hunter Davis
Jason Stotts
Jennifer McGrail
Jonathan Holt
Josh Fowler
Josh Smith
Keith Moore
Kristin Fowler
Kyle Cannady
Mary Jane Fawcett
Nick Eastman
Rebekah Blauer
Robert Begley
Sarah Biddle
Stewart Margolis
Susie Rawlins
Synneva Ramsey
Tom Jones

About the Author

Tim White is an author, editor, writing coach, and game designer in Phoenix, Arizona. He started writing fiction in 1996 and nonfiction in 2006. As of 2023, he has published more than 1,000 nonfiction articles and three nonfiction books. Although *The Nightmare Machine* is his first published novel, he has also written two other novels, four novellas, dozens of tabletop role-playing game (TTRPG) scripts, and hundreds of short stories.

Tim is a zealous crusader for the power of storytelling to promote human flourishing. He writes fiction in several genres, particularly one that he calls "Romantic horror" (as in "Romantic-era novelists" such as Victor Hugo and Alexandre Dumas, not as in "romance novel"). This little-known genre is unique in that it uses fear as a backdrop against which heroism is sharply contrasted, dramatized, and elevated.

Tim's storytelling philosophy is summed up eloquently by one of his favorite authors:

> "I often hear people say that they read to escape reality, but I believe that what they're really doing is reading to find reason for hope, to find strength. While a bad book leaves readers with a sense of hopelessness and despair, a good novel, through stories of values realized, of wrongs righted, can bring to readers a connection to the wonder of life. A good novel shows how life can and ought to be lived. It not only entertains but energizes and uplifts readers."

— Terry Goodkind

Before transitioning to writing full time, Tim was an Army combat medic and, later, a nurse paramedic specializing in trauma and surgery. He is a lifelong shooter and has ranked moderately well in state-level 3-gun competitions. He loves board games, video games, and role-playing games; cats; Pembroke Corgis; good coffee; good books; and escape rooms. He owns an escape room venue in Arizona, where he designs and builds every prop and puzzle in-house.

For more information, please visit TimWhiteWriting.com